PATMOS

Πάτμος

PATMOS

A NOVEL

David Stoeckl

Cover design by Dave Stoeckl
Front Cover Painting by A. N. Mironov
Interior design by Dave Stoeckl

Library of Congress Cataloging-in-Publication data
Stoeckl, David

Patmos – an Apostle in Exile – A Planet on Trial

p.cm.

ISBN: 978-1-967695-00-3 *

Library of Congress Control Number: 2019900749

For further information, contact Albedo Books at:
albedobooks@gmail.com

To Amy
My beautiful wife
whose undying love and support
inspires me every day.
(PS – I still loveth youeth moreth)

"And when I do it well,
help me to never seek a crown
for my reward
is giving glory to You."
-   Keith Green

Introduction and Acknowledgements

First, I need to say this was a scary book to write. Everybody and their mum has an opinion about the Book of Revelation. Even John himself warned to not add or take away a word of the Revelation, and as a devout believer in Christ, I feared crossing that line; something I discussed with my pastor early on. In turn, I will say that this is a novelized version of the true story of John the Apostle when he was exiled to the Greek island of Patmos for failure to worship Domitian Caesar and for spreading the Good News of Jesus Christ. It was here as a prisoner of Rome that Jesus gave him what we call The Book of Revelation. Remarkably, that is just part of the story of John on Patmos. In turn, this book is **_not_** a commentary on the Book of Revelation. There are already plenty of those, and the Revelation is not received until late in the book.

First, I wanted to let you know that the name John does <u>not</u> appear in this book beyond this Introduction. He is mostly called by his Greek name Ionnes, sometimes by his Hebrew name Yochanan, and the Romans call him by his Latin name, Giovanni. He was around 85-86 years old at the time.

Similarly, you'll see other alliterative names. Jesus Christ is commonly called Yeshua Christos. James is Yaakov. Jerusalem is Ierusalem. Israel is Yisra'el. Rome is Roma. You get the idea. The letter 'J' did not exist at that time, so I avoided using it for most of the names. With that said, the word Jew is still used instead of Iew or Yew. Iew seemed to me as possibly confusing to the reader, and in English, the word Yew is type of a tree.

Late first-century Patmos was a society of Christians, Jews, Greeks, Romans and others I did not even try to include. So, some of the alliterative names changed, depending on who was talking. For example, the Greek word for LORD is Kurios. In Latin, it's Dominus. Similarly, the names of Greek gods and goddesses were different from the Roman names. For example, the Greeks would say Aphrodite, Zeus and Hera, versus the Romans who called them Venus, Jupiter and Juno.

John wrote five books of the New Testament, but we know little about his personal life. When compared to the Apostle Paul who wrote about himself a whole bunch, John seemed to me to be humbler and much more self-effacing. Even in his gospel, he does not identify himself by name, but calls himself "the disciple whom Jesus loved." He also appears in the other three New Testament gospels as well as the Book of Acts. Paul mentioned him once in Galatians 2:9. John also named himself a few times in the Book of Revelation.

The internet was wonderful for providing additional resources, but the other two books I must acknowledge are the writings of Eusebius, who was the first official Christian Church historian, and a small book written by Prochorus, who was St. John's scribe and close friend. Prochorus is listed with Stephen and the other deacons in Acts 6:5, so probably knew Jesus personally. Most of the miracles accounted in Patmos came from this book which was kept in the St. John the Evangelist monastery on Patmos. It was brought forth in the 17th century and translated from its original Greek. I have a Kindle copy I poured over as part of the research for this book.

From this book and other sources, I learned about some of the people in history who dwelled on Patmos during Ionnes' imprisonment:
- The Roman governor, Laurentius,
- His wife, Chryspippe,
- Her brother, Apollonides,
- Their parents, Myron and Fona,
- Kynops the Magician,
- Roman Proconsul, Makrinos

Likewise, the Apostolic Fathers lived at that time, who would carry the torch of Christ's church into the second century. Most of the Apostolic Fathers were converts of Paul, John and Peter. They included Ignatius of Antioch, Clement of Rome, Papias of Hierapolis and Polycarp of Smyrna, all part of this story. Even Timothy, Paul's protégé, was bishop of Ephesus at that time, and would be martyred about a year after this book closed.

With that said, there are characters I had to make-up, including the prisoners and Roman soldiers. Between 2,000 to

3,000 people, estimated, lived on Patmos at the time. There were three Greek temples already built, to Artemis, Apollo and Aphrodite. The island, though remote, was already somewhat developed and not just tribal encampments. Being biographical, I must acknowledge some works and people who helped make this book what it is:

- The Bible, the holy and inspired Word of God, certainly provided much to the book.
- "Acts of John, According to Prochorus", written by Prochorus, compiled by Margarita Grillis, and edited by Dr. James Corr.
- The writings of Eusebius, the first, official Christian church historian.
- Keith Green, my favorite Christian songwriter and performer, who died in 1982. His words and music shone as part of this book throughout.
- Internet research for first century, AD life answered questions like 'when were crayons invented?' How to make tallow? Parts of a loom. What dog and horse breeds were in ancient Rome, etc.? Greek gods vs. Roman gods? Things like that.
- Special thanks to Martha Ireland, editor. Her corrections and suggestions were perfect, totally appreciated and re-taught me a few things about English grammar that I'd apparently forgotten or ignored when attending high school and college.
- My Pastor, Jerry Luengen, in Sequim, WA, who I discussed the project with throughout its composition.
- The Olympic Peninsula Christian Writers, a wonderful group of believers I am blessed to know.
- A few others by name who gave me insights and suggestions during the book's composition. These include my brother John Stoeckl, whose early readings helped set the direction for the book. David Merrikin, my musical brother in Christ, who created a sounding board for me as

the book progressed. Also, Ken and Jacquie Bradford, my Aquilla and Priscilla, who suggested some really great edits and feedback late in the project.

- And, of course, to Amy, my wife who supported the project from start to finish, and to whom this book is lovingly dedicated.

It's also good to mention that there are various old world expressions, including Greek and Roman/Latin and Hebrew words throughout the book, so I put a small **Glossary** at the end.

This book has brought many tears of joy to my eyes many, many times, both when composing and during the numerous reedits. I wrote it and it still overwhelms me with emotion as I read. I learned so much about the early Christian church. How did the apostles die? Who else was martyred? How do their sacrifices contribute to my walk with my LORD today? What became of the Christian Church after Christ, Pentecost and the Book of Acts? I hope to continue with more First and Second Century novels about the early Christian Church.

I pray this book blesses you equally as much as I was blessed to read and learn and ponder the early church at the end of the first century.

PATMOS
by David Stoeckl

CHAPTER 1

"Crack!" shouted the matte gray marble sheet. The men atop, bathed in sunshine and sweat, continued to pound with sledgehammers onto flattened spatula spikes with power and purpose and rhythmic precision. A fissure formed in the rock and widened as the men nimbly stepped along the solid side of the hill. Dim, a brick mason from Pergamos stolen away from his wife and two boys, grabbed a quick glance at the Roman guards. Whips in one hand and the other on their sheathed swords, they watched for any opportunity to use either. Most of the shirtless workers displayed wild scribblings of scar tissue all over their bodies. They never did anything without a wary eye out for their captors.

Dim continued hammering in sync with the others. The neutral, gray stone, peppered with sparkles and mineral glitter, reflected the harsh, unfettered sunlight to pierce and stab and gouge their eyes with Oedipal intensity. Squinting to reduce the glare, he focused on the spike, still held up by young Talor, a whipped puppy teen from Knidos who should not even be there. A miss with that big sledge could certainly injure the youth - even break an arm. If that serious, he would be no good for mining and the guards would likely beat him until he was no more.

"Who picked this vein?" demanded Minos, opposite Dim, whacking the spike but making little impact in the marble. A farm hand from Knosos, Creta, with a countenance commonly moribund, he lacked any ticklish sense of humor. The Roman soldiers sometimes called him by his Latin name Minus.

"Hippocrates," answered Jack, a Spartan who had been a spice merchant. He landed another crushing blow with his sledge. "No one knows more about veins than Hippocrates."

A few men smirked. Most did not get the joke any more than Minos.

Big Seth, a Jewish fisherman from Cæsarea, came up to check Minos' spike. Singing a song of Moses, he brushed away the dirt and dust to expose the layering in the marble, not completely unlike wood grain. A papyrus thin layer of clay appeared between the marblish layers suggesting the best place to drive. Seth moved Minos' spike and held it as Minos gave it a whack.

"You break my arm and I will break you," warned Seth. Minos glanced at his helper long enough to not glance at him anymore. Already he had enough foul and loathsome sores of his own. It took a few tries with Seth cursing as each blow rattled the metal spike in his hand, but finally the metal pressed itself into the metamorphic rock.

The prisoners stood atop a cliff little over a dozen feet high and hoped to separate a section of rock the entire height. If accomplished, it would be both a dozen or so feet wide and tall and between two to three feet thick.

Four ropes were secured to spikes, driven in at the bottom of the rock sheet. The ropes rose topside, up and over, held by many hands to keep the marble from toppling. Once it started to go, it would take every ounce of strength the men could combine to keep the heavy rock from crashing and breaking into many pieces. Nobody wanted to again be pulled over the new made cliff - not that it was a serious precipice that would cause injury or death. Many had made similar jumps, even that same day, but their captors were always quick to bring down the whips if the marble was damaged or wasted.

Back on top, the men kept splitting the rock until the cliff found its fracture. As the fissure widened, longer metal pry bars replaced the flattened spikes. The men applied leverage to further widen the marble sheet. Sometimes horses were used for additional pull and strength, but horses pulling often caused too much stress and splintered the rock. The veteran miners could see what was needed to separate the marble and make immediate adjustments.

"Dim!" yelled Jack. "Give your side a whack. It is begging to crumble."

"Ho," Dim answered and glanced over at Jack in acknowledgement.

Talor grabbed a longer flattened spike made for just such a task and brought it to Dim. The two men carefully dropped the long spike down into the fissure. A knot in the rock showed itself.

"Knot," yelled Dim, positioning the spike to the outer side. Another long spike, positioned by Seth and Gallo, was positioned on the inner side of the knot. Both bigger men then grabbed sledge hammers. Seth, the stronger, took the inner side and Dim the outer. The rope tenders prepared to pull back in case the rock suddenly gave way. It had happened before and they wanted no accidents or mistakes. Oftentimes, the bored guards would whip one of them if they thought he was not watching.

Each resounding clang hung in the air like cranky, buzzing bees before your nose. The fissure widened as the knot let go of the cliff side.

"Freedom," called Dim to his coworkers. "Freedom" - their tongue in cheek code word for such rocky release. None of the men were free and how well they knew it. Dim resisted peeking quickly towards a couple of guards who stared back at him intently. They knew the codeword, too. Each stood with a hand on his sword ready to chop down even the slightest indication of revolt or rebellion.

The pry bars were again shoved into the fissure. The men grunted and strained as they applied leverage to increase their torque and separate the stone from its long, long time mountainous home. Each small crack echoed forth in declaration as the stone continued to give way. There was no final, decisive SNAP. As a whole piece, the rock seldom gave way without continued pressure. Pushing and prying and such and the large stone eventually surrendered to separate from its ageless home. Its own weight and gravity took over to finally finish the job.

"Lines," directed Pterrkee, a thief from Helikassos on Asia Minor. The workers already well knew what to do. They also knew Pterrkee's common yearning to give orders. An angry man always ready for a fight, Prerrkee found himself a prisoner after intentionally tripping a drunken Roman soldier in a bar. Those prying dropped their tools and went to man the lines with the others for the farther forward the rock wall leaned, the heavier it became. Down, down, down.

Four men at the bottom pushed against the marble with long poles. The poles scraped along the ground for added drag.

The heavy wall approached the flat ground.

Euæmon, a young adventurer from Nemesis who had been arrested for drunkenly helping a slave escape, stood at the bottom of the cliff with a sledge hammer during the entire process, watching the spikes and ropes. If one of the spikes gave way or shifted, the wall could fall. He would keep the spikes driven and the ropes in place. It was the most dangerous place to be, and well he knew it. Rock could tumble down from the top or the wall could suddenly give way and fall on him full force to be dashed to pieces like the potter's vessel. Even the guards gave Euæmon plenty of room to work.

Ropes and poles did their jobs as the sizable chunk turned on its new, broad side like a slice of freshly baked bread.

Euæmon slipped out from under in the last seconds.

"Touchdown," yelled the men from the bottom, arms raised, moving their large poles away to stand on different long poles placed horizontally under the wall atop a fulcrum. Leverage again would soften the landing plus make it possible to raise and move the wall more easily to move it once flat on the ground.

Dim stood atop the cliff, looking down at their latest prize. Not that it was his anymore than it belonged to any other penal colony tenants, or even the Roman soldiers for that matter. Yet, grasping and rubbing the small, marble carving of a dolphin tied around his neck with a stretch of leather, he looked with tinges of both pleasure and deep mourning as his personal little flames of reason and purpose and fulfillment rolled across his mind.

The terrible sound of ripping flesh distracted his muse. Two soldiers kicked Gallo to the ground. A Roman citizen sent there for possibly sleeping with a Centurion's wife, Gallo, the new whipping boy, received the most brutal brunt from the guards.

"Where are the tools given to you?" yelled one guard. He tightly held Gallo's hair while the other kicked him down to his knees. Then the lash, wrapped around Gallo's face, landed with the couple dozen tentacles attached to the short, woven handle. The tips had no chance to rest for the soldier ripped away the whip to bring another and another and another.

"I do not know," yelled Gallo, his voice a gargle, his hand out to try to stop the sting.

The guard drew back intentionally just far enough to whip the offending hand. Gallo yelped and pulled his now throbbing hand away just long enough to feel the whip again across his body. Head. Neck. Back. Front. Arms. Legs. Feet. It did not matter. The guards knew well how to torment and cause pain.

"Where are they?" yelled the burly guard.

"I do not know," Gallo pled, sobbing.

Dim walked off, head down, as Gallo's wails continued to echo back and forth, over and over through his ears. Every convict knew tools, especially metal tools could be weapons. They were checked out and checked back in for every specific assignment.

Dim well knew the rules. He had been there close to three years. He had already lived through Gallo's spot - the newcomer who got it from both sides - from both the guards as well as the persons who sent him there. Patmos. Little Greek island in the Ægean Sea about thirty-seven miles from Asia Minor. A person could easily walk its length, top to bottom, in less than a day.

A beautiful piece of real estate, really. Remarkable stone structures and beaches against the azure waves - much bluer than the Mediterranean. Fortunately, it had its own freshwater spring, but also had pale soil that resisted any healthy growth of crops. Not much to eat certain times of the year.

Roma had taken it over well before Dimetrius cried his first. The marble quarry had only been around for the last decade or so. Not the best marble in the Greek islands, Dim had been told. Paros was famed to be better with its white stone, pure as ivory, but Patmos still offered decent quality marble for most needs.

As a prison, it was not the worst place in the Empire they could send a man, but most Roman penal colonies were probably better.

Gallo's screams subsided, either by distance or the guards were done tormenting him. Dim knew the tools were already gathered and stored. The guards grabbed any easy excuse to castigate Gallo who had arrived seven, or maybe eight days past. The Laurelheads in Roma who sent someone to Patmos usually checked up on their quarry over the first couple/few months. Satisfied he was being adequately mistreated, they usually lost interest and Patmos never heard from them again. Similarly, the guards regularly tormented all newcomers, to control and break his spirit. Broken men were much easier to control. Dim could tell Gallo would not take long to defeat; if he did not kill himself first. There always simmered that final escape clause, alive and dwelling deeply inside each and every man. Dim recalled how some had died with a wry, little smile on his face as Dim fingered his own cloth belt. He recalled his own moments of suicidal contemplation and the very real, hope filled reasons he chose to remain alive.

He passed a large bucket of drinking water for the workers. He felt hot and stopped for a long, deep gulp. He wanted to dunk his entire head in the bucket to cool off but knew all too well to not.

He had done it once, a few months after he arrived as the first hot days of summer began. No one had forbade or warned him. First, they beat him with fists and feet and a dozen odd implements. Then they half-drowned him, sticking his head in the bucket over and over. Then, they tied him to a large, deep post for a couple days and nights without food, water, sanitation or anything else. Neither sitting nor lying down, half on his back with his hands tied a couple dozen inches or so above the ground, he had prayed to the gods for death countless times before they released him, whipped him a few more times, and sent him dehydrated and bleeding to his cell.

Others brought him water but not much else. No dressed wounds. No words of sympathy or encouragement. Nothing more, for they had already given from what little any of them had and water was the last thing they had to give. After Dim drank as much as he could hold, he laid on his side, closed his eyes and appreciated the shady rest. He imagined his life before Patmos with wife and children. What had happened to that life before the beatings? Before the pain? Before the quarry? Before the prison with gates made of glorious blue saltwater? Perhaps that was partly why the guards regularly beat them. If any actually tried to swim away, their wounds would attract sharks with gruesome certainty. The salt water might burn in the wounds for a few minutes, but even small flecks of dried blood would bring certain death in such waters.

Opening his eyes from his bedroll, he peered out the open door. A hedgerow rose before them, and there was not much to see. He could not see the sky or the town or the Acropolis Kastelli or the fig trees or the Ægean Sea, mottled with emerald sparkles. He could not see Apollo's Temple without first climbing the hill. Lying there, he cursed the god as much as he cursed his own life. For two days, Apollo had sucked the life out of him with his fiery chariot. He took another gutful of water before closing his eyes to try to sleep. It was not yet dark, but he had not slept much either day or night, and despite his wounds, he knew that they would expect him out there tomorrow to cut stone.

"Roma," he muttered angrily. No curse felt worse than to say the word, "Roma." It filled one's mouth with the worst taste imaginable. The soft R. The broad O. The flattened M. The A with Arrogant Attitude. It still spewed forth from Dim's mouth like caustic, bile filled lava and he wondered why Vesuvius could not have buried Roma instead of Pompeii or Herculaneum?

As the day's work ended, Dim noted the gentle warmth of midspring breezes as he departed the quarry for dinner. Just as the sun set, the elements stirred up a little fresh air to announce the oncoming nightfall. Some others were already eating as he approached. Entering the large tent, he accepted his scrap of dinner then exited to join the others. The men always wanted more to eat, but to be honest, were seldom hungry. Living on such rations, the stomach had adjusted to the personal famine. Dim knew well his captors. They were not inclined towards any sense of mercy or compassion, yet their dinners commonly seemed like more than he would have expected for prison fodder. He had dwelled on the why for some time after arrival. It became something to think about - a game. A motivating puzzle to be solved. Why would they feed us this much? If they could, they would feed us nothing. He kept this musing to himself, partially to not draw attention lest the soldiers reduce their rations, and partially just the personal challenge to figure it out by himself.

He expected they fed them to prevent revolt, but that rationale never settled well. The guards commonly provoked the men towards revolt. They often even beat the men just for something to do - to offset their own boredom. Pressing others to revolt would be a welcome change for some of the Roman guards.

Then, it occurred to him one day, sitting with the group under an olive tree. The Romans had marble quotas to meet. They had to cut marble, and they needed strong men to do the job. If they fed them too little, the men would famish, and marble would not be hewn. They needed them to be this strong, however much it galled them. He felt a personal sense of pride and triumph but dared not share his insight. Again, they might take away what little the men had.

He took a small nibble on his bread so it would last longer.

"SATURN, TAKE MINE!" yelled a surprising but familiar voice. A screaming figure entered amongst the prisoners. The guards, ever ready to go to war, pushed back their swords in sheath and exhaled exasperation. "Apollonides," one whispered and rolled his eyes.

"Here they are," continued the stranger. "Take them. They are yours anyway." He bounced around with a strange and jerky dance, from man to man. Gallo screamed when

Apollonides slapped Gallo's legs and knees and feet. Still licking his wounds after the beating from the guards, he kept to himself, such was his shame and fear and hopelessness.

Talor sat up to lean towards Dim. "Who is that?" he asked.

"Oh ho," laughed Dimetrius and whispered, "Thas' Apollonides, the Govner's brother-n-law."

Apollonides leapt away from Gallo to fall back. He rolled around on the ground, then grabbed a handful of dirt and tried to toss it in the eyes of someone no one else could see. "Bring your scythe. The chicks are waiting," he screamed at the sky, lying back, legs spread.

"Is he mad?" checked Talor.

"More than the muses. Even more than Orestes."

Still rolling on the sand, Apollonides tried to make it stick to his arm. It slid off, so he spit on his arm repeatedly, rolled the sand against it, then loosely wrote his name on his arm.

"SATURNNNNNNNN!"

He sat up and looked at Guard Julius. "Where is a Titan when you need one?" He raised his arm towards Julius and the sky to display his name, then just as abruptly jumped to his feet.

"You!" he turned violently towards Gallo, pointing with purpose and menace.

Gallo's eyes widened.

"You have hidden Saturn from me."

Gallo knew it was not true. He knew everyone else knew it was not true. Even Saturn knew it was not true, but Gallo dared not answer lest he invoke another beating from the guards.

Then, Phranc appeared unexpectedly. Phranc, a Roman from Asisium, landed on Patmos a year earlier regarding a dispute over his vineyard.

"Can I help?" he asked, placing a hand on Apollonides' back.

Apollonides screamed and jumped away as though Phranc's touch burned like a hot branding iron.

"Holy Zeus!" he beheld, his eyes wide saucers.

18

"Can I get you some water?" Phranc asked, and walked over to the bucket.

Apollonides continued to watch Phranc furtively. He knew he could be invisible at times, but he also knew Phranc could be invisible, too. That had to be how Phranc snuck up on him so easily. He licked his dry lips.

"Only if it was drawn from Neptune's hand."

"Oh, it was," assured Phranc. "He brought it to me fresh this morning."

Apollonides cleared his raspy throat and straightened up to his regal best. "Then, yes, I shalt accept your water."

Phranc lifted the ladle. Actually, not much water lined the bottom of the bucket, but enough to give Apollonides to quench his thirst. The madman slurped it gladly. He wanted more but restrained himself. He knew the dangers of too much water, and never wanted to drown in his thirst.

"What brings you to our camp?" asked Phranc, replacing the ladle with a thud in the wooden bucket.

Apollonides looked around the evening sky as he mindlessly answered, "Music."

"What music?" challenged Minos with his usual cynical spirit.

"The music of the chain," answered Apollonides, closing his eyes to feel the melodies, then he looked at Phranc, smiled and placed a hand on his shoulder. "Yours sings so pretty."

"Yes, it does," agreed Phranc, somewhat sadly.

Looking at Gallo, he declared, "Yours is clatter."

Gallo seized up but feared moving lest his chains make more noise.

Apollonides looked around at all the men. Drooling, he reported, "Saturn sent me to Vulcan to forge him the musical chains." Drool was good. The leaves liked it enough to stick to it.

"And, did you make them - the musical chains?" asked Phranc.

Apollonides closed his eyes and dropped his head. Tears appeared, mingling with his spittle. "No," he admitted, ashamed and broken. "Vulcan was not home."

"Was anybody home?" asked Phranc.

"Was anybody home?" mocked Pterrkee.

"Was anybody home?" imitated Dim. Pterrkee shot him a mean glance. Dim smiled.

"Just Venus," answered Apollonides, "but she knows not the chains."

"Well, we have chains here," jingled Phranc. "Perhaps Saturn would like our chains. I would be glad to lend them to him."

Most of the men chuckled. Minos spit. Pterrkee wanted to strangle him.

"Tell him to leave," said Guard Julius. The Roman guards were not allowed to forcibly remove Apollonides except to save his life, being Myron's son and the governor's brother-in-law. Apollonides jiggled Phranc's chains, then Dim's, then Talor's and others, sometimes licking them. Again, he told Gallo, "Yours are clatter," then to the rest, "I cannot bring these to Saturn. Your chains need tuning. Their music has gone sour." "Perhaps we just do not play them as sweetly as you," suggested Phranc.

Apollonides fell forward to his knees beside Phranc and uttered, "Sometimes things are so sweet, they are sour. Or bitter, like a bittern, or porcupinecone." He took Phranc's chains in hand and examined them up close, studying each link, enthralled at the beauty of the workmanship and wondered which link he would be. "Many parts are edible," he added, still talking about the porcupinecone, but everyone thought he meant the chain.

He peered up at the twilight sky and sighed. Fatigue reminded him he had not slept the previous night, perplexed with wondering what happened to the sun. He brooded on the question throughout the long night until it dawned on him...

Then, the sounds of horses and hooves arose, approaching the camp. Some of the men slipped back into twilight shadows to avoid notice until they saw who came up at so strange a time. Even Apollonides tried hiding behind a tree until he remembered that he was invisible.

Three men rode up, a sort of nobleman, and two Roman guards. Guard Octavius attended to the leader's horse, holding the stallion steady as the man dismounted. The leader, wearing a white linen tunic and long, black cloak, nodded to the guards before moving towards Apollonides, his face dark with intent and totally put upon.

"Who is that?" whispered Talor to Dim.

"Kynops, the Magician."

"Why does he wear makeup?" asked Talor, "especially around his eyes."

"No idea," admitted Dim. "Perhaps t' look more like an Egyptian."

"Apollonides. Let us go," ordered Kynops, his eyes afire.

Apollonides remained invisibly seated.

"Let us go," ordered Kynops. "Your father awaits. He is very unhappy with you."

Apollonides almost spoke but held his tongue. He did not want to give away his position and he definitely did not want to go home.

"Move it," said Kynops. "On your feet." He approached the young man with plodding, indignant purpose. He was Kynops, the Great Magician of Patmos. Who was he to play nursemaid, even if it fulfilled the governor's wish? He still had not admitted to himself his motives to regain the governor's good grace and favor after the last debacle.

Apollonides remained still and in his mind, undetected.

Kynops bent over in front of Apollonides, practically nose to nose, and said in his deep voice, "You are not invisible. I can see you. Now move it."

Apollonides remained stone.

"I assure you, if I could make you disappear forever, that would be my greatest wish."

Apollonides finally moved, his eyes making contact. They can always see you when your eyes make contact. He rose from his hiding place behind nothing, walked around Kynops and took hold of Kynops' horse.

"No, you do not!" yelled Kynops. "Do not let him mount," yelling to Guard Octavius. The guard responded, leading the horse in a spiraling circle to keep Apollonides from mounting. Apollonides hopped around behind the horse, one foot in the air and one hand on its mane. Men laughed to themselves.   They all remembered the last time when Apollonides took Kynops' horse and rode off in flight.

"You walked up here. You can walk back. In irons if I have to."

"Why do not you just send him there," suggested Guard Octavius, flipping his head back and forth towards the sorcerer as the horse continued its gyrations. "...With your magic?" Octavius always hoped to see Kynops perform some magic.

Kynops shoved Apollonides aside as he took hold of his horse to answer the impudent guard, "If you want to see some magic, I will turn you into a skink."

The guard backed away, his eyes widening.

Phranc wanted to help. He stood idly, uncertain what he could do. Even he feared Kynops' sorcery and temperament to some degree. Phranc knew magicians, sorcerers and shamans to typically be unpredictable and moody creatures.

Dim, Talor and a few others, including the other guards just sat back to mutely and cautiously enjoy the show. This was a good one as they go. Usually the guards made the prisoners leave or turn their backs, but even they were more so distracted.

"I will have Diana on you," threatened Apollonides to Kynops. "My sister knows your ways."

"Your sister and I broke fast this morning. She wants you back at home, too."

Apollonides stalled, a hand on the horse's haunch. "Then, I shall go," he decided, "if only for Diana," and he bounded down the hill towards home.

"Follow him," ordered Kynops to his escorts. "Make sure he does not stray."

The two guards complied and rode off down the hill behind Apollonides who was singing a song of unrequited love to the tortoise he had just skipped past.

Kynops turned towards the Roman guards with a vengeance.

"Why did not you tell me he was here?"

"What is that?" questioned Guard Ernesto, standing taller, but still ready to take a quick step or two back.

"Why did not you get me?"

"We did not know it was your turn to watch him."

"It was not."

"Sir?" The soldiers suddenly did not know where the conversation strayed - nothing unusual with Kynops the Magician. Everything about him had to have mystique, or at least a confounding.

"Have you not been instructed to contact Governor Laurentius if Apollonides showed up?"

The guards all looked at each other. The truth was not always the best option at times like this.

"It is our duty to carry out the governor's orders," opened Guard Julius. "To the best of our knowledge, if he ordered us to report the whereabouts of the governor's brother-in-law, we were not informed."

"Impudence!" yelled Kynops and still holding the reins, raised his left hand menacingly.

Guard Julius led the others as they all took a leaning step back.

Kynops stood erect and menacing for a few seconds, then brought his loaded hand back down. No spell would be ejected this time, but they never could guess with certainty what he might have done. He had been known to turn people and even animals into other objects. That always seemed like a lot of trouble to Guard Julius since it was typically easier just to kill something. If you are going to take it out of commission anyway, might as well be the permanence of death.

Kynops separated the reins to mount his horse. Just as he prepared to jump up, someone flipped a sharp rock against the horse's nose. It reared up suddenly and backed away. In course, Kynops was thrown onto his back atop the hard ground. Stifled laughter filled the air. Kynops scampered to his feet, looked around from face to face, settled on Dim, and walked forward as into a headwind.

"You did it," he accused.

"Did what?" defended Dim, still amused by the fall.

"You spooked my horse."

Dim looked at his compadres. "Not me, Mr. Nops. I do not even know what happened."

Kynops pressed him. "So, you are a worm?"

Dim looked surprised.

"Cowards like you always make good worms."

Dim rose and looked at him questioningly. He glanced over at Talor, brow furrowed.

"Worms," said Kynops, getting louder and louder and louder, repeating the word, "WORMS," and moving towards Dim with each ominous step. Dim stood his ground, not out of revolt as much as out of curiosity and puzzlement. Kynops yelled, "WORMS!" one more time, his deep voice shrieking, then he suddenly pushed against the prisoner's chest with all his might. Dim was much stronger, but already leaning back an inch or two, still fell back, hit the ground and vanished. Only a small earthworm slithered where Dim had crashed. His shackles fell over, empty.

Everyone gasped except Guard Octavius who had waited so long for such a moment. He had often wished the Grand Wizard would teach him how to do that.

"Hmph!" declared Kynops, then turned towards his steed with gale force authority.

The small group of men parted quickly and fearfully. Gallo's sobs could be heard behind them. Kynops fancied himself as not one with whom to be trifled. He mounted and rode off down the hill.

Talor and Phranc turned first to seek Dim. Talor picked up the earthworm next to the shackles. It wriggled in his fingers as they do. He looked around for a place to store the critter but saw nothing. Even in his short time there, he well knew to keep the worm from the guards if possible. They would make a game of it, toss it around and eventually kill it. He did not know how long Dimetrius would be an earthworm, but needed to give him every consideration, just in case...

Phranc took the worm from Talor.

"I have a place for it," he assured, and placed it in his breast pocket.

As the last rays of daylight slid away, the guards sent the men to their quarters.

"I told you Dim would get it some day," barked Minos as they entered their hold. "He always had a little too much spark for Roman swine to handle."

"Quiet!" ordered Seth. The Jewish fisherman from Cæsarea had an idea to help Dim.

"Take him to Yosef. The Rabbi may have an answer." Entering their dirt floor shelter, Talor and Phranc saw the old Rabbi Yosef. Talor, a Greek kid from Knidos knew little about the Jewish faith or lifestyle. Phranc knew much of Jewish ways. Plus, he personally loved all creatures as flowed his nature, despite the brutal, tormenting Roman guards. He had been a compassionate man in his former life, and only imprisoned on Patmos because he owned a small vineyard wanted by a land baron named Cato. When Phranc would not sell, the baron formally charged Phranc with robbery of his niece and bribed the magistrate to get rid of him. Phranc saw the writing on the walls and signed a quit deed over to his uncle in Roma who could not be so easily intimidated or pressed by Cato. Of course, the one condition was to never, ever sell the vineyard to Cato. His uncle was not a particularly giving or compassionate man but was a sensible businessman. He would take good care of the vineyard and possibly return it to Phranc when and if he returned. And, best of all, Cato would not reap its rewards.

Cato shrieked with fury, of course, but still mocked and laughed as he saw Phranc board the boat in chains for Patmos. Phranc had sent him a bottle of bitter wine vinegar as a parting gift to be delivered after he sailed away. Cato found it on his dining table as he entered his villa. The inscription on the bottle read *Aceto di Cato.*

Yosef had just retired to his bed when Talor and Phranc found him. He looked at both warily, then relaxed when Phranc presented the earthworm. They explained what happened.

"What can I do?" asked Yosef, throwing his hands in the air. "I am but an old man. What do you expect me to do?"

Talor was not shy with his answer. "We were hoping you could change him back."

"Why me?"

"Are not you like a holy man of God?" asked Phranc. "We pray your patience that you could ask this God of yours to help." Yosef felt a tad beside himself but closed his eyes in a holy nod. Talor felt tears rising for Dim. He swallowed them back hard. Tears always invited mockery with this group. He went over to his bed and laid down, saddened and alone in his thoughts; the worm next to his head. He feared falling asleep and the worm be gone in the morning. Even more, he feared the worm burrowing underground then changing back to a man. He would never survive in such a tight spot, void of air space.

Phranc and the others let him be. They did not have any answers anyway.

Better part of an hour later, against the quiet, the door opened to their barracks. The men looked and saw Guard Octavius enter holding a torch. Most turned away, so did not notice the man with him in chains. Those that did look were amazed.

"DIM!" yelled big Seth, sitting up.

The others looked. Guard Octavius pushed him towards his bedroll then left the room, scowling, and relocking them all inside for the night.

"What happened?" asked most of the men. "We saw you changed into an earthworm by Kynops." Talor checked. The earthworm was still next to him moving slowly away. It would find the dirt floor and make its final exit.

"Know not 'bout any earthworm," admitted Dim, "but when I fell down, I sudd'nly found meself in an olive tree on Gov'ner Laurentius' estate. I had t' grab any branch t' keep from fallin' out. After I got back my wits, I was gonna jus' hop down & walk out, but there were guards 'round the grounds, & there was no way they were gonna believe I was sent there by Kynops. Perhaps that is the very reason he sent me there."

"Astral projection?" asked Euæmon.

"No idea what that is, but that explains it 'bout as well as anythin' else."

Dim held up his manacles. "Man, it felt good t' be out o' chains. Yeah, we don' usually work in them, but it was totally different. So, I watched the guards for a spell, saw a chance t' make my break, slipped out over the wall & walked right int' Octavius. You would o' thought he saw a ghost. Also, a good thing I was not shackled. No way I coulda snuck off the property with chains jinglin' all over the place."

"Did you see Kynops?" asked Pterrkee?

"Nope," answered Dim, glad for the avoidance. Before that moment, he had forgotten that they were heading for Myron's estate. Good chance they would have passed.

"Apollonides probably took 'em on 'nother goose chase. For that matter, he pro'bly thought he became a goose." The men laughed.

"An invisible goose," added Euæmon who rose honking and waddled like a shackled goose around the gloomy room. More laughter, though not too loud, lest the guards on watch happened by.

"By the way," said Dim. "What spooked the horse?" None of the men knew. Or, were not admitting it. Probably the former.

"Maybe Gallo?" Dim thought aloud. No. He was behind the horse and too far away.

"Octavius," suggested Mothcrates, an aging Athenæn who fancied himself a colleague to the philosophers of old. "He always wants to see Kynops do some magic and what better way than to anger him?"

"He could have tossed something at the horse," suggested Seth. "I have seen that rat flick a pebble with one finger sharp enough to make it skip on water."

The men nodded and muttered affirmation, but most knew they would never really know.

Talor started to speak, then held back.

"What?" asked the others.

"Um, I never saw Kynops before today, but I never want to get on his bad side."

"We are already on Kynops' bad side," hissed Pterrkee.

"Uh huh," agreed Talor, "but he still scares me. When I saw Dim disappear..."

The men all muttered and/or indicated their personal responses. Dim cleared his throat the loudest. "I agree he is someone t' avoid, but lemme tell you, he is not the big shot he pretends t' be. Yes, pretends. He is the Master Magician - on *Patmos*. Little, ol' Patmos. That is it. He would be at most a Class Beta hustler in Athenæ, Sparta or even Ephesus. That makes him no more than the big frog on a small, small pond. More bluster & bluff than blood or blight."

"Blimey!" exclaimed Euæmon.

"Exactly," smiled Dim. "But, like I was sayin', Octavius brought me back up t' the barracks, locked me in some shackles and brought me here."

"Too bad you did not get away," judged Minos.

Dim looked at him through the gloom and answered, "If I ever aim t' make a break for it, I will have a clear plan. T' go without a plan is t' get caught & punished & beaten & prob'bly killed."

Minos knew it to be true as did all the others. Still, he might have followed the temptation to its limit.

"Not like I could not outrun Octavius," boasted Dim. "One against one, we might have a chance. But he starts yellin' & the whole town comes out. Would not have a chance. Again, I needed a clear hole t' get through their webs."

He sat down on his bedroll and laid back, turning towards the wall. The 'maybes' and 'what ifs' started replaying through his mind like they tended to do. He did have a chance to escape. The perfect diversion. They maybe think you are dead already. Even turned into a worm, and the blowfish Kynops would never claim his magic was anything less than the best. Maybe he should have found a boat to steal. It is only a couple/ few hours to the next island, depending on wind and wave. Maybe he could have found what happened to his wife and children...

The others returned to their beds as well to share the same dream. Freedom. They always wished it but seldom actually said the word.

"But that is not the worst of it," Dim added, turning back toward the others. "We were walkin' back up the hill. We stopped by the barracks where I was chained again, so we are ploddin' along. The sun is gone and the moon has risen, mostly full, so the trail is pretty easy t' see. Octavius wants t' push me forward every now & then but he is huffin' & puffin' a bit himself climbing the hill. Then, I sees somethin' & I stop. Octavius pushes me, but I look at him & point t' the sycamore tree. We see a man hanging there, his belt around his neck."

"Who? Who? Who?" most asked.

"Could you tell?"

"Yes," answered Dim. Tears shamelessly filled his eyes.

"Gallo?" asked Rabbi Yosef from his bed.

"Gallo," Dim nodded to the invisibly black ceiling.

Solemn silence quickly filled each head.

PATMOS

CHAPTER 2

Aphrodite, the bright and morning star, shone starkly in the early morning sky as dawn's twilight leaked over the Taurus Mountains across the water on the Asia Minor mainland. Dim always liked seeing the planet in the mornings and evenings. He had been told the morning and evening planet was the same one, but he had never felt sure that was right. One appeared in the east and the other in the west. One brought the morning and the other closed the evening leading into night. Two totally different functions for the same wandering planet? How could Pythagoras know? Did he shoot an arrow into Aphrodite at evening and check the next morning to see his arrow still stuck out of her?

The Roman soldiers tended to call her Venus. Dim did not know why and definitely did not like the name as well as Aphrodite. Dim knew he was not the brightest dye on the urn, but he never found his Roman captors to be all that sharp. Heading to the quarry, he spied a new ship in the harbor. Probably arrived overnight. Nothing unusual. He noted it only briefly - a Roman craft made for crossing the Mediterranean. The Romans called the Mediterranean *Mare Nostrum* - "Our Sea", such displayed their arrogance.

She probably held upwards of eighty people plus oarsmen. He was not that close, but she looked anchored without much activity happening on deck as yet. She disappeared from sight around the next turn and Dim thought nothing more about her. They had a huge stone slab to try to move today.

He saw Minos and Phranc ahead - a common pair, silent, but total opposites. Minos always head down to face the day. Phranc looked around, taking in the cool breeze, the feathery sounds of trees and the sight of pelicans flying over. Filling himself with the sweet morning air, perhaps he could be any and all. It seemed always so funny that the two became friends.

Jack chattered from behind Dim.

"Put it back in the cave, child," he said to young Talor. "There be no use for your manhood here. The maidens are forbidden to even talk to us, much less mingle. And, beware. Those Roman swine can gawk at the dancers all they want, but if they see you enjoy it, you had better turn into a celtic vertragus and flee."

"Or, better yet, a bird - a seagull - or cuckoo...like Zeus...," added the teen, "...and just fly away from here."

"Then, do not change form when the archers are practicing."

Talor sighed. "Zeus became a cuckoo to woo Hera. Maybe I should insult a few gods. They might turn me into a bird. Or a warthog. Or, even a bug."

"You would do better to learn to throw lightning bolts," laughed Jack.

"Quiet!" ordered Guard Mucius as the prisoners stood in line to have their irons removed.

"Work!"

Heading to the rock, Talor whispered to Jack, "If I could chuck bolts, I would get us all out of here."

Jack planted a supporting hand on the youth and grabbed hold of a large pole to start raising the heavy block of rock. Others joined in. Most knew their roles throughout the day, including the guards who lashed workers at random as it suited them. The pain was never welcome but considered a regular part of the routine. They stayed the course, whip or no whip. Thus, the prisoners mostly tried to avoid the mistakes that would bring down wrath, torture, extreme correction and other madness.

The block was placed upon rolling logs. The workers knew if someone wanted the entire chunk intact, it would be a face of wall for some temple or large public building and would take a ship to transport much larger than the one they saw in harbor that morning. On the other hand, the block could be cut and shaped into thinner sheets and used as a veneer over brick and mortar. Domitian's palace on the Palatina Hill had been made that way.

The long poles again worked together to push the block whatever direction they needed. Some manned the rolling logs.

Some kept the ground as clear and flat as they could. Some pushed the heavy stone inches at a time with leverage and teamwork. As the sun rose, the heat pressed against them with increasing pressure and hindrance. It was always amazing how welcome a tiny breeze or shade could suddenly feel. Water was brought often by a prisoner. The guards, however brutal, still wanted the work done.

Strangers entered the quarry. Dim glanced at them briefly; apparently long enough to invite the whip. He writhed with trained theatrics and pressed all the harder against his pole, not even looking to see which guard whipped him. Most of the inmates who had been there some time knew well each Roman guard's way of whipping. As unique as a man's ears. Some things in life definitely did not matter or require a second look, and in that fashion all the guards were considered repulsive equals.

The newcomers approached. The quarry workers pretended they were not there and kept to their tasks. Lucius, the Captain of the Guard, met the visitors.

"Got two more for you," opened Cap, the sea captain, as his deck hands pushed two men in irons forward.

Lucius eyed the two prisoners quickly, sizing them up as was his habit. One was prime-of-his-life tall and slender. Probably strong and agile. The second was older than the old Rabbi Yosef. Lucius spit. Why send such an ancient to mine rock? They had no strength or stamina. They were surely the first to die under the lash - likely Roma's intent.

Handing two papyrus scrolls to the Captain, the sea captain continued, "This one's Arion. He's from Thorikos. A thief. He was caught stealing weaponry from the armory. Apparently, this one loves anything armament, so watch him.

"The old man is Giovanni, also known by Ionnes. A religious zealot. We brought him from Roma, but he was already a prisoner, from Ephesus I hear, though he's not from there, either. Says he's originally from Capernaum in Galilee."

"A zealot, eh?" noted Lucius.

"Talk your ear off," assured the sea captain.

"They usually do," grumbled Lucius, studying the old man who looked back at him straight and true as the finest crafted arrow. His gray-brown eyes stood out from his weathered wrinkles and thinning white hair. Lucius stared intently at the old man, eye to eye for a few seconds. Neither man spoke. Neither man flinched - until Ionnes' facial features slowly metamorphosed into a deep and genuine smile.

Lucius, the Roman soldier, felt repulse. Obviously, this man was deeply disturbed.

Lucius, the man, felt a softening stir aroused somewhere deep inside.

His well-practiced coldness remained as he turned to carry on his duties.

"Join the prisoners," he ordered Arion with a flip of his head. Arion lifted the shackles towards the Captain. In response, the Captain clubbed Arion side the head with a metal bracelet made for such a moment. "I said join the prisoners," repeated the Captain sternly. Arion straightened up, wiped some blood from his throbbing ear and shuffled towards the team of workers.

Lucius watched him as he then heard Ionnes muttering something. A prayer of praise? A petition to some foreign deity? The old man's lips quivered and flowed with each whispered word. It sounded like gibberish to Lucius who had an ear for most languages in that region of the Mediterranean. He glanced at the prisoner. His eyes were closed calmly in total trust - something so uncommon on Patmos. The Captain noted it, considered also clubbing him, withheld his attack, then looked towards the workers.

"Teos. Side." A man turned from the pack of prisoners. "Front and center," ordered the Captain. Guard Octavius smacked Teos or Side as he headed for the Captain to hasten him along. Arion approached and was directed towards Seth, Jack and the other pole bearers.

Teos was from Side, or was it Side from Teos? Nobody could quite remember. He was a bit of a simpleton either way and did not much care what anyone called him. For Teos or Side, the fact that they called him by his name most of the time pleased him as an improvement.

"Take this one down to the salt ropes," ordered Lucius. "Then, get right back up here."

The two men departed, shuffling slowly towards the coast, slowed by Ionnes' chains.

"Be aware," warned Cap, motioning towards Ionnes. "That one's gonna be your greater challenge."

"How so?" smiled Lucius, amused by the sea captain's caution. "He looks well harmless enough."

"Oh, he won't put up a fight. He's not a killer. Wouldn't even spit on the deck. Not a violent bone in his body, but he'll weave his flesh and blood deity into this island faster than you can say, 'Patmos,' I tell you."

"Made you a member of his sect, did he?" chided Lucius.

"Tried to. Some of my crew and other passengers had better part of a month with nothing else to do than listen to that old man tell story after story about some fellow named Yeshua. He made his impact on some of them."

"A Christian zealot," cursed the Captain of the Guard. "I have dealt with them before."

"Perhaps," agreed the sea captain, "but he's one of Yeshua's first followers. I doubt it'll take long for you to see how dangerous he really is."

Lucius unrolled Ionnes' tallow sealed scroll to read the report. He read it over a few times, his brow furrowing deeper and deeper.

"This cannot be right," he declared.

Cap wanted to move around to see what Lucius read, but knew that could be his last bold act on Earth. He waited and smiled, then spouted, "If it's what I hear'd, I don't believe it, neither."

"It says the man was boiled in oil in the Flavian Amphitheater before Titus Flavius Domitianus Cæsar. Now they have sent him to me."

"That is what I hear'd," acknowledged the sea captain.

"And, he did not die?"

"Not even scalded as far as I could tell after our weeks in close company."

Lucius reread the words in the scroll another time. Same meaning. There was no date when the attempted execution occurred.

"Do you know when he was dipped?"

"No," admitted the sea captain. "But, couldn'ta been long before I arrived in port 'n was commissioned to bring 'im to Patmos. It was all anyone could talk about in Roma that week - on the docks and in the town. I wasn't even going to Patmos, but some centurion chartered my boat to bring him here. They paid me well. Apparently, twas that 'portant to them."

"Anything else?" questioned Lucius.

Cap paused for quite a spell, looking up and twiddling his fingers on his chin.

"Well?" pressed the Captain of the Guard.

"Sorry sir. Jus' don't wanna bore ya with the chatter of old ladies."

"I noticed no women on board."

"They unloaded in Creta."

Cap still appeared quite hesitant.

"Out with it," order Lucius.

"I ain't sayin' anythin' happened," started Cap, hands moving for emphasis. "I been on the sea my whole, sorry life and I seen more than my share o' weird. This one jus' be another one, sir."

Lucius showed his patience wearing thin. He knew how to get information out of people when he needed. He wasn't about to torture the sea captain, but it didn't make him all that much more patient.

"You saw that storm a few nights back?" Lucius nodded.

"Well, weze got caught by it. It weren't the worst I'd had, so I weren't too worried, but it tossed us around a bit. Well, we sent the passengers below, but some kid jus' hadda be on deck. I twas too busy tyin' sails to tell him to get below when a big wave washed over the deck. Dumb kid. He didn't know the sea and it took 'im overboard."

"What did you do?"

"Me?" Cap looked surprised. "I didn' do nothin'."

"Nothing?" checked Lucius.

"I didn' see 'im, Cap'n. I twas still tyin' the line, but my hands started yellin', 'Man overboard. Man overboard.' Then, I sees an old man come up on deck yellin' and screamin' and grabbing hold a the rail to look for his son over the side. That grabs my attention and I don' see his boy no more. The storm's still pouring its wind and wrath on my little boat and I keep tending the line. Then, I sees old Giovanni come racin' up, chains and shackles and all. Now that really grabs my attention. All that metal he haulin', he'd sink faster than one a your rocks. He runs past me and goes to the stern, and yells over the side. I can't hear nothin' he's sayin', not that I thought it mattered, when suddenly another wave rose like a blow hole and washes right over old Giovanni. I see the old man still holdin' on but, then I sees another - the kid, floppin' around on the deck like an old fish catchin' its last breath, and I said, 'No way!'"

"So," Lucius checked, "you are saying Giovanni magically brought the kid back on board?"

"I dunno," admitted the sea captain. "I jus' knows what I seen."

Lucius looked perturbed as he glanced again at the still open scroll. If Giovanni had been that magical, he could have stopped the storm with just a word. For that matter, perhaps he could have walked to Patmos over the water. That would have been the best trick of all for someone trying to escape. Lucius mused, if someone could walk to Asia Minor atop the water, he would not even try to stop him.

Rereading the Latin words for the nth time, he continued to ponder the report.

"He-WmmmNmmmKmmmmm," mumbled the soldier, reading.

"What's that, Captain?" asked Cap. "Did you say something?"

"Nothing," uttered Lucius, not much louder than his mumble. He reread the scroll one more time, dwelling on some of the last words near the bottom.

"He would not cook."

Ionnes and Teos (or Side) slowly moved towards the coast. Chains and shackles slowed a man's movements pretty much the same as old age. Ionnes had both and complained about neither. The morning clouds contributed to a slight chill in the air. Most expected the low clouds would burn off by mid-morn. With Ionnes' shackled, he plodded along slowly but felt no hurry. He had visited some of the Ægean islands over the years, but never Patmos and breathed in his new digs. His ragged, dirty clothing, seldom washed since he had entered captivity, along with his unkempt hair and beard added to his appearance as being a new prisoner, but his demeanor seemed more like a visitor on holiday.

"Well," thought Ionnes, "my passage and board were paid for by the generosity of the Roman government." It was not the first time he had been in chains for the everlasting gospel and his miraculous performance in Roma made the trip to Patmos all that much sweeter. He might be expected to 'pay the bill' now that he was here, but he knew that worked both ways. Always!!!!!

"Where are you from?" Ionnes asked his chaperone.

"Side," answered Teos.

"Which one?" asked Ionnes. He knew of at least five or six.

"I dunno," admitted Teos. "It is just across the water."

He pointed out east of the bay."

"Near Mylasa?"

"Uh-huh."

"I have been through there. I lived in Ephesus for many years."

Teos did not even try to shake off the feeling of loss and sadness that filled him for that moment and every other time he thought of his long, lost home.

"Why are you here?" asked Ionnes.

"I stole'd some bread," he uttered, still lost in his memories.

Ionnes thought that quite a severe punishment for petty thievery.

"How much bread did you steal?"

"Oh, just a couple of loaves. My mama died. She always took care of me, but she could not make me dinner, so I went into town. Nobody I knew could help. I asked some other people for help, but they could not help me, either. Then, I saw the bread in the window, so asked the man if he had any bread for me. He got me the loaves. It was so good. I was so hungry. I ate them down right there. Then, he said, 'Where is your money?' and I did not have any. So, he started yelling at me and calling me names and pushed me out of his store. He found a Greek soldier and told him I had stole'd the bread and had me 'rested. And, now I am here."

Ionnes felt rising compassion for the young man.

"How long have you been here?"

Teos thought long and hard and finally answered, "I dunno. Long time, I guess." He kicked a rock, one of many, along the footpath.

"He said I stole'd it with a knife. I dunno what knife he meant. I never owned a knife in my life. He had a big knife right there on the table. Maybe he meant that knife."

"Robbery," thought Ionnes. The crime and punishment made a little more sense.

Walking along, they saw four men in a field - two prisoners and two Roman guards. The prisoners worked diligently, digging a large hole.

Ionnes stopped.

"What is that?" wondered the elder. Teos did not know. Ionnes left the trail to investigate.

"No, no, no," urged Teos, trying to block Ionnes. "The guards will beat us."

"Then, stay here," said Ionnes, still walking towards the scene with chain music to announce his approach. Teos followed, but at a distance. He also noticed a white horse, alone, prancing across the sloped field.

Approaching, Ionnes saw the limp body lying on the dirt, obviously dead for some hours. No burial wrap. Just a naked corpse lining the ground.

"Gallo," Ionnes could hear Teos say from behind him. Ionnes wondered how he died. The marks on his neck suggested strangulation but could not tell the whole story.

"Move on," ordered Guard Octavius, actually removing his sword. Guard Mucius followed suit. The diggers stopped for a moment. Bloodshed appeared imminent. Talor started to move forward with a shovel. Dim placed a hand out to steady the young man.

Ionnes smiled at the two guards - an old man in chains. Not like he presented any sort of threat.

"I came to pay last respects," he told the guards. The guards both laughed and were incredulous. Dim and Talor looked at each other questioningly.

"I said, 'Move on,'" Guard Octavius re-commanded, raising his sword.

Ionnes seemed to not hear him nor notice the guards at all. He knelt on the dirt beside the deceased and closed his eyes for a long minute. His mouth muttered what sounded like Hebrew to the guards. The guards were not big on patience, but this held some intrigue. Then, Ionnes touched the dead man. Almost immediately, his chest moved as it refilled with air. Gallo gradually turned his head towards the sky, slowly exhaling and drawing in another deep breath behind little gasps. The sickly blue colors throughout his body started to fade and change to red. He gulped another breath, and another. The other five watching gasped with horror and disbelief.

"Gallo," greeted Ionnes.

Gallo peered at Ionnes, perplexed, then after a spell saw the others there, settling on Dim. "Wormmm?" he mouthed. His eyes closed wryly. Pain filled his thoughts. "Letmedieagain," he uttered. "Thereisnothingformehere."

Ionnes wanted to invite him to sit up and even to stand, but his discernment suggested otherwise. Listening to the Spirit, he said, "Yeshua, the Jewish Messiah, has raised you. You are brought back to Earth by His holy name."

Gallo looked at Ionnes. He understood but said nothing. Ionnes continued, "He does not want you to die in darkness. Ask, and He will give you eternal life."

Gallo closed his eyes. A tear appeared on the lower left side.

"ThankYouYeshua," he whispered. "Forgiveme. Bringme home." Then, he turned his head away and his breath again left him.

Ionnes watched him a moment longer as his pink features waned. The old, bound man then struggled to stand, and saying a final, "Amen," turned to go.

"What was that?" demanded Guard Mucius, smacking the old man side the head with the flat side of his sword blade.

"I did not want him to die to eternal darkness or Hellfire."

Mucius responded angrily, swinging his large sword across Ionnes' gut, running him through. Ionnes cringed, spilling his entrails on the ground before him, then gasped as the pain filled him to overflowing. He crumpled into a heap, in total pain but praising God in everything. Then, he rested in lifeless relief. Mucius pushed the dead body beside Gallo's.

"Keep digging," he shouted towards Dim and Talor. "Looks like we will need a bigger hole."

About that moment, Mucius awoke from his daydream and with Guard Octavius, watched the old man in chains and Teos return to the trail to continue on their way.

Speechless is Speechless, and that is all a person can say about it.

Passing through Phora, the town was now alive and open for business. Ionnes greeted various shopkeepers and shoppers throughout the Acropolis Kastelli. Their response was typically cold and barely civil if at all. Most folks parted to let them pass with ample room on the narrow streets. He spied a lame woman across the square, begging near the gate. He started to go towards her when some adolescents raced around him, taunting him and spitting on him. He thought of Elisha and held his tongue. There probably were no bears to be summoned on Patmos, female or otherwise.

He then recalled Yeshua and the twelve heading for Ierusalem. They passed through a part of Samaria. It always seemed odd for Ionnes, back when he walked with Yeshua, to keep his judgments of Samaritans in check. Yeshua, growing up in Nazareth, had been taught like everyone else that the Samaritans were their lessers and to not associate with them. Somehow Yeshua totally shed that practice, but it still plagued the rest of the apostles the first year or two.

The most direct route between Galilee and Iudea took them straight through Samaria. They knew another main road between Galilee and Iudea around Samaria, or they could have detoured over the Jordan to go through Perea, but Yeshua seemed focused on getting to Ierusalem as fast as their feet would take them.

The Samaritans were thrilled to have Yeshua there. They asked Him to stay. He declined only because He had to get to Ierusalem. Ionnes saw their faces. Another rejection from a Jew. Typical. Begone Yeshua the Jew.

Then, just about that moment when a man thinks he has overcome his prejudices and foolish hates, Ionnes and his older brother Yaakov slid right back into old habits.

"Lord," Yaakov said, "do you want us to command fire to come down from Heaven and consume them?"

"Just as Elijah did?" added Ionnes. Ionnes liked adding that last line. It was so copacetic to do great things like Elijah or one of the other prophets.

"NO!" answered Yeshua, rebuking both of them. "You do not know what manner of spirit you are of…"

Ionnes suddenly felt more like Jonah than Elijah.

"…For the Son of Man did not come to destroy men's lives but to save them." And, they went on a little more silently to the next village while Yaakov and Ionnes wondered what spirit still plagued them like a cold that kept hanging on and would not get better or a nasty habit they had both tried to overcome yet continued to dwell deeply within each of them. Yeshua did not even stop to wipe the dust from His feet.

As expected, the low clouds had begun to thin out promising another warm, sunny spring day. Beyond the Acropolis, heading down towards the water, Ionnes and Teos passed by two temples to Artemis and Apollo. Ionnes watched the priests and patrons seated and chatting on the marble. A sculpture of Apollo stood amidst a still fountain. The temple prostitutes would still be in bed. They passed without notice, entering narrow streets between whitewashed buildings. Teos moved away from the road to the beach, leading to undeveloped coastline. Four other men stood waist deep in water tending the salt ropes. Ionnes had heard of the salt ropes before but had never seen them. Strong ropes dipped in salt water, then left to dry, then dipped a second time, pulled up, left to dry, then dipped again and dried and dipped and dried however many times it took to make the rope a formidable saw, strong enough to cut and shape marble. The ropes could be retreated at least a few more times after they lost their salt.

The salt ropers always watched the sky. The morning sun promised a blessing. Rain the opposite as they always packed the salt ropes safely away before the rains came. Coastal salting was easy duty compared with cutting the rock; an enviable position, and one not typically assigned to newcomers - even eighty-something year old newcomers.

Ionnes was shown the ropes as Teos ran back to the quarry. The old apostle sang hymns of praise as he learned to braid rope, then dip it thoroughly in the sea and lay it out on the rocks to dry. He had grown up to work the sea. In that fashion, he enjoyed the duties given him. He felt the merriness of one whose hands belonged in the water. At times, words of praise and thanksgiving flowed from his lips. The other workers and Roman guards thought him a daft old man.

"Too bad the Dead Sea is so far," Ionnes suddenly spoke quite aloud. "We would get these done in less than half the time."

One or two may have nodded, but none answered or otherwise acknowledged. They were puppets. They were not allowed to think. Thinking brought them trouble. This newcomer needed to learn that and quickly. That was Lesson Number One. And, Lesson Number Two took too much brain power if he was still thinking and ignoring Lesson Number One.

Whips came down to quiet the newbie. Ionnes again encountered the old, familiar sting. He'd been a prisoner on and off over the years and knew the lash by some guards more than others. Even a new arrival could recognize the more cruel and sadistic guards. They were the only ones happy to be on Patmos where they were free to inflict pain any time, day or night. Sometime around midafternoon while the sun was still quite high, Ionnes stood waist deep in the surf, a salt rope in his hands. He heard a faint yell from up shore. Looking around, he eventually saw a man near the hill holding his left leg. He kept yelling. Others joined him. Ionnes also left the water to attend if needed, tossing the rope on the beach beside the others. Approaching, he saw the man full of fear and agony.

"I am going to die," screamed the victim frantically, holding his leg and rocking back and forth; his face a freakish mask. The Roman guard grabbed a young jack rabbit of a man named Atticus and said, "Flee. Bring Dim." The boy immediately obeyed and shot up the hill towards town and the quarry.

"Quintus, stop being an infant," scolded the guard. "Didja see the snake?"

Quintus looked up at the guard like he did not even know he was there. Tearfully, he nodded.

"Describe it."

"Gray body. Black markings crisscrossed on its back."

"Coastal viper," assessed the guard. "Good thing. If a cobra, you would already be dead." The Roman guard looked at two other prisoners. "Put him in the water. It may dilute the venom a bit."

Two grabbed the young man, standing him up. Each placed an arm around their shoulders and brought him down to the surf. He hopped along on his unbitten leg. Just over knee deep with the surf washing back and forth a bit, they tried to wash the leg with briny water and squeeze out a bit of the poison.

Before they even left the water, the victim started to feel nauseous. Bringing him out of the water, they laid him on the rocky beach. He turned to his side to hold his stomach, eyes closed, fear still totally present. No one knew what else to do.

Ionnes knelt beside him praying.

"Back to work," yelled the guard, not just to Ionnes.

Ionnes placed a hand on the young man as he committed him to Adonai's ever-present love. He rose, acknowledged the guard and returned to his rope and the sea.

Another half hour passed before Atticus reappeared with Dim some distance behind him. Dim spied the situation. All of the other prisoners stopped working to watch. Some came closer to 'help' if needed. Dim knelt beside Quintus, looking a bit more bloated. He recognized the effects of the venom and placed a hand in Quintus' dark, curly hair, stroking it a bit. It was not quite as sweetly relaxing as Dim had hoped for his fingers occasionally snagged Quintus' large curls.

"Relax," he urged. "Ya have t' relax."

Quintus tried, but fear still gripped him tightly.

"Relax yer muscles," pressed Dim. "Calm yer heart. Yer agitation will kill you."

That got through and Quintus took a deep breath, then another and another to relax.

"This is terrible, but ya have t' do it," Dim told him and moved him to lie quietly on his back.

"Open yer mouth."

Quintus did so.

"Wider."

Wider.

"Wider. Far as ya can open it."

Quintus questioned him with his eyes but complied as Dim continued to stroke his hair.

"Perfect," applauded Dim, a bit of spittle escaping down the side of his mouth.

Suddenly, with one coordinated motion, Dim grabbed hold of Quintus' hair in one hand and his beard in the other and hawked a huge ball of spit in Quintus' mouth, aiming for the back of his throat.

Quintus gasped and tried to spit it out, but Dim held his mouth and yelled, "Swallow it! It is antivenom. It will help & probably save yer life." Peripherally, Dim saw the guard turn away and squirm.

Quintus tried to swallow, but repulsion kept it lodged and oozing down the back of his soft palate.

"Pretend ya jus' kissed a maiden. Nothin' bad 'bout that. &, RELAX, RELAX, RELAX! Fightin' me spreads the venom thru yer whole body."

Quintus snorted through his nose but forced the vile antidote down his throat.

Dim rose. He read the guard's face. "I been bitten by coastal vipers four times since I been here. They tell me my spit become an antivenom."

The guard spied him with a look of disbelief. "Well, if I am bitten, you may never do that to me. I would rather die." The two men nodded. Dim smiled to himself. He felt the same way the first time someone did it to him.

An old man standing by added, "We took him down to the surf to wash out the wound and clean out the venom."

Dim spoke plainly as he answered, "Not a good choice. The more ya move him other than completely carry him, the more the venom moves thru his body. Ya probably washed it with yer fingers as well?"

"Well, not me," answered the old man.

Dim looked at the other faces. One nodded yes.

"Massagin' the wound also spreads the venom."

No one dared say, "The guard told me to," but every one of them thought it.

Then, Dim noticed Ionnes. It took him right back to that morning and seeing Gallo come back for that minute. He visibly shook, head to toe, from the memory.

"Pack it in," yelled another guard walking down beach.

"You. You," pointed the first guard. "Get a stretcher and take snake bite to his bed."

"&, make sure he drinks plenty o' water all night," said Dim, (then, "if he lives," to himself).

They did as ordered as the others stowed gear for the night. Dim stayed to help, remaining close to Ionnes. He had worked the salt ropes on and off over the years and could say the newcomer needed training. Of course, he mostly needed to ask this old man about the morning miracle.

"Ionnes," said Ionnes.

"Dimetrius," answered Dim, coiling a rope. "They call me Dim."

"Where are you from?" asked Ionnes.

"Pergamos,"

"Ah," smiled Ionnes. "I have been there many times."

"&, you?"

"Ephesus."

"Ya do not sound like a Greek from Ephesus."

Ionnes laughed. "You are right, my friend. I am from Capernaum."

"Capernaum?" thought Dim a moment then queried, "A Jew?"

"Yes, - and more."

As the sun began its last hour of daylight, the prisoners were escorted to the barracks, shackled and sent to the penal colony for dinner and sleep. They shuffled up from the sea for the evening trek. One man's chain snagged on a rock and he almost fell. Some near him laughed.

"One would think you would have learned by now," one chided.

"Shut up," came the tripper's reply and pushed his friend. It was not long before Dim said to Ionnes, "That was amazin' this mornin'."

"Yeshua's plan is always amazing," replied Ionnes. "I mean," stressed Dim, "Gallo was dead. I know. I had t' carry him t' the cem'tary with Talor. The Roman swine..." Dim turned his head to make sure the guard was out of earshot. He lucked out this time. It surprised him, being so careless. He certainly knew better than to be that foolish and reckless.

"Ev'ry time someone dies, they make us carry the bodies & souls of men almost two miles while they ride horses. We even had t' carry our shovels & pickaxe. No way they would make one o' their precious horses carry a body."

"Tells you how much they value you, does it?" acknowledged Ionnes.

"Totally," answered Dim. "But, I still wanna know how ya did it?"

Ionnes smiled as they shuffled along slowly.

"I did nothing. I am only a vessel for Theos' mighty power."

"Like a channel?"

Ionnes knew the word to be technically correct, but he steered away from it because of its regular use with idol worshipers.

"Not exactly," he answered. "More like a dance."

Dim did not expect that answer or comparison.

Ionnes continued, "To channel is to be used by whatever power is passed through you. Theos is love, and we are His children, so He would never merely channel His power and grace. He touches us and lives within us, so His power manifests itself when He is one with us and we are one with Him. A dance."

Dim admitted, "Well, I still know not how ya did it, but it blew me away more than a desert scirocco."

Ionnes laughed. "Yes, yes," he agreed. "and hopefully it will always touch you that way. I assure you, it does me."

"Can we expect any more surprises in the near future?" Ionnes shrugged. "That is not for me to know until it is revealed by His Spirit."

Dim repeated those words to himself but suspected he did not really know what they meant. "Seen anyone else brought back to life?"

Ionnes nodded. "Yeshua," he first said aloud. "And Jarius' daughter. And, the widow's son at Nain. Many others. And Lazarus." He paused. *Lazarus.*

"We were out in the wilderness. Yeshua was telling us more about the kingdom of Theos.

"Yeshua liked hilltops. It is true. He would go help the people in the towns and He would walk through the groves and He would row across the Sea of Galilee, but when He came to the quiet with us twelve, He would often pick a hilltop. Lots of sun. Good view of everything around you. Hard for someone to sneak-up on you.

"He wanted to talk about Heaven one day. We all knew He was Messiah."

"What is a Messiah?"

Ionnes thought a moment. "Christos. An anointed one. A person promised by Theos to bring deliverance to the world. We knew Him as Messiah who came to us from Heaven. This was one of those times when a 'Witness of One' was quite enough. Most sufficient.

"Not like His baptism. I wish I had been there. You know how they say a matter must be established by the witness of two or three testimonies?"

Dim nodded. Everyone knew that.

"First, Yeshua came out of the water. Then, the Holy Spirit appeared over Him looking like a dove."

"A dove?" checked Dim.

"You heard me right."

"Why a dove? Why not a eagle or a owl? Or another animal? Or even His own form?"

Ionnes loved these questions. "Why not?" he answered, knowing that answer razzed the asker. "Okay, quick answer," Ionnes said. "First, Theos is Spirit. We cannot typically see Spirit with our own eyes, so His own form would not work. But, Theos is also Creator. He made all this." Ionnes stomped on the ground with his sandals. "So, He could choose to look like whatever He wants. Why choose a dove? Because it is not aggressive. You would not fear a dove so much as one of the predators you named. And, the dove points to Noah."

"Who is Noah?"

Ionnes ribbed himself when he sometimes forgot he was talking to a very pagan Greek and not a Jew.

"You recall mention of a great flood that destroyed the Earth many, many centuries past?"

"Perhaps."

"Noah built a large boat - an ark. Theos placed all the animals on it, one male and one female, then flooded the Earth with rain. After many days of floating on the water, Noah sent out a dove which came back with an olive branch in its beak. That showed him that the water was receding, and since then the dove has been a symbol of peace and promise for the Jews. So, He appeared as a real dove and alit onto Yeshua.

"Then, Abba Theos spoke from the clouds above. Three witnessses to the truth, and for that matter, I could include Yochanan the Baptist and lots of others. That was three years before Lazarus.

"So, now it is three years later. The previous week, we had to leave Ierusalem. Yeshua told the Jewish leaders and priests, 'The Father and I are One.' Woah! The priests and Jewish leaders violently shook like lightnings, noises, thunderings and earthquake and great hail all in one. They definitely understood Yeshua's inference. Flesh begets flesh. Spirit begets Spirit. They grabbed stones to kill him. If He had just said, 'The Father and I are One in purpose or mission or duty,' nobody would have gotten upset, but that is not what He said, and He had to make an escape for His time had not yet come..." He trailed off, gazing down.

"Take ye heed. Watch and pray, for ye know not when the time is." His face showed he was very far away.

Dim waited as they slowly walked. The sounds of their chains kept cadence.

"You were right, Ionnes Marcos." Ionnes sighed one more time, then looked up towards Dim and their surroundings.

"Who is Ionnes Marcos?"

"Later," smiled Ionnes. "I will get off track again.

"So, where was I? That is right. We departed Ierusalem and went a ways from the city. I believe we were still in Iudea, but it is not that far from Samaria. The wilderness is the wilderness, and I really did not care where the hill was from. Yeshua talked to us about Heaven. You know, for all that He said about Heaven, I still have a feeling or belief that when I die, I will still get to Theos' Kingdom and say, 'Wow! This is not at all how I imagined it.'"

He laughed at himself and shook his head, then continued.

"We saw a friend named Isaac coming up the hill to us. He went straight to Yeshua to report that the one Yeshua loved was dying. To be honest, most of us, including myself, did not hear Isaac's message until later. He stayed with us for the night, so we learned Lazarus was dying, then Isaac headed down the next day. It was really good to see him again.

"We stayed another day, then another. We had enough food to stay there over another week at least, but then Yeshua said that it was time to go.

"As I recall, we had one major objection. They had tried to stone Him in Ierusalem just days earlier, and now He decided to go back. We were like children to Him, but still felt a desire to protect Him.

"Then, He told us Lazarus was sleeping. With Isaac's report of his sickness, Bartholomew suggested sleep would do more good than a bunch of us invading his home. I still laugh at us. We were so dense. So thick headed. It is truly the eighth wonder of the world that Yeshua kept all of us the entire three years and thereafter. Notably and totally, we were there for Him. Not like Moses who had a huge number of rebellious and uncooperative followers. Is that not a strange expression – 'rebellious and uncooperative followers'? If they are uncooperative or rebellious, how are they followers?"

"Who is Moses?" asked Dim, then wanted to rescind his question so he could hear the rest of the Lazarus story.

Ionnes nodded. Later for Moses, too.

"I also scold myself," continued Ionnes. "Yeshua healed so many people. I cannot begin to count how many. I am certain He healed some while we were not there. People born blind could then see. A woman with an issue of blood for like twelve years just touched his cloak and He felt healing power go out of Him. So, when He said, 'Let us go see our sick friend,' you would think even one of us had a clue, but somehow we did not. We were such knuckleheads.

"Then, Yeshua said it plainly to us. 'Lazarus is dead.' I recall wondering how He knew. Isaac was long gone. Nobody else came to us with that message. Like I just said, we really could be so thick headed.

"I also recall that lump in my throat almost gagged me when He said Lazarus was dead. I loved him, too. We all did. We were all concerned about being stoned or arrested or who knows what not, but we also knew that we had to see our friend – and see to Martha and Maryam. Lazarus' two spinster sisters had opened their home to us so many times. We had to go.
"For the most part, I loved Jewish ways. I still do. You may not think so, but I know Jews to be a rare and wonderful people. Still, there is one practice that always irritates me and that is the mourners. They came to your home, ate your bread and fish and figs and whatever else and yelled loudly, over and over, mourning whomever it is in your home who died. They

50

did not love Lazarus. I expect some did not even know him at all, but they are there creating this cacophony of artificial travail at a time when many want to be alone with family and close friends to grieve. The Jews really can be the most honest people but may ignore honesty and consideration with this foolish practice.

"So, we approached Bethany. The "House of Figs" is usually a delight this time of year. Then, we stopped by a well near town and Yeshua sent two of us to Martha and Maryam's home. One delivered the message to Martha and one stayed with Maryam while the other brought Martha back to Yeshua. You could see by her face she had not slept much over the last few days.

Yeshua greeted her with a hug. He seemed so sad - not like Him. Very emotional and shaken.

"Martha accepted His words of comfort. I ever chide myself, even to this day, how often Yeshua would tell us something really amazing and we either thought He meant something totally different or we saw it as a bad or even dangerous decision. "I still make that mistake, by the way. For all my years with Him and then Him sending the Paraclete and all these decades gone by still serving Abba Theos, Yeshua and His church, I still totally misunderstand His lessons and directions more often than I think I should. Not always, but it is not unusual."

Dim wondered about the Parakeet but said nothing.

"I recall laughing appreciably the first time I read Paulos' letter to Corinth. 'The wisdom of men is foolishness to God' and vice versa. 'Yessiree!' I prayed and gave a few sermons over the next year specifically on that very subject. But, I am also sad I never got to see Paulos after I read that. He was already in Roma. He was technically a prisoner, but lived in a comfortable, little villa and had regular visitors. You know how it is. He had been under someone's lock and key before. This was nothing new or unusual. He had received thirty-nine lashings five times, I believe, if memory serves. We totally expected him to sail away from Roma some day. No one was more stunned and saddened than I when I heard Paulos had been beheaded by Nero. I had put off coming to see him many times and wept when I heard and could not be consoled for some days."

"Ya loved Paulos?" asked Dim.

"Just as much as I disliked him. He mellowed or matured or something his latter years, but before that he could be quite unbearable. It is no coincidence you never heard of Paulos traveling around Greece and Asia Minor without one of us original eleven apostles. We were very impressed by him and he helped the church grow in places and ways we had not yet imagined. His example inspired all of us. When Yeshua gave us His final commandment to baptize in His name to the ends of the Earth, Paulos went farther from Ierusalem than any of us up to that point. He also brought offerings from Macedonia and Aigeira - no, that is wrong. Not Aigeira. From where? Um. Um, Achaia. That is it. Macedonia and Achaia, brought to the disciples in Ierusalem. My brother Yaakov was in charge then, but I was also there when the men brought in a king's ransom to help the persecuted church in Ierusalem.

"Still, if there is one thing I could change, it would be to go to Roma to see Paulos before he was killed. Then, Yeshua's Holy Spirit reminded me why He did not send me to Roma. Good chance I also would have been arrested and detained.

"Wow!" said Ionnes, stopping and looking at Dim with self bemusement and stupefaction. "I am so far off topic. More of 'the foolishness of men', eh? Forgive me. Was not I talking about Lazarus?

"So, um, Martha left and Yeshua sent for Maryam. Martha returned to their home and Maryam ran out to meet Him, still by the well. Martha and Maryam really loved their brother, of course. He took such good care of them and saw to their needs. As I recall, He resisted Yeshua when first they met. Typical Jewish stubbornness. I could shake my finger at Lazarus (and others), if I was not so much like them.

"We waited by the well. Some prayed. Some prophesied. Some fixed lunch. Then, we saw Maryam running towards us with the mourners following. I was saying, 'Oh no,' but Yeshua seemed glad for the crowd. Not that He was happy. I have seen Yeshua come and go from indignant to angry to joyous jubilation to silly jokes to transfigured radiance, but I never had seen Him weep more than He wept for Lazarus, except at Gethsemane just a few nights later. He did not weep even once when they flogged Him and the Romans are not inclined to stop at thirtynine lashings. That is a Jewish standard. I was not there and know not how many times He was whipped. Yeshua did not weep during the trial nor when carrying His cross nor when they hung Him upon the cross. But, he wept for Lazarus, such is His love.

"Cephas put an arm around Him to console Him and Maryam. But, just the opposite happened and big, brawny Cephas - the 'Rock' we called him, a hearty and manly fisherman also cried like a hungry baby. Then, my brother Yaakov joined them. Then, I and others and we all wept for Lazarus. "Yeshua said, 'Show me where he was buried.'

"As you know, people get buried very quickly, especially during warmer days and seasons of the year. Get them in the ground before they start to stink. It does not take long.

"We trekked together to the grave caves. We were all amazed when Yeshua said, 'Remove the stone.' Someone four days dead was going to be a ripe and bloated stench. I did not want to, but I was the youngest apostle so went to move the stone."

"How old were ya?" asked Dim.

"Twenty-three. Andrew and I together pushed the large stone aside and yes, putrescence. Made me want to puke. I would like to say we all knew what was going to happen by that time, but to be completely and bluntly honest, Dimetrius, I believe none of us truly saw it coming.

"Yeshua approached the cave. Tears were still wetting His eyes and He could hardly see at times. He wiped them away and others immediately appeared. He closed both eyes, squeezed tight, like He was in great pain. Everyone of us watched Him intently. Looking back, I think only Maryam really had a clue.

"Then, He relaxed a bit. His eyes opened. The pain and grieving began to drain. He took a deep breath, found His voice and shouted towards the cave, 'Lazarus, Come Forth!' I recall peripherally seeing just about everyone turn towards the cave entrance. It was dark in there - darker because of the bright sunlight around us, but I detected some movement and a moment later Lazarus emerged.

"You wanna talk about a Spirit of elation coming upon us like a cloudburst. Everyone saw it but few quickly believed it. And, there was poor, old Lazarus, stiff from being dead a few days, wrapped head to foot with like another fifty pounds of embalming spices in his linens.

'Unwrap him,' ordered Yeshua. I was right there by the cave, so I helped remove the cloth wrapped around him. He looked a bit haggard but had good color. No blue at all. I did not say anything, but he still stunk. I expect a bath never felt so good.

"Yeshua welcomed him with a bear hug. Martha and Maryam went to him, weeping new tears of joy. Oddly, or at least I thought it odd at the time, most of the mourners left. Their reason to be there suddenly ended. If I wanted to be loud and obnoxious about anything, it would be for a man's recreated life. Now that is a reason to shout and shake rafters. And, we all went back to Martha and Maryam's and had a party. Lazarus did not stay late, I noticed. Apparently, four days of death takes a lot out of a person."

Ionnes looked at Dim. It was obvious the Greek prisoner did not believe a word he was saying. He was about to assure Dim of his authenticity, when he suddenly remembered something he had not thought about for quite some years.

"I just remembered," he began. "Something. It was around six years after Yeshua died, resurrected and ascended."

"Yeshua died, resurrected & ascended?" asked Dim.

"Yes," glowed Ionnes, "and that is another excellent story you will want to hear. But I just recalled a Roman named Matthias who was on some sort of investigation to find the body of Yeshua. He even questioned me at length. At one point, he was convinced Yeshua lay in the vacant grave of Lazarus. He pushed aside the large stone all by himself - an impressive task.

You could tell he was not used to physical labor."

"So, did he find Yeshua's body in there?"

Ionnes seemed to not hear, then turned toward Dim.

"Of course not. Not at all. Not at all. There is no body to find. Well, almost. The grave was for Lazarus' family. Some other older family members were there long before Lazarus. Lazarus teased Yeshua a few times thereafter – 'Good thing You did not call out their names.'"

<>< ><> <>< ><> <>< ><> <>< ><> <>< ><>

The road took them back through the middle of Phora. The day's light seemed to hang around a little longer than usual that eve as they migrated through the center of the settlement. The towns folks were well accustomed to the evening line of convicts shuffling through their town. To them, the prisoners could have been a herd of three toed sloths slowly moving and bothering none. Just so long as they kept moving.

Ionnes was surprised to notice most of his fellow prisoners spitting near the Temple of Artemis. To them, was not this her island? Then, she could take the blame for them being there. If she was the goddess of virginity, then she is the one responsible for their involuntary chastity.

Approaching the Acropolis, Ionnes saw numerous men and women exiting. Most dressed in finery, it appeared they had attended a civic banquet of some sort. With usual practice, they ignored the prisoners. Their slaves likewise spurned the prisoners. Some slaves attended to their masters who had had a little too much wine. Some slaves brought horses and carts to transport their masters. Some drivers would bring their carts dangerously close to the prisoners as a boast - to make them move out of their way. It was truly an amazing arrogance, even for a slave, for there is always an interesting and intriguing social ladder when one encounters arrogant slaves. Depending on whom they belonged to, they could likewise shun Roman soldiers. And, every slave on Earth wanted to shun Roman soldiers. Ionnes shuffled along with the rest but studied the people as he entered the town square. No head down like the others. He was very tired from his day of labor but wanted to absorb and remember each and every face for when he might meet them at a later time. Stuck in a cell or chained to a boat, he had not had to work like that for quite some time. He expected dinner awaited up the hill and realized he did not even know where he would be sleeping.

"I have not been assigned a bed," he alerted Dim.

"Yes, you have," corrected Dim. "Same barracks we all get locked in for the night.

"Perfect," said Ionnes as they began to pass the townsfolk.

"I cannot wait to get home," said one middle-aged woman to her husband. "My hair pin has poked me all evening."

"Did you kill all the beetles?" asked another man to his slave.

The slave nodded affirmation.

"If I find one beetle in my chambers, that is all you will be eating for a week."

"Where is our chariot?" demanded a portly matron. "Philo has been late all week. You will absolutely have to have him flogged when we get home."

"The wine is not as good as last year," noted a man in full toga.

His friend placed his hand on a shoulder and leaned in close. "I already told you the grape crop is not as good this year as previous years."

"Well, then you shall come by my estate tomorrow. I made some almond nectar like you have never before tasted."

A bright shooting star flashed from the western dusk to the eastern dark sky. Those who saw it reacted favorably, regardless of rank or social status. Zeus glowed brighter in the southwest sky than an Ægean sparkle. Yellow Cronus would faintly appear later for the stargazers and astrologists.

"Jupiter was afraid of fire before Prometheus got to him," someone said. "Remember when Olympus caught fire? That was the first time Jupiter touched off a spark. Bolts would come later."

"Please hold your tongue," said his sister, a woman barely past the beauty of her youth.

"Like this?" he mumbled, both hands attached to his mouth.

"Brother!" she said a bit more forcefully.

He let go of his tongue with one hand to slap hard the top of his head repeatedly - something he did when his sister ordered him to behave.

"Oh yeah," he continued, still slapping his head, "Jupiter would not have even a candlelight dinner with Juno before Prometheus got involved. But then Juno loved Jupiter more than Jupiter loved Juno when you consider his lovers and trysts. It is a wonder they are still together. Good thing they are immortal.

I expect they would have killed each other by now."

"Apollonides!" she pressed, tugging him by the arm to try to get him home.

"Fret not," assured a man in purple. "A man is prone to say things when he has had too much wine."

"Wine!" spun Apollonides towards the man in purple.

"Wine?" He smiled and held up an imaginary goblet. "I only drink wine when the clams tell me. Do not you love their little tongues, the precious hatchlings? You should see how they hold theirs." He drank the rest of his mimed wine, sticking out his tongue to get the last tasty drops. The man in purple shook disapprovingly, then turned towards another figure exiting the Acropolis.

"Governor," he bowed. Others also turned to give their respects and salutes as Governor Laurentius entered the square accompanied by Myron and Fona, his in-laws, and Makrinos, his proconsul.

"Problem?" asked the Governor.

"Just the usual," answered his wife, Chryspippe. "Apollonides showing off."

"The devil!" declared the Governor.

"The devil?" Apollonides repeated loudly from within the sea of bodies. He stretched out his arms and twirled around and around, running into patrons, slaves and even prisoners.

Ionnes came close enough to smell his spikenard and alum. Myron tried to catch his son, but the younger, sprier man flew away on the wind.

"Devil! Devil! Devil! Devil!" yelled Apollonides. "I am a dust devil. Spin me around baby tornado. Only when one lies in the eye of the tornado and looks up can he see Isis." He continued his tour, bouncing off anything in his path, living or static.

"Apollonides!" commanded the Governor by just the one word of his name.

Apollonides stopped and started slapping his head again, harder and harder. Tears came to his eyes. He ripped his tunic practically in half and shouted, "No! No! No! I am not a fig. She is! She is the chrysolite fig." He pointed to a woman in green.

"Get him home," commanded the governor to his slaves.

"I recommend chains," said the Roman Proconsul Makrinos impatiently, looking down upon the entire episode.

The servants went to grab hold of Apollonides who docilely remained seated on the stone square. As they picked him up, he wriggled his feet in the air and yelled, "Look everyone. I fly like Mercury. And, I am the messenger. I brought all of you here. Not my father or my brother or my sister or Roma itself. I am the reason you are here. And, I am the reason you may stay."

His voice grew hoarse from shrieking louder and louder. "Everyday I sweep the sand and rock up from the surf so Patmos will not slip into the sea."

He writhed and struggled to be free of his detainers.

"I shaved Hercules when he was not looking and I will do the same to you."

Suddenly, he broke free and rolled under legs and carts, springing up near Ionnes and Dim. He stopped to look at the old man, adding, "Today I dug my grave on the beach, then realized I am too young to use it. So, I give it to you." He looked towards Dim. "And you, too."

The slaves grabbed hold again. This time he did not immediately resist. Chryspippe approached her brother and placed a hand on his cheek. It was an old technique - one she had used since they were teens. It used to work. Not so much in recent years.

"You should have your thyroid checked," he said to his sister. "I will get you some pomegranate. And pillars of gray salt."

"Father is here," assured Chryspippe. "Let us go home and we will share our stories with father."

Apollonides smiled, then said, "He told me I was fat, so I ate him." He started laughing uncontrollably, even with the firm hold of the slaves. "Something I learned from Saturn," he added almost unintelligibly and once again suddenly spun out of their hands with amazing strength and verve. His escape replayed, he grabbed a knife from Makrinos' belt and put it to this throat.

Makrinos stepped back to distance himself from any potential stabbing, but then smiled with approval to see Apollonides begin slashing his own throat. Laughing and crying at the same time, Apollonides looked at Chryspippe and threw her a kiss, ready to plunge the blade into his throat. Just then, a single word crossed the city square, bouncing off the whitewashed walls.

"WAIT!"

Everyone in the square stopped as if the order was directed personally to each and every one of them. Even the governor stopped and waited. Makrinos said either, "Do it," or "Knew it," disapprovingly, only to himself.

Apollonides froze as though he could not move his arm. Or, his other arm. Or his legs. Or even swivel his head.

The old prisoner Ionnes, gray and dirty, with chaffed wrists and ankles from being chained all day, approached Apollonides. The young man saw the prisoner. He started to speak, but instead dropped the dagger and fell to his knees, eyes never leaving the old man's.

Chryspippe watched her brother. She wanted to go to his side, but felt the deep, mysterious compulsion to watch, wait and see.

Myron waited next to his son-in-law. He did not even know why. Everyone stood where they were. Patrons. Slaves. Prisoners. Even the Roman guards, each enthralled by the episode as it played out. Only a lilting spring breeze seemed to measure the passage of time around them.

Ionnes words were direct. He did not shout, but all there could hear.

"Demon, in the name of Christos Yeshua, depart from him and leave this island."

Apollonides began to shake and shiver and shudder, becoming more and more violent. It lasted maybe half a minute but seemed like a teeny eternity.

"Ahhhrrrrr!" he shouted, gasping loudly and succinct, then fell forward, kissing the pavement, breathing hard like a man purposely refusing to die.

Ionnes knelt beside him and placed a manacled hand against the young man's back. Apollonides heard the music of the chains singing behind him. Chryspippe found her feet and joined Ionnes, also kneeling beside her brother. She glanced at Ionnes with puzzlement, then placed her arms and attention around her brother.

Others also moved around them, mostly to get a better look.

"M'God!" muttered Dim, not realizing the total significance of his words. He knew they were crossing the lines and disobeying the rules and whatever else, but at that moment he really did not care. The crowd around them whispered to each other in amazement, or thought they whispered.

Apollonides' panting abated as he started to raise his hind half. Shoulders and head followed, and he took seat on the pavement, one leg folded down; the other leg folded up.

"Apollonides?" beckoned Chryspippe, now stooping to hold her gown off the pavement. Some strands of her preened hair had come undone in the episode.

He looked at his sister and smiled - a tired, haggard smile like one who has just completed a long trek on foot, or like one whose fever finally broke. The strange marathon completed, he felt weak. Streaks of sweat on his brow and forehead and upper cheeks already showed signs of drying by the breeze. His breathing came and went in long, deep breaths.

"Sister," he finally said and leaned his head against her. She cuddled and cradled him and he accepted her loving caresses. Ionnes stood and backed away, praising God with manacled hands raised. Dim felt like he should be doing something but had no idea what.

"Apollonides?" Their father, Myron, strode up to lean towards the couple. Fona stood back behind her husband a bit, keeping her distance.

They broke embrace and Chryspippe stood.

"How do you feel, my boy?"

Apollonides hung his head forward, then up as he smiled at his father. "I feel good, papa. Better than I have felt for a long, long time." He slowly stood to face his father full on, placed a hand on his shoulder and said, "I am very sorry. I know not who I was, and I wish never to be again." The two men hugged, father and son alike.

Chryspippe looked around. Her husband, the Governor, remained aloof as the drama unfolded. She knew that to be typical, yet she could also tell that he seemed pleased with the changes. He certainly could be a very hard man, but this time looked at her with patience and loving relief.

The sounds of silence broke by voices exiting the Acropolis.

"I pulled him from the sea as easily as one collects shells," boasted Kynops. "His escape was as easily thwarted as one swats a fly or mosquito." He waved his hand flamboyantly before his face. "Begone knave." He stood that much taller. "And, take not my personal boat. The dolphins brought him back to me and tossed him on the beach by my command."

The two men laughed, then saw everyone looking at them. Kynops quickly felt a sense of pride well up. All eyes were on him - like one would behave for the governor. Or Cæsar himself if ever he ventured to their small island.

Then, he spied Dim - the one he had sent away last night. He narrowed his eyes towards the lowly prisoner, standing next to another very old prisoner he had never before seen. That man stood with hands raised and praising God. Kynops thought his pose ridiculous - a shackled man praising some broken deity. The thought was too delicious. He would have to exploit that vision sometime.

Then, he noticed Governor Laurentius. And Proconsul Makrinos sporting his usual frown. And Myron. And Chryspippe, and Apollonides with his tunic half ripped to shreds.

"Typical," he shrugged to himself - the crazy son of Myron. Nothing new, but then, even in the twilight and public torches, he could tell something differed. Apollonides seemed calm. And, quiet. He stood by his father and sister.

"Kynops," then called Apollonides and approached him.

"Since I am cured, I must also apologize to you for my behavior."

"Cured?" questioned Kynops, brow furrowed. "How? By whom?"

"By the old prisoner," answered Myron.

Kynops peered at the young man with firm, confident acknowledgement, but was actually somewhat puzzled. He thought of the old Jewish Rabbi. He knew not most of their names, nor cared to for he was the great Kynops, the Magician of Patmos. He and he alone ruled the spirits that dwelt there.

Then, his eyes returned to the old prisoner with hands raised. He scoffed his disapproval at such explanation.

"And, why was I not consulted?" he puffed up.

The question proved unexpected, and none knew the answer for that next moment.

"It happened very quickly, before anyone would know it would happen," answered Chryspippe.

Kynops stood very still for a spell. His following movements were very slow and deliberate.

"I am glad for your cure," he spoke. "We shall see if it lasts."

He stared intently at Apollonides a moment, then bowed slightly to the governor to take his leave. Daggers filled his eyes as he departed, staring intently at Ionnes who knew that look and the demons that lived behind it. He felt their presence depart with the magician. Sighing, he looked to Dim. The pair turned to go.

Chryspippe kept eyes on Kynops. She never could trust him. The Greek sorcerer played the part of homage to Cæsar because he liked his head where it stood. He could create much havoc, but still live as a mortal man. She never liked him before and disliked him even more at that moment. Had he not squandered many opportunities to cure Apollonides over the last year and more?

She wrapped an arm around her brother as they moved towards the carriage to take them home. Governor Laurentius placed a supportive hand on Apollonides and a glowing expression of appreciation and love for his wife. She had helped her brother when everyone else thought him a lost cause. She smiled back at her husband as she turned to her parents.

"Good night, papa, mama," she said, giving each a quick kiss and entering the carriage behind her husband. As they took off, she looked for the aged prisoner who had freed her brother. He was not hard to find, still walking away with hands raised in prayer and praise. She wanted to go to him for some reason though she knew not what she might say. And, her husband would never approve. Nor would anyone else there, not that any other rules of etiquette had been followed during the evening's event. What does one wear to an exorcism? Does one serve white wine or red?

Still, she waited and watched as the pair joined the rest of the prisoners and guards and disappeared from sight into the fading twilight of the young night.

PATMOS

CHAPTER 3

The harsh SNAP of the lock always said a cold good night, no matter the weather for the men held within. The stone structure had no windows - only the door. During the summer it could be suffocating. There were small slits at the top of the wall between stone and the wooden eaves supporting the roof. They served as its only circulation and light after the door was locked. The men became adept at moving around in the gloomy, dank room. During the rare occurrence when one of their own entered the room late, the fresh air rushing in for that brief moment from the open door felt better than a rub down after the day's labors.

It had no fireplace or chimney. During the winter it chilled the bones and froze their blood. The men would gather together to share body heat. The guards razzed them in the morning, but it never stopped them. What little coverings they had on their bodies would not keep a krikri warm. The barren ground they slept on sapped the heat from their bodies within the first hour or two, much less all night. Everything within felt cold and got colder as the night plodded along. The ground. The stone. The air. When it rained, the stale, damp air made all worse.

And, that did not account for those who snored worse than a cyclops.

The toilet bucket in the front corner could be gross and sickening, especially during the warm nights.

Complaints were dealt with harshly by their captors, and hence expressed at most with subtle, non-verbal methods.

Entering the encampment, the men dined in the dark. Dim noticed his compadres were quieter than usual. Not that they were prone to chatter, but the air just seemed emptier than usual. Then, he looked at Ionnes. The old man received not the usual silent treatment for new inductees. It seemed more like caution - even fearful reverence. He had certainly made a big splash his first day there.

"Come," said Dim to Ionnes after they had finished eating. The two men entered the cramped cabin to help Ionnes set-up his bed roll before they were locked in for the night. Ionnes, well accustomed to Roman 'hospitality,' appreciated this lodging to be better than any of the prisons in Roma. The spring night air seemed not yet too cold for comfort. His weary, old bones would rest well in <u>this</u> strange place.

"They are scared o' you," said Dim, looking down, unfolding the blanket. He wondered why he helped Ionnes at all. The old man had 'troublemaker' written all over him. One that would be viciously dealt. Any in his company would surely receive the same fate.

"I know," answered Ionnes. "Take heart, my friend. It will not last long."

"Are ya certain?"

Ionnes smiled and nodded in the gloom. Only his semi-white teeth and hair could be seen, lit up by the flecks of moon and star light meekly entering the room. "My God is not a God of fear. He is a God of Love."

"Are ya certain?" joked Dim, not sure what else to say.

"More than you know," assured Ionnes. "More than you know."

They finished the bedroll and proceeded to exit the cabin when, "Bed!" yelled Guard Mucius, now that the men had finished eating.

The men were well familiar with Mucius' one word commands. He only said it once and punished you if you did not respond right away whether you heard or not. The men heard and headed for their respective lodging.

"Julius, you get prettier every time I see you," joked Jack before entering the cabin.

"Move it," ordered Guard Julius, his head jerking towards the cabin. Over a year back, Jack created then accepted the personal challenge to make Julius laugh. The cruel and heartless soldier never smiled, but Jack knew some day he would succeed.

"Moving it as ordered," acknowledged Jack grabbing his rear and heading through the door.

Julius gave the barest of chuckles, then straightened up. The men inside and the door locked, the familiar click announced their incarceration for another night. Some hated that sound at night and preferred the opposite sound in the morning allowing them to take part in the day. They may have been enslaved prisoners, but they still appreciated being needed for the job. The lazier prisoners preferred the nighttime lock. Notably, it felt like the one sanctuary from the guards. It may have been an illusionary impression, but one's illusions commonly helped them deal with the hardships and pains. Still, one fear often tickled the ears of their psyche. What if the cabin caught fire? Stone or not, they would never place their confidence in the Roman guards for their deliverance.

Closed in, they all could die by smoke just as well as fire.

As the footsteps outside announced their relative privacy, whispered conversations began.

"I'm telling you, Guard Mucius has it out for me," griped Minos.

"Mucius has it out for everyone," said Seth. Some uttered affirmation and agreement.

"Is it supposed to rain tomorrow?" wondered Rabbi Yosef. "My joints feel like we shall see rain."

"With a nose like that, it is a wonder you cannot smell the rain," spouted Jack.

"Judge not the afflicted," counseled Mothcrates.

Some laughed.

"What?" puzzled Mothcrates.

"Shut up!" ordered Pterrkee.

"Or what?" challenged Euæmon. Pterrkee's nasty outburst had become a regular occurrence each night. Euæmon loved tormenting the sourpuss. Sometimes Euæmon would call him Galinthias.

"We should try to sleep," suggested Phranc - also part of the nightly ritual, right on cue within the queue.

"Did you hear about Gallo this morning?" Teos piped up.

"Side. Shhhh."

"What?" asked Teos. "I saw it myself. So did you, Dim. And Talor. Were not you there?"

The following silence was deafening as each knew they were avoiding the subject most on each of their minds, except Teos who could not understand why anyone would hush him. This morning had been BIG news. This evening BIG news, too. He complied out of obedience - for the moment - and, not out of recognition or understanding.

"I heard they might pull some of us off the quarry for olive duty this year," said young Talor, changing the subject.

"They say that every year," answered Dim. "I will believe it when I see it."

"Thomas," muttered Ionnes.

More silence until Teos could contain himself no longer.

"Did you hear about Apollonides?"

"Shhhh!"

Teos sat up in the darkness, unable to really see anyone, but well familiar with the layout and sleeping arrangements of the barren barracks.

"I saw them," urged Teos. "This morning, Gallo was dead and then he was not and then he was again."

"That is not what happened," snapped Pterrkee.

Teos thought about it for a bit, then added, "Yes it did. I am sure I saw right. It was the newcomer, Ionnes. He spoke and Gallo came back to life."

"Skybalon!" scoffed Rabbi Yosef with disgust.

"Uh-huh. I was there."

"Let us ask him," Jack jumped in, "So, Ionnes, on your first day here, it is said that you have resurrected one slave if only for a minute or two, then you cast a demon out of another person - a Roman no less? I'm guessing that one is for more than a minute or two. Anything else we should know about you?"

"Leave him alone," defended Dim.

"Why?" teased Jack. "You have been attending to his every need all day. Looks like the Romans taught you well."

"Watch it, Jack," Dim sat up to face the jokester. Sometimes his jokes could go too far.

"Enough," said Ionnes, touching what he hoped was Dim's arm in the gloom. "What troubles you, son?"

"Troubles?" laughed Jack. "The only troubles I got right now are right outside that door. I just heard you did some hocus pocus magic today and wanted details."

"I assure you, it was not hocus-pocus or any other kind of magic."

"Then it was real?" challenged Jack.

"Yeah?" said others.

Minos spoke. "Even Kynops could not do what you did today."

"So," questioned Jack, "that makes you a magic man? Or, a god?"

Ionnes sighed. "I assure you I am neither."

"So, you were not boiled in oil in Roma?" challenged Arion.

The others had all heard tell something like that happened. Arion, who arrived with Ionnes, as the newcomer kept it to himself, but the sailors shared the story and rumors with some of the townsfolk who told their neighbors who told other neighbors, etc. Euæmon and Minos also overheard them talking about it, such be the rapidly spreading wildfire called gossip.

"I am thinking," added Jack, "we would all like to make sure who we are sleeping with in here."

"I would feel the same way," acknowledged Ionnes, lying back on his bedroll. His thoughts took him a fortnight or two back.

<>< ><> <>< ><> <>< ><> <>< ><> <>< ><>

Tears filled Ionnes' eyes. He had been in the prison awaiting his execution in the Flavian Amphitheater, but his tears shed not for himself or his fate. He wept for the others there with him. How could people treat each other so horribly? They knew it was wrong. They _knew_ it for they knew how they would feel if someone did it to them.

And, to make a public spectacle in this huge theater shown ever more barbaric. Obviously, the partial purpose was to scare and intimidate in order to control the Christian sect; not that Christians were the only group being killed that day.

Jews. Greeks. Criminals, of course. Public executions were very popular and not just with the Romans. All cities of decent size could persecute and execute, but none were anywhere nearly so flamboyant and ostentatious in modern times as Roma. Ionnes knelt in the holding cell awaiting his turn. He always knew it would come but knew not what form it would take. He recalled Yeshua being beaten, crowned with thorns, flogged, carrying that huge cross piece, then nailed and dropped into the ground to hang there like a hideous ornament, warning others to beware the wrath of Roma. It still caused his heart to drop a beat or two when he relived those hours. How much he loved Yeshua! How much he had wanted to save Him but stood there utterly helpless. Yet, even during unbearable pain, Ionnes had seen so many amazing events with Yeshua including the dozen-odd times He, Yeshua, should have been stoned or thrown off a cliff or starved to death. And, Yeshua always brought all of them through. He gave the cat nine lives.

How many more might the Son of Adonai possess?

He recalled the apprehensive joy in the Upper Room when Maryam Magdalene brought news of Yeshua's resurrection. Always a little crazy, they feared the disappointments to believe her. Still, he ran with all he was worth to the grave to see for himself. Lying there, he again wondered for the thousandth time or so why he stopped at the cave entrance and waited for Cephas to first go in.

He recalled the miracle before them even if Cephas still clung tightly to his grief. It was not until Yeshua stood amongst them that their grief became replaced with glorious jubilation and their tears changed to gladness.

"I will believe it when I see it," Ionnes had heard Dim say.

He recalled how they told Thomas who refused to believe until he saw and touched Yeshua. How obstinate Thomas had seemed until Ionnes realized all the apostles and disciples in the Upper Room did not fully believe before Yeshua appeared to them. Only then, when they could see and touch Him did they believe. Thomas just had had the "unfortunate" timing to be absent that day.

Yeshua told Thomas, "Blessed are they who have not seen and yet believe." Ionnes suddenly realized He had said that not just to Thomas but to all present who had not believed any better than Thomas.

"I am the Way, the Truth and the Life," said Yeshua, specifically to Thomas over a year earlier. "No man comes unto the Father, but by Me."

Ionnes recalled Thomas' face, following Yeshua's face into a knowing smile. The Way was not a road or a shipping lane. It meant Yeshua Himself. Those moments of insight in introspection were the moments of his life that Ionnes always loved and cherished the most.

Then, his mind jumped ahead to the news that his brother Yaakov had died by the sword. Herod displayed his brother's head outside the palace in Ierusalem. The first of the twelve to be executed for serving Yeshua. Was not it enough that Roma killed so many of the people of Iudea, Jews and Christians alike?

Suddenly Jews wanted to kill Jews who followed The Way.

Herod even forbad Yaakov a proper burial, lest he come back to life like Yeshua. He wanted not another empty tomb like Yeshua - or Lazarus. And, there his brother rested in a common tomb with criminals, slaves, indentured servants, and other nameless corpses. Ionnes shed more tears at first for Herod's final insult to his brother. Then, Ionnes reconsidered and treasured his brother's grave. He could think of no greater honor.

"The first shall be last the last shall be first," uttered Ionnes to himself.

"What?" asked Dim and some others.

Ionnes words hung around them in the darkness while his mind continued down its long road.

Right after that, Herod tried to kill Cephas as well, but Yeshua sent an angel to free him from captivity. He recalled wondering why Yeshua did not spare his brother in similar fashion? The question plagued him from time to time - probably the devil trying to shake his faith. Then, Cephas met the same fate as Yeshua. Cephas counted himself unworthy such a martyr's fate and urged them to crucify him upside down. They complied, mostly out of brutal humor and taunted Cephas as he hung there. Cephas praised Yeshua and sang hymns of thanksgiving until his voice failed him. Even then, his lips continued to move in prayerful diligence. Unlike regular crucifixion where the arms and chest cut off the air to his lungs, Cephas could continue to witness to the guards. He would not deny Yeshua again and counted his unique demise as a blessing.

Ionnes wondered that the Roman soldiers even considered Cephas' request. They had to fashion a different cross for the special request. Cephas, a prisoner, certainly had no position to make such a request. To hang him upside down clearly attested to their brutal heartlessness.

After that, Ionnes seldom questioned Adonai's purposes and relished the means of his brother's demise. The sword was not the most painful way to die. He embraced the opportunities to bring light to a dark world - to be the one truth against so many lies - to be sin forgiven before those who commonly could not even see their sin.

Other impressions came and went as news of another apostle was killed, then another and another, mostly by Roman hands - killed by cross or stone or sword or spear or... It was by such a people and society that Ionnes found himself leaving Ephesus for Roma to face Domitian Cæsar.

And, there he stood in the Emperor's throne room. Many, many Romans surrounded him, filling the seats of the gallery - officials, citizens and guards gathered. When the emperor entered the chamber, those in attendance bowed low - some even dropping to knees to bow before the self-proclaimed deity, Titus Flavius Domitianus, now Cæsar Domitian Augustus.

Ionnes' chains scraped along the marble floor as he entered the room. The guards expected to have to drag him, holding each of his arms tightly, yet Ionnes, old and creaking, stayed upright on his own feet as he approached the center of the large room. Guards stopped him with a hand on each shoulder, then flung him forward to his knees before the emperor.

Domitian glared at the filthy, unkempt prisoner. A Sage standing beside the ruler spoke. "A Christian zealot." Then, he added with emphasis, "One of their primary leaders."

Ionnes tried to stand. The guards shoved him back down and kept hands on his shoulders.

"What is your name?" barked Domitian between slurps of strong wine.

"Giovanni," answered the Sage.

"Thee Giovanni?" laughed Domitian from over the rim of his goblet. "This old fossil? Surely not." All in the room joined in the laughter, but briefly lest they miss whatever would come next.

"The same," assured the Sage. "One of the founding members of the sect."

"So, Giovanni. I hear that you worship only one God?"

Ionnes nodded. "That is true."

"And, this God of yours was a flesh and blood man?"

"Yes. For a brief time. Adonai is Spirit and we worship Him in spirit and in truth."

"And, did you know Roman emperors are also gods?"

"I have heard them claim that is so."

The guard to the right prepared to club Ionnes. The Sage raised a hand to stop him.

"But you disagree?" further questioned the emperor.

Ionnes did not hesitate a second. "There is only one God."

Most attendees in the room gasped. A few smiled with villainous glee.

Domitian glared at Ionnes.

"One God is all you Iudæan zealots can afford." He stood and stepped down the steps to approach Ionnes who noticed the bright, scarlet stripes lining his toga.

"I have seen your sect rise over the years though its founder has been dead for decades. I have heard tell of wonders and miracles. I have heard stories beyond belief. So, I already know your answer, but I will grant you an amnesty. You may go free before the sun sets. All you need...."

"... is to worship you as a god," finished Ionnes.

"Yes," Domitian answered, deliciously towering over the kneeling apostle, then turned to return to his throne. He knew the outcome before Ionnes entered the room.

"Well?" Domitian loudly demanded, theatrically swinging around as he sat.

"You know my answer."

"I want to hear it from your own lips." Domitian often loved this moment between himself and such prisoners.

"I am still upright," answered Ionnes, stiff and still and tall from his knees. The soldiers pressed down hard on the old man's shoulders. Ionnes resisted but could be forced down until his nose pressed against the cold stone.

"Yeshua is LORD!" yelled Ionnes. "There is only one God and LORD in Heaven and on Earth. That is the God I serve..."

The soldiers stopped pushing down. Ionnes raised his head up enough to look towards the emperor, positioned further up from the main floor.

"... and, you are not Him, little Cæsar."

Domitian watched the scene unhurried. He let the weight of the moment settle in on itself.

"Cupbearer," he eventually summoned with a smirk. A small, young man came forward, a golden cup in his hands.

"Serve our guest."

The cupbearer did not hesitate, but also did not hurry. The best kind of drama! The room held rapt and dared hardly breathe. This was the moment many had come for.

The cupbearer approached Ionnes who prayed aloud as he rose back to his knees.

"LORD Yeshua, into Your hands I commit my spirit." Ionnes struggled to stand, then took the ornate goblet. He paused briefly, then drank the sour, caustic fluid. The cupbearer took the goblet back in hand, turned towards his emperor and turned over the goblet. It was empty save a few baby drops. He then returned to his place in the throne room. All eyes stayed on Ionnes. The soldiers had let go. They moved away as to not block the witnesses. All eyes watched what seemed a long time and then a longer time. Then, a longer time still, yet Ionnes stood to his feet, still in prayer and, well, quite relaxed.

Domitian Cæsar felt his anger rise - something he was not accustomed to restraining. Most Cæsars quickly became accustomed to having their own way, and Domitian definitely showed no exception.

"Cupbearer," he shrieked.

Shuddering, but just as prompt, the cupbearer stepped forward. He kept head and eyes down. All knew it to be death to face the emperor when he blustered like this.

"Cupbearer, did you not give him the poison?"

"Hail, Cæsar," answered the cupbearer. His voice cracked. "Before Cæsar's eyes, I gave him the goblet and watched him drink all."

"Was the goblet full?"

"Half full, O Cæsar. More than enough to impose death."

Domitian tapped his fingers on his knee - a common behavior when he felt perplexed or miffed.

"What poison?"

"Cyanidus," answered the shaking cupbearer.

"Full potency? Not medicinal?"

"Emperor Nero's recipe." Everyone in the room, including Ionnes, were well familiar with the late emperor's love of cyanidus.

"Refill the goblet. Same amount as you gave the prisoner."

The cupbearer followed orders without question. He retrieved a small, clay pot on a table and filled the same cup exactly as ordered. The cupbearer always had his own table in the throne room. The attendees knew better than to drink anything from that table, and not just because they might be supping down some poisonous concoction. The cupbearer returned to the center of the room and stood, now a quarter turn towards Ionnes, his young head and eyes still down.

Domitian stared at the servant, brooding.

"Drink it," he finally said.

The cupbearer hesitated.

"Drink the cup," ordered Domitian intensely. "All of it."

The cupbearer then looked at his emperor. He could argue, then Domitian would only up the dose. He could try to flee, but where or how? He could "accidentally" drop the goblet. Yeah - right! He knew well the potency of the poison. He had mixed it himself the night before. He looked at Ionnes who said, "Do not."

"Silence!" yelled Domitian to Ionnes, then "Drink it now, cupbearer. All of it. Now."

The cupbearer visibly shook with fear as he slowly raised the cup to his lips. Just the smell irritated his nostrils and sinuses.

Ionnes again pleaded with him. "Do not give in."

The cupbearer barely glanced away from the goblet to Ionnes, then obeyed his emperor. He knew himself a dead man anyway by this point. He tasted the sour concoction. It numbed his lips on impact. He tipped and gulped down the rest, feeling its toxins rake the walls of his throat and esophagus all the way to his stomach. Some fluid slid down both cheeks, but he drank more than enough. He faced Domitian, held forth the goblet and turned it upside down. Empty.

The poison rapidly took hold. His stomach knotted and head became light. He plopped to his knees. He knew he had consumed enough to kill even ten men.

Setting on the floor, then lying on his side, he coughed and hacked and groaned more and more until the poison claimed his final breath and he lay limp on the marble. Caustic drool escaped out the side of his mouth.

The room remained mostly quiet until his breath departed. Then, the personal commentaries arose like white background noise. Most approved of the death.

Yet, Domitian Cæsar, ruler of the mighty Roman empire, sat brooding. He eyed his quarry. Giovanni the zealot still stood before the ruler, old and creaky and perfectly healthy. He stared shamelessly at Domitian - a practice not common for the emperor. Most feared and avoided him.

"Take him away," Domitian presently ordered.

The two guards stepped forward, ready to grab Ionnes, but then the old man slipped down under their grasp more slippery than an anguilla eel, scaled and dipped in olive oil. The guards paused with surprise. Ionnes never displayed cooperation with his captors, nor certain fear, but he had never moved away like that.

He knelt before the dead cupbearer. The dead eyes half open. The blue lips and freshly dead hands still sporting an occasional twitch. With hands still manacled, the old man fell forward across the limp body. His chains echoed across the chamber as all became quiet to watch him. He prayed in Aramaic. Tears filled his eyes. His breathing became shallow, yet he prayed all the harder.

Domitian, the Sage, the guards and who knew who else were ready to stop the episode, but still waited to see this little drama unfold.

Ionnes rose, struggling to push his old bones up off the floor. He wiped the tears away from his eyes with his shoulders and laughed, "Thank You, Yeshua. Thank You."

Back on Patmos, Dim and the others watched Ionnes wipe away the tears from his eyes in the gloomy lodge. "Thank You, Yeshua," he whispered. "Thank You."

They continued to wait more seconds for an answer to Jack's question from this unexpected comrade.

With all eyes on Ionnes, it took a few extra seconds before Domitian and others noticed the cupbearer breathing. He groaned and turned over, looking up at Ionnes. His muscles relaxed from the earlier cramps, and he sat up and wiped his mouth with the edge of his tunic.

"Welcome back," greeted Ionnes. "How was your journey to the other side and back?"

The cupbearer's eyes widened. He looked at Ionnes.

"Horrible. Such creatures." He shuddered and buried his head.

"No River Styx, was there?"

The cupbearer suddenly looked up. "No," he croaked.

"No, I was here. I could see all of you, but I was also apart. It felt cold and then fearful creatures ripped me away from here and dragged me down a deep pit. I screamed but had no mouth.

No air. There was nothing inside me to come out."

Ionnes smiled and placed his forehead against the cupbearer's shoulder. "Praise Yeshua of Nazareth. He brought you back. Not me."

"Enough!" Domitian stood - an emperor in defiance. An emperor faced with a greater power than he could muster? Emperors do not usually like that, especially rulers with a god complex.

"Take him away," ordered Domitian.

"Who?" asked one guard. "Which one?"

Domitian felt a temper tantrum coming on. He took a couple of deep breaths and answered, "The prisoner," he pointed towards Ionnes. The two men locked eyes - Ionnes and the emperor, until Ionnes was forcibly removed. Neither broke gaze before Ionnes left the large throne room. He praised Yeshua aloud the entire time, through Roman halls and past Senate chambers and across the court and down the avenue to the prison. Many thought him mad. Ionnes knew better.

They proceeded off Palatina Hill towards the Forum district. Ionnes looked to the left, hoping to see the Tiber. Not this time. He envisioned thousands upon thousands of Christian converts baptized in that river. A few more turns and the Carcer Tullianum loomed ahead. The prison, older than Roma itself, welcomed Ionnes back with ominous resolve. Ionnes stopped at the doorway to touch the stone. He was not the first Christian to grace these walls and he yearned to feel the love and strength of Cephas and Paulos and others he knew and loved who had been here before him. He again thanked Yeshua for His deliverance for no one stayed at the Carcer Tullianum for very long. Returned to his cell, Ionnes smiled under the buoyancy of a spirit-full heart. His chains never felt so light.

Sleep evaded Domitian. Not typically a man of deep convictions or considerations for anyone besides himself, he seldom spent his nights restlessly. A couple/ three quick goblets of strong wine usually helped when needed, but tonight no go. Tossing and turning, he eventually rose to exit his bed chamber, another goblet of wine in hand.

"Hail Cæsar," spouted the two guards as Domitian appeared. He ignored them. Proceeding down the hall in bedclothes, he entered the throne room. Dark and quiet, lit only by lanterns in the hallway. He seldom saw it that way. He wandered over to his throne, perhaps out of habit, and sat down. It felt empty and a bit hollow without all the world at his feet. For a brief, brief moment, he missed the freedoms of his youth. His father Vespasian and brother Titus had worn this crown. For fourteen years he had carried the torch - now longer than both of them combined. When first he became Cæsar, he had sought to bring the republic to the greatness of Augustus Cæsar. Oh, to have collected and brought together the crumbs of Roma back together into one loaf.

He had been just a young man when Nero fled Roma, only to take his own life. Not yet seventeen, Domitian could not see or be privy to the power plays and chaos in the Senate. The Prætorium searched the empire for the next emperor. Generals became the obvious choice. Domitian's father and brother engaged such a long distance campaign to take back control of Galilee, Samaria and ultimately Iudæa and their stronghold Ierusalem. In the twelfth year of Nero's reign in Roma, the father and son led over eighty-thousand soldiers who took out Jewish strongholds one by one, eventually setting siege of Ierusalem in 69 AD, challenging the Jewish rebellion. General Vespasian left the battle unto his son, Titus, when he was deemed Cæsar in 69. The following year, Titus ransacked Ierusalem worse than ancient Tyre or Sidon. Even the Hebrews' beloved Temple became first looted, then burned, then destroyed, brick by brick. The Roman hammer came down hard on insolent Ierusalem. In turn, Domitian had never been close with either his father or brother. They had always been about the business of Roma as he aged and grew into a man. He had sought military greatness like they had, but he proved inadequate to such ambitions. He displayed better molding for battles in the Senate than military conquests. His father's position with the empire paved many roads for Domitian into the Senate.

No other general commanded more troops than General Vespasian. After giving the job of Cæsar to three other generals that year, the Senate finally threw in their lot with Vespasian.

Domitian had been pleased his father would be so close, and it had been good those first few months, but Roma made its bottomless list of insatiable demands, and his father's heart served the empire more than his family.

Then, ten years hence, his father died suddenly. The Senate gave the throne to his son Titus - the first time any emperor's son had taken the Roman throne after his father.

Titus took the laurels to heart like his father and fulfilled some of his father's endeavors including completion of the Flavian Amphitheater. Vesuvius erupted during his reign, burying Pompeii, Herculaneum and more. Then, after just two short years in office, he died from a severe fever. Domitian sat with his brother as his life ebbed, partly to protect him.

Domitian remembered seeing his brother, always so strong and sure of himself, succumb to such a simple fate. Domitian never foresaw his brother's death the entire vigil until he deceased. The fever came on so suddenly with vicious intent until Titus breathed his last, forever gone.

Seated in the throne room that night, Domitian recalled visiting his father and brother in their throne rooms or banquet halls. Each shared stories of their conquests and battles and victories. Not surprising, neither had anything good to say about the mule stubborn Iudeans. That was for sure and for certain; a lesson Domitian never forgot during his reign.

To everyone's surprise, the Senate elected Domitian to rule after Titus' untimely death. A bit of a cad and womanizer, he may not have been everybody's first choice, but fortunately he remained not anybody's last choice; a compromise who had served in the Roman Senate most of his adult life so he knew the ins and outs of Roman politics including the long list of who's who in Roma. His father and brother had both been good emperors, so Domitian had seemed a good choice and far, far better than the chaos of the late 60s after Nero's death.

Thus Domitian, now forty-four years of age, ruled the greatest kingdom on Earth. It would not be fair to say that the emperor began his reign as a humble yearling. His ego and confidence already well established, he became more so inflated each passing year. They treated him like a deity and after a spell he came to believe it and expected others to embrace it as well. To say he showed cognitive awareness of the seduction of power would be an uneducated guess. It was not like there were many who could tell him he was being a jerk without elevating the emperor's ire.

Thus, he sat alone in the gloom on this throne in the middle of the night unable to sleep.

A lighted figure entered.

"I heard you were in here," entered the Sage.

"Could not sleep."

"Nor I, my lord."

"Why could you not sleep?" asked Domitian.

The Sage took a chair a few feet from Domitian. The seasoned ruler made sure his main advisor held no arms.

"I suspect for the same reason as you, my lord."

"The Christian zealot?"

The Sage nodded. "He made quite a show, did not he?"

Domitian nodded, staring forward intently to the blank spot Ionnes had occupied not so many hours prior.

"Brood not," urged the Sage.

Domitian looked at him without turning his head. "The empire will not fall because you destroyed one of its rebellious leaders. Previous Cæsars have removed their founders, yet the empire stands, strong as ever. Another dead zealot will not the empire miss."

Domitian did not look convinced.

"You doubt that which recent histories have attested?"

The emperor started to speak, paused, again imagined the old apostle before him and folded his hands contemplatively.

"Who led the last purge?" Domitian eventually asked. He thought he knew but wanted to make sure. It was late.

The Sage thought a moment. "Claudius Cæsar? Or, Nero?" he considered.

"Nero," Domitian answered his own question. "Did not he crucify their leader?"

"Petros," remembered the Sage. "Upside down. That is the only reason I recall."

Domitian nodded. He was around fifteen then as he recalled hearing the news in passing. Petros would not die like Yeshua, his leader, so the guards hung him head down. Something like that. It had created quite the gossippy chatter that week.

"So," brooded Domitian, "What to do with one we cannot poison?"

The Sage waited before giving answer. A tactical move. Learn what the emperor wanted before telling him what he wanted to hear. Only that way could he better guide Domitian and not say something that might irk a cranky emperor on a sleepless night. The truth be told, he had been sleeping most soundly when servants banged upon his door, rousing his servants who roused him reporting that the emperor was up and could not sleep.

"We need something that will truly make an impact on the people."

The Sage nodded and sat in a thoughtful stance.

"So, are we in agreement that he must die?"

Domitian peered at the Sage. Was he serious? What a lame question.

"The man made quite an impression in your court today, did he not?"

Another lame statement. Domitian wondered that this man ever achieved the role as counsel to the emperor.

"If so," continued the Sage, "may I suggest you dispose of him in a rare and painful and permanent manner."

"I am listening," said Domitian, shifting in his seat.

The Sage furrowed a brow. "Another crucifixion?"

"No," answered Domitian without reservation. Of late, crucifixions had become somewhat commonplace to the Roman citizens on the street who mostly ignored them and went about their business of life. Of course, the real, targeted audience were the other zealots or criminals who might think twice if they saw their compadres executed on display.

He considered feeding him to lions. A gladiator would chop him up faster than the prisoner could raise his sword. No, it had to be something big.

"Oil," said the Sage.

Domitian glanced up.

"Boil him. Dip him slowly. More pain that way. The people will flock for miles to see it."

"In the Flavian Amphitheater?" thought Domitian.

"Or, the Latin Gate."

"No," the emperor sat up. "Flavian Amphitheater. Are not there games this weekend?"

The Sage nodded.

"Then, we shall add one more event."

Domitian still scowled. He had never known a prisoner fried.

He asked, "Do you recall the last time Roma executed one in this manner?"

"No," admitted the Sage. "I recall not even once in my long life and service to Roma."

"Then, it is long overdue," decided Domitian.

"I will make the arrangements," assured the Sage.

"Good," agreed the emperor, finished his wine and left the room without another word. The Sage had become used to such behavior. Most Cæsars behave much the same in some ways. Grabbing his lantern, he headed for home and his now cooled bed.

And, Domitian laid back down on his bed. He expected sleep to come, but it kept its distance most of the rest of the night.

Ionnes likewise did not sleep well that night, though his reasons weighed far differently from Domitian. The dark, cold prison was made to be uncomfortable. Between the chains, an occasional but regular drip somewhere down the hall and the guards talking just outside his cell, he had difficulty closing all of it out enough to go to sleep. Still, he had learned over the years that if he laid down quietly and did not stress over not sleeping that his mind would be refreshed the next day as though he had gotten a full night's sleep. Just relaxing and clearing his mind gave him the rest he needed.

Prayer? He chuckled from his bed. Prayer NEVER strayed far from his lips and half that distance on sleepless nights.

An image of Paulos came to mind. Had not Paulos begun his stay in Roma here in the Carcer Tullianum? The prison not designed for long term stays, Nero had given Paulos, a Roman citizen, a simple, little home to dwell - a rental house arrest with decent food to eat and friends who could come and go. Paulos occupied the comfortable home for two years until one day Nero had Paulos beheaded.

Thus, Ionnes spent the time in prayer - for the church in Roma, and Ephesus, and even Ierusalem, and - he laughed merrily. He could not even remember all the Christian churches built that century since Yeshua's resurrection and ascension. What a truly glorious profession of faith. What an expression of Adonai's love on the world. What a silly example of Ionnes as the oldest and most revered administrator of the church at that time.

He thanked Adonai for those praying for him. He was not Yeshua. He could not feel the prayers of the saints, but the day's miracles attested to and complemented the prayers of the Church. Ionnes did not believe for even one second that the day's miracles occurred only between himself and risen Yeshua. The saints praying with him made their major impact as well, not to also mention the divine effect on the Roman court.

Next, he prayed for the Roman guards that they would find Christos. That had become a much easier prayer since some of them already had converted over the years. "So, why stop there?" thought Ionnes. He prayed for the emperor and the Roman Senate. Yeshua had urged them to pray for their leaders. Paulos wrote it as well. Domitian's attitude spoke scrolls and scrolls that he needed Yeshua at least as much if not more than anybody else.

Ionnes wearied at the sense of hopelessness for such a prayer. A Christian Cæsar? Why not? Regardless of Cæsar's self-proclamations of himself, he verily lived still as just a man with knees for bowing and a tongue for confessing Christos. If Domitian who tortured The Way could be baptized, what an amazing wave of Yeshua's love that would ripple, over and over like a pond or a flag to unfurl and flutter in the Spirit of the Wind.

Ionnes wondered if Yeshua would someday knock Domitian off his chariot some sunny day, ("...some Sonny day?" he again laughed to himself). It got Saul's attention during his campaign to arrest and execute Christians, but the other part of Ionnes' brain knew that answer before he even asked. Adonai is not a God of fear, but a God of Love. Saul recognized Yeshua's loving mercies when the LORD appeared to him and knocked him off his horse.

"Saul. Saul. Why do you persecute Me?"

If Yeshua did the same for Domitian, the emperor would only respond in fear. That scenario clashed totally against Saul's divine visitation; and Saul's special calling who himself zealously sought the same God that the Christians loved, served and gave their lives for. Saul simply had to be shown in a fashion that got his attention. He had been introduced to Messiah lots of times before. That time, Saul finally really saw Him.

And, what an amazing disciple he thereby grew to be. Ionnes praised Yeshua for Saul, really the first to genuinely follow Yeshua's last instructions and begin to fulfill the Great Commission way beyond Ierusalem. Ionnes recalled his own initial resistance to gentile converts. It was not until after the LORD appeared to Cephas and gave him the vision regarding no unclean foods then sent him to the home of a gentile to preach and baptize and disciple that Ionnes pressed past another prejudice of his youth. He laughed again, this time at himself. The Hellenists were now as much like him as he like them.

So, why not a Christian Cæsar? Even if not Domitian, perhaps some day... In the meantime, Ionnes praised Yeshua for using Roma to His purposes. Hundreds of years now past, Adonai had sent the Assyrians to judge Yisra'el and later Babylon to judge Iudæa. Then, he sent the equally pagan Medes and Persians to judge Babylon the Great for being pagan. That idea assured Ionnes that Yeshua, the LORD of Hosts, still dwelled with them and for those who truly served Him, Amen.

Some days later, Ionnes heard soldiers coming. Many soldiers. Around twenty, at first count. The door to his cell flew open and his chains detached from the wall to be led out. He passed Guard Marcellus, a young warrior who screwed up in battle. His punishment - prison duty. Intrigued by Ionnes, he had conversed with the zealous apostle those few nights and secretly accepted Yeshua, the Anointed One. Ionnes noticed the severe concern and fear on his face as they passed. It foretold a terrible fate to come.

Though puffy clouds spread across the sky, the daylight still blinded him after days below in the prison. It felt good to be out and he breathed more deeply. Regardless what lay ahead, he took the present moment to feel the beauty of the world around him. Lots of people walking through the streets stopped and gave way to the small parade heading through. Ionnes stood no taller than the men around him, but he sought out the faces of pedestrians, all created in Adonai's image. It was not unusual for folks to take note of prisoners and other celebrities as they passed, but Ionnes detected more of an interest than normal.

He noticed the gasps and mutterings of Romans as he passed.

"Is that him? Is that the one they poisoned?" Other similar whispers feathered through. Ionnes praised Adonai for that moment t'where the holy and powerful name of Yeshua would be advanced.

Then, he spied a familiar face. Urbanus? Ionnes had not visited the Roman church for quite some years. The man's face had certainly aged, but still unmistakably Urbanus. He saw three others beside Urbanus he did not know, but then saw Persis. Then, Rufus. Then, Nereus and his sister. He could not quite remember her name. Olivia or something like that.

Then, he saw Prochorus. What a welcome sight? His aide. His scribe. His friend. And, certainly his brother in the LORD. He had not known if Prochorus had made it to Roma after him.

Prochorus played the part of a gawking tourist as their eyes met - a knowing welcome - a protected love. They did not have long to exchange deep silence and expressive body language, but Prochorus raised brows and eyes to the left, up the wall of the narrow street. Ionnes followed his gaze, and there he saw Clement, Bishop of Roma. Peter's protege'. Older and a bit balder, but he still had that stubborn, little hairy tuft in the middle of his head.

The kindly bishop looked sternly but compassionately at the last apostle. Seconds passed and they were out of sight from one another. Ionnes wondered if they had planned a rescue attempt. It would not have been the first time, but likely they did not expect twenty guards surrounding Ionnes. He would be chopped dead before they even got to him.

Rounding the next corner, he thought for a brief moment that he saw Priscilla and Aquila. He spied them for only a flash, but the vision totally surprised him. He knew of their martyrdom many years earlier.

Continuing along, the group turned towards the Flavian Amphitheater. Ionnes had heard of its enormity. The descriptions did not do it justice. What an extraordinary structure! Even a blind man could not miss it, it was so big. And for Ionnes in chains, the structure seemed perhaps the most amazing he had ever seen, and he had certainly seen some amazing chunks of architecture. The Parthenon in the Acropolis in Athenæ, built to worship Athena, may have had the Flavian Amphitheater beat, but being in chains added its impressive heaviness to the moment.

They entered through a large door, big enough for horses, carts, chariots and such. He could hear the sounds of swords crashing and clashing and clanging somewhere nearby but could not tell if it was in a nearby chamber or out on the battle field. Probably not on the battlefield. He would also hear the whoops and hollers and ahs of the audience attending; the choir of those voices unheard.

Eventually, they came to a large cage filled with prisoners. Some paced. Some sat, alone and scared. Ionnes joined them and sat on the floor along one side. He could hear some of the activity outside as the games began.

"Ha!" taunted a large, bearded fellow of around twenty, pacing along the front. If he was to die in the arena, he had to badger as many Romans as he could until then.

Ionnes watched him some minutes, then his mission suddenly became clear, at least for the immediate moment. He rose and stood patiently by the pacing figure.

"What?" the pacer finally turned.

Ionnes held apart his hands showing himself unarmed. Of course, he held no weapon. Was not he in a prison holding cell in the Flavian Amphitheater awaiting a bloody fate like all the rest in there? Still, Ionnes knew it to be an effective introduction.

"Ready to die?"

The big man stopped. Others in the room took notice.

"I asked if you were ready to die?" Ionnes leaned his back against a wall. He coughed a bit to clear his throat.

"Are you?" the man finally answered.

Ionnes smiled. "You bet."

"Then, today is your lucky day," he retorted and resumed pacing.

"It can be your lucky day, too." Ionnes looked around at all the prisoners. "All of you face the same fate. We may be gone and dead before the sun sets today. Is your spirit ready to go? Is your soul ready to face the other side of life?"

"Shut-up," came answer for a couple men, but Ionnes saw others who had sat up to listen.

"And," continued Ionnes, "It matters not what you have done in life for there is One ready to receive you into His Heavenly Kingdom." He paused and looked around from face to face.

"So, you can go to your death forgiven and free."

"Free!" scoffed the pacer. "Your 'One' did not keep you out of this place."

"Yes," agreed Ionnes, "but I know that He brought me here to help bring all of you to Him. Any who wish to go."

The prisoners were silent for some moments. The sounds of the crowds and the activities outside seemed louder.

A voice broke the silent chain.

"I wish to go."

Ionnes turned towards the voice. A young woman remained seated on the floor.

"Why are you here?" asked Ionnes.

She hesitated, but soon answered, "The guards tried to rape me. My husband fought. He killed one and maimed another. Now he is gone and I am here."

Ionnes felt her pain and tears filled his eyes. He smiled through the watery blindness to assure her.

"Have you heard of Yeshua the Messiah?"

"Only stories," she answered. Some around them scoffed and turned away. Others waited to hear more, if only to pass the time until their fated turns. Ionnes could usually read those no longer willing to hope.

"The Romans killed him, too," Ionnes said of Yeshua, "but he came back to life three days later."

Some cursed to ridicule.

"Impossible."

"No way."

"You lie."

"Not I," spoke Ionnes to all. "You are indeed wise to disagree, but that does not mean you are not wrong. I know for fact it is true because I was there. I saw Him crucified in Ierusalem. I saw Him die. I saw Him buried and three days later, just as He foretold to us many times, He rose to live again."

More scoffed. Some snickered. Some wanted to hear more. Some cared not either way.

"Silence," yelled the pacer. He wanted to both smack Ionnes between the eyes to shut up and still get up to tell him more.

"And," continued Ionnes, "after His resurrection, I saw Him, ate with Him, and touched Him."

"You touched Him?" asked an older man, a Greek, still seated on the rock floor.

"Touched Him?" grinned Ionnes. "He gave the greatest hugs. His hugs could take all the fear and friction out of my life faster than a crashing wave." Ionnes nodded and smiled at the man in the most sincere and reassuring expression that man had EVER seen or encountered. He sat up a little more.

"Then, I saw Him ascend on the clouds to Heaven and now I look for the day when He will come again to Earth. So, I have faced death for His name many, many times, and today I face it again. But I face it gladly and without fear, and you can face it, too. And, if today I die, I know that I will be with Him and I offer you the same chance for eternal life with Yeshua."

The guards came.

"You. You. You." Three taken to the yard.

"Remember what I said," Ionnes yelled to the three, "and seek Yeshua before you die."

"Stupid old man," grumped the pacer.

Ionnes turned towards the pacer. "And, what you offer them is better?"

The pacer started breathing heavily, glaring at Ionnes.

"Your fear is killing your thoughts."

The pacer became more agitated.

"Yeshua has already gone this way to death. He came back and now leads me forth this very day. I am never alone."

The punch came sudden and quick, right in the face. Old Ionnes stumbled backwards by the blow. The woman tried to catch him, but both went down. Ionnes laid there a moment, letting his senses regroup. He felt the blood slithering down his nostrils and wash through his mustache and beard. The red blood against the white hair added to the effect. He would have wiped it away with a cloth or even water if either were to be had in the holding cell.

He stood, slowly, but directly and faced the pacer who stood straight on with teeth and fists clenched. His hand rose to wipe the blood away from his nose and mouth and beard. He looked at the dark ruby red liquid of life in his calloused hand, then held it up towards the pacer.

"Yeshua shed His own blood for you so you could have eternal life with him. He shed His own blood for your sins."

"Then, he was a madman or a fool."

"Or," smiled Ionnes through the throbbing pain in his face, "He showed you how much He loved you by giving His life for you."

The pacer looked at the old man, still bloody. He peered at the bloody hand. The blood on Ionnes' face added to the effect. A spark of life touched him. The effect of hope scared him, and he turned away.

"Just leave me alone," he muttered, but the words sounded hollow.

"Are you a father?" asked Ionnes. Somehow he already knew the answer to the question.

The pacer turned back towards Ionnes, puzzled by the question.

"Yes," he reluctantly answered.

"One child? Two? More? Sons or daughters?"

"Both," the pacer answered. "One girl. One boy."

"Would not you give your life for them?"

The pacer nodded.

"Why?" The pacer looked perplexed, though he certainly understood the question.

"If your children were doing something that would cause them great harm, even everlasting harm, would not you do what you could to help them and protect them? Even save them, if needed? Even if it cost you your life?"

"Definitely," answered the pacer. "It would break my heart if anything happened to them."

Ionnes smiled, even as the blood congealed on his facial hair.

"You have just described the love Yeshua has for you. It is just as real as your love for your children."

"Truly?"

Ionnes nodded and continued to talk about Yeshua to the pacer and the others. Not that everyone welcomed his words, but most of the sneers had since melted away. Ionnes knew he had little time to share the good spiel. He spoke with passion and urgency. He spoke of saving grace from death and Hades.

Heads nodded at his words. Some even prayed with him. Barely minutes passed before the guards returned. They took four more. The three did not return. Ionnes prayed for their souls.

"Why pray for dead men?" belittled the pacer and others nodded agreement. They knew there were questions no mortal man could answer.

"Why pray for dead men?" considered Ionnes as he picked the dried blood out of his beard and mustache.

"Because prayers for one already gone can be given to him by God, even before he has left this life. God can get those prayers to their destination at any time, past or present or future. That is the God I love and serve."

The pacer scoffed again but stopped pacing and went over to the corner to lean against the wall and brood. Figuring she had nothing to lose, the woman came to Yeshua that hour. The older Greek and two others joined in as well.

Soon the guards took others, including the pacing man.

"Call out to Yeshua," urged Ionnes. The pacer looked back briefly, then they were gone. Ionnes prayed and others waited with him until they also were taken to the games. It failed not Ionnes' notice that he became the last man waiting.

He needed not guess when the guards came for him. His heart felt heavy - not for himself but for all the others who had gone before him. He had prayed the martyr's prayer before, but still shuddered as he reached the arena.

Then, even with his earlier injury, his nose detected it first. The smell of cooking oil. Led by soldiers, he saw the great cauldron filled with oil. The fire beneath blazed high as though built by Hell itself. A wooden crane stood right next to the cauldron.

They led Ionnes to near the center of the field. He stood, weary but still praising Yeshua. Tears filled his old brown and gray eyes. Flecks of dark red blood still dressed his face and beard.

"Giovanni of Ephesus," called a voice. Ionnes turned towards the sound. A herald stood next to Emperor Domitian Cæsar, his wife Domitia, the Sage and others in the Senate, many also accompanied by their wives. The emperor, dressed in full toga with a fancy purple stripe border and laurels, smiled at the old man, so small on the huge field. The hungry crowd filled almost every seat for this, the Main Event.

The herald continued. "You have been charged and convicted of treason for failure to give praise and worship to Cæsar Domitian - god on Earth."

The audience waited though many farther down could not hear the yelling herald.

"You have been sentenced to death by boiling oil. But also, Emperor Domitian Cæsar offers you clemency if you will bow and worship him, here and now, before all these witnesses."

Ionnes continued to weep as he saw those before him, now dead, being piled up near the wall. The pacer lay upside down, his face a blue scowl. The young woman draped beside him, covered in her blood; one of her arms missing. The weight of the world pressed mercilessly upon him. Then, he swallowed. It would soon be over. He would be with Yeshua. Perhaps he would see brother Yaakov and their father Zebedee - and Cephas - and Paulos - and Antipas – and so many others. Yeshua's resurrection had opened again the Gates of Heaven. Like so many times before, Ionnes could not wait to see it all as he again wondered what Heaven looked like.

His thoughts flitted over to his friend and spiritual brother Ignatius of Antiochus. They had broken bread just the last month or so before Ionnes' arrest, but it seemed like so long past. Ionnes had always been inspired by Ignatius' boldness and total surrender to Yeshua.

One time Ignatius said to Ionnes, "My devotion to Christos cannot be complete lest I be martyred. Only then shalt my faith reach the ultimate test."

Ionnes accepted a deep, deep breath into his old lungs. The air smelled sweet. Clouds still covered the sky with ominous gloom. He looked to the audience - so many men and women so blind to their fates. His tears poured out like a bowl for them, too. Then, he looked skyward just in case Yeshua took this moment for triumphal return. He turned back towards the emperor.

"I pray FOR you, Domitian. Not TO you." His tears gave way to Spirit-filled boldness. He stared straight as a marksman's arrow at the ruler with sadness and pity. Such a small man after all. "I pray for you to find Yeshua as Messiah. Yeshua Christos loves you, emperor. His life is still yours to receive."

Domitian kept eyes on Ionnes.

"Now," he said, eyes still on Ionnes.

The herald waved hand towards the guards who pushed the prisoner to the crane. They stripped his garments to only a loin cloth, tied his bound hands to the board and raised him up.

Then, they hung heavy iron balls from the chains on his feet.

"In the beginning was the Word, and the Word was with God and was God," yelled Ionnes. "He was in the beginning with God." The ropes hurt his thin, wrinkled wrists as they raised him up. "And, the Word became flesh and dwelt among all of us, and we beheld His glory, the glory as the Only Begotten of the Father, full of grace and truth." The crane swung around over the large, smoky pot. The oil almost to flash point, small bursts of flame flared here and there over the fluid surface.

"Eternal life can be yours with Elohim and Yeshua in Heaven. And of His fullness we have all received, and grace for grace. Grace and truth came through Yeshua Dominus." Caustic smoke rose from the hot oil, barely beneath the metal weights attached to his ankles.

"Hey, Giovanni," called a guard beneath him. "Watch this."

Ionnes looked down as the guard tossed a few loaves of bread into the hot oil. Immediately, they sizzled and fried. More smoke arose. Within the next minute as Ionnes hung two short feet above it all, the loaves turned black.

"Roma, do not give in to your fears," continued Ionnes, as loudly as his voice could travel while hanging, arms up. "Yeshua wants you to be free. You know that Roma hung Him on a cross, but He died for you to no longer be prisoner of your fears. Then, He rose from the dead for you that you could dwell with Him forever."

Some of the crowd started booing. Others enjoyed the spectacle and the anticipation of the pain that would change the words of the zealot to screams of torment.

Domitian motioned to the herald who yelled. "Now. Slowly."

The ultimate torture. Frying feet and legs would not kill a man. He could remain alive and suffering even after major organs were destroyed. Not until the oil reached heart and lungs would the man achieve mortality - if he did not first pass out from the pain. That was always part of the hat trick. Keep him just short of death. The drama, spelled out best on the dying man's face, would be the last to be dunked save the arms from which he hung. He might pass out from the pain before the torso, but what fun would that be?

Three guards manned the crane to control the descent. Ionnes felt the crane move him closer. The heat and smoke continued to rise. He lifted his legs, pulling up against one-hundred-plus pounds of extra weight on his ankles and feet.

The metal went into the oil.

"Yeshua, I am Yours," he said quietly, looking at one of the guards beside the cauldron as he relaxed and the bottoms of his feet reached the oil. "LORD, forgive them for they know not what they do."

The guards paused momentarily, perplexed by those last words. As one abruptly awakened, they returned to the task at hand to gradually lowered him down.

Most of the crowd cheered or held breath. The anticipated moment had finally arrived.

Ionnes looked skyward.

"Roma," he yelled, "love one another, for love is of God, and every one that loves is born of God and knows God. He that loves not knows not God, for God is love."

The soles of his feet entered the oil. Then, his ankles and calves.

"God sent His only begotten Son into the world, that we might live through Him. He knows your ways and your sins and your heart's intent. Repent."

The oil reached his knees.

"His name is Yeshua and He loves you, Roma. He loves all of you dearly. He seeks all of you to come to Him. Be baptized. He will set you free."

The oil reached his groin and waist. At this point, Ionnes' feet stood upon the bottom of the pot. The fire continued to violently rage directly underneath. The crane went down further, giving the old Apostle some freedom of movement. Ionnes did not know, of course, this instruction by Domitian and the Roman Prefect of the Army. As the legs boiled to death, they could no longer hold up the weight of the body. He would continue to descend into the terrible burn no matter how much a man tried to stand.

Instead, Ionnes kept standing and moved as much as he could, his wrists still connected to the crane.

"Thank You, Yeshua," he laughed and danced a bit in the steaming oil.

"HE IS NOT BOILING!" gasped the lead guard.

"No!" stood Domitian. For that matter, all stood and waited. The hush in the Flavian Amphitheater expressed everyone's amazement, such was their awe.

"Bread," yelled Domitian. It took a moment for the herald to decipher Cæsar. He turned to the guards.

"Throw more bread into the oil."

They had no more, lifting empty hands to the emperor.

"Bread," called the herald to the audience. "Give us bread."

After some moments, some pieces were produced by the crowd, tossed down onto the dirt. The guards gathered everything up, went to the cauldron and threw in the food. All immediately wildly boiled and bubbled. Ionnes watched it boil right next to him and it reminded him that his own body stood, not boiling or sizzling. He watched a grape or an olive thrown in, boiling furiously before him. He wanted to reach down to pick it up; to examine it, not that his hands were free. Then he chided himself why any man would put more body parts like his fingers into boiling oil, even if he stood as a living miracle before all?

"Amen," he said, quietly to himself and his LORD, then turned his attention to the emperor.

"Domitian Cæsar. The LORD of lords and KING of kings calls to you. Yeshua is His name and I am His forgiven servant."

They waited some minutes longer, but no further progress for Ionnes as the flames raged up the sides of the huge pot.

"Pull him out," Domitian finally said. The herald barked out the order. Ionnes arose, wet and dripping hot oil as they placed him upon the Earth and released him from the crane.

Some of the guards showed fear to approach him. As one guard released Ionnes from the crane, the apostle immediately fell forward upon his spindly knees. The crowd gasped as they saw this little man fall, but he smiled and raised manacled hands in euphoric praise for his Savior. Some clapped. Less sneered.

Most were too much in awe to do or say anything. The guards approached to remove the weights from his ankles.

"Ow!" yelled a guard, jumping back and putting his burned fingers in his mouth. Others checked it. The metal radiated, boiling hot and the oil burned as it clung to their skin. They waited quite some minutes until he became cool enough to be able to remove the ankle weights.

The mighty Emperor Domitian had the prisoner taken back to the holding cell. Leaving the stands of the arena, he could hear the footsteps of the Sage and others behind him. They entered a room, adorned with whitish-green chalcedony where the resurrected cupbearer served the emperor more wine.

"It did not work," yelled Domitian, slugging down a gulp and expecting a quick refill.

"I was there," assured the Sage.

Domitian looked hard at his counselor for answer.

"I also have no explanation and do not believe what I just saw." Both men were quite unwilling to actually admit to each other what had just transpired in the colosseum. Domitian downed more wine. He emptied the cup and threw it, then plopped down on an old, wooden chair.

He waited quite a spell, numb and quiet. No one dared speak or do anything but await the emperor's next move. The Flavian Amphitheater slowly emptied out. Half an hour plus passed. He rose, and still waited, not speaking. Eventually, he marched out of the room to enter the arena and approached the cauldron, followed by the usual hive of attendees. The fire had died down some, but still displayed an impressive collection of coals. He touched the side of the pot. Immediately, he felt the pain spread and blister his finger. He dipped quickly another finger into the oil - quickly enough to feel the heat but not get terribly burned. Bubbles filled the spot he touched. The self-proclaimed god admitted only to himself he would not have survived the bath. It was still too hot, even now. He left the blood-stained battle field quite a bit slower than he entered. He walked down to the road and awaited his chariot. Stepping up, again looking at his blistered fingers and placing them in his mouth, he leaned towards the Sage and said with exasperation, "You too saw it. He would not cook!"

Ionnes turned towards his fellow inmates. Barely a minute had passed since Arion's question, "So, you were not boiled in oil in Roma?"

"No," answered Ionnes, still lying on his bedroll. "You are incorrect, young man. I was indeed lowered into a huge pot of heated oil. And, poisoned, too. Cyanidus."

"And, you were not harmed?" asked Euæmon.

"Not at all."

The men muttered varying expressions of disbelief, except Teos who said, "Wow, man! Wish I had been there."

"Me, too," whispered Ionnes. "Me, too."

"And?" urged Talor.

"And, that is why the emperor sent me here." Ionnes sighed, feeling the weight of the day's labors.

"Why?" asked Seth. "Why would he send you to this God forsaken island?"

Ionnes smiled. "No place is forsaken by God, my Jewish brother. But it is my guess that many in Roma were seized with fear, so the emperor wanted me far away from Roma. And, quickly. Not another day passed, and I was taken, even accompanied by a garrison led by a Roman Centurion who paid my passage to Patmos. Yet, I found it odd that not one Roman soldier sailed with me. The captain and his deck hands became my guardians."

"How did that work?" asked Dim.

"Mostly they just put extra chains on me so if I jumped overboard, I would surely sink. And, quickly."

"That is a truly incredible story," said Mothcrates. The old Greek philosopher from Athenæ always loved hearing new ideas, thoughts and accounts.

Ionnes nodded, but then added with a yawn, "What is truly incredible, my friend, is not that I was spared, but that Yeshua was glorified through me. The LORD God omnipotent reigns. I see no greater delight."

The prisoners thought about that for a moment. A few more questions came to mind right about the moment they realized they could hear Ionnes quietly snoring.

PATMOS

CHAPTER 4

Chryspippe awoke with a start. Fitfully asleep before, then suddenly eyes wide open. Breathing hard, a sense of fear filled and consumed her, grating the interior walls of her brain. Lying in her bed alone, the familiar sounds and smells of the usual morning seemed alien. Birds sang loudly outside her window. Two slaves chattered about their husbands. The smells of burning wood and boiling something or other permeated the salty sea air. Still, nothing felt right.

The sense of alarm slowly abated like water in a leaking tub making it that much harder to make sense of anything. She knew not the source of the alarm. Her breathing gradually relaxed but left her with a sense of despair and disconnection with her familiar surroundings.

Her husband would already be gone to work. The governor kept his own bedroom. They had not slept together since arriving on Patmos and not much for some years before that.

Herself a socialite, Chryspippe would get together with other bored wives that afternoon for tea, olives and raisin cakes. She did not need anything but might spend the morning shopping before her luncheon. "Need" and "Shopping" were two words that seldom shared the same sentence in her experience.

The sunlight always fooled her as the spring days got longer and longer. It became harder to sleep when morning's brightness filled her window. Sundials did not work at night and roosters were often too early risers. She knew aristocratic families in Roma who kept a slave or two to specifically keep time. She always wished they could have their own time slave as well, even if it was an indecent luxury.

"Lorin?" she called.

A young woman rapidly arrived.

"Miss?"

"Shopping and tea," said Chryspippe.

The slave girl ran to the closet to help her mistress dress for the day. She picked three outfits to present - one white, one green and one blue. Chryspippe would make the final decision.

"Not white. Not blue."

The losers were laid upon the bed as Lorin helped Chryspippe prepare for the day. Seated at her vanity while Lorin brushed her hair, Chryspippe suddenly saw Apollonides' face pop up in her mind like the sparks of a hellacious campfire. It was ugly and bent and twisted as one in great torment. The harsh fear which roused her from her slumbers tumbled and bounced all over her mind like a disturbed nest of crazed hornets. Each new impression stung and throbbed. Nothing would ease that pain.

Lorin stopped preening as her mistress started shaking and shivering. The tormenting images of Apollonides continued to bombard her mind.

"What is wrong, Miss Chrys?"

Chryspippe did not seem to hear her.

"Sisters," called Lorin. "There is something wrong with Miss Chryspippe."

Two women dropped what they were doing and ran to the bed chamber. The room felt cold to them as they entered. The heaviness weighed down each of their steps with ball and chain madness. They arrived just in time to be just as puzzled and confused as Lorin.

"Get water," said Lorin, grabbing a quilt to cover and warm Chryspippe. "Help me get her to bed."

Chryspippe accepted their help and laid her head back when suddenly Apollonides' grotesque features appeared beside her on her pillows. She screamed and jumped up, backing away.

The slaves let her move backwards while staying with her.

"No," she commanded and straightened up.

The slaves let go.

"Where is my husband?" her voice squeaked.

"To work," answered Lorin.

"What was he wearing? Uniform or toga? Or tunic?" The three girls looked at each other to remember.

"Uniform," one of them said.

"I must find him," she said, an order implied in her words.

"Yes, mistress," answered Lorin and the three prepared to accompany Chryspippe to the military post. Apollonides' scary face kept appearing out of nowhere - across the wall, on the door, over a chair, in the garden and pond outside... Common places stretched like potter's clay into his repulsive form. At one point, Chryspippe looked back at her servants to see if they saw the same thing. She recognized that they saw nothing. If they had seen it, they already would have said something.

Shortly thereafter, outside, the quartet hastened down the hill. Apollonides' malformed face mockingly laughed at them from the hillside. Chryspippe hastened all the quicker, seeking a sense of relief to put distance between herself and the visions. Apollonides' face did not appear again after the hill, but she felt far from safe or assured.

"Seek the protection of the gods," her mother told her one time. "Artemis will protect you."

Chryspippe shook her head violently at the thought. She had never known the gods to care about anyone besides themselves. Even Prometheus' gift of fire sometimes seemed like an act of defiance against Jupiter rather than a benevolent, caring gift to mankind. She had been to the temples many, many times and not once did she feel any caring regard from any of the gods.

She knew the godly stories about as well as anyone. Such readings had been part of her education. She was one of the few women she knew who were formally taught to read and write and more. She treasured that gift, though to be honest, she had done very little with it since marrying Laurentius. When they were young and in love, he had claimed it was one of the features he most treasured about her. Yet, as he climbed the Roman hills of success, he expected her to be more an ornament and brainless support than an intellectual equal.

Perhaps it might have been different if they had been blessed with children....

Reaching the Castra Legionaria military outpost, the four women entered without a challenge. The Roman soldiers all knew Chryspippe on sight, even if most believed that she, a woman, had no business being there.

"I seek the governor," she told one young soldier.

"I believe he is in the armory," answered the soldier. Glad to hear he was there, she then tilted her head as an order for him to take her.

"If it pleases your governess, I am on guard duty here, but can call another to take you to the governor.

"Very good," she said, then added, "And 'hastatus,' the wife of a governor is not called a governess."

"Apologies, m'am," the young soldier corrected, a little too timid to ask her what the wife of a governor was called and hoped she would volunteer that information. She did not.

The young guard whistled loudly. Helmeted heads appeared. He waved, signaling for some to come. Two complied immediately.

"Please escort the governor's wife to the governor." "Begging your pardon," answered one soldier. "We know not where the governor has gone."

"Check the armory or the Legate."

Entering the compound, they first stopped by the armory.

The governor had already left.

They stepped out into the shady side of the building to head to the Legate. A prisoner in chains stood nearby, looking at them. Chryspippe barely saw him as was her custom, but the corner of her eye demanded a closer look. She turned and gasped without breaking stride with her chaperones. The old prisoner who had cured her brother watched her shamelessly, a warm smile adding to the sunshine.

She watched him and briefly wanted to stop and thank him, but that was unthinkable according to her station, and she continued on to the parade field.

Crossing the parade field, they targeted the offices of the Legate. Chryspippe wondered about the old man until she slowly realized the sense of fear which had so mercilessly attacked her not an hour earlier seemed distant and somewhat foolish to admit to her husband. Leaving the parade field and about to enter the command center, she felt compelled to tell them to stop and never mind when Laurentius and the Legate exited the building. The governor noted his wife, nodded to the Legate and stepped down the stone stairs to meet her.

At this point, their guide saluted Laurentius, then hastened back to his other duties and assignments. The three slaves waited a fair and respectful distance from the couple.

"What is wrong?" asked Laurentius.

Chryspippe suddenly felt a bit embarrassed to admit what had happened. She paused, unable to coherently speak.

"Chryspippe?" said Laurentius, as much a statement as a question.

Besides her reluctance and apparent confusion, as well as the untimely arrival, he also noticed her appearance. Dressed for the day, but not as kempt as usual. Her face barely painted. Her hair a bit untucked. Her collar and sleeves not straight. Out of breath and perspiring from her trek to find him.

Coming with three handmaidens instead of just Lorin.

"Chryspippe?" he repeated more directly.

She wanted to run to him, hug him and have him take away all the fear and angst and woe. He would reassure her in his manly, protective embrace and look into her face.

"Gimme those tears," he used to say with slurpy kisses to playfully bring her spinning head back to Earth. But those days were long past, and she restrained her impulses to run up and grab hold of him, using trained and ever restrained control.

Was not that the way the cultured Roman woman behaved?

"Chrys?" Laurentius called as they drew near.

They both stood a moment, gazing at one another; she fearful and embarrassed, and him questioning about something he might never understand.

"Um," she finally managed to say. "Apollonides."

"Is Apollonides alright? What is wrong with Apollonides?" He almost sounded disappointed.

"No," she blurted. "At home. It----" The dam broke abruptly. She lurched forward and grabbed hold of him with resolve to never let go. He almost gasped with surprise. Her handmaidens did gasp. They had never seen her act in this manner towards her husband over the previous year or three that they had been in bondage.

"I do not know," Chryspippe answered, tears filling her eyes. "I was in bed when I saw his face. It was twisted and ugly, and I feared first for him. Then, I saw him again and again, distorted and freakish, and I feared for myself. Even after I left the house, I saw him again on the hill."

"You saw Apollonides?"

"NO," she shouted. "Not really. I just saw his face on my wall and in my bed and in my toilet and wall and other places in the house."

"Like a dream?"

She paused. "No," she finally said. "It was more than a dream but less than really seeing. And, it scared me greatly." He stood still while she continued to hold to him tightly. Finally, he looked down at her and admitted, "That would be terrible. It would scare me, too."

She felt some relief for he at least seemed to understand. He was not typically a tender man and compassion flowed not from him a common trait. She had learned to rely on her own strength or perhaps a strong matriarch or two over the years. With Apollonides' madness, she had had to be strong at times she would have preferred otherwise. After all that life behind her, she wondered that she could not be stronger now, but she had never encountered such visions - visions that started by pounding first her brain, filling her with fear, then next appearing throughout her home. Even next to her husband, her frame shuddered as the experiences replayed through her thoughts.

"I am sorry to bother you, m'lord, but I have never felt such fear. In turn, I had to see you."

"Are you past your fears, now?" She looked up at him.

"Yes," she whispered.

He smiled. "Then, for now we shall expect it is passed and you are safe."

She waited briefly, not quite ready to let go.

"Woman!" he said more loudly.

She knew that voice. She always hated that tone, but she knew and accepted its meaning.

"I am sorry, m'lord." She broke embrace.

He felt the ice quickly form between them again. He never liked it, but had grown accustomed to its patterns, like the frozen gatherings on winter windows and other ornate etchings in glass.

She turned to go, returning to Lorin's care and attendance. The four women walked in step as they departed. Chryspippe turned one more time towards her husband. He had remained, watching them those few seconds, perhaps to see his wife safely on her way, or more likely, perplexed by her behaviors and reports. They gazed at one another those few seconds. She thought to ask what he wanted for dinner or would he like a bath when he got home, but her lips remained sewn. She nodded and turned to leave.

An impression caught her eye and she turned back. Apollonides' horrid features replaced her husband's hard face. Her eyes widened. It was only there for a second or so, but unmistakable. She gasped but dared say nothing. He noticed her repose, but also did not ask or call to her. She turned, walked a dozen more steps, then looked back. Laurentius' face answered her returned look. She continued, and when she looked back one more time, he strode towards the Legate, his back to them.

"Come," she ordered. As they left the base, she ordered Lorin to accompany her to town, and the others to resume their duties at home. The pair departed, somewhat ready for normalcy to return. Neither coveted Lorin's day with their mistress.

"We must find Mallia," she said, speeding her pace.

Few noticed Chryspippe as she entered town, though she felt terribly conspicuous, being so unkempt. Mallia would fix that and the pair beelined to her salon.

"Mallia," she called as she entered.

Mallia looked up from the hair she curled. Chryspippe recognized the elderly woman being attended to - a Greek somewhat beneath her socially. "I need your help," she directed.

"I should say so," agreed Mallia. "I have another coming shortly, but she will just have to wait." The wife of the governor would seldom be expected to wait and usually could cut in line ahead of everyone else. Mallia knew the rules as well as anyone in town. She finished up the matron quickly and sent her on her way.

"Please my dear. Come and sit."

"Mallia, my day has been absolutely frightful," said Chryspippe as she was seated before her hairdresser.

"Well, I will take care of everything," assured Mallia. "Ugh!" she added. "Who brushed your hair this morning? It is like trying to brush a bird's nest." She looked up towards Lorin. "Was it you?"

The slave gulped and sort of nodded.

"Well, it is awful," growled Mallia.

Lorin looked shamefully at Mallia, then at Chryspippe.

"Please," interrupted Chryspippe, "it is not her fault. Not totally. I had a scare this morning and needed to leave my house before I was ready."

Mallia's features softened, but only slightly.

"So," continued Chryspippe, "I have come to town for shopping and a luncheon with the ladies."

"Sounds glorious," applauded Mallia and meant it as she deftly pulled hair back to mold and decorate.

Another woman entered - the next appointment. Seeing Chryspippe, she knew she would have to wait, and sat to join in. She smiled. Not every day came that she got to visit with the governor's wife.

"Lisa," called Mallia. "I will be with you soon." The women chatted about this and that. Chryspippe became surprised that no one mentioned her brother Apollonides and the amazing occurrences of the previous night. Then, it occurred to her that these people were probably afraid to ask. She knew she would have been, even if only out of charm and politeness. Then the women, loaded with no more information than before Chryspippe entered the room, would all cackle and chatter as soon as Chryspippe left. She loved being the most important and respected woman on the island. Being the target of gossip was just part of the gig. She totally accepted it and oftentimes cherished it. Gossip can work for a person just as well as it can work against.

"There," finished Mallia. New hair. New face. Washed feet. She re-attained the presentable status as the governor's wife, ready to enjoy her day in town. Rising, Lorin stepped forth to attend. The unkempt young slave girl seemed so plain and crude next to her primped mistress. She sighed to herself.

"Mallia, you are a miracle worker," applauded Chryspippe, admiring her image in the wax buffed and polished metal, then she moved to a large, dark bowl full of water near the window to see her reflected image there. She paused, and almost declined to look, suddenly wondering if she would see the twisted face of Apollonides in the water. She did not want to have another scene like she had had that morning, especially here in the shoppe. They would surely all gaggle that she took over the madness of her brother. She sighed bravely to herself and looked towards her reflection in the water. Her fears abated as she looked down upon herself, perfectly adorned. She looked away quickly just in case the image changed.

"Lorin," she called.

Her slave girl approached and waited.

"Come," ordered Chryspippe to follow as they exited. "Our day is already half wasted." Then, she spun around towards Mallia. "Thank you again, my dear. Your skills will not go unrewarded...."

The three women chatted further, on and on. Lorin watched and listened a minute or two then took the moment to gaze at her own image in the water. A tear touched her eye. She blinked quickly and dared not wipe. The image beneath her looked back with deep sadness. She knew she could jiggle the table with a small bump and destroy the image, but she kept eye contact with herself.

She recalled the first time she saw her reflection. She was perhaps ten or eleven. Maybe even twelve. The first time she saw what her face looked like. She had seen her shadow countless times, of course, but shadows only tell part of the story. She recalled the time she discovered her eyelashes, poking out of her shadow as it slouched against a white marble wall. She moved them and touched them and rotated her head against the sunlight to make sure they were really hers. Still gazing at her reflection below, she cracked a smile, nudging up her left cheek. She paused only briefly to admire, daring to go no further.

"Lorin," snapped Chryspippe. "I said, 'Come.'" It did not matter that she had said that some minutes earlier then had stopped to prattle.

The smiling reflection in water disappeared to morph back to somber sadness as Lorin turned to attend to her mistress. The two women entered the narrow walkway, turning towards the town square. Lorin respectfully followed a few steps behind but kept her eyes and ears a step or two ahead. Entering the public square, Chryspippe suddenly stopped. There he was again. The old prisoner walking under guard toward the sea. He did not notice her, though he seemed to notice just about everyone else. He smiled, or his lips quivered together as though lost in a whisper. And then, barely a minute later and he was gone, behind a building.

Chryspippe wanted to chase him down. She did not even know why. The compulsion had not yet reached the cognition of words, but pressed her with a compelling, unspeakable flow. Again, she restrained herself. It was a totally different matter to lose all control to one's husband versus chasing a complete stranger. And, a prisoner no less. Even if he did heal her brother, he was still an untouchable. She knew her place and his. She knew her thoughts, but it was the first time in a very long time - if ever, she felt a twinge to question a person's station in life. Something deeper down than she had as yet experienced started to simmer and churn and question her lifelong held beliefs. She felt a moment of something - guilt perhaps? Uncertainty, at very least? Whatever it was, it pricked as a completely unaccustomed feeling and that fact added to her unsettled thoughts.

She vaguely recalled reading something like this long ago.

Socrates perhaps? Or Marcus Aurelius?

"Chryspippe," greeted Madame Her. The large, matronly woman grabbed both Chryspippe's green clad shoulders to touch cheeks. "What a beautiful gown!" she cooed with typical flamboyant flair. "Darling. We feared we had missed you." Other women joined them.

"Madame Her," Chryspippe managed to say and nodded to the others.

"Please, my friend. Join us. Let us go. I found a new sweet cake at the bakery that you just have to try."

Chryspippe smiled and turned to go with the ladies. Walking in stride with the other women, she nonchalantly looked back again towards the wall the mysterious prisoner disappeared behind. The spot still empty, she returned her attentions to the women.

None of the women seemed to notice except Lorin who shared her mistress's watch but knew not why.

PATMOS

CHAPTER 5

Splat!

He killed a fly.

Splat!

Another.

Scooping them up and placing them in a stone bowl, Kynops kept eyes alert for another. The recipe called for sixteen. Five more to go.

His flat, far outside of town, seemed more like a cave than a manmade structure. He had dug a huge hole in the hillside, built his house in it, then practically buried it. The cold, dank walls sometimes sweated like the outside of a cool goblet of water on a hot day. No windows anywhere in the structure, but the earthen insulation kept temperatures coolly constant year round. He needed that for his potions. Only one thick, wooden door led in or out. Inside there were some partitions, but in actuality, it was pretty much just one large room. He lived alone, though at times he might have had an apprentice to learn his dark arts. They never stayed long, probably because of the shadows.

Sometimes shrieks and hollers and painful wails could be heard coming from his home at night. Nobody dared enter uninvited, and most declined when they were invited. Kynops was not one given to entertaining guests and visitors.

He recited a repetitive mantra to coerce the demonic census he sought. Who was still out there? Which spirits could he still rely on?

Dogs outside his house started howling as he began his incantations. The dogs always knew when he set about his work. He had felt a great disturbance in the source of his power and wanted to expel it or make the disturbance his own if it would serve his purposes. Early indications suggested the former would be his only choice. Something had recently changed the spiritual flow around Patmos. The spirits he bridled now avoided him, along with the power they wielded.

They still came forward when called, but with less flow and intensity.

"What is it, my shadows?" He closed his eyes to block out the physical. He covered his ears for the same reason. One did not only rely on the five or more natural senses to talk to the dead.

Changes in the spiritual world were not unusual. Actually, it happened every day, to be sure, for one who cared to check. Kynops noted the flow and ebb like a sailor watching the sky. His cold heart could measure any increase in the ethereal temperatures. His closed eyes saw the afterimages of his unholy vassals. His nostrils detected their decaying, sulfurous stench. His fingertips tingled like the countless jabbing needles after a limb fell asleep then became aroused.

Splat!

Four more to go.

He flicked the insect off his prickling fingers into the marble bowl.

His thoughts returned to the previous night. How he had walked into the square to see Apollonides cured; his sanity regained. He knew not the cause. A part of him reveled. He had long past grown weary of the governor's brother-in-law and his rants and raves. He did not relish being Apollonides' babysitter anytime further. In that, he could applaud. But, the source of the healing? That arose as the unanswered question which plagued and bothered him. He had not heard of any physician recently coming to Patmos. And, what doctor practices in the town square at night? Something was amiss. He needed to know what.

Splat!

Down to three.

"Are you sure you cannot mend him?" asked Laurentius.

Chryspippe looked up from her knitting.

Kynops stood from his seat for a loftier stature. He peered at the new governor and his wife with an expression of knowing confidence. Whatever the source of that insight, implied or real, he would never have to actually verbalize. They had been on Patmos but a month. This was their first meeting - one he had put-off to add to his mystique and importance. The governor would undoubtedly test and quiz Kynops to see what he could be capable of and whether he would use his powers for Roma.

Apollonides had already etched his nonsensical mark on the small island. Laurentius had wanted to leave him back in Roma, but Chryspippe insisted her family come with them. Laurentius loved and respected her father, Myron. The elder had helped mentor his young son-in-law. Now neither man young, Laurentius still valued Myron's insights and was pleased to have him and his wife Fona join them. But that meant the lunatic Apollonides would also accompany them. Laurentius had to choose between either both men or neither.

He had literally flipped a golden Aureus that he owned with the pressed image of Augustus Cæsar on the front and a dolphin on the back. If Cæsar landed upside, Myron and son would join them. Not that he truly relied on the flip of a coin to decide. He would use it to gage his own reaction. If he hedged, not sure which way to decide, he would flip the coin. If he felt relief at the coin's landing, he knew that to be what he wanted. If he felt dissatisfaction or disappointment at the coin's choice, he knew to decide the other way. The system actually worked consistently and quite well for him. When the August face gave thumbs up for Myron and son, Laurentius felt relief. From that, he knew their accompaniment to be ultimately the right choice. Fortunately, neither Myron nor Apollonides were present when Kynops received summons to the governor's mansion. "It is not mine to take away," Kynops soon answered regarding Apollonides. He still stood, admiring his long fingernails. "His mind shouts forth like a gift from the gods."

"Well, that 'gift' has long ago slayed my patience. I'm ready to reassign it to another - say a prisoner or an untouchable. Or, even a Hebrew."

"Indeed," considered Kynops. He looked through the governor like a specter as he added, "Like the owl, I shall intercede as the matter overtakes me."

112

Kynops' voice crackled like a cranky fire as he paced back and forth throughout his gloomy dwelling. The shadows followed him. He had been surprised by the presence of the shadows many years earlier. They knew his every move and followed him as shadows should. But they were not always his body's shadows.

He might be sitting on the floor eating as the shadows swayed back and forth together like underwater reeds on a breezy day. He could seek a scroll of spells. The shadows sometimes knew and pointed where to look. He slept under their layers, piled high like a weightless blanket of icy stones. He could read their mute lips and feel their loss and hopelessness. He welcomed their dark, blinding ways and distractions, for all that he commanded they were compelled to do. Kynops treasured the power they provided and no more. No kinship. No sweet attachment. No compassion. And, certainly no love. He never questioned why they would do his bidding. He never questioned that he had authority to order them. He only knew it to be true. The why did not matter, and as far as Kynops lived, probably better left unanswered. Day or night. Inside or out. He could order them about almost as directly as the Legate ordered a soldier.

So, it grabbed his notice when on this day the shadows shuddered or faded in and out. He summoned and they came but disappeared most quickly if not ordered to some task. He sought answers. The shadows remained elusive. The spiritual tide had ebbed out, much deeper than usual. As he paced, he repeated age old mantras as he sought answers from unholy tide pools. No harbinger came to his aid. No enchantment danced or teased before him. He, the Kynops, the key mystic on the island, found no answer to satisfy him as yet.

"The dogs do not speak Latin - or Greek. If they did, we would better understand them otherwise."

Apollonides sat on the sandy shore petting their white alopekis, Skylos, who loved to be petted and loved Apollonides the most. The canine had been part of the family over seven years. Although Apollonides could suddenly go from calm to crazy at the wag of a tail, she still loved his scent, touch and melodic tenor voice.

Apollonides felt the eyes of the whole family upon him. His father, Myron, who kept him hidden from the real world and never understood him. His sister, Chryspippe, who was the only other person in the world to know his self-christened secret name - Heliotrope. His brother-in-law, Laurentius, who better knew the use of a dagger than a bragger or nagger or flagger or badger. And certainly not a wagger like Skylos - a fact which always made Apollonides stagger.

He saw the usual Roman soldiers in attendance as well as the family slaves. Lorin looked at him curiously, but she often did that, and he smiled towards her as he kissed Skylos' hairy forehead.

And, now this new face. Kynops. He wanted to call him Skysnots but knew that would be rude. The magician loomed over him menacingly which Apollonides considered rude. So, he gazed numbly out over the water towards the mainland. The Taurus islands stood hazily and lazily just out of reach.

"I used to walk on the water," muttered Apollonides, "but Neptune stopped me. Now the Ægean hates me. No longer does the Mediterranean current move me. I asked Neptune why. He shrugged, but in that shrug I could see Juno. Her wrath pushed my brother Neptune against me and now I am just as much a prisoner here as all of you."

"The gods never speak to you," challenged Kynops. "They told me so."

Apollonides peered up towards the strange fellow, Skysnots with the painted eyes and long earlobes. The sky was blinding, but he liked the red, crooked scar on Kynop's chin. The magician's chin always smiled even when his mouth wore a frown.

"Ah, but they do," challenged Apollonides. "One time Jupiter asked me to die, so I did. He may have been upset that I called Juno a HAG. I had to explain from the underworld that

HAG meant Happy And Gay. So, Jupiter brought me back to this life. You should have seen Pluto's face as I slid out from under his grasp. Charon already loved me and would take me back over the River Styx."

"Charon loves no man."

"He does when you bring him dolmathes. Everyone brings him a gold coin. You cannot eat a gold coin, and there is nothing for him to buy down there. Next time I go, I promised to bring spanikopita."

Kynops felt the venom in his veins for this one. He wanted to turn him into a lame dwarf but withheld any mystical mischief.

"Jupiter was waiting when I exited the underworld. He explained, when he had asked me to die, he did not mean literally or right then and there but was asking for my love and servitude - that I would be willing to die for him. He apologized for his miscommunication."

"A god never apologizes or asks forgiveness - least of all the king of all gods. Even less to any mortal."

Apollonides giggled as he watched the waves. "They do when you make them laugh. All gods love to laugh, but they seldom get a chance to do it."

"Death does not let go," added Kynops. "If you were dead once, you would not now be here."

Apollonides seemed to not hear for some time, barely petting the dog who looked at him longingly. Then, he started singing,

> "I wish I was on Styxie.
> Hooray! Hooray!
> On Styxie's Boat I'll stay Afloat,
> To die and live on Styxie.
> Away, away, away down down on Styxie!
> Away, away, away down down on Styxie!"

"Quiet," shouted Kynops.

Apollonides looked up at him and smiled again. This was too easy. Skylos growled. Apollonides could hear his family muttering around him, but he did not have to listen. He already knew all too well what they were saying. Their voices were chaff against the lapping waves and feathery breeze which foremost drew his ears to listen.

"I am building a canal between here and the mainland," he continued. "It is not made out of water. It is made out of land. You know. Dirt. Rock."

"You mean a bridge?" said someone. Apollonides thought it could have been Kynops, though such details to that personal query did not really matter.

"A bridge? Yes. A bridge," thought Apollonides aloud, still staring at the mountains across the water. "But I just like the word 'canal' better."

Kynops started muttering something. Apollonides knew not the meanings of the odd words but perked his ears only slightly. Stylos started getting antsy. She whined to move away.

Apollonides kept hold and tried to soothe her.

"Where are their horns?" wondered Apollonides. He pointed across the water towards the mountains. "The mountains," he added, more to himself than anyone there. "They used to have horns. Where did they go? Nobody knows." He sighed. A tear appeared. "One day they were there. Another day, they were gone."

His voice choked as the emotions of sadness and loss pushed through him.

"Where did they go? Nobody knows."

Kynops kept muttering his strange words. Skylos started howling. Apollonides suddenly tossed Skylos from his lap, jumped up and ran to the shoreline. He entered the surf, up to his knees in water, then hips, then waist. He stopped and turned back. The others followed him. Then, he turned and fled from the water before Neptune could strike him.

He looked at his family, face to face there on the shore.

"Nobody knows." He looked at Laurentius who looked back and forth between Apollonides and Kynops. "Not even you." Raising both hands, he yelled, "NOBODY KNOWWSSSSS," his voice reaching high for the sky; or any gods who might have been listening.

Then, he turned again to Laurentius, "But, I do." He smiled impishly. "I do. I pulled them off. Those nasty, impudent horns, each with a little snarling face that talked to you like you were stupid." He pointed towards the mountains across the channel. "I pulled them off and buried them beneath the quarry. Some day you may dig them up."

Kynops raised a hand towards Apollonides.

"Oh! Oh!" He bent over and grabbed hold of his bitter stomach. "I think I am going to throw up. Whoops! Let us see if it comes back to Earth thereafter." He turned his head sideways to make sure no vomit was returning to Earth where he stood.

"Sister," he called. The pain on his face became obvious. She leaned down and placed her hand on his shoulder.

"I would rather be a hammer than a nail."

"As would I," assured Chryspippe.

"Apollonides," approached his father. Kynops continued his chant and he paced around his quarry. Laurentius kept watch over all and the Roman guards not far off kept watch over the governor.

"Father," Apollonides answered, the pain still filling his face and features.

"Let it go," urged Myron.

"Father," Apollonides repeated. "I tried to teach Mercury to fly. It was hopeless. The wings behind his ears made him an airhead."

"Let it go," repeated Myron as Chryspippe placed her arm around her brother, kneeling down together on the moist sand. He looked at his sister and pressed a weak smile.

"I do not like to beg. I would rather be the person that people beg from."

She nodded, partially because it was the sanest thing she had heard him say for a long time.

"My, my, my," she assured.

He looked deep in her green eyes. "I think that is the most selfish and self-centered sentence any person on Earth can ever say."

She grinned. "Brother, you may be right."

He laughed, though still in pain. He looked up at Kynops, still pointing those long fingers towards him. No comfort there, so he turned attention to his father.

"The gods have spoken and that is why I am broken." He leaned forward, pressing his forehead into the gravelly sand. He raised his hands up to slap the back of his head while it pressed into the sandy beach.

"If their chatter would end, then perhaps I could mend." He coughed.

"If the gods were all mute, I could be a flute. I surely would try it, if the gods would be quiet."

He started drawing two eyes and a singing mouth in the sand. Raising up a bit, still on his knees, he stared at the flecks of sand on his fingers and those falling from his forehead.

"Look sister. I am a crayon of many colors made from the finest Roman tallow. Even the bees are envious."

He looked at Chryspippe. "Remember when we were children, how I used to draw on the walls with my crayon fingers."

She nodded acknowledgement.

"Remember how mad that used to make mama? I had to stop after awhile because it is hard to eat with no fingers."

Chryspippe burst out with a little laugh. Part of her knew he was sick, but every now and then he said something that absolutely caught her off guard and made her laugh.

He looked up at papa Myron who gave a supporting smile. Then, a quick glance at Kynops who glared at him intensely with the friendly, red smile still on his chin.

"Still trying to put the chariot before the horse, are you?"

Kynops answered, "It matters not as long as I find a bit that fits your mouth." He continued to stab the air between them with his long fingers. Then, he abruptly stopped. He peered at Apollonides intently for what seemed a long time. His chant changed as he saw the shadow covering the man like a sheer mesh. He knew at last how to free Apollonides, but his shadows did not wish it. He just knew that. And, even as their earthly commander, he also knew when best to not challenge their wishes.

He snorted as he announced, "I must stop. I could cure him, but the cost would be too great."

"Why?" demanded Myron, rising to face him. "What worse fate could become of him?"

"I am not willing to risk it."

"What?" pressed Myron.

"He would be like a snail on this salty sand."

"I would rather be a sparrow than a snail," said Apollonides.

"What would happen to my brother?" asked Chryspippe. Kynops looked at her with a deathly stare. Fear seized her as her eyes met his, and she emotionally backed away as she saw images of Apollonides lost and gone from them forever.

"Father let him be," she urged.

"Woman?"

"Forgive me, father, but let him be."

Myron huffed with disgust. Skylos again howled, then slipped behind Chryspippe to glare and snarl at Kynops. Apollonides rose up, still on his knees, as the tormenting pain eased. He looked out over the water and thought he could smell a Roma from there but opted to keep silent. He stood and sneezed, driving a bit of sand from his nose.

"I have to get out of this sun," he said. "My skin is too sparkly. It makes everyone think I am a god." He grabbed a new lungful of air. "That is not always a bad thing."

Laurentius finally stepped forward and scoffed. "Be gone," he ordered Kynops.

"My pay for service?" reminded Kynops.

"What service?" barked the governor. "You wasted my time and day with your ineptness. I pay for results, not excuses or failures."

Kynops stood ground until Laurentius added, "Guards."

Three men stepped forward, spears in hand or swords drawn. Kynops sort of bowed with little more than a head nod and turned away.

"I shall not destroy art," he said as he turned to go, "nor loiter for your entertainment." Mounting his horse, he trotted off.

"What a waste of time!" Myron said to Laurentius. The governor nodded and headed with decisive purpose for his horse. He would waste no more effort towards this foolishness.

The term, "It was worth a try," did not even try to sneak into his thoughts.

"Take them home," he ordered the soldiers. "And, make sure Apollonides does not stray." He rode off towards town, two soldiers on horse following as escorts.

"Come, brother," Chryspippe took Apollonides' hand. "Let us go home."

"Did you leave your husband and move back home with papa and mama?"

"No," she giggled. "But our parents' home is always a home to us, no matter where we are in life. Is not that right, papa?"

Myron took hold and hugged his daughter around her shoulders. The day was a disappointment, but otherwise no harm done. It certainly fared not as the first time someone had tried to heal their kin and failed. The three mounted a horse drawn cart to go. Their slaves and Skylos would follow behind on foot.

Apollonides sat numbly as his sister stroked his dark hair. He watched the shoreline behind him shrink. He watched the hill before him grow. He closed his eyes, but it did no good. "I try to be blind," he uttered, eyes still closed, "but my eyelids are transparent. Makes it difficult to sleep sometimes." He leaned his head against Chryspippe. "I got that way from eating fish."

Another little laugh snorted through her nose.

The slow, steady movement, led by the clomping of horse hooves, shouted louder than their silence. Each considered the activities of the day and made their own personal assessments. Apollonides looked aside at the small grove of olive trees. He smiled towards the bluegreen leaves like beryl and tiny fruit as he muttered, "I would rather be a forest than a street," then looked up at his sister and smiled. "Yes, I would. If I could, I surely would."

"Speak to me," Kynops ordered one from his company of shadows. This one had assisted him time and time again.

"What powers cause you to quiver? Speak to me apparition."
The shadow quaked but remained silent.

"SPEAK!" ordered the magician.

The shadow started to fade.

"NO!" yelled Kynops. "Remain."

The unholy spirit froze.

"Remain until I pray you leave."

The grotesque predicament of both mortal and immortal remained at stalemate or an unlikely tug-o-war. Neither moved. If Kynops moved forward towards the ethereal being, it shrank back. He stopped, and it stopped, but nothing seemed to be able to bring him the answers he sought.

Splat!

Fifteen.

The spirit saw its chance and fled.

Kynops stood, the smashed housefly in his hand, alone in his cold, dark dungeon of a dwelling. It was oddly colder than usual to be alone there. The walls felt still. He swatted his sixteenth fly and placed the dead pair in the bowl with the others. Grabbing his pestle, he mashed and ground and pulverized the little creatures. Adding some herbs and leaves, he continued the process until the blackish paste became complete. Grabbing a freshly made flat of pita, he spread the paste across the surface, folded it in two and took a bite. It tasted good to him. He must have been hungrier than usual.

Still eating, he stopped chewing mid bite.

"How could I be so blind?"

The pictures of logic flashed across his mind forming one bold answer he should have seen from the start. A divine presence had to have arrived. That supported the only plausible explanation. He did not know who, but he would find out.

"Eternal judgment," he swore.

"Chryspippe," he added. She was there last night. If anyone knew what cured Apollonides, she would know. Something cast away the spirit from that one. No wonder the shadows all shuddered. He finished his meal and sat brooding. He poured a glass of blood red wine. Taking a gulp, he knew what he must do. The rancid, cling-on liquid toured his pallet before swishing down the gnarly drain called his throat.

The first question plagued him as to who interfered? The next question was harder. Much harder. What to do about it?

And, quickly.

PATMOS

CHAPTER 6

"Shalom," greeted Ionnes, entering the barracks. Only three as yet inside for the night - Teos, Mothcrates and Rabbi Yosef.

"What is Shuh-lome?" asked Teos.

"It means Peace," answered Ionnes. "It is a Hebrew word. We use it as a way to greet someone such as 'The Peace of the LORD be with you'."

Rabbi Yosef cleared his throat in a most obnoxious and grumpy fashion. Ionnes recognized the rabbi's noisy disapproval.

"You disagree rabbi?" Ionnes turned face towards Yosef. For the last month since Ionnes arrival, Yosef had kept watch of the older apostle who acted like the only witness to the One True God on the island.

"My good fellow," Yosef began, "Shalom means much more than just 'peace' as any devout Jew would know."

"Only Elohim is good," interjected Ionnes.

"Scribed," nodded Yosef, "and, you are right to say so, but that is beside my point and I will not be deterred."

"My apologies," said Ionnes, sitting on the floor near the rabbi.

"And, what is good?" Mothcrates threw in to join the discussion.

"I said I will not be deterred!" groused the old rabbi.

Mothcrates acknowledged though he truly still would have liked to hear their answers to his question.

Yosef looked first at Teos, then Ionnes, then back at Teos.

"Shalom can mean 'peace', but it comes from the word Shalam which means to be of sound mind; completeness; fullness. When I say 'Shalom' to someone, I am also wishing them fullness and well-being, particularly in Elohim's care."

"Does that make sense, Teos?" asked Ionnes.

Teos looked at the two men a moment, then answered, "Uh-huh. It means 'peace'."

"Um-," started Yosef, then looked at Ionnes and had to smile at the young man's simple way of understanding. He had been a rabbi long enough to understand the depth and beauty of simple faith and understanding. He nodded at Teos, then looked at Ionnes.

"Do you know the Aaronic Blessing?"

Ionnes knew the Blessing pretty much as well as any Jewish rabbi. For Yosef, it was like asking someone if a person knew his own birthday. Every rabbi knew the Aaronic Blessing from rote. He did not wait for Ionnes to answer.

"Speak to Aaron and to his sons, saying, 'Thus you shall bless the sons of Yisra'el. You shall say to them: The LORD bless you, and keep you; The LORD make His face shine on you, And be gracious to you; The LORD lift up His countenance on you, And give you peace."

"From Numbers," added Ionnes.

Yosef continued, "Aaron said, 'And give you peace.' Give you Shalom. What were they about to do?"

"Enter the Promised Land."

"Yes," agreed Yosef, then added, "So why would Aaron wish upon them God's peace when they were about to go to war?"

"Sounds like a good way to lose a war," said Mothcrates, not familiar with the story of Joshua and the Yisra'elites entering Canaan.

"True," agreed Yosef, "if that is what God meant, but He wished for them His Peace for doing what He directed. Have not you ever felt that way? You want to do something, and your mind can tell you why it is okay, but your discernment and heart tells you it is wrong. You know it is God speaking to you, and if you are wise, you choose to listen not to your own reason which can misguide a man, but God's holy voice. When one follows God's laws and precepts, may he always find God's peace within."

Dim entered the barracks. Nobody looked at him except Teos who always smiled and nodded when he saw Dim.

"They's fighting," whispered Teos, cuppng his hand next to his cheek so the others would not hear, or so he thought.

"Like Daniel," said Ionnes.

Rabbi Yosef nodded.

"And, Yosef."

Rabbi Yosef really nodded.

"And, even Moses, though he did not want to follow God's direction and return to Egypt. But still he went, and Adonai blessed him mightily."

Dim noticed that name, Moses, again spoken by Ionnes, so hunkered down to see if he could learn more. He knew these two had a history all their own. It often felt like trying to learn a foreign language talking to them.

"*The LORD shall fight for you, and you shall hold your peace*," Yosef said, quoting from Exodus.

Ionnes was not sure of the reference. "The LORD shall fight for you," he muttered, the list of scriptural books flying through his sharp mind.

"Could be David."

"No," answered Yosef.

"Not even in the Psalms?"

"Not this time."

Ionnes thought hard.

"Gideon?"

Yosef shook his head.

"Moses?"

"Correct," said Yosef.

"Where? What was happening?"

"It had to be either Moses before Pharaoh, or after the Yisra'elites had left Egypt and Pharaoh ordered the army to pursue them."

"The latter," answered Yosef, "just before Elohim divided the Sea."

"That is a very complete Shalom," said Ionnes. "Adonai destroys their enemy and they are certainly left with Shalom. Most convenient."

Jack and Talor entered.

Talor said with purpose, "I am telling you, Jack, she thought I was something."

"You are something," agreed Jack, "but this time, you are the jailbait."

Everyone stopped to look at each other. Jack saw the two old men sitting side-by-side and perceived something was up with them.

"Ooh! A holy rock, papyrus, scissors match. Anyone taking bets?" not that any of them had anything to bet.

Pterrkee the sourpuss also entered, saw the set-up, shook his head with disapproval, flopped down on his bedroll and turned away from everyone.

"That is how Alexander achieved peace," interjected Mothcrates. "By destroying his enemies before they destroyed Greece."

"And, yet he died without knowing the true Prince of Peace," commented Ionnes – an interesting statement in that Alexander died before Yeshua walked the Earth.

Rabbi Yosef sat up taller. He well knew the reference in Isaiah.

"The one Prince of Peace has not yet come."

"Who is the one Prince o' Peace?" asked Dim.

Yosef looked at Dim, almost startled like he knew not anyone else was still there.

"Yeshua," answered Ionnes before Yosef could add his two mites.

"Rubbish," challenged the old rabbi, shaking his head - his hair and beard swishing back and forth with the motion.

"You are saying the Prince of Peace is rubbish?" teased Ionnes, "Or, Rubbish is the name of the Prince of Peace?"

"Neither," blustered Yosef as some around them giggled. "And, plague me not, Christian. I will not be denied."

Ionnes looked towards Dim. "Yeshua is the Prince of Peace," he firmly said.

"Rubbi..." Yosef stopped himself. "Foolishness," he corrected.

Ionnes accepted the invitation. The door had been flung open wide. It was a most familiar road for him, arguing the cause for Christos, including with his Jewish brethren. He knew what they thought better than most for he had already been in their sandals.

"Why is it foolishness?" *'The wisdom of men is foolishness to God,'* he thought, again recalling Paulos' letter to the Church in Corinth. First letter? Second letter? Third or fourth? He was not sure anymore and silently scolded himself for not remembering.

"Because it just is," dismissed Yosef.

"Rubbish," teased Ionnes. "You really do not have an opinion about Messiah?"

"Of course, I do," defended Yosef. "But I have never been swayed by the fables and parables of your Nazarene bastard. His name has brought only grief and suffering to my people."

"That is as good a place to start as any," Ionnes thought aloud. "What if I told you His birth was not borne in sin but a miraculous conception and beginning?"

"You refer to the virgin conceived. I have heard that nonsense."

"Why is it nonsense?" checked Ionnes.

"Because," Yosef stiffened up, "I have heard virgins who conceived give their reasons and excuses, but never have I heard one claim Elohim lay with her."

"Um," considered Ionnes, "I do not think any ever said that Elohim knew her. In fact, Elohim did not appear before her. Rather, an angel of the LORD named Gabriel brought her the news she would conceive and bear a son and call Him Yeshua."

"The same Gabriel that Daniel encountered?"

"As far as I know," acknowledged Ionnes, "and she said to Gabriel, 'God's will be done,' and it was done, and her womb was touched by Elohim's Spirit to conceive."

"Then, Yeshua cannot be Messiah by your own words," challenged Yosef.

Ionnes waited for the rabbi to continue, though he already figured what Yosef would say. He had been down these roads countless times already.

"Does not scripture foretell that the Anointed One will be a direct descendent of David? And, thereby even Abraham?"

"It does," agreed Ionnes. He well knew the prophesy in Isaiah:

Then a shoot will spring from the stem of Jesse,
and a branch from his roots will bear fruit.

Ionnes always thought that an odd scripture to point to only King David since Jesse had multiple sons.

"Then," pressed Yosef, "the virgin would have to conceive from a man who is descendant of David."

"Maryam, Yeshua's mother, was a descendant of David, as was Yosef, Maryam's husband who reared Him."

"But Yosef was not his father by blood?"

"No," Ionnes answered bluntly.

"Then, Yeshua cannot be Messiah for the prophesy is not fulfilled."

"True," confessed Ionnes, "unless you also look at what Isaiah wrote earlier:

Therefore, the Lord Himself shall give you a sign,
Behold, a virgin shall conceive, and bear a Son, and shall
call His name Immanuel."

"A VIRGIN shall conceive," Ionnes repeated. Adonai is not mocked. He said it clearly that though the Messiah be born of a virgin, He shall likewise be of the line of David. And, funniest of all are those who believe in Genesis where our Creator who made the heavens and the Earth including all the living plants and animals and finally Adam and Eve but deny Adonai's ability to divinely conceive a virgin."

Yosef had read the word many times over the years under different considerations. He withheld his concession here until he could re-read the holy scrolls.

"What else?" challenged Ionnes.

"He was a Nazarene, but Micah clearly said Messiah would be born in Bethlehem."

"Yeshua did enter this life in Bethlehem.," said Ionnes. "Do you recall hearing when Herod the Great went crazy and had all young boys killed in Bethlehem?"

Yosef remembered hearing the account which happened so many years back - twenty years or so before his own birth.

For Jews, such events were told and retold and grieved as though they had happened only yesterday.

"Yeshua's earthly father, Yosef, received a dream from Adonai commanding him to take Yeshua and Maryam away from Bethlehem. They fled that night for Egypt where they lived until Herod died. Then, they returned, quite unnoticed, to settle in Nazareth."

"How did they afford such a journey?" wondered Yosef.

"I do not know for sure," admitted Ionnes, "though I do recall that shortly before they fled to Egypt, they received a visit from a caravan of kings and astrologers from the East who brought gifts, including gold, frankincense and myrrh. I would expect that would be more than enough to cover their travel expenses and give them a good start in Egypt."

"That sounds like a convenient provision."

Ionnes nodded. "Would Adonai let His newborn Promised One be killed by sword? And, did not Isaiah also clearly write that Messiah would not be born to privilege and affluence?"

Yosef nodded as his eyes filled with tears. "I weep also for those many children who did die by the sword."

"As do I," agreed Ionnes, tears also filling his eyes. "And, their parents - and families. It is liken to Pharaoh trying to kill infant Moses."

"Oy!" agreed Yosef, leaning forward to bereave. "We are a downtrodden people."

Dim noticed the name Moses again. Why always Moses?

"As much as we are a people of victory. YHWH's chosen." Ionnes put hands together prayerfully.

Then, they heard laughter from across the room. It was an odd laugh. Not a sound any of them had heard before. Heads turning, and ears cocked, the guffaw increased until almost giddy. None could speak.

Pterrkee turned over, still laughing hysterically. None had ever encountered so much as a smile, much less uncontrollable laughter from the cranky crab.

"This is too rich," he blurted out between heaving breaths of laughter. "This is sooooo rich!"

"What?" asked Teos.

Pterrkee let the hanging moment dangle before answering. Between his giggles, he looked at their faces and laughed some more as he said, "Two old holy fools arguing over the same God." His laughter resumed. "It is too rich for words." Some others started laughing a bit, mostly out of humor to see Pterrkee actually losing it.

Ionnes and Rabbi Yosef also looked at each other in the gloom. A shared smile touched each of them.

"Maspik!" whispered Rabbi Yosef and laid back on his bedroll.

The others turned away, ready to sleep. It had, of course, been a hard day and would be a hard day tomorrow. Some already slept, only briefly disturbed by Pterrkee's outburst. The lodge grew quiet for the first time all evening. The words of the two old men played through their minds, but only briefly for most as sleep overtook them. Only Dim felt the weight of the words more than the others, and he laid there, looking up at the darkness, taking it all in and sorting it out into smaller pieces. Rather like cutting chunks of meat or vegetables into bite-sized pieces. He felt like their words needed to be cut up even smaller to be able to take them in and not choke on them. Bare starlight came in through the small openings near the ceiling. The flecks of light commanded his eyes' attentions. Two eyes, each seeing its own image, yet the image became to him as one, not unlike the two old men in debate, each with his unique point of view, yet coming together as one.

He turned towards Ionnes who had already found sleep. Dim wanted to ask him more questions, but nothing he wondered compelled him enough to disturb the old man. Perhaps they would talk again tomorrow. Tomorrow counted not that far off and would already come too quickly.

Closing his eyes, he cleared his mind. Touching his sculpted dolphin ever hanging around his neck, images of his wife and boys filtered through the holy rhetoric, as well as the day's events of the quarry and the fresher slices of pain in his back from the lash. The visions of family seemed less powerful tonight. Some nights, he could reach out and touch them, but tonight they merely kissed him goodnight.

"Shalom," he uttered to his lost loved ones and eventually drifted off to sleep.

PATMOS

CHAPTER 7

Myron entered his home, a little weary with the day's journey and labors. He had risen early to meet friends at the palæstra for handball. Myron became renowned as the only person on Patmos with handballs made of pig's bladders, thereby the envy of them all. After their workout, some of the men dined on dried fish and figs in the arboretum. Myron later met with the temple priests to discuss repairs to Artemis' temple. Part of his afternoon he spent playing latrunculi and/or tali, (aka, knucklebones). He oversaw a slave execution, then walked up the hill to his home. It had been a very good day, especially beating Lucius, the Captain of the Guard, at handball. Groin pull or not, he still beat Lucius.

Myron's home was not the biggest on the island, but it was easily bigger than most. Upon arriving on Patmos, he and wife Fona had been disenchanted with the selection of homes for them. The Governor and Chryspippe had the largest home - that was expected, but he needed one suitable for a gentleman of Roma. After numerous tours of the area, the only villas they fancied were already taken. He could have pulled rank and strings and whatever else he wanted to yank to make those grander homes his primary dwelling during his stay on the island - not that that would be their only home. They had three other places he could hang his togas besides Roma.

Point of fact, Myron already had begun the process to unload his home in the capital city. He had never liked Roma that well to begin with and Fona's family wanted them closer. He was an old man, so had few ambitions to pursue in Roma. The money from the sale would be far better to add to his inheritance. Plus, Tuscana was much more to his liking. Nowhere else on Earth compared with Florentia, though they spent most of their years there some miles south in the vineyard region.

Their other home really was a modest dwelling of barely four walls in Ariminum. They spent the least amount of time there and used it primarily for its seaport on the Adriatic, or to temporarily house relatives they really did not like.

And now this fourth home on Patmos for the short year or two they would be on the island. Since they could not find any house to their liking, they bought two smaller villas and connected them into one larger home. Fona thought her husband daft when he suggested it. It had its peculiarities, of course, including a large banquet area where the two homes had been conjoined. Being separate dwellings, Apollonides' bedroom could be on the opposite side. Their son had not kept a consistent sleep schedule until very recently. Myron enjoyed the grand view of the town down below, spreading out to the sea. Out his back atrium he had a bit of a view of Mt. Elias. Barely an ant hill compared with the Alps, he had often wished to climb it someday, as all men wish when they see a mountain, but so often leave such inspirations for some other forever unnamed day. Both villas included slave's quarters in the back. One of the slave's quarters had the perfect wine cellar, now with a newly added lock. They moved out of their daughter's home before reconstruction was complete, stating that they could better supervise details by being there, but everyone knew Myron wished to not be too long a guest of his daughter and son-in-law. Not that they were not good people, but he definitely preferred his own home where he could be quite himself and supremely more comfortable. One additional advantage – even if Roma fell, he knew he could sell it for more than he paid when that time came.

Tobie met his master as he entered the door.

"Did you get the supplies I ordered?" asked Myron.

"Of course," answered Tobie, "but prices of grain have increased."

Myron waited for Tobie to go on.

"Uh, prices almost doubled for both wheat and barley."

"Did they say why?"

"Something about a lost cargo ship."

Myron suddenly recalled hearing news of a lost ship. What was its name? Perseus? Something like that.

"Eyore!" he swore. "Next thing you know they will be charging us a full day's wage for a sorry quart of half ground wheat."

"How much?" Myron mocked as though speaking with the grocer. "A denarius? For what? Just a quart?"

(Imitating the grocer), "I can give you three quarts of barley for the same price."

Myron peered at Tobie and sighed. "Well, what of the wine and the olive oil?"

"No harm - so far," answered Tobie.

Myron sighed again wearily and continued into his lounge. The delightful day suddenly weighed in a bit heavier.

"Papa?"

He turned, mildly surprised. Chryspippe rose to come to him. He had seen her just out of the corner of his eye as he entered and unconsciously thought she was a slave.

"My favorite daughter," he said to his only daughter, taking her arms by the elbows and kissing her forehead. "What brings you to this part of the island?"

She smiled as they separated and took a seat on pillows. Two slaves entered to serve. Myron looked at his daughter who moved her head 'no'. He raised an arm and they backed out.

"Mom said to tell you she would be home within the hour."

"Where did she go?" Myron asked, not really caring.

"The Acropolis. She has been invited to a special dinner in her honor."

"Another one?"

Chryspippe nodded and smiled. Myron shook his head. The welcome committee of Patmos was sometimes a little too enthusiastic.

"How is Apollonides?" asked Chryspippe.

"Apollonides?" Myron looked up. "I do not know today. I have not seen him as yet."

She shook her head again. "I do not mean just today. How has he been since his recovery?"

"Fine," answered Myron. "He is more the son I recall, and I can sleep better at night because of it."

"Quieter?"

"That, too."

She bit her lip.

"So, what troubles you, my dear?"

She feared sounding like a foolish woman even if that was oftentimes expected by Roman men. Still, she knew she would be crossing into new territories of incredulity if she babbled all that had occurred recently. She crafted her words carefully.

"It is just a feeling I had. I wanted to make sure that he was okay."

"If anything had happened - a relapse - or even just a foot down the wrong fork, you would be one of the first to know."

She sighed, pleased and a little relieved, but the visions yesterday morning were not going to be airily dismissed for a long time. Even when Laurentius came home to Chryspippe the previous night, she kept to herself. If he had wondered about her visit to the base that morning, he did not inquire further. Their distance had become commonplace and her solitude seemed to suit him just fine.

"I am glad," she said, but her expression drooped.

"You do not look glad," he said.

They were close - a closeness she treasured - the primary reason she had wanted them on the island with her, and not just Apollonides' condition. If her two other brothers could have come, it would have been even better. They got along well enough, but one loved Roma and the other Tuscana. Both were good venues for orators and perfect to oversee family affairs at each location.

"Is Apollonides here?"

"You know, I know not. I just returned home myself, as I am sure you do know. Tobie?"

The slave appeared.

"Is Master Apollonides home?"

"No, sir. Master Apollonides departed this late morning."

"Did he give any indication of where he was going or when he would return?"

"No, Mr. Myron."

It was never a slave's place to ask, though they had been given more liberty by Myron to keep eyes on Apollonides when he was out of his mind. It had not been that long since he had resumed his sanity. Tobie might have asked but would not press his master's son.

"That is all Tobie." The slave disappeared.

"They are just feelings," she lied. "Probably old feelings and concerns for my brother. It has been a long time, has it not?"

"Yes, it has," he answered, most fatherly. "Your mother is still beside herself with joy."

Chryspippe paused, not sure she should continue. He raised his brows inquiringly. She well knew that look and relied on her trust and his love.

"Have you seen the prisoner who healed my brother?"

Myron was surprised. No, he had not. It had not occurred to him to look or wonder. She recognized his answer without the need for words.

"Well, I have. A few times, now. And in the oddest places."

Myron shrugged. What of it?

"I wanted to thank him for helping Apollonides, but it would be socially inappropriate for me to approach him alone."

It took an extra moment for Myron to wrap his thoughts around such a concept. One did not thank a slave or prisoner for anything. Everyone knew that.

"Papa?"

"You want me to find this prisoner?"

"Yes."

"And, do what?"

Now faced with the real question, she wondered how her father would take her suggestion. This was soupy quicksand for a Roman where the men ruled with a harsh hand. Still, it seemed a reasonable request for such a grand gift as they had received in the healing of her brother. She had to ask, even if she feared his consternation. In her father's home she was Chryspippe the daughter, but on Patmos she lived as the governor's wife, and she liked having firm answers where social etiquette and decency reigned. Still, such a question had not come up often. Slaves and prisoners served. The gods designed it that way. One does not thank any creature beneath them for doing what they were predestined to do. Everyone knew that - even the most dense and foolish slave.

"Would not we thank the doctor who healed our beloved?" she eventually said.

"A prisoner is not a doctor."

"Would not we?"

Myron pondered the question. He knew doctors could become prisoners, though he personally knew of none. Still, it seemed possible. But he also knew his son had been healed in ways doctors typically did not practice. Even Kynops the Magician could not heal him.

Not six months back, they had taken Apollonides to the *Asklepion* in Pergamos. The hacks! They only gave him a sedative, put him to sleep, and let harmless snakes climb around all over him. When he awoke, he reported his dreams. The "doctor" listened, offered some insights and told him he was healed.

As Myron recalled, Apollonides relayed the dream where he stood on the Appian Way selling its cobblestones. "Want more?" he would spout and stooped down to dig up a dozen more bricks. "WITH THESE BRICKS, WE COULD BUILD A WALL AROUND ROMA," he yelled to the uncounted many who passed.

The 'doctor' said he was disillusioned with Roma and wanted to warn others to avoid it. He also said Apollonides was rebelling against Roma, destroying it in a way so all roads would not lead to the capital.

"Poppycock!" cursed Myron at the time and took his disturbed son back home to Patmos. Grabbing a charter out of Smyrna, Apollonides one time jumped in the water to race the boat. Another time he started digging a hole in the hull to see the fish underneath, or so he said. Secretly, he really needed a window to keep an eye on Neptune. Mostly, he just planted himself on the prow of the ship alongside the carved figurehead, facing forward, bouncing up and down, feeling the wind and the splash.

Six months later, a man - a prisoner no less, appeared out of nowhere and with only the power of his Word, healed

Apollonides. Some magic or sorcery came from this old man in chains. Perhaps he felt a little fear of this magic that conveniently kept Myron from pursuing any such contact with him.

"Would not we?" repeated Chryspippe.

He took his daughter's hand. "Yes, I guess we would."

She smiled and dimpled, and Myron recognized his little girl again.

"We should invite him to dinner," she tweeted.

Myron just about spit up his wine or would have if he had been drinking any. He did cough and clear his throat and feel like he had just sizably bet against the wrong roll of the knuckles or the wrong charioteer.

"Tobie. Wine," he called.

Tobie already had a goblet at the ready. Myron gulped down a couple swallows, coughed some more and grabbed another swig. The red fluid could have been vinegar, but Myron knew his palate soured the nectar and not the vintner. Tobie refilled the cup, then exited the room.

"That is preposterous," he blustered.

"Papa," she coyly cooed. "It is fine. He has given us a great gift - a gift no one else could have given us. The least we could do is show him our appreciation." She paused, then added, "And, mama said it would be good as well."

He sighed. Though he felt it foolish to bestow any manner of gratuity on any prisoner or slave, another smaller part of his mind thought it right, or at least reasonable. Only his daughter's love could tip that balance, making that non-substantial, featherweight idea heavier. He sighed again and resigned.

"When?" he said, saying yes without saying yes.

"Whenever you would like, Dad."

"Sly answer," he thought. "I will look into the matter."

"Tomorrow?"

He looked up briefly. "Yes. Tomorrow I will look into the matter."

"And dinner? Tomorrow? Or, the day after? Mama and I already planned what to have prepared."

He sighed again and smiled. "If you wish. (Sounds like it has already been decided by you and your mother.)"

"Thank you, Papa. Thank you." She leaned to give him the hug he knew was coming and always welcomed.

Rising, he walked her to the door. Lorin appeared. Neither gave her even a first look.

The sun had already set behind the mountains, but still promised much daylight to see her home. She hugged him again to say good-bye.

"This may not be a good thing," he warned.

She nodded but did not believe it. Something inside told her this was the best thing. That same feeling compelled her to want to see again the old prisoner. That same feeling compelled her to reach out to her father for help. She knew fully well, this was more than just the right thing to do.

"Give Apollonides my love and tell him I want to see him tomorrow."

"Tobie?" called Myron.

The slave appeared as one who walks through walls. "If I am gone before Apollonides arrives, would you give him word to contact Miss Chryspippe tomorrow?"

"Of course, sir," bowed Tobie.

"Thank you, papa." She seemed most pleased. Almost giddy. It warmed the old man's heart to see his daughter so happy. He had not seen her this happy for many a year. He would inquire about the old prisoner tomorrow.

"He may be dangerous," Myron warned. "Or a raving lunatic. Most are full of anger."

She remained unswayed, but answered, "I know, and I will trust your judgment."

He knew a lie when he heard one, especially a loving one.

She hugged him again and turned to go. Lorin followed behind as usual. He watched the pair turn past his gate. He considered sending an escort with them, but they would be home well before dark. Despite the penal colony, so prevalent on the island, and a few other lowly figures, Patmos excelled as not a place one walked in fear, even at night. That fared not so for Roma, or even Florentia. Even outside Phora in the countryside, few brigands and robbers lay waiting on Patmos. It was not like one needed to travel by caravan or with armed guards.

"Tobie," he yelled, entering his home. "I need a rub down before dinner."

Tobie already had the cushions, towels and olive oil ready for his master.

PATMOS

CHAPTER 8

Two nights later, at the evening meal between the gusts of breeze and wind, Ionnes could be heard talking with Euæmon about Yeshua. The carefree young man listened like one who would rather discuss visiting flamingo flocks in Africa. Ionnes always knew two things – one, that even one who held minimal interest in Yeshua still came closer to His Spirit and second, that though he spoke to one person, others would be there to listen and learn. He trusted God's Holy Spirit to complete His work of molding thoughts and filling empty hearts with His love.

Even more than slaves, prisoners could be his best audience.

Ionnes and Rabbi Yosef had hardly spoken to one another those two days, easily dismissed as the demands of their imprisonment and the quarry wedged widely between them. That day, many of the prisoners had been sent to collect pieces of marble from a crumbled chunk. Those pieces would make good goblets and plates and bowls. The prisoners owned little to nothing, but most had at least one or two marble pieces, sculpted and shaped into a useful item. The Romans not only allowed, but also encouraged the men to work and fashion the rock. They would better learn how the marble could be cut which definitely would help them in the quarry.

So, many had formed beautiful pieces. He watched Euæmon forming the stone with another stone. A chunk of granite, broken to have a jagged edge.

"Arion made it for me," said Euaumon. He held up the chunk of granite.

"How did he chip it away so cleanly?" asked Ionnes.

"With his hands," answered Euæmon.

"Of course," agreed Ionnes, "but, what tools did he use?"

"His hands," repeated Euæmon. "He is new here. He has no tools, but he fancies himself a warrior as you know. For some years now, he has been breaking river rocks with only his hands. He says the smaller rocks can be harder to break than the larger rocks."

Ionnes wondered briefly if the young vagabond pulled his beard.

"When he made this, Arion told me he broke river rocks as part of his training. Toughens him up. I did not believe him, but shortly thereafter I saw him breaking rocks we found along the roadside with his hands. He pounds them together forcefully enough to make a man step back. It hurt my hands just watching him."

Ionnes noted early on that all of the prisoners' sculptings had a chunk or a chip on them or were made from pieces too small to quite complete the item. All of their handiwork had at least one very noticeable flaw. He asked Dim about it one time as he watched Dim sculpting a bowl shaped like a seashell. His metal tool no bigger than a fingernail, yet he scraped away the rock with patient, repetitive motions or chipped tiny fragments away using a rock as a hammer. The small chunk of marble took shape under his trained hands.

Talor sat nearby carving his own chunk of rock. He remained quiet, working intently, carving a human facial image. His craftmanship in no way compared with Dim's, but he kept at it as though it was the most beautiful creation on the island. Like his skill levels, his hands were becoming more and more calloused the longer he worked and lived on Patmos.

"Why are all of these pieces you make less than perfect?" asked Ionnes to Dim. "You do such beautiful work, yet it seems intentional."

Dim looked up from the piece he was forming. "Ya are right." He went back to task. "I am told before my time here that they used t' make perfect items, but the Romans would take 'em away & sell 'em t' others. Of course, they kept the money for our work. So, we make 'em less than perfect. They fill our needs, & the Romans cannot sell 'em."

Ionnes knew his words to be right. He knew well the rare sense of pride and ownership by men who owned nothing. The men all knew too well that their Roman captors could collect all the pieces and destroy them that day. Still, Ionnes also recognized that powerful part of each person to have something of his own.

Then, he remembered Yeshua. Often overlooked, that was another thing that Yeshua had over most everyone else he had ever met. Yeshua owned nothing for as long as Ionnes knew him. He put others in charge of the expenses. He assigned Matthew to be his scribe. He never took anything with Him - not a bag or scroll or tool. Just the clothes on His back, and Ionnes watched as even those were taken at the end and gambled away right under Yeshua's bleeding feet as He hung against the coarse wood of a Roman cross. Ionnes suddenly wondered for the first time what had become of Yeshua's sandals? It surprised him that he had never considered that question before now. And, who on Earth, or even in Heaven, could fill those sandals?

"Bed," yelled Guard Mucius.

Prisoners stopped talking or sculpting or whatever, rose and went to the barracks. Shackled, of course, they entered the room and took their regular places on the floor. Ionnes nodded towards Seth and Rabbi Yosef as he entered.

"Who took my doll?" said Minos, searching through his bedroll in the gloom. The door still stood open and enough light slid in to illuminate the room. His doll was nowhere to be found.

"Shut-up," said Pterrkee, lying down and turning over towards the wall.

"Phranc, did you see anyone take my doll?"

"Sorry," said Phranc, and searched through the blanket again with his friend.

"What is wrong, Minos?" teased Jack. "Someone take your little dolly?"

"This is serious," pressed Minos.

"Minos cannot sleep without his dolly," chided Euæmon.

"Here it is," said Talor, tossing it towards Minos. It had been hidden in the back corner by who knows who?

The men regularly teased Minos about his doll, but they all knew it to be an intended gift for his daughter if ever he left Patmos. The figurine was made of quartz, crafted by melancholy Minos' fatherly hand. Ever on the lookout, he sought someone heading for Knosos on Creta, his hometown, who might be willing to deliver it. A few other prisoners also had keepsakes for their families should their deep yearnings to be reunited ever come true. Still, that never stopped some from teasing Minos about his doll.

Phranc had promised to deliver it if possible in the chance that Minos died. How well they all knew that any of them could be history any given day. Minos took it and laid it on his bedroll, flopping himself down dramatically on his bed to ward off any further teasing intent by the men.

With the dolly found, everyone settled down to his own bed. The door closed, and the lock clicked, just like all the other nights. The air grew quiet, and some started to turn over to sleep.

"It is written," said Rabbi Yosef to Seth, piercing the silence, "that the Messiah would reign on David's throne and over his kingdom, establishing and upholding it with justice and righteousness from that time forward and forever."

"So," added Seth, "you are telling me that Yeshua could not be Messiah because David's throne has not been reestablished?"

"Yes," Yosef answered firmly.

Most of the men groaned.

"Go to sleep," snapped Pterrkee.

"You crazy zealots," moaned Minos.

"You crazy zealots," teased Phranc.

"Such a Messiah is always here, always has been and always will be," philosophized Mothcrates. He sighed fitfully. That sounded so clever. If only he had known how truly clever his words.

"Like all the gods," he added. (Oops! Screwed that one up, Moth.)

"You mean Yeshua is not Messiah?" asked Teos, bewildered and fretting to sort it out in his simple mind.

"No," repeated Rabbi Yosef.

"Who is David?" asked Dim to anyone in the darkness.

Silence.

More silence.

Then, even more silence - to get the men thinking.

Dim turned his head towards Ionnes. Most realized Yosef and Seth were baiting him. Ionnes peered briefly at Dim with his characteristic smile on his face. Dim could see his few white teeth in the gloom. He knew that Ionnes knew as well as any there that this old fisherman was being baited.

"What?" blustered Seth. "What did you say?"

More silence.

"I love Isaiah," whispered Ionnes, his words swiftly bouncing around the barracks. "Do not you?"

"Yes," said Seth.

Yosef considered his answer more careful, but also answered, "Yes, of course."

"And, you know well his prophesies about Messiah?" asked Ionnes.

"Yes," answered Yosef, a little more quickly.

"And, you believe this verse you just recited?"

"Yes."

Ionnes sighed pleasantly. "Me, too."

Yosef waited a spell before saying the needless, "So, it proves Yeshua could not be Messiah."

"How so?" challenged Ionnes.

The old rabbi sat up, beside himself. It seemed so obvious to him. He knew this Christian apostate to be no fool, so this had to be a game, but he went forward with his answer.

"If Yeshua had been the Messiah, he would have reestablished David's throne. Roma would have been conquered and we would have been a free Yisra'el once again. That did not happen. I do not know what Yeshua was - prophet or good man or madman, but I do know that He was not Messiah." And, with that, he knew the matter was settled as he turned over.

Still, Yosef waited.

Silence again. His neck cricked and popped as he turned towards the center of the room and across to Ionnes.

Dim laughed to himself. As little as some of these men cared about these religious types, he knew nobody there was sleeping.

Ionnes secretly shared his humor.

"So, my dear Rabbi," Ionnes words so quietly shouting across the room, "the LORD of Hosts is holy and the whole Earth is filled with His glory?"

"Yes," muttered Yosef.

"How do you know?"

"What do you mean how do I know?"

Ionnes turned towards Yosef. "What glory to the LORD do you see from a prisoner's life on Patmos?"

Yosef, unmoved in his faith, readily answered, "These chains I wear, I wear for Him. These chains I wear because of those who oppose the LORD of Hosts."

"Amen," agreed Ionnes, "You and I share that same fate, but you wear these chains for God's judgment for your sins, and I wear them for His glory. So, if His glory fills the whole Earth including Patmos, how do you see it? What here shows you His glory?"

Yosef took quite a bit more time to consider the same question.

"All his creation - the Earth and the sky reflect His glory."

"True," agreed Ionnes, "So, God's glory is here in ways we cannot always see it?"

"Of course," nodded Yosef on his rolled-up shred of cloth he used for a pillow. "Like the ladder of angels that Jacob beheld. Like the army of angels Elisha showed to his servant. Like the fiery presence of the LORD holding back Pharaoh's army."

Dim wonder who some of these people were but held his tongue. He would ask Ionnes later. At least, they did not again mention Moses.

Ionnes gave Yosef a moment to finish and dwell upon what he had just said. The moment satisfied, Ionnes added to Yosef's list, "And, the only way David's throne could be established is forever?"

Yosef's brow furrowed deep. His elation switched to frown.

"Forever," repeated Ionnes with urgency. "FOREVER." The old rabbi understood Ionnes' intent - mostly. Ionnes continued.

"David sat on his throne only until he died. Solomon sat on that same throne - only until he died. Then, Rehoboam, and Abijah and Asa and all the others, all the way to Josiah. Some served God. Some did not. And, they all died.

"So, Messiah comes. If He stays a man, He may establish David's throne on Earth, but it only remains until He dies. And, that makes God a liar. A mockery. Or, God is not a liar, and David's throne could only be in Heaven at the Right Hand of God where there is not rust or aging or death. Only there could David's throne be forever."

Yosef wanted to speak, but his mind was playing too many thoughts to carefully pick any one, so after some seconds, Ionnes continued.

"For which of the angels did God say, "Sit at my right hand until I make thine enemies your footstool?"

Yosef immediately recognized the Psalm of David.

"None," answered Yosef. "Only the Messiah can be there, but that does not mean Yeshua."

"Perhaps," agreed Ionnes, "but consider this. Much is made of David. The House of David. The City of David. David's throne. How many chapters of scripture are devoted to David?"

"Sixty-five," readily answered Yosef. "More than any other patriarch."

"Right. And, how many additional volumes and volumes have been written about David over the centuries?"

"I could not even guess," admitted Yosef.

"Nor I," said Ionnes, "and David has always been a king above all other kings of Yisra'el in Judah - one who inspires me and you and all who seek the LORD. But..." he lowered his brows, "... David was still just a man. He died and stayed dead. He did not create the Heavens and the Earth. This man after God's own heart sinned grievously. Parts of Yisra'el literally died for his sins. He was Not the Messiah."

Ionnes again paused a moment, then added, "And, the same is said of Moses..."

"Moses again," Dim repeated to himself. Ionnes heard him and smiled.

"... or Abraham or Elijah or Isaiah or Solomon or Yaakov's son Yosef or any others."

Yosef laid there feeling the crusty, Jewish law hold him in its staunch grip.

"So, what is your word?" he asked. The question sounded foolish, even to himself.

"My word," considered Ionnes (who also suddenly remembered that 'In the beginning was the Word and the Word was with God and the Word was God'), "was that if the Messiah is going to reign forever on David's throne, He also has to live forever. And, thus far, no one under Adonai's creation has come close. So, I follow the One of the House of David who died and rose again, then ascended to live forever with His Father in Heaven, and to reign forever on David's throne at His Father's right hand."

Rabbi Yosef felt the truth of his words, but still knew his doubts about Yeshua.

"So, if Yeshua was all that you claim, why did He leave us to serve the Romans?"

"For our sins," answered Ionnes. "Is not that the way it has been for our people so many centuries? Again, you my good teacher know the scriptures as well as any man. To defeat the Romans with the sword will NEVER make an everlasting throne. So, I must choose to worship the Thronemaker who sent His Son to Earth for a short while to bring new life and a new covenant with His people. And, now His Spirit dwells within me as well as all who seek Him."

Rabbi Yosef hmmph'd, turned over and said no more unto sleep. His mind thought what to say, but he held his tongue until he could further weigh his words.

"Bravo," whispered Dim. Talor patted the old man's foot, then laid back down. The room again became quiet. Ionnes closed his eyes to rest. He could hear the mighty rushing wind outside, some of which refreshingly forced its way into their little barracks. Ionnes took a deep breath and praised Yeshua for His words. He knew he never could have said any of this without help and direction from His Holiest Spirit. Amen.

PATMOS

CHAPTER 9

"I recall Yeshua of Nazareth," spouted Yosef, seated in the unlit corner of the camp some days after their previous discussion. Darkness surrounded the man - a voice without a figure, but all knew the sounds of his voice. Dim and Ionnes looked towards the night clad rabbi.

"Oh, He was big news around Ierusalem," continued Yosef. "I was around nine or ten, as I recall. I had heard about Him but had not been granted privilege to see Him. Then, we heard He came into the city, Ierusalem. It seemed like everyone in town knew all at once, such flowed the wildfire of announcements. 'Yeshua is coming. Yeshua is here.' You would have thought Moses came down with the two tablets."

"What are the two tablets?" asked Dim. Others nearby also wondered.

"God's commandments He carved into stone on Mount Sinai," answered Ionnes.

"And who was Noses?" added Dim, smiling and sort of winked at Ionnes.

Yosef shuddered and took a deep breath. Stroking his beard to calm himself, he answered, "Moses, not Noses! One of our greatest prophets. He led the Yisra'elites out of slavery in Egypt. Pharaoh's army followed to force them back to slavery. Jehovah held back the army with a pillar of fire, then using Moses, parted the Red Sea so Elohim's chosen with all their carts and children and herds and belongings could cross on dry land. When they had safely crossed, Elohim removed the pillar of fire. Pharaoh's army saw the opening in the sea and also tried to cross and pursue. Their chariots lost wheels, trapping them on the bed of the sea. Then, the water crashed in, sending them to mortality."

Dim looked at Ionnes. "When did this happen?"

"A long time ago - over a thousand years back," answered Ionnes.

"It is a mainstream of our history," added Yosef.

"And, you believe it to be true?" verified Dim.

Ionnes nodded and smiled.

"Absolutely," assured Yosef, void of any doubt. "The two tablets were still intact in the Ierusalem temple until twenty-three years ago. I know not what has happened to them since the scourge."

The rabbi rubbed his eyes, then continued, "So, where was I? That is right. Um, Yeshua of Nazareth entering Ierusalem. My mother had told me to clean the goat pen. I grew up an impressionable and adventurous youth, of course. Chores were never my favorite. There, with the goats, collecting their droppings for the garden, I saw my neighbors and others, passing, excited and shouting, 'He is here. He is coming.'

"I wanted to go, but mother forbad me. Not before the pen was cleaned properly. I knew she had other chores for me after that. Others raced past with the news, 'Yeshua is here!' I kept to my task until I could contain it no further, dropped my shovel and joined the race towards the East Gate. I heard my mother calling me, but ignored her, as though I could not hear her voice through the crowd. Silly, of course. The lamb can always hear mama ewe and knows her voice no matter how large the herd."

Ionnes was about to speak, but instead smiled. Since he had been there, too, he knew what he had seen and done with full clarity but wanted to hear the old rabbi's account. ("Old Rabbi!" Ionnes teased himself. He himself was around a dozen years older than Yosef.)

It had been quite some time since anyone had spoken of the Triumphal Entry Sunday. The weight of the week suddenly pressed upon the old apostle. The memories flooded through faster than Pharaoh's army became drowndead. The entrance through the gate. The people celebrating and welcoming. Yeshua heading straight to the Temple to again overturn tables and drive the merchants out of the Outer Temple. The sound of Yeshua's voice as He taught and shared those few weekdays as the Jewish leaders closed in their vile, evil net around Yeshua. The Thursday preparation for Passover. Judas Iscariot betraying their friend and teacher and LORD. The Passover meal, including the bread and wine divine. The night in Gethsemane. Yeshua arrested before Friday's light arose. Ionnes briefly dwelled on the facial expressions of Malchus the servant getting his ear miraculously healed by Yeshua after Cephas lopped it off. Malchus jumped from pain to joy to doubt in what they were doing.

Then, the Friday trials and crucifixion. Ionnes looked to Cephas who also became just as lost and fearful. Cephas fled, but Ionnes stayed, seeing Yeshua on the cross until He gave up His Spirit, and Ionnes taking mother Maryam with him as they descended Golgotha, barely able to see through the tears and horrors replaying constantly over and over through their minds. How long that sleepless night, gathered with his friends, fearfully mourning in that Upper Room!

Then, Saturday next morning arose gray and drab with an eerie stillness, even with the swell of pilgrims and visitors for the Feast of Unleavened Bread. Sabbaths were typically quieter than most days of the week, but after such a week with Yeshua, the excitement of the city suddenly flopped and laid still like a woebegone fish on the sand, gasping its last breath. That week had passed so quickly. The following few days of grieving passed so slowly and terribly, as though the sun lost a wheel but was still being slowly dragged across the sky. He returned his attention to the rabbi.

Yosef continued, "I became part of the crowd, racing towards the Golden Gate. Pardon me. In those day, we called it the East Gate. We filled the broad road, then all parted to make room for Him. Some laid their coats on the street ahead of Yeshua. Others without coats started pulling off palm branches. I found one by the wall. It was damaged, but I took it and laid it on the road with the others. I will declare, we ate less dates that year than usual.

"Yeshua passed me riding a poor, little donkey colt. No might. No splendor. A few cloaks laid across its back as a saddle. The colt could not run and the Rider showed no hurry. Yeshua looked at all of us. He did not wave or say much, but His smile gave back as much as He took in. He looked at me as He passed. I cannot say it proved life changing or that I had found my vocation at that moment. I am a Levite, so always knew that I would be a rabbi. Still, I clearly recall Him smiling at me. I often pondered that I always thought of Him whenever I read Isaiah."

Yosef looked around at the night and sighed. The stars burned through a very light haze. The three-quarter moon, big and yellow, prepared to set for the night. It would be wise to bed down before its light was gone.

"I was so happy that day," he muttered. "I do not even know why."

"You met Messiah," said Ionnes.

Rabbi Yosef peered angrily at the Apostle through the gloom. His intense eyes reflected a far-off bonfire.

"I met another hope for deliverance destroyed by Roma. I cannot see a Messiah who is weaker than men. Our captors killed Him, like all the others. That is not my Messiah."

Ionnes praised God - a quiet prayer ever on his lips.

"I know I shoulda asked before now," thought Dim, "but 'xactly what is a Messiah?" He had a pretty good idea he already knew the answer from talking to Ionnes, but wanted to hear what Rabbi Yosef thought.

Yosef raised his brows as he spouted, "The Promised One. The King that Jehovah promised to deliver us. Our prophets commonly wrote about Him."

"Christos," added Ionnes, again using a Greek word Dimetrius would likely understand. "The Anointed One."

Then, Ionnes peered at Rabbi Yosef as the twilight took over. "Did you not hear of Yeshua's resurrection from the grave?"

"As a lad, no," answered the old Rabbi. "I heard that nonsense some years later."

"From whom?" Ionnes hoped the Rabbi would remember.

Rabbi Yosef thought long and hard before settling on an answer.

"In the synagogue?" he considered. "Or, the temple," his eyebrows dipped low. "Synagogue," he decided. "We were warned to beware of your sect and its teachings."

"Who warned you?" asked Ionnes.

Yosef thought hard. "A visitor. A remarkable young man. A student of Gamaliel. Saul? Yes, Saul was his name."

Ionnes smiled. "Saul from Tarsus? I knew Saul. I knew him very well."

Rabbi Yosef felt surprise. "How did you come to know Saul of Tarsus?"

"He fought against Yeshua as Messiah for years. Then, Yeshua called him personally, and he became one of our strongest and most zealous disciples."

Rabbi Yosef paused, unsure he had heard correctly. This Saul he had met hated The Way. He found nothing but lies and deceptions in their cause. Ionnes must mean someone different.

"Nope," assured Ionnes, deducing the rabbi's thoughts. He died for Yeshua, in Roma, almost thirty years back. Beheaded."

The old rabbi made his usual noise of disapproval, but Ionnes could see the questions bouncing around the back of his head. If stubborn Saul changed to follow Yeshua, what did he see that Yosef could not yet see? He fretted, still unsure he truly sought the answer to such a question.

PATMOS

CHAPTER 10

Whack!
    Whack!
        Whack!
            Whack!
                    went the sledge against the huge spike.

Euæmon spied the wobble of the spike in the rock. Far left side. It was beginning to bend a bit by the weight of the stone against the ropes. He Whacked it again and again, trying to get it in deep enough, bent or not.

"She's begging to crumble," someone yelled from above. He could hear the music of metal tools clinking around above him.

He checked the other three spikes. Firm, as best he could tell. The taut ropes may have made the spikes press upward against the pulling of men against rock and gravity. He glanced back to make sure the manned poles were at the ready to catch the huge slab of deadly stone.

A concise snap croaked from beneath the marble wall. Euæmon had never heard or noticed that noise as yet for the dozen odd times he had manned this post. The bent spike shifted outward just a quarter inch, but Euæmon noticed it. He watched the wall carefully as he raced back to try to keep the spike deeply enough within the rock.

He had used an old hole to start that spike. Sometimes the wall split into more of a wedge t'where the top side was wider than the bottom. As the rock teetered and rocked its way to the ground, it might crack just above the spikes. It could come sliding down into the ropes suddenly. That was never a good scenario, and Euæmon had been warned if he saw that to get away as fast as he could. Then, the next time, the spike might already be in, hard and secure as can be. Usually, the spike fell out with the tumbling wall. But, if a hole still showed for the next wall, Euæmon would drive the new spike into that small, leftover hole. It was typically easier than starting a new hole and should be equally secure.

Should be.

It started out holding just fine, but then created its own small fissure allowing play in the spike. Euæmon jumped in well before the spike came fully loose. He pounded for all he was worth to affix the spike securely once again. It seemed fine as the men above continued to loosen the huge chunk of gray marble.

Another snap resonated within. Euæmon knew that sound. That was the sound he had anticipated as the wall began to loosen from its last firm hold.

He watched overhead. Sometimes rocks came down from the face or above, especially from this point on. One time he had asked for his own Roman helmet for the task, his request denied. He wore a turban someone gave him and hoped that would make the difference he needed between life and death if a chunk of rock came tumbling down.

This time it did not help.

The piece, about the size of a Roman helmet, hit him before he knew it was coming. He collapsed in a heap on the hard earth.

"Hold!" yelled the men below, but the wall already began its descent.

Polemen tried to catch it. Euæmon remained in fetal position, still stunned.

"Euæmon," yelled Phranc. "Move." He pressed against the wooden pole with all his might. If he had not had the pole, he would have run in to pull Euæmon out. Every prisoner tried with all they had to hold the rock wall up just a little longer. No soldier even considered diving in to drag the prisoner out of harm's way.

Another vertical crack shot up the wall, this one on the left side by the bent spike. Only a single rope held a third of the wall which slipped towards its loose side, insisting to topple.

Its bottom pressed against the rest of the wall as it pivoted to the left. No ropes. No poles. The chunk of marble landed hard, breaking into uncountable many pieces.

Crumbling rocks of freshly exposed cliff dropped all around Euæmon, miraculously missing him. He started to move, almost to a crawling position to escape the remaining slice of wall. The other two thirds continued to drop down. The men did all they could to hold the side up, but they all knew, even with a third gone, all they could do was keep it from falling too fast. Down it came with Euæmon still beneath.

"Euæmon!" everyone yelled as he continued to crawl forward. Equally, all knew it was too late.

From final crack to its resting place on the ground of the quarry only took a minute at most. The poles never could quite stop the descent. Such rock remains just too heavy. The dust hid Euæmon away as the huge layer of stone touched down. A hideous silence swept through the quarry. Even some soldiers appeared stunned. The rough but flat sea of gray lay before them. One by one, they checked around it to see and assess the damage. Mothcrates came around the back side of the wall, looking up more than down at times, expecting to see Euæmon's feet sticking out of the bottom of the wall. Nothing there. He hung his head and said a prayer of extinction to the gods.

"Yo," yelled a voice.

Mothcrates looked across the marble to see who was yelling from the other side. Phranc stood there numbly. Pterrkee searched around the perimeter of the rock like a sniffing dog. Teos felt old tears of loss, setting his head against the huge stone. Euæmon never liked Teos, but he still felt great sadness to lose another.

"Yo," repeated the voice. Teos looked up to see who was calling. Mothcrates looked around. Everyone else was looking around, too.

"Euæmon?" he dared call.

"Yeah." Weak voice muffled by a ton or more of stone.

"He is alive!" yelled Mothcrates. The old Greek was beside himself. "I know not how, but he is alive. Oh, Apollo! Oh, Artemis!"

The others ran over to the right side by Mothcrates. The men topside were already dropping down, most jumping the precipice, of course landing at least some feet from the rock wall. The guards stood together at a short distance, their swords drawn. Death of a prisoner often led to at least one or two prisoners attacking with angry revolt. Or, just as likely, the prisoners became seized with fear and fled. One guard was sent running to bring other guards.

"Arion," called Phranc.

The wiry youth came forth.

"You are nimble. See what you can see between the cliff and this fallen wall."

Arion understood and practically became part of the cliff wall as he moved spritely between the stones. He stayed clear of the fallen wall but considered if the weight of this great stone did not kill Euæmon, Arion's extra hundred pounds would make little difference. Still, to mount the rock would feel like walking over someone's fresh grave. Prisoners deserved better than that, regardless what any Roman dog would have said.

Dim laid down flat to look under the stone. He noticed a small bulge in the rock. Not much, but it perhaps pointed to Euæmon.

"Come on," he yelled, grabbing wooden poles.

"Wait!" yelled Seth to Dim and pointed. The two men looked at one another. Dim nodded. Seth was right.

"This way," corrected Dim.

"What?" Guard Ernesto finally stepped forth.

"We have t' break it," yelled Dim.

"You do and you will be broken far worse. All of you."

"If not, Euæmon will die."

"You heard me," pressed Ernesto, sword still drawn and ready to take down any who opposed him. He stood not alone. Better one dead prisoner than one broken sheet of marble.

"Yo!" yelled Euæmon.

Dim approached Ernesto. He put his hands out, then parked them on his head.

"We have t' try." He looked at Ernesto earnestly. "Will do what we can't save the sheet."

Ernesto spit and flipped his head – a sign of permission to proceed.

"Seth," yelled Dim, briefly glancing at Ernesto in thanks before turning back to the task at hand.

"Arion, did you find him?"

Arion waved. He had.

Dim and Seth both nodded. There was not enough room to lift the wall from cliff side. That required leverage. The cliff blocked them. Dragging it like it was typically moved would only crush the man underneath.

They could lift from the side, but the 'grain' of the stone ran vertically. If they tried to lift from one side of the other, the rock would split and Euæmon probably crushed, not to mention Roman guards taking out their disapproval on the prisoners for damaging the goods.

Three poles had been placed under the rock – standard procedure to hold up the rock after it landed. They provided ways to move the rock and start to roll it to the docks. That method would not work with a living man underneath. So, they had to try something else.

If they lifted the rock from its side farthest from the cliff, even just a few inches, it would crush Euæmon for sure. That pointed back to lifting from the side.

"Perhaps," Seth wondered aloud, "we could lift both sides at once near the cliff. That would use the grain to help hold it together." Dim measured the distance between the sides with his eyes and experience.

"Yo," coughed Euæmon.

"They are working on it," assured Arion. He looked under the stone and could see Euæmon, just a few feet away. Something caused the stone to not fall flat, providing just enough space, but he was clearly pinned.

Dim and Seth took opposite sides of the wall near the cliff. All available wooden poles were divided between them. Pry bars were also brought down from topside. Dim dug into the dirt under the wall with the pry bar far enough to get a wooden pole under it. He checked. Seth did the same. They both planted the long poles under the stone a full foot in and used the pry bars for a low fulcrum. Coordinating with the other side, both sides of prisoners slowly pressed down on the pole. They all knew, not only could the rock break, but the poles could break, too, causing the rock to drop. One pole was not made to support that much weight. Two? Maybe...

The rock wall started to move. They lifted just enough to get another pole placed underneath it to hold it up. Then, they replaced the pry bar with another chunk of wood for a higher fulcrum and lifted again. All efforts coordinated, they felt the rock wall move again, a little higher. Again, they placed thicker pieces of wood under the wall to hold it up on the one side. So far, so good. Nothing broken, yet, but the higher the wall was raised, the more points of stress could cause it to break and even crumble.

The third lift brought the stone even farther off the ground.

"I feel like I am building a pyramid," grunted Seth to Rabbi Yosef right behind him on the pole.

Chunks of rock and whatever else could be found were tossed and pressed under the rock sheet to hold it up. It groaned as they let it down on the new mounts. Everyone's breath stopped for a moment. No, it did not break, but it did complain.

"He is moving," yelled Arion. "The center sinks, and he is still trapped, but he has a little more room to move."

"Is it holdin' steady?" yelled Dim.

Arion looked at the rock.

"I think so."

"Talor," yelled Dim to Seth's side. "Bring the pry bar." Seth looked at Dim questioningly. Talor complied immediately.

Dim picked up his own pry bar to hand to Talor as the youth approached. "Go join Arion & dig 'im out. We dare not lift it any higher. Go." He swatted the youth as he went to the side of the cliff.

"And, be careful," Phranc added needlessly.

"More stones or logs or whatever," called Dim. His fellow prisoners scavenged whatever they could to add to the supports.

"Try to add a little more support along the cliffside. Just a couple more pieces could save the piece as well as Euæmon."

They could all see and hear the two young men digging. It seemed like slow going; deadly slow progress. There was little room for them between the cliff and the wall, but they continued to work together to make a space large enough for a man to crawl out or be pulled out. They expected the latter.

Rocks were placed on each side to hold up that side of the wall. It took over an hour, but Arion finally slithered underneath to Euæmon to continue digging him out. He tried to turn. The pain in his face was obvious. He swore again at the sharp pain.

The digging continued as afternoon arrived. Water was brought for the workers. They kept at it until a cheer arose across the whole quarry when the two could be seen pulling the broken and bleeding but breathing body of Euæmon from the rocky grave. All covered with more dirt than any man should carry, they smiled ear to ear as they turned Euæmon around. He did not have the deftness to move between rock and the hard, stone cliff, so they placed his body right atop the wall. They would take a step or two and move him again. A step or two and move him again. Groaning and limp with bones broken, he tried to help move himself in careful ways with each step in the process, mostly to prevent or deal with the dozen odd places of stabbing pains. As he approached the side of the wall, others carefully reached out to bring him over.

Euæmon cried-out with pain as many hands brought him to the side of the slab. Dried, speckled blood covered various parts of his body and clothing, especially around his face. He gladly gulped a dusty drink of water.

Dim applauded. "Last time we had somethin' like this, we had t' drag 'im over the side o' the wall with a rope while he held on."

"How did the wall not crush you?" asked Rabbi Yosef.

The others all nodded. They also wanted to know.

Euæmon looked at them, still very weak.

"My sledge."

He saw they did not understand. It took him much time to explain, but they were all ears.

"I saw the wall dropping over me. I was woozy, but knew I had to do something or die. I grabbed my sledgehammer and held it upright to catch the wall. I had no time to think about it. If I had, I might have just given up. The handle is wood. It could never hold that much weight. And it did not. I saw it bow so grabbed the bottom half by the head. It broke and as it dropped, I kept hold of the bottom half upright with the metal against the dirt. I felt the weight press me down, but I kept hold of that half hammer. The shorter piece of wood held along with some rocks that had earlier fallen. My head was not crushed, but I was clearly pinned. Pains shot through me everywhere, especially my hips and legs, but I could not move. I looked up at the stone, not much more than an inch from my face, and I wondered why I was still alive."

"We were amazed when you called for help," said Mothcrates. "We all were sure you were dead."

"So was I," admitted Euæmon.

Teos stood by, looking a bit timid.

"What is it, Side?" asked Phranc.

Teos kept looking down at the dirt, but soon said, "Um, I was so scared when I heard you say 'Yo!'"

"Yo?" asked Euæmon, his brow furrowed a bit.

"Uh-huh. We all heard you say, 'Yo!' a few times." Others nodded in agreement.

"Um, I was not saying, 'Yo!'" corrected Euæmon. "I was saying, 'Eyore!'"

"Aha!" exclaimed Teos, less confused and the others laughed.

"Get him to the shack," yelled Guard Ernesto. "Dim."

Everyone understood. Each took hold to carefully lift Euæmon. Pain was inevitable, but they did the best they could. So many hands could help make his journey that much lighter. They brought him into the makeshift shack, onsite for just such emergencies and a good place to store shackles. Laying him on a table, Dim began to examine his wounds more closely. He looked at Guard Ernesto.

"I need Ionnes."

The Roman nodded.

"Fly," Dim said to Talor. The teen looked at the guard for confirmation and took off on jack rabbit legs for the salt ropes.

<>< ><> <>< ><> <>< ><> <>< ><> <>< ><>

"Where did you learn to do that?" asked Ionnes.

"Pergamos," answered Dim, still attending to Euæmon's wounds. Broken legs almost crushed from the knees down.

Concussion. Other scrapes and bruises. Still a miracle, really. Ionnes smiled, helping to clean the body and let Euæmon sleep. They had given him more than enough opium to knock him out.

"Ah," he said, "the healing center of Asia Minor. Is that where you are from?" Pergamos thrived, right in his neighborhood, some miles north of Ephesus.

"Yup," answered Dim. "Not that I am or ever could be a doctor, or even one o' those brainless attendees who lead ya down t' the healin' spas."

"Why do you call them brainless?"

"Have ya ever been t' the spas?"

Ionnes nodded. He had, a few times over the years.

"Pergamos has those natural springs of invigoratin' & even healin' waters. So, someone built a shop around it, called himself a doctor, hired his nephew or granddaughter or someone t' take you t' the springs. They point, ya enter the cool water, then just about the moment yer body finally gets used t' the water & ya can relax, they return & tell ya yer times up."

"And?"

"The one time I went, I paid for an hour. I am sure not half an hour passed before I was bein' ejected. Then, the lazy louses would not even bring me a towel. They was right there, & I got t' shiver a bit before I wrapped up."

Ionnes laughed, his head nodding in agreement.

"It happened to me, too, just like you said." He looked at the injured man as he added, "But, they are not all like that in Pergamos."

"Whom did ya go to?"

"Two of them. Alistair was on duty the first time I went. Even though he was recommended, his was just as you described. Probably a relative recommended him. The other was Paisley. He was far better and after that, I saw him almost every time I visited Pergamos."

Dim stared at Ionnes.

"Why does a divine healer like ya need any time in a spa? Cannot ya merely heal yerself?"

Ionnes chuckled. Good question. "If only it worked that way, my friend. I stub my toe just like you. I cut myself while gutting fish. I get hungry and thirsty and feel when the Romans and others in my life cause me pain and harm."

"Like gettin' poisoned or boiled in oil?"

"Okay - most of the pain. And, like you and everyone else, there are exceptions. Some more amazing than others."

Dim did not look convinced. Ionnes always wondered with awe when and how a holy and miraculous blessing could become a negative event.

"So, where in Pergamos did you learn to care for the sick and injured?"

"I jus' picked it up here & there," answered Dim. "Not hard when ya live so close."

"So then, what were you?"

Dim became more intense, brought to face his former life.

His jaw started to twitch. His breathing increased.

"Forgive me," said Ionnes. "It is okay if you do not want to talk about it."

Dim took the next moment to settle down before answering.

"I miss my home," he eventually confessed. "And, it kills me sometimes t' think about it. Yet, it is the very reason I do what I do."

Ionnes did not pretend he could fully understand and waited for Dim to continue. The Paraclete seemed content to let the occasion uncover itself naturally.

"I worked as a brick layer. A mason. It seems my life's callin' is t' work with rock. Perhaps that is why they sent me here." He looked out the door at the quarry wall. The men continued working within close sight, collecting smaller pieces of marble to finish their workday.

Dim clutched his dolphin necklace a moment and took a deep breath.

"I am married," he added. "Two children; both boys. I wish I knew what happened t' them. Are they still alive? Are they okay? Were they sold inta slav'ry? I do not know. So, I work the quarry as hard as I can. It is not a huge vein of marble. It will be gone within a few years. I saw that as the only way t' truly escape – t' mine all there is t' take, then maybe Roma would let me go."

Ionnes prayed quietly to himself as he heard Dim's story, asking Yeshua for His insightful wisdom.

"What are you here for?" he finally asked.

"Theft," Dim answered curtly.

"What did you steal?" asked Ionnes.

"Not a thing. Not a thing," Dim stressed. "I was a mason, hired t' build a walled garden by some laurelheads..."

"Laurelheads?" interrupted Ionnes.

"That is my name for them - the Roman arist'cracy."

Ionnes had to laugh. He knew he would recall that nickname.

Dim continued, "So, I am there levelin' the land, makin' brick, heatin' the kiln, & so forth. I had this reed I used t' measure the layout. Had not done much on the actual wall as yet when the matriarch o' the house started yellin' somethin'. I paid it no mind at first & kept t' my task. It is not unusual for my employers t' yell at their slaves or kids or friends or whoever. Suddenly, all o' the slaves are bein' rounded up. There are like twelve or fifteen of them. Even then, I am no doofus & jus' kept workin' on my wall.

"Suddenly, two soldiers came over & grabbed me. Ya know how it is. Ya say, 'What are ya doin?' & they never listen. So, now I am lined up with the slaves o' the house."

"You told them you were not a slave?"

"Of course. One of the first, middle & last things I said."

"So," asked Ionnes, "what for was the roll call?"

"Someone stole some o' her jewelry."

"What jewelry? What pieces?"

"Flogged if I know. I still do not know. For all I know, she misplaced it. So, ya know how it is. A bunch o' Roman soldiers come. First, they interrogate everyone. I was whipped & beaten til I was black & blue throughout."

"And?"

"It is so frustrating. You cannot tell 'em anythin' ya do not know. They tortured each one of us. Two of them - slaves - I do not know which two, 'pparently told the guards I was in the villa & rummagin' through madam's possessions."

"Were you?"

"Never entered the house before that day & even t' this day. I expect it was either those two or another slave they was tryin' t' protect."

"Did you tell your prosecutors that?"

"You think? I told 'em everythin' - maybe even more than I knew. Next, I am before the Roman court. I am not a Roman citizen. Most days I am glad o' that, but I had nothin' t' defend myself & no one t' speak for me. So, I got convicted of a theft I never did & here I am."

"Just like that."

"Jus' like that." Dim laid his hands on his head. "I lost everythin' that day. My wife. My sons. Even my home & all I possessed. When they convict ya, ya are taken right then t' serve yer sentence. Well, ya know...."

Ionnes definitely knew.

"I could not see or say good-bye t' my wife. As ya know, women are not allowed in court unless they are the one on trial. I looked for her, but no success. I looked for her as I was taken in chains t' the cell. Next day, I am on a boat to Patmos. From the dock I looked but could not see her, even then. And, that tears me up most o' all. What if they was already captured t' be sold as slaves? I have seen it happen before."

Tears had already made their way across his eyes. He sniffed a bit. Grief afforded no man its company in this place. The tears came anyway. He felt weak. He felt beaten. He felt the weight of his loss, perhaps more than any time recently.

"They take everythin', do not they?" He choked down the pain. "Ya do not even get t' make out a will. Any rights & priv'leges as a Greek citizen that I thought I had was gone. I became a prisoner; lower than a slave while my sentence reigns. Expendable. Replaceable. Nothin' t' them."

"When I feel that way," began Ionnes.

"Ya NEVER feel that way," accused Dim.

Ionnes paused, then reassured, "Of course I do. Look where we are. Who here does not know great loss?"

"I thought ya had yer God - this Yeshua, t' help ya."

"Aye," agreed Ionnes. "You are right, but when He died, it was the greatest loss I have ever felt. And, for three days, nothing could take away that pain."

Dim looked up at Ionnes. That was an odd expression - 'for three days'. "So, what happened after three days?"

The visions and impressions of those days, now so long ago in a man's life, came back with a resurrected flash as though current affairs. Ionnes looked at Dim intensely as he answered, "Yeshua rose from His grave. He came to us, alive and breathing. We felt His touch. We saw His wounds. We knew His scars."

Dim stared at Ionnes briefly, then bluntly retorted, "I do not believe ya."

Ionnes was unmoved. "I know," he admitted. "Most people do not, even though I am a witness. I saw them flog Him within an inchworm of His life. I saw Him carry His cross up the hill. I saw Him nailed and left to die, hung there like a common thief. I SAW HIM!" Ionnes pressed with purpose. "I saw Him die and I saw Him after He rose, and I saw Him ascend to Heaven. These are not just stories. I was there."

The two men stared at each other, barely a few feet apart. Then, Ionnes leaned towards Dim to add, "So, yes, I

166

know great loss, but I also know great redemption. My loss was replaced with His great Love."

Ionnes straightened up to take a gulp of water. He had not noticed how dry he had become until the water blazed its trail down his parched, nagging throat, filling his chest and stomach with its coolness. Setting down the marble cup, he stated, "And, I also knew it is your loss that presses you to work so hard. That has been your only hope, and that is a sad hope, indeed."

Dim's face admitted the truth of those words, but he still feared letting any other man know. Like most secrets, his could also be used as his weakness, and weakness flaunted a luxury no prisoner on Patmos could afford. He rose and walked to the open door. The day felt refreshing against his stinging senses. Part of him wanted to flee, but he remained. Still leaning against the door frame, he said, "At least I am still alive t' hope. Even a worn & tattered hope is better 'n no hope at all." His thoughts still swirled around the day of his trial.

"There was another man on trial that mornin' accused o' killin' his father-in-law."

"Patricide?" asked Ionnes.

"Yup."

Dim shuddered. "I saw the whole thing, start t' finish. He was stripped naked right there before the judge, then blindfolded, never allowed t' see the day ever again. Then, they kicked & smacked & tripped him as they led him out with the rest of us, dressed in nothin' but a blindfold. They took him out into the courtyard t' be beaten & flogged. We all stood there, chained t' one another where we had t' watch.

"He was cryin' but his tears could not escape. On his knees, cryin' out in pain & humiliation, one guard lit'rally whipped his tongue. Blood gushed from his mouth & he coughed & wheezed. Tied t' the post, he could not fall forward - or backward or any other way. Those Roman swine laughed.

'Good one,' they yelled.

"He tried again & missed.

"'Two out of three. Two out of three.'

"They all laughed while the rest of us died. Some puked. Some turned away as best they could, closin' eyes or droppin' heads. I stayed & watched. I needed t' know my enemy." His thoughts went to the boat.

"I felt great sadness for him. Like all o' us over the age o' two or three, I had seen Roman cruelty & barbarism, but this one vexed me more than most. I know not why, except I heard his voice in the courtroom. His father-in-law was not a good man t' know & had both tormented & infuriated his son-in-law. His murderin' sounded more like self-defense t' me.

"So, they brought him on board the boat with us, still naked as the day we were born. The blindfold was still tightly wound 'round his head & leavin' its mark like a tourniquet. He was bloody from the floggin' & could hardly move."

"Why did you not go to him?" challenged Ionnes.

Dim looked at him frostily. Then, hostilely.

"You could not stop his sentence, perhaps," said Ionnes, "but you could have eased his pain, even a little."

"Or joined him."

Ionnes knew that to be possibly true, but during his life also had stepped up to try to help nameless others many times before. Over the many years, he had seen countless brutalities, and always stepped forth to help or comfort where he could. Sometimes he received a harsh blow. Sometimes he reached the hurting soul. He never knew until he tried, and he noted to date, he had not as yet been given the same fate as the sufferer. Likewise, he usually brought some comfort, if only for the moment.

Then, he recalled Yeshua after a few hours on the cross.

"I thirst," He said.

Young Ionnes stood, seized by his apprehensions, whether and how to bring Yeshua some water. He watched as the soldiers filled a sponge with vinegar, attached it to a wimpy hyssop stalk and raised it to His face. Yeshua grabbed a quick taste, then turned away and gave up His Spirit not long after that. Even with everything else Ionnes did to remain with His LORD during the execution, Ionnes often wished he had at least tried to bring Yeshua some water.

"Do not get me wrong," added Dim, bringing Ionnes back to present day, "There was not a Greek on board who did not feel his pain & wanted t' help. We sat there grieving, also chained & beaten, as they cast off. The parricide man, still in chains, hardly moved, groanin' & still bleedin' & already half dead. He looked t' me like one who had never met the lash.

"We was barely a few miles out when the guards came up with a large sheet of leather, sewn together from more than one bull. They laid it on the deck, dumped the man on it, still in his chains, then folded it over him & sewed up each side. He did not even try t' fight or struggle at first. Then, they tied a rope t' each side & raised it up so the opening was on top. I could see the lump that was the man at the bottom of the huge bag. Then, they brought out the animals. A viper, a dog, a monkey & a rooster. They tossed each one in then tied up the top. The critters all start t' squabble, of course. The guards are laughin' at the sight, like it was a circus performance. I felt ire and repulsion.

"Then, they dropped it off the ropes, grabbed the movin' bag on all sides & tossed it overboard. As terrible as it was, we all watched. All the animals inside started bouncin' around tryin' t' escape. The captain had even dropped sail t' watch the spectacle. We were still quite close & we could hear the cries & howls & fightin'. It still curdles my blood when I think o' those sounds. Death has such a hauntin' cry.

"It must have taken even ten minutes t' fill with water enough t' sink. Jus' as the sack is mostly underwater, we were all shocked t' see his manacled arm come forth through the top o' the sack, grippin' at nothing but the deadly water. It flailed back & forth out o' the water til it went limp as it went under the surface."

Dim looked at Ionnes. He was surprised to see the tears in the old man's eyes. He wondered that he himself had become so calloused to be untouched by another man's violent death. The memory of Gallo arose as he recalled walking away from the young Roman as he was beaten. He recalled that he did nothing for Gallo even after the beatings were over. He recalled the face of the dead man as they carried him to his grave. Then, he recalled with a terrible and haunting shiver, the cold voice of the man resurrected by this old holy man. Gallo's puzzled expression as he looked at Dim, the Worm. His wish to re-enter mortality. His last breath given without remorse. Only then did Dim start to catch the barest glimpse of the saving grace of Yeshua for Gallo and the reality of why Ionnes brought a dead man back to call on the name of Yeshua then slip back into death.

Dim recalled as he buried Gallo, the look of peace on his face that had not been there connected with his first death. Dead is dead. He turned blue and pasty and the beauty that is life departed him, but perhaps he left the body a little less fearful and hopeless the second time.

Dim looked very far away as he said, "As that bag disappeared under the surface o' the blue water, we watched the spot for some time. I know there burned a place in my heart that hoped he would come back up from the depths. That wish remained empty & lost. I watched for sharks but saw none. The captain stayed there some time t' make sure, then weighed anchor, set sails & off we went. Even as we felt the motion of the boat on the sea speed up, I still watched the spot as long as my eyes could strain. And, the last image o' the man's struggles still cling t' me like a giant leech."

Dim did not cry, but his eyes became moist as his hard face replayed and displayed the pain of the moment.

"Dear Yeshua!" sympathized Ionnes. "I have heard of that torturous death but am glad to say that I have never seen it."

"Changes a man's heart, & not for the better," decided Dim. Then, the tears dried more quickly than they appeared. A self-condemning thought occurred to him; that he eased his own terrible loss and pain on Patmos by distracting it with the death sentence of another. How cold-hearted and ruthless he felt that moment, but he had learned to bronze his heart during his years of captivity and grueling labor. In turn, he feared the stark truth about himself. Even if they released him, who would he be if he found his family? The plaguing question remained one he ever hoped to explore if given the chance, but it likewise scared him more than all others.

"A man's heart holds the treasure he values most."

Dim looked back at Ionnes. "What did ya say, old man?"

"A man's heart holds the treasure he values most," Ionnes answered. "Now what 'treasures' have you stored within since you have been here? Or, what treasures did you come here with that have been replaced?"

Dim quickly realized he knew not those answers. He wished he could open his chest as easily as one opens the neck of a tunic to look inside. He had not considered anytime recently what he would find. If he had such a knife, he might be tempted to skin himself to see the man inside. The self-condemning idea did not scare him as much as it should have - and would have in his former life. And, he realized that stony insensitivity answered the question for him. His hardened heart shied not to answer. He shuddered under its icy beat.

"What is in yer heart, old man?" demanded Dim, thinking that question would reverse the focus back towards Ionnes, (or anywhere else besides on Dim).

"Yeshua's love," Ionnes answered most readily. "Yeshua is love."

Dim cursed.

A few times.

Vulgarities slid forth like his tongue resembled a long, slippery chute.

"That does not make it less so, my friend," assured Ionnes.

Dim paused from his tirade briefly to wonder what he would find skinned under the old man's tunic. Dim's old self hoped from afar such love truly existed. For those briefly passing seconds, he missed his old self. The present man repelled anyone's love, save his weary love for his missing family. Even that felt at times more like habit than conviction if ever he cared to look closer. He clutched his dolphin necklace through his tunic. His beautiful love for his family, once so vibrant and alive, had been demoted to a mere motive for survival.

He shook and shivered as the thoughts and impressions of his past life washed over him. He saw the passionate smile of his wife. He repaired the sandals of his children. He felt their hugs in his mind and heart like a lost treasure newly found. How he missed his family. How he missed the laughter and tomfoolery of his boys.

He suddenly felt cold. Very cold. Encased in ice as the cruelty of hopelessness and despair suddenly descended and tried to crush him. He shook violently under the horrible, blood sucking burden.

"BE GONE!" shouted Ionnes.

Dim jumped.

"IN YESHUA'S NAME."

Dim turned and rose up with a start.

"What happened?" he said, fumbling and stumbling over his raw emotions.

"Demons," answered Ionnes. "Just demons, up to their old tricks. Feel better?"

Dim thought the old man a bit crazy there, but he also realized, yes, he did feel better.

"What? What do you mean?" asked Dim.

"Evil spirits abound on this island," answered Ionnes. "I have detected them since before we made port."

"I do not believe in evil spirits, either," Dim said, somewhat automatically.

"Oh, I can tell," admitted Ionnes, "but that does not mean they do not believe in you."

Dim blinked, unsure what to think.

"Demons are just as real as the One True God," attested Ionnes. "And, the differences between the two are obvious."

Dim had a good idea of the differences, but remained mute, awaiting Ionnes to continue. He had already learned from this Christian zealot at least a few things he had never considered before.

Ionnes continued, "Adonai creates. Demons do not. Adonai made all things that are alive. Demons cannot make anything alive. Adonai can make everything and everyone in this world do His bidding but loves us more than enough to let us decide for ourselves. Demons cannot make anyone do anything, and love is never why they do anything."

"So," interjected Dim, "if demons cannot make things move, or create anythin', what do they do?"

"They tell people what to do and those with tickling ears who listen to them do their biddings. Most of the soldiers from Roma carry at least a demon or three with them, compelling them to cruelty. The demon does not move their arms or legs, nor their words, but they do infiltrate their thoughts. The demons only see and seize the opportunities to suggest and steer those who blindly and foolishly listen."

"Like a ship's rudder," Dim thought aloud.

"Yes," affirmed Ionnes, "or, an evil demon-stration."

Dim groaned though actually he liked the pun more than he wanted to permit. "The demon made me do it," was an old expression. He had never considered its reality quite so literally as he did at that moment. He still shrugged inside, not sure he believed in demons, but their reality seemed a bit more possible than he had considered for most of his life.

He had grown up in a society of many gods. One of Pergamos' main attractions was the spa and temple to Ascleplus, the god of healing, but there were plenty of other temples and sanctuaries - such as to Demeter, Dionysus, Athena and Hera. Being a mason, he had enjoyed studying the temple grandeur and architecture, visited them as was expected by society, and had drank too much celebrating their holy days. But, for the most part, the gods were just hollow names with exciting stories. He did not disbelieve in them, but their reality did not touch his everyday life. Therefore, many commonly understood that the gods had sent him and the others to Patmos to forget them. With that in mind, Dim wondered that he would give this holy man any consideration that there be only one single God. Ionnes saw the young man thinking and sat back to let the ideas feather through his head.

"So," Dim wondered aloud, "These demons cannot actually control me or anyone else?"

"Aye," answered Ionnes. "Just speak to you, or even take over your body if you let them. They need a person's body to do their dirty works. But, Yeshua has risen and ascended back to Heaven where He touches my life in amazing and wonderful ways each and every day."

"Are you finished?" interrupted Guard Octavius. "Get back out here."

Dim jumped as he checked his patient one more time. The injured man laid there sleeping, his breathing labored. Dim gathered up his few supplies as he and Ionnes headed for the door.

"So," double checked Dim, "demons cannot make ya do anythin' ya do not want t' do?"

"The demon never made Eve eat the fruit," added Ionnes. "She did that on her own."

"Who is Eve?"

Ionnes shook his head with bemusement. "That, my friend, is another story."

PATMOS

CHAPTER 11

"*Eyore!*" cursed a guard.

The second guard nodded agreement. No other word said it better.

Climbing the hill covered with fancy buildings, they passed the homes of the upper crust. Neither had spent much time in this neighborhood. For both, it felt awkward and out of place. They were used to the barracks, or the quarry, or the docks. This neighborhood made them uneasy as they passed marble fences around carved granite homes.

There were sculptures of gods and goddesses throughout. Some they recognized. Some they did not. Passing a replica of the Discus Thrower, one tipped his spear its direction.

"From that stance, no one could throw a discus more than half the distance." Both of them laughed. Both men well knew how to throw a discus and apparently The Discus Thrower did not.

They both looked down the hill towards the town. The beauty of the view touched one and not the other.

As they rounded the corner, both were unsure where they were going. Their instructions were implicit, but the one who could read wished he had written them down. One home had torches lit out front though it was not yet close to dark. That may have been indicative they were expecting someone.

"One home made out of two," the second said, suddenly remembering what they had been told.

The house with torches was not the one. They continued as the leader looked back towards their prisoner. "Move it, dog!" he yelled to the old man in chains.

Chains were meant to slow down a man's movements, but the guards never seemed to understand or appreciate that fact.

Ionnes had been surprised by the invitation. He had been sloshing through the sea on a wavy day, making salt ropes, when a Roman guard called him in from the surf. A well dressed, elderly Roman stood beside the guard, accompanied by his slave. He looked familiar to Ionnes, but the apostle did not immediately know from where.

"I am Myron," he said, speaking Latin.

Ionnes nodded, slicking back his salty, wet hair. "Ionnes. But you prefer Giovanni." He smiled. "And, what is your name?" Ionnes asked, looking at the slave.

Tobie stood frozen, unsure whether to answer. It was not customary for someone to make introduction to a slave, plus this man was an inmate. Double jeopardy.

Tobie, tell him your name," said Myron, humoring Ionnes.

His voice cracked a bit, but he answered, "Tobias. I am called Tobie. Tobie Gillius."

"Shalom, Tobias. It is a sweet blessing to meet you."

Ionnes started to move towards the slave, but the Roman guard took a step forward to intervene. Ionnes stopped and backed up, creating a social vacuum. Myron moved forward to fill the void.

"Are you the one who healed my son a few nights back outside the Acropolis?"

"Perhaps," answered Ionnes, not toying with the man at all though he did wonder where such an inquiry as this would lead. It could be only very good or very bad.

"Praise You, Yeshua," slipped through his lips. His fate flourished Always in the LORD's hands. He seldom believed otherwise and found only his own folly when he did.

"I shall speak with you," ordered Myron.

Ionnes nodded and smiled to continue.

The men took seats and conversed for some time, mostly Myron asking Ionnes where he was from, what he had been before his arrest and why he was in Patmos. Tobie remained on the outskirts of the conversation though Ionnes looked at him and spoke to him just as plainly as he spoke to Tobie's master.

"Oh!" exclaimed Myron. "So, you are the one?"

Lucius had shown Laurentius who had shown Myron the scroll from Roma after Ionnes arrived. Its message reported quite clearly, yet it created quite a debate between the two Roman elders. Now here, meeting Ionnes, Myron felt even more unsure this could be the same man described in the scroll. Apparently, he expected someone bigger, or heartier, or more arrogant. Roman floggings can tame a man, but there always exists some men who can never be tamed. In Myron's mind, this old man did not fit that 'never be tamed' image. Ragged and dirty and unkempt. Well, he was a prisoner who had already been working today for some hours. Fortunately, Myron's nature knew better than to believe every first impression he thought or imagined. Mostly, he fretted over having such a sorcerer in his home, (not to mention what Fona would say). Ionnes neither admitted nor denied Myron's question. He still waited to see what Myron wanted. Elderly Roman aristocrats did not seek the company of prisoners without good reason, but Ionnes well knew if their intents were nefarious, Ionnes already would have been dragged forth by Roman guards like a sack of moldy grain and dumped on the floor before whomever to face charges and fate. That was not the case here, at least not yet. Ionnes responded to Myron with his signature, inoffensive smile. And, to be honest, he just liked this old Roman, Myron. One of those inexplicable human things. He hoped someday they would be friends. This meeting was already a good start that direction.

"My family and I would like to thank you for your service to my son. My daughter has asked that you join us for dinner. Tomorrow?"

"I do not think I am busy," answered Ionnes humorously, genuinely surprised by the invitation, but still smiling.

"Then, I will have you brought to my home."

"I look forward to it," Ionnes answered. It would be nothing short of a divine blessing to eat something besides prisoner food. In that fashion, he also wished his fellow prisoners could join him. And, even the guards. He saw what they ate most nights, and it honestly was not much better than the prisoners. Maybe that partially explained why they were so vicious.

"I will arrange for your transfer," closed Myron and turned to go.

He walked away like one who typically ignores nobodies with his own slave in tow. His noble gait unmistakable, especially when you were the slave or prisoner. Over his many occasions of captivity, Ionnes had become well accustomed to the custom.

He returned to his duties with rope and salt and sea.

Now, walking up the hill, Ionnes noticed an oddly made home, like it had been made from two homes. Both were granite, but detectably not from the same quarry. The guards were about to pass it when Ionnes said, "Could this be the villa?"

One of the guards turned to thump Ionnes, but they both looked and knew they had found the place. They brought him forth and pounded on the front door.

Tobie answered and ushered the three inside. The guards felt aghast at the opulence and beauty of the home as both wondered if they had pursued the wrong profession.

Myron appeared.

"Remove his chains," he ordered.

The two guards stood briefly. The order was clear enough, but they still wanted to make sure that they had heard right.

"Remove his chains. He will be our guest for the evening."

The first guard pulled out his keys and unlocked Ionnes shackles. Ionnes shivered. It always felt good to remove the cold iron.

"That is all," added Myron. "Tobie, take them to the slave's quarters. Did not you see to the extra portions for their dinner?"

"Yessir," answered Tobie and walked away, expecting the guards to follow. They were a bit slow, wanting to make sure their prisoner did not try to escape. He may have been a humble, old man, but they would be severely punished if they lost him. They had no reason to believe the old Roman would stand up for them to the Captain of the Guard and report that he ordered the stocks removed.

"Come this way," ordered Myron. "You may want to clean up after your day on the beach."

He led Ionnes to a private room with a basin. Beside the basin stood no pitcher of water, but Ionnes saw something odd attached to the basin he had never seen before. It had a handle, but Ionnes did not assess for what.

Myron read Ionnes' face and stepped forward to turn on the water.

Ionnes laughed. He had heard of such homes but had not as yet actually seen one. My! My! My! What a modern world.

Myron explained. "When I rebuilt this home, I opted for running water. The water tower is right out back and filled weekly by the slaves. We were fortunately able to import lead pipes. They do not rust, and adds a tangy, slightly sweet flavor to the water."

Myron removed a tunic hanging on the wall. "Here is a tunic to change into. I saw yesterday you were in need of new clothing."

Ionnes smiled appreciably as Myron turned to go. Cleaning up, he used the water sparingly, but took his time. It had been so long since he could properly clean up. He remembered the days of his youth when ceremonial cleaning was the norm, even for lowly fishermen.

He knew it to be quite a haul from the one island spring of fresh water to here, no doubt done with donkey and cart. Two prisoners did water duty daily for the guards and prisoners. Ionnes took one more sip before exiting. Yes, the water did have a slightly sweeter, savory flavor.

The tunic fit well enough. It felt odd, the scratchiness of the new fabric against his flesh. He checked his appearance in the small, polished metal mirror. It showed not a clear reflection; in this case clearly the better.

Exiting the private room, another servant awaited to take Ionnes to the banquet hall. Ionnes, awed and pleased by what he saw, noted the dimensions of the room to be larger than most Christian churches, or even synagogues. Only four people, including Myron, sat on the floor before one end of a very large table. Two men and two women. The table could easily seat twenty or more. Though slightly larger, it reminded Ionnes of a large table he sat at in an upper room all those years ago. Plush and beautiful cushions and pillows abounded framing the table. Six slaves stood nearby in the sizable room. Large windows and skylights allowed in tons of sunlight. The room felt quite warm from the beams of sunlight displaying the dancing, frolicking bits of dust and lint in the air. Ten trees bordered the room's perimeter, some potted and others planted in the ground, bringing life as all reached merrily for the skylights.

A matronly woman arose - the younger of the two women.

Much younger than Myron, but she still could have been his wife. Such arrangements were common. No, she had been seated next to the younger man. Ionnes glanced at the young man. He gazed at Ionnes intensely. Ionnes recognized him right away.

"Welcome Giovanni," approached the younger matron. "I am Chryspippe. We are so glad you could join us." She motioned for him to join them at the table.

He nodded and followed. She introduced her brother as Ionnes sat himself next to Myron. Apollonides barely nodded. His expression never wavered as he kept narrowed eyes fixed on the prisoner.

"And, this is my mother, Fona.".

Ionnes smiled and bowed his head. She smiled politely and felt less sure of the invitation than when Chryspippe asked. Ionnes seated next to Myron, he could easily converse with the three across the table.

Even before plopping down, Ionnes noticed that no one sat at the head of the table - the place where Myron would have sat. Myron sat to the right of the head, Chryspippe to the left, Fona next to Chryspippe and Apollonides next to his sister. He wondered that Chryspippe did not sit next to her husband. That may have been common practice, he thought, but not everyone on Earth followed common practice.

On the table sat a bowl of fruit, a small bowl of olives, pistachios with a tool to crack the shell, and a plate of bread, but the servants went into motion as soon as everyone sat. Leaving the room, they soon reappeared with five steaming plates of food. Another followed bearing a pitcher of wine and goblet for Ionnes.

The winebearer poured a scant amount of wine into each goblet for the diners to taste. If approved, he would fill glasses. Myron and Chryspippe downed their samples and nodded for more. Even if they intently watched Ionnes, wine's regular ritual at Roman meals demanded one's attention fully.

Nobody had to tell Ionnes to eat, but he took a moment with head bowed to thank Yeshua for this feast, and then another to keep him humble.

"Esau," muttered Ionnes, strictly to himself, almost in place of "Amen" to keep his faith focused.

With freshly cleaned hands, the apostle took hold of a crust of flat bread. He praised God and gave Him thanks, broke the bread and muttered, "This is my body." He slowly ate the bread. Then, he took the goblet of wine and whispered, "This is my blood." He finished the sample and thanked the slaves for more.

Ready to dig in, it tasted better than it smelled. He had been on prisoner's rations for months. He knew he would never be able to consume the whole plate and more. He would not even try.

He may have grown up in Galilee, but had learned table manners later in life, first as a follower of Yeshua, and more so as the bishop in Ephesus. Likewise, he wished to savor each bite while it lasted.

Ionnes dipped some strange and wonderful root in hummus. It tasted tangy and spicy all by itself and he relished the strong flavor.

His eyes never far from his hosts, he noticed very little conversation while they ate. Most Roman households he had visited were the exact opposite. Meal time each day seemed like a major family affair to come together and work out the world's woes. He found it an Italian exception, the family who kept something hidden from the rest of the clan, so Ionnes took the initiative. He looked directly at Apollonides.

"How have you been since I last saw you?"

Apollonides did not immediately realize Ionnes spoke to him. When he looked up, he saw all eyes on him. His eyes again narrowed towards Ionnes.

"Well," he said, done with that part of the conversation.

"You look well," agreed Ionnes, "although you may have gotten a little more boring."

Myron, Chryspippe and Fona, (as well as the slaves) all gasped a moment before the three bursted into laughter.

"I do not see what is so funny," defended Apollonides.

"I am sure you do not," giggled his father. "But, I - we are glad for it."

"I see no reason to sit here and be insulted," snapped Apollonides, starting to stand.

Ionnes raised a buttered hand. "My apologies. Please. No insult intended. Please remain."

Apollonides settled back down and returned to his dinner. "You are not the only antagonist," he said to his plate and Ionnes. "I am more than glad Kynops is not here."

"Who is Kyknots?" asked Ionnes.

Apollonides did not answer quickly, so Myron answered, "Kynops. He is the Magician of Patmos. A great sorcerer. He has never been Apollonides' favorite."

"It appears he still is not," suggested Ionnes, "and sorcery does not make one great."

The three nodded in unison.

"Yes," grumbled Apollonides, "the night would be just perfect if Kynops had come."

Ionnes waited and Myron sighed mightily. In turn, Chryspippe gathered the threads of dissention to make a loving tapestry.

"Apollonides," she cooed, "we are here to honor this man for helping you. That is the very reason why he is now here."

"And, I already told you, it is unnecessary." He looked directly at Ionnes as he added, "We always knew the gods would eventually favor us. This man's presence is no more than a mere coincidence. I felt fine before."

"Honey," wooed Fona.

"You were not fine," said Myron boldly.

"I was," insisted Apollonides, glaring at his father, "and I must say, also much happier."

"Were you?" challenged Chryspippe. "Brother, you were seldom happy."

Fona felt and watched the tears blur her vision.

Apollonides stayed his course. "Not while I felt like a prisoner in my own home." He looked over at their prisoner guest and realized it was probably a poor choice of words, not that he would come anywhere close to an apology or even slight embarrassment.

"I will not thank some prisoner who happened to whimsically wave his magic hand. And, I will not make a mockery of a gift of the gods."

"It was just one God who touched you," corrected Ionnes.

Apollonides turned his glare towards Ionnes. "Which god? Jupiter? Mercury? Perhaps my name sake - Apollo? He is a god of healing. I always knew he would find me."

Ionnes stopped eating to look intently at Apollonides. The staring match followed, neither man flinching for some seconds, like a bold and intense silence in Heaven for half an hour or more. Myron and Chryspippe watched, he intrigued and she anxious. Fona started to speak but Myron's hand ordered her silence. She complied. Chryspippe looked back and forth at each of them, then placed her hand on Apollonides' shoulder.

"Brother, what is important is that you are well."

Apollonides broke gaze with Ionnes to look at his sister. He nodded, eyes closing with the motion of his head, and said nothing. He looked again at Ionnes, stubborn but less intense. "I know you disagree, prisoner. I have heard you are a follower of The Way."

"You have heard correctly," relaxed Ionnes and resumed eating.

"Christians!" barked Apollonides, "and you Jews. Only one God."

He looked at his father with an insight he had forgotten - something his father told him at least once.

"And, where is your temple?"

Ionnes' face drooped. "The temple stood in Ierusalem. Now it is no more."

"Only one temple?" chided Apollonides. "You Jews cannot even afford more than one God - or one temple."

Ionnes encountered an old, familiar sadness, remembering the destruction of the temple, now well over twenty years past, but his spirit would not be slapped around much by this old chastisement.

Apollonides looked at his father. "Did not you once tell me that before he became Cæsar, General Titus put down their uprising, leveling Ierusalem as well as destroying their one temple?"

Myron nodded.

"And, as I recall, Titus declined the praise and rewards which go with such victories. They tried to give him a Wreath of Victory, but he said there was no honor in destroying a people who had been abandoned by their God. That he merely served as the instrument of their God's wrath."

Myron almost glowed in Roman pride but kept his temperament even. Chryspippe wondered with surprise at her brother's coldness and insolence towards the man who had healed him. And, it surprised her just as much that she cared. In the old apostle, Giovanni, though just a prisoner, she suddenly saw something more that she had never quite seen or recognized before that moment.

Ionnes still looked downtrodden, remembering the loss of Ierusalem, but he had become well accustomed with Roman arrogance.

"Do you believe their God abandoned them?" he asked, looking up from the table.

"Yes," answered Apollonides firmly.

"And, that Titus was an instrument of Almighty God's wrath."

"Yes," repeated Apollonides.

"I am glad to hear you say that you believe in the One True God," said Ionnes. His old smile returned to his face. He raised his wine goblet and took a drink to commemorate the occasion.

Apollonides, flustered, made some awkward noises trying to form words. Eventually, he said, "No. That is not what I meant."

"But it is," assured Ionnes. "Your own mouth is witness."

Chryspippe snickered to see her brother suddenly squirm and struggle; an orator without words.

Apollonides looked at his family, stood and excused himself.

"Apollonides," called Ionnes. Apollonides stopped to look back defiantly towards the old man who had no worldly business being in his home. It disgraced his father to have him here. His father well knew better. Whatever demon possessed Apollonides must have moved into his father.

"Yeshua purged the demon that filled you," stressed Ionnes. "I urge you to open your heart to Him."

"Tough," rejected Apollonides, again turning to go.

"Apollonides," commanded Myron, but his son was gone. Ionnes knew it polite to ask forgiveness for upsetting his host's son, but such politeness seemed wasted. It seemed clearly obvious that Apollonides planned to storm out first chance.

Myron looked at Ionnes, then at his daughter and said, "He will live."

Chryspippe nodded to her father, then looked at Ionnes. She also would have apologized for her brother's behavior - then remembered Ionnes was still a prisoner. It surprised her that she had to remind herself. That façade was beginning to give way to the man beneath.

"But, father," she started to protest.

"Apollonides led us to the battle ground. He knew the challenge he created. He started the contest and lost. Hopefully, he will be wiser for it."

Then, Myron turned towards Ionnes. "Giovanni, now that the niceties are out of the way," he smiled at his own humor, "would you share again your experiences in Roma which brought you here?"

Ionnes felt glad to share how Yeshua had delivered him. Some stories would never get old. He spoke with eloquence and authority. Myron made his points, and Ionnes allowed his host his dignity without compromising the gospel. His own accounts, starting from the shores of the Sea of Galilee, (before it was called the Sea of Tiberius by the Romans), to present times. He had so much to tell, but he encapsulated and summarized and whet appetites regarding the power and deliverance which laid groundwork for his life's work.

The slaves stayed close by. One scoffed, not loudly, but the four heard when Ionnes mentioned Yeshua walking on water and calming the stormy sea. It had failed Myron's notice, but not Ionnes that he bore witness of Yeshua not just to Myron, Fona and Chryspippe.

At times Myron sounded more like a Greek, openly discussing the life of Yeshua on Earth and the greater life thereafter. Many leading Romans tried to repress any suggestion of a greater life outside of Roman rule and worship of their gods. It became the grand arena there at the oversized table. Myron challenged Ionnes at times. He pulled no punches and rolled with Ionnes'. It reminded Ionnes of the early days of his now pal Ignatius, in Antiochus, arguing against the deity of the Christ only to find his arguments thinner than high mountain air against Ionnes' loving testimonies and teachings. The Syrian born Ignatius always loved a good debate.

The ongoing theme throughout Ionnes' talk remained the love of Yeshua.

"He (Yeshua) loved His own who were in the world. He loved them to the end."

Ionnes had long since finished eating and savored another sip of wine. The goblet, held by its bowl with two fingers, slightly rocked back and forth as he spoke - an old habit. Sometimes Fona watched the glass more than heard the words of their guest.

For Ionnes, the best part of the evening was Chryspippe's face. Ionnes relished her rapt interest. She absorbed every word like a hungry bath towel. She did not yet know it, but for the first time in years - perhaps the first time in her life, she began to detect the reality of a God. She could not yet put her thoughts into cognitive words, but clearly showed a spiritual hunger and yearning she had never before noticed or recognized as being fed for the first time in her life.

As the evening drew to a close, Myron rose. He nodded towards the guards who had been summoned. They came forward, chains in hand.

"That will not be necessary," ordered Myron.

"Sir?"

"Chains will not be necessary to transport the prisoner."

"But, sir," argued a guard, "we shall be slayed by the Captain of the Guard for transporting any prisoner without chains."

Myron knew it to be true. He motioned for the men to wait and left the room. A few minutes later, he returned, a sheet of fancy papyrus in his hand.

"Give this to your commander."

They took the notice. Only one could read and looked at Myron with fearful awe.

Myron added, "If you cannot transport this prisoner without chains, you are no soldiers of Roma."

The first guard saluted, followed by the next.

Chryspippe stepped forward to Ionnes. He held his old tunic, carefully folded and tucked under his left arm.

"You desire your old tunic?" asked Chryspippe, a bit puzzled.

"I am glad for your gift," answered Ionnes, fingering his new attire, "but, there are others in my life whose clothing is worse than this one. Far worse. If it can be of use, then it would be a wise and perfect blessing to someone."

Chryspippe nodded, again perplexed at the extraordinary attitudes of this little man.

"I am so glad you could come," she said, the governor's wife never forgetting her manners.

"We are honored with your visit," added Fona, then almost gasped. She also had briefly forgotten his station in life. Ionnes happily accepted her gracious words. She smiled with embarrassment and left the room.

"It has been a sincere blessing to meet all of you, - and you, too Tobie." He looked over at the slave, then added looking past Tobie, "And, the others." Two nodded. They had enjoyed this man's outlandish stories and demeanor more than they enjoyed most of Myron's other visitors.

"And, it has also been a blessing to become acquainted with Apollonides. Truly."

Chryspippe took his free hand with both of her's - a very forward and unusual act. "Please forgive my brother. He is not always this way."

"I already knew," confirmed Ionnes.

"We hope to see you again soon," she added.

Ionnes smiled. He started to turn, then stopped. "I must confess," he began, "when I arrived, I thought the two of you were married.

The surprise on their faces was immediate. Both Chryspippe and Myron began to laugh.

"This is my father," she said between chuckles. "And, the Governor Laurentius is my husband. We waited for him, but he apparently could not be here tonight. We saved his spot at the head of the table just in case he came."

Ionnes nodded his approval, adding, "Then, I shall pray for your marital union."

She seemed unsure exactly what that meant or what form it would take, but mouthed, "Thank you." If she had to pick anyone on the island whose prayer might actually be heard and acted upon, she would pick Giovanni.

The trio turned to go. The slaves saw them out the gate. As they departed, Ionnes suddenly recalled Myron's words yesterday; that his daughter had requested Ionnes' presence for dinner. Duh, Yochanan!

When they were down the road still in sight of the villa, the illiterate second guard asked, "What did that paper say?" The first guard felt the refined scroll of papyrus, gingerly handled to keep it from being creased or crumpled.

"The governor's father-in-law made an edict. We are to not shackle this prisoner. He has been a guest of the House of Myron and is to be treated as such."

"For just tonight?" asked the second Roman.

"It does not say. But it has his seal at the bottom, so it is official."

"*Eyore!*" swore the second guard.

"Uh-huh," answered the first as the night overtook the walk towards the penal colony barracks.

PATMOS

CHAPTER 12

Chryspippe entered her home. The Roman guards who escorted her saluted the governor, then departed for home base, the barracks and a swig or two. Her husband, still in uniform, greeted her. It was getting late, but likely he had not been home long.

"How was your dinner with the prisoner?"

Chryspippe smiled. "It was very nice. He is well educated and very knowledgeable. We enjoyed his visit very much."

Laurentius frowned at that answer.

"Is something wrong?" She immediately wished she had not asked, but then realized it mattered not. He would speak anyway.

He ordered wine before answering. Taking his own swig, he set his glass down and sighed heavily.

"He is a prisoner of Roma. His rights have been stripped, and for good cause. Now, you honor him, and it is never good for a prisoner to be honored or dressed up or placed above his station. It makes only trouble for the guards, and not just from the one prisoner. Others reveal their jealousy towards the favored man. Even my soldiers become restless. Then, arguments and even fights between the men are a safe bet. If it goes unchecked, the guards may face an uprising. Many would die, and the quarry would not mine marble as ordered."

He stopped though not finished, mostly making sure his wife became pressed down by the weight of his words.

"My dear," soothed Chryspippe, "we only wanted to honor the man who healed my brother. Would not you also thank anyone if they had healed your brother, or father, or mother or any other close to you? What if I had been the one he healed? Would not you wish to thank or at least acknowledge his favor? And, does not it help you and your career as well to have my brother well? Did not that show cause enough to break with protocol?"

"No," answered Laurentius curtly.

He stared at her more intently, his voice much louder, his face more twisted. "He was sentenced here by Cæsar Domitian himself. Personally. *Personally!* Domitian will be keeping tabs on him - Especially this one, and I cannot have any report returned telling the emperor that his prisoner is being honored and fed and wined by the governor's wife - or any other person on this island."

Chryspippe, keeping eye contact with her husband, felt her body fill with paralyzing fear - even panic, similar to the craven fear she had felt when Apollinides' faces appeared in her bed chambers. She swallowed hard to maintain composure and from her own station in life knew her husband was right. Or, at least partially right.

Then, the face of the prisoner, Giovanni, and his stories of Yeshua came to mind. The impressions were so fresh and real, she felt like he had just left her at her door. She tried to imagine the love of Yeshua. Those images, imposed on her thoughts and emotions with the impact of a mighty ocean wave, just as quickly dissolved her fears and warmed her heart. She became completely off guard with surprise by such a striking change of emotions - such deliverance!

For the first time in her life she uttered the word, "Yeshua", barely audible, even to her own ears.

Laurentius noticed his wife's change of demeanor, but kept on, his face hard as his sword's steel.

"I do not care if he is some sort of magician or holy man or shaman or whatever he thinks he is. It did not protect him from capture and sentence. He is a prisoner of Roma, and therefore subject to the whims of his captors."

He went to grab his goblet but did not drink. His face paled as it lost a little blood. His head turned downward.

"It would not surprise me if one of Domitian's spies has not already left Patmos for Roma. The Eagle of Roma wields a large sword and hammer." He took his intended gulp or two and again set down his glass. He paused again, looking far away before adding, "For all I know, Makrinos has already sent report to Roma of your dinner tonight."

"He would do that?" she checked. She had met the proconsul and adjudged him just another shapeless, stuffed toga of Roma.

"I would not be surprised and would kill him myself if I ever found out," he answered, breathing hard. "But that is not the point. Whether Makrinos or any other stooge, I want not their selfish, backstabbing accounts to be sent to Domitian. No assassin's blade is more honed."

So, what?" yelled Chryspippe, eyebrows down turned. "The emperor is not here."

"Cæsar is everywhere."

"Cæsar is never everywhere," bantered Chryspippe just as loudly. She knew well the rules of the game. Cæsar ruled on high, like one of the gods on Olympus - or demigods. He had his wide array of soldiers, minions and informants to do his every bidding, spread out throughout the empire. In that sense, Cæsar lived as more than a god, for she had seen more accomplished from Palantine Hill than any or all the temples to any god. But, even with all that, the Cæsar never dwelt everywhere. Never would he peek out under every nook and cranny.

Laurentius stepped forth in response to her defiance, closing the distance. She knew that look in his eyes, and he knew hers. The blow cometh. Perhaps more than one. He grabbed her in rough, mighty hands, then shoved her against the wall. Every good soldier knew a wall reduced their adversary a way to retreat. The blow across her face came harsh and quick, knocking her to the ground. She held her cheek. Blood oozed inside the back of her nasal cavity but did not spring forth.

"Cæsar is everywhere," he corrected.

"Cæsar is everywhere," she echoed from the floor. She spoke the words with hollow voice. Her hand stayed planted against her throbbing cheek as she sat up. She knew it would bruise. This certainly was not the first time he had struck her and would not be the last. Women of all station knew the value of beatings by their husbands. Some covered the bruising with make-up and avoided appearing publicly. Others wore their bruises like trophies, as though it displayed their husband's affections. Chryspippe did neither but went forth with dignity just as expected by the governor's wife.

"And, he is no fool," added Laurentius. "Nor is the emperor as forgiving as your zealot, I have no doubt."

Chryspippe, still on the floor, paused for serious consideration. She truly liked her role as the governor's wife, however empty and fruitless it had become. She did not need some new Legate showing up one day, announce himself and introduce the new governor while she and her husband were ordered journey back to Roma to face Domitian. Domitian gave Laurentius this island, and he could take it away just as easily. She took a deep breath and spoke more calmly, with a controlled coldness as she rose and faced her husband. Her hand dropped to her side as she looked at Laurentius.

"I only wished to thank someone who healed my kin. But I will refrain from such charitable and civilized activities henceforth, just as the governor demands."

Her hand returned to her cheek as she moved past him to her bedchamber and closed the door with a quiet, unmistakable click. Lorin followed in right after her mistress.

Laurentius looked at the closed door. He picked up his glass, took a loud sip, then threw it hard against the fireplace. The pottery shattered. The remaining wine splashed in all directions at once. He cursed and went to his own room, slamming the door. He said nothing to the slaves who all knew they would clean up whatever messes the governor made. None followed him into his room.

Once inside, the governor sat on a wooden chair and untied his leather bodice. It was not the first fight he had struck or beaten his wife by any stretch, but this one ended on a more disturbing note than he had previously encountered, and he wondered what on Earth she was thinking. Changing clothes for the evening, he also rejected her words inferring him a barbarian. They played through his brain over and over as he corrected her with his own words and fists; his logic undeniable; her finally seeing true and sober reason.

He stopped dressing a moment to speak, though none were there to reply.

"Giovanni," he cursed, every muscle in his body and face tense and tight. "You shall finally learn the wrath of Roma or watch it from your grave." No matter what words reached Domitian, the loudest would be Laurentius' judgment.

PATMOS

CHAPTER 13

Myron sat outside the cafe, sipping wine and enjoying the last hour of the late spring sunshine. It had been a nice day - not quite summer, but appreciably warmer. Only moments earlier, some friends had taken their leave to head to their homes. Myron enjoyed his status in this little community. As the father-in-law of the governor, no one quite knew how much preferential treatment they should offer. They knew him an affluent Roman. Most gave him at least a little more than his due share of privilege and rank. Better a little too much than a little too little.

In turn, Myron loved that part of his life. All the celebrity with none of the responsibilities.

Oh, he was seldom idle. He had heard leisure could be the hardest work of all. He deplored boredom. He was a learned man and liked his mind sharp. A little wine to season the palate, but not enough to dim the wits. A little time to seize on the talent, but not enough to trim the wicks.

The evening migration began. You always heard them before you saw them. Chains on cobbled rock or dirt, dragged along by plodding feet. Everyone noticed, though never made any ado about it. As the prisoners increased in number passing through the square, voices of the townsfolk increased to be heard over the noise, like happens at parties and dances and on windy days.

Myron watched the sky paint its darker hues more than he noted the prisoners and slaves until one caught his eye. A young man he did not recognize, not that he knew many of the prisoners, but this one wore a newer tunic, golden brown topaz in color. It took but a few seconds before Myron recognized it as the tunic he had given Giovanni just two nights earlier. He considered and puzzled over what he saw.

The young man did not look vicious. It seemed unlikely he took the clothing by force. If another had bullied it away from Giovanni, it seemed unlikely they would give it to this young fool.

The young man did not look popular. He walked alone, notably behind most of the others who traveled in twos or threes.

The young man did not look devious or sly. He would not have stolen it.

To be honest, the young man looked like one more likely to be robbed if any other fancied the garment.

He watched the slow gait of the young man until he disappeared. Myron's curiosity was not such that he would leave his seat to question the young man. It was only a prisoner, and without thinking it aloud, he probably valued the tunic more than the prisoner.

His last thought on the subject settled as the answer, whether truth or false. He could see the prisoner Giovanni giving it to another with greater need. Such behavior was not alien to his experience, but he also knew he never fully understood it. He had helped out many a friend over the years, but most of his friends were also well-to-do, so his assistance was never purely charitable.

He had seen slaves help one another, but seldom in such a material manner. He had seen gladiators sacrifice themselves, usually when they were already mortally wounded, to help another to win. And, of course, many in the Senate and the royal seats of government had been helped by others, but that was purely selfish ambition by the giver. No, he knew how little Giovanni had, and it intrigued him that any man, including Giovanni, would give up the one intrinsically valuable possession he had.

A voice interrupted his musings.

"Hi papa."

Myron smiled as his head turned towards the familiar and welcome greeting of his oldest son.

"Apollonides. What brings you to town?"

Apollonides sat as he answered, "A maiden, of course." He turned to the owner to order red wine. Myron delighted to see his son's smile again. It filled the patio with its richness.

"Is that her?" pointed Myron.

Apollonides spied the old hag. An old joke for his father.

"Why not?" answered Apollonides and rose like he would venture forth. He stepped down onto the cobblestones, then whirled around.

"No! My eyesight failed me. She cannot be the one. My heart is already smitten for another."

"Smitten?" chided his father. He knew better. "It takes more than a maiden to smite the house of Myron."

Apollonides smiled.

Myron also smiled.

"It is so good to see my son again. I know I have said it too much these last few days, but it fills my heart again and again to have my son back."

Apollonides wanted to say, "Enough". His Papa had been worse than a brooding hen since his recovery. It was okay at first, but he wondered how much longer to remain patiently silent. Even worse, the whole town treated him like a leper. Well, not really a leper. They did not scream, "Leper!" and throw stones at him. They did not cast him out of the town or make him dress in sackcloth, pour ashes over himself and walk through the town crying, "Unclean! Unclean!"

Well, not yet anyway.

Maybe now was the time after all. And, compared to his behavior not so many days past, such leprous rantings rated more socially acceptable.

"Papa, I appreciate your concern. I am the gladdest of all but let us move forward - not dwell on that which lies behind us."

Myron nodded. Most wise. He held himself from adding, "Well, I am just glad to have you back."

"So, what shall you do now?"

Apollonides smiled again. "To woo some unsuspecting maiden?"

Myron enjoyed the answer, but said, "You know what I mean. Where does life lead you from here?"

"From here?" mused Apollonides. "Uh, Antonia? Drusilla? Sabina? Julia?"

"I am serious," urged Myron.

"As am I," teased his son.

"Besides," added Myron, "those are all Roman women. Back in Italia. Did you hire a ship to have them all brought to Patmos?"

"Not hardly," answered Apollonides, "but it is a grand idea. May I use one of your crafts?"

"Not hardly," echoed Myron.

The never-ending slight breeze moseyed in as the sun set. It increased a tad - not badly but added a little pre-twilight chill. Townfolks closed shops to head for home and dinner. The last of the prisoners passed - except for one talking with two of the young men. They conversed in Greek and Apollonides' heart and head hardened like dirty water into ice. He glared at the prisoner who had not yet seemed to notice Apollonides or Myron.

Myron noted his son's reaction.

"Why the anger, my son? What violation has he afforded thee?"

"You know perfectly well," clenched Apollonides.

"I know what you have said," admitted Myron, "but, I still cannot see his offense."

Apollonides peered at his father. "Then, I fear you shall never see it."

Both men sat silent for a spell. The cafe owner approached indicating a 'last call'. Myron brought forth his purse and paid for the drinks. He would have to get home. Fona would be anxious; of this he had no doubt.

"Perhaps he speaks from the Unknown god," suggested Myron.

Apollonides snorted. "That is in Athenæ, papa. Not Roma."

"Still..."

"No."

The men were silent again. Apollonides rose to leave. He appeared ready to storm off but turned and placed a loving hand on his father's shoulder.

"Fear not," he relaxed. "I am just unsure how to accept this gift." He stretched as he added, "Some gifts you cannot give back to the sender." He started across the square.

"Will you be home tonight?" called Myron.

"Probably," Apollonides called back. "Wait! Better make that maybe. Minerva invited me to dine with her." And with that, he turned to hasten along the way towards the beach.

Myron watched the back of his son moving away. Old apprehensions filled him all over again. If his son joked, he chose bad timing and very poor taste.

PATMOS

CHAPTER 14

"That is never good," observed Phranc as they arrived at the quarry for their day of work. Minos scowled and nodded in agreement, as did other veteran prisoners.

"What is that?" asked Talor. He followed the direction of glances but saw nothing except the usual guards heading their way.

"Meetin'," answered Dim.

"Meeting?" repeated Talor.

"When the Roman guards come from a meetin' with Lucius, they always got special orders, usually to destroy at least one of us."

Talor wondered who would be targeted as he feared and hoped for himself. Most of the men certainly shared that same fear. They lined up to have their chains removed for the day's work. One by one, they went to their assigned tasks with a small sense of relief. Oftentimes, the targeted prisoner remained shackled, lest he try to fight back or run, but this time none wore iron to begin work.

They prepared to drop another huge slab of marble. Dim, Seth and others grabbed tools and climbed to the top. Others positioned at the bottom.

"Arion," yelled Guard Mucius.

Arion turned towards the voice. Sledgehammer in hand, he stood at the bottom of the cliff driving the spikes to fasten ropes.

"Top," ordered Mucius, nodding upward towards the cliff.

"You want me on top?" checked Arion. He had never worked that side as yet.

Mucius nodded and stepped forward as if to whip him if he did not get a move on. Arion did not have to be told twice, leaning the sledge against the wall.

The men at the bottom all looked at one another, wondering what gave. Tools in hand, they prepared for the slab to give way, but waited for the ropes to be secured and Arion had thus pounded in only one spike of the four. They all waited, certain one of them would be picked for this most dangerous task.

"Giovanni," yelled Mucius.

Ionnes turned with a long, wooden pole in his hands.

"Spikes," yelled Mucius and pointed towards the sledge hammer.

Ionnes put away the pole from the other workers and stepped forward to grab the heavy sledge. It was heavier than he expected. He was reasonably strong for a man his age, but certainly nowhere as strong as he had been in younger years. Still, in typical, Christos-like service, he stepped forward to drive the huge spikes into stubborn rock.

He stood a moment looking at the large spike. It always felt odd to hold such an object in his hands as he recalled the terrible uses such an item could be enlisted. He could not help but remember the feeling inside as he watched them driven through hands and feet. And, not just Yeshua's even if that moment hurt the most. He had seen many crucifixions by heartless Roman hands over the decades of his life, and each one crushed him most deeply.

"Who shall hold the spike?" called Ionnes, standing under the wall.

All the guards glared at him and remained silent.

"Who shall hold the spike?" repeated Ionnes.

Guard Julius stepped forward, sword drawn and yelled, "Do it yourself, miracle man."

Ionnes turned towards the stone as a man well accustomed to the foolish intent of others. He stooped down to grab the spike when Julius sent whipping cords through the air with a vengeance. The tips snapped against the bones protruding from his lower back. Not totally prepared for the attack, Ionnes jerked his body up in response, stressing other vertebrae and muscles along his back. The new pains moved in, worse than an angry wasp's sting. He looked at Julius questioningly and saw only the demon within him. He turned back to the spike and wall.

The lash landed again, this time across his neck. He rose and faced Guard Julius.

"Do you want me to drive this spike or not?"

Julius replied with the whip. Ionnes ducked, but it still touched his left ear. The entire side of his head filled with the pain. He moved his hand from his back to his ear. Some blood. Fortunately, not much, but he already knew he would lose much more before the day ended. As his ear bled, he quickly prayed for Yeshua's help and healing and strength. Not that it was the first time that morning that he had lifted voice of praise to his Savior.

He also thought of Malchus and the time Cephas lopped off his ear. Then, Yeshua healed it before Temple Guards led him off to stand trial before the Sanhedrin. The memory gave him comfort and hope. He smiled, just a little. Malchus became an amazing believer and brother thereafter.

He turned again to attend to the spike. He felt Julius' presence, but kept to task. If the lash came again, he would stop, deal with the pain, and continue. The pain did not arrive before he tried to drive the spike into the hard rock. He had not worked the quarry long enough to learn the best places to drive a spike. Comparing Arion's first spike, he sought similar vein lines. Clumsily, he struggled to pound metal against metal. The rock silently laughed at his efforts. He tried again. The whip came down.

"Hurry," yelled Mucius.

Ionnes straightened up with the pain. He felt fresh blood trailing down the back of one leg. He ignored it as best he could and tried to pound the spike again. No success, though he caused a couple chipped pieces. The whip struck again, across his right arm. He winced but kept to task.

"Rock of ages," Ionnes muttered, recalling Isaiah's words. "For You, the LORD, is everlasting strength. Rock of ages." The sledge struck again and again and again until his arm greatly ached. The spike made its way into the rock. When it felt secure enough, he stood to drive it more.

Another blow, this time from Mucius.

Ionnes looked back at Mucius with less compassion than he typically preferred. Then, he saw the faces of his fellow prisoners. They looked at him with pity, but their eyes kept distance. Only Phranc's eyes seem to share the pain Ionnes endured. The others, not so much.

Ionnes knew the display came not only to punish him and try to put him in some sort of crooked line, but also to drop him down more than a few notches to the other prisoners. Ionnes had been down this road before. The pattern seldom waivered. Usually, their first efforts were to arouse his anger. They wanted all to see him as a mere human and nothing special.

Ionnes laughed.

Mucius struck him again and again, then Julius a few lashes. Ionnes laughed between flinches.

He looked at the two guards and said, "Did not you know that all are special? Including you, Mucius and Julius." He turned back to the next spike. Both soldiers stood dumbly and mute, looking at each other and not getting answer. To be honest, neither felt sure what those words meant for the other.

Ionnes struck the spike a dozen odd times before it broke surface and began to drive in. He kept at his task, both physically and spiritually.

Mucius moved past his personal confusion and continued to flog Ionnes at times. Ionnes perceived the whippings perhaps a little less severe.

The third spike became fastened and he moved to the fourth.

"Here?" he asked, turning to Julius while pointing to a spot on the wall.

Julius's right hand dropped down as he stopped to think. "I know not how wide the wall. Will this work?"

The soldier looked up, then back to Ionnes, then nodded.

Ionnes wiped the sweat spread across his brow and went to work on the final spike.

Oddly, the whippings also replaced the petty jealousies and snide remarks the men made the night Ionnes returned from Myron's. Ionnes had replied in love. He first asked how many of them would have declined invitation to dinner at Myron's? They were mostly silent, or at most grumbled to themselves. He assured them he wished all of them could have been there. The place was certainly big enough.

Then, Ionnes took off his new tunic and put on his old one. He stood before Teos and said, "Brother, your tunic is far worse than mine. Here."

Teos, already so easily confused by this living apostle, took the new tunic gratefully though it scared him. It was soft and warm. He liked the warm, golden color. His tunic was indeed a rag, hardly suitable to make even a patchwork quilt. He looked at Dim who nodded and smiled. Teos smiled back as he excitedly changed clothes. He felt very special and looked to see who was admiring him.

Looking down at his old garment, he wondered what should be done with it? Ionnes took it and rolled it tightly, placing it on Teos' bedroll as a pillow. Teos was elated, and some of the men wondered why they had hated Ionnes so quickly just minutes past.

Driving the fourth spike, Ionnes sang, "*God will appoint salvation for walls and bulwarks*," - a song he sang at times during his youth. He delighted to recall the tune though he could not remember the last time he had thought of it. Many years past to be certain.

"*YHWH Tsuri*," he then sang, making up words and melody in beat with the sledge.

Ropes hung down from the top. Others had already secured the three ropes to the first spikes and stepped forth when the fourth was driven.

"Now what?" asked Ionnes to some nearby.

"Keep the spikes hot," answered Pterrkee, long pole in hand.

"And, we will lay it down like a sleeping baby," added Phranc.

Ionnes nodded.

"Silence," yelled Julius, striking Ionnes twice for his alleged sins.

The sounds of activity above kept them all focused. They watched and waited. Ionnes checked the spikes, though he felt more inclined to watch above him. Any of a countless number of rocks and stones could slip over the side and fall atop his head if he kept not watch.

After many minutes, the great wall of stone began to move. The feeling took away Ionnes' breath as he watched the great wall, so immovable minutes earlier, begin to falter. He smacked the spikes again. One seemed to be coming loose already.

As the wall cracked and sent out its screams of protest, Julius and the other Roman guards backed away. They knew the power above them and had just seen it crumble, burying the previous sledge and spike man. Ionnes would be the only one they wanted under there, or such stood the plan. Well, joked Guard Ernesto months earlier, Jews preferred stonings to crucifixions. The wisecrack made its way through the ranks over and over, specially immortalized just for times like these.

Ionnes drove the loose spike with renewed force. He felt selfish, mild amusement that Arion's spike showed first to come loose. Rock moved and crumbled around him. He moved away slightly and dared look skyward. No sizable chunks heading his way, but that could change very quickly.

He briefly thought of Stephanos, his brother in Christos. He then thought of Yaakov, Son of Alphæus. Both had met their death by raining stones.

He sighed, and a tear tried to wet his eye against the quarry dust and sweat. He praised Yeshua for being in the most blessed of company.

The wall gave way and fell forward, caught barely by the four ropes. Ionnes looked up and danced away from two falling stones, not huge, but big enough to want to avoid. He checked the ropes and the spikes as the deadly wall started to fold his way. The poles were already all around him, pressing against the rock. He ducked as he moved back and forth, giving the wall its respectful room. As it approached forty-five degrees, someone yelled, "Ionnes - MOVE!"

The apostle did not have to be told twice. He dropped the sledge and sprinted as fast as his old bones would take him. The whoosh of air blasted from behind him as the great wall of stone knuckled during its journey down. The ropes and wood kept it from breaking, but just barely. It groaned briefly like an undecided beached whale as it found its whole new place of rest. The guards did not wait. They leapt forward and brought their whips down hard on the old apostle.

"Where's the sledge?" yelled Guard Julius.

"You buried it," accused Guard Ernesto.

The whips burned, one by one by one against the old, weathered flesh. It sprung leaks all over like an old, cracking wineskin. Guards grabbed hold of Ionnes and dragged him through the quarry to a secure and sizable wooden pole near the entrance. There they stripped him bare and tied him to the post. One guard kicked his legs with heavy boots. He wondered if one leg had not just broke as he schlumped against the coarse, harsh wood. Two guards posted, one on each side, to flog him until he was dead or at least wished he was. It grew quiet as the guards waited, baiting him, letting him anticipate the greater pain that would surely come.

In the lull, Ionnes looked past the guards to his fellow prisoners. They stopped and watched. Some showed compassion. Some anger. Some had become too hollow to feel anything. Ionnes noted each face, committed to memory, to bless and pray for them - if he survived.

The first lashing came with soulless vengeance. Partially congealed blood exploded from his skin by the impact. The pain drove deep into his muscles.

The second one followed. He had been whipped before, more than once. The scar tissue provided some protection, at first. The guards knew this well as they directed their torture. Soon the scartissue gave way to expose fresh meat. Ionnes spoke prayers of pain. He himself had heard Yeshua cry these prayers. He felt apostle Bartholomew's pain as they skinned him before crucifying him.

Still, he ever shared their blessed company. He persisted in his prayers.

He recalled Cephas. They were together flogged by the Sanhedrin. That had been a hand slap compared with this. Between the tears and the blood, he suddenly spied faces in the yard. They surprised him, these faces. He knew none of them. Another bite of the lash. He winced, then opened his eyes. The faces were still there, raising hands and rising over the flurry of red and brown uniforms. The whip came down again. He heard singing. Beautiful singing, like never before encountered. The sounds filled his ears to flow within. The whip again. He felt peace fill him. It warmed him. It overwhelmed his senses like a warm blanket in winter. The whip fell once again. He looked at his visitors, thanking Yeshua, and closed his eyes. The peace of death would come to him finally. He would rest with his fathers. Better, he would rest with his brethren. Even better, he would again rest upon Yeshua's bosom.

"The pain is for a moment." He heard Ignatius' voice. "I would happily endure the pain for a moment, certain to find peace and love and joy forever in the beyond with Yeshua."

No one knew this better than Yeshua. Ionnes saw Him beaten far worse, even before they nailed Him to that cross. The thought gave Ionnes courage. Courage to endure, and another thought passed through his mind. Or a couple of thoughts, really. The first was that unlike Yeshua's gruesome death, Ionnes did not suffer for the sins of all. Yeshua was the Sacrificial Pascal Lamb - not Ionnes. This sacrifice Ionnes faced stood as the ultimate testament to the love and truth for Christos.

The second thought comforted Ionnes even more. He knew that all those years back, Yeshua could have stopped the beatings and floggings and torture and crucifixion at any time. It took years for Ionnes to understand the reality of those words. Yeshua went to the cross by His own choice and in obedience to His Father. Ionnes had heard Yeshua crying out in Gethsemane to His Heavenly Father. The words were not loud, but Ionnes could hear them, for a spell, before he nodded off to sleep.

Ionnes did not have that power. Or, so he wondered. He swallowed hard; his throat so dry. His neck felt like it was half missing. He croaked the words, "*He will swallow up death forever, and the LORD God will wipe away tears from all faces.*"

"Silence!" shouted Guard Julius, witnessing the torture, "or I will keep you there, bound for a thousand years." He winked and snickered at Guard Ernesto, covered in the zealot's splattered, sardonyx hued blood, grabbing a breath between swings.

Ionnes cringed against the pain as his lips muttered, "Amen."

Another whip and another.

"Ready to say I am your favorite uncle?" taunted one flogger.

"No, I am your favorite uncle," urged the second.

Ionnes could barely move but opened an eye. It took a moment. He thought himself alone again, but then he saw the faces. He watched them and felt their sadness. One grabbed his attention over the others. They looked eye to eye, and the compassionate face said, "Demons."

Ionnes jerked. Demons? Demon? What had he known before he even reached harbor?

"Yeshua," he spit, wheezing and coughing. "Yeshua." He strained to look around at his captors, one by one by one. Facing the post while filling his lungs with dusty air, he proclaimed in a loud voice, "In the name and blood of Yeshua, demons be gone from this island - forever."

His strength left him for the moment thereafter, and he slumped down again against the coarse pole. He hung there uncounted moments before he noticed the quiet. Silence filled the air more than the dirty dust. It sounded so empty compared with the ravaging wolves who had just surrounded him. He still could smell the dust, nudging him to open his eyes. To his surprise, he hung alone. He spied only a couple soldiers, far off, attending to the quarry. The workers strove to move the heavy wall they had just cut, but near Ionnes, all sounded very quiet.

The faces also disappeared yet he felt not alone.

For a moment he felt terrible disappointment. He had been so ready to go home to Yeshua. The reality weighed upon him and for that moment felt worse than the terrible beatings he had so recently endured. Tears made their way out his eyes and down his cheeks. Some landed on the parched dirt. Some mixed with his own blood, rolled over his thinning mustache and tried to quench his vicious thirst. He wept shamelessly, as nakedly as the man attached to the pole.

Eventually his emotions settled. Assessing his condition, his hands and wrists felt nothing, suspending him by the tight rope. He stood, still bent towards the pole, and found his leg bones not broken. He wiped the tears from his eyes with the backs of his dirty hands as they tingled sharply with new feeling. He knew not how long he would be tied to this post but expected it would still be for quite a spell. He knew men who had died of thirst and exposure tied to a Roman pole. That seemed unlikely. Unlike crucifixion, they used this torture more to compel obedience than as a means of death. It also served to dispense fear to others; in this case the other prisoners. He leaned his forehead against the post, expecting they were going to be close friends for the next day or two.

Tied close enough to the ground to settle onto his knees, he leaned his head against the post as he prayed. He always prayed fervently and sought genuine devotion, but despite his great pain and fatigue, he treasured the urgent love he felt when he prayed during persecutions. How often raw pain could make the prayers of man that much more real.

He looked down at his deeply reddened body. The scars still throbbed. The blood felt cold and sticky against his skin, even under the warm sun.

"Isaiah," he said aloud. He had always loved Isaiah, perhaps more than any other prophet of old. "Did not Isaiah spend three years naked?" he thought to himself. He recalled it as symbolic for the Egyptians and Cushites who would be dragged away by Assyria, naked and bleeding with buttocks uncovered to their shame.

Then, he wondered what Isaiah's wife said when he went to leave their house unclad for the first time. Isaiah did not say. The day passed slowly, but still it passed. The final hour of the workday approached. The men would have to pass by him. He remained on his knees in prayer and psalm for most of that last hour.

The stinging senses of pain had given way to the deeper aches. Ionnes had no illusions it would not come, and soon. The sun set, and the men began to collect their tools to be locked away for the night. One by one they passed him. Most behaved like Ionnes was not even there. Teos watched him openly, taking in every gash and lash left by the Roman soldiers. Ionnes saw Teos wanted to go to him, to talk to him, perhaps to help him. Ionnes said no, his head following. Teos understood enough to keep walking.

Phranc went near Ionnes.

"I tried to get you some water. They said no."

"Thank you," yawped Ionnes as Phranc kept walking. "Adonai will remember your efforts," but Phranc already departed.

Dim walked by as though he did not care what happened to Ionnes. Ionnes watched him. He recognized the fear. He recognized the coldness. And, Ionnes recalled that Dim had already been in his place.

The others also passed without incidence and Ionnes waited alone. Even the guards passed by without a word, and he had expected another round or two of torture before day's end.

Alone, likely for all night, Ionnes persisted in prayer though his voice hoarse and garbled. He prayed for the prisoners and even for the Roman guards. He prayed for Myron and Chryspippe and Fona. And Apollonides. His span of prayers widened as he added his regular, daily prayers for the church. The chill of the evening attacked without mercy and he began to shiver but persisted with his prayers and praised Yeshua it was not winter.

He recalled Cephas, imprisoned when God unlocked his chains and led him out of the prison. He recalled Paulos and Silas freed of their chains inside a very different Roman prison. God added an earthquake to that miracle which brought the jailer to his knees asking what he needed to do to be saved. In turn, Ionnes wondered if Yeshua would free him of these bonds. He asked, but his discernment suggested not. Yeshua was not through with him, yet. He should have died, yet here he remained. No compassion or mercy of Roman guards kept him alive. Nope. Papa Adonai's will kept moving, to where Ionnes not yet knew, but he recognized its certainty all the same. The sky darkened. The deep, dark blue, rich as sapphires, overtook the warmer oranges and reds. The cool spring air chilled him. His old body, terribly weakened by the day's beatings and exposure, feared to shiver against the thousand and one aches. Ionnes tried walking in place to move his body for warmth. The edgy pain argued otherwise.

He watched the stars pop out, one by one. Aphrodite brightly blazed behind the twilight. The stars kept coming as they wove their sweet tapestry across the cosmos. Aphrodite disappeared behind trees and then landed. A southern breeze stirred. At first, Ionnes became chilled by the fresh air, but soon its warmth embraced him. Clouds moved in from over the water. The cold sky supported its cloudy blanket, holding in the day's sun warmed radiance of the ground. Still, he could see the glow of a few fires off in varying distances and wished to be close to their glow.

He leaned against the post. He could not quite sit down, so remained on his knees, his body pressed up against the wood. As his knees tired, he tried stooping, but it stretched his tender skin. Not good. If he could not rest against the ground, he would rest against the post. His hands felt numb and his arms ached from being held up by his bonds. He wondered at life, for barely twenty-four hours earlier he enjoyed hospitality as guest in a home of opulence and affluence. The next day, the extreme opposite. He labored not to distinguish which came from God and which came from demons. And in that, he praised Yeshua for when the attacks came at their worst, God stood at His closest to breaking through the demonic strongholds. He saw it not as a time of retreat, nor did he see it as a time of judgment, but of pending victory and justice.

Long lost to the never-ending night, a modest noise caught his attention. It became footsteps - almost too quiet to hear - yet more than one as best as he could tell. He could not see anyone through the gloom but waited. Fear tried to move in.

He rebuked it. Adonai would not be mocked.

Two dark figures appeared, still approaching. They did not waver. Their direction showed certain as they moved towards Ionnes. He pulled up on his ropes to stand, painfully twisting partially around to see who came to him in the dark.

He recognized the helmet of a Roman soldier. The other with him wore only a tunic and belt. The two moved quickly, and Ionnes wondered that a Roman soldier would not bring a lit torch. It probably had already burned out.

"Ionnes," said a whispering voice.

"Still here," answered Ionnes, still uncertain who it was, but they used his Greek name, not his Latin name. That lent to some hope.

The two men came close. Even in the dark with clouds covering the stars, Ionnes easily recognized Dim.

"Thirsty?" said Dim. He held up a leather wine skin. Ionnes recognized it as one Dim had made but used only for water. Ionnes recommended filling the bag with vinegar for a full day to remove the flavor of the old wine, then filled with water for a day to remove the taste of the vinegar. Dim chided, "Ya got any vinegar I can borrow?" It was not like he could drop everything and head to the store. "Besides," Dim added, "a little bit o' wine makes the world a little lighter, even if it is just for flavor - a bitterish flavor - not very appealin' anymore, but still a flavor."

They helped Ionnes up. He faired weaker than he realized.

"Careful," Dim urged, and tipped the water into the parched, open mouth. The water pressed through the layers of pain and blood and dust, blazing a trail of blessed bliss for Ionnes. He drank both eagerly and thankfully.

The soldier covered Ionnes with a woven cloth. It was not especially thick but provided some warmth from the cool night.

"And, you are?" asked Ionnes to the Roman soldier. He knew for certain he had not yet seen him.

"Best you not know," came answer. Best to remain ignorant if they questioned him later about who helped him.

Ionnes nodded and accepted a second drink. Weak as he was, the water began its strengthening revival.

Dim smiled at Ionnes. He moved in to examine the apostle.

"Hard t' tell in the dark," noted Dim, "but they beat ya worse than usual. Not the worst I seen, but worse than most. Ya look more blue than red."

He fingered a couple of the more protruding sores. No pus - yet.

"When ya passed out, we all thought ya dead." Dim spoke in hushed tones.

"I passed out?"

"Hung like a ragged, old cloak."

As much as he tried, Ionnes could not remember either passing out nor awakening.

"Yeah," continued Dim, "ya stood up & yelled something. I would bet we all heard ya hollerin' at that moment 'cuz lots o' heads turned. Not that we could tell what ya said, but ya stood up on those skinny spider web legs o' yours & stood taller than I ever seen ya. Ya raised yer voice, then collapsed lifeless."

Ionnes tried to recall what he had said. Something - rebuking demons? It was still hazy.

"What happened next?"

"I dunno," admitted Dim. "Ev'ry one o' the guards just stopped right where they was. One even dropped his whip. They stood there a moment, then all walked away. I never seen nothin' like it. They ALWAYS whip ya at least a coupla more times in case they think ya playin' a Greek tragedy. But, they did not. They jus' walked away. They did not even look at ya."

Ionnes' brow furrowed to understand even if the other two could not see in the gloom.

"I was not there," added the mystery Roman. "I wish I had, and I am glad I was not."

"Hil----." Dim stopped. He looked briefly at the Roman, then back to Ionnes. "This, my friend here, told me the guards got orders from the gov'ner hisself to beat ya within a thumb's width o' yer life."

"And, if you died," added the Roman, "that would not be bad, either."

"So, why did they stop?"

"I do not know," both nodded, "but," observed Dim, "they all acted like the air got knocked out o' them."

"No one said nothing back at base," added the guard. "It felt like they did not know themselves that anything had happened."

"So, ya just hung limp there & looked like the greatest escape we get." Dim placed hands on hips. "Ya old goat. I even caught myself prayin' t' yer lonely God."

Ionnes grinned and suddenly felt better than he had felt since the torturous event began, if only for the moment.

"Obviously, it helped," complimented Ionnes.

"Perhaps," thought Dim, but said nothing. The man was still tied to a post. It was not over, yet. He ran over to the shed and grabbed a basket. Returning, he turned it over for Ionnes to sit upon. The apostle still had to face the post, his legs straddled around it.

"I will return before dawn," said the soldier.

"And, do not drop yer blanket," added Dim. "It be a bugger t' get it back on." He made sure the blanket was securely wrapped over and around Ionnes before they slipped away.

"Thank you," said Ionnes, answered only by their departing footsteps.

He laid his head against the post and closed his eyes. It was still chilly, but he shivered not, and was able to find sleep. Perhaps God would give him sleep to quickly pass the night.

A few hours later, he felt a hand upon his shoulder awakening him. Startled, he felt relief to see the young soldier. Still mostly dark, the first sparks of morning started to touch the sky. The mystery soldier carefully lifted Ionnes and removed the basket. He ran it back to the shed. Returning, he took the blanket, still draped over Ionnes' shoulders. Only at that moment did Ionnes realize it was his red cape.

"Sorry," he said, then walked around dragging the cape on the ground.

"I used to bring a branch to hide our footprints," he explained, "but a branch makes its own trail. This cloth swishes away our steps as easily as a Sahara sandstorm."

Satisfied their footsteps were gone, he shook then reattached the cape to his uniform and grabbed a bag of water to give Ionnes another drink.

"I must go," he said, leaving the naked man to the cool start of his day.

"Look pathetic," the soldier added. "They like to see you suffer. If you look too strong, they will leave you tied there."

"Yeshua be with you," whispered Ionnes as the man turned to go.

Stopping, the young Roman turned and looked down as though dwelling upon Ionnes' closing endearment. He nodded to the ground, then looked up at the old apostle, smiled and replied with unfettered affection.

"And, also with you, Yochanan."

Ionnes on his knees, felt the coldest part of the morning attack his naked skin. He leaned his head against the post, eyes closed, as always in prayer. It brought him comfort from his throbbing sores and kept the shivers at bay. The shivers caused the fresh sores across his back and sides to slice him with new pain. For so many years now, prayer came as naturally as breathing.

The light of day continued to approach, soon lighting the ground around him. He kept to his vigil, a half hour or longer, until he heard those approaching. Friend or foe? He knew the answer without opening his eyes. His foes, or more accurately, his would be foes save the strengthening grace given him by the Love of Yeshua. He prayed for further strength if they repeated yesterday's tortures. His prayers included petitions to be delivered into the loving arms of Yeshua. He yearned to again place his head on his Savior's breast. Why would he want to sit beside Yeshua, right hand or left, when he could be cuddled and given full healing in the bosom of his Messiah?

He heard laughter. Opening eyes, he saw three soldiers. No one else with them. They walked by Ionnes towards the quarry like he was invisible. Not even a glance.

Ionnes' head, still stationed against the post, looked downward. His splashed and dripping blood of yesterday still stained the ground around him; its stiff mud a scarlet crust. It spread out a formidable distance from the whipping post. He raised a brow in question. Lifting his head from the post, he studied the ground more carefully. Not a footprint anywhere around him. He could see the three sets of footprints of the

214

guards who just passed, but no signs of his compassionate visitors last night or this morning. The young Roman did sweep and swish away their footprints, but then he came back to give Ionnes another drink of water. Where were those footprints? Great fatigue filled him from his ordeal and painful night attached to a pole, but he could clearly see no prints on the blood crusted dirt and rock. He laughed, just a bit to himself. Yeshua brought him comfort in form of an angel dressed as a Roman soldier. And Dim? He had wondered how Dim left the locked barracks. He had already planned to ask. He still would but expected to learn his friend never came to Ionnes at night.

PATMOS

CHAPTER 15

Lorin washed her face and brushed her hair for the day. The house rested quietly after the earlier eruptions. The governor had already departed for the day; storm clouds following his exit. As his horse was brought, he grabbed the reins with urgency and resentment. Even the stallion noticed his rider's mood and shook his head with disapproval. Governor Laurentius yanked on the reins forcefully, wheeling the horse about, then kicking heels hard to make the animal fly off faster than Pegasus. He had been in a mood since the cold war with his wife, begun three nights back.

Lorin watched the governor's dramatic departure. Her friends entered the home with silent mouths and knowing eyes, keeping personal opinions stowed until the masters were gone and repercussions minimized. Then, and only then would they speak candidly, and even then, with caution. In the world of slaves, some had bigger mouths than ears, perhaps to curry favor with their masters. Some might support Laurentius. Some Chryspippe. Some neither. Some both. And, some just blabbermouths.

Lorin prepared to serve her mistress, though it remained uncertain exactly when that would begin. Chryspippe often slept in past midmorning, but also might rise to meet the morning sunrise without notice.

Lorin did not treasure her life as a slave. Silly to consider, of course, though she knew some who did. Still, she did value her assigned duties. She knew far too many slaves who worked the fields or oared ships or served more barbaric masters. Some were kept to sexually serve their masters. Even more odd, some slaves cruelly oversaw the other slaves; as quick with the whip as any Roman soldier or cranky scorpion. They rose to positions of menial power yet could be themselves lashed for even the smallest misdemeanor.

So, however Lorin may have wished for her freedom, she also saw the good in her service. Chryspippe seemed as good a mistress as one could hope for. Lorin and the other slaves had good food to eat and a decent bed to rest. Lorin kept personal possessions and her own space to keep them. Chryspippe was not completely above having her slaves flogged, but it was not as common as most other slaveowners. With that said, if she felt a slave needed correction, she would typically leave that to her husband's hand. His hands felt much rougher than his wife's.

Sometimes Lorin wondered what she would do if she was suddenly no longer a bondservant. Such musings were typically tickled only when she rested at night before falling asleep, or those dozen odd occasions throughout each year when Chryspippe said or did something Lorin seriously disliked. Lorin possessed no education, so she would surely be working a trade to survive. For that matter, her main qualification was to wait on and serve others such as she was already doing. Good chance, free or not, this is how she would be living her life. That fact never deterred her wish for freedom - the prime wish of every slave. Such wishes, knitted in the fabric of each human being, remained commonly suppressed. The gods deigned she be a slave and a slave she would be. Everybody knew that. Her station in life began even before she could talk or knew the word 'slave'. She knew her station and her station demanded she know it.

At this time of her life she wished for marriage and a family. Not that slaves did not marry. Most did, but families always interfered with the masters' wishes. Always. Nonetheless, she wished for the closeness and intimacy that could come with marriage. She wished for it with all her heart at times, even when she saw her own owners seldom sharing such as she herself wished for. In that way, she knew their freedoms did not bring them the loving satisfaction she knew at least Chryspippe yearned for.

Some slaves had shown interest in her. She felt pleased, but never ready to give her heart to any of them. Her main hope at that time of her life was to allure the attraction of one not enslaved - even a freedman, who would buy her freedom, so they could be together. It was not a very common practice, but still it floated to the top of her main hopes and fears.

To wed another slave would mean to bear slave children who could be sold by their masters. Laurentius had already done that to other slaves. Such crushing heartbreak kept her deepest yearnings in check.

She heard Chryspippe stir. Quietly setting down her hairbrush, she moved silently to the bedchamber. Her mistress turned but did not rise. The moment starting her day had not yet arrived. Lorin returned to the vanity and her hair.

When first brought to the governor's home in Roma, she seldom washed or bathed or brushed her hair. Her earlier life in the scullery did not require such grooming or hygiene. Her master, a lecherous, old coot died, and his family sent her to the slave auctions. She was not as attractive or shapely as other young women. Likely she would not be bought as a sex slave. Some homes preferred physically attractive slaves, but most, especially those with a jealous mistress, preferred a female slave that would not tempt her husband or maturing sons. Lorin tolled that bell for the house of Laurentius.

She started by cleaning everything throughout the house with two other slaves. As she filled the needs of the household, her duties pressed her to attend to Chryspippe. There never heralded a momentous day or official announcement of Lorin's swing of duties. (One would never call it a promotion.) She waited on her mistress more and more, started attending to Chryspippe when she left the house, and became the preferred attendee over the other slaves. Habits formed as they always do, like where to sit when dining or a favorite wine goblet. Household expectations became more firmly rooted as Lorin rose to the task. She preferred it far better than her earlier duties of house cleaning, though she still helped there, and she greatly preferred it over scullery to a lewd old goat.

When the governor became assigned to Patmos, Lorin feared for the change, but still packed and loaded their household belonging into stowage for the lengthy trip. She discovered for the first time the feeling of seasickness. Sickly green with nausea, it fortunately passed after the first day or so. One of the other slaves moved in to help, but Lorin would not give up her station. Green or not, she would do her best to serve her mistress.

The trip took over two months to complete. The actual sailing not much more than a week or so, but she felt like they stopped at every island they passed, and there were an abundance of islands from the Tyrrhenian to the Mediterranean to the Ægean Seas. They would stay for at least a day, and often three to five days. They stayed eight days in Syracusæ on Sicilia, and a day or two at most ports on Creta, practically encircling the island. They aided survivors of a shipwreck and made harbor to wait out as storms blew through. The duties of the slaves were reduced during the journey and only three were kept in chains. Supplies were replenished as needed, and the two small families with a couple dozen slaves finally stepped onto the shores of Patmos.

More the homebody, Lorin less yearned to see the world than some of her shipmates. The trip had been an extraordinary adventure for most of them, but as they unloaded the ship and headed through Phora for the first time on loaded carts to their new home, Lorin thought Patmos looked pretty much like most of the other islands she had just left. Some of her peers stated the same. She heard the Greek music from the cafes. It seemed rather alien then. Now, it filled regular parts of her life, and though she sometimes still missed and yearned for her home in Italia, she had grown to love the salty air and balmy breezes. The Greek architecture had become commonplace. The people of Patmos welcomed them everywhere. It mattered not whether their amicable words were genuine or because Laurentius governed as the ruling hand of Roma. Just so long as they were friendly.

In short, the House of Laurentius, as so often happens, started becoming one with the island.

Chryspippe stirred. For real this time. Lorin entered and stood bedside, ready to attend.

Chryspippe's cheek showed more bruising than when she reclined to sleep. She would wish for it to be covered, or not go out at all.

Suddenly, Chryspippe arose with a start. She looked around the bedchamber in one panoramic sweep, then relaxed a bit and looked up towards Lorin. The two women locked their gaze.

"I had a dream," Chryspippe said, moving her eyes away to nowhere.

Lorin waited, then asked, "A nightmare?"

Chryspippe also waited, as if entranced. The doors to her ears had been closed, but the muffled voice of her slave eventually filtered through. She looked up at Lorin again.

"No. Not a nightmare. More like a daymare." She paused. That word did not make sense, but it still described the impressions of her mind better than any other word she could conjure. "Help me dress," she ordered, yanking aside bedsheets and blankets and dragging her nightgown over the feathery bedside to stand. In typical pattern, Lorin stepped forth to help. Chryspippe dashed off to the pot, then threw off her bed garments. Lorin had already set down three outfits on the bed. White, yellow and lavender.

"Yellow," pointed Chryspippe, re-entering the chamber. Lorin was not yet convinced, but Chryspippe had picked the middle color every time since Lorin had started counting. Not yet a moon's cycle had passed since she started counting, so not for certain, but true to form thus far. She had not yet placed Chryspippe's less common outfits into the mix. She did not want to be that obvious. She picked up and fluffed the yellow dress before masterfully wrapping it around her mistress. Chryspippe checked the placement of the garment, then sat at the vanity. Lorin never would have noticed as a scullery slave, but since picking outfits for Chryspippe and accompanying her to her regular social engagements, she grew to appreciate the broad choice of colorful outfits Chryspippe owned. Most Roman women, however affluent, tended to prefer less color. It set her mistress apart to be sure. Colored cloth could be so much more expensive and therefore a tad peacocky. Lorin started with the hair. At first impatient, Lorin noticed Chryspippe's exuberance ebb away like cupped hands full of water. Soon, she sat numbly, looking without seeing. The morning sounds of birds abated. Chryspippe tilted her head. A new sound slid through the doorway to her chambers. Grinding. She heard again her no night daymare. She rose and stood by the door. She must have heard this before, but today it seemed more noticeable than usual.

"The upper and the nether," she muttered as she sat back down for Lorin to finish.

"Miss?" asked Lorin, replaying the words through her mind. What did her mistress mean by naming millstones? But then, at that moment, she also noticed the sounds of grinding grain.

Chryspippe did not seem to hear her slave. Lorin finished her hair and knelt down to begin applying makeup. The bruise on the left cheek continued to darken and would take some doing to cover up without making it look like it was being covered up. Lorin appreciated her mistresses dumbfoundish ways this morning. She could be most temperamental and frankly a big baby when it came to dressing her husband's bruises. Lorin dabbed and lightly brushed the bruise beyond invisible.

"I was in the mill," Chryspippe muttered to nobody. Lorin paused and waited. Chryspippe continued.

"I watched the flour squeeze out of the millstone. I had never seen such grain - it was not wheat or barley or millet or.... I do not know. They were perhaps like pearl snowflakes fed into the mill. It made the finest flour I have ever seen. None needed to be milled again."

She stopped to swallow. She looked at Lorin, kneeling before her, and smiled at her favorite slave. Lorin dodged the compliment to attend to her task. If she did a poor job with makeup, she would not see her mistress again smiling at her that day. Mostly, at that moment Lorin just wished her now chatty mistress would just hold still.

"And, the baker came. Or, so I thought it was the baker. I knew it was the baker though all I saw were hands - and sometimes wrists. They grabbed a huge sifter. It was rather like a kite shape - I think. I was amazed when I saw its shape. Like a kite but pressed in towards the center - the crossing part between the four points."

She stopped. Lorin stopped. A goblet of water sat upon the vanity. Chryspippe took a sip and continued.

"There was nothing that did not sift through. The flour was that fine. The hands mixed in olive oil and wine. A light colored wine. And, just one drop of water. I gazed at the drop for such a long time, dangling from one finger. I thought I saw my reflection in that drop just before it let go of the finger. I wondered in my dream what that one drop meant. The white dough kneaded and flattened out to be placed in the oven. I thought I would have to wait long, but there were the loaves, hot and beautiful. I bent over to smell the steam which rose. It smelled fresh and pleasant and sweet.

"The hands took a loaf right off the hot pan, tore it in half and gave me half. I took a bite. It was so tasty and reminded me of wafers made with honey. I wanted the other half.

The hands already offered it to me.

"Then, I saw another - a flask of wine beside the still steaming loaves. I wanted a drink but did not take one. Quail the color of jacinth appeared on the table - briefly, running in their single file line, and then were gone. But I knew they were not far, and their visit did not seem at all odd."

Chryspippe looked at Lorin who had to wait sometimes as Chryspippe recounted her dream.

"Then, the strangest thing occurred," her brow furrowed worse than a newly plowed field. "I know I left, but do not recall the journey. I just remember standing by the sea with the upper millstone tied around my neck, hanging like a medallion. It was heavy, but not as heavy as I expected. Being right next to the water, I knew I was in danger, but felt amazingly calm and more afraid of losing the stone in the surf. Then, the stone was lifted off of me and I was eating more bread - or maybe could just taste the bread, and then I awoke."

She looked at Lorin.

"What do you think it means?"

Lorin shrugged. "Dreams can be very strange."

Chryspippe looked at Lorin, eye to eye.

"Simple girl you are," she smiled. "Are you finished? There is something I have to do today."

"No, Miss Chrys," Lorin answered. "You have been moving more than usual this morning."

"Yes, I have," admitted Chryspippe. A shiver overtook her body. Lorin waited, then put on finishing touches as Chryspippe became more and more fidgety.

"You are perfect, Miss Chrys."

"If only that were true," answered Chryspippe and jumped up to leave right away.

"Your breakfast is waiting," said Lorin.

"Then, it can wait longer. We must go."

Lorin grabbed shawls as she raced straight for the door after Chryspippe. Outside, the wind blew. Clouds bounced around in the upper atmospheres, some going east and others much higher heading southwest. Sunshine came and went, following the whims of the clouds. Lorin wrapped the wool shawl around her mistress, covering her brushed hair, then donned her own shawl. The briny wind smelled fresh and welcoming as it flowed into nostrils. Lorin breathed in deeply the fresh morning gusts, glad for the temperate climate as winter's bite no longer sharpened or gnashed its teeth.

Chryspippe continued without hesitation past the street where dwelt her parents and brother. She well knew neither would understand her mission or urgency. The sloping descent hastened their steps, leaving the houses for the business district. Chryspippe paused only briefly in the town square, looking around all 360 degrees. (Chryspippe did not know that number, even if Euclid did 360 years or so earlier). She apparently did not see what she sought and walked quickly towards the Roman base and marble quarry.

Lorin noted the usual society matriarchs wandering through town to see whom they might chance to meet. They always called to Chryspippe, but this time saw her urgency, perhaps, and did no more than raise a hand of summons that flipped into a wave as the governor's wife continued on her way. Not a word or acknowledgement from the governor's wife? Were they snubbed? Was she in trouble? Did she have a lover she was racing to? Or away from? Was that a bruise on her cheek? What about the other cheek they could not see? Perhaps she covered the rest of the blows with that shawl. The possibilities were endless and would occupy the women's guesses and conjectures the rest of the day.

Chryspippe headed up the hill towards the quarry. Lorin still followed. Chryspippe may have been moving with urgency, but she was unaccustomed to such rigorous movements. Her stamina waned faster than an eclipsing moon as the slope increased. Lorin kept pace. They stopped to rest a moment, Chryspippe, panting worse than younger Lorin, rested against a post. Her yellow dress billowed in the breeze as it even outshone the yellow, dried grass of the hill.

They very seldom took this road. Lorin looked around at the hill before them, and the town and water below them. She saw a hole in the rock to their right along a modest cliff wall. It rather looked like a cave, but she was not close enough to tell for sure.

Chryspippe righted herself to continue. She pressed on, not quite so quickly, respecting the incline she fully intended to overcome. They could hear the sounds of men and rock and tools pounding and creaking and grinding up ahead. Dust clouds rose higher and higher as they approached. Without hesitation, Chryspippe turned in and entered the quarry, passing Roman guards, the soldiers totally perplexed by this unexpected visit.

"May I help you, Miss Chryspippe?" called Guard Julius, racing to catch up.

"I seek someone," she answered loudly and kept moving. She passed the empty whipping post.

"Whom do you seek?" he asked. Lorin still had no idea. She wondered if her mistress even knew for whom to ask. Chryspippe continued to move towards the worker's arena of activity.

"Ouch!" she yelled. A stone slipped into her sandal. She stopped, held onto Lorin' shoulder and bent over to dislodge it. Tossing it in disgust, she continued to ignore Guard Julius and hasten towards the quarry wall.

"Miss Chryspippe," pressed Guard Julius right alongside her. Guard Octavius joined them. ·

She continued to search through the workers as moving air swirled about redirecting the dust. Most stopped working as she approached.

"I do not see him," she said to Lorin.

"Who is that?" asked Lorin, glad to perhaps get a clue what all this was about.

"The old zealot of The Way, Giovanni."

Guard Julius stopped, not sure he had heard correctly.

"Where is he?" turned Chryspippe.

Both Roman guards also peered across the yard and did not see the ancient prisoner. Dim, Talor and Minos stood closest.

"Dim," called Guard Julius. "Where is Giovanni working today?"

"Do not know," answered Dim. The inmates looked at Chryspippe and Lorin. They were not usually that close to females with whom they could actually converse. It reigned as a special moment that would stay with them all the rest of the day and beyond.

"Salt ropes," answered Talor. He spoke to the guard, but his eyes could not leave the women.

"Salt ropes. On the shore," Guard Julius began to say, but Chryspippe interrupted, "I know where that is."

The two guards bowed to the governor's wife. They had all heard she was being a bit eccentric of late.

Chryspippe immediately turned to go. Lorin gazed at the prisoners a moment longer - taking in the sight of each, Dim and Talor and then Minos. They looked so dirty and repulsive, yet shirtless and strong with tight muscles that reminded her of Hercules or Apollo or some other masterly sculpted marble protecting the temples or city gates, even with the stripes of the scourge. She noticed the blue eyes of the younger one.

The pair departed with equal haste as their entrance. Guard Julius offered to have them escorted. Guard Octavius just wanted to do something - anything that might be memorable to the governor's wife. Chryspippe did not hesitate, but kept moving, leaving the quarry in her lovely yellow gown. This time as they entered town, Chryspippe realized she was wearing down a bit. She wanted to find Ionnes, but they were still some distance and time from the beach where the salt ropes were made. However much she wanted to continue, she knew it would be prudent to stop, have something to drink and maybe a late breakfast.

Entering town, the few cafes all seemed the wrong place to go. Most were too slow to serve. She did not want to take the time.

The invisible wind persisted, increasing in speed as it squeezed between the whitewashed buildings. She stopped in the bakery. She had not realized how chilled she had become until it felt good to be out of the brisk wind. As usual, the baker's wife who tended shoppe stopped talking to whomever was there to promptly attend to the governor's wife. The patron was mildly irritated until he saw Chryspippe. He knew he would have done exactly the same if they had entered his tannery.

The cakes and loaves were all setting out for her to see, but still she said, "We are in haste. What is ready?"

"Is this to eat right away or later today?"

"Both," answered Chryspippe, suddenly deciding this could be something to take home as well though the slaves usually did their grocery shopping. She looked over the baked goods.

She saw white loaves of bread on a shelf. The visions of her dream suddenly resurfaced.

"I will take two of those," she pointed as the baker's wife followed her direction.

"May I taste one?"

"Of course," answered the baker's wife, handing the entire flat loaf to Chryspippe.

Chryspippe broke off a section to taste it. It was good but did not come close to the impressions within her dream.

"Do you have hummus?" she asked.

"Of course."

"Fresh?"

"Made it myself this morning."

"Two of those pitas with hummus. And, four more of the barleys to take home for tonight." She went to the bucket of water, lifted the ladle and took a drink. Lorin followed suit.

The baker's wife attended to their order and handed the extra loaves with the hummus filled pair. Lorin stepped forth with a woven bag to place the loaves and the purse to pay the baker. Chryspippe thanked her and they headed back out into the windy sunshine.

"If it was not for the wind, this would be a pleasant day," yelled Chryspippe.

Lorin said nothing but agreed. They stopped by the well and filled two decent sized leather purses with water for drinking. A lame beggarwoman sat nearby. She called to them for alms, but both ignored her.

The wind changed form as they left the rows of buildings. The salty air felt a tad warmer, but also a bit clammier. Chryspippe paused, not exactly sure where the salt ropers would be, but replayed their trail up from the beach from their nightly migration over the uncounted occasions she saw them. She got a bit turned around as well as a bit exasperated, but eventually found the prisoners. The sand and rock beach rolled under their sandals like irritated marbles. She thought that she could see old Giovanni just beyond the surf. She noted and wondered that he worked far, far farther down beach from everyone else in the water. As the two women approached she realized why. The red welts of the whip still covered him head to toe. She could not be sure how old those new scars, but he had dined with her only four days earlier. Such severe sores he had not received before he dined as their guest.

Walking down beach, she called to him as they approached. The wind carried away her words before reaching his ears. The sun and wind blew surf and spray about the coastline. As the two women approached, they saw what looked like a rainbow around his head. Chryspippe called again. He looked up and smiled, tended to his rope a moment longer then waded out of the water. He walked slowly; carefully, yet smiled his customary greeting, standing on the sand and the sea.

"To what do I owe the honor of your visit?" called Ionnes on approach.

Chryspippe waited until he came closer. She saw the brutal scars, looking worse and worse with each closing step.

He also greeted Lorin with a smile and a nod. The bondservant returned his greeting with her rarely shown shy smile.

"What happened?" asked Chryspippe.

Ionnes looked at her with an obvious expression. She knew just as well as anyone there.

"It is amazing you are not consumed," she said.

"Amen," agreed Ionnes. "My God and His delightful Spirit have kept the sharks away.

All knew the common practice to send a whipped prisoner to the salt ropes to be attacked by ravenous sharks. Their spread of blood, however dry, always promised a brutal death at some point unknown but with certain expectation. If the prisoner refused, he became chained to a large stone that other prisoners tossed in the water to keep him waist deep. Both soldiers and prisoners were equally in awe that Ionnes continued to survive. Still, none of them would enter the water anywhere near him. One guard boldly tried yesterday to give Ionnes a few new open sores and was devoured in knee deep water before his first strike. Ionnes tried to help, but the guard dropped below without another word. Ionnes prayed fervently as he still wept for the lost man. He did not even try to flee the water as the feeding frenzy reddened the water barely thirty feet away, between himself and the beach. He prayed the sharks to depart, but Adonai's judgment and Word reigned. He could only stand in gut deep water adding his own tears to the tide and accepting whatever judgments Yeshua wished. When the sharks soon swam off, Ionnes slowly walked to the shore to fall upon old hands and knees, shivering and broken with grief. Other guards ran up but were swept with great fear and kept distance from this holy man whom even the sharks respected. One picked up the now empty helmet as it rolled up with the lapping surf to the shoreline. He fingered the teeth marks that scraped the side of the metal.

Ionnes did not tell Chryspippe about yesterday's loss. He perceived she did not already know.

"What purpose brings you to the salt ropes?"

Chryspippe stood a moment, almost as if she herself did not know, but the morning's thoughts that pressed her forth so urgently came back to mind. It began all so clearly during the morning. She accepted the moment to bring that clarity back rather than fear the moment.

"I wish to be baptized," she eventually yelled, bluntly.

Ionnes smiled. Lorin dropped their bag of bread.

"Lorin!" scolded Chryspippe. She took the bag Lorin picked up to dust off the sand. "Oh, and we brought you some bread." She handed him a flat loaf filled with hummus. He took a bite and thanked her, Lorin and Yeshua.

"When?" he asked as he swallowed.

"Right away," she answered. "Right here."

"Why?" he asked.

Harder question to answer, but she already felt somewhat acquainted and comfortable with her thoughts, considerations and deliberations.

"I cannot say it fully in words," she began, "but since you delivered my brother, you have shown me a road I never before saw."

She paused again to choose words carefully.

"Then, as I heard you tell tales of Yeshua and the marvelous miracles He performed, and that Spirit of Yeshua continues to shine in you, I wanted to know it for myself."

She felt a sense of fear rise though she knew not why. Fear of disappointment? Fear of rejection from her family and peers? Fear of loss or retribution by Cæsar Domitian? Fear of looking foolish? Fear of losing her husband? All of the above? Overthrowing all the other fears prevailed a fear that Yeshua did not baptize Romans.

"And, now," she drew a breath to continue, "I see a man who should have been attacked by sharks and who raises people from the dead and is not a fool but loves those who hate him. I have seen shamans and sorcerers and even temple priests before. They always filled me with repulsion and even fear, but I touch your life and feel warmth and trust and even unknown love. You say it is Yeshua. I cannot explain it, but I know I want something different and more real than what I have always had."

The air blew coolly against his wet body causing him to shiver, but Ionnes felt warm tears of joy well forth and praised Yeshua for this moment. Nothing certain as yet, but to his never-ending amazement, life ever moved him down the right direction. He chuckled to himself. He knew with full certainty he would find converts on Patmos. He never doubted Yeshua, himself or the message of Christos' love, but he never imagined the first to be the Roman governor's wife. Adonai's grand sense of humor surely withheld that prophesy.

He took a welcome bite of his freshly made sandwich. Despite Roma's efforts to strip away everything and make a follower of The Way into walking death, Yeshua still shone most brightly. Ionnes long knew when the things and matters and fears and concerns of the world were taken away, the realities and presence of Adonai became much easier to see and hold. He praised Yeshua and the Spirit who prepared hearts before Ionnes knew they would meet. In that way, Chryspippe's holy conversion shone as bright a miracle as any mortal resurrection.

"My daughter," said Ionnes. Chryspippe's face showed shock to be called such. "My daughter, there is more than just baptism. That is the outward act for one who wants to give her life to Christos Yeshua. Do you confess that Yeshua is Dominus? That is, your LORD?"

She examined the question carefully before answering.

"Yes," she nodded.

"Do you want His gift of eternal life in Heaven?"

She thought for another moment, trying to precisely recall his words over dinner the other night. His description of life in an eternal Heaven with Yeshua definitely outshone her lifelong expectations of Styx and Pluto. She always slept with a gold coin for Charon in case she failed to awaken. She sighed. The Plain of Asphondel always sounded a bit dreary. And boring. And crowded. She looked at Ionnes. She had not been expecting a quiz when she played this out in her mind before coming.

"I think so." She shuddered, but it felt good. "I am trying to recall how you explained it at my parent's home. I knew then I did not fully understand it, but also felt the call to find out more."

"Amen," applauded Ionnes. "Amen." He looked over to Lorin and took another bite of his sandwich.

"And, what of you, Lorin my child? You also heard me the other night? Do you share also Ms. Chryspippe's desire to know better Yeshua as LORD?"

Lorin suddenly felt that old fear well up - the fear most all slaves share - when their own wants may not mesh with their master's. She had been alongside the entire trek as her mistress became more and more erratic and distressed, uncertain of the search - only to bring them to this moment.

Now she was offered equal footing, if only for a lonely minute. That always scared her. What would her mistress think?

Or say? Or do?

And, what should she say to this old man for whom she felt both awe and fear? He stood so far above anyone she had ever seen yet stood before her also a slave. She took the safe slave answer as she knelt down and bowed low to worship him. Only a god could do the marvels Giovanni had done. Worship was the right course.

"Lorin!" he called. "Rise, child."

Still bowed low, she looked up at him.

"Worship me not," he urged without chastisement. "Rise. I am only a mere man and not a god - not one to be worshipped. Rise and stand. We are both slaves. I am a slave to Yeshua but with one big difference. My Master gives me His freedom. And, the closer I am to my Master, Yeshua, the more His freedom flourishes within me. So, rise, my child."

He offered her a hand up. She declined, but still rose and moved slightly behind Chryspippe.

Ionnes looked at Chryspippe. "I know you can order your slaves to be baptized. Please do not. It is their decision. Let Yeshua call each Himself, through your example and as they see the glorious strength your life will become."

She nodded. That had been her plan once she was baptized - to also have them baptized. That was what slave owners did - demand their slaves worship their same gods. Everyone knew that. Still, she also knew Laurentius did not yet share her faith in Yeshua. She expected he would not allow his household to be converted or baptized, but before today she never expected to be standing on this beach before this amazing apostle. Changes were suddenly more possible than she had yet dared imagine.

Ionnes set down his sandwich and knelt on the sand. With a head nod, he invited Chryspippe to join him.

She looked over to the guards, a fair distance, who she knew had watched the entire encounter.

"Do I have to kneel?" she asked.

"No, of course not," answered Ionnes.

It was inappropriate to kneel before this man, this slave, especially since she was married, but positioned beside him would be odd yet still socially acceptable. She took advantage of that stance and knelt to his side where she could still keep an eye on the guards. She looked up at her slave who immediately followed, kneeling next to Chryspippe in well-practiced subservience.

Ionnes bowed his old head in what looked to the women like a tired and well-worn pose. Or...? No. They were wrong. He easily turned upwards and smiled with every fiber of his being. He let Adonai's Holy Spirit move the moment. Hearts were open to His receiving. Angelic choirs were briefly silenced to be witnesses to God's glory. The prayers of Heaven and Earth are for these moments answered.

He prayed, first silently then a bit louder. He turned his head towards her.

"Chryspippe of Patmos, do you wish for Yeshua to be your LORD and Savior?"

She nodded.

He said some other words she did not understand, then said, "When we spoke a few nights back, I spoke of the love of Yeshua - a love that is mighty - a love that is everlasting. It is this love that sustains me during my greatest trials. Do you wish to have this love also in you?"

She nodded again. Lorin may have nodded, too.

He prayed some more. The agape of Yeshua filled the beach. Chryspippe felt it. She took Lorin's hand. It trembled. Lorin felt it, too. They heard faint laughter far off up the beach but did not look up.

"Praise You, Yeshua," closed Ionnes and slowly stood. Each year the ground became harder to rise from, as though calling those old bones back to where they were formed. Lorin rose and helped her mistress to her feet.

"Now what about baptism?" perked Chryspippe.

Ionnes laughed. New converts were absolutely adorable. "We could meet at the harbor," he offered. "That should be safe. I would not dare bring you down to this water right now. I am one who everyday expects to die in my faith, but I would hope if you met that same fate, it would not be during your baptism."

She looked woeful at that thought.

"My daughter, you already well know not all sharks live in the water."

She felt comfort and had to agree. She had always lived in a world that included sharks.

Ionnes thought about the area. "Also, did not I see a fountain near the Acropolis? And, one near the Temple of Apollo? I have not been here long, so I am sure you know of others. Pick your pool, and you shall be baptized." He looked at Lorin, "And, you too, I hope."

Lorin withheld answer. She had always been expected to worship the Roman gods. She suddenly realized her interesting week would continue.

Ionnes sat down on the rocky sand and continued eating his meal, still shivering at times though it still felt good to get off his feet. Chryspippe looked at Lorin, removed her shawl, laid it on the ground and sat before Ionnes. He looked at the slave girl. She felt odd but followed in harmony with her mistress. And, there they sat for the next hour or so for Ionnes to share the love of Yeshua and the meaning of baptism. He told of Yeshua's baptism by His cousin Yochanan who called on the Jews to repent. Repent! Repent! That was Yochanan's main message. And, likewise the message Yeshua began when He baptized, (though Yeshua Himself baptized not, but His disciples). How amazing! Yeshua never needed to repent, yet He sought to be baptized. Then, it was even more amazing to see Him being lifted out of the water by the Father and the Spirit.

Ionnes spoke of Adonai Abba's love to send His only begotten Son. He spoke of Yeshua's sacrifice on the cross for her sins, resolved by His resurrection three days hence. Ionnes spoke of Yeshua's ascension forty days later. He, Ionnes, spoke as personal witness to all.

"We have some bread," said Ionnes. "Did you happen to bring some wine?"

"No," answered Chryspippe, almost apologetically. "We have water."

"We could make do with water, but we will wait. When we have bread and wine, I will share the greater gift of Yeshua in the breaking of the bread."

Then, he laughed. "Please, give me the water," he said. Lorin brought forth the leather purses they had filled in town.

"Yeshua's first miracle was turning water into wine."

Chryspippe looked at him oddly. "Really?"

"Yes," assured Ionnes. "It was for a wedding. They ran out of wine, and Yeshua's mother told her Son to do something. He told her it was not yet His time, but she would not hear of it. You know how mothers can be."

Chryspippe still was not sure she believed. It seemed contrary to everything else she had heard from Ionnes, and frankly sounded more like something a Roman or Greek god like Bacchus would do.

"Verily," stressed Ionnes, "His mother Maryam told the servants to do whatever Yeshua ordered them. He had them fill six large pots. These were big pots, made to store grain - no, wait - for ceremonial washing and purification. Well, the servants took Yeshua literally. They filled the pots all the way to the brim. I think some were mocking Him, but He did not miss a step. He did nothing unusual. He did not touch the pots or wave His hands over them or add anything to the water. Nothing. I still well remember the look of their faces when He told one of the servants to take a cup of the water to the chief steward. The servants all stood there like someone just told them to stab the wedding party. Finally, one took a cup, and dipped it in the pot to take to the steward. Of course, some of the water spilled out over the side, and the cup was dripping as he took it away. He gave the chief steward the cup acting like he had just asked for a cup of water. The chief steward accepted the full cup, sniffed it, took a sip and another and then another. I loved his face. It said it all."

"What?" asked Lorin, then looked embarrassedly at Chryspippe who disapproved, but could not help but understand. She also wanted to know the same answer.

Ionnes smiled at both of them as he continued, "The chief steward went straight to the groom with the glass and gave him a drink. He smiled in approval. The water had been changed to wine - a delicate and flavorful white. Light tannins. Just dry enough for most Jewish palates. The chief steward did not know the miracle and chastised the groom."

"Why? How?" demanded Chryspippe. She looked at Lorin who also wanted the answer to those questions.

"He asked why the groom had saved the best wine for later? As you know, at any party you usually serve the best wine first, then when everyone has had some and are feeling more relaxed, you can bring out the lesser wine. Nobody will complain."

Chryspippe knew that to be true and had done that herself for dinner parties, weddings and week-long family gatherings.

Ionnes shook his head with a smile, remembering that day. "I went back into the kitchen. Word was already being spread about the miracle, and all the servants were dipping into all six pots to check. They never became less amazed. All six pots held this delightful fruit of the vine."

"So," considered Chryspippe, "can you change water into wine?"

Ionnes smiled. "I have never succeeded, yet. And, yes, I have tried a few times, but Adonai is not mocked. It might have been given to Ionnes' glory and not Yeshua's. In that, I am ever thankful that I failed."

He took the leather in his hands, raised it to Heaven and spoke very simply. "Yeshua, may we have some wine to share in your communion?"

He lowered the bag and gave it to Chryspippe who took a sip. Her face also said it all. Still water.

Ionnes showed no disappointment and kept his smile genuine. He had given all. He could give no more. And, all included his trust in Yeshua's loving wisdom. If right, the small pouch of water would have been miraculously changed. "It is not time to share the LORD's supper with you," assured Ionnes. A thought occurred to him. "Do you still wish to be baptized?"

"Yes," Chryspippe automatically answered, but then wondered. The miracle did not work. Perhaps Ionnes was not who he said he was. No, she still decided. Apollonides was proof enough. A little bag of wine weighed nothing compared with her brother's deliverance.

"Yes," she said again, more firmly, "but only if you can baptize me in water changed to wine." She smiled.

Ionnes giggled at that. "I will work on it," he promised. His face showed his mind playing around with that idea. "I would have them lining up down the block to be baptized if I could do that."

All three laughed, then Ionnes' brow turned down as he restudied the bruise on her cheek.

"What does your husband say?"

She paused and the smile that lit up her face quickly faded. Ionnes recognized the obvious.

"Do you plan to not tell him?"

"If I could, yes - for now," she answered, "but I know it would not work. I see my own foolishness here." She sighed. "I know not what to do. Or say."

Ionnes thought a moment.

"Have you ever heard of Esther?"

Her blank face gave answer, so he shared the account from scriptures. Her features softened as he relayed the tale, including the victory over Naaman.

"You have your own Ahasuerus," he stated. She agreed she would give it a try.

"Sunday, then?"

She nodded.

"Where?"

"I will let you know," she answered rising. Lorin rose as well, of course.

"Then, Yeshua be with you, my daughter." He strained to get up and accepted her hand on his arm. "Thank you. The ground gets farther and farther away every year."

She understood, even though she shared maybe half his age. She noticed the terrible lashes again.

"I pray that you heal quickly."

"That is always welcome," agreed Ionnes. "Yeshua told us where two or more of us are gathered in His name, there He also would be."

He watched them depart, then headed back to the water to face the wind and the wave and resume dipping the ropes.

The afternoon felt cooler than the morning. Rains would surely soon follow. Chryspippe feared not getting caught in the rain. It was not that imminent, but they still hurried to get home. Passing through town, other women noticed the governor's wife, again in haste as she passed through. Their tongues wagged away all the more as the two women continued up the hill towards the governor's villa. Reaching home, Lorin saw to her mistress's needs before removing her own shawl and delivering the loaves to the kitchen.

"For dinner," she said to another slave. She left the kitchen to find the toilet when she heard her name called from behind. She sighed but returned to the kitchen. Two slaves stood with the two leather purses.

"Where did you get this wine?" one asked. "It must be the finest I have ever tasted.

Lorin furrowed brow as she took hold of the waterbag. She sniffed. It definitely smelled like wine. She took a sip. Sure enough, it was an amazing flavor as it spread across her palate and warmed her wonderfully as the fluid moved down her throat and across her chilled bosom.

"Miss Chrys," she yelled, grabbing a goblet and hastening out.

Chryspippe was already in the lounge, her feet up and head back to rest. It had been a physically demanding day.

"Taste this."

She poured the water changed to wine into the goblet.

Chryspippe looked at her slave questioningly but accepted the goblet and took a sip.

"Are you playing a trick on me?"

"No Miss Chrys. If so, someone plays the trick on both of us." She explained what had just transpired. Chryspippe took another drink and let the fluid melt in her mouth before swallowing. She did not want to swallow, it tasted so good. The two women looked at each other and for a brief moment with knowing smiles to share. For that moment, in their own lives and experiences, they were equals in the same room.

PATMOS

CHAPTER 16

"No," said Myron.

"Chryspippe!" added Fona.

Standing in her parent's home, Chrypippe felt an old wonder come to mind - something she had wondered since her teen years. How is it someone can say just your name, but it means something completely different at times? This time her mother meant, "Chryspippe, what do you mean you are getting baptized? How could you?"

Chryspippe had not expected her parents to understand. Still, she wanted them there. She wanted her family there almost as much as she had wanted anything ever in her life. She pondered that desire. No satisfactory explanations seemed to scratch that itch, so she accepted the yen as it was, pressed upon her, naked and exposed. Her family needed to be there.

"Mother," she answered, totally explaining in one word.

Myron heard the word, "Mother."

Fona heard her daughter say, "Mother, how could I not? I am not a child any longer and have been on my own for quite some years. I certainly know what you are thinking, but I have not lost my mind. We have a prophet among us - a real skin and bone holy man unlike anyone we have ever yet encountered. How could we not follow him and his teachings? Who else have we ever seen perform the wonders this Giovanni has done? These were no tricks. No illusions. Even Apollonides knows that, more than any of us. I know this Yeshua is considered an enemy of Roma. He is not, I tell you. He is not. So, fear not Mother. I know the dangers of this path I have chosen. All the more reason I want my family with me tomorrow."

Fona looked woeful. Chryspippe went forward to give her mom a hug. It was at such a moment as this that

Chryspippe noted how much smaller her mother's stature than her own. Carried away by their emotions, the tears gushed out.

Still ahold of her mom, Chryspippe looked towards her dad.

"Papa, did you not tell me that very night after Giovanni departed that you had never met such an extraordinary man, and believed it unlikely to meet someone so special ever again?"

"Chryspippe," he answered in one-word protest.

"Papa," she retorted thoroughly.

He felt the bindings tighten around the truth of his own words. He looked at his wife. Her tears expressed her fears for their daughter. In the changing glance towards his daughter, her tears followed a different vein; one of joy. The only fear he saw in her was fear of losing the love of her family.

Facing his own retrospective reality, he himself knew firsthand the attraction his daughter felt for this Yeshua. He likewise felt His invitation when Giovanni dined with them. That night, the old prophet's words drove wide spikes in his marble-hard heart. He felt the structure give way to expose that part of him which had been encrusted and forgotten for many a decade. Expecting the fissure to heal and reseal, it only widened as he witnessed his own daughter's courage.

He nodded and approached his wife and daughter and bent down to put his big arms around both of them. Together they strengthened each other with their love.

"Woah!" entered a voice. "Looks like I missed the party." The three turned towards Apollonides' familiar voice. "Did someone die?" He stepped close like he might join the group hug.

Myron broke hold and faced his son.

"You sister has an announcement."

Apollonides looked at Chryspippe with anticipation.

"What, sis? Are you with child?"

Her womb had been closed all her years with Laurentius. It was a sad and sensitive subject - not one that Apollonides would typically spout. Chryspippe might have teared up at this moment, but she felt more peace than expected, and answered her brother.

"I am to be baptized tomorrow."

Apollonides looked at her perplexed. Baptized? Washed?

What? Then, his expression turned as he saw the giddy excitement not far under the surface of her moist eyes. He wanted to make sure but was already there.

"The old zealot?"

She nodded.

He stopped to compose himself. Before his madness, he had been a successful orator in Roma, so gathered the loose pieces and debris of Roman logic scattered about his mind to address his sister. His love for her could not cloud this moment.

He saw an Alpine avalanche he had to stop.

Why? the obvious first question. He ignored it. Are you mad? the second question. He squelched that one, too. He played the big brother, even though she was older than he - a common practice in the Roman patriarchy.

"My sister, please consider." He took her hand. "I have loved you from the moment I first saw you. We shared a good life together in Italia. We - father, mother and I came to Patmos at your entreaty, even leaving our two younger brothers in Italia. Have you considered how this decision will affect all of us?"

She again nodded. Actually, she had considered it most carefully.

"Then, you know what will become of the House of Myron if you continue down this Way. The emperor may strip us of all. Our homes and our lands. Our vineyards. Our high position in the nobility. All could be lost with just a snap of the emperor's divine fingers. You know Domitian readily jumps at the chance to execute any, no matter their station, if he can seize their assets to pay his debts within the government. Treason and insurrection are his favorite flavors. How odd that our lives are no stronger than a thin thread on your loom. Are you truly willing to take all of us to ruin with you?"

"You exaggerate, my brother," she answered, though all Roman nobility truly shared concerns of Domitian's fearful lunacies, made worse after an assassination attempt. It took very little rumor to tip his scale against any of them.

"Do I?" said Apollonides.

He let her think about that one a few seconds before continuing.

Her breath abated, and new fears slithered in to retake a stranglehold on her newfound faith. Well she knew the tales of Domitian's cold fingers which she felt clamping down on her heart. Only recently had she learned a new insight and expectation for her divine soul. Her brother's words tried to rip and shred beyond recognition that joyous expectation right there within her.

Her right hand found her left. She felt her fingers clutch one another. She looked over at Lorin. Just yesterday, they had held hands as a love indescribable filled them both. Her hands felt the same trembling clutch.

And, she smiled as she recalled the nectar of a miracle brought home. Her newfound faith would not to be the ruin of her family, but its deliverance. Her brother, love him, could never speak what he had never seen or experienced.

"Yes," she said to answer his question. "You cannot tell me what you do not know. And, you should know better than I. Your sanity was misplaced. All our hours together to care for you could not pile as high as one word spoken by Giovanni. The old zealot and his God brought your reason back to you. They found it for you like one finds a key under the rock by the door. Do not judge me as misled or uncaring. I have been nothing but caring for you all these years. And, now I ask for you to support me in my time of need. Please, come. Come and see for yourself."

His eyes became intense, and his jaw twitched, but he nodded. As completely insane and off target he believed his sister, she still warranted his care and consideration, at least for this one day.

Myron stepped forward.

"Chryspippe, what does Laurentius say?"

She paused, then boldly admitted, "He knows nothing."

"Nothing?" checked Myron. "My dear, is that wise?"

Chrypippe did not answer. The chasm between her and her husband had widened immeasurably over those few preceding days. She recalled the fresh scars all over Ionnes. What could she possibly say to her husband that would help in any way? He would kill Ionnes that day if he thought it would stop her baptism. Her only hope came from Ionnes' suggestion on the beach yesterday.

Myron leaned towards his daughter. "He is your husband and master. This is not a petty matter; not like it will not bring Cæsar crashing down upon him like an angry tidal wave."

"You know that not," defended Chryspippe.

"No, I do not," admitted Myron, "but, I am not so naive to ignore the possibility."

She looked at both of her parents. And, then her brother. Then, back at her father.

"Then, I shall not ignore the possibility, either," she assured, "but I shall not give this up just on what might occur nor fear the future that might happen."

Myron sighed. He knew his daughter's headstrong ways. Even if the governor could completely destroy his wife without retribution, even to death, Myron had to resign himself to be supportive and let his daughter make her own decisions, including her own mistakes. He and Fona had not always reared her that way, but that was how she turned out and they were not about to change her now.

The three failed to notice Apollonides had already departed their company. None but the slaves noticed his departure. His head down, he marched through town deep in thought and purpose to what end none of them could tell. He muttered angrily to himself as he left. Lorin, Tobie and the others looked at each other as they replayed his words as he headed out the door.

"Wait until Jupiter hears about this!

PATMOS

CHAPTER 17

Riding up the hill, he wondered what laid ahead. Something suspicious? Something disturbing? Or, it could be just his accursed Roman training, staining his thoughts like an old, worn out dyer's wheel. The invitation had been clear enough. In years past he would have welcomed such an invitation. In yesteryears, the gaps between them were never this wide, but now, those early days somehow transformed into these last days of confusion and uncertainty where the butterfly became the caterpillar, or the toad a drowning tadpole. Would he exhale to find no next breath waiting, or find a tunnel at the end of the light? He sighed and reflected upon his younger days when life moved honestly easier, and each day filled with love and hope and naïve pleasures. Where did they go? How in Jupiter's name did he let them slip away so unnoticed?

He told himself he could have more easily held back the tide as contained the changes of the years, but that admission never settled quite right. He knew he bore not all the blame for the present problems of his life, but the specific parts and ways he had contributed were not always so clear, like trying to write outside on wet papyrus while the rain fell, or like the chipped and faded words on older Macedonian ruins. Still, he wondered that he wondered about today's invitation. He looked at the callouses on his hands and wondered what other parts of his mind, body and spirit shared that feature.

Just a few hours earlier, in the Governor's Forum, while he met with the leaders of the Metalworker's Guild, he was surprised to see his wife standing in the doorway. They had hardly spoken since their fight a few evenings back. The cold war that followed laid siege, ever threatening to keep them far, far apart. Many, many years ago and many Roman governor's before Laurentius, the Governor's Forum had originally doubled as the governor's home. He could step across the atrium right into the workplace. It seemed ideal.

Then, the old Greek Erastus passed away. His plush and elegant home had been the envy of Patmos for many years. Childless, his home became easy seizure by the present Roman governor who had always fancied it. He kept tabs on old Erastus approaching mortality, and no sooner had the old man passed when the governor promptly took possession and moved in with his family. And, just like that, it became the Governor's Mansion. Seldom counted years had passed since Erastus' passing. Even the oldest Patmosites now called it the Governor's Mansion or Home.

Still, the old dwellings at the Governor's Forum were maintained and kept available; typically used for love affairs and trysts or lodging for visiting family members and friends. Not that there were many visiting family members to Patmos. Most were glad to avoid it, but the governors always kept it ready for occupancy at a moment's notice. With the cold war between Laurentius and Chryspippe, he had remained there the previous two nights, so it surprised him all the more to see his wife there.

She seemed content to wait until he completed business with the guild members. That weighed strange enough all by itself. She typically displayed more patience than Laurentius, but not by much. He looked over at proconsul Makrinos, considering whether to let him finish the business meeting. He rejected that idea, and instead did rush the meeting a bit, but as soon as all points had been addressed, he excused both his visitors and Makrinos for his next 'appointment'.

She entered when called – but not until he called – also an oddity. And, Lorin waited in the hall. It surprised him how pleased he felt to see her. She looked lovely. Even the bruise on her left cheek was starting to fade, or Lorin did a better job covering it up. He was not sure. Maybe both.

"It is good to see you," he opened.

She smiled and nodded but kept some distance from him.

"You surprise me."

"I had to come," she said. "You look well."

"So do you."

She smiled again.

He wanted to say something like, "So, now you are speaking to me again?" but opted for wiser words.

"Um, why did you have to come?"

"To invite you to dinner."

"You could have sent one of the slaves to tell me."

She nodded, but answered, "It seemed better to come invite you myself."

Actually, he could not argue with that at all. After the last few days with hardly a word between them, her words and presence spoke far more compelling than anything any slave could have relayed.

He nodded. He felt like he should have said something else, but no words materialized. He wondered briefly if she invited him to dinner to poison him? Nah. Where did that idea come from? They had argued many times over the years, and she did not need some formal invitation to take his life. There may be something she wanted, but it was not his head.

"Then, you will come?" she asked.

He nodded again.

"Good," she twittered. "I will see you tonight." Unhurried, she turned to go. He watched her as she left the room. Her footsteps left no tap. He felt glad to see her, but still wondered if he missed something. Likewise, an impression tickled his senses whispering to him this is how it felt when mortal man received a visit by a goddess.

His horse moved along quickly. The gray Arabian which he had named Caput Bove, knew the way home and always increased his gait when he knew stable, and dinner awaited. Laurentius let the animal move along as quickly as he wanted. The governor still pondered what might be to come but felt content that the answers would come quickly enough.

Arriving home, dismounting, one of the slaves came out to attend to his horse. Another came out to attend to the master.

"Hi dear," greeted Chryspippe.

"Oops!" thought Laurentius. The second was not a slave.

"Thirsty?" She had both a goblet of water and one of wine in her hands. She walked to him and presented both. He took a sip of the water, then accepted the wine.

"Please," she invited, "rest after your long day. Dinner will be done soon." She took his sleeve and led him inside to lounge on the cushions. Sitting down, he sat beside her. She had even lit the golden censer.

"What is this about?" he asked.

She looked hurt. "Do I have to have a reason to have my husband home and sharing time with him before dinner?"

"Oops!" he thought again, though he was not one to suffer guilt gladly. Then, his next thought. "I wonder what she wants? I know she wants something," (or so he would have thought if the smells of dinner did not interrupt his suspicions).

"Is that roasted lamb?" His favorite.

She smiled affirming.

"I cooked it myself," she said, or would have said if it were true. She recalled the compassionate words of their cook a few hours earlier as she entered the kitchen with the generous raw cut of meat freshly purchased from the town butcher. She immediately went to work to prepare the meat. It was about that moment everything went south. She could not find the seasonings. She put too much on and had to wash it off. She heated the oven too hot. She dropped the pans. She almost cut the cook with a kitchen knife. It was then the cook most considerately said, "Out of my kitchen!"

She would have argued and played the head of the house mistress but knew her cook's words were only right. She had wanted to make the dinner for her husband, but too many years had passed since she owned the kitchen. She thought cooking would come back to her as easily as swimming, but some skills apparently, could be misplaced with the passing of the years. In turn, she reminded herself the end result was far more important. She would take at least *part* of the credit for the day's feast.

Her next words took her by surprise.

"I cooked it myself," she announced, disregarding everything she had just thought and recalled.

Laurentius looked at her with *that look* over his goblet of wine.

"Cook helped," she added.

Next, she rose and knelt behind him on a pillow. Her hands began to rub his broad shoulders. She may have needed a refresher course in the kitchen, but this part she still remembered well. Every sore muscle. Loosening the tight ones. Every place he loved to be scratched.

Now he *Knew* she was up to something, but at the moment did not care. She could almost hear him purr.

Dinner came and was a success. The more he drank, the more they laughed. It had been so long. Too long. And, as he rested upon his bed, his head still spinning a bit from the wine, he looked at Chryspippe with an old expression not used for years.

"So, what do you want?" he slurred.

She looked down at him, kissed him passionately on the lips, and smiled. "Nothing, my husband."

"Nothing?"

"Rest."

He closed his eyes and sighed, feeling a little too good as she continued to caress him. There he rested and when he awoke the next day, she still laid beside him. She looked so lovely in the morning light.

He arose to prepare for the day. Tertius, his slave, came forth to assist. Chryspippe stayed reclined, eyes closed, ears open.

He shaved and dressed and sat beside her before leaving. Bending to kiss her, she turned towards him in response. A quick kiss and she smiled as she covered her mouth. She was sure her breath smelled as badly as his.

"When will you be home?" she whispered.

"Not late."

"Good," she applauded. "I have a special dinner in mind for you tonight."

He knew with untarnished certainty that something was up. This only verified it. Quite the game, but one that was certainly fun to play. He glanced at her belly beneath the blanket. No, that was not it. Something else. Guess he would wait and see. He kissed her and rose to leave.

"Love you," she said.

He paused. Rare words to hear of late. He turned back towards her.

"Love you, too," he smiled, then headed to face the day quite a bit happier than he had been in a long time.

<>< ><> <>< ><> <>< ><> <>< ><> <>< ><>

Chryspippe gasped. Like yesterday, holding vigil, watching for Laurentius coming home, she saw he rode not alone.

Another rode by his side, his companion not a welcome sight.

"Send word," she spoke to Lorin. "We may have a guest for dinner."

Lorin beelined straight to the kitchen, alerting the other slaves along the way.

The two men dismounted. Horses were taken and led away.

"Welcome home, my dear," she greeted with a kiss. "I see we have a guest."

Laurentius nodded, perhaps a little intensely.

"Kynops," greeted Chryspippe with practiced warmth. "Welcome to our home."

He barely bowed with an ominous nod of his head. Laurentius boldly led the way in. Kynops kept narrow eyes on Chryspippe.

"Kynops," said Laurentius, "met me on the road on the way home. He wished to discuss security matters on the island. He persisted, so I invited him to dine with us this evening."

Chryspippe smiled outwardly, cringed inwardly.

"You are welcome, sir," she lied. "Would you like something - wine? Water? Milk?"

"Wine," answered the magician.

Lorin and Tertius entered, wine in hand. All three accepted a glass. Kynops drank his down, throat wide open, in one gulp. Tertius looked to Laurentius. The governor allowed their guest his oddity. The goblet was promptly refilled. Kynops repeated the ritual. The goblet was again filled. This time, he plopped down on a cushion without spilling a drop, his back against a wall, taking a sip as the 'magic' of the wine took its effect. Long fingers clutched the shadows on the wall beside him. He kept eyes on Chryspippe, save once when a housefly landed nearby.

Dinner was served. Quail wrapped in salted pork belly.

Everyone knew, (except perhaps the Jews), salted pork belly made everything taste better. Laurentius' favorite. And, the most flavorful white wine Laurentius had ever tasted to wash it down. He could not help but relax and indulge.

With the presence of a sorcerer, the repast, oddly enough, could still be enjoyed and wine flowed freely. Kynops stayed by his wall, enjoying the hot meal and watching the couple interact.

"So," he said, his voice emerging from his perch on the floor, "what is this I hear about you Chryspippe?" He licked the liquid fat off his long, slender fingers.

Both heads turned questioningly towards Kynops.

"You and your family have invited a prisoner into your home?"

Both looked at one another. It was not like secrets could be kept for long on such a small island, not that Giovanni's visit was a secret, but what concern could Kynops have?

"And," Kynops continued, "I hear that he is a wizard."

Chrypippe was about to speak, but Laurentius beat her to it.

"Why does Kynops ask? What is Kynops' interest in the affairs of the governor's wife?"

Kynops was not deterred.

"Concern," he said, his brow deeply furrowed. "Concern for the house of Myron - and yours as well, governor. Wizards are known to cast spells - spells created to delude and remove the guarding layers of your souls. I hear he, this Giovanni, is most seductive."

"Your concern is noted," dismissed Laurentius, and took another drink from his goblet. He recalled their last encounter when Kynops could not heal Apollonides. He did not get paid that day, and surely begrudged the governor and her wife, at least a little, and likely more.

"So, he has enchanted you, governor?"

Laurentius set down his goblet, set upright and glared at Kynops.

"Why do you say that?"

Kynops watched the governor carefully; cautiously, but he was far from done with his evening's focus.

"If I saw that possibility, would not I be delinquent to remain mute? To bridle my tongue? Nay! You, m'lord, would compel me to speak. Well, speak I am. I have seen this Giovanni spread his enchantments throughout your penal colony and quarry, even seducing your soldiers. Also, it seems the townsfolk can talk of nothing else. Already, he has infected all. Who is this sorcerer – this necromancer that Cæsar Domitian has sent to you?"

In that brief moment between sentences, they heard the slaves giggling to themselves like children. Three heads turned to the new sounds of silence as the slaves just as quickly clammed up.

"You were saying?" returned Laurentius.

"That is all, governor." He finished the wine and lifted his goblet for a refill.

"So, you think the House of Laurentius is bewitched?"

"I fear for the worst."

"You fear...?"

"...for the worst," finished Kynops. "I have seen such men before. More ravenous than a pride of lions and equally more destructive than a stampede of wildebeest."

Laurentius drummed fingers across his knee and swirled the pale wine around his goblet hypnotically as he thought. He looked at his wife. She remained subserviently silent but looked like an old wine bag ready to burst. It was not her place to interrupt the sober talk of men. In that, her silence seemed not uncommon, but it appeared quite obvious, at least to Laurentius, her silence involved more than mere social mores.

He grabbed another sip of his wine. Even three goblets later, it still tasted fresh and delightful. He had never encountered such flavorful drink. He let the fluid tour his mouth and pallet. He did not want to swallow. Kynops did not seem to delight in the flavor of the wine as much, but as Tertius refilled the magician's glass, Laurentius saw he was drinking red. He seemed to recall hearing the magician preferred red wine to white – the bloodier the better. Fair enough. It mattered very little to the governor. Very few sorcerers he had met showed themselves as cultured, and thus would not appreciate this exquisite wine. He hoped they could get more.

"As I said," answered Laurentius, "your concern is noted.

Anything else?"

Kynops ran his finger along the rim of his goblet. No sound would ring though the surface was smooth – smoother than most pottery.

Kynops looked towards Chryspippe – that same intense gaze he had when entering their home.

Chryspippe was accustomed to being noticed and looked at, by men and women alike, but this was different and much more disturbing.

Laurentius sat up, about to confront Kynops when the magician muttered strange words under his breath, then broke gaze. He rose, finished his wine, and headed for the door.

Slaves came forth.

"You are leaving," said Laurentius, more a statement than question.

"Aye," answered the sorcerer. Slaves raced off to retrieve his horse. "I believe the governess has something to tell you." Then, he spun around violently and disappeared.

Initially shocked, both Laurentius and Chryspippe took the moment to catch breath.

"At least he is gone," Chryspippe finally said. "What a horrible man."

They soon heard the sound of galloping hooves outside growing fainter as distance increased.

Laurentius looked around the room. Such magicians were famous for leaving some sort of memento most sane folks preferred they not leave behind. Nothing seemed out of the ordinary. He looked over at Chryspippe.

Chryspippe followed her husband's examination of the room.

"What a horrible man!" she repeated.

Laurentius nodded in agreement.

"It is like everything he touches quickly turns to wormwood."

He nodded again, but then asked, "What did he mean you have something to tell me?"

Chryspippe almost lied. Almost. She wanted to. The night had been a total disaster. Her Esther plans were trampled underfoot by this unwanted intruder. She thought to request dessert, but nothing would salvage the shipwrecked evening.

The dinner became rocks and waves and darkness. No beacon lit. No flotsam or jetsam to cling to. She sighed.

"I do not know what Kynops thought I had to tell you," she began, "but he is right. I wanted tonight to be special. And, last night as well. I made a decision and wanted to find the best way to tell you. Now, it is what will be, my husband."

Laurentius would only allow her cryptic descriptions for so long. She knew it well, and unconsciously had it timed. Not all roads regularly walked in life were made of dirt or rock or brick.

"Good news or bad news?" he asked.

She smiled. "I think it is good news. Very good news."

Her face fell, "But, I fear you will not share my joy."

"Then, spit it out," he said. She had cast her nets thirty or so hours earlier to lure him. He was more than ready to get some clear answers or shove her down and go to bed. He did not work tomorrow but was still tired and ready to retire for the night.

She bit her lip. "What think you of Giovanni? Do you think him an enchanter? A sorcerer who has us under his spell?"

"He is a prisoner."

"Yes," she agreed, "but, you know him to be an unusual prisoner."

"So, I hear."

"Then, you have never met him?" she asked earnestly. He scoffed. The governor did not patronize with prisoners.

"Well, as you know, I have met him and even invited him to dinner at my father's house."

"Yes, yes," he knew. Was not that the reason for their fight a few days back?

"I do not believe I am enchanted or under a spell, by Giovanni or anyone else, but I am convinced he is a holy man – one who needs to be reckoned with."

"That is why he is here," barked Laurentius with a little more snap than he meant to speak.

"And, so my husband, I make an earnest request."

He knew he was not going to like it.

"Would you please meet with Giovanni? Just once is all I ask."

"And, then what?" Actually, he felt minor relief. Her request was much tamer than other matters she had buttered him up for over the past years.

"Then, we will talk further. Anything I say to you tonight you will see with closed eyes and ears."

He studied her. Her request seemed odd, but not unreasonable. And, she was probably right. He already knew his prerequisite expectations for any prisoner under his jurisdiction. He may have been the governor, but this prisoner had already stood before Cæsar Domitian. Laurentius had never found audience with Cæsar. If nothing else, they could talk about that.

"Yes, I will meet him."

"When?"

"Soon."

"Is tomorrow too soon? You work not."

He sighed. Yes, he would see him tomorrow, mostly out of curiosity of his wife's motives.

She bounced up on her toes a bit and gave him a big hug.

He stood unmoved – for a moment, then put an arm around her. His calloused hands did not seem quite so rough. If it was that important to her...

She smiled, her cheek against his. "Thank you, Esther," she whispered.

"Who is Esther?" he asked.

She thought for a moment. "Um, no one you know, but a very special woman."

"Does she live on Patmos?"

Chryspippe giggled to herself.

"Kind of."

Lorin brushed Chryspippe's long hair before bed. At least C strokes. Chryspippe felt the tension in her brain give in to each stroke. A question occurred to her.

"Lorin, during dinner, why did all of you laugh?"

Lorin stopped brushing only briefly.

"Kynops," she answered.

"Yes?" Chryspippe urged her to continue as the brushing continued.

"He said he would bridle his tongue, then neighed like a horse."

Chryspippe barely remembered.

"Then, Tertius slipped into the kitchen, put his finger in his mouth like a horse's bit and neighed."

"Ah," Chryspippe accepted and smiled almost to a laugh.

PATMOS

CHAPTER 18

"So, what did you think?" asked Chryspippe.

Laurentius handed over the reins to Tertius who handed them to another slave. She stood before him at the door with water and wine and a welcome home smile.

He looked at her with mixed impressions. She seemed obsessed with this Christian zealot, but he appreciated her attentions anew, even if they were only because she wanted something. That had to be the only explanation for her newfound subservience and attendance. If Giovanni was not so old, he would undoubtedly have other concerns for her attractions.

"You mean the old lunatic?" he answered, entering his home, taking both goblets from her hands. Like before, he drank water to wash down the dusty road, then the wine to wash down the water. He saw the red fluid – not the same as yesterday's treat. He would ask, but totally expected the skin would be empty. He sipped. A favorite vintage, but after yesterday's offering it might as well have been melted, rancid tallow and old vinegar.

She knew his answer to be serious but pretended otherwise.

"Yes. You met with him?"

"Aye."

"And?"

He plopped down on his favorite pillows. She moved behind him to unfasten his cape and leathers and rub his shoulders.

"First tell me why it seems to matter so much to you."

Following silent, deep breaths, she answered, practically whispering in his ear, "Simple my husband. My father and I took time to honor him for healing my brother. You were displeased, even enough to have him flogged. I am amazed he still stands. It upset me greatly, of course, but I realized part of your anger must come from your own failed impressions. If you had met him before, I doubt you would have reacted so strongly. So, rather than see a sweet, old man beaten again because he was asked to dinner and because you were upset with me, I wanted you to meet and know him yourself."

Laurentius took a bigger drink of his wine. Still swill, but better than the first taste.

"He is old. I will give him that. But, sweet?"

She sat beside him, looked him in the eyes and asked, "Please, share with me your meeting."

He glanced at her, but mostly looked out the window. The tanned lines of his face stood out darker than usual.

"Governor?"

Captain of the Guard Lucius entered the Forum 'throne room' with two other soldiers and their prisoner.

Laurentius had heard the harmonic clanging of the chains before they entered the building. He looked at Giovanni who looked at him. Two things he noted right off – well the same feature twice. Most prisoners were either burning with rage against him or too scared to look him in the face. This ancient man in rags was neither. If they had been in a café, he would have expected Giovanni to ask to see a menu. The freshly inflicted sores across his neck and legs still bore clear witness of the governor's orders.

"Leave us," he stood.

Lucius saluted, turned and left the room followed by the two soldiers. They would remain close for immediate summons.

"Kneel if you wish," opened the governor.

Ionnes remained standing.

"As you wish," muttered Laurentius and returned to his seat.

Ionnes noticed the similar way the governor turned and seated himself, just like Cæsar Domitian, his cape twirling around behind him as his back side descended. Then, he wondered if it was mimicry of the emperor, or just a Roman thing. Probably both. He also noted, for any leader to turn back to a prisoner, even for a quick second, screamed of arrogant surety.

"Why are you here?" asked Laurentius.

"Because you summoned me."

"On Patmos."

"Oh. Um, I expect you have already read the official report," answered Ionnes.

"I have," assured the governor. "Quite the story. Quite unbelievable, to be honest."

Ionnes nodded. He was used to such spurning.

"Then," continued Laurentius, "I am told you add to the incredible saga since your arrival."

Ionnes nodded again.

"So, why are you here?"

"For my love and commitment to Yeshua, my Messiah; my Dominus. And, to spread His good news to all in His name, as He commanded." He paused then added, "And, apparently to work the quarry."

"How is that working for you – the quarry?"

Ionnes answered ever truthfully, "It is hard, of course. I am not such a young man anymore. But, while we are on the subject, perhaps you can direct your guards a way to make the salt ropes more efficiently."

Laurentius nodded to continue.

"You know how we make the salt ropes?"

"Of course."

"Well, the Ægean Sea provides the salt, but I considered right after I arrived here that the Dead Sea in Iudæa would work better for saturating the ropes with salt."

Laurentius looked a bit perturbed. "You want me to move salt rope operations to Iudæa?"

"No, no, no," answered Ionnes. "That would be terrible. But, the same effect as the Dead Sea can be imitated on Patmos. In smaller pools, of course."

"I am listening," said the governor.

"It is very simple," explained Ionnes. "We dig out areas to make large pools close by the sea. The pools must be lower than the sea. Fill it up with salt water when the tide is high, then as the tide recedes, close it off and leave it to partially dry up for some days. The salt will be stronger, make the ropes both better and salted in half the time. Then, after much water has gone down, take away some stones and dirt and such and refill the pools next high tide. Close them off again. Give them a few days for the water to go down and start again in the stronger brine. We would need multiple pools lest the pool become rancid and stinky. Part of the time a pool would need to have the tidal waters wash in and out for a couple of days."

"How can you speak with your mouth so overloaded with words?" said Laurentius, staring at Ionnes thoughtfully. Despite his gristle, the plan actually seemed plausible.

Ionnes shrugged.

"Did you suggest this to the soldiers?"

"Most soldiers have closed ears," answered Ionnes. "I made the suggestion more than once. Each time I was whipped and sent back to the surf."

Laurentius rubbed his chin. He was glad to hear the soldiers were following his orders. "I will suggest it to the Captain of the Guard."

"That would be appreciated," said Ionnes. He bowed his head and closed eyes prayerfully.

Laurentius watched him briefly. In his experience, one religious zealot was pretty much like every other. That included the temple priests and other fools following one of the gods or goddesses, but none he had encountered had such stories attached to him.

"So," said Laurentius, changing the subject, "in Roma, were you actually boiled in oil?"

Ionnes' smile remained as he answered, "Governor, I am a humble servant of God. It is not my place to point attention to myself, for all I do I do for the glory of my Heavenly Father."

"So, you do not deny being boiled in oil?"

Ionnes answered with silence. Not even a head nod or diversion of his gray-brown eyes, locked like a wrestler's embrace on the governor.

Laurentius shook his head in tired consternation. "If I had a cauldron, I would boil you myself right here and now."

He looked up at Ionnes. "And, if I had the authority, I would send you to Pergamum for execution like your friend Antipas."

Ionnes expression changed to remorse, and he dropped his head. The sadness of that execution suddenly weighed upon him worse than a marble rockslide. "Antipas, oh Antipas!" he cried within. His eyes felt the tears flow freely and painfully. Not yet three years past since that horrid execution, Laurentius had already taken governorship of Patmos. He surely heard the report across the Ægean of the execution of the Bishop of Pergamos.

When Ionnes heard Antipas had been arrested pending execution, he hastened with Prochorus, Papias and others from Ephesus northward. Roman executions typically came quickly and Pergamos was close to a three-day journey from Ephesus.

As feared, they arrived too late.

"Too late for what?" Ionnes uttered to himself before Laurentius. How could he have stopped anything? But he had to try.

As they entered the city, they passed the Asklepion, the mystic healing center of Pergamos. Farther on, in blind sadness, he entered the Temple to Zeus. The throne there empty, but the bull still smoldered with its latest execution. Fashioned the size of a regular bull made it big enough for three or four human bodies. The animal's haunches showed a simple door with outside twist locks. Inside its snout and horns included small, acoustical pipes to make the dying man's wails resemble sounds of the raging bull. It reeked from the smell of roasted human flesh. Ionnes strode to the bull and carefully opened the door to look in. Charred remains and flesh oil coated the inside bottom of the bull. He reached in a hand, not to touch, but to be closer as he prayed. More tears showered his face and beard. More painful remorse filled him through and through. He shuddered under its dead weight and frantically prayed for Antipas' resurrection. Just as he thought he could bear no more, he heard the voice like many waters, rushing over his head and under his feet. He closed his eyes. His breathing relaxed. He praised Yeshua for the voice and its comfort as the voice said,

"Thanks to you, my child, but he does not want to go back."

A smile redirected the tears. He slowly closed the door and recalled the time long ago when he left an open grave with empty burial clothes.

"Were you here?" he asked some with him. They nodded, and leaving the "Throne of Satan," those from the Pergamos church relayed account.

Together they celebrated the life of their friend and brother. Ionnes recalled youthful Antipas with such a bright face, ever wishing to draw closer and closer to Yeshua. At times, Ionnes secretly wished he had had a little more Antipas in him when he was that age. His disciple's growth in the Spirit never wavered, even when Ionnes ordained him to be bishop of Pergamos.

The Holy Spirit moved through him like water through a clean fountain. By the power of Yeshua, the demons in Pergamos fled in droves. The priests of Asklepion feared the changes surrounding them as this new faith in Christos Yeshua grew and daily added converts while their "spirit guides" departed. Some demons wailed as they bolted, "Remove Antipas," or "Begone Antipas." The priests of Asklepion applied an age-old solution to such problems. Approaching the hated Roman governor of Pergamos, they whined and complained how this new Christian movement, and specifically the prayers of Antipas, expelled the spirits of the city which in turn hindered the worship of their gods.

Ionnes immediately recalled the same tactic used by the Jewish leaders to crucify their LORD Yeshua.

The Roman governor, already compelled by his dislike towards followers of The Way, arrested Antipas. The bishop, beaten but still praising Yeshua, received orders to offer wine and incense to the Roman emperors and declare them as gods. There were no less than three temples in Pergamos built to deify Roman emperors. They brought Antipas before all three temples to compel him to pagan worship. Antipas refused each time, well knowing he faced the penalty of death.

Thereby, they brought him to the Temple of Zeus to force him into the large and hollow Brazen Bull. A great fire was lit beneath the bull, eventually roasting the prisoner to death. Antipas' head had been intentionally bound inside the head of the bull to capture the sounds of the bellowing bovine. Despite their sorrows, Ionnes and the others praised Yeshua for they were told how Antipas prayed for all of them and the church continually during his execution. Those attending heard the pagan bull praising the name of Yeshua.

"I wish that I could have taken his place," said Ionnes, raising his head, eyes reset on Laurentius.

"As do I," assured Laurentius. "As do I."

A silence rose between them. At first a thick fog of contention, Ionnes breathed in deeply strength and love from the Holy Spirit and, for him, the contention faded into the grace of peace.

"So, governor," spoke Ionnes, "we both seek to serve a higher power."

Laurentius nodded.

Ionnes continued, "I choose to serve the higher power which made your higher power."

"Yet, you are the prisoner," countered Laurentius.

"Yes, I am," admitted Ionnes, "but only my body. My spirit soars far beyond any lock or key by which you may burden me." He paused for effect. "And, sir, you know perfectly well, not all prisoners wear chains." He raised his arms to jingle his own black chains.

Laurentius sighed his admission of those words.

"Besides," Ionnes added, "More than once I heard my DOMINUS Yeshua tell us to love one another as He loved us. Then, right after that He said, "Greater love has no one than this, than to lay down one's life for his friends."

"You believe that?"

Ionnes grinned. "Governor, were not you on the field of battle some years past? Did not you see the greatest sacrifice – friends laying down their lives for others? Of course, you have. There is no deeply hidden mystery in those words."

"Agreed," admitted Laurentius, "but, I expect we both apply those words unequally."

"I am sure." Ionnes smiled again. "You are here, in part, to keep the peace. I am here because I serve the Prince of Peace.

Same purpose. Different bull's eyes."

"Well, for someone who supports the cause for peace, you seem to rile and stir things up far too easily."

"I hope so," he winked, still smiling. "True peace often requires the cost of a battle. Perhaps many battles. I see within you, governor, that peace evades you."

"And, why do you say that, Zealot?"

"Ask Apollonides."

Laurentius raised his head like a dog sniffing the air. "Yes, yes," he recalled. "I was there."

"I did not see you," admitted Ionnes, "but it was only my first day on Patmos. How is Apollonides doing?"

"I know not," said Laurentius. "I scarcely see my brother-in-law, although I hear you are not his favorite person."

"You are correct, I am sad to say. He is faced with a dilemma. No longer does the demon drive him. His own faith is put to the test, and for the first time, perhaps ever, he must stand on his own two feet."

Laurentius wrestled a bit with the words, weighing their accuracies. He would not come to that same pronouncement for some time. Possibly never. Then, just as he felt ready to shove talk of Apollonides and his demons out the door, Ionnes asked, "And, what of your demons, governor?"

The question caught him totally off guard and disarmed him.

"What demons?" He almost sputtered.

"I know that you do not know," assured Ionnes, "but that does not mean they are not there. Would you want to know?"

"How?" asked Laurentius, intrigued but not really believing the old Christian.

"Easily," answered Ionnes, "if you wish them gone. If you cling to them, I can do little."

Laurentius furrowed brow. Impressions inside his mind dismissed the invitation. It was foolish to be sure. And, was not he the governor? Do not forget that this is a prisoner – a nobody, in Roma and the world.

Ionnes shared a disarming smile, but his countenance felt the urgency to go forward, whatever the cost.

"Your demons are afraid and telling you to refuse."

"How would you know?" challenged Laurentius, his temper suddenly gaining elevation.

"I can see it," Ionnes answered plainly. He knew telling the governor, or most people for that matter, that their demons were making them angry typically made them even more angry. It was an old demonic defense tactic – as old as Cain and Abel, Jacob and Esau, or David and King Saul. And even more oddly, in the day-to-day activities of life, most people became at least somewhat comfortable with their demons.

It took a moment for Laurentius to settle down. He seemed ready to call the guards and have Ionnes taken away; even put in the stocks for the night. Eventually, his passion cooled, and his reason warmed up. There was truly something intriguing in this old man's invitation and what sane man would not want to lose his demons?

"Have you expelled your demons?"

Ionnes did not hesitate. "Every day. Seeking the will of Yeshua has certainly made me a target."

Laurentius decided to play along, partially because he expected nothing to happen. He would not be drawn along by his emotions like so many fools he had seen. Strangely, only the recollection of Apollonides being delivered actually gave him real cause to fear. That moment made the old man's offer more real, and thereby possibly something Laurentius could not control.

Ionnes stepped forward within feet of Laurentius. The birds chirping away outside filled the quiet between them. The tile floor suddenly seemed harder and cooler. Swords could be heard being drawn in the next room. The demons present certainly were not only in the governor. Ionnes knew they would only come if they saw certain danger for their leader.

Ionnes might have asked him to close his eyes but knew that would never go over in the presence of a prisoner.

"Two items," said Ionnes, closing his eyes and raising his chiming chained hands to Heaven. "Laurentius of Patmos, do you wish for your demons to be expelled?"

Laurentius weighed the word carefully before answering, "Yes."

"Good," applauded Ionnes, looking intently at Laurentius. "Consider your answer carefully. Laurentius, in the name of Yeshua, demons be gone. Flee. You are not welcome. Leave Patmos forever." Ionnes kept eyes on the man though a perpetual prayer continued to shudder his lips.

Laurentius looked at Ionnes like he was a madman. What in the world? Did he truly believe that was all it took? He was about to call the guards to have this lunatic taken away, but instead he chuckled. Just a quick snicker followed by another then another, then a smile of contentment. Warmth quickly filled him like freshly baked bread wrapped in a blanket brought in fresh off the line. Any anger he had moments earlier disappeared like steam over a boiling pot.

"You did what?" laughed Chryspippe.

"I played along with his game."

"Having your demons expelled is a game?"

"Yes," said Laurentius, "for most shamans I have ever met, yes."

"How did it feel?"

"Like I always thought the womb must feel to one not yet born."

"Laurentius of Patmos," said Ionnes, placing a hand on the governor's shoulder, "you have asked me many questions. May I ask one of you?"

Laurentius still felt the amazing effects of demon deliverance. It was sweet, but also awkward. He was not sure how well he would walk if he stood, but he also wondered that he scarcely cared.

"What?" asked Laurentius.

"Do you believe the mortal Cæsars to be gods on Earth? Does not that violate the immortality you have always believed in the gods?"

Laurentius felt a nagging fear try to take hold. Fortunately, it could not upset the sense of satisfaction he had never before encountered since teen years. Perhaps even earlier in life.

"I do not know," he admitted. Even that answer could have been heresy to some Cæsars, but he did not feel compelled to take it back.

"I could tell you do not," stressed Ionnes. "You go through the motions of worship, but it is not hard to see your true beliefs to be honest, so hear me," urged Ionnes. "Yeshua brought you to rule over Patmos before you knew it would happen. He knew you would be here when I was delivered by Cæsar Domitian to you. And, I for one praise Yeshua that I am here, and I praise Him that you are here."

Laurentius took his words as something a zealot would say. Or would he? Most zealots were inflexible in their beliefs. In this he saw Ionnes no different. But most zealots did not wrap their beliefs and words in so much love. In that way, this old Giovanni had them totally beat. He smiled and allowed Giovanni's words to be the truth for that moment between them.

They spoke little more when the guards were summoned.

"Yeshua be with you," said Ionnes as he turned to go.

A young Roman couple entered the chamber. Laurentius had been expecting them. They were early. He had planned a quick bite before they arrived. For that matter, his meeting with Ionnes went much longer than expected. Still, he expected to move the pair along in short order.

Still manacled, Ionnes stopped before the couple. He touched the woman's slender stomach with his right hand. The young man looked briefly at Governor Laurentius, then turned sharply to object, but held his tongue as Ionnes said to the woman, "Be blessed, sister. Your womb has been opened. You will have a son by this time next year."

He smiled and departed with the three soldiers.

"What the infernum was that?" arrogantly asked the young man to greet his governor.

"A Christian holy man," answered Laurentius. "Fear not. He is harmless, and perhaps his word is right. I know you have long wished for a child."

"How did he know that?"

Laurentius shrugged. Despite the affairs just minutes earlier and his own demons still released, he still was not ready to admit Giovanni had the one direct Appian Way to God. To be honest, he did not fully believe the miracles attached to this old zealot, net, rope and sinkers, but he had wondered if Giovanni might perform some acts of magic when they met. Little did he know Ionnes came from the side of one who was expected to perform before King Herod just hours before He was sent to be crucified. Ionnes would not have entertained Laurentius any more than Yeshua entertained Herod.

"After all that, you still think he is an old fool?" asked Chryspippe.

"Verily," answered Laurentius.

"And, you believe he has no special place with his God? This Yeshua?"

Same answer.

Chryspippe dropped her head with sadness.

"I had wanted you to meet him that you could perhaps see even a little bit of what I find so amazing."

"And, why does it matter to you?" he asked.

Her breath held back until she could hold it no longer. Exhaling, she said, "Because I wish to be baptized by him."

There! She finally said it. Pressing forcefully for days on the tips of her tongue and teeth, it found sweet release to finally say the words.

Laurentius sat a bit stunned. He knew Chryspippe to admire the old man, but he did not expect her to convert. She added to her explanation.

"Please forgive me, my dear, but I believe it is the right thing. After Apollonides was delivered, it was no secret I wanted to know more about the man who could heal my brother. Then, when I heard he brought a man back to life who had been dead for many hours, that added to my interest in him. Then, I understand one of the prisoners almost died by crumbling marble and he was made whole. Then, even the sharks would not dispose of him even after you had him flogged."

The next moment's pause felt longer than it really measured.

A fierceness threatened to rise, but he let it pass as he answered, "I know." He knew not why Giovanni was still with them, and that made the man like no other Laurentius had ever seen.

"I cannot condone," he calmly answered. "I am the Roman governor of Patmos, but I will not forbid you from this baptism. Perhaps that is what it will take for you to see it is nothing, and if I am wrong," he paused, weighing his words, "then I am wrong."

She about tackled him with her hug. She had expected to enter the water with new bruises or be forbade to ever see Giovanni again if her husband did not execute him. She kissed and hugged her husband with the greatest of gratitude, and he let her have the moment. It was good to see her so happy. He firmly feared such joy would be turned to sorrow when and if word got back to Cæsar Domitian, but it did not and could not overcome the sense of contentment and happiness he had found with the world since the day's meeting with the old zealot. He did not want to sleep to awaken tomorrow with his same, old demons back within. No. No. He fervently hoped this newfound peace would last, if only for a little bit longer.

PATMOS

CHAPTER 19

"Giovanni," yelled Guard Mucius.

Ionnes left the crowd of prisoners to answer the guard. Now late morning, the rains had fallen over night and the quarry was still a bit muddy. Shards of sunlight snuck in between the clouds whenever allowed. The air occasionally swirled around them, but most wisps could be heard shaking the taller treetops.

Mucius took hold of Ionnes, presented a key and removed his chains. He turned towards another young soldier to hang the chains with the others.

"Harbor," he pointed.

Glancing past the soldier, Ionnes noticed Dim's questioning expression. A thought occurred, and he did not hesitate to ask.

"Dim should come with me."

Guard Mucius looked at Ionnes like he had just asked to use the latrine, then nodded and flipped his head towards the quarry entrance.

Dim remained in place, a bit dumbfounded. His impressions became even more confused as Mucius stepped forward to also remove his chains. Their musical jingle filled his ears as they fell away from his wrists.

"Harbor," the soldier repeated.

Dim acknowledged and joined Ionnes, leaving the quarry. He could feel the questioning gazes of their fellow prisoners trailing behind them. Would nothing ever make sense? First, you NEVER asked a guard to go with someone else, (unless you were Jack from Sparta who probably could sell snowballs in the Alps). Second, they were released without explanation. Was this another emergency like Euæmon crushed by marble or Quintus when stung by the snake? Maybe somebody died?

Third, why the harbor? They often loaded or unloaded boats, but nobody, even Mucius, would have sent the old man alone to such a task. Usually, they sent at least seven or eight men at any time to load or unload. Nope. None of this made sense, making conjecture that much more of a dissatisfying mystery.

"Ya got any idea what is goin' on?" asked Dim as they proceeded down the hill towards town and harbor.

Ionnes smiled and took a deep breath. The air was sweet as it filled his nostrils; the flavor just as sweet as it burped from lungs.

"Just another blessing when we least expect it," he answered, happy to leave his friend in the dark just a little bit longer. The surprise would not be far off.

Entering the rows of whitewashed houses, the smells of baking pita or blanched grape leaves filled the air. One dwelling shared the smell of freshly applied pitch, sealing the roof for the winter and rainy season. Ionnes waved to the workmen on the roof who started to wave back, then stopped. Oops! They looked like prisoners, even if they were not shackled.

Ionnes seemed to be healing from his severe beating, only days past. He was not up to full speed, even for his age, but presently seemed to have a funny, little spring in his step as they continued down the dirt road. He held up his arms as though to capture and catch even more of the beauty of the morning to save for later. He stopped to look at Dim.

"Would you check to see if any of my sores are still bleeding?"

Dim moved his tunic around to see the old man's skin. He saw nothing new that had not already been cleansed in the surf and now barely clean, baby scabs covering the shrinking welts.

"Good," applauded Ionnes. "You recall how I mentioned how Adonai brings opportunities to us, sometimes with little warning?"

"Yeah."

"This may be one of those moments."

"So, ya do know what is goin' on."

"We shall see. We shall see," winked Ionnes and hastened his steps.

Both the space and quiet moment between them did not last long.

Dim caught up. "Tell me," he urged, "how can ya do all this magic stuff?"

"Magic?" checked Ionnes.

"Yeah. Ya know – healin' the sick. Raisin' the dead."

"Miracles," corrected Ionnes.

"Yeah. Miracles. What other miracles have ya done?"

"Oh, lots," admitted Ionnes without admitting anything.

"Have ya, um, healed a blind man?"

"Yes."

"More than once?"

"Yes."

"How 'bout a deaf man?"

"Yes, and women, too."

"Oh, yeah," corrected Dim. "& women, too." He rolled his eyes, not that he thought women should not be miraculously healed. More a feeling of "what have not you done?"

"Do ya ever fail?"

Ionnes stopped, looking down the road a ways before turning towards Dim.

"Of course. Every day." He resumed walking.

"Like when?"

Ionnes sighed to go along with his deep, heaving breath.

"I pray for Yeshua, the Prince of Peace, to reign here on Patmos as well as Roma, Ierusalem, Ephesus and, well, the rest of the world. I am here by Yeshua's grace, so I pray for all of you here to find Yeshua, and I weep for I know most of you will reject Him."

"Ya pray for us?"

"Of course," assured Ionnes. "Of course. I pray for all of you - for Rabbi Yosef and Seth and Pterrkee and Phranc and Teos." He stopped and placed a hand on Dim's shoulder. "And, you too, brother Dim. I pray for you every day."

He resumed the walk. "But, will any of you answer the call of Yeshua? Like all mortals here, I can pray and direct and expect, but mostly must wait and see. So yes, Dim, I fail often -

even each and every day, but I will likewise tell you that my prayers are also woven with hope. Hope like a large basket a man carries, full of goodness. Fullness he can share. Blessings he wishes to give away, freely. I pray most when my basket of hope needs to be refilled."

He walked in silence for a bit, then muttered, "My heart pants, my strength fails me; as for the light of mine eyes, it also is gone from me."

"What?" asked Dim. "What was that?"

Ionnes sighed again. "Just a Psalm of David."

"Who is David?"

"Yisra'el's greatest king," Ionnes grinned and placed his hand on Dim's shoulder to continue their journey. Ionnes replayed the verse through his mind as he wondered what melody King David had composed for such a Psalm. The Phora streets became more crowded with people as they approached the business district.

"I will tell ya what I do not get," thought Dim.

Ionnes peered over at Dim while continuing to walk. "If ya can do what ya do, why would this Yeshua - your Kurios, send ya t' Patmos?

"What do you mean what I do?" asked Ionnes.

"Ya know," answered Dim, "if ya are such a holy man, why are ya a pris'ner? Why does not yer God protect ya? Does not He care 'bout ya?"

"The Spirit of Yeshua does protect me, and yes, He does care about me. I encounter His love every day. And, not just me. He loves and cares about all of us - even the Greeks - even the Romans - and more. There are peoples I have never seen or heard of, I am certain, that Yeshua died for and knows each of them by name."

"But, ya are still a pris'ner."

"Yes." Facing Dim, Ionnes took hold of his friend's wrists. "I am a prisoner of Roma, for the present. I will not lie. I welcome the day when my chains will be removed, but my life is abnegated."

Dim raised his brows, "Yer what?"

"Um - selfless. Dutiful. Willing to give up for others. Committed to a cause."

Dim understood that. He clutched his marble dolphin a moment in his mind.

"Um," Dim wondered, "Somethin' else I do not get."

Ionnes waited for him to continue.

"You was a leader in Ephesus - at the church there?"

"Yes."

"So, why have they not come t' yer aid? Why are ya here alone?"

"Good question," commended Ionnes. "My first guess is they do not know where I am. I was taken from Roma quickly on a boat hired on the spot. I did not see my brothers on the docks, so they surely did not know I was taken away. I have complete faith they are trying to find me, or at least see if I am still alive."

"And then?"

"And then?"

"Will they rescue ya? We are on an island, not a fortress. At least a coupla times each week that one o' us could slip away if others came t' help."

"True. True," admitted Ionnes. "But I will wait on Yeshua's guidance and word before I flee from this land. You may see me as another prisoner," he pulled his tunic neck down to expose his newly received scars, "but, I am blessed to be beaten for the cause of Christos. And, I will tell you, young man, I am a weak man. I could endure none of this if it were not for the Spirit of Yeshua living within me."

"If ya are a weak man, why would ya place yerself on Roma's trail t' be run down by their chariots?"

Ionnes did not hesitate to answer. "Because the cause of Christos is the one cause worth dying for - even if the world loves its sin. Yeshua gave every one of us His forgiveness from those sins. New life. New light. New love. To see and touch and hear Adonai like never before. Still, I miss His hugs. I used to place my head on His chest and listen to His heart. That sound still beats inside me like a song replaying through my mind, over and over and over, but in Yeshua, I never tire of the beat. It fills me. It paces me. I am made strong in my weakness because of that beat."

He smiled larger than life. Larger than Dim had ever seen.

"And, I must tell you my friend - Yeshua has a Big Heart."

Entering the town square, Ionnes nodded greetings to the townsfolk. Some started to nod back, unlike the first few weeks after Ionnes arrived. His reputation and holy walk had been the hottest of topics on the small island all month. None dared join him, but the people found themselves esteeming Ionnes highly. Many disbelieved or suggested 'rational' explanations, of course, but even many of those were eager to see what marvels the old nonconformant might perform next.

Crossing the town square, Ionnes noted the beggar woman. A few steps further, he recalled seeing her during his first days on Patmos. She sat upon the cobblestones. Her face showed the wear of the hard years. Her clothes displayed her poverty. Her frame slender save her distended stomach. Her feet showed callouses where they were dragged behind legs that had never worked. She sat begging. Her dry hands were empty.

"Do you know her?" asked Ionnes.

Dim looked towards Ionnes, then direction of his gaze.

"That is Barbara," he answered.

She sat near the way to the Acropolis against a white post, calling out for help. The townsfolk knew her well. Not many would still help her.

Ionnes rerouted to speak to her. She noticed the two men on approach - prisoners, at best. Dim she sort of recognized. The old man, not so. She knew they had nothing to give. She would waste no time on either.

Ionnes stopped before her.

"Move," she ordered. "You are blocking my way."

"Oh, I am sorry," he responded and moved closer to the post as not to block others passing who might give her enough bread to fill the day.

She ignored them until Ionnes stooped down beside her. Seated on a small, straw mat, she turned her head towards him, wary of his intentions. She had been kicked before. Some had covered her with the mud on their feet. Children had thrown stones or worse at her, certain she could do no more harm than yell at them. She knew she had nothing of value, but prisoners often had less. Dim had never accosted her, but that did not mean he never would. She was a lame woman - lowly beyond measure. Worthless to most. A burden who made Patmos a little drearier.

"What do you want?" she demanded, looking at both men.

Ionnes did not deter by her words. That made her all the more suspicious.

"To help," he answered.

A couple passing by stopped. Noting Ionnes, they sensed a scene worthy of their attention about to emerge. Another woman followed their lead. Then, another...

"I need not your help," she spit, "nor your pity."

"Fine," rose Ionnes. He looked to Dim and started to walk away.

"Unless you have money to give," she suddenly added.

Both men turned back towards her, taking position before her, like when they had arrived.

"Move," she repeated, but Ionnes stayed before her.

"Move," she said again, louder, then stopped and looked in the old man's eyes. Something stirred in her - a feeling she had long forgotten, like a nursery rhyme her mother recited to her broken child. The feeling swirled around inside her, bouncing around inside her head like the panic of a fleeing mouse.

"You asked for money?" asked Ionnes.

She nodded.

"May I give you something of greater value?"

"What has greater value than money?" she challenged, her eyes narrowing. She peered back and forth at both men.

Ionnes kept his eye on her.

"Freedom," he answered.

"And, what do you know of freedom, slave?" she challenged.

"Much," he answered, "and much I can share with you."

She sat unconvinced, easily cramming back any hope that might dare try to rise.

He stooped down beside her. She drew back her tattered clothing and held her arms over her bosom.

"Barbara," said Ionnes, "neither bread nor money have I to give to you, but in the name of Yeshua, be healed. Rise, take-up your mat and walk."

He stood. She sat there a tad dumbfounded. Who was this strange man telling her to leave? Could not he see that she was lame? Could not he recognize her useless legs?

He waited a moment, then put out his right hand to help her up.

Still she sat, unmoved and perplexed by his offer.

When she did not respond, he stooped down again, this time reaching a calloused hand towards her ankle. He grabbed hold of skin and pinched.

"Ouch!" she cried, then looked at him amazed. She looked towards her feet. Both stood at attention like a Roman field inspection. She had never felt sensation there before.

They looked stronger. Not so atrophied.

"Rise," urged Ionnes, standing again and offering a hand up.

Still looking at her legs, she aimlessly raised her hand. Ionnes took hold and pulled upwards. Her knees bent, this time straightly. They responded to the call to stand. She gave him her other hand as she felt her feet take hold beneath. She had never felt the stones against her heels. Her toes started to tingle. She responded to his pull though she still did not know how to stand. She had never done it before, and fear gripped her. A little cramped hope wriggled out between her ears as her body began to ascend. Her knees shook under the strain. Another moment, and she was upright, standing to full height for the first time in her life.

She had no words as she continued to hold onto Ionnes' right hand. Gently, he pulled her forward. Her body leaned but her feet stayed put.

"You have to move your feet," teased Ionnes.

She looked at him, still puzzled, but soon tried to move her right leg forward. The leg obeyed such a command for the first time. The untwisted foot found new ground. Looking down, she felt the pull against her back leg, so moved it forward to overtake the right like she had seen others do so many times past. It responded, finding firm footing ahead of her. The right leg followed, then the left. A pebble poked the bottom of her left foot. She stopped pressing down, moved a bit to the right and finished her next step. She looked up at Ionnes, then over at Dim who waited, equally speechless. They smiled at one another. Looking back towards Ionnes, she suddenly realized he had let go. She was standing on her own. A lifetime crawling over the hard dust still felt right. She found new altitude. She found new height, and it felt scarier than she had ever dreamed or imagined. She put out her hand to him. He stayed just out of reach before her. One step, and she would reach him again.

So, that one step she took.

A cheer went up around the crowd. Grabbing Ionnes' hand, she looked around. It seemed half of Phora was there. When did they gather? She had not seen or noticed them, but they had certainly noticed her. A part of her wanted to hide, not used to such attention.

"Come," urged Ionnes. "You have been made whole. Find your new path."

She looked at Ionnes as tears rose to block her vision. The floodgates of hope happily erupted. A smile again cracked across her face as she took another step, then another. Soon she accepted no help from Ionnes as she continued to learn new steps. The steps came easier. She started bouncing a bit - a dance in the making. The crowd parted to make room for them. She learned to turn for the first time, almost losing her balance in the move. Ionnes, Dim and others made ready to catch her, but their hands were not needed after all, and she smiled and teared all the more.

"Look," she finally spoke. "Look at me."

Her words were hardly necessary, but she needed to say them, anyway.

"Barbara," called Ionnes, "What is the first word you said to me?"

She stopped moving a moment to look at him and replay the past moments of their meeting.

"Move?" she squeaked, wriggling her nose.

"Yes," he smiled and nodded, "but Yeshua, our Christos gave you the chance to Move instead."

PATMOS

CHAPTER 20

The large crowd snaked through narrow Phora streets towards the harbor. Only a couple thousand people actually lived on the island. You would have thought most of them had shown up for the procession. Passing Roman guards, the soldiers totally gawked at the sight. The head guard sent for reinforcements. Children leapt and danced out front. Old Ionnes and Dim followed them. Barbara followed Ionnes also with a charming, awkward dance in her steps. The rest of the island could have been following thereafter.

The procession bubbled forth with celebration and joy; even more than when a new shipment arrived with delicacies or a harvest celebration. More like the birth of an honored child or the time Nikias the Publican took everyone for rides on his new chariot.

"Did ya plan this?" yelled Dim.

"In my name? No. In Yeshua's Name? Yes."

"This cannot be coincidence," urged Dim. "Ya knew this would happen."

Ionnes placed his hand on Dim's shoulder.

"Divine coincidence is never a coincidence, my friend."

The harbor workers heard the approaching parade. They stopped working to see, to their amazement, the throng of bodies who kept coming and coming then to spread out as room allowed along the docks.

Seven sets of eyes widened most of all at the coming human stampede. The flock headed directly towards them with uncertain purpose until Myron spotted the small man at the epicenter.

"I should have known," said Myron.

"What?" asked Fona, looking towards him.

"Giovanni."

"Where?" craned Fona. "I do not see him."

"Mom, he is right there," pointed Chryspippe.

"Where?"

"Coming right towards us," added Apollonides.

"I do not see him."

Myron rolled his eyes. His wife would see the old man soon enough.

Chryspippe noticed some of the women approaching, led by Madame Her. No way they would approve or understand. Surprisingly, that fact swiftly struck her as trivial and nonconsequential.

Then, she saw Mallia, her hairdresser, looking at bit perplexed by it all, but still sharing her signature smile as her eyes caught hold of Chryspippe.

The procession continued to spread out around the docks. Ionnes beelined straight to the foursome.

"Chryspippe," called Ionnes upon approach. He looked at her family. "Myron. Fona. Apollonides. I am so glad you all came." He also greeted Lorin, Tobie and another slave he did not know.

Apollonides made noises of disgust and disapproval, but none could hear, drowned out by the flood of people.

"Everyone, this is Dimetrius."

They all looked curiously at another prisoner they might have to be nice to.

"And, this is Barbara."

Barbara stepped forth, her smile almost too wide to fit down narrow streets.

Chryspippe and Fona greeted her. She looked familiar, but not sure where. It was Myron who realized the miracle.

"This is not???"

"It is," she laughed.

Myron furrowed his brow but had a good laugh.

"What?" checked Apollonides. The women wanted to know, too.

"Look a little closer," answered Myron.

"Oh my!" said Chryspippe.

Apollonides cursed.

Only Fona did not know, but she did not travel into town as often as the others.

"You have new feet," said Myron, almost as a question.

She bounced in response.

"I never imagined," she started. There were no words she could collect to make her joy adequately shared.

"Nor I," said Chryspippe. "But, how?"

She looked at Ionnes.

"Yeshua," he smiled and pointed both upwards and inwards. "Ready to get baptized?"

She suddenly felt most conspicuous with the hundreds in audience. This certainly was not how she imagined it. She would never absolutely know for the rest of her life, but without Barbara miraculously standing before her, she might have backed out, at least for the day, from so many gawking witnesses to her holy conversion. She looked at her family. What advice could any of them possibly say to dissuade her at this moment? She nodded at Ionnes and turned towards the water.

Some years back a pool had been built in the harbor shallows by stacking rocks to build a rock wall, creating an eddy. It was perfect for wading and playing during the six months of warm weather on Patmos. The women regularly brought their young children down there to play. Chryspippe sometimes joined them when asked. She loved the feeling of the salty water on her feet and ankles as they watched the children play.

This felt like the perfect spot for a baptism.

Ionnes waded out into the knee-deep water. Chryspippe joined him. He stared for some length at Myron. The elder puzzled a moment at the zealot's gaze, then recognized the invitation. He spent a few hard seconds of soul searching before answering. Ionnes kept his eyes on Myron who returned the gaze. He nodded and joined the pair in the water on the other side of his daughter. Fona and Apollonides stood speechless. He felt his mother take hold of his arm seeking a steadier relative to support herself.

As Myron joined Ionnes and Chryspippe, he turned to face the shore, not that many feet off. Some children joined them in the water. All others remained on shore. Even the dock workers all stopped to watch the spectacle.

Ionnes wasted no time.

"Friends," he yelled, "thank you all for coming. I am Ionnes, a Jew from Capernaum. I have spent most of my life in Ephesus, but I was born in Galilee, north of Iudæa. It was there that I came to know Yeshua of Nazareth Who showed Himself to be the promised Messiah, not just of the Jews, but also of the Gentiles. That means all of you. I know most of you have heard many of the tales of Yeshua by this time and are at in some way familiar with The Way. I was one of Yeshua's closest followers – an Apostle. One of His chosen twelve who worked with Him the whole three-and-a-half years He walked and ministered in Iudæa and Galilee and Samaria.

"This is the Savior I serve Who brought all of you here this late morning. I saw Him executed on a Roman cross where He died, but then arose from the grave three days later. This is no fiction but rather an account. I was there and am witness to this truth. And he who has seen has testified, and his testimony is true, and he knows that he is telling the truth, so that you may believe. Then, before Yeshua was taken up to Heaven, He commanded all of His disciples to baptize in His Holy Name. So, we are gathered here today for the first baptism on Patmos." He turned towards Chryspippe.

"Chryspippe of Patmos, do you ransom your life to Yeshua Christos?"

She felt some fear but nodded at Ionnes.

"And, do you seek eternal life with Yeshua in Heaven after you complete this life?"

Again, she shyly nodded.

"Then, as Yeshua commanded, I baptize you in the name of the Father and of the Son and of the Holy Spirit." He cupped his hands, filled them with water, raised it over her head and gracefully poured the water over her head.

She held her hands together and felt a rush of joy as the bit of cold water cascaded over her. The last drizzle of briny love tickled her ears and shoulders. She started giggling with delight.

Myron, still standing in the water, looked forth. Over the heads of the crowd, he could see two of the three Greek temples – one to Artemis and one to Apollo. It seemed odd to start a new following not far from their revered shadows but looking towards his daughter, he saw more joy bubbling forth from her than he ever imagined seeing again - certainly more than he had ever witnessed by her in any god's temple. As her father, he could not help but feel the utmost support for her.

He looked at Fona. She almost looked like she wanted to join him in the water. That look surprised him just about as much as his daughter's baptism.

"Thank you, Giovanni," teehee'd Chryspippe. She wanted to give him a hug but accepted his hand towards the shore.

Suddenly, a woman dashed forward.

"I wanna be baptized. Can I be baptized, too?"

Ionnes smiled. "Of course, Barbara. Come down."

Leaping forth like a young buck in the throes of first rut, she led the race, no one would have guessed that she was virtually unable to stand or walk not an hour earlier. She shivered gratefully as her legs felt for the first time, cold sea water. He repeated invitation to her. She had not heard the gospel as Chryspippe, so he took the chance to quickly explain the gift of eternal and abundant life from Yeshua and the purpose of baptism. Besides, he had a rapt crowd to hear the good news. Barbara glowed ever so brightly as a very special witness to the power of Christos.

Barbara sloshed around the water, almost distracted by her toes digging in the rocky sand and enjoying the new experience of floating sand over her feet.

Myron was about to leave, but Ionnes touched his sleeve. Myron already felt so conspicuous, but respected old Giovanni's request. Ionnes baptized Barbara in similar fashion to Chryspippe, and shortly thereafter led her from the water.

"Anyone else?" yelled Ionnes, then he looked at Myron.

The old man's face clearly answered. Clearly no. Ionnes smiled, nodded and turned towards Dim.

Dim's face said it all. He did not think for one solitary minute that he understood the depth of the invitation, but he was privy enough to figure out no one else did, either. He entered the water without reservation. Not that he had seriously considered baptism any time before that morning. It was not something Ionnes and he had discussed that much, but watching the others, and seeing the power of God instilled in this crazy, old man, he readily recognized that same Yeshua calling him forth. He wallowed forth like a kid who was told by his folks to stay out of the water and not get wet.

"Dimetrius of Pergamos, do you accept Christos Yeshua as Furios?"

"Yeah," smiled Dim.

"And, do you want Yeshua to forgive you your sins?"

"O' course," answered Dim.

Ionnes grabbed hold of Dim and motioned for Myron to do the same.

"Then, in the Name of the Father and of the Son and of the Holy Spirit, I baptize you." He wrapped skinny arms around the younger man's shoulders to tip him backwards as he dipped him down in the water. Myron caught on quickly and helped. Dim almost resisted, but virtually told himself to let it happen. He grabbed a breath as well as a hold of his nose as they submerged him for a second or two, then lifted him back to his feet. Drenched, he was more surprised than anyone what had just happened. He expected drops of water over his head like the women. It would not occur to him for another hour or two that Ionnes chose that fashion of baptism out of chaste respect for the women. Drenching their clothing would have been bad form and considered inappropriate bodily exposure throughout both Greece and the Roman empire. More so for the aristocrat Chryspippe, even if Ionnes did not seem to give much respect to societal class positions. Barbara he would not dunk for exactly the same reasons as Chryspippe. But for Dim, a man, and for that matter, a prisoner/slave – social etiquette or decency mattered far less.

Dim also later wondered if he let himself be dunked out of desperation. Was he looking for a magic formula to gain him freedom from Roman bondage? Perhaps, but God knew not blindness to the heart of this lowly prisoner who befriended His disciple. Despite the pain and loss and injustice, Dim lived not forgotten by Yeshua, but rather bought and *redeemed* just the same as everyone else on Earth.

"What does it mean t' be redeemed?" Dim asked Ionnes one night while they laid heads down to sleep for the night. The prisoners had grown accustomed to these nightly discussions. The quiet words whispered a hope that all of them had previously lost somewhere along the way. Now hope found itself ushered right into their little barracks, complete with his own bedroll. Hope could be locked behind the door, same as all of them, but amazingly rose above the pain and fear and floggings and chains. Many had come to fear hope more than the whip. Ionnes showed them the foolishness of such practice. Some accepted the newfound hope easier than others, but all still felt its effects.

"What is redeemed?" thought Ionnes. "It has quite a strong meaning for both Jews and Christians. And, the meanings have wonderful similarities. Like when Adam and Eve sinned and were expelled from Eden."

"Who are Adam & Eve?" He had asked about Eve before when they were nursing Euæmon.

"The first man and woman. Adonai's first created people."

"Okay," accepted Dim.

"So, after their exile from Eden, a garden of unspeakable beauty, they lost all because of their sin, but Adonai promised them a Savior who would redeem them from their loss and sin.

"Then, Adonai made a covenant with Moses and the Yisra'elites."

(*"Moses," thought Dim. "There is that name again."*)

They were bound by slavery in Egypt. Adonai led them out in mighty and miraculous ways. It is an amazing story. That was an amazing redemption. Then, in our holy writings, others received redemption from Adonai - David from King Saul; the prophet Elijah from King Ahab and his wife Jezebel; others. And, all those point to the greatest redemption of all, when Yeshua was sacrificed like an unblemished, sinless lamb on a Roman cross for your sins. If you accept His love, you too may be redeemed."

"But what does redeem mean?" pressed Dim. His original question.

"Oh," paused Ionnes. "Um, I am sorry. Let me see. Let us say one of your relatives died. You could be in line to get the land. If you qualify, you could redeem the land. It then becomes yours. In similar fashion, when your old self dies to sin, Yeshua steps up to redeem you and make you His."

Ionnes grinned to himself. He just remembered something one of his students said…

"Not long before I was arrested, I was teaching a group of young men in Ephesus. I had one special student who absorbed the good news of Yeshua like thirsty ground sucks in the rain. He could never be saturated.

We spoke of redemption, and he said it in a way I had never considered before." Ionnes turned over to his side and lifted head to face Dim as he rested on one arm. Dim looked at Ionnes, barely a shadow within a shadow in the dark hut.

"What did he say?"

Ionnes replayed the words through his mind as he spoke. "My student broke down the word into two sections. "RE" meant to do it again. "DEEM" meant to give it value. We deem a boat a worthy vessel to take us from the island. We deem each other as worthy of the labors given us. So, to be redeemed is to be valued once again. For Yeshua to remove our sins gives each of us new value in His kingdom. I will tell you, it gave me shivers that day I first heard that."

Dim remained silent.

"Does that answer your questions?"

"Uh-huh," he sighed then wondered, "What became o' yer student?"

"Oh, he lives in Smyrna. He may have returned there. I pray I will see him again before I depart this world. He has blessed my life more ways than I can count on fingers and toes and teeth combined."

"What is his name?"

"Polycarpus."

"Polycarpus," repeated Dim. He never knew whom he would need help from when and if he ever left Patmos. It was good to know a name that might help him. He clutched his little dolphin necklace as he turned over.

"Polycarpus," he repeated, then added, "Goodnight, Ionnes."

"Goodnight, Dim."

<>< >< >< >< >< >< >< >< >< ><

Now baptized, Dim left the pool in the harbor a little wetter and a lot more blessed.

"Anyone else?" called Ionnes.

The audience stood restlessly. None came forth. The sounds of Roman soldiers on horses could be heard approaching. Some quickly disbanded before they might be seen. Others watched, then turned away as the soldiers came into view.

Ionnes and Myron waded out of the water and stood by Myron's family. Dim stayed close by, as did Barbara for different reasons. She did not understand what she had just received but knew that she wanted more. She also feared if she offended Ionnes that he might take away her healing.

"What is going on here?" demanded Lucius, the Captain of the Guard, briskly riding up on his horse.

"Just a religious gathering," answered Ionnes.

Lucius was about to draw his sword for effect. The other soldiers behind him would take his lead and unsheathe their swords. A bloodbath could ignite like a spark on tinder, but then Lucius saw Myron. And Chryspippe.

"Are you in any danger?" he asked them.

"Not hardly," answered Myron. "We invited the gathering." He moved his arm across the docks as he added, "But, I will admit, it was more like the Circus Maximus than I expected."

Lucius dropped down from his horse, his hands still on the reins. The horse tried to dislodge and spit out the bit with his tongue at times.

"Pardon me, m'Lord Myron. I received report of a mob heading to the harbor."

"It was more like a parade," corrected Myron, then consoled, "In your place, I would have feared the same."

"Yes sir," nodded Lucius. His horse continued to shake his head.

The crowds were already disbanding, most heading back towards the town square or their homes; most chattering away to one another about what they had just seen. Only a couple known informants stayed behind to see if anyone got arrested or disemboweled. The sun came forth from behind clouds. The sparkles on the harbor blinded those who looked forth. It felt amazing to behold. Even the Captain of the Guard became touched by the glorious sights.

Then, he eyed Ionnes, the old Christian zealot and knew somehow this involved him.

"And, what mischief are you up to here, Giovanni?"

The old man took a couple of steps forth towards the Captain.

"Just fulfilling my mission here on Patmos."

"That is what I am afraid of," admitted the Captain. "Are we done?"

"Yes," answered Ionnes, though he knew for a fact they were just getting started.

The Captain knew he had no authority over the governor's wife or her family. His job was to protect Romans and squelch any rebellious intent. He saw the seeds of such in Ionnes, but accompanied by Chryspippe and family, he would leave well enough alone - for now. It occurred to him what might be going on in the home of the governor that Laurentius ordered they flog old Ionnes. Even that episode had strange details attaching themselves like horsehair to his kilt.

"Thank you, Captain," said Myron.

The Captain saluted with right arm across his chest, then remounted his steed. Turning to his troops, he yelled, "Make sure all is secure, and nothing is disturbed, broken or stolen. It appears the mob has disbanded but check the town and report anything that seems suspicious." And, with that he rode off.

The soldiers went off to follow orders.

"Thank you," said Ionnes.

Myron looked at Ionnes. "I should drown you myself for bringing that crowd."

"Aye," agreed Ionnes and the two men smiled. "I would tell you it was not my doing, but I doubt you would believe me."

"Aye," answered Myron.

"Where is Apollonides?" said Chryspippe.

The group looked around. Chryspippe had already scanned the area. They only verified what she already knew. He had departed them again – behavior that had become common most recently. What they could not see as they left the harbor for home was Apollonides on foot, hastening to the Temple of Artemis. The temple priests wondered what caused the grand commotion. Apollonides approached, more than glad to give report. The priests showed concern. They had already heard reports on the mainland of disturbances caused by these Christian zealots. One temple priest began his vocation in Ephesus. When a young novitiate, he recalled a Christian disciple – oh, what was his name? It began with P. Panos? Peter? Not, not Peter. Paulos? Yes, Paulos. He recalled the name by its oddity – a Roman name attached to a Jewish man. What was it Paulos did? That's right. He disrupted the Temple to Diana in Ephesus. Some silversmith riled up the people. To his best recollection, it wound up not amounting to much, but he knew that would not be the end of such troubles from this group. It concerned him all the more to hear such a missionary had come to Patmos. The gods had blessed them up until now, and they prayed for deliverance from this cult.

Apollonides thanked them, then headed on to the Temple of Apollo.

PATMOS

CHAPTER 21

The rain fell like a legion of leaky wooden buckets. The wind oftentimes blew it all sideways. Prisoners pressed on, drenched. The best shower any of them had had all year. The cold water stung their senses and made them shiver as well as made the stone more slippery. Huge drops wrung from beards and hair. Euæmon looked upwards to the sky and drank in the torrent. Phranc praised the gods for the water though he never liked being wet. Jack walked past Rabbi Yosef and Ionnes to say, "Hope you brought your ark."

Others grumbled, their words hidden by the rhythmic patter of the weather. Roman guards watched, but the prisoners had to screw up pretty badly before one of them would step out from under a shelter to flog. The players understood the rules of the game and all played their parts perfectly; better than a scene in any Greek drama.

Ionnes moved logs with Rabbi Yosef. It was foolish to put the two old men together, but that was how they were assigned, so each took advantage of the other's advanced age to work a bit slower.

"So," started Ionnes, lifting his side of the log, "Do you sin?"

"My sins are not your matter, apostate," grumbled the old Jew.

"Of course not," agreed Ionnes. "That was not the question. I merely asked if you sinned?"

"Of course, I am guilty of sin, much to my shame."

"As am I," confessed Ionnes. "So, how do you atone for your sins - however big or small?"

The chunk of wood pressed hard against their brittle arms. The rabbi still had some meat on him from before his arrest. Ionnes' looked more like winter twigs. The chunk of wood preferred the ground. The two old men would have liked it better that way, too if given the option. The rain made it no easier, making the barkless poles more slippery as well as heavier.

"That is my affair alone," heaved Yosef. "There." He pitched his head to where they would go with the log.

"The LORD's temple is gone," said Ionnes with perhaps the most compassion he had shown since arriving. "The sacrifices were destroyed with the bricks."

"Gimme that, Old Man," appeared Seth, and picked up the entire log by himself. Impatience ruled. He walked some steps then dropped it right where he wanted it. Ionnes and Yosef stayed with him just in case he needed the help, but knew they were more in the way.

"Thank you," said Ionnes.

"Bah," answered Seth, and went back to the pit. The old men waited to attend to their pole when the slab rolled forth and over.

"Your friend is a sheep," chided Ionnes. Yosef looked at him perplexed and a bit vexed.

"Did not you hear him? Baa."

Yosef rolled his eyes and turned away with well-practiced long suffering.

Ionnes laughed as he watched and waited for their turn. It would come soon.

"Quiet," yelled Guard Mucius.

The two old men glanced towards the sound. Mucius was addressing Minos and Phranc. Both turned and separated, adding space between them and the crusty guard.

Yosef looked at Ionnes who looked to him more like a half-drowned cat.

"I wait," he eventually said. "I wait for the temple to be rebuilt. Someday it shall be. I will make atonement for my sins then."

"What if it is not rebuilt before you depart this world? Moses was very specific. Sins are forgiven only with blood sacrifice. And, it had to be at the temple."

"What about your sins?" barked Yosef. "Where is your blood atonement? Where is your temple?"

Ionnes stood a little taller as he smiled and said, "Messiah Yeshua shed His blood, once for all, for our sins. His death on the cross is His sacrifice - the sacrificial Lamb."

"And of the temple?"

"His body is the temple. I heard him tell the Jewish Authorities in Ierusalem more than once – '*Destroy this temple and in three days I will raise it up.*' They did not know His words or their meaning. He spoke not of the temple in Ierusalem, but the temple of His body. And, on the third day after his sacrificial death wrought and brought by their destruction, he rebuilt that temple and returned to this life."

The huge slab came close and they pressed in to guide it along with the rest of the men. The wet ground bogged down the rolling logs, making the journey that much harder. Yosef got his fingers stuck under the log for a second, and pulled away quickly, the wince of pain filling his fingers. No permanent damage, but a lot of pain for the moment. He mostly ignored it and kept to task lest the guards jumped in. He thought he heard their chuckles behind him.

"I pray for you," Yosef finally said between heaving breaths.

"And, I you, my brother," answered Ionnes, equally gasping for air.

"Just make sure you know to which God you are praying."

"There is only One," nodded Ionnes. "Only One that I know."

PATMOS

CHAPTER 22

"Why do not you just kill him and be done with it?"

Governor Laurentius peered intently at Makrinos as he dwelled upon his proconsul's question.

Makrinos continued, "I know not why you put up with him. He stands against all that Roma and the empire holds precious. I say run him through and be done with him."

Birds ever chirped away outside the governor's office, louder by the pause of the two men. Laurentius had heard Makrino's side comments throughout the months after Ionnes' arrival, ever disapproving of the apostle and perhaps also indirectly towards the governor.

"Do not you fear the gods?" challenged Laurentius.

"No more than they fear the words of this charlatan. Even the spiders of Roma could learn from this one."

"Perhaps," nodded Laurentius, then looked intently at Makrinos. "Is that your fear, sir? That I am caught in his web?"

"No, my governor," lied Makrinos. "Your wisdom and guidance are not in question. I challenge you not and forgive me if I harbored that impression. Nay. I only ask to understand better your intentions. As you know, it is commonly Roma's way to deal harshly with those of his pedigree and motive, yet he even as a prisoner of Roma continues to labor to the very purpose that brought him to us in chains."

Laurentius felt the stiffness in his jaw set in. "The emperor himself sent him to us to work the quarry and that he does."

"Yet," checked Makrinos, "does not he still preach the ways of his crucified God?"

"That is what zealots do," declared Laurentius, his voice rising in volume. "You can blind him, deafen him and cut out his tongue and a zealot will still seek to please his God."

"True, true," admitted Makrinos, "but if you seek to maim him, why stop there?"

"You know his account," bantered Laurentius. "Domitian had him poisoned, then boiled him to death, yet here he lives, untouched and unharmed by Roma's best."

"Never heard I of one returned after lopping away his head."

"Nor I," admitted Laurentius, his head and eyes drooping a bit, donning a faraway look as he imagined such an execution. Old Ionnes' head kept talking from the ground praising Yeshua as his body found its top and reattached it. If the governor could imagine such a miracle, he knew the gods could, too.

He glanced towards Makrinos. Many Romans sought to take down their superiors. Best way to create vacancies they could fill. Makrinos fit that mold as well as any Laurentius had known.

"Keep your eyes pared upon the zealot," directed Laurentius, "and report your observations."

"Of course, my governor," subserviently nodded Makrinos. "It is only my will to serve."

Laurentius returned the nod. "That is all."

Makrinos stood, then paused like one considering whether to say any more. Keeping his tongue, he turned to go.

"Oh," called Laurentius before Makrinos reached the archway. The proconsul turned. "I need to know I can count on you."

"Of course," again lied Makrinos.

"And, that means no reports to Cæsar Domitian without my approval."

"Uh," Makrinos took a moment to weigh his words, laboring through a suddenly thick silence between them. Laurentius did not await any two-faced response.

"If word gets back to me that you contacted Domitian or the Senate without my authorization, regardless of the outcome, I will run you through quicker than a speared fish."

Makrinos remained frozen by the arch.

"Do I make myself clear?"

"Perfectly," dryly answered Makrinos, then turned to go.

Laurentius felt amused satisfaction to see his conniving proconsul depart the governor's chamber with quick, stiff steps slapping floor tiles, but the entertainment lasted not long. Makrinos knew well the dagger's best place in a man's back.

"Et tu Makrinos?" misquoted the governor with a mutter and a sip of wine. "Et tu Makrinos."

PATMOS

CHAPTER 23

The flames bounced all around him as he swam through thick, swampy murk. To the left hungry lava. To the right bottomless bubbling tar. Sulfurous stench pierced and divided each nostril. His eyes burned as though poked with orange glowing rods. He gasped for breath without avail. His joints terribly ached, each threatening to seize up or shut down. Waves of filth washed over him, on and on. No sooner did he spit the muck out of his mouth when more took its place with the next pounding wave.

Figures ahead fiercely loomed like fiery mountains. They knew his name and he knew their venomous intent. He absorbed their nefarious wishes. During his life, evil was neither friend nor foe. It just was, though it more often resembled foe. He continued in his struggles to swim but knew his efforts to be wasted as the noxious current led him directly wherever it wanted. Choking from the sludge and heat and poisonous wind, he coughed for the last moment, expelling all air from his lungs just in time to be pulled under. Whirlpool? Talons yanking down on his ankles? It mattered not. Down and down he submerged with no air in his lungs left to scream. His vacant lungs refilled with the slurry mire. Each pore and crevasse of his being absorbed the toxins, consuming and corroding his flesh. He knew not if he was blind or all light extinguished. It likewise mattered not as his brain measured its last flicker of being.

Darkness became complete.

Kynops awoke.

The sweat continued to pour out as he reassessed his surroundings. His cool home with the taunting shadows. Shaking, he arose, felt around for his tinder box and made the small flame – enough to light a lantern. His trembling hands could scarcely bring the flame to the wick. He adjusted the wick, then lit another. The flames flickered in unison. He saw the shadows on the walls, dancing to avoid the presence of light.

Biting an apple, he chewed and thought.

"What to do? What to do?" he fumed as the nightmare continued to replay between his thoughts. It frightened him beyond measure. Fortunately, it was not as bad as some of the other nightmares that recently visited him.

He coughed a bit, choking on a small chunk of apple. From that, the idea took hold. He struggled to focus for a bit, but the concepts eventually strung together like a twisted seashell necklace.

"Ionnes," he spit, grinding the sweet pulp with the last of his yellowy-bronze teeth. What weakness could he exploit?

"Chryspippe," he added. His incantations in their home just nights back were repelled and came back to him. How could she do this? She had not the power of Kynops!

"Apollonides," he then whispered to the shadows. They jolted. An incantation formed on his lips and he pointed from shadow to shadow.

"Go," he ordered. They obeyed, quaking as they disappeared.

He sat alone in the gloom, finishing his apple as he considered his next strategic moves.

PATMOS

CHAPTER 24

"Oy!" grumbled Rabbi Yosef at workday's end, walking back to the barracks. "Sometimes I wish Elohim would just take me away from all this for good. I never felt such love for our people enslaved in Egypt as I have since the day I came to Patmos."

"Tough day?" asked Seth.

"You were there," snapped the old rabbi. "The rock begged for mercy the whole day. Everything we touched crumbled to dust. No man could spit without getting the lash."

"Oy!" agreed Seth, dropping his head while rubbing his ridged and rippled shoulders. Each man's back had a combination of floggings, some fresh that day, some yesterday, some the day before and so on. Each day had its degrees of healing. Everything throbbed or itched all the time. Sleep never came easy but was still the only true form of escape during each twenty-four hours.

Both heard the clicking of Euæmon behind them. His walking stick ever close by, he continued to limp as the weeks passed.

"Never have I heard of half a miraculous healing," grumbled the old rabbi.

"So, you think Euæmon is faking his limp?"

"I think Yochanan is not the holiest of prophets he proclaims."

A snort of laughter burst out of Seth's nose.

"What?" challenged Yosef, daring an answer.

"The man was crushed under a wall of stone. It is a miracle he is alive, much less up and walking. I love Elohim with all my heart, but I have never seen such miracles from my own words."

Yosef deflated a bit.

"And, neither have you," added Seth.

"Oy vey!" admitted Yosef, feeling even more the weight of his years.

They entered the encampment, accepted their dinner, and sat to eat. Sometimes it felt better than food in the belly to get off their feet and finally sit for the first time all day. Others followed; Euæmon and Phranc and Talor. Others. Eating. Some talking. Some keeping to themselves.

Ionnes entered the group, passing by the food. He took a bold drink of water from the bucket, staring at the water for some moments before he replaced the ladle. The patterns to watch the old saint had become well-worn and hard to break. Ionnes acknowledged none, but went to a place apart from the others, still within view of the guards. There with his back to the party, he dropped to his knees and sunk down deep. His back started to bounce and heave, showing a man in deep grief. All watched from afar but kept distance. Even Phranc seemed to be wary to disturb Ionnes.

"Where's Dim?" asked Talor, looking around.

The group joined him, looking from face to face. No Dim. A sense of panic, not unlike when a parent loses a child in the marketplace, began to move through the prisoners. Talor went to the guards.

"Did anything happen to Dim today?"

They shrugged.

He bit his lip, and moved over to Ionnes, still weeping on the ground. He placed a hand on Ionnes' back and asked, "Is Dim okay?"

"He is," answered Ionnes without looking. Then, he said something else, but Talor was not sure he heard correctly or what it meant.

"What is that?" he asked, but Ionnes withheld answer, keeping his vigil against the dirt.

Talor stayed a few more moments before returning to the group.

"What did he say?" asked Phranc.

"He said Dim was okay. That much I got out of him."

"So, that is not why he weeps?" asked Minos.

"I think not," answered Talor.

They all stopped to wonder awhile.

"Did he say anything else?" asked Phranc.

"Um. I think so, but I may not have heard him right."

"What did he say?"

Talor replayed the broken words through his mind a bit to try to make the sounds emulate Ionnes.

"He said – something like – um – the ninth of something. Ninth of Ov. Ninth of Oaf. Something like that."

Suddenly, Rabbi Yosef fell forward beside them, dropping his dinner on the dirt. Seth grabbed hold of him, then realized the rabbi was not ill, but joining Yochanan in his grieving.

"Av," corrected Seth, tears starting to well in the big man's eyes. "The ninth of Av. We did not realize today's date." He turned away to kneel and join Rabbi Yosef on the ground. Both threw dust on their heads as they wailed.

The others sat stunned, not sure what to make of the spectacle, and understanding little more than before. Conversations waned. Most sat feeling compassion for their fellow prisoners without even knowing why.

Dim came up the hill.

"What is goin' on?" he asked, looking around.

Talor nodded towards Ionnes, off away from the group.

"Of course," he said, looking at Ionnes, Yosef and Seth as he went for dinner.

The others started to fidget.

"Do you know what is wrong?" asked Minos, more an impatient demand than a question.

"Yes," answered Dim seriously.

Their faces pressed him for more.

"Ionnes asked the date to one in town on his way here from the salt ropes. He discovered it was the ninth of Av in their Ierusalem calendar. That is the date their temple was destroyed over twenty years back."

"Hah!" criticized Pterrkee. "He seeks to topple Apollo's temple, then weeps for his own." None seemed as impressed with Pterrkee's insight. He hmmph'd and went into the lodge to his bed even though full daylight would be with them a couple more hours.

Another hour and the deep grief passed. Ionnes stood, brushed off himself, then went to Rabbi Yosef, still beating his breast. He knelt next to the rabbi to place an arm around him.

Yosef leaned into Ionnes and accepted the comfort of this one fallen from the faith.

Teos brought them water. All accepted a drink, then rose to sit upon stumps and rocks, each man still numb in the aftermath of deep grieving.

Yosef looked at Ionnes with new eyes.

"I was there," he said, eyes filled with pain and tears in rapid order. He laid his head forward towards his knees as tragic and ruthless memories pounced upon his emotions.

Ionnes placed a hand on the old man's shoulder. He had been hundreds of miles away as Bishop of the Ephesus church, but his heart broke knowing the pain and torment filling his beloved Iudæa and especially Ierusalem.

"Tell me," urged Ionnes. "I truly wish to know." Yosef looked up, his eyes meeting the old apostle, but his lips moved not.

<>< ><> <>< ><> <>< ><> <>< ><> <>< ><>

Some days passed with nary a word from the old rabbi. His broken heart stubbornly refused to heal or lap up his grief. He worked the quarry with soulless intent, moving through the motions; barely responding to the whip. He neither ate nor slept and replied not to Seth's concerns.

"Another one gone," nodded Guard Ernesto with a grin to his *amicis*. They could readily tell when one gave up on life. He would be gone within the week or so, usually run through by Roman steel for apathetic noncompliance.

"I know not what to do," fretted Seth.

"Pray," suggested Ionnes, "as well as attend to him."

"I have done both unceasing," said Seth. "He looks at me with dead eyes and tells me he is well."

"Persist," added Ionnes. "You are not alone in your prayers. We share your pain and despair."

Seth opened mouth to object, but found the words hollow and easily broken. He nodded acknowledgement and turned to attend to his rabbi.

The next two days passed with similar lethargic slowness.

The prisoners collected marble like wilted flowers, piling them onto an old wooden cart. Dim ever worked with verve and purpose, already seeing signs of the marble tapering down. Hefting a large rock upon the cart, he noted Ionnes coming alongside.

"There is one thing I still do not get 'bout Yeshua," opened Dim to Ionnes.

"Join the palæstra," quipped Jack walking past. They smiled but otherwise ignored him and kept working in sync to continue their chat.

Dim said, "Ya told me the Jewish leaders had Yeshua killed."

"Aye."

"But He died attached t' a cross – a Roman ex'cution."

"Verily," answered Ionnes as they passed Rabbi Yosef and Seth, each toting a chunk of marble. "The Jews feared Yeshua's acclaim; that He might lead the people to revolt and bloodshed. The high priest that year, Caiaphas, decided Yeshua should die - to protect the nation. He thought it better One should die than many."

"Caiaphas always scared me," said a voice. Ionnes and Dim turned towards the source.

Rabbi Yosef placed a stone on the cart as he looked at them and repeated, "Caiaphas always scared me."

Ionnes glanced over at Seth who looked as surprised as the other two.

Rabbi Yosef looked at each but still spoke to none in particular, "He commanded our fear. By time I completed Hebrew school, and also my internship as a scribe to take on the role of Rabbi, he had retired. His younger brother Theophilus became high priest, but Caiaphas still kept his bed made in the temple. When he coughed, we all still brought him a kerchief."

Awaiting no acknowledgement of his words, he turned to get another rock. Seth shrugged at Ionnes as he also turned to kept pace with Yosef who seemed to speed up a bit.

"The hope of freedom blossomed all over Iudæa like pink or white petals covering the fruit tree," entered Rabbi Yosef plunking down onto his favorite rock in camp next to Ionnes, Dim and others. Seth followed. Yosef glanced over at him almost perturbed with a leave-an-old-man-alone expression – a response Seth knew oh so well and wisely ignored.

"It seemed like everyone came to arms overnight, ready to finish the cause and expel Roma forever. It reminded me of the Jews' return from Babylonian exile, working to rebuild the wall around Ierusalem under Nehemiah. Each wore his sword at his side as he worked."

"Who is Neh'miah?" Dim whispered to Ionnes. Ionnes placed his hand of Dim's shoulder clearly answering, "Later."

"Then," muttered Rabbi Yosef, "the attack at Beth Horon surprised all. None ever expected to overcome a Roman Legate so easily, and for the first time I could recall, Roma felt like a foe we could conquer. Yet, for all our verve and commitment, when Roma sent uncounted thousands of troops, we quickly became no match. They did not try to destroy us all at once, but took us piece by piece, like we were a large chunk of old jerky that they could not eat all at once. But, once they started gnawing on it, the end was inevitable."

"So," asked Ionnes, "you were in Ierusalem during the initial attacks?"

"Oh, no, no, no," Yosef shook his head. "I came not to Ierusalem until much later, keeping to my synagogue in Gazara. The home of the Macabees seemed like the perfect place to rebel against the tyrant Roma. Of course, Gazara was nothing like its former glory."

"Where is Gazara?" asked Talor.

"Roughly halfway between Ierusalem and Ioppa which is on the Great Sea, it filled the plain with its glory and gladness. Barley and flax and vineyards with grapes the size of Solomon's nose made the sweetest wine I ever sipped. Solomon received it as a wedding gift from Pharaoh – oh, I forget which one, as dowry for his princess daughter. But, fallen from its glorious beginnings, it was little more than a humble, little farming community by time I settled there as rabbi. I would not say we were without our share of Roman atrocities and cruelties, but our little berg became the place the soldiers would rest and take vacation before heading to the beaches and brothels of Ioppa.

"I would love to tell you that as soon as I received the news that Ierusalem was free of Roman tyranny, that I raced there right that day to see for myself and celebrate with my Jewish brethren, but that is not what happened. I knew Roma would retaliate, so like a coward, kept my distance.

"Then, when our people destroyed Gallus' forces at Beth Horon, I finally ventured to Ierusalem. And, I am so glad that I did. No man alive could believe the difference. For the first time in our lives, we lived under the rule of no other power save our own and the power of Elohim. There was dancing in the streets for weeks. Even as they worked, the holiday within continued. The streets were quiet as peace at night. Each man felt the Hand of God upon his shoulder. I would ever call it amazing.

"The calm before the storm," interjected Seth.

"Aye," agreed the rabbi and others with a sigh. "Revolution ever rumbles and froths under the surface of every Jew throughout Iudæa. You can still feel those turbulent rumblings today, even here on Patmos, but they never create a chasm big enough to entrap all of Roma, and so our mourning and travail remains ever our companion."

He sighed again as one who has been beaten a few too many times. Eyes first fixed on the dirt before him, he suddenly looked up and saw the others around him, wondering if there would be more to hear.

"So," the rabbi straightened up, "none felt more surprise than myself when I heard Ierusalem had been cleansed of all Romans."

"No Romans in Ierusalem?" challenged Pterrkee, entering the circle of men. "Impossible. Ridiculous, in our lifetimes."

"You are wrong," answered Yosef.

"Yes, it was so," assured Ionnes.

"How did you know, holy man? Were you there?"

"No, I am sorry to say," answered Ionnes. "I lived in Ephesus during those years, but word traveled to us quickly of the revolt."

They looked towards Seth who shrugged those big shoulders.

"I was only an infant at the time. I recall nothing of leaving our home in Cæsarea. My earliest memories take me to the coast south of Tyre where papa could tend his nets and act like he knew nothing when Romans faced him. Years later, after we returned to Cæsarea, he said to his shame most of his catch went to Roman mouths."

Seth felt the weight of the years and his father's shame piled upon. His head down, those big shoulders drooped under the weight.

"I read of your rebellion," interrupted Mothcrates. "A Jewish historian, as I recall; Josephus I think was his name."

"Yosefus the traitor," violently scoffed Rabbi Yosef. "Worse than a Samaritan dog. Believe nothing you read of him. He writes for Roma. He begs on Roma's leash."

"The Jews no longer speak his name," added Seth.

"Pray, do tell," requested Mothcrates. "What terrible atrocities did such a man do? You Jews make craggy mountains out of the easiest knolls. You would stone a man for the smallest violations of your laws. Even in this last year with you, I have heard you condemn men who caused no more than a minor nuisance to you or your culture."

"Like who? Or, when?" challenged Yosef. "Give me one example."

Mothcrates paused. "Um, no one occasion comes to mind, but when it does, I shall make declaration."

"Bah," answered Yosef.

"You curse the Romans," said Seth.

Yosef gave him a 'Whose side are you on?' glance, then said, "Every man here curses the Romans." He then looked face to face at his fellow prisoners, his gaze pausing a moment on Ionnes. Then, Phranc. Then he added, "Perhap."

"So," returned Mothcrates, "This Josephus. What terrible things did he do to deserve your condemnation?"

Rabbi Yosef spat to begin his answer.

"First, let me tell you, I personally knew Yosefus, the son of Matthias, so my testimony of the turn-tunic dog is not merely hearsay.

We met in Ierusalem around a decade before the revolt. My, he was full of himself. More egotistical than most teens. He had recently returned from a three-year sabbatical, living in a hermitage in the wilderness where Moses and the Yisra'elites spent forty years before entering Canaan…"

"Moses again," whispered Dim to Ionnes. The elder smiled.

"One would think after such a spiritual sojourn, the partaker would have found humility and grown in age and wisdom. For Yosefus it showed not so. He boasted of his devout years without restraint or forbearance. I was never impressed, and others pressed upon him temperance of his ego and pride. All such fell on deaf ears.

Like me, he was a Pharisee."

"A Pharisee?" checked Mothcrates.

"The Jewish sect with the most political members who maintained control of Ierusalem and all of Iudæa for many years.

As the years continued, we went our ways – me to Gazara and Yosefus remained in Ierusalem, serving Elohim and sometimes serving as a judge of the people."

"Is not that young for a judge?"

"Yes," answered Yosef, "Typically, but even at fourteen the Jewish fathers sought his insights and counsel. He was a brilliant young man. Too bad he also knew it." He sighed, deeply and sorrowfully.

"I can be a weak man," said the rabbi. "Elohim knows. I can be the worst, and I sometimes wonder if Elohim did not judge Yisra'el for my sins alone. Was not Roman occupation judgment enough for our sins? Scripture is so clear on this, yet we Jews never seemed to learn. 'Trust in the LORD with All of your heart. Lean not on your own understanding. Acknowledge the LORD in All of His ways and He will make your paths straight.' Elohim said that for each man, but also for our entire nation. His covenant with us He made clear and without fault. If I stubbed my toe, my entire body reacted and felt the pain. If I sinned, all of Yisra'el reacted and felt the pain.

"It is there that I understand Yosefus the least. He well knew the law and the prophets as well as any man alive, I would say, and he supported the rebellion. They gave him the militia over Galilee to defend, and he went to war against Roma. I know all this to be true. But it is what came thereafter that I cannot fathom or truly understand. Perhaps we were wrong to send him. He knew the law as well as any man, but that did not make him a general, prepared for war and leading men into battle. Then, I think that is what this sinful world would have me believe, and I recall Jehoshaphat beginning the march into battle with the temple priests in the lead."

The old man started dancing around gayly, singing, "Praise be the LORD. His mercy endures forever and ever. Praise be the LORD, His mercy endures forever and ever."

The others enjoyed the spectacle, laughing and smiling.

Even Minos cracked a thin, dry smile.

"Or, even Gideon," he stopped, catching his breath, "defeating the Midianites army with only three-hundred men. Oh my! So, I can totally appreciate and support the decision to make Yosefus leader to defend Galilee. But, when Elohim's judgment is decided, our prayers of repentance and mercy still stumble through the dark."

"Too little, too late?" suggested Mothcrates.

"Yes," affirmed Yosef. "Vespasian's troops marched from the north, taking back town after town right on to Capernaum. We all expect Yosefus knew not what to think or do, filled with fear and ever retreating. I am ever plagued with the vision in my mind of Yosefus, cornered and hiding in a cave with thirty others, instilling me first with fear, then repulsion. I see them cowering, knowing the fate for those who surrendered to Vespasian. Roma loves a slow, torturous death."

He peered with perplexity at Ionnes.

"It amazes me beyond understanding when I think that Domitian Cæsar first chose to have you poisoned. Most men I know would have far preferred that manner of execution over crucifixion or other barbaric manners."

Ionnes nodded. He had wondered at that, too. As the only one of the twelve who stood before Yeshua dying on the cross, Yeshua had often protected him, and in that, while he stood before Domitian, swilling poison, he believed a swift death to be equal to God's mercy. His spiritual discernment suggested differently, but drinking the caustic cocktail seemed to possibly be Yeshua's plan. Then, when he did not die from the deadly poison, he instead lived to be boiled. Even then, Yeshua foiled that plan of execution, creating the perfect platform from which Ionnes could preach His Word. Many Romans surely believed in Yeshua after that display, some aloud; most silently."

"Hmmmmmph!" replied Rabbi Yosef. "As I recall, we were talking about Yosefus, trapped by Vespasian's troops in some cave."

Ionnes was about to point out who changed the subject to himself, but let it lie.

Rabbi Yosef continued, "As you know, it is dreadfully wrong for a Jew to commit suicide. Suicide is a sin from the deepest trench. Still, I can appreciate not surrendering to those who would truly torture a man before they killed him. I was told that Yosefus convinced them to kill one another, one at a time. That way, they did not face the sin of suicide as their spirit departed the body. I weep for them, having to make that sacrifice. And, I would weep for Yosephus as well, but the Samaritan dog was one of the last two left, and instead of choosing death, he surrendered."

"But," objected Mothcrates, "if I understood you, the men were in a quandary. The last would have to take his own life. Suicide would still befall at least one."

"True," admitted Yosef, "unless they arranged to kill each other at the same time. It has happened in battle more times than a man can count. I have little doubt they could do the same if both agreed."

"I, II, III, go? Like when we were children?"

"Exactly. But that is not what they did. Yosefus killed his friend, then surrendered and played the prophet, telling Vespasian he would be emperor someday."

"He foretold Vespasian becoming emperor?" snarled Pterrkee. "How did he know that?"

"Maybe he really could see the future," said Teos.

"No, he is no prophet," corrected Rabbi Yosef. "He merely schmoozed the general to save his neck, then by an amazing twist of fate, Nero poisoned himself, and Vespasian eventually became emperor over all Roma."

"Weird," said Arion.

"That it is," agreed Yosef. "That it is. So, then Yosefus tried being a liaison between the Romans and the Jews, especially during the siege of Ierusalem. Of course, the Jews washed their hands of him. After the war, there was no way he could stay in Iudæa, so Vespasian's son, Titus who became emperor after his father, took him back to Roma where he married, had children and still lives a comfortable life, I am told.

"So, my dear Mothcrates, that is why I believe nothing he writes. His words are made for a Roman audience alone. His lies have kept him alive all these years, and I have nothing good to say of such a turn-tunic."

As the dinner basket came around, each man accepted his portion. Habitually, they ate slowly to make it last. "Was there Christians in Ierusalem at that time?" asked Dim, breaking the silence.

"Um, yes," answered Ionnes. "Many. Yaakov, the brother of Yeshua acted as their bishop and spiritual leader until he was stoned, just three or four short years before the rebellion."

"I thought ya said Yaakov had been killed by the sword," questioned Dim.

"No, that was my brother, Yaakov. Herod Antipas executed my brother. The Jews seemed to like it, and the Herods were never popular with most of the Jews, so anything that made them happy the Herods might do. When Yaakov was killed, Herod had Cephas, our leader, arrested with plans to execute him."

"So, he died there, too?" asked Dim.

"No. Miraculously no. An angel opened every lock in the prison, unchained him and led him out to the street, untouched, unnoticed and unharmed. From there he left Ierusalem for a spell. As I recall, he went home to Galilee, but it has been so long, I am no longer exactly sure.

"But, Yaakov, Yeshua's brother, received an invitation from the High Priest himself to stand upon the top of the Jewish temple and tell the people Yeshua was not Messiah. To this day, I know not what the Jewish leaders were thinking.

Yaakov accepted their invitation to speak from the top of the temple, but he told everyone that Yeshua was indeed the Messiah. He had an earnest audience and the best spot to preach in the city."

"So, what happened?" asked Teos.

"Oh, the Jewish leaders were furious. They yelled for him to stop and rent their garments, but he kept preaching, so some raced up to the roof and literally pushed him off. He fell to the ground but did not die. Then, the Jewish leaders who were still on the ground started beating him, then stoning him. One man with a club used to beat rugs was there. He hit Yaakov on the head just once I am told, but it was enough to kill him."

Ionnes took a moment of respect to mourn his fallen brother.

"I am ever perplexed by such behavior," he muttered, first to himself. "In all the years I have served Yeshua, I have never struck a blow against another man, woman or child. Yeshua never did, either. None of my friends except Cephas did, and when he did, Yeshua rebuked him, then healed the servant's ear. All these years of responding with love and truth has still martyred all the other apostles, and many disciples."

"So, why try?" challenged Minos, his head ever pointed earthward. "Sounds like the cause of losers."

"Easy," answered Ionnes looking directly at Minos as though he stood transparent. "Because, the more death and violence we must encounter, the more I see that the world needs Yeshua. He is the only answer to cure the madness of men.

"And, though I am a prisoner on Patmos and regularly in chains, I still see the uncounted, abundant blessings Yeshua has provided all of us here on Patmos, as well as throughout the world. No, no. no, my friend. Love and truth shall always, always, always be worth fighting for. And, the power of Yeshua's Spirit within me gives me the power, not just to heal those in need, or dislodge demons, but also gives me the internal strength to endure terrible persecutions, beatings, floggings, stonings and more. I would have crumbled and given up long ago save the power of Yeshua's Holy Spirit ever fills and guides me." Ionnes paused a moment.

"Since Yaakov died just a few short years before Ierusalem was liberated from Roman rule, I have often wondered if anything in Ierusalem would have been different if he had been there during the siege? But, Ierusalem killed another one of God's chosen, securing the final avenue for its destruction hence."

<>< ><> <>< ><> <>< ><> <>< ><> <>< ><>

Rain fell like Gethsemane, hard and terrible, drenching the men right down to their spirits. The day dragged on. Even dinner could not escape the deluge. The men ate in shivering pain, their chattering teeth practically chewing the food effortlessly. Each sought the sheltering barracks well before the last lock of the door would be felt. Each dried himself with the edges of his blanket, not wishing to wet the mid sections of the cloth where warmth would be sought later that evening.

"You never finished last night," Talor said to Rabbi Yosef.

"Finished?" questioned Rabbi Yosef.

"Your story," answered Talor.

"That is right," said Phranc. "You told of Ierusalem right after the soldiers were cleansed from the city. Then, spoke of one named Josephus."

Rabbi Yosef replayed the previous night's conversation a few times, checking for omissions and errors.

"Yosefus," he mumbled to himself. "Yeshua's followers in Ierusalem." He continued the checklist in his mind until he announced, "You speak truth. There truly is much more to tell." He wrung out his bushy beard and adjusted his still damp and clinging clothing to sit up a bit.

"Where am I? That is right. The Beloved City." All illumination slipped in through the open door. He let the raucous sounds of the rain on the roof and walls and ground fill each pore lining each man's soul.

"Word came of Vespasian's march. We mobilized, but it would never be enough. I have always been a man of prayer, but this time I prayed harder than any other time of my life. Word of Vespasian's troops destroying our strongholds one by one came from those who fled to Ierusalem.

"I stayed in Ierusalem as long as I dared. When I heard that Emmaus and Jericho fell, I knew I had to leave before I would not be able to leave. We fled, thinking we would return to our beloved Gezara and its peaceful valleys. Alas! We found our mistake all too quickly. Not many miles west of Ierusalem, we saw much smoke far off in the distance ahead. Not good, but we still proceeded towards Gezara. Not another mile forward when we encountered many Jews heading towards us in haste.

"'Go back,' they urged. 'Go back. Gezara has fallen. Gezer and the Maccabees weep. Vespasian has taken Ioppa.'

"I can still feel the pit in my stomach pinching the knot in my throat. I feared to see my little synagogue reduced to ashes. I wondered how many had fought and futilely died. Perhaps the smoke we saw were the flames from bodies immolated. I will never know, and I believe that ignorance plagues me more than if I had seen the burning bodies myself.

"So, we tried to turn south towards Gaza rather than return to Ierusalem, but topping a hill, we could see the Roman flags afar off. I had seen no Roman for over a year. Seeing our nemesis returned in full fury and force fills a righteous man with hopeless anger. One part of me wanted to face my enemy head on. The other man took me by the beard and led us back to Ierusalem's walls.

"When we arrived, the city showed greater chaos than when we left, just two short days earlier. We knelt and wept as we saw our brethren fighting amongst one another. You would have thought Roma was Gideon and we were the Midianites.

"I have read countless times the accounts in scripture when Ierusalem fell to Babylon. I wondered at Isaiah and Jeremiah and looked to see if those in the spirits of Isaiah or Jeremiah came to us with Elohim's pronouncements and prophesies. Alas! I could not see even a glimmer of prophetic voice amidst the anger and fear and chaos of those days and weeks and months. Each and every time I read those holy words of old, I wondered how I would have done facing Babylon, struggling to survive with only my faith to sustain me against the hopelessness. There, back in Ierusalem's bosom, I received my painful answer a hundredfold.

"Even before I left for Gezara, Ierusalem was already being divided into factions. The Zealots wanted to fight. The refugees wanted revenge. The Jewish leaders feared Roma's retaliation and saw our efforts as futile. Their counsel said to surrender, placing us all at Vespasian's mercy in effort to save our lives and our city. In turn, most Jewish leaders met mortality, not by Roman swords, but by their fellow Jews for not standing against Roma.

"I watched from the outer wall as Vespasian and Titus arrived with the largest army I had ever seen. I reminded myself that they were only mortal men who were given authority and power only by Elohim, Himself. And, there we waited as the siege kept us prisoners within our own home. Each day more were killed by their own brother's hand. Oh, Cain, how could you kill Abel? Oh, Esau, know ye not your brother Jacob?

"I feared for my life each day. Seated outside the temple one morning, I saw Rabbi Yochanan ben Zakkai pass by. He saw me and stopping, grabbed hold of both of my hands like a man lifting you off the ground.

'Adonai has heard our cry,' he said, comforting my fears. 'We are judged for our sins. We must stand as one people before Adonai and confess our sin. Is Roma truly greater than Philistia of old? Only then will Adonai turn away our provocation. It is to Him that we must surrender. We must be the four lepers before the Arameans. We must stand as one, as our fathers did against the Assyrians. We will not strip the temple like King Hezekiah. We need not pray the bruised reed that is Egypt to come to our aid, for we are the chosen people. Our sins brought this army and our repentance will take them away.' He dipped his thumb in a small bottle of olive oil and anointed me, placing the *tav* upon my forehead, my lips, my hands and my heart.

"I nodded to this wise rabbi. We had shared many a Passover together. We had taught our people as best we knew how. We knew they needed us more than ever, and we would not abandon them. Or, so I thought.

"One morning, news came to me which shocked me to the core. I fell flat, weeping and in fear. A scribe told me Rabbi Yochanan ben Zakkai had escaped that night, disguised as a corpse. Worse, he did not try to sneak past the troops, but brought himself, bound and helpless, before Vespasian to negotiate his surrender. I was sure he would face execution that day. It was some years later that I learned Vespasian gave him leniency and let him live.

"But on that day, I rent my robe in grief, and shamelessly wailed before all. I prayed for Elohim's angels to come and blind the Roman army. I prayed for manna to come to us to feed us. I prayed for Elijah or the Prophet to appear. I prayed every prayer of deliverance I could conjure or remember. Others joined me in Solomon's Court, but for all our petitions and confessions and prayers, nothing would appease the wrath of Elohim.

"Then, something happened to take away our grief, if only for a season. News came slowly to us, but we noticed the Roman army backing away and less aggressive. We knew not why, but eventually learned that Cæsar Nero had killed himself. We praised Elohim for this news, and the Roman siege seemed to be breaking apart. Perhaps Elohim would deliver us after all.

"Our hope lasted only a few months. Still unable to escape the walls which protected us, we learned Vespasian had been recalled to Roma. Most never lived to learn the Senate gave to him the throne and laurels. He left his son, Titus, as general over his army. Titus did not share his father's patience. Attacks increased. Night times when the sky was dark, and a man could not see his hand before his face, we strained through the gloom to see if the Romans were on the attack.

"One night I was awakened by a great flame within the city. I arose to find the Zealots had set fire to our grain. Our storehouses were still quite full. We could have withstood the Roman siege even years, but the Zealots challenged us to stand and fight against Roma and believed taking away our food would press us into fighting.

"They were wrong. Starvation became our enemy. Some ate animals forbidden by Elohim such as horses and pigs. Soon, some ate feces. Such became our sins. We grew weak, and our faith waned. As I already confessed, I sometimes wonder if my sin alone was enough to bring Elohim's judgment on Ierusalem.

"For over two years I awaited the Roman crucible to crush us. For over two years, I prayed with full and earnest fear. For over two years I barely slept, wondering if that night would be my last. And, in the name of our sins, I watched us destroy ourselves from within. When Roma finally breached our walls, it was as much a blessing as a curse. Elohim's judgment became complete, and we would all be taken to our final rest."

"So, why are you here?" asked Mothcrates.

"Yeah," added Minos. "How did you escape the Roman cross?"

More tears flooded Yosef's eyes.

"By Elohim's grace," he answered with hopeless shrugs.

"Explain," demanded Minos. "You turned cloak, too, did not you?"

"Nay," argued the old rabbi, his fire returning. "I was led out with the rest of the remaining prisoners. We were weak from starvation and were brought out to face our execution, mostly by crucifixion. They beat us and flogged us, of course. There were not enough shackles for all of us, so many of us were tied together by rope as we were marched to our doom. I know not if the soldier who bound my hands did so poorly, or whether he chose to make a bad knot, I know not. I only know that my ropes seemed to come loose. I continued to march along near the rear of the line, knowing I would be promptly killed if I ran.

"Then, my foot tripped on a rock along the trail. I fell forward, landing in a bush of small, red wildflowers. A couple young palm trees on either side as well, and with no plan to escape, I suddenly became hidden and by Elohim's Word, seemingly unnoticed. I stayed down and imagined David in En Gedi, hiding from King Saul. I felt certain I would be missed; that they would return to find me, but no one came. I felt sure someone would thresh out the brush, but of those that passed me, no one gave me a second look. I felt completely conspicuous and was amazed no one saw me from my foolish hiding place.

"Then, I sat up, alone as night drew near. I needed to relieve myself. Still no captors anywhere I could see. Seated here before all of you, I testify and maintain that it can be worse wondering than knowing where the enemy are at. I stood by a tree to relieve myself, then moved very slowly and with stealth along the trail. Darkness became both my ally and my enemy. I knew I would see soldiers coming up the trail at any moment. Still, I went forward. I could see the dome of the Mount of Olives in the distance against the stars, so made that my goal. No moon arose to expose me. Torches or fires announced Roman positions, and I stayed clear. Here I am, a man of forty-six years moving slowly through a somewhat familiar region at night with no further plan of escape. I felt no guidance or direction from Elohim, but apparently, He took me along His right path, and by morning I could lie down and sleep a few hours nearby a stream. Berries, full and ripe, tasted ever more wonderful. I loaded up a few to continue, took another drink and continued up the mountain. Before nightfall, others found me, signaling for me to join them. The warm, summer nights kept us alive for we dared not light a fire. We continued inland, away from the Romans. Their garrisons showed fewer and fewer as we trekked unnoticed into Moab. And, that is how I escaped from Ierusalem."

Yosef stepped out to drink from the bucket. His mouth had been parched for some minutes as he spoke. He felt odd sharing the story with this mixed group of gentiles. Only Seth had heard the account before.

"Did you ever go back?" asked Talor, looking up from his bed on the floor.

Yosef nodded gravely.

"With great caution we watched helplessly as the Romans mounted crosses to execute the prisoners. One scout returned one night, claiming he had seen over three-thousand of our people upon the rough, wooden cross. Imagine that? Three-thousand of our people at the same time, living a torturous death, calling out to each other for support and sharing their final moments of love for one another in a pain-filled blur. Not even the Flavian Amphitheater could contain it.

"Some crosses were *tav*. Some were *chi*. One told me how the chi crosses were close to the ground. A man died helpless, barely inches above the ground. Most remained silent during their execution, but some in their anger and frustration would curse the guards as they patrolled past. If their words upset the soldiers, they were spread eagle and could be kicked anywhere – even between the legs. I have never donned a cross, so have never been kicked thus, but I still shudder at the thought of such torture. Our executioners lacked enough crosses to execute an entire city, so at times they would place a second person on the opposite side of the cross. Not even murderers and thieves meet disgrace in such a manner."

He felt tears returning again, so stopped his narrative to mourn some minutes. The sun likewise dropped low, peeking at them beneath the veil of clouds to share in the vigil.

"Bunk," yelled Guard Mucius though all had already entered the barracks. Lying down, listening through the patter of raindrops for the click of the lock, the group expected another lesson between Ionnes and Dim, but quiet ruled the moment. Only sounds of breathing filled the stale containment.

"Never once," opened a voice. Rabbi Yosef looked upwards to the faint starlight seeping through the rafters as he repeated, "Never once."

The silence thereafter left the question dangling between the men, daring any to ask.

"Never once?" asked Teos. The simple man never could keep his mouth to himself when he wanted to know something.

Rabbi Yosef rose upon one arm, looking over at Teos and Ionnes.

"Never once," he again said, "did I sit in the temple. It always held for me special awe as though I was Moses himself walking barefoot on holy ground. As if I could see the ladder of Jacob descend upwards from the rooftops.

"I never forgot the crushing blow of Babylon when Solomon's Temple was destroyed. Ierusalem always thought Elohim would save them and Ierusalem would never fall. Yet, fall it did, to pagan Babylon. So, as I stood before Zerubbabel's temple, with or without the splendor of Solomon's, I prayed that we had learned our lessons from the first destruction. But, alas, we never learn, for the temple did fall, stone by stone. As the flames raged, flecks of pure gold, melted and molten, dripped between the stones. It was said the Romans destroyed the temple, brick by brick, not to punish so much as to get that gold. I could not say. I later fled back to Gezara and my scattered flock, that being the only comfort I could perform. Even there, I knew not if I was truly safe. I would not have been surprised to find myself tied to a Roman cross any given day.

"I heard it said that when Titus returned to Roma, they tried to decorate him for his victory, but he declined, stating no honor in defeating a nation whose God had abandoned them.

"And now, the question which ever crosses my mind is whatever happened to the Ark of the Covenant? I expect the Roman swine destroyed it or carried off the gold. In that, I fear the LORD's greatest abandonment. How could He let them destroy His most precious home?"

He looked through the gloom at Ionnes.

"Were our sins truly greater than our righteousness? Did we finally lose Elohim's mercies forever?" The following moment's silence heard his sighs turn to sobs.

Ionnes crawled over to the sound of Yosef's broken voice and brought his forehead against the shuddering rabbi's.

"No," he whispered, wrapping his arm over Yosef's shoulders and around the back of his neck. "He is not our Abaddon. He is our ABBA and we are His children. My love, my life. The love of our ABBA is what shines oh SO Splendidly in each of us against this sinful world of sin and hate and fear. ABBA abandoned not his children after Babylon, and He abandons you not, even now. He says, 'I have been waiting for you.' When all is said and done, He is ever willing to take a chance on me and you. Because of Him, I have a dream – one we may share – one that will never slip through my fingers. Ever seek His love and you can withstand even a thousand-fold sieges. ABBA ever loves each one of us, His children. He abides in each of us; knowing me; knowing you, and day by day His love is perfected in us."

Some minutes passed, and Yosef felt new breath fill him.

He released hold on Ionnes. Sitting back on his bedroll, he sighed, no longer as one fretful, but as one who had finally come full circle to confront the hollow backside of his fears and grief.

"ABBA, Papa," he uttered, more to himself, then bushy brows pressed upwards as he raised eyes towards Ionnes, a barely visible outline in the darkness. "Despite our despair, you still know the love of our ABBA?"

"Yes, I do," nodded Ionnes. "I do, and our ABBA loves you just as much."

The old rabbi sighed again, taking Ionnes' hand. The firm squeeze connected them.

"Thank you, Yochanan ben Zebedee," he whispered, then released hold and rolled back onto his bedroll to let new sleep fill him with more rest than he had found in many years.

PATMOS

CHAPTER 25

"Giovanni," yelled Chryspippe, running down the beach. "Giovanni!"

Waist high in the surf and waves, he heard not her call. Only as she approached did he catch sight of her out of the corner of his eye. Immediately, he saw the frantic fear filling her face. Lorin beside her mistress, of course, also looked worried. He came forth from the water.

"What has happened?"

"It is Apollonides," she yelled.

He nodded for her to continue.

"The sickness is back, but far worse than before."

"Where is he?" asked Ionnes.

"I know not. He ran off into the hills."

"What did he say? Were you there? Did you hear him?"

"No. Father told me. He was home when Apollonides suddenly ran out of his room screaming. Papa did not recognize his words. They were gibberish - not even real words, he said. Apollonides looked at dad, his eyes wide with fear. He bit into his clothing, tearing it. Sometimes he bit his own skin, ripping it.

"Papa called the slaves to hold him, but he broke away with amazing strength. He fled to the wilderness, up and away towards the hills. Papa sent two slaves to catch him, or at least watch him. When they were out of the town on the mountain, Apollonides turned and attacked them both, throwing rocks and trying to bite them like a wild beast."

She looked at Ionnes. His eyes down, he wept in prayer for discernment and understanding.

"What should we do?" she asked. He held up a hand as he kept his head down and eyes closed. Two Roman guards approached.

"I need to take the prisoner with me," said Chryspippe.

"Not without direct orders from the governor," said one.

"It is an emergency. I need this prisoner for his special gifts."

"Not without direct orders from the governor," he repeated. He kept a hand on his sword, not to be used against the governor's wife, but in case the prisoner tried to go with her.

She humph'd as she turned to go. "You will have your governor's orders and I will have your heads."

The soldiers watched as she stormed up the beach for the Governor's Forum.

"Maybe we should have let him go," said the second.

"Then, the governor would have our heads," said the first. He looked at Ionnes. "BACK TO WORK."

It appeared Ionnes heard neither. The guard was about to jab Ionnes with his sword point, but a sense of fear slithered in, holding him back. This was still the strange zealot who had power from his solo God. He looked up towards the sky just in case any clouds were rubbing together their hands to make lightning. For a moment, he thought he saw the face of Jupiter in the clouds. Just a moment, then it was gone.

"Back to work," repeated the second guard.

Ionnes opened his eyes, looked at the two men and turned back towards the beach.

"I am coming quickly," he muttered though he did not hurry. The first guard was about to give Ionnes the lash, but the second held him back.

"He is going," he said.

Ionnes hobbled back to the ropes, his prayers continuing throughout. Not an hour passed when a chariot appeared at the beach, one soldier driving, Chryspippe and Lorin riding along. The soldier stopped before the two soldiers Chryspippe had pointed out and handed the first one a small scroll. Opened and read, the soldier nodded.

"Bring the prisoner," he said to the second guard. He did not have to say which prisoner. The second guard trotted down sand and rock to the surf and summoned Ionnes.

"Put away your ropes. Wait! Belay that. Lay aside your ropes. You are required elsewhere." He would have the other prisoners retrieve Ionnes' ropes.

The two men walked up beach. No hurry, as Ionnes had been feeling his age of late. They helped him up into the chariot and off they went.

"It is good to see you again," shivered Ionnes, still wet from the salt water. "And you, too," he greeted Lorin. "And, also you," he said to the Roman soldier driving the chariot who did not know he was also being addressed.

The chariot bounced around as they do on unpaved roads. All inside held onto the sides, lest they make an unscheduled stop and watch from an uncomfortable posture as the chariot continued without them.

Handing Ionnes a cloth to wrap up, then pita and water, she yelled, "The driver is to help us find Apollonides. Others were sent on horseback to find him. Watch for their signals." Ionnes nodded and grinned. He figured they would go after him on foot and Ionnes on foot was not a speedy journey anymore, to say the least. But he also knew the Power of Yeshua's Spirit found no limits by distance. His prayers paved the way ahead of them.

"You be praying, too," Ionnes told Chryspippe. "And you too, little Lorin." His expression glowed for her, especially since her baptism the week past. Ionnes had requested Chryspippe to not have her slaves baptized by command, but by their own request and conversion. Lorin saw the change in her mistress after her baptism and went to the water willingly. Ionnes almost lost footing as the chariot flew over a sizable bump in the road but kept his appreciable smile to her, then went back to his vigil.

The two women felt awkward and really did not know what to say but tried to follow Ionnes' instructions. Lorin remembered how Giovanni said it was as easy as talking to an old friend. Just be honest for Yeshua is ever honest with you.

Much of the day passed, riding along the roads through the hill country. For all anyone knew, Apollonides could have returned to the city.

"You should have brought your dog," suggested Ionnes.

"Skylos?" checked Chryspippe.

Ionnes nodded. "As I recall, he loves Apollonides. His nose would find him faster than our eyes."

Later in the afternoon, they spied a man atop a hill waving his arms. A signaler. They turned towards him. As they approached, he pointed the way to the right heading down a hill into a small ravine. The shadows covered the ravine floor and the charioteer had to slow down lest he lose a wheel and throw them all. Others waved and pointed the way. Not half a mile farther, they saw half-a-dozen soldiers with spears pointed at a single figure. Chryspippe gasped as she saw her brother. He looked not like himself at all.

Almost naked, he hunched over like a crimped chimp. He repeatedly smacked the back of his head with a rock. He hissed at the soldiers who had him pinned against a rock wall. They had tried to shackle him, but Apollonides thrashed them so madly. Two were pounded aside the head by their own manacles. They backed off and waited for they knew not what.

Chryspippe, the first to jump out of the chariot, almost stumbled. It was not something society ladies did most days. Lorin jumped down behind her to help. Waiting until it stopped, Ionnes gradually sat down on the edge of the chariot to give his legs less distance to the ground.

The trio came up through the brush to approach from behind the soldiers. Not slowing down a bit, Chryspippe walked past the line of spears to her brother.

"Har Megiddo," he hissed to her and crashed his head full strength into the cliff behind him. Stunned, he turned back towards his sister.

"Middad," he yelled, then looked at all.

"Brother," she urged and put out a hand to touch him. He pounced on her, swatting her away and later biting her until she retreated back behind the guards and spears. Apollonides retreated but a moment, then leapt forward advancing and again felt the harsh points of metal start to pierce him. He withdrew just far enough.

"I do not understand," she said to Ionnes. Tears came, but also anger. Anger at Ionnes. Anger at the world. Anger at Yeshua and His God. And, anger at herself for ever listening to this old codger. She felt the dirt of the world piling over the top of her, burying her, overwhelming and destroying any cleansing baptism.

"You were baptized to Yeshua," explained Ionnes. "the devil's revenge took back your brother."

Apollonides continued to scream words none there could understand save Ionnes.

"What do we do?" begged Chryspippe.

"Same as before," answered Ionnes. "In the holy Name of Yeshua, we drive the demons out of him."

"Then pray, come forward," she pleaded.

"As you wish," he answered, then added, "but, you have the same Spirit in you who dwells in me. You also have the power to command these spirits to depart."

Chryspippe looked scared. This was a new experience for her, and she likewise feared for her brother who continued to scream and rant and smash rocks against his head and feet. She looked at Ionnes incredulous. His confidence shown back. She realized her trust for him beyond anything she would have given any man before this. His nod gave her strength and resolve as she rose and turned to face the demons holding her brother.

Moving forward of the soldiers beside their spears, she yelled, "Demons depart in the name of Yeshua."

Apollonides looked at her and laughed. An insidious, evil laugh.

"I am sealed with wrath and chaos," he answered. "Abaddon has called me. Middad."

She repeated her words, this time louder and more forcefully.

Apollonides still laughed.

"I fear only the trumpets," he said, and blasphemies came from his mouth. Chryspippe had never heard such vile words from her brother. It was not even his voice.

As the blasphemies began, Ionnes stepped forward and said, "Demons depart in the name of Yeshua."

Immediately, Apollonides fell back against the ground.

He writhed and twisted, his face most hideous.

"Depart," repeated Ionnes, "in the Holy Name of Yeshua."

Apollonides screamed, long and hard. Even after his breath was spent, he kept trying to scream. Only until he began to turn blue did his breath return. Immediately exhausted, he laid still as death a spell, then awoke, struggling to sit up on the cold dirt. He sunk his bleeding head forward, leaning it on his bloody hand, red against red. Chryspippe ran forward and knelt before him, checked his response, then laid his head in her bosom. He rested there uncounted minutes.

"I am thirsty," he finally said. "And, hungry."

They rose and a soldier brought water. He drank as much as he could hold.

"Thank you," he said, then looked at Ionnes. His brow sank in practiced consternation, but then relaxed.

"You," he pointed with his eyes. "You brought me back."

"Aye," answered Ionnes.

Apollonides wiped something off his brow. It was dirty blood.

"I am a mess," he said, stepping away from Chryspippe to examine himself. He looked again at Ionnes.

"Can you tell me what happened?"

Ionnes went up against the stone cliff which had contained the wild man. He ran his hand along its rough edges and felt the beauty their Creator God had made. He continued to feel the wall as he answered, "You invited the demons back."

Both Apollonides and Chryspippe looked at the old apostle with astonishment.

"No," said Chryspippe, then looked at her brother. He had uttered no, too.

"Yes," answered Ionnes. "Yes, you did." Then, he looked at Chryspippe. "And, you did good, woman."

She puzzled over his words as she answered, "But, it did not work when I spoke."

"No," he agreed, "but, let me tell you a quick story. Many years back when I was a young man, Yeshua and the rest of us were traveling when a man came to us and begged us to help him. His young son was possessed and always hurting himself, even unto death. We disciples tried to cast out the evil spirit but failed. All twelve of us together could not drive out the demon. Then, Yeshua came forward, rebuked the devil and the child was cured.

"Well, later we asked Yeshua what happened. 'Why could we not repel the demon?' we all asked. I did not sleep well for the next few nights after I heard His answer. He said, 'Because of your unbelief.' That was tough to accept, especially since all of us had given up all and followed him. Then, He added that if we had the faith of a mustard seed, we could move mountains.

Nothing is impossible.

"We heard his words but were still a bit confused how to have that kind of faith. We understood His directions but stumbled like deaf and blind mice how to make them ours. Yeshua never missed a moment. He answered us most directly, 'Howbeit, this kind goes not out but by prayer and fasting.' I never forgot those words. As I learned to share the gospel of Dominus Yeshua, I further learned the value of prayer and fasting."

He chuckled.

"As a prisoner, fasting is less hard. Some nights, the bread is like stone. We fast often. And, of course, prayer is never far from my lips. You did well, young woman. Hopefully, you will learn more."

He looked at Apollonides, "And you, young man. Rise."

Apollonides looked at the old man with modest dread but arose.

"Yeshua also told us the account of a man possessed by a demon. We drove the demon out and it wandered through the wilderness for some time. Then, it returned to the man and found his soul clean and swept out, but not filled with the Spirit of the Living God. So, the unclean spirit went off and found seven other spirits worse than itself and they possessed the man anew and far, far worse than the first time. I believe that is what happened to you. Your soul became a target and as long as you refuse the gifts of eternal and abundant life with Yeshua, you may be filled with even more demons the next time."

Apollonides shuddered at the thought. He started to ask, but Ionnes cut him off to make answer.

"Commit to Yeshua and His Spirit will ever protect you. Be baptized, like your sister. No demon will ever take you over again. Oh, they will taunt and hurt you, mostly through others – your friends and family and foes but be strong and courageous."

Apollonides felt the tug on his heart and responding, knelt down, hung his head and let Ionnes lead him to Yeshua.

"Mea Culpa. Mea Culpa. Mea Culpa."

The guilt drained away to be replaced by the Love of the Spirit. In turn, Apollonides' spirit rose, and he felt giddy. He wanted to leap and dance. He bounced around all of them. The guards thought his behavior similar to before the first exorcism, but Ionnes could easily tell the difference. No, this was elevation by Yeshua's Holy Spirit.

Together, they rode home on the chariot as the sun started to set. They rode to the House of Myron where all could join in for a bite to eat before Chryspippe went home to her husband and Ionnes returned to the penal colony.

PATMOS

CHAPTER 26

The bag of money landed with musical clang on the wooden table.

Kynops ignored it. He remained intent on the small fire needed to make his next potion. If too hot, it would burn and be useless. If not hot enough, it would not blend.

"Please, sir," pleaded the priest.

Kynops glanced at the bag of money. Gold, silver and even some gems. A generous amount and much, much more than he typically made in uncounted years.

"You are the only one who can help us," added another priest.

He peered over his left shoulder at the three men who invaded his home, all head priests. Artemis, Apollo and Aphrodite. Some called them Triple A. The temple to Artemis, the virgin hunter, stood as the lead deity to whom the island had been devoted. Apollo's temple, not far down the same street from Artemis, was smaller but had a larger façade. Aphrodite's temple stood outside of town near the sea. The smallest, it better resembled a shrine than a temple.

Still attending to his small fire, Kynops said, "Did you not cast me out of your beloved Temple to Artemis around this time last year?"

The first priest nodded. Known by his haughty and arrogant demeanor, he was the one who had confronted Kynops when he made the priest's daughter disappear last year. She came home soaked and freezing, having materialized offshore the better part of a mile and had to swim back to Patmos.

"We were wrong," he buttered. "We did not see your greatness."

Nice lie.

"And, now you come to Kynops for help with this intruder - this prisoner - this one in exile?"

"Yes," they all answered and nodded.

Kynops ignored them for some time as he mixed together his concoction. He moved it up and down over the small flame so as to keep it from getting too hot.

"Why me?" he asked, not really caring what they answered. The gold made any answer a mere formality. He knew what they wanted, and why.

"Sir," answered Artemis' priest, "we know well that for years you have been helping this island, so your holiness Kynops, we ask for your help now in this difficult situation created by Ionnes, the foreigner exiled to this island..." The Artemis priest continued painting the picture he sought with his own colors and hues to suit his petitions.

"The governor will do nothing," added Apollo's priest. "The prisoner has bewitched him, we are sure. He arrested the prisoner when we petitioned him, but now the prisoner moves about more and more like a freeman."

"How can the governor arrest one who is already a prisoner?"

The three men stopped to question this. None really had an answer, but the third priest said, "We know not, but it was not a full day before we again saw him walking through Phora.

"And, now the destruction of the temple..."

Kynops turned head to peer at them. He had heard nothing about the temple.

"What of the temple?" he asked. "Which temple?"

"Mine. Um, Apollo's," answered the second priest.

Kynops waved his long fingers for him to continue. The priest looked at his colleagues before continuing.

"We have seen this type of sorcery before, but never to this degree. His presence disrupts the island, and we see the beginnings of a following. We have heard tales of this cult who call themselves disciples of Yeshua Christos, their dead leader whom they say came back from the grave. They have many churches on the mainland, and now this prisoner is trying to establish one here on Patmos."

"No doubt," agreed Kynops, "but, what about the temple?"

They all looked at one another nervously. The second priest finally said, "We know it sounds impossible, but this prisoner destroyed the temple to Apollo with just a word."

Finished with his potion, Kynops fed and stoked up the fire a bit to warm the room. Taking a seat, he stared at each man for quite a spell.

"How does any man destroy a building with just his word?" challenged Kynops. He knew that he could not do it. He had checked into it many times and always found more impossible than possible. Even his shadows could not level a well-made stone building.

The second priest continued talking. As the priest passionately droned, Kynops closed his eyes and listened just enough to get this much of the picture:

Late summer felt good that day as the sun made its glorious appearance. After windy rains all week, the cooler northern wind gave way to African breezes bringing its signature warm, drier air. Blossoms furled in full bloom. Even the little arbutus forest swayed together mightily and in unison. Ground cover flourished with flowers. Insects abounded. Typical summer sunny feelings when not just the body is warmed, but also the souls of the people, young and old, slave or free, lifting their sprits to feel and celebrate the glory of the day.

Temple priests witnessed the spiritual weather changes from their pinnacles, not liking what they saw. This little sect of Christians showed growth, it seemed, every day. Starting with the governor's wife and a lame woman magically healed, the citizens of Patmos drew towards this old prisoner like mold on pita. The priests spoke against this intruder who called himself a Christian, but many still sought him. They might as well have been trying to sharpen a sword with a magnetic rock.

The priests of all three temples conspired to gather the townsfolk together as the evening migration of prisoners would approach. They created a gala event with much mirth and food and just enough wine to merry hearts without blocking all reason. On cue, they stood upon the steps of Apollo's Temple to address the people.

"Quiet!" they yelled, repeatedly, with clapping hands or sticks beaten together. The ruckus would garner attention from all. The partiers turned attention to the priests.

"Thank you all for coming," yelled the Apollo temple priest, his hands raised. "We celebrate the feast day of the great god, Apollo, and we see that our worship pleases the sun god, for he has brought us a day of great joy to celebrate him.

"All of you here certainly know the other priests with me here." He pointed to his left. "The priests from the temple of Artemis." The priests waved or slightly bowed. "And the priests from the temple of Aphrodite." Those three priests also waved and slightly bowed.

"We gather to thank Apollo for today's music. For today's poetry. And, perhaps most of all, for the miraculous healings that have recently taken place on Patmos. For all of us here know it is the gods who grant such miracles to occur. All other gods named are counterfeit. I, Apollo's humble servant, speak from Apollo's mouth his truth and prophesy. It cannot be denied."

The prisoners from the sea started to move past the crowd in their nightly makeshift parade. If noticed by the crowd at the gala, none were given attention. Passing Artemis' temple, many, as per usual, spit on the pavement towards the temple.

After some minutes' passing, a disciple of Apollo raised arms from the back of the crowd, signaling the priests.

"And so, my people, I must seek your counsel and advice."

The revelers murmured amongst themselves, what counsel and advice could a head priest of the temple even ask? This was certainly a first for all of them.

"We have amongst us an outcast who stirs up the island with his illusions. Worse, he takes due credit away from the gods for his miraculous doings. If we could, we would stone him for his lies and heresies right here. Look! The charlatan approaches."

330

As he spoke, the wine-gullible partiers suddenly felt the call to justice. What mortal man had the gall to perform works of wonders and take credit away from the gods who made them? Their anger and indignation grew bit by bit as the priests spoke and stoked.

Suddenly, stubby hands and fingers flew forth dramatically from his priestly garb, pointing towards the line of prisoners passing.

"I see the fraud now. There is our latest false prophet who must be purged. Bring him to me."

Three temple guards moved around the crowd to confront Ionnes. The crowd, stirred by priestly anger and inebriated sense of justice, turned towards the action, ready for the hostilities to begin. This was quite a party! Food. Wine. Music. And now a show.

The guards said not a word as they grabbed old Ionnes, one on each side gripping an arm, and the third behind to pick up the pieces as needed. As the trio plus one wedged through the middle of the crowd, Ionnes saw again the anger and disapproval of the crowd. Many there had seen the miracles and wonders of this self-claimed prophet of God. Now, the priests had him brought forth to expose as a fraud.

Ionnes glanced up at the temple; its steps, its fountain and ornate garden all leading to the carved stone pillars and structure. The sculpted figure of Apollo, naked and strong, stood in the middle of the fountain.

He also noticed a pile of large rocks close enough for everyone to grab one.

Some of the prisoners, including Mothcrates and Minos stopped to see what would happen. Neither stepped forward to help or hinder. Guard Octavius drew sword, about to pounce on them to keep everyone moving, then seeing Ionnes grabbed, stepped up grinning to watch. Maybe he would finally see some more magic.

"Prisoner," addressed the Apollo priest.

"Ionnes," corrected Ionnes.

"Prisoner," repeated the Apollo Temple Priest in loud voice to be heard by all. "You are charged with fraud. You are charged with intentionally deceiving the good citizens of

Patmos with your words and promises of a dead Savior. You are also charged with taking credit for the supposed miracles you have touted during your first months on Patmos - credit due to the divine gods and goddesses of Patmos. Thereby, you are charged with desecration to our sacred temples. How do you make answer to these charges?"

Ionnes looked at his fingernails, cleaning them with other nails, or scraping the tips with his front teeth to file them down. He continued this silent project for some moments until everyone, including the priests started to shift uneasily.

"Prisoner," the priest yelled all the louder.

"Ionnes," corrected Ionnes, not looking up while breaking his silence.

"Prisoner," he screeched, "how do you make answer to these charges?"

Ionnes continued cleaning his fingernails. Perhaps finishing, he lifted the front of a foot to examine his toenails. Nah. Back to the fingernails.

"PRISONER!"

"Ionnes." He looked at the priests, one by one. Each glared at the old apostle, some with arrogance; some with fitful anger; their murderous intents so easy to pick out. Ionnes had seen that look in the eyes of men more times than he could count - for that matter, more times than he could count since his arrest at Ephesus. His eyes came to rest on the Apollo priest.

"What did you say?" He chewed another fingernail and was tempted to pick up one of the rougher stones close by to finish filing, shaping and smoothing it.

"I said, how do you answer to these charges?"

"Charges?" repeated Ionnes, looking upwards in thought. "Charges? The only wrongdoing I see is you keeping an old man from his dinner. Where are your manners?"

The priests would not be deterred again.

"Dog! What brought you to Patmos? You are an exile, are you not?" He extended his arm upwards to the bright sky. "Behold our beloved Apollo, crossing the sky above us. He sees and loves what he sees. Bow dog. Bow before the Temple of Apollo. The sun god demands your worship."

Ionnes extended his arms to the sky, mocking the priest, then pointing at the image over the fountain.

There were countless Scriptures regarding idol worship, but for whatever reason or prompting he thought of Habakkuk as he answered, *"What profit is the image, that its maker should carve it? The molded image, a teacher of lies, that the maker of its mold should trust in it to make mute idols? Woe to him who says to wood, 'Awake!' To silent stone, 'Arise! I shall teach!' Behold, it is overlaid with gold and silver, yet in it there is not breath at all."*

The crowd stood stunned. Ionnes recognized the effect when one first hears the divine words of scripture. It drives to the heart and touches the soul with its unequalled love.

"You dare desecrate the temples with your lies?" yelled the priest, his voice cracking. The other priests joined-in, each face its own personal consternation. Ionnes saw some grab stones and position themselves amidst the crowd of lightheaded partiers.

"Answer me this question," challenged Ionnes, feeling the boldness of the Spirit fill him. "You claimed the miracles of my hand came from the gods and goddesses of Patmos?"

The priests all nodded.

"Then, answer me this. Before I came, what miracles and wonders did your gods and goddesses perform on Patmos?"

The wordless pause answered most loudly.

"Cannot you name even one miracle?"

Same answer.

"Then, why would your gods allegedly choose now to…"

"Silence!" screamed the Apollo priest, racing down the steps to Ionnes. Reaching the apostle, he slapped him hard across the face.

"Silence slave! You have no voice here."

Ionnes felt the sting across the left side of his face. He flinched not, but let the moment pass and the initial sharpness of the pain subside. Compared with his flogging, this was nothing, but it was always so odd how a slap across the face held that special sense of correction, perhaps left over from lessons from a person's youth. With raised brows, he let the warm afternoon air fill his lungs a few times as he prepared answer.

"It is not for you to silence the gospel. Yeshua is not mocked. I will no longer quibble with you with mere words." He looked up at the temple.

"Is it empty?"

The priest looked a bit stunned at the question.

"Is what empty?"

"The temple, man," answered Ionnes, pointing. "Is there anyone inside?"

"That is no affair of yours."

Ionnes was persistent. "Are there no souls still within? If so, get them out, now."

The priest felt his authority rapidly slipping away though he did not fully see it. He started again to protest.

"NOW!" stressed Ionnes.

The priests remained unmoved.

Ionnes said to all present, "God made the walls of Jericho come down that His people might enter the Promised Land. And, now the same Yeshua will show you the same might of His right hand."

He looked at the priests a moment. "Is the temple empty?"

They stood unmoved.

Ionnes continued, "You claim that I am a fraud and that the marvels and miracles I do are from the hand of Apollo or one of the other gods but let me show you. Would Apollo destroy his own temple? If I show you the might of Yeshua and His Father in Heaven, will you then believe?"

The priests looked around and saw the faces of the crowd. They could see the spell this old prophet had placed. These men, so ready to kill Ionnes only minutes passed, now looked more like docile sheep. The Apollo priest walked through the crowd shouting, "Men, why do you bow to this fraud, who is exiled here because of his sorcery? Why are you letting yourselves be misguided by this despicable man, an exile, who here insults the immortal gods and their house?"

Ionnes looked at the priest as he drew back before him. Via a side glance, Ionnes saw six quickly exiting the temple, holding hands over ears. The building was empty. The apostle felt the Spirit fill him, giving him the next words that came forth like distant thunder from his mouth.

"May - your - house - be - desolate."

It started as a low rumble. The temple priests looked down at the ground or at each other. At that same moment the temple collapsed in on itself. All stones turned in as though a crushing hand came down upon a lazy nomad's tent. The sounds of crumbling stones rattled all in attendance. Stunned, all stood helpless as they watched their beloved temple become rubble, mightily adding to the pile of stones at their feet. The fountain with its image of Apollo became crushed by the stony avalanche. Those with stones in hand also dropped them and leapt back. The following silence of awe was deafening, replaced only by the sounds of birds and gurgling waters.

"Get him," yelled a priest on the steps. Ionnes saw the arrogant priest from Artemis' temple pointing, (as though anyone verily needed him to point). The priests started down the steps. Some disciples joined them, rushing Ionnes, grabbing him every which way but loose. Fists joined the fury, again pounding the apostle, knocking him to the ground. Most stood back to watch the furious display.

Sufficiently bloodied, they grabbed Ionnes to have him arrested. Guard Octavius had already entered the scene along with other soldiers.

"Take him to the governor," ordered the priests though none were letting go, pushing him towards the forum. Guard Octavius drew sword and entered the mob to take Ionnes. Only then did they let go but kept close company as they hastened the few blocks to the governor's forum. Laurentius had already left for the day.

"Lock him up," yelled the priests as one. Guard Octavius motioned to the others, and Ionnes was placed in a holding cell for the night. Satisfied he would be contained for the night, they returned to the fallen temple. Some hoped they would round the corner and find it still intact. A dusty cloud still hovered above the pile that was the temple. The priests could then enter the temple court, kneel down among the rubble and let the tears flow. The wailing could be heard for blocks and continued throughout the night.

Laurentius had been informed of what happened by soldiers and townsfolk soon after its collapse. He stayed away until the next morning. In awe, he inspected the destruction and marveled how any man could have done this by the power of his word. As the temple priests relayed the account, he noted how the details of the story changed overnight to make Giovanni the aggressor. After his audience had been completed, the priests returned to their mourning and tears. Laurentius returned to the forum and declined to question the prisoner, pre-playing their entire, inevitable conversation in his head. Grabbing his golden coin, he flipped. It landed to send Giovanni back to the quarry. His senses knew this to be the best option and accepted the counsel of the Augustine coin.

Now Kynops looked at the three priests, kneeling and bowing before him in veneration. He smiled inwardly at the irony of this situation.

"The governor did nothing?"

"Nothing," all three answered.

"And," asked Kynops, "you were expecting at least a flogging if not death?"

"Verily," the three priests answered.

Kynops sat brooding a spell before he said, "Leave me."

"Sir?" they questioned, rising.

He stood, opened the door to his little home and said, "I must prepare."

The priests rose and nodded respectfully as they headed for the door. The Apollo priest stopped at the door to say, "Your services will ever be rewarded," and with that they departed. Kynops barely watched them as they turned off his yard. Closing his door, he laid flat faced on the floor, speaking the unutterable for some hours. To anyone present, it would have been gibberish. To Kynops, it was part of the pact he shared with the shadows. Still facing the floor, he felt the stirring darkness around him, both inside and outside the dwelling. Briefly distracted by the sounds of howling dogs, his mind examined his list of demons. He needed one very special to carry out his next task. More than one came to mind, yet he chose one most nimble who had always shown unusual cunning and resourcefulness.

Rising, he called upon the demon. It came forward like a quivering arrow.

"Tarrow, prepare," ordered Kynops. "Seek the prisoner called Ionnes. Blind both of his eyes, remove from him his soul and bring it to me that I may judge it as I wish."

The demon tarried.

"GO!" he shouted and with that, the quivering arrow shot off.

Kynops sat to wait, though his vigil would be far from passive. He continued his evil words as he watched the shadows around him and felt their cold responses. They would alert him to the assigned demon's approaching return.

Ionnes felt the weight of the day's labors as he laid calmly upon his bedroll. The prisoners were unusually quiet. Ionnes counted it to fear or perhaps awe. Minos and Mothcrates were especially receptive to Ionnes – every step he took. They spoke not, but neither would take an eye away from him. Pterrkee muttered away to himself whether to face the wall or keep watchful eyes on Ionnes. Neither felt safe as he opted for cold stone. Even Dim seemed lost in thought and unwilling to engage in their nightly discussions and teachings.

Ionnes' presence in the holding tank the previous night left the barracks to open discussions about him or whatever. Reducing temples to ruins would be the hot new topic, no doubt. In the holding cell, Ionnes heard the guards talking about it all night. Throughout the day, everyone, prisoners and guards alike, gave him distance. Only one came to befriend. Myron brought him lunch. The two sat under an olive tree talking. Even Myron showed a bit of awkward pretentions, but he openly admitted his concerns.

"So then, why are you here?" asked Ionnes.

"I knew you needed a friend," answered Myron.

Ionnes' eyes expressed his deep gratitude.

Myron noticed. This standalone apostle who most days seemed more like a lone mountain than part of a range showed that most human frailty of appreciation and connection. It was beautiful and made the apostle seem much more approachable than ever before.

Evening came and Ionnes sat alone as he ate. Only Jack came up at one point and said, "Hey zealot, howizit you can topple a temple but cannot break a barrack?"

Ionnes just shrugged. He knew any words he used would sound arrogant and had to remind himself the temple was not destroyed for Ionnes but for the glory of Yeshua. Always and all things for the glory of almighty Yeshua.

The click of the barrack's lock seemed more like being sewn into a large leather bag. Who would be the dog? Who would be the cock? The snake? The monkey? The drowning water?

Ionnes kept to his prayers as sleep overtook him. He slept fitfully enough until a sense of alarm shook him from his slumbers. Only briefly did he consider it a dream, for the depths of Yeshua's Holy Spirit filled him anew as he detected a new evil presence enter the mason's box. It was dark, but eyes were not needed. His ears turned up, he could faintly hear the outside sounds of wind and surf and the song of the cricket. Inside, some men snored or itched or talked to themselves as they slept.

Yeshua's Spirit spoke, "Yochanan, keep closed your eyes – just for the moment."

The apostle heard and obeyed without question. A quivering arrow appeared in the black and white images behind his eyes. He knew not its meaning or intent but prayed for Yeshua to open his spiritual eyes to clearly see. The Holiest Spirit readily responded, and Ionnes spoke aloud to the air, "In Yeshua's name, freeze unclean spirit." He opened his eyes and sat up. There above him, stationed against the gloom of night shuddered a presence of lost darkness.

"Remain demon," ordered Ionnes, "in the holy Name of Yeshua until I order you away."

The dark shape remained as though netted by the stale air of the barracks.

Ionnes had endured such invaders before.

"Tell me, unclean spirit, why have you come into this building?"

Some moments passed, but Ionnes knew he needed not tap the stone twice to produce water. He waited as the prayers continued to pour off his lips.

Just as the darkness was about to cave in on itself, without breath or vocal chords or lips, it spoke.

"Apollo's priests came to Kynops and spoke blasphemies against you. They begged him to come to you and bring about your death. So, he sent me, his cunning messenger, to blind you then glean your soul and bring it to Kynops for his condemnation."

Ionnes felt from within himself that the demon spoke truth, for so often they knew lies far more than honest truth and in wise counsel, a disciple always double checked anything spoken from the pits of Hell.

"Have you ever before gleaned a man's soul and taken it to your master?"

Tarrow shuddered above a moment before giving answer.

"I have before been sent to kill a man. I have never before been sent to deliver his soul."

"Then, why do you submit to him – this Kynops?"

The demon was quick to reply. "Satan's whole strength and depths resides in him. He has made covenants with our unclean rulers so Kynops obeys us and we in turn obey him."

Ionnes felt a flash of remorse as the Holy Spirit gave him a very brief picture in his mind what Tarrow, this fallen angel, used to be before he became in league with Lucifer. The beauty was dazzling, and he thanked Yeshua for His love and mercy.

"Unclean spirit," said Ionne, "you are ordered by Yochanan, the Apostle of Yeshua, the Son of God, to never come out and encroach on any human. You are never to return to Kynops, but rather to depart from this island forever."

Immediately, the malevolent spirit fled from Patmos, cursing and blaspheming.

"Wow!" said Dim.

Ionnes turned towards the voice.

"Sorry to wake you."

"Like anyone could sleep through that?" complained Pterrkee, still facing his wall.

"So, everyone is awake?"

"Yeah."

"Aye."

"Uh-huh."

Well, one slept, his snores crowding the room.

"Yosef," shook Seth. "Rabbi."

"Please," urged Ionnes. "Let him sleep." He laid back. "As I recall, that was what I was doing before madness aroused me."

Quiet resumed and most fell back to sleep. Dim felt the pull to sleep, too, but laying on his back, parked his locked fingers under his head and put together the events above him in the dark. None of it made sense at times, but somehow he still treasured how it all unfolded around him.

Kynops watched from the starless gloom until dawn's breaking. An inordinate amount of time had passed since sending Tarrow to retrieve the soul of Ionnes. His discernment itched and could not be scratched. Something must have gone wrong. Further he waited, brooding, until his patience prickled. Closing eyes, he whistled and called another demon. Named Bruiser, it resembled a mass of bruises. Kynops repeated the order to blind Ionnes in both eyes, then extract his soul and bring it to Kynops to send it to eternal judgment.

Bruiser raced away with bold determination. He knew not for certain whether he could remove the soul, but he was well practiced roughing them up. He raced across the countryside a ways before he realized he had no idea whom or what he was looking for. Still, he searched. Lesser imps growled and derided as they pointed the way. Bruiser became flustered, distracted by his critics, trying to hear them to follow their directions while knowing full well any or all could be lying to ridicule the demon. Touring Patmos in zigzag motions, he suddenly took note of the ever-present Light of Heaven, touching down or glowing, here and there, around the island.

Some Lights came and went. One Light held steady, so putting II and II together, he headed for that one.

Reaching the shore and surf, he saw an old man tending to various ropes. The strength of the Light frightened him. Patmos had been under almost perpetual darkness before he had arrived. Lidless, the demon still tried to squint as the Light grew in brightness and intensity and power upon his approach.

The old man tended to his work. Bruiser saw the soul of the man, soaking in the Light like rain channeled into a bottomless barrel. He cursed the man as he considered how to steal his soul. He knew souls to be grafted and woven tightly to their human by design. As death overtook the body, the soul then and only then disconnected, like a placenta from uterine walls. He could kill the body and try to grab the soul upon its exit, but that was not Kynops' instructions. He pondered how the body would survive without the soul? He had never seen it be so. Perhaps he should just take the whole man and let Kynops do the duty.

Then, it occurred to Bruiser this man could repel the demon with just a word. He would have to be silenced before delivery. The answer spread out before him. He would garner the waves to drown the man, just enough to render him silent, then steal away his body to deliver to Kynops. Would not Kynops be pleased to bring him the whole person? He shuddered with evil glee at the prospect and prepared to enter the water just as Ionnes spoke.

"Stop demon!" he shouted.

Bruiser tried to move but found he could not. He tried to look around, but even that was taken from him. He detected God's holy angels soaring around him and he knew one gripped his entire being in its right hand. The hold tightened the more he struggled.

The human still tended his ropes as he said, "Why are you here?"

Bruiser tried to answer, but his ability to speak failed in angelic grip and suspension.

"In the holy Name of Yeshua, speak demon."

"Kynops sent one of the rulers of the demons to kill you. He did not return, so called upon me and said, 'Go and kill Ionnes.' That is why I am here."

Ionnes flexed a rope to gather more salt.

"Salt and Light," he muttered to himself and smiled at the beautiful memory of his LORD when incarnate. Then, he looked up. Not that his eyes could 'see' the demon. For that he praised Yeshua with gladness. They were typically quite repulsive when the Holy Spirit allowed such vision. He reached up with a hand and Bruiser tried to withdraw, trying to wriggle its way out of captivity. It who thought nothing of capturing others somehow never saw the hypocrisy to struggle against its own capture. And Bruiser totally feared the warm, healing touch of this apostle.

Ionnes felt the wave press him from behind.

"Yes, yes," he muttered, his spirit ever alive in Christos. His hand gripped to a fist as he said, "Demon, I order you in the name of Yeshua Christos to depart from this island. Do not return to Kynops. Do not impose your evil upon any other man or woman. And, begone from Patmos forever."

Bruiser felt the power of the Light pressing upon him like the wielding sledge upon the anvil. The powerful grip which held him eased. He struggled to escape. He looked in all directions, but none mattered as he scampered away as quickly as his broken being could go. Heading out over the Ægean, he glanced back at Ionnes, still in the surf, and glimpsed for the first time since his expulsion from Heaven the equality of God's merciful judgment. An eye for an eye. He could have received what he had been sent to do to Ionnes.

PATMOS

CHAPTER 27

Reactions to the Demon Attack the Night Before

Mothcrates from Athenæ: The world is a dizzy place. I cannot say whether the apparition was real or not. All I saw was darkness and my eyes now fail me. I did hear a noise from above which I had never heard before. It did behave as a voice and its message eerie but clear. Still, I know that my senses can be fooled – that even the evidence of my own old eyes and ears can be false witness to the truth. With that said, the event left me speechless and hardly able to sleep the rest of the night. Tonight, I feel no greater comfort of what may come. For even if my eyes failed me in the darkness, they did not fail me when he brought down the temple to a pile of empty stones.

"Any more devils on attack today?" joked Dim nervously as Ionnes sat to eat. The barley loaves were surprisingly good. Someone said they came from the Phora bakery; just too old to sell. Each man got a handful of raisins, and the fish head nectar tasted like the heads were not too old.

Ionnes saw Dim's self-sculpted marble cup filled near the top with hot fish water. The Greek from Pergamos savored as he slurped. They even added a touch of lemon for flavor. All the men wondered what gave. Was it the governor's birthday or what? As per usual, they dared not say a word lest what little they received be taken away.

Ionnes answered with silence, considering it better to keep the second episode in the surf to himself for right now. Lots of fear already floating around them tonight.

"How are you doing?" asked Ionnes.

"Weird," answered Dim, honest and lacking words to explain what he felt.

"Most encounter fear," counseled Ionnes, "but you have power from on high to combat any demons."

343

Dim looked a bit encouraged as he singly and purposely ate each raisin, savoring each morsel to the last.

Teos from Side: I never seen no demon before. I did not know what it was, but it sure scared me. Then, Ionnes said, "Go away," and it went away. I love Ionnes so much.

"What was that?" sat Teos from his bed. "That was scary."

"Yes, it was," agreed Ionnes. "That is how you can tell it is not of Adonai. Yeshua is not a God of fear but is a God of love."

Teos loved that warm, fuzzy feeling he received at times listening to Ionnes talk.

Talor from Knidos: It really scared me. Tingles and goosebumps up and down my spine, over and over. I almost peed my tunic.

"What did the spirit want?" asked Talor, swallowing hard to have courage to ask. He had been silent all day fretting if another demon would enter their barracks tonight. The small group of prisoners sitting together felt Talor's question leave their lips at the same moment. They all knew they would again be locked in with this prophet for the night as well as many nights to come. Would this be a nightly visitation? Oddly, the old man did not seem threatened by the demons, but did not demons come from burning and eternal torment? What if the next one tried to set their barracks on fire?

"Did you hear it?" answered Ionnes to Talor.

"Uh-huh, but I could not understand all of its words."

Ionnes pointed towards the hills. "The demon said Kynops sent it to me to bring me to him."

"Can they do that?" asked Dim.

"Only if you let them," answered Ionnes. "Mostly, they possess others..." he looked around at the present company of soldiers, "... and have the humans do their destruction."

"But this one came straight at you?" questioned Minos, seated next to Mothcrates. "Is not that more powerful?"

"It can be," admitted Ionnes. "All the more reason to give your life to the divine God in Heaven who will always give you power and authority to protect yourself from such attacks. And yes, they are always attacks."

Minos from Knosos, Creta: I have seen it all, or so I thought. How does anyone topple a temple with just a few words out of his mouth? I was not that far from him yet did not even hear him but figured it out very quickly what had happened when they began to beat up Ionnes. Then, to be awakened by a demon? At first, I thought the demon was brought within by Ionnes, and that maybe explained how he toppled the temple, but then the demon said that Kynops sent it. I dared not breathe. There was nowhere to run and all any of us could do was wrap-up in our threadbare blankets for protection like little children. Surely, does not the ostrich hide its head beneath the sand? I do not recall being that afraid since I was ten when I fell in the pond and knew not how to swim. The water filled my lungs like a – like a - flood. Wait! That sounds foolish, does not it? Of course, it was a flood.

Pterrkee from Helikarroses: I finally get to sleep. Finally! Then, I get aroused by this barbaric presence. Yes, you heard me. Uncouth barbarians, all of them, attacking a working man in his own bed. Waking him from his slumbers. I cannot think of anything more barbaric.

"Well, I want not you sleeping in my lockup," announced Pterrkee.

"Where do you suggest I go?"

"I do not care. Just stay away from me."

Dim defended, "Like he gotta choice where he sleeps? Like any o' us gotta choice?"

"Shut-up, Dim," Pterrkee yelled.

"You shut-up," Dim yelled back. "Yer the one talkin' crazy. If there is no one I want sleepin' near me, it is you."

The two men ready to go to blows, the conniver Pterrkee backed down.

"Just stay away from me, or else," he warned.

"Brothers," called Ionnes, raising his hands to comfort and stop further aggressions. "Brothers, I understand your fears. Verily I do. I promise, as assuredly as Yeshua lives, no harm will come to any of you by any of Kynops' unclean spirits."

"Humph!" humphed Rabbi Yosef.

Ionnes looked at his biggest critic.

"You have something to add?"

The old rabbi muttered illegibly to himself, then raised his old, bearded head high and announced, "I knew you were a charlatan."

"By what words?"

"My own," stressed the rabbi. "I slept fitfully night last, then this morning received report of a demon invasion within our quarters. It stands by the testimony of more than two witnesses. Still, I cannot but believe some trickery has been played."

"To what purpose?" asked Ionnes.

"A ruse," he answered without hesitation. "A sham. To tie bales of wool over our eyes to fool all that you have such authority over demons in the name of your dead Savior. I still will not be thus fooled. If anything, I declare only a demon can order another demon. And, you Yochanan, are a worse demon than a Samaritan dog."

Ionnes recalled similar insults leveled at Yeshua by the Jewish leaders and Pharisees.

"So, you are saying I cast away a demon from Patmos because I am a demon?"

"Exactly," answered Rabbi Yosef. "You may even be the prince of demons..." His eyes turned down right after his answer.

"That sounds like a house divided," noted Ionnes.

Rabbi Yosef had already expected those words.

"And, it cannot stand," he muttered, finishing the Scripture mostly to himself, recalling the throne of David under Rehoboam when the ten tribes split off from Judah creating two kingdoms. What a sad day for Yisra'el that day. What a fool to be Rehoboam. How could he not glean from the wisdom and strength of his father Solomon? Did Elohim not likewise invite him his heart's wish like his father? Yosef did not know, but if so, whatever Rehoboam may have asked of Elohim, the young king did not seek wisdom.

Rabbi Yosef did not know how incarnate Yeshua answered that same charge all those years back. Such account was not common knowledge among exiled rabbis.

Seth from Cæsarea: I have been a devout Jew and rock-hard fisherman my whole life. Sometimes I miss the sea and the nets and the breeze and the rock of the boat. I have heard tell of this Yeshua over the years. I even met a few Jews who thought Him Messiah. I was never convinced, and the rabbis always swayed me away from that man, but now I see amazing miracles and wonders coming out of this decrepit old man who knew Yeshua personally. I hear his words. I see how the world changes after his touch, and now I start to wonder if the rabbis really were right.

"So," continued Ionnes, "how else am I a fraud?"

"What?" perked Rabbi Yosef, looking up from deeper in thought.

"You said I was a charlatan - a false prophet. How else am I a fraud? I am sure casting away a demon is not your only evidence. Or testimony. We might as well get it all out in the open. You tell the others what you think of me. You might as well also tell me."

"Oh, uh, yes," Rabbi Yosef regathered his thoughts, "you mean besides your claim of the Promised One who has come and left His people enslaved to the Romans." He looked over at their guards who were gleaning every word. They knew the old rabbi wanted to add a few more insulting descriptions to the word, 'Romans.'

"I thought we already went over this," considered Ionnes.

"Yes," admitted Rabbi Yosef, "but my position has not changed."

"Nor has my response changed," affirmed Ionnes.

Phranc from Asisium: I have always sought compassion and to look for the good in others, but the cold hate radiating from that presence – from that black hearted being. Well, it made my blood turn colder than salted ice. Colder than the snowy Alps. All my years in Italia and now Patmos never prepared me for that surprise attack. And, after it ended, I found myself happy. Oh, yes. Happy, but happy in part that the demon did not come for me. I say this to my shame.

"Bed," yelled Guard Mucius. The men rose to enter the large cell. Locked in, the men were brought face to face with their earlier fears. Would Ionnes be visited by another demon? What if the demon included any of them in its invasion this time around?

Most laid there, eyes wide open searching the dark. Some scooted their bedrolls a little farther from Ionnes. Only Teos scooted a little closer. The northwest breeze continued to blow, rattling the rafters. The men had heard those sounds countless times before, but now they checked in case some demon would be the cause. Even Rabbi Yosef watched the darkness, partially to not miss the show and perhaps find Yochanan's deception.

Minutes turned over slowly. The vigils wore on and lost watchers, one by one, as repose demanded each man's attention.

Ionnes had already found the depth of sleep; a comfort to some. If he worried not, they should not, either.

Arion from Thorikos: Here we all are, locked into the small space with only our hands and feet for weapons – and maybe a blanket or towel. Give me a sharp sword. Give me a long spear, or the finest long bow and arrow. I would have made wine pulp out of the intruder in no time. Achilles fought demons. But then I remembered how Ulysses fought monsters armed only with his wits, and given the chance to engage fantastic battle, so would I.

Kynops saw the end of the day approach. Still no word from Bruiser. The dolt. He chided himself severely for even trying to send such a halfwit. Thrashing, he stormed about, pounding and kicking and cursing. Almost nothing in his home was safe. Only when his need to breathe exceeded his anger did he stop to think as well as catch breath. Which should he send now? What should he do differently?

"Legion?" he muttered. If only, but it had been years since he heard from the Legion of demons. The last he had heard they were in Roma, and that was at the court of Cæsar Nero. Never before did he feel a need to command the Legion, but it had always been his ambition. He checked his shadows. Nowhere near two thousand. He would need others. His mind and eye watched the shadows.

"Ponos," he finally said.

The demon slipped out of the pack, moving deftly towards Kynops like a rancorous avalanche.

"Talaiporia," summoned Kynops.

A second demon left the pack, swirling and twirling, sometimes tornado, caging its quarry; sometimes whirlpool, sucking its prey down to hell.

"I need answers," said Kynops. "One of you go in. The other remain outside and listen. If the first succeeds, both bring the Christian zealot to me. If the first fails, report to me what occurred. That will tell me how to defeat him. Together we can bring down this man. He is only a man. He is not a god. Now, away."

The two bowed as they departed, swift and silent like fierce, oiled felines. The nighttime split to let them through as they hastened to the barracks. Seconds passed, and they saw the stone box holding the prisoners.

"I will wait for you," hissed Talaiporia.

"No, I await you," replied Ponos. "Kynops said you to go first."

"Wrong," answered Talaiporia.

Back and forth the two argued, both fearing to go in first. Hours passed, and they grew no closer than when they arrived. They tried to pick a number, but neither would trust the other to not cheat. They battled, but neither could overcome the other. Distracted, Talaiporia accidentally entered the holy light connecting Ionnes with Heaven. It screamed as though suddenly covered with festering boils. Ponos guffawed, even as Talaiporia retaliated, stuffing it into the smoldering firepit.

Both knew the only deciding answer. They would have to return to Kynops to ask which should go in first. And, both knew his wrath for such insolence. So, off they flew and within seconds were back at Kynops' dwelling. The two demons faced one another.

"Well, go in," hissed Ponos.

"You go in first."

"No, you."

Again, the argument engaged, neither willing to give in even one eternal second of torment. The argument would have continued, but they heard the voice of their master.

"Ponos! Talaiporia! Appear before me. Now!"

Each blamed the other as they entered to appear before Kynops. As darkness against darkness they shuddered openly before Kynops who sat upon the side of his bed, somewhat cranky from lack of sleep.

"Ponos, you bring Ionnes to me."

Ponos shook like the leaves on the autumn olive tree. The core of its being now rooted in fear, it had long since lost the sense of holy love by which it had been created by Elohim. It expected Tarrow and Bruiser had been exiled from Patmos by Yeshua through Ionnes and feared the same fate. A demon wandering alone became a terrible target by the other dark powers filling the Earth. Worse, it could also be subdued and held forever by the Heavenly Host. As much as it hated answering to Kynops, it much more feared and hated being expelled.

Kynops continued, "Ponos, you fall upon your prey like an avalanche and wrap around him worse than the python, squeezing the breath from him before he has any chance to speak. Silence Ionnes and he will be unable to overpower you or send you away with just his voice."

Ponos knew the truth of those words. Still, it felt not comfort. It looked at Talaiporia who heckled with barely an expression.

"And you, Talaiporia," turned Kynops, "foolish spirit. Tax me not with your selfishness or I will expel you from Patmos myself."

The demon rage swelled, and it wanted to pounce upon this flesh and blood man to suck the breath out of him faster than a cobra, but still shook with fear and homage. It knew Kynops said only what he meant and would send it away without hesitation or remorse.

Kynops continued, "You wait outside. I know your hearing to be large, so listen to what transpires, and if Ponos fails, report back to me. But, be alert, for if you hear a struggle between Ponos and the zealot, hesitate not to rush in and help. He is only a man. Together you should overcome him."

Talaiporia answered not but raced away as ordered. Ponos followed, less enthusiastic. The pair raced forth, arriving back at the barracks. The men inside slept. No guards could be immediately seen. Talaiporia peered at Ponos as they set up position. Ponos carefully entered the chamber, ever ready to flee. It viewed the men below. Some nurtured their own demons. The presence of the living God clearly shone upon one soul. Another soul beside him also shone the light of Christos, and dimmer lights touched three others. Ponos rolled shards of glowing sulfur between his folds as he prepared to pounce. With undiluted evil, it moved into position, each layer tensing like a cat on the hunt, ready to pounce. The figure still slept, undisturbed by its presence.

Ponos counted the seconds down to zero, then attacked – hard and fast and strong, like a lion seeking the one to devour. It wrapped around hard and covered the human man's mouth and nose. No words would be spoken by him for sure this time. No chance to escape. No chance to exile Panos from Patmos. It squeezed as hard as it could, giving everything to trap and contain. The man must not utter even so much as a grunt or a groan. The man struggled, but it was too late.

Keeping its hold, it looked around and prepared to make the jump to dark speed. Talaiporia, the coward, never ventured in to help as directed. It would chastise the skulker later, but for now, the triumph belonged to Ponos and only Ponos. Rising, it headed straight for the ceiling. Piercing through the roof, it saw Talaiporia, lying across the roof like a sunbathing lizard.

"Come," ordered Ponos, but Talaiporia failed to move.

"Hurry," added Ponos, but Talaiporia turned not.

Ponos began to depart without the other. It was never unusual when any demon left the wounded behind, whether flesh or spirit. Ready. Set. Stop!

Ponos checked its prey. It found nothing, Ionnes not held within its folds. How had Ionnes escaped without notice?

Or, had he?

Peeking back in the barracks, it saw Ionnes, turning over, but sleeping soundly. Backing out, it hovered, pondering what illusions had been played upon it and preparing to reenter and capture the sleeping prophet when it felt the warm arms of solid light encapsulate and capture the unclean spirit. It looked over at Talaiporia and realized it had already been caught. Angels filled the cosmos around them, some with swords drawn, some touching the lives of those around Ionnes in answer to his prayers, and some singing praises to the LORD. It screamed but could not get free. In its struggles, it suddenly saw Ionnes, kneeling in prayer on the roof. He looked at the demon and said, "Begone from Patmos in the name of Christos Yeshua. No longer plague another man, woman or child ever."

Ponos felt the grip loosen as it scampered to race away from the island, screaming and cursing as it choked over its own wails.

Talaiporia knew the same fate awaited him. It looked at Ionnes, defiant but fearful. The old apostle stood and faced the demon.

"Unclean spirit," he said, "what is your name?"

"Talaiporia."

"Then, in suffering I send you," answered Ionnes. "Return to Kynops and tell him the LORD Yeshua lives and that on Patmos, every knee will bow, and every tongue confess that Yeshua is LORD. Now, begone."

The first light of dawn touched the eastern sky, silhouetting the distant mainland mountains as Talaiporia raced back to Kynops. Looking back, he saw not Ionnes on the roof, and realized the apostle still slept inside while Yeshua brought forth his spirit to the roof to deal with his attackers. For Ionnes, the incident would be only as real as a dream to him, yet the commands from his mouth held equal authority, compelling obedience as if his body's mouth spoke them aloud.

Returned, Talaiporia spoke to Kynops all that transpired. Kynops thrashed about his home again in unrighteous anger. The shadows all shuddered at his tirade.

"Must I do everything myself?" he shouted, looking at the shadows. Then, he stopped as an idea took hold deep within.

He weighed the scheme as the shadows strained to eavesdrop. "I will need your help, my shadows," he said.

The shadows tried to withdraw until he added, "Prepare," then laid his head back upon his bed to finally rest.

Jack from Sparta: Most of these holy joes cannot get a whole basket full of gods to give them the power that Ionnes' one God gives him. Does not make sense to me, partially because what god would want those old bones? I know I certainly would not, but I also admit, if I had all the answers, I would become a god, or at least give one a day off.

PATMOS

CHAPTER 28

Roman Guard Julius stood at his post, somewhat confused. Or, perhaps perplexed sported a better word. At least one or two big questions presently plagued him, hovering over perhaps a half dozen lesser questions. He looked over at Octavius. His fellow soldier and friend watched the proceedings without much thought. He was not someone Julius could discuss any questions with any depth. Octavius only volunteered for today's duties because he knew the zealot Giovanni did amazing things at times, and he hoped today he would see some more magic. But hardened Julius watched everyone, studying face to face to face, seeking clues to answer his questions.

The first big question was why this Christian zealot was even here? Why did not someone execute him years ago? Julius paused to recall the flogging, and how oddly it had ended. One moment, splattered in the man's blood, he laughed at the flavor filling his mouth. The next second, he stood like one dazed by a solid smack to the head during battle.

"Odd," he muttered. It seemed that word could be attached to this Christian over and over and still not become common. He had heard the account of being both poisoned and boiled in oil in Roma before Cæsar Domitian without success - a story too fantastic to be true even if it came from Cæsar Domitian himself. But, what about the sword? Or the spear? A dangling rope? A few extra minutes underwater?

With that said, who would dare execute Giovanni? He would have bet none from his ranks. Julius, for all his godless ways, still recognized a fear, or at least a caution for dealing with this prisoner. No man, Roman or otherwise, wishes to be personally cursed for the rest of his life by any man's God - especially if that God seems to be in town at the time. Giovanni may not have called down fire from Heaven as yet, but that did not mean he could not do it. Inaudible voices inside his head seemed to say leave well enough alone with this one. Dare not take the risk.

His second big question surrounded the governor's family. Both his wife and her brother now supported the prisoner, and Julius was not so sure about their father and mother. He had never heard of such tomfoolery in his life. Why the attraction? He could not see it but had to respect it. Sure, he had seen Apollonides not right in his mind, and he had heard Giovanni prayed for his deliverance, but that still seemed a poor reason to give homage to this prisoner and his companionless God.

So, here they all stood under two olive trees atop the hill to the southwest of main Phora City on a Sunday for a time of worship to Giovanni's God. The word "Odd" popped again into his head. Not that this was the first time Giovanni led others in prayer and worship since he had arrived. Right from the start, the old zealot asked to know the day of the week. Thereafter, every Sunday, he sought even a few minutes for a special time of prayer. He would sing as he worked. He would pray for others, sometimes laying his old, spotted hands atop their heads. One time, he overheard Giovanni mention Sunday as a weekly anniversary for worship, but he could not make out what they were honoring.

The summer sun shone brightly on the congregation. One of Julius' little, nagging questions was why they had trekked all this way up the hill? Old Giovanni panted hard the whole way up. His brittle bones made the journey, but it seemed an unnecessary effort. Well sure, these holy types did seem to like worshipping on high places.

"Brings them closer to their gods?" he muttered to himself. Octavius glanced over at him but did not understand. Growing up in mountainous Pescara, right in the middle of Italia, he well knew that Romans did not have a specific, weekly day of worship of the gods. There were special holidays each year for each god and many families worshipped their favorite gods in home daily. It seemed odd to Julius, and to many Romans for that matter, for Christians and Jews to have a special day each week to come together to worship their solitary God.

A few years earlier, in Roma, Julius had a chance meeting and discussion with Flores Postumius, the Rex Sacrorum - the "King of Sacred Things," ie, head priest in Roma. Not that anyone ever called him by his given name Flores anymore, not even his wife. Even she carried the title Regina Sacrorum instead of Ovidia, the name of her birth. Like so many, his job and title became his identity. A patrician directly from the Collegium Pontificum, he most commonly visited the Roma Temple of Jupiter. A portly man, he was, of course, the ultimate bureaucrat. One does not rise to such prominence in Roma without appeasing some very commanding people.

In spiritual affairs, he stood second only to Cæsar, the Pontifex Maximus - a position originally held by a pontificum of the Collegium Pontificum until Julius Cæsar seized the title for himself some one-hundred-and-fifty years earlier. After Julius' assassination, the position went back to a patrician of the Collegium Pontificum, but shortly thereafter Augustus Cæsar reassigned the title to himself It continued to pass to each emperor thereafter, reasoning that if Cæsar was god, then he would be the divine spiritual leader of the land – and the world. By design, he would need to be the Pontifex Maximus.

Julius did not bring it up to the Rex Sacrorum, but later overheard him talking to other patricians about the evergrowing Christian church. The Christian church was still something of a curiosity at the time. Some still considered it a branch of the Jews though they had already well spread outside of Iudæa into Greece, Italia and even Asia and Africa. Many were known more for their miracles than the messages they shared or the source of their powers. Flores withheld comments of the accounts he had heard. He had seen many extraordinary events during his tenure as Rex Sacrorum, but nothing compared to the accounts shared surrounding followers of The Way and their executed then reportedly resurrected leader, Jeshua.

That day Julius went away thinking he would snuff the breath out of every Christian he found. Now he stood on a Greek hillside following direct orders to oversee one of their meetings of worship led by their last living apostle, of all people. Shaking his head, he looked back down the hill to the

Temple of Artemis. It seemed so small from this vantage. Likewise, further below, the crumbled pile of the Apollo Temple still remained untouched as though priestly prayers and offerings would rebuild the structure. He had always been a good soldier, following orders to the max, but never had he encountered a greater temptation to disobey orders by killing Giovanni. Temptation or not, his sense of duty was only exceeded by his sense of fear of this holy man. He loved his empire and his home but not enough to risk a curse upon his own life or the empire.

He watched as Ionnes knelt and stacked a pile of stones before him with the largest, flattest rock on top. Chryspippe stepped forward, unfolding a cloth to reveal a flat loaf of bread. Ionnes took both. He flattened out the cloth on the stone, then set the loaf atop. Resting a moment, he closed eyes, sighed, muttered near silent prayers, said, "Amen," and stood.

He picked-up the small loaf of unleavened bread. Made from wheat, he dwelt upon the beauty of the loaf – its little, burst bubbles and cinnamon-brown sides, cooked upon heated stone. Freshly baked, its yummy scent reached that old nose with a tantalizing tease. Bread was the mainstay diet for the prisoners, the loaves usually made from barley. This savory wheat became all that much more special to Ionnes.

He looked over and smiled at Chyspippe to thank the benefactor for the day's remembrance as Yeshua directed. She smiled as she recalled the look on their cook's face at home when directed to make a loaf without leavening.

Standing next to her brother, both smiled back. Apollonides held a bottle of red wine and some clay goblets for the service.

Ionnes looked back at the bread, still in his hands. Old fingers clutched the bread like a newborn infant premie. Eying his hands, he smiled to himself. His hands had seldom been this clean since he had arrived on Patmos – or even since he had been arrested in Ephesus, now about a year past. In anticipation to the day's gathering to worship Yeshua, he scrubbed fingers and palms, expecting the LORD's Supper would be shared.

The summer sun shone brightly upon all there, but a welcome northeastern breeze blew over them from off the water, keeping the sun from roasting them.

Ionnes looked back at the congregation. Chryspippe and Apollonides stood closest to Ionnes. Barbara next to them.

From the penal colony, Dim, Talor, Euæmon, Teos and Phranc. Lorin and Tobie took servant positions slightly apart from the crowd. Talor could not take his eyes off either Chryspippe or Lorin. Also, a few seekers from Phora, Skala, and surrounding regions heard rumor of a gathering and came to investigate.

Finally, a few Roman soldiers completed the assembly.

Ionnes welcomed each of them as he said, "Not all of Yeshua's miracles are grand and glorious affairs to men. Often – perhaps more often, they are smaller moments like this one, here and now, where a holy group of believers like us come together for the first time. Who here foresaw this gathering a year ago? Not even I, I admit."

He glanced at each of them with his signature smile. His eyes settled on Teos. The initial prisoner to guide him through Patmos smiled back and recalled the first time he had seen Ionnes worship. Teos thought it had been so odd at the time.

Not many days after Ionnes arrived on Patmos, he asked if anyone knew the day of the week. None of the prisoners knew including the rabbi. He found no synagogue on Patmos. None of the guards knew either, or they would not answer.

Nothing unusual there, so he went with his most educated guess. The crew thought it Wednesday when they landed. He personally held his devotionals most days anyway, but always wished to make sure he shared in the LORD's supper on the LORD's Day. A Jew by birth, it seemed an odd change from the Sabbath day of rest, visiting the synagogues or making the annual trip to Ierusalem and the temple. But, with the resurrection of Yeshua on Sunday, the triumphant entry into Ierusalem on Sunday and more, the weekly celebration of Christos became more and more a Sunday occasion. Not that

Ionnes cared what day they prayed. Every day was the right day to worship together the Son of Man.

One evening after dinner, Ionnes looked around at his fellow prisoners as well as the soldiers. So little happened there, that when anyone did anything, everyone noticed. Ionnes depended on that fact as he took a few steps forward and fell to his knees on the dirt.

"Abba LORD - Redeemer Yeshua - beautiful Spirit, good evening."

He did not have to look. He knew he immediately had a rapt audience.

He raised hands and head to the heavens. The twilight had not yet quite started. His steamy breath could be seen in the last light of day, puffing up like a chimney coughing up greenwood.

"We come to You with praise and thanksgiving, for You are the LORD who made all and are in all."

He could hear breathing increase around him, detectable each moment the breeze briefly abated. The guards might jump in, but well acquainted with Roman guards, they typically did nothing as long as insurrection was not being instilled.

"Whatcha doin'? asked Teos, seated close by on a rock.

Ionnes looked around at the simpleminded man.

"Praying."

"That loud?"

"Uh-huh."

"Does your God have bad hearing?"

The men all laughed, including Ionnes.

"Good question. Good question, my friend. No, God does not have bad hearing. Sometimes I just like to make more noise. You are welcome to join me," Ionnes invited, still enjoying the special mood set by the unintentional joke. "Adonai likes it when more of us make noise for Him."

Teos wanted to jump down and join in, but instead watched the guards. Of course, he had little to zero experience compared with Ionnes on Roman guard reactions to prayer and worship.

Ionnes recognized the apprehensions and went back to praying. Though not absolutely sure, he still went forward as though they shared the LORD's Day.

This day, Teos watched Ionnes lifting the little flat loaf of bread.

"What is the bread for?" he asked. He felt hungry and hoped the old man had more. Or, maybe he would eat it all right in front of them. That would be terrible.

Ionnes smiled at Teos. "It is for each of us to eat, but just a little bit."

"What for?"

"It helps us to remember Yeshua."

"Ionnes, you know I never met Yeshua. How can I remember Him?"

"We can remember Him in different ways." Ionnes looked at the congregation. "How about all of you? What can you say Yeshua has done for you?"

The group started to move and shift around awkwardly.

All except Barbara. She stepped forward boldly and happily.

"Because of Yeshua, I can walk. And run. And dance," her mirth irrepressible.

"Amen!" said Ionnes, still smiling. The others nodded appreciably.

"Barbara, you really have no idea how much joy each step you take brings to me. Each day, I praise Yeshua for you."

In response, she stepped forward and gave her friend a hug. After a lifetime of crawling on her belly in the dirt, hugs had been alien to her since childhood. Now that she could stand, she hugged anyone she could, such was her joy. Ionnes saw the change in her heart, as real as the change in her legs and feet. He loved her hugs and was warmed to the core to share her elation.

"Anyone else?" asked Ionnes.

"He healed my brother," added Chryspippe. Apollonides nudged his sister with a shoulder but appreciated what she said.

A moment's silence then Dim said, "He broughtcha t' all us here on Patmos."

"Yes," went out, spoken by most there. Heads nodded, sharing that grateful fact. Ionnes looked again at Teos.

"So, Teos, why might you remember Yeshua? What did He do for you?"

Teos wanted to repeat Dim's answer but thought he should say something new. His mind stumbled along, but in the unhurried group, he eventually found his answer.

"You made Gallo come back."

Guard Octavius grunted with agitation.

"That was amazing," spouted Talor, looking away from the women, suddenly reminded how stunned he had been that first day. Somehow it is different and all that much more remarkable, the first miracle - when a man anticipated nothing and suddenly everything appeared before him.

"I wish he was still here," added Teos, looking down embarrassedly.

Ionnes felt more tears. He wondered if he had not shed more tears on Patmos than in recent years in Ephesus? Regardless of his history with Yeshua, he was still a man with his weaknesses and struggles and shortcomings, as had been all his brother apostles. Yes, he had grown so much over the years, but that did not mean he was not still growing.

"I might wish he was also here," he answered, "but, more I am glad he is now with Yeshua. That is the best news of all."

The prisoners shared the gladness, some more than others.

"So, when do we get to eat the bread?" asked Teos.

Ionnes again smiled at Teos whose basic faith both gave him great glee and helped to keep his own faith on track.

"In a few minutes," he assured, "but, please allow me to talk about this bread. Would that be alright?" He asked everyone. None objected. He set the bread down on the cloth covered rock altar. He led all in prayer, then looking up, he said, "Apollonides?"

Apollonides kind of jerked up in response.

Ionnes motioned to the bottle of wine and goblets. Apollonides stepped forward and presented all to Ionnes who poured some into one glass. He then set the glass beside the bread and the bottle on the ground beside the table.

"When Yeshua walked the Earth," he began, "I recall a time when we, the twelve, had been with Him for over two years. He fed five thousand men plus their families miraculously, starting with only five barley loaves and two small fish. I still am awed when I recall that day. The fish and bread just kept being there for everyone to eat. Have you ever played a game that you tried to lose so you could quit, but kept winning? It reminded me of that. No matter what we did, there kept being more and more bread and fish for everyone.

"Thereafter, the people all wanted to make Yeshua their king. He would not entertain their persistent requests. I love Yeshua so much, and this was one of those times I could love Him more. He would not be a king because He already was the King of kings. His kingdom was not of this world and He would never be the warring king so many prayed for. So, He departed their company and went off to the mountains to pray – something He did often. Sometimes we prayed with Him, and sometimes He needed to be alone. This time, He went off on His own towards the mountains. He told us if He arrived not back by nightfall to take the boat across the Sea of Galilee to Capernaum. Well, we waited. As the dinner hour approached, we would dine on the extra bread. We had taken twelve full baskets of bread after everyone had their fill.

"Well, evening approached, so Cephas recommended we go. I recall watching the mountains, searching for anyone who might be heading our way. My gazes produced nothing, and I entered the boat. I knew we had to get going, so we said our good-byes to those on the beach to shove off and set sail. It seemed like a good evening's run when the wind suddenly came up like someone suddenly opened all the windows to Heaven. Clouds rolled in, covering the stars. We took down the sail and all started rowing hard. The storm gained strength and after a spell we were not even sure where we were rowing or whether we would make it. We just wanted to get to safe land. Then, Andrew saw something that took us all to fright. I can still feel the shivers up and down my spine." He paused.

The listeners waited only so long.

"What?" Phranc finally said.

Ionnes closed his eyes a moment as though collecting thoughts before letting them flow forth from his mouth.

"We saw Yeshua coming towards us."

He paused again, then added, "but, He had no boat."

"Was He swimmin'?" asked Dim.

"Did His boat capsize, and you found Him hanging to floating wreckage?" asked Apollonides.

"Are you gonna tell us He was riding a big fish?" asked someone from the town.

"No," answered Ionnes. "Good guesses all, but none correct."

He watched their yearning faces as he answered, "We saw Yeshua walking on top of the water towards us."

"No way!" said Guard Octavius, then looked at Julius and the others and shrank back a bit.

"Hard to believe, is it?" Ionnes called to Octavius. "I might agree if I was you, but I saw Him with my own eyes, walking on the water as if it were dry land. And, it scared all of us worse than seeing a pack of hungry sharks.

"He knew all of us were scared, so He said, 'It is I; do not be afraid,' (1) and He climbed into the boat with us. Perhaps all of us were stunned, but it seemed like the next moment we reached the shore. It felt so odd to be afraid of the waves, then afraid of a vision of Yeshua, then afraid for He was real, then find all was good and fine and perfect as soon as He entered our boat.

"It was late, but we found a place to lodge for the night and caught some sleep. The next day, we saw boats coming in and started to recognize some of the people whom we had seen the day before. Some who ate with us when Yeshua fed the five thousand. So, we met them on the beach.

"I loved the look on some of their faces. They saw Yeshua, but many knew He had not departed with us and they saw no other boat tied there. Yeshua's name was already well known in Capernaum and many there joined us on the beach. Our brethren from Capernaum invited Yeshua to synagogue, so we marched up the beach together to town. On the road, Yeshua first addressed the visitors who sailed to us that morning. *He said, 'Truly, truly, I say to you, you seek Me, not because you saw signs, but because you ate of the loaves and were filled.'* (2) Some said, 'No,' but many nodded in agreement.

"So, Yeshua said, *'Don't work for the food that perishes but for the food that lasts for eternal life, which the Son of Man will give you, because God the Father has set His seal of approval on Him.'* (3)

"Someone asked, *'What shall we do that we may work the works of God?'* (4) and the others nodded to ask the same.

I loved His answer. It was sooooo simple a blind man could see it and a man born with no arms could carry it. *He said, 'This is the work of God, that you should believe in Him whom He has sent.'* (5) That was it. Just believe. Now, I am not so foolish to not see how difficult that can be for some people. Many are not used to trusting, even if it is God Himself in the flesh asking for that trust.

"But what amazed me was their answer. First, Yeshua said, 'Just believe,' and they said, *'What sign shewest thou then, that we may see, and believe thee?'* (6) Just yesterday, He had fed five thousand of them plus their families with a truly amazing miracle, and they still sought a 'sign.' They also heard of the miracle that brought Him across the water, but that was not sign enough, either. Some people! You would think they wanted the LORD Adonai Himself to perform for them like a circus juggler. Of course, walking through town attracted the attentions of others who joined us. Even the Rabbi was honored to have Yeshua teach in his synagogue." Ionnes paused and sighed.

"Sometimes nowhere else on Earth feels more like home to me than synagogue. We all grew up there, just as much as at home or on the sea. It was our place of meeting, of sharing, of community and love. We were taught right from wrong. As baby boys, we were circumcised there - something I praise God I do not remember."

Everyone chuckled.

(Some days back, Apollonides asked Ionnes about circumcision. With full knowledge of Jewish requirements, he wondered if Christians likewise demanded such from grown men. Ionnes assured him circumcision was not required and thereby a personal choice.   Apollonides answered, "Good, 'cause it ain't never ever gonna happen.")

"We prayed there," continued Ionnes, "but also we laughed there, and we cried there. I was a rambunctious boy in my youth, both my brother and I. We were called the Sons of Thunder for good reason. Our father, Zebedee, never spared the rod and we both were seldom shy to give him good reason to use it. But it shaped us into men of strength, knowing right from wrong. Each of us started working the nets with our father as fishers before we turned ten. I well recall falling asleep while trying to complete my Hebrew lessons. Of course, I never could foresee what fate Adonai placed for me - like all of us. Even now, at times I scarcely believe the life that lays behind me, but I treasure it in my heart with more loving wisdom than Solomon ever conjured. Adonai knew the calling upon all of our lives with Yeshua, so reared us accordingly."

He took another moment to reminisce and enjoy, then looked again at the group as he asked, "Now, do any of you know what manna is?"

None did except Dim.

"A long time ago, my ancestors, the Yisra'elites were slaves in Egypt. A great leader named Moses came to set them free."

"Moses again," thought Dim, though Ionnes had already told him all about Moses.

"Adonai was with him, leading many towards Iudæa - it was called Canaan at the time. Have any of you ever been to that region?"

Guard Julius wanted to say that he had but kept his tongue. To his surprise, Ionnes looked directly at him a bit as he continued.

"There was no food for them. Certainly not enough to feed over a million people, yet Adonai kept them out in the wilderness for forty years."

"Why," asked Phranc, "would your God keep a group He had just delivered in the wilderness for so long?"

"Good question," answered Ionnes. "There is more than one answer, but I will say that the Yisra'elites had lived in Egypt many generations, so Adonai wanted to shake Egyptian ways off of them a bit before they entered their Promised Land. And, we could talk about that question for the rest of the day if I let myself get distracted. I asked if you knew about manna. Adonai fed them with manna for all those years in the wilderness."

"So, what is it?" asked Chryspippe.

"It is like bread. Every morning, they would go out and collect just enough manna for the day. On Fridays, they would gather twice as much so they would not have to gather any on the Sabbath - a day of rest."

"Why not gather enough for the entire week?" asked Apollonides.

"Because Adonai made it so it would not last. If they gathered too much, it turned rotten by the next day - except for on Fridays. That day, they were to collect enough for the Sabbath, so none would have to work. Adonai miraculously made the manna that day last for two days."

Most wondered at such a story. Oh well, every faith had its folklore.

Chryspippe suddenly recalled her dream with the tastiest bread.

Ionnes continued, "As I recall, the Jews in Capernaum told Yeshua that Moses gave them manna, and Yeshua corrected them. He said, *'Truly, truly, I say to you, it is not Moses who has given you the bread out of heaven, but it is My Father who gives you the true bread out of heaven.'* (7)

"So, they said, *'Sir, give us this bread always.'* (8) Who would not say that? We apostles wanted that, too, and we were with Yeshua every day. We also had eaten His bread and fish only yesterday, so we were not as surprised as the crowd when He said, *'I am the bread of life: he that cometh to Me shall not hunger, and he that believeth on Me shall never thirst.'* (9)

"Yeshua saw their faces. He knew what you were thinking before you did, but this time even we disciples could see what was going on, and I am here to tell you, sometimes we could be so thick-headed and dense. He told them that they had seen Him but still did not believe, so He kind of repeated what He had just told them.

"He said, '*All those the Father gives Me will come to me, and whoever comes to Me I will never drive away. For I have come down from heaven not to do My will but to do the will of Him who sent Me. And, this is the will of Him who sent Me, that I shall lose none* of all those He has given Me but raise them up at the last day.' (10) Then, He added, '*For this is the will of My Father, that everyone who looks on the Son and believes in Him should have eternal life, and I will raise him up on the last day.*' (11)

"I recall being a bit astonished by the crowd. Yeshua just told them that He would raise them up on the last day, and all they could hear was that He said He came down from Heaven. Well, some there did know that He grew up in Nazareth. They knew His parents, Yosef and Maryam."

"Like Rabbi Yosef?" asked Teos.

"Same name. Different person," answered Ionnes. "Uncle Yosef was a wonderful man. I loved him so much. And, though he lived as a working carpenter, he was still one of the wisest men I ever knew."

"He was yer uncle? Yer real uncle?" asked Dim.

"Yes," answered Ionnes, though he knew Yosef was not related by blood. "Maryam, Yeshua's mother and my mother were sisters.

"So, Yeshua just told them to not murmur amongst themselves. He repeated, '*No man can come to Me, except the Father which hath sent Me draw him: and I will raise him up at the last day.*' (12) Then, Yeshua said more to address their disbelief and possible stubbornness as He added, '*It is written in the prophets, 'AND THEY WILL ALL BE TAUGHT OF GOD.' Everyone who has listened to and learned from the Father, comes to Me. (13) Not that anyone has seen the Father, except He [who was with the Father and] who is from God; He [alone] has seen the Father. I assure you and most solemnly say to you, he who believes [in Me as Savior—whoever adheres to, trusts in, relies on, and has faith in Me—already] has eternal life [that is, now possesses it].*' (14)

"We could tell they were still unsure, so Yeshua continued by reminding them, '*I am the bread of life.*' (15) It was the perfect thing to say after yesterday's miraculous feast, but He did not stop there. No. No. No. He went back to their claims about Moses as He said, *'Your fathers did eat manna in the desert, and are dead. This is the bread which cometh down from heaven; that if any man eat of it, he may not die.'* (16)

As I recall, it seemed like literally everyone there just had this dumbfounded look on their faces. They could not quite put II and II together to reach IV. I know Yeshua could confound many with His words. He confounded me many times, but this time I think most people were starting to get what He said but were not sure they heard Him right."

"Why?" asked Apollonides.

"Because He just told them He was the bread of life, then said that one may eat of it and not die."

"So, what?" asked Apollonides. "He was being rhetorical. Symbolic."

Ionnes nodded to acknowledge the Roman, but insisted, "Please be patient. There is more to tell."

Apollonides started to speak but stopped. His training as an orator kept trying to take center stage, but he knew this as one time he was definitely the student and not the teacher.

"You have a good point," applauded Ionnes, "but, it is incomplete. Yeshua next told them, *'I am the living bread that came down from heaven. Anyone who eats this bread will live forever; and this bread, which I will offer so the world may live, is my flesh.'* (17)"

The group stood a bit stunned, trying to see if they heard correct. Ionnes looked at each one. Even the Roman soldiers.

"I see in all of your faces the same questions I always receive when I share this teaching. And, rightfully so. The Jews tried to make sense of it, same as all of us, but it felt wrong. Some started quarreling amongst themselves about it asking, *'How can this man give us His flesh to eat?'* (18) To tell you all the truth, I wondered the very same thing the first time I heard Yeshua talk about this.

"Moreso, His answer disturbed them even more. He said, *'Verily, verily, I say unto you, except ye eat the flesh of the Son of Man, and drink His blood, ye have no life in you. Whoso eateth My flesh, and drinketh My blood, hath eternal life; and I will raise him up at the last day.'* (19)

"Well, that certainly did not stop the quarrelling. Verily, it made it worse. Eat someone's flesh? Drink their blood?"

Ionnes shook his entire body as though repelling such a ridiculous idea.

"Brrrrr! The crowd was getting more and more upset. Then, it got worse, and Apollonides, this answers your question. Yeshua then said, *'For My body truly is food, and My blood truly is drink. Whoever eats My body and drinks My blood abides in Me and I in him. Just as The Living Father has sent Me, and I am living because of The Father, whoever will eat Me, he also will live because of Me. THIS is the bread that came down from Heaven. It is not as your forefathers who ate manna and have died; whoever eats this bread shall live for eternity.'*" (20)

"So," adjudged Apollonides, "your Yeshua wanted everyone to eat His flesh and drink His blood? That is sick!"

"And, you would be correct," agreed Ionnes, "so much so that many disciples departed following Yeshua shortly thereafter. It was a teaching which sounded of lunacy."

"Then, why did He say it?" asked Chryspippe and Phranc together in sync. They looked at one another a bit amused. Chryspippe still felt odd to be sharing time on this hill with some prisoners, but sharing the same question made it less odd.

Apollonides looked at Ionnes, then smiled, "But, you are going to tell us why and how it made sense."

"Already, you know me too well," complimented Ionnes. "Honestly, all twelve of us brooded about that teaching. It was hard for us to fathom as well. Then, just before Yeshua was tried and crucified, He showed us the answer. It was Passover, and as Jews, we were celebrating and honoring one of our stories of old from the time of Moses."

"Moses again?" said Dim, this time aloud. Ionnes nodded to him.

"About, oh, three-fourths of the way through the meal, Yeshua took bread into His hands." Ionnes picked up the bread before him.

"He broke the bread, ripping it in half." Ionnes did the same. "He did not cut it, but let it be pulled apart by His hands.

Then, he passed it around the table, instructing each of us to take off a chunk." Ionnes tore off a piece for himself, then handed it to Chryspippe to do the same. She broke off a small piece of bread, then looked at Ionnes questioningly as she passed the loaf to her brother.

"It does not matter how big or small a piece you take," answered Ionnes. "Just make sure there is enough for everyone." Each took some bread, then returned the rest to Ionnes.

He looked at the Roman guards and held up the bread to them. Octavius almost said, 'Yes,' but waited for others. When no other stepped forward, he remained in position.

Ionnes held up His piece of bread as He continued, "Next, Yeshua took the rest of the loaf, held it up high for all twelve of us to see, and said, *'THIS is My body which is given for you: this do in remembrance of Me.'* (21) Then, He told all of us to eat that part of the whole loaf, and instructed us to do this regularly in remembrance of Him.

"I can still remember sitting there right beside Yeshua, and suddenly seeing the answer so clearly. It was like when your ears are clogged then suddenly open, and you did not even know they were clogged. Or, like when you cannot stay awake, so nod off for a short nap, then when you awaken, you feel so alert, and your mind is so much clearer. I realized the answer to the body and blood. The Bread of Life wanted us to eat the real food of the unleavened bread."

Raising his piece of bread over his head, Ionnes looked at the gathering. Three had raised their bread up as well, Teos up over his head like Ionnes. The apostle smiled, then noticed something. He tore his shard of bread in half and handed one part to Teos. Teos did not understand, but that was nothing unusual, and he happily smiled to have more. Ionnes returned to the front, then said, "Thank You, Yeshua." He put the bread in his mouth and the others did the same.

Chewing, Apollonides watched Ionnes. The old man kept his eyes closed tightly, his brow furrowed a bit. He waited a spell, not even chewing, then opened his eyes and continued the service.

"Next, He took the cup of wine." He lifted up the goblet set before them, "and said, *'This cup [is] the new covenant in My blood, which is poured out for you.'* (22) Yeshua took a sip, then passed it around to all of us to do the same."

Ionnes took a sip, savoring the red liquid that the prisoners could not typically indulge. He passed it around, this time starting with Apollonides. The young Roman raised the cup to his lips when he stopped and offered it first to Barbara who stood beside him.

"You first," he said. She could not believe her eyes; that this Roman would give her first consideration. She took the goblet, took barely a sip and handed it back. Apollonides took a sizable gulp, then passed it to his sister.

"So, it is symbolic like I said," he addressed Ionnes as others continued to sip the wine.

Ionnes was about to answer, then put up a couple fingers, requesting a moment, his eyes pointing towards the activity behind them. He watched the goblet move around. Phranc was the last to take a sip.

"Finish it," said Ionnes.

Phranc looked in the cup. There was not much left, but more than some others had consumed. He sniffed the cup and rolled around the scant amount of wine, watching the hues and legs. He touched his lips to the glass and let a little fluid seep in. The flavor gradually spread around his mouth and palate. He let it season his practiced taste buds, then took the bigger drink. The fluid toured the whole of his mouth for some time before he swallowed. The winemaker could not have asked for a better moment than that one.

"Thank you," said Ionnes to Apollonides. "And, the answer is still No. It is not just symbolic, for when Yeshua said, *'My flesh is the true food, and my blood is the true drink.'* (23) He was giving us a divine peek into Heaven. It is His real body and blood that looks, feels and tastes like bread and wine. That is one of those little miracles I mentioned when we first arrived here today – the divine presence of Yeshua in a humble chunk of bread and a sip of wine. So no, my brother, it is not just symbolic."

Apollonides nodded, but he knew he would have to take some time to digest the day's teaching, no pun intended. This was something he had never heard about the Christians and had a very good idea most Romans shared that ignorance.

After another prayer and a song, Ionnes went around and gave hugs to whomever desired. Even Chryspippe, the married woman and socialite, accepted a polite hug from her teacher. She felt thanks he was not as stinky as many of the other prisoners, probably because he spent so much more time in the salty water.

"Tell me," asked Apollonides as they all began the descent down the hill, "are you always so – um, holy?"

Ionnes was about to answer No but thought better to ask for clarification.

"I mean," continued Apollonides, "after you ate the bread, you took more time than anyone else, perhaps to savor the food, or more likely to give further thanks to Yeshua?"

Ionnes smiled sheepingly. "To tell the truth, you are only partially right. Yes, I did savor, and yes, I did give thanks, but well – um – erm, I paused mostly because I bit my tongue."

It took a moment for everyone to start laughing, starting with Apollonides and Teos.

"You bit your tongue?"

"Uh-huh. Hard."

"Um, yes," Apollonides still chuckled, so struggled to get out the words. "Now I know beyond any doubt or shadows that you are a man of God. You use not the words I use when I bite my tongue."

"We shall see," acknowledged Ionnes, "the next time you bite your tongue, being a new creature in Christos and all..."

"Perhaps," Apollonides answered though not convinced. "I have already discerned my life with Yeshua is a journey more than a destination."

"You perceive correctly," Ionnes smiled as he internally praised Yeshua for this moment, sharing the LORD's Day with a new convert from Florentia. The splendor of Yeshua's never ceased to amaze him.

Guard Julius kept a warrior's pace near the walkers. Peaceful it appeared, but he knew that anything could change in an instant. He glanced at Octavius close by.

"What is wrong?"

Octavius looked up at Julius like he had slapped him. He even placed his palm against his cheek. He knew his answer to be foolishness to his fellow guards, so kept his tongue. After a fashion, Julius asked, "No magic, eh?"

Octavius nodded – barely and looked down.

"Do not hold your breath, my friend. Likely will never happen again."

"That would be bad," muttered Octavius.

Julius paused and placed a hand on the soldier's shoulder.

"Wrong! That would be very good. That would be best for Roma."

(1)	English Standard Version, et al
(2)	New American Standard
(3)	Holman Christian Standard Bible
(4)	New American Standard 1977
(5)	Berean Literal Bible
(6)	King James Version
(7)	New American Standard
(8)	Christian Standard Bible
(9)	American Standard Version
(10)	New International Version
(11)	English Standard Version
(12)	Webster's Bible Translation
(13)	Holman Christian Standard Bible
(14)	Amplified Bible
(15)	Et al
(16)	Douay-Rheims Bible
(17)	New Living Translation
(18)	Et al
(19)	King James Version
(20)	Aramaic Bible in Plain English
(21)	Et al
(22)	New International Version, et al
(23)	NET Bible

PATMOS

CHAPTER 29

Kynops awoke with a start. Though it was warm and sunny outside, he felt cold and wrapped his blanket tightly around him. He peered around his dreary dwelling under the covers. The shadows. They darted about, clearly agitated. Were they powerless lest Kynops do something? He had never seen them this way. He listened to the wind outside, then realized the gale blew inside. Cold and frosty. His breath spelled out the cold as it escaped his mouth. He knew the day had well begun. They knew it, too, nudging him like wheedled needles to go forth. He ignored them, as was his way, lest they start to act as if they would be in charge.

Soon, but not too soon, he rose. Still seated upon his cot, he checked the walls. No Legion. Via incantations and spells, he had asked much and often throughout the night, but no answer. Nonetheless, his plan would not be diverted and thereby continue with the shadows present.

"Pridæ. Katastrofi. Skotadi. You know what to do - as do all of you."

He rose to dress, eat and head out. Dogs barked furiously outside as the bright sunlight pierced his eyes right down to the temples. He squinted to avoid the blinding pain. It attacked eyeballs with violent vengeance. It seemed to get brighter, as though his eyes forgot how to adjust. The shadows could not be counted on to help here. Some time waddled by until he could open eyes and continue his plan of action.

Heading to the shed, he found hay to feed, then bridle and blanket to dress his horse. He rested against a post as the horse dined. It seemed to take forever, and as his head cleared and his eyes finally adjusted to the daylight, he turned anxious to get on to town. He had so much to do.

The animal shook its head as he donned the bridle. The blanket flowed over the animals back perfectly. Kynops mounted. Again, he spoke to the shadows. "You all know what to do. Falter not."

He rode off towards Phora, mood intent. His eyebrows furrowed, practically touched. Entering the town, he rode past stone dwellings. Commoners noticed him and started to follow. What could Kynops be doing in town? Kynops never came to town without urgent cause. The Magician felt the fear filling the citizens as he passed. His demons touched pagan souls, empty save the ingrained fears that compelled people to follow. What started as a line of four or five townsfolk quickly grew. The more that followed, the more that would follow. The mob filled the trail behind him. The shadows virtually saw to that. The parade advanced upon the city center, talking and chattering and making enough racket to draw others to join them.

Kynops kept moving as though no one followed, occasionally jerking the rein harshly, directing his horse to dawdle, lest they go too fast and get too far ahead of the crowd. Vile words of death and destruction inaudibly wheezed and squeezed out his lips with each equine bounce, damning the land and its people to turn hearts against the Christian prophet.

Roman soldiers noted the oncoming crowd and took position, sending for additional enforcements. Some encountered awe to see Kynops, high atop his steed like Hercules come to town. Kynops regarded none, knowing with complete certainty that the fools would follow him. Though reclusive most days, his reputation stood him apart from any others on the island; as a man to be feared and revered – a status he had enjoyed for over two decades. Seldom did he feel the need to exploit his renown, and so it promised to work in his favor as evidenced by the crowd promptly forming behind and around him. Now he merely needed to sway them back to Kynops and away from the zealot. Now he merely needed to make his own miracles.

Moving to the open square, he stopped, still stationed on his horse, and let the followers catch up. All moved forward, creating a large circle around him. As the stragglers moved in, he raised both hands, then curled them around, bent tightly at the wrist to a menacing stance like an Egyptian asp ready to strike. Hands still upheld, he looked around sternly at the crowd. Fear had always been his ally and he would not behave differently now.

"You ask why Kynops comes to Phora," he spoke, loudly that all would hear. "You follow your Magician with expectation. You seek his company and his counsel. This be your day. I have come to expose the great evil that condemns Patmos. I come to challenge a liar among you. I come to challenge a fraud; a charlatan. Come with Kynops, and you will see great and powerful things."

He turned the horse in a full three-sixty of which Euclid would have been proud. His shadow etched its sundial image on all it passed over.

"Now," he continued, "go to the homes and shops seeking anyone that you can find and bring them out. They must see how Kynops will cleanse this our island. The purge must come, or we will all die, either at the hand of Roma, or at the hand of a foreign God who seeks the destruction of our lives. Our temples show the temperament of this false God. But, hear me now! Kynops will expose the fraud for all to see. Open your eyes. Turn to me your ears. Gather all who seek the truth and you shall see and hear before this day ends. To this, I swear. Now go."

He stayed upon his horse as he looked at the crowd around him. Few if any moved away.

"I said now go!" he yelled all the louder, "and find all others. Scatter to be gathered. Bring all back with you to this square. We await your harvest. NOW GO!"

Most raced off, then soon the square started to fill again. Kynops dismounted, not to rest his horse, but to continue his incantations on solid ground. Horses commonly reacted strongly when he practiced his spells. He did not care to be atop one when it did. His horse got more agitated the longer he spoke, and he tied up the steed for distance between them.

Within that hour, the number of islanders increased, filling the town square practically to capacity. Not all within the city limits stopped their lives to pursue Kynops, but most considered it possible as more and more familiar faces arrived. The wizard felt pleased with the audience. This had never been his way - that of the showman, but he knew fully well he needed to make the bigger and lasting impact on the people.

As the hour passed, someone offered him a glass of wine. He took a drink of the wine, laced with terebinth for flavor. The vino tasted warm and dry, but a bit watered down - obviously for family consumption during meals. Another wine, seldom available on Patmos, Kynops once tasted wine laced with lead. The lead added a pleasant flavor, and agreeably altered the feeling of the fluid in a man's mouth. It also preserved the wine for longer storage. He would have preferred something stronger and leaded, but still quickly finished the offered glass given him.

He viewed the mass of people around him. Satisfied, he remounted his horse and led the way through the sea of humanity. The flow followed in to tail Kynops as he headed for the beach. He almost gasped and stopped to gop at the rubble that had been the Temple to Apollo. He maintained his stoic posture as he passed the two temples. No one noticed the slight nod Kynops made to the priests. Their blank answer meant business while the procession of followers bowed or at least waved to their priests. To their laity, they replied with a wave and grim smile.

"What is this all about?" yelled Daniel, the tanner, pushing through the crowd like one in a logjam.

"A purging," answered Kynops from on high, piercing eyes narrowed towards the intruder. If Kynops could not subdue or destroy this upstart, all would be lost before the people and his devious plan.

"You do not need the whole town to do a purging," challenged the tanner. "My customers walked out of my shop to see the cause of the commotion. And, who are you purging anyway?"

"The deceiver," Kynops boldly answered so all would hear. "The vile deceptions stop today. Kynops must act or Patmos will be lost. Now, join us or be purged as well."

The tanner stood ground - for a moment, then left, grumbling. He passed the two men who had hastened from his shop.

"Come see me after you are done here. Daniel will take good care of you."

Kynops wasted no further time. The mob was his to use or lose.

"To the purge," he shouted, over and over and over, like a broken Psittacula Parrot. Some joined in with the chant, then more, then even more voices, filling the day with its tumultuous roar. Roman reinforcements arrived, ready to disband the mob by force, if necessary. Lucius, the Captain of the Guard, rode up upon his horse, able to clearly see Kynops. He knew not the magician's intent but held his troops at bay. If this was what he thought it was....

Wedging through the sea of flesh, Kynops led the way to the beach. Few, if any failed to follow. He watched the sky, seeking guidance and direction to his prey. Clouds gathered more and more, the closer to the coast they drew. The crowd continued to call out, ignorant of the plan, or even the target, but certain they were doing the right thing.

As the narrow streets opened up to the coastline, Lucius hurried through, followed by five soldiers, all on horse. Riding up to Kynops, he called, "What is this about?"

Kynops had heard the horse hooves approaching from behind and without looking deduced their riders.

"Captain?" he answered, still not looking.

Lucius cut-off his direction, halting the horse.

"I do not care if you are the Great Magician of Patmos. When I call you, you better stop and stop now. Do I make myself clear?" Veins lined his neck and temples. All swords already drawn.

As Kynops stopped, so did his flock. He could not lose control here. This moment also meant everything.

"Captain," he repeated coldly, yet his lips kept moving. The men locked eyes. Kynops considered his best options. Make him disappear? Stun his senses? Blind him? All of the above? All those would bring the entire regiment to his front door. He had never worn chains and knew today would not be the first day.

"Fear," he said to himself. Fear promised to be the superior weapon of choice. Besides, he would have wagered the Romans assigned there wanted the zealot gone, too.

"Captain, I gather these here as witnesses to challenge the Christian zealot and expose his lies. He is a fraud and after the destruction of the Temple to Apollo, I knew I could no longer be idle. So, we seek the zealot to bring to judgment and justice."

His eyes remained narrow and riveting as though trying to pierce or stab through the crusty exterior called Lucius. The Captain of the Guard, a long-time warrior who shared in no less than six warring campaigns for Roma, stared back with equal ice. Intimidation would not work so easily for Kynops. He uttered further words of incantation. Lucius did not flinch so much as move aside, slowly, but truly, and Kynops could readily imagine what Lucius suddenly was thinking. Kynops tarried no longer and strode around the captain without further discussion.

He checked the sky again.

"Votrys?" he uttered to himself.

His shadows pointed the way. His evil eyes could not see the Holy Light which rose high up to Heaven itself from the small, old man soaking ropes. But, Ionnes felt the tidings of Yeshua's Spirit warning him of the oncoming duel. He knew not as yet what form it would take. He received no names, nor could he yet see Kynops or his mob, but he knew with full certainty something quickly approached.

The beauty of Yeshua's love filled the old apostle, ever preparing him for any attacks to come.

A half hour plus passed when he saw the hoard on approach. His old eyes could not yet tell who led the pack. He saw Roman soldiers, but they better resembled army ants or Canaan sheep dogs keeping the flock moving forward to not stray.

The leader rode on horse. Ionnes had never before seen him, but his clothing and demeanor gave away the truth. Kynops the Magician clearly sought conference with Yeshua's Holy Apostle.

"Perhaps he seeks me to be baptized," said Ionnes, fully certain such could only be dreamt. But, what a dream! Baptize the leader and the hundreds with him would follow. Ionnes prayed for guidance and the Spirit's direction, mixed with words of praise and thanksgiving for the Holy Spirit's preparation. He continued to attend to his ropes while remaining deep in prayer as the parade approached.

"Ionnes of Ephesus," called Kynops, still mounted, reaching the calm edge of the sea.

"I am he," said Ionnes, "and by who am I addressed?"

Some of the crowd laughed. Others felt more fear. They had been awed by this old man. Now Kynops challenged him? Some had secretly prayed to Yeshua just to see if He answered. Some wondered that none of the temple priests attended. Some just came for a good, old-fashioned showdown. This could be better than taking in the theater in Pergamos.

"Kynops the Magician," he answered and dismounted.

"A magician of what?" challenged Ionnes. Bringing his ropes to shore, he unhurriedly and carefully laid them to dry on the beach.

Kynops almost let himself be swayed towards distraction. Dodging the question, he loudly announced, "I come to berid us of the fraud that is Ionnes of Ephesus. You deceive the good people of Patmos..."

"... God's truth is never deceptive."

"... and where Roma has failed, Kynops will triumph."

Ionnes hedged not. "I stand on the Rock of Salvation," he said loudly. "Yeshua Christos is His name. He is the chief cornerstone. His kingdom endures forever. I am His humble servant, and in His name, I will not falter."

"Then," announced Kynops, "I am here to send your soul to eternal judgment."

"I fear not your judgment," countered Ionnes, "only your foolishness."

Kynops kept eyes locked with Ionnes long enough to make the crowd uncomfortable. Boldly staring into those old gray-brown eyes, he saw strength uncommon. This was not some man's façade for power and holiness in those eyes. As the line of sight still stretched taut between them, Kynops suddenly wondered if this challenge might become a mistake? His certainty of success up until that minute provided him inertia driven conviction. Suddenly, he faced the possibility and even reality of failure. Even cataclysmic failure. He felt all eyes of the island upon him. He felt all eyes of Roma as well. The challenge he delivered. His witnesses attended. He knew his plan of attack to now be graphically played out. No exit existed. All bets in one basket. He had to succeed – the reality he well knew even before he departed his home this morning.

Turning towards the crowd, Kynops announced, "Men, blind and deluded, listen to me! If Ionnes is righteous, and what he says is righteous, let him do what I tell him to do and then I will believe in what he says."

He turned towards a young man a few faces back in the crowd.

"You," he pointed. "Come to me."

All stayed frozen.

"You," Kynops pointed. "Step forward."

The young man shuddered but dared not disobey.

"I know you," said Kynops.

"S-S-Sir?" the young man stammered, fearful of the sorcerer.

"I know your pain."

The boy thought that sounded very bad.

Kynops closed his eyes as though deep in thought, ready to see the beyond with eyes closed. He showed no hurry.

"Your father," he eventually said, opening eyes to look at the young man. "Tell me about your father. Is he alive or dead?"

The young man immediately looked like someone had kicked him in the gut.

"Dead," he said, the weight of timeless sadness renewed. "My father was a sailor. His ship went down at sea, and he drowned."

"You father a sailor? His ship went down at sea, and he drowned?" Kynops repeated loudly for all to hear.

"Yes," whimpered the young man, still wracked with regurgitated grief. Head down, shoulders slouched, his countenance broken, none there needed to hear his answer. His demeanor answered loudly enough. He wiped his nose with the sleeve of his tunic.

"When did he die?"

"Oh," thought the young man, "Three years, at least and maybe a half."

Kynops turned towards Ionnes.

"What say you, Ionnes of Ephesus? I declare to all here you are a fraud and a deceiver lest you can prove otherwise. I beseech you, return this boy's father to him, alive and well, and I, Kynops will worship and follow you and your God."

Still addressing Ionnes, Kynops turned slightly to better include the crowd. "But, if you cannot resurrect him, you shall be shown to be a fraud to the people here and dealt with severely."

Ionnes waited a moment to receive counsel of Yeshua's Holy Spirit. With the challenge spoken, complete and real, Ionnes felt the Spirit's presence assure him. The warm wind blew through his hair and beard. He breathed in deeply, then looking at Kynops answered in a loud voice, "Yeshua is not mocked, nor to be tested by one as yourself. Your intent is not for the glory of God, but to deceive these good people who have come forth."

He looked past Kynops to the crowd, "Men of Patmos, of Phora and Skala, of Kastelli, Kipoi Osiou and Diakofti, be not deceived by this sorcerer. I was not sent here by Christos Yeshua to entertain like a trained pony."

Kynops smiled as he said to those gathered, "He speaks as one who cannot deliver. If you believe, you who live on Patmos, that Ionnes is a fraud and that he deceives you with fraudulent magic, then keep him here till I bring up the boy's father and present him to you."

Some men in the crowd stepped forward to hold Ionnes and keep him from fleeing – an act the apostle had no intention of attempting.

Kynops stepped towards the shoreline, his back to the crowd. He removed his robe, laying it on the sand. Extending both arms, he clapped hands loudly. Suddenly, all beheld a loud crashing sound from above. Startled, all in the crowd jumped save one, then gasped as Kynops vanished before them.

"Great is Kynops!" declared one of the men holding Ionnes. "There is no one like you." Others in the crowd nodded and started repeating the same. Even more joined in, paying fearful homage to the wizard.

The crashing sound blasted again. Some placed hands over ears. The water near shore started churning. They watched intently to see Kynops rising from the sea with a man, a sailor, trudging up out of the water beside him.

Kynops redonned his robe as he found the boy and asked,

"Is this your father?"

The young man started crying uncontrollably as he struggled to answer, "Yes m'lord." He bounced forward and took hold of his father, holding on tight. The man felt cold, but he did not care. He returned the hug with substantial strength, and the young man never wanted to let go.

He spied Kynops. The magician watched the pair intently, a narrow smile prodding his cheek. The young man let loose of his father and ran to hug Kynops, falling forward and sliding down the full length of the man. Once down on the sand and rock, the boy worshipped Kynops. Others joined him, casting themselves to the ground to pay veneration to this man who had resurrected the boy's father.

Kynops took it in a moment, then stepped forward through the crowd to a man lying face forward.

"Rise," said the wizard.

The man immediately obeyed.

"Do you have a son?" asked Kynops.

"I did," answered the man. "Another man coveted his success with horses and murdered him."

"What was his name?" asked Kynops.

"Ascopius."

Kynops placed a hand on the man's shoulder and said, "Despair no longer. Your son will be resurrected." He twirled around, his robe spreading out widely, pressing the crowd back to gain extra room. Again, clapping hands loudly, he called loudly, "Ascopius, draw nigh – and also you, his murderer."

Some seconds passed when two men suddenly appeared as out of nowhere. The crowd again felt awe with the sight of the two materialized.

Kynops took hold of the younger man and brought him before the man.

"Is this your son? And, is this his murderer?"

"Aye," answered the father, moving before his son, barely able to speak and less able to believe his eyes. Grabbing hold of Ascopius, the two shared a long hug. Still embraced, the father looked at the murderer who stood defiantly.

"Truly it is them," the father choked out the words.

"Truly it is them," yelled Kynops. The crowd dropped down once again to worship the wizard. He stepped over prostrate bodies to return to Ionnes.

"Are not you also in awe?" asked Kynops for all to hear.

Ionnes showed disapproval. "No," he answered just as loudly. "These are not the men you claim they are. They are part of your deception – your ruse."

Kynops countered, "Greater works than these you shall soon see, and you shall know that Kynops is the champion of the people of Patmos. No longer will they bow or pay homage to your dead Savior. No longer will they be fooled by you. No longer will you be here to fool the people."

Ionnes said intently and clearly, "Your displays and false miracles will be annihilated along with you to soon disappear and never return."

The crowd gasped at Ionnes words of insubordination and misconduct towards Kynops. One man stepped forward, speaking for the people.

"Why do you blaspheme the blessed Kynops? You are but an exile and a prisoner. Where is your God that you should be punished thus?" Others added to the accusations, getting more and more agitated until the mob rushed towards Ionnes with singular purpose. Grabbing the saint, they threw him to the ground and beat him savagely. Some became like savage beasts and started biting and chewing on Ionnes' skin. Barely minutes passed until Ionnes' blood-covered body went limp and lifeless.

As the attackers stepped away, Kynops studied the body of Ionnes some moments until he announced, "Good. Very good, you fine people. This one is too evil to bury. Leave him, on the beach, and let the birds and dogs and rodents eat his flesh. Let us see if his precious Christos will resurrect him."

Kynops pushed his way through the human sea, too full to part quickly, but as he grabbed the reins of his mount, the crowd disbanded. Everything had gone off without a hitch – even better than he had expected. The foolish sheep had turned to wolves. He smiled to himself, climbed atop his steed, and yelled, "This day Patmos may celebrate. The purge is complete." Most followed, departing the beach, cheering and celebrating, pleased that Ionnes was dead. The young man kept ahold of his father and the father whose son was murdered kept hold lest he be taken from him again.

Evening approached. The prisoners laying aside their tools looked over at the body of Ionnes but did not approach. The guards who had seen the entire display from afar kept to their duties, and saw the prisoners move on towards their dinner and barracks. Few others toured the beach, perhaps intentionally staying clear.

A few from the crowd remained on the beach until the mob cleared away. Fearful they would also be attacked or punished by Kynops, they waited until the dusk drove away the light to hide their actions.

"No birds have come," noted one.

"Nor dogs – or rodents."

"Even the sharks would not attack him," reminded a third.

The fourth stood and approached the body. Kneeling down, he felt the arm. It was cool, but not blue. Ionnes seemed unaware of his presence, but the fourth placed his ear by Ionnes' nose.

"He breathes," he said to the others.

It was a warm evening, but the fourth removed his cloak and placed it over Ionnes. The others joined and knelt around him. They checked his head and neck, his back and shoulders, his arms, then his hips and legs and feet. He was bathed in his own dried blood, but amazingly nothing seemed broken.

After a spell Ionnes groaned.

"Rest," said the first.

"You are among friends," said the third.

With some struggles, Ionnes opened one swollen eye, then the other to see his caregivers. All four were dressed in white robes. None looked familiar in the gloom. He groaned again as he tried to turn over.

"Rest," repeated the first.

"I have been resting – too long," answered Ionnes, most crochety. "Please, help me up."

Four pairs of hands moved upon the man to help him rise to a sitting position. He placed his hands on his head and pulled his knees up to his ears. Tears started flooding forth, and he wept shamelessly.

"Are you in pain?" asked the second.

After a spell, Ionnes answered, "Of course I am in pain, but that is not why I weep."

"Why for?" asked the fourth.

"Because you are here. You four whom I have never laid eyes on have come to my aid. That is why I weep. Tears of thanksgiving."

The four looked at one another. The first smiled. The others nodded and smiled back.

"Can you walk?" asked the second after a spell.

"Let us find out," answered Ionnes, putting out his hands to be pulled up. Once on his feet, his legs wobbled, from not just the beatings but also lack of water, not to mention his age. He took moments to steady himself and gratefully accepted the help of strangers. They moved slowly up the beach. Once upon the dirt road, the walk became a little easier.

They stopped beside a dwelling, the first man, peering around the corner of the building, raised his hand behind them to stop the small parade. Ionnes felt need to inquire, but another placed fingers against his lips. Silence, please. The first man kept vigil. After a spell, two soldiers on horses rode through the quiet street, their horses' clop filling the night. Once well past the group, they all advanced forward.

"We see the Roman soldiers come through most nights around this time. Unless there is trouble, they will not be back for at least an hour."

They continued along, staying close to the buildings. Music and loud voices arose at times from a couple of bars. Some maybe celebrated Ionnes' demise.

"I am sorry we have no horse or cart," said the fourth.

"So am I," nodded Ionnes. "So am I."

He stopped occasionally to rest but was able to keep going with less assistance by time they reached the Acropolis. Heading towards the bakery, the fourth asked, "Can you climb some stairs?"

"I think so," answered Ionnes, but after a couple shaky steps, he paused.

Two moved up with hands intertwined and connected to become a seat. The other two helped Ionnes to sit atop the human transport and provided additional support to make the climb to the top safely. A woman opened a door. Two children watched from a doorway further in the small dwelling. They set Ionnes down upon a mat and laid him back, a feather pillow stationed under his head. The woman brought a bowl of tepid water and cloths to clean the wounds of the apostle. He thankfully accepted their care. Another brought goblets of water and wine and broth - first the water to quench thirst, then the wine to help numb his aches, then the broth to strengthen. As they completed dining on fluids, bread was also offered. They helped Ionnes sit up again. The stiffness and achiness had had time to settle in since the beatings, but he was pleased for the bread and praised Yeshua for both the feast and attending company.

"Animals," snapped the woman with disgust. "They be all cowards."

"Verily," agreed the second and the others nodded.

The first sat beside Ionnes. "This is my home," he said. "This is my wife, and you saw both of my children. We run the bakery downstairs. I will have to rise early to begin the day's baking, but we could not leave you on the beach all night."

Ionnes acknowledged, but still felt a bit puzzled. He looked at the plate holding small loaves. They were all in the shape something like scrolls. He looked at the first man, the baker.

"Many of my customers are amused when I shape my loaves into simple objects. Good for business."

Ionnes nodded agreement and ate the small book. It tasted a bit sweet, glazed with honey.

Swallowing, he added, "One thing still puzzles me. Why did you help me?"

They looked from one to the other until the third, sitting opposite Ionnes said, "We are all followers of Yeshua Christos. New followers I must add."

"How new?" asked Ionnes, eating more bread.

They again all looked at each other, then the first said, "Maybe two months, now. We were there when you and Yeshua healed Barbara. We have known Barbara all of our lives, so when she stood for the first time, we were all in utter awe. We all talked among ourselves that such a miracle could only be performed by one blessed by God.

"Even then, we waited. Over a month."

"What for?" asked Ionnes.

"To see if Barbara's healing was real. Weeks passed. Then one day when we saw her skipping through the square past my shoppe, I called to her and invited her to dine with us that evening. She was suspicious, of course, and I said that I wanted to hear more about you and your God. She smiled and seemed satisfied with that answer, and shortly after nightfall, she came to our home and told the story of you, Ionnes, and your God."

"Did you believe her?"

"Not quite," the fourth honestly answered. "If not for her own healing, we would have kept to our doubts."

"Still," continued the first, "some weeks or so after that, we accepted her invitation to be joined with Yeshua, the Anointed One."

"Where is Barbara?" asked Ionnes. "I have not seen her some days."

"Visiting family on Kos, I think she said," answered the woman. "If she had been here today, she would have clawed the eyes out of Kynops or died trying."

"I am sure," agreed Ionnes.

"But," said the first, "we are honored and pleased to have the last living apostle of Yeshua under my roof." All the others nodded and felt the holy glow of the divine bless that moment. "And, we pray for Yeshua's blessing to challenge Kynops, bring him to his knees that he might ask Yeshua's forgiveness as well as bring the others who live in this town to our Savior."

"Amen," agreed Ionnes, sipping the wine and feeling its warmth fill his torso. He praised Yeshua for just such moments - when one felt the most alone, Yeshua opened a new door Ionnes did not even know existed to show His eternal love.

"I am sorry," said the first, "for not coming to your aid when the mob attacked."

Ionnes knew the danger as well as anyone. Also, he knew the power of the Almighty against not just mobs, but nations and armies. Yet, he had not one word of criticism to cast upon his benefactors. He never forgot the lessons of his youth and the many, many mistakes he and his closest friends made when Yeshua first called them.

"Our God is not a God of guilt, but of love," Ionnes comforted. "You have been exactly the blessing Yeshua sought to provide and exactly what I needed."

His hosts still seemed unsure, so he added, "Consider where I would be right now if you had not come to my aid. Likely still on that beach, beaten and weak. I am Yeshua's apostle, but I am still an old man with human frailties and weaknesses. Your gifts to me are beyond measure."

He continued to speak, sharing the gospel and learning what Barbara had told them about Yeshua. As the evening wore on, children were put to bed. He blessed each before they departed.

Then, he asked, "You have not been baptized?"

"Not yet," answered the second. "We continue to live in fear, not just of the Romans, but also our own neighbors and even friends who feel dread and angst and even anger towards you when you destroyed the Temple of Apollo. I know not for sure but believe that truly prompted the crowd to attack so vehemently in trepidation, both of you and Kynops' anger."

"I know it upset many," admitted Ionnes. "Typically, it takes small actions or even merely words of truth to open a man's eyes, but Adonai well knows and has shared that it may take great feats to open many eyes at once. Destroying the temple of His adversary certainly provided that effect."

"The people truly fear you."

"Our God is not a God of fear, but of Love," Ionnes replied. "The certainty of their fear can be changed to divine love more easily than people typically adjudge. You shall see."

He smiled again, for the first time since he had arrived in their care. His wounds ached, of course, but this was nothing new or unusual. He (again) praised Yeshua to be worthy to suffer for the gospel and had long since learned to praise Yeshua in everything.

"How would you see that change?" asked the fourth. "Lots of people really love to cling to their fears. It empowers them. And, the fears of others give them something to talk about."

"Amazing, is it not?" agreed Ionnes. "And, as to how I would see that change, I have already seen it in you. And, tomorrow I shall go forth to preach the good news of Christos again as though today did not happen."

"And, what of Kynops?"

Ionnes looked at all of them intently.

"Kynops is a deceiver – a sorcerer who controls demons. That is his power, and it is a pitiful power, indeed."

"But he raised three from the dead," objected the first.

"We saw him," the others chimed in.

"No!" said Ionnes. "Did I not just tell you he is a deceiver? His resurrections are also deceptions. Those you saw raised from the dead are not men, but no more than demons obeying his commands. They shall be cast away as surely as we are here together tonight."

"Then, why did you not cast them away today?"

"I know not," said Ionnes, "but, sometimes – even oftentimes Yeshua's Holy Spirit urges me to remain mute and let the madness play out. Kynops claimed he would show his power, and that he has done. He also said he would worship my God if I raised those from the dead. That was a lie, of course. Finally, he wanted to completely destroy my status on Patmos and my testimony of Christos Yeshua. He wanted me dead, but he did not want my words to live on after me. So, he had to try to strip away everything before the crowd."

"But you said nothing."

"Again, I know not why, but I also remember when Yeshua was tried, both before the Jewish authorities and before Pontius Pilate, the Roman Procurator to Ierusalem many years ago - now just over sixty years past, He also remained mute through most of the trials. And, the testimonies of lies could not stand against Him. Once His execution was imminent, only then did He finally break His silence, leading Pilate to the question which I am told plagued the Roman leader to the day of his death."

"What question?" asked the blank faces before Ionnes.

"What is truth?"

Ionnes gave them a minute or two to let it sink in. The third started to speak but stopped to reconsider his words.

Ionnes nodded to each one. All five sat on the edge of their floor to hear more.

"Yeshua had already said, over a year earlier, *'I am the Way and the Truth and the Life. No man comes to the Father but by Me.'* The Truth that became flesh had already spoken."

Ionnes considered his next words. "As we have already discussed and what you learned from Barbara, Yeshua came to Earth to remove our sins by His sacrifice on the cross. He also came to share the ways of His Father in Heaven, and to send His Holy Spirit, so take note. The living God in Heaven laid aside His divinity for a spell to become mortal man, and in doing so, made the Creator of all more real than ever before.

"Compare that to the temple and the gods you previously worshipped. They never lived. Never. The breath of life never filled them, and they certainly never created all the world and those in it. They never stood up to Adonai for they have no substance or being or thought. They never existed at all yet were made real by the stories and imaginations of men. In that, they became real to those who worshipped them, to those who serve them in the temples, and even to those who do not believe. I know the Truth and the Truth has set me free. The false gods and idols of both the Greeks and Romans (and others) are carried only by the words and actions of men and women. Only Yeshua stands with His almighty power which He gives to us freely."

The group pondered those words. It had never occurred to them the gods were never real. They had not thought it through to that degree as yet and wondered anew the loving power of Christos Yeshua touching each of their lives. Each had felt the change when they prayed to Yeshua with Barbara. Now, they wondered at this loving power of which Ionnes spoke.

"What power is this?" asked the woman.

"It is the power of the Holy Spirit. You told me you have not yet been baptized?"

No, none had.

"The baptism of water is to be cleansed of your sins. All of us have sinned."

"Even you?" asked the second.

"Even me," confessed Ionnes. "Grievously at times, I will testify. But there is another baptism which is not for the cleansing of sins, but rather for Yeshua's divine touch on your lives, day to day. In that, you live lives of divine holiness, not by your power, but by the power of His Holy Spirit."

"So, what baptism is this?" they all asked.

"The Baptism of the Holy Spirit," answered Ionnes.

"How do we perform this baptism? Do we need to be immersed again?"

"No," answered Ionnes. He loved moments like this – when new converts could discover for the first time the Love of Yeshua in all His Spiritual glory and power.

"No. It would be silly to baptize you in water a second time. But, by the laying of hands of the saints can you receive the free gift of the Holy Spirit. He will fill your lives and take away any remnant of that God-shaped void you may still hold in your previous life."

They were amazed at the simplicity of the answer. It sounded too easy.

"I understand," answered Ionnes. "It sounded too easy to me, too, but the Holy Spirit came upon one-hundred-and-twenty of us one day as we gathered in an upper room to pray and worship Yeshua. Yeshua had just recently ascended and returned to His Father in Heaven. We remained some days, deep in prayer. Suddenly one morning we felt a mighty, rushing wind blowing inside of our large room. Scared all of us out of our wits, I will tell you. Then, if that was not enough, the room became brighter. We looked up at the source of the light and saw many tongues of fire, suspended in the air, all brightly burning. I recall feeling my own fear rise at the sight. Then, those tongues of fire started to move about the room and one by one, dropped down upon each man there. One landed upon my head, and I will tell you, I had never felt more intoxicated, and giddy in my life. Mine immediately filled me through and through with a feeling I never encounter anywhere else in the world or my life. Nowhere. I cannot explain it or tell you what to compare it with. No words are adequate. No words will explain it to you any more than if I tried to tell you how something tasted. Only after you have tasted it will you truly know its flavor.

"Yeshua told us many times that He had to depart so that the Holy Spirit could come. Until that blessed day of Pentecost where each became filled to overflowing with His Spirit, we finally understood the strength and power of His words. The Baptism of the Holy Spirit completed that Word."

"Then, how soon can we receive this gift?" asked the woman.

"Now, if you wish," answered Ionnes and raised off the floor to land upon his knees. He positioned himself before his host, the baker, and prayed for him. Turning to the others there, he flipped his head as if to say, "Join me." One responded and the others followed, all laying hands on the baker.

It took not long, and he felt the giddy love of Yeshua's Holy Spirit fill him. They went about the room, praying together. All responded in like manner, yet still were unique in words and personal traits as the breath of life from God entered each of them. The fourth started to prophesy. He knew not even what he said. The third started to weep and confessed many sins he had committed, some even after he had given himself to Yeshua. The woman could not stop laughing and their children came forth wondering about the source of all the noise. She kissed them, prayed for them, kept laughing and sent them back to bed.

"We have all started meeting together on the LORD's Day," said Ionnes. "Perhaps you will join us? Just this last Sunday, we met atop Phora hill."

"That may be good for the summer, but what about after the rains return and the weather turns cold?" asked the second.

"We shall see what Yeshua provides," assured Ionnes. "Fear not. You will see greater works than these. And, even more so, you will find glory and strength in places and times you never before imagined. Even my presence in your home supports the truth of my words. Yeshua's loving and living proof."

He excused himself to find the bathroom.

"What do you think?" asked the first to his new friends.

They all looked at one another again until the fourth dreamily said, "Best day of my life."

The others enthusiastically agreed.

The next morning, Ionnes' sleep was disturbed by the creaking sounds of feet around him. The baker prepared to head downstairs to his ovens. His host noticed.

"It was funny," whispered the baker to Ionnes just before he headed downstairs. "Since I rise so early, sometimes I get the time wrong. I may sleep in, of course, but also, I may nap for only an hour or two and widely awaken, ready to start my day. I have been known to head to the ovens closer to the eighteenth hour instead of the twenty-second. If there are no clouds, I can check the stars to help me count the hours, but as you know, many early mornings have no sky a man can see."

He slipped out and Ionnes enjoyed a few more moments of prayer and thanksgiving until he nodded off back to achy sleep.

Stirred by sounds downstairs, Ionnes sat up. The baker had already departed nearly two hours earlier to begin his day's baking. His wife saw to the children and would be down to run the shop within the hour. It seemed every muscle connected to his bones throbbed and ached like some sort of pain contest. None seemed to be winning at that moment, but he knew the jabs of pain would come and go as he tried to move. Those moments of certain pain and weariness had been his companions for many years, appended by his age. He pressed against the pain to find his feet, standing and immediately putting away his host's bedroll.

The baker's wife peeked around from her bedroom door. Dressed in nightclothes, both knew it improper for her to appear wearing anything besides their day clothing.

"Must you go?"

"I must," answered Ionnes.

"Then, see my husband before you leave. I know he awaits you down at the shop."

"I shall," nodded Ionnes. "Thank you again for your loving care. I pray Yeshua continue to be with you. You have a beautiful family."

She acknowledged and slipped back to bed with her children. She knew she had another hour before she would have to start her day.

Ionnes slowly crept down the stairs but heard the door open at the bottom. The baker stepped into the stairwell with a smile and invited the apostle in. Ionnes followed.

"You do not look well, my friend."

"In Yeshua's good time, I shall heal. I always do." Sighing, he smiled. "Still in white, I see."

The baker laughed and slapped the flour all over his clothing. White whiffs of floury dust went everywhere.

"Are you certain you have to go?" asked the baker. "You may remain as long as you need."

"You know I must go now that first light approaches," said Ionnes. "You have harbored a prisoner in your home. I would not bring the wrath or blight of Roma upon your household.

"Of course," he knew the truth of those words. He headed to the racks to grab two barley loaves.

"Breakfast," he said, handing the bread to Ionnes.

Ionnes accepted the loaves, then peered perceptively at the baker.

"It was you?" he said. "I should have known."

The baker shrugged with no idea what the old man meant.

"You came to Yeshua by Barbara's healing and words. In turn, you started bringing your extra bread to the penal colony for the prisoners."

"And, even the guards," admitted the baker. "The guards would share none if there was only enough for them."

"But it must become a great expense."

"Not so much," the baker assured. "We have unbought bread each and every day. We try to sell the next day, but even then, we often still have way too much bread to sell. So, rather than feed the hogs, we decided to give it to the prisoners. The hogtenders never gave us much for it, anyway."

"It has been appreciated more than you know," applauded Ionnes, raising the two loaves. "Proud to be in their number, I can testify with full authority how special your offerings have been received."

The baker was pleased. Up until that moment, he truly had no certainty his bread ever made it to the mouths of the prisoners.

"Do you think Yeshua will help me gauge how much bread to make each day, so I have less waste?" He paused. "Belay that. If I only make what will sell, I can never give my excess to those who need but cannot buy."

He smiled again. The two shared a hug.

An idea occurred to Ionnes.

"Do you ever get to the mainland?"

"Me? No. Not very often. I have the bakery to run, but one of those with me last night sails over often."

"Does he sail to Ephesus? Or Smyrna?"

"Yes, I am sure. Often even."

Ionnes felt tears of gladness well up.

"Do you think he would deliver a message for me?"

The baker thought briefly, but only briefly. He knew the answer just about as quickly as it took him to decipher the question.

"I am sure he would."

"Then, ask him if on his next journey to Ephesus if he would seek Prochorus? He has traveled with me over the years and often assisted as my assistant and scribe. My message is simple. Please pass along that Ionnes lives and is in chains on Patmos. That is all he needs to hear."

"I think I can do that," answered the baker. "But Ephesus is a big place. Where should he go?"

"To the north part of town," answered Ionnes, "Demetrius the Silversmith will know where to find him." Ionnes paused as the recollections gathered, crossing his thoughts like stampeding cattle. "*Demetrius*. His father hated the church, but then his son took over the family business after Demetrius the elder passed. He had learned his trade from his father making silver idols. Praise Yeshua, He showed Demetrius the younger the sins of his idolatry. Now he loves Yeshua as much as any man I have ever known and makes beautiful articles out of that same grade of silver for the home and the churches."

He thought another moment. "Or tell Timotheos if Prochorus is not there."

"Anything else?" asked the baker.

"Oh, um, tell him to avoid Alexander the Coppersmith. He has always been hostile to our faith. He did much evil and the LORD rewarded him according to his works. Sadly, his heart only became harder."

Ionnes' thoughts went up the mainland coast.

"If your friend goes to Smyrna, please ask him to find Papias – or young Polycarpus. Same message. The church meets just a few doors down from the synagogue. You will see the fish symbol by the door – if nothing has significantly changed. I have been away over a year."

His head drooped, but only for a few seconds, taking in the pain of that reality. Then, his spirits rose just as quickly to again thank his new friend. Grabbing his two loaves and looking outside first to make sure the coast was clear, Ionnes headed out to the beach and the salt ropes. He walked in painful stiffness but with renewed life and purpose as he praised Yeshua for his breakfast. He also praised Him for his life. Next, he praised Him that he could spend the night with new friends and not in chains. Finally, he prayed for his brethren who wore those chains over the last night, first naming his companions on Patmos; Dim and Teos and the others, then for those in chains for Christos throughout the world.

Traversing the narrow streets, a couple passed. They paused in amazement as he passed.

"We thought...." said the man.

"Yeshua lives - my life is in His loving hands," answered Ionnes, bit off a chaw of breakfast, and continued his snail pace trek to the water, nourished for a time and times and half a time.

<>< ><> <>< ><> <>< ><> <>< ><> <>< ><>

Kynops thrashed about his home again, angrier than last time. The shadows quivered at his rage and slunk to hide beneath the uneven floor tiles. His tirade continued until he became winded and flopped down on his one chair.

"Everything," he blithered. "Must I do everything?"

He felt the shadows shudder beneath his feet.

"Eyore!" he swore and rose to prepare for his next performance. Picking up pieces of potsherd, he laid them on the table then looked at the wall.

"You are sure he is alive?"

The demons filled him with yes.

"Never dead or resurrected?"

The demons did not know. Kynops hoped the former. It would be easier to kill a man who was almost dead the previous day than one who had been miraculously resurrected. They always came back from resurrections healthier than before they died, whereas a man beaten but did not die was still a man beaten. Pain and weakness should still fill his bones.

"Locusts," he spouted.

"Or scorpions."

His mind a bottomless pit, he peered down deeply to find the greater combatant power of evil. Hot, putrid breaths arose. Sulfurous smoke surrounded him. His anger arose again, peaking beyond to mindless hatred. He shuddered and quaked as the darkness filled him. He grabbed a blade to cut both his forearms. He expected black blood to ooze forth but looked down to see the selfsame dark redness. He had hoped for the black blood many times. Only the masters of sorcery had black blood.

Incantations, repeated over and over, he rose off the floor briefly, hovering like a wriggling worm caught in a thin spider web. He soon descended, as if his exhaling breath brought him back to Earth. Finding his footing, he called out to the shadows to come forth. They had to finish this.

Stepping outside, his horse zipped to the back of the small corral. It would not come forth and moved away as Kynops tried to grab it. After numerous failed attempts, he closed his eyes to seek spiritual assistance. The stallion started kicking hard against the wooden borders of his pen. Kynops was not so naïve to believe himself invulnerable to the horse's attacks. Likewise, he did not need another horse kick to the side of his head in his lifetime, but he still needed his horse. He turned to the shadows.

"Go away." They started to disappear.

"Not far," he yelled.

Wailing grumbles.

The horse settled down, but still would not let Kynops near him. After further failures, including trying to lure him with hay, Kynops stopped, leaning against the crude fence to strategize. The stallion kept distance across the limited space.

An abhorrent thought crossed his mind. He knew not where from it came. Like a bad taste in his mouth, he tried to expel the idea, but it would just rise again to the top of his thoughts like cork in water, as soon as his mind rested. He watched his steed. Its eyes, ever watchful, never left Kynops. Kynops widened his Egyptian painted eyes, but no avail. Turning, he leaned arms on the fence.

The abhorrent thought came to the surface.

"Yeshua," he said absentmindedly.

He stood dumbfounded a moment, wondering why or how his mouth could utter such a despicable name. He would have played out the thought a bit more save the nibble on the back of his neck. Turning, he saw his horse, large and alive, standing docilely before him. He lifted the bridle to the horse's nose without protest. The animal donned the ropes. He placed the blanket, then led his steed out of the corral, climbed aboard and headed for town. He rejected the obvious explanation for the horse's agreeable change in favor of unknown, unproven rationalizations.

"Come," he called to the shadows. The horse became testy but did not buck. They moved towards town, and like the day before, many came to follow. Everyone knew perfectly well why Kynops had returned. The news had already rapidly spread of Ionnes' miraculous recovery from yesterday's beating, promising another toe-to-toe standoff. All gathered near the Acropolis. Roman soldiers beefed up security. Temple priests stood stoically along the sidelines. The young man with his risen father, and the old man with his risen son came forth. Everything played out as if merely rehearsed the day before.

Ionnes heard them coming and left the water and his ropes to kneel and pray. He praised Yeshua, certain his prayers arose not alone today. Another left the water some yards down to join him in prayer.

"I have missed you, Dim, my brother," said Ionnes.

"Thought ya could use a extra hand – 'specially if ya get beat up again."

"I hope not," admitted Ionnes, still black and blue throughout. "I am not sure my old bones could take another beating like that so soon."

Dim nodded. He had already feared that truth but dared not say such a thing out loud. When Ionnes said it aloud himself, Dim felt a deep and inexplicable respect and admiration for this strange old man who had turned their lives upside down and inside out since he arrived. Mob or no mob, the two of them would stand together against any other attack from cowardly rioters.

As soon as the crowd reached the beach, Kynops dug heels into haunches to hasten his beeline to Ionnes. The crowd would catch up soon enough. The man beside him was of no consequence to the magician.

"So, you still live?" Kynops rode up.

"Obviously," answered Ionnes, standing most upright; adorning his fresh bruises. Dim followed beside him.

Both glanced over as the crowd trotted down to them. Ionnes looked for the corporeal demons masquerading as lost loved ones. Two of the three appeared. The 'murderer' went ethereal or at best kept distance in the crowd. Probably the former, thought Ionnes. The old man fretted not for he knew the unholy cad would show itself at the appointed moment.

"Are you ready to worship Kynops?" Kynops yelled.

"Are you ready to worship Yeshua?" Ionnes yelled all the louder, "the One True God."

"Hah!" chided Kynops. "You live today only by Kynops' will. Prepare to be expelled to greater eternal judgment."

Ionnes shook his head in disgust. "Yeshua is the only true judge. You have no power to send me or anyone else anywhere."

Kynops considered sending Ionnes elsewhere on the island as a display of his power before the people as well as to silence the disciple. Maybe he should send him out to sea or onto another island, but they would only have to do this again tomorrow. He knew he could not hold the crowd forever; their interests always so fickle and short lived.

Dim wanted to punch the wizard. The strong impression surprised him. Not generally prone to violence, he considered today's occasion a good exception. Ionnes placed a delicate hand on Dim's arm, looked at Dim and smiled. Nodding his head, Dim gazed at the old man, saw what Ionnes saw, and soon shared the smile. There they were, the church, gathered and moving through the hoard of watchers and wall flowers and goppers. Chryspippe led the small but determined group.

Ionnes greeted each with a holy kiss as they drew near.

"Pray unceasing," he coached, then added as he turned to the crowd, "This is not over, yet." He looked at all present, seeing the fear in so many faces. Yesterday's attacks replayed mentally, still so fresh in his mind. The mob attacked in fear. Only fear. Not out of valor or any noble cause. Only fear, compelling them to destroy that which they feared. He knew that any wrong word from his mouth could bring a repeat of the fear-filled wrath. The crowd had already started to mumble and grumble between themselves.

"Kynops," he yelled so all could hear. "Kynops. You have despised the Almighty God of Heaven and His Holy Son, Yeshua, for all your life. But I offer you the one chance to come to Him and be changed forever. His Spirit may live fully within you, if only you would accept Him. You, too, may have eternal life in Christos."

"Never!" screamed Kynops.

"By your own word," answered Ionnes. He peered at the magician. The fear in his eyes was clear and obvious. The façade would fool the people only little longer. He turned away from Kynops.

"Numbered. Numbered. Weighed. Divided," said Ionnes, not loudly, but Dim and others close by heard.

"You," yelled Ionnes, pointing. "The young man stood paralyzed the next moment, uncertain what this old man would say to him. Just yesterday he had seen him for the first time as a fraud. It seemed unthinkable then. Now, he did not know.

Ionnes pushed through the crowd to the young man. His "father" stood beside him, an angry scowl upon his face.

"This be your father?" called Ionnes.

"You know it to be so," answered the young man.

"I know this not," confronted Ionnes, "for I see only one who deceives in the name of Kynops."

"You lie," cried the young man, feeling the pit in his stomach form right beneath the new knot in his throat.

"Verily, I do not," answered Ionnes. He looked upon the young man with compassion. He knew well the pain he would cause this boy very shortly - a pain the boy would soon meet without doubt even if Ionnes did nothing for the demon would not remain corporeally his father forever.

"How do you know this is your father?" asked Ionnes.

"How do you know it is not?" challenged Kynops.

Ionnes ignored him.

"I can plainly see he is my father," answered the young man.

"But you have already seen changes, have you not?"

The young man paused. He seemed unsure how to answer. Ionnes pursued the truth as he continued.

"What has he said? What words has he used? Does he remember everything you brought up from years past?"

The young man remained silent, but his face displayed the truth of Ionnes' words.

Ionnes turned to the "father".

"Say one thing for me," charged Ionnes. "Just one little thing."

"What be that?" hissed the "father."

"Declare Yeshua as LORD."

The "father" started to shake.

"Just once," said Ionnes. "Loud enough for all hear."

The "father" folded arms and stepped back a short distance.

"Just once," urged Ionnes. "Come forth. Yeshua is LORD."

"No," said the "father."

"Then, in the name of Yeshua, our LORD, show your true self to the boy, and after you do, be gone from Patmos forever."

The young man looked at his "father" oddly as his eyes turned to horror and disgust.

"Yes," acknowledged Ionnes. "Demon, depart. Leave Patmos and never return to fool the people."

The demon's angry scowl remained, then it yelled obscenities and blasphemies as his physical form faded from everyone's sight.

"No," cried the young man. "No. Father. Come back." He turned to Ionnes. "Bring back my father."

"He was never here," Ionnes said compassionately. "You were deceived, by Kynops."

"Do not listen," yelled Kynops.

Ionnes turned to Kynops.

"Silence. You are mute for now."

Kynops tried to speak but could conjure no more than a whisper.

"You shall not speak again until you declare Yeshua is LORD."

Kynops' anger filled every pore in his being. He tried to curse the apostle. Nothing came out. He tried incantations. No power behind no words. He felt like a man stripped of all riches.

He kept standing only to keep from kneeling.

"No," cried out the young man, beside them, losing control. "Bring back my father."

Ionnes turned. He tried to place a supporting hand on the young man's shoulder, but he moved away.

"Your father died at sea three years past. I am sorry for your loss, but this being was not your father, no matter how it looked. Kynops commanded it, no demon can create or resurrect life, but I serve the greater power in Yeshua. The demons tremble before Him, for He truly has the only power over life and death."

The young man wept shamelessly as he schlumped down in a heap on the sand and rock. Ionnes looked at Chryspippe who fell to her knees beside him and held him as he again wept the loss of his father.

"And you," turned Ionnes.

The crowd looked towards the point of his fingers.

"In the name of Yeshua, come forth."

The "murdered son" stepped forth, shuddering.

"In the name of Yeshua, depart Patmos and never come back."

The demon stood ground as long as it could, but the greater power of Almighty God compelled it to flee. The "murdered son" promptly disappeared. His father gasped and threw himself at the feet of Ionnes.

"Bring back my son," he both pleaded and demanded.

Ionnes placed hands on the father's shoulders. The father looked up at the apostle who said, "Your son never returned to you. I am sorry and weep with you for your loss, but that was not your son. I have sent another of Kynops' deceiving demons away from Patmos. Kynops tried to use you to destroy me."

"No," cried the father, refusing to believe.

"Watch," yelled Ionnes. He raised his hands. "In the holy Name of Yeshua, you will see only truth." He turned towards one way back in the crowd.

"Demon come forth."

The demon resisted but moved towards Ionnes as though pushed from behind.

"What is your name?" Ionnes asked.

The demon shook but remained mute.

"Your name, deceptive spirit" pressed Ionnes, "that all here shall see you as you really are."

The demon stood ground a moment before finally blasting out an answer.

"Skotadi," it said.

"Louder," commanded Ionnes.

"SKOTADI."

Ionnes turned to the father. "Was that the name of your son's murderer?"

The father, just rising off the sand, looked dumbfounded a moment, but finally answered, "No."

"Skotadi," called Ionnes, "be gone in the name of Yeshua Christos. Flee Patmos to enter the abyss. Never come back to Patmos to plague or possess or destroy the good people here."

The demon shook violently, then crumbled into small pieces, falling to and being absorbed into the ground.

The crowd murmured amongst themselves. They yielded today, so different from yesterday's resolves that compelled them to attack this old man. Yet, here he stood, displaying powers greater than the mighty Kynops.

"People of Patmos," yelled Ionnes. "Be ye not deceived. The LORD Almighty lives, and His name is Yeshua. He calls to each of you in His love. He sacrificed Himself that all of you might live in Him. Hear His call and respond. Hear His call and come forth to eternal life in Him."

Ionnes looked over the crowd of faces. Some nodded to receive his invitation. Some still appeared hostile, but less sure. He prayed quick prayers for each as they crossed his vision. He raised hands high to Yeshua, then turned just in time to see Kynops try to crush him with a melon-sized rock.

Dim intercepted. The slave, strengthened by years of molding stone, easily disarmed and knocked down the sorcerer. He looked at Ionnes just in case the apostle wanted him to crush the magician's skull.

"It is finished for you, Kynops," yelled Ionnes. "I still pray that you would find it in your heart to serve Yeshua. But also, I pray that Yeshua may strip you of your power over the demons. And, finally I pray that Yeshua would open the eyes of the people to see clearly your deceptions and frauds."

Kynops rose. He brushed himself off as he spied the crowd around him, watching his every move. He peered at Dim, assessing, then rushed at Ionnes with uncontrollable anger. Dim jumped to intercept, but his efforts found other hands rushing in to help. Human walls surrounded and protected Ionnes. Kynops tried to push through the crowd; his efforts useless and wasted.

"Be not deceived!" he yelled to the crowd or would have if he had any voice. Facing off with the very people who worshipped him only an hour earlier, he saw their faith in him fall off like damp sand drying against skin.

"Fools," he tried to say, and stormed off to his horse to take his leave. This was not over, yet. Kynops would have the last victory over the old zealot.

"Apollyon," he mouthed as he pressed through the crowd.

He stopped. Where went his horse? It stood there just a moment earlier. Looking around, he saw the animal moving through the crowd as if to avoid him.

"Grab my horse," he barely squeaked and pointed. None could hear him. None moved to help him. He pressed through. It seemed the sea of bodies became thicker and harder to push through. It seemed the faces before him became harder. It seemed those who feared him found new boldness. Pushing through, he found one who pushed back. He paused, indignant. Few if any turned away or backed off. He looked again for his horse. It trotted even farther off. Pressing through again, others started pushing him, left and right, back and forth.

"Stop," he barely hissed. "I am the great Kynops." He raised his hands high and menacing, as if to topple them like a stumbling rockslide, but his voice could make nothing happen, and those beside him brought him down, arms first. He would destroy none today. Others pushed, becoming bolder.

"Hey Kynops," yelled a tall man behind him wearing a turban.

Kynops turned just in time to receive a two-handed punch across his face. He fell back into the crowd who joined in, striking and punching and kicking.

"Guards, help!" he tried to yell.

He saw some on the outskirts of the crowd, watching with amused interest.

"Shadows," he called. Even with no voice, his summons seemed more than empty, and between the blows, the words of Ionnes rang through his being.

"But, also I pray that Yeshua may strip you of your power over the demons."

The unfettered demons would turn on him with a rage. He shuddered with great fear as the mob tried to steal from him his life. He felt the blows and kicks cover every inch of his body. His nose bled. His eyes puffed and swelled, blackened and bruised. His jaw snapped on the left side, snagged on a random sandal. His arms became useless to stop the attacker's blows but wrapped around his bleeding head as he rolled up into a ball. He felt his backbone snap and wondered if it broke.

Then, a voice cut through the mob's angry attacks. Some were pulled away. Sunlight found its way to the ground around him. Kynops peered up through half blinded eyes to see the mass of bodies part. Ionnes moved forward and stooped down before the broken form. Dim, Chryspippe, Apollonides and others stood with the apostle. Kynops saw compassion in their eyes. It looked so alien against the backdrop of hostile faces.

Ionnes stooped down and touched the broken man.

Tears touched Kynops' eyes, but he turned away to refuse Ionnes' help.

"Let me die," he spoke only to himself against the gravelly sand.

Ionnes stood to address the crowd.

"The true deceiver has been exposed. Fear him no longer. His power has been stripped. But I serve a compassionate God who still offers him New Life. This is the same New Life which Yeshua offers to all of you. If you seek The Way to Heaven, come with me now and be baptized. Find in Yeshua Christos your peace, your joy, and your eternal and abundant life. Come." He looked down at Kynops.

"You are welcome, too."

"So, you can feed me to the sharks?" hissed Kynops.

Ionnes understood, but only repeated his offer then stood to head to the shore with the others. He needed not look back but placed hands upon the shoulders of his friends who made a human wall, plowing a holy furrow to the briny water. Many followed. Less entered the water, but many were added that day to their number. Ionnes preached to those present as Dim, Apollonides, Teos and others baptized. Even the man with the murdered son came forward to be baptized. The young man did not. Still, those present felt a warm delight, like the effects after a thunderstorm, enhanced all the more as Yeshua's Holy Spirit reveled and welcomed the new converts.

"Hungry?" asked a familiar voice as Ionnes came up out of the water. He was very tired from the day but could not be happier. And, now stood Myron. The day kept getting better.

"When did you get here?"

"Same time as Apollonides and Chryspippe."

"I did not see you."

"You did not need me before now."

Ionnes laughed. "And, how is it I need you now?"

Myron winked. "So, you are not hungry?"

"Starved."

"Then, come home. Fona already has everything prepared." He looked at the crowd still around Ionnes. "That invitation extends to all of you."

"Then, I will gladly join you," accepted Ionnes. He smiled, but then looked over at the lump of humanity still piled upon the beach. He had been that lump just twenty-four hours earlier. He went back to Kynops, certain he might find him dead. Approaching, he saw the sorcerer still breathed and stooped down before the fallen man.

"May we help?"

"Damn you," mouthed Kynops through barely pursed lips, still unable to speak.

"And, damn your pride," answered Ionnes. "It will do nothing here to save you."

Kynops moved his mouth a bit, but again no discernable words or ideas came forth.

"I told you what you had to do to speak again," reminded Ionnes.

Kynops finally looked up at him, a question attached to his swollen features.

"Yeshua has called you and declared that you shall not speak again until you say that Yeshua is LORD."

Kynops preferred silent curses and blasphemies.

Ionnes rose.

"Yeshua's offer will stand, anytime, day or night. His spirit shall be ever watchful. And, I will always come to pray with you if you want."

Kynops turned away towards the ground. Ionnes sighed, and departed with Myron, Dim and the others.

The late afternoon summer sun continued to beat down on them. However hot, it somehow felt perfect. Myron invited Ionnes into his chariot. Ionnes saw there was not room for all, so declined the ride to walk with the new converts. His spirit soared with joy as he met each and every new disciple.

"Bear with me," he pleaded. "It will take me a while to learn all of your names." He looked over at Dim. Practically from his first day on Patmos he had felt a special place in his heart for this fellow prisoner, but at that moment the agape love filled him to overflowing. He hoped that Dim and others shared the same loving flow of the Spirit.

Myron's home, such a welcome sight. The doors opened up to the back atrium. Fona fretted as she saw the crowd, much larger than expected, but clapped hands to hasten her servants to find more to eat and drink. She kissed her husband, daughter and son as they entered. Before Ionnes, she took his right hand in hers, knelt down and placed his hand against her forehead.

"Silly sister," he lovingly scolded, urging her to stand. "I keep telling you, I am merely a man, and not one to be revered or worshipped. I am only a servant, like all of us. We all may be blessed and part of the same body in Christos."

She rose, though she still felt like she should hold this old apostle in high esteem. Even as an aristocrat, she knew her place in Roman society as a woman and just as well respected her place that the gods might smile upon her. This man tore down so many of her presuppositions and lessons of life, yet she saw the truth in his words. Her husband shared her struggles with this new truth – a journey which brought them closer together than they had been in years. She saw the beautiful changes in her daughter, and the deliverance of her son. How could she not appreciate this strange Galilean with his foreign Greek dialect and even more broken Latin who declared his Jewish Messiah had come and backed it up with more divine miracles than Fona had ever imagined. He stood not as a sorcerer, but as a servant of the one crucified then resurrected. She still questioned that story, as any sane woman would, but nonetheless found a spot of belief in her being made real by that risen Savior's Spirit guiding and blessing a lowly political prisoner who had turned his exile into his thriving home.

Even with all that going through her head, she admitted she had not cohesive words to express her awe and respect of Ionnes.

Many dined as the sun moved west, disappearing behind Phora hill well before nightfall. Ionnes took opportunity to teach those new converts, then blessed each of them as they headed for home. They would come together again Sunday.

"We must go, too," said Ionnes.

"Still the prisoner for Christos?" said Myron.

"Amen," answered Ionnes, pointing upwards and adding, "until He says otherwise."

The two men shared a cheek-to-cheek hug, yet Myron did not let go. Close and in front of Ionnes, he became very serious as he said, "There truly is one thing I do not get about you."

Ionnes waited.

"Kynops tried to have you killed. And, worse, to slander you and make you a fraud to the people. And, in doing so, he also slandered the God whom you serve. Yet, when he showed himself to be the deceiver, and his own words became his undoing, you went to him in the name of your Yeshua and invited him to be forgiven and join with you."

Ionnes nodded. "So, what is your question?"

Myron considered that a moment, then just answered, "No question, other than why. Like I said, verily I do not get it."

Ionnes smiled as he conveyed, "Yeshua's short time among us brought His new life and covenant, first to the Jews, then to everyone else. In His own words, 'Repentance and remission of sins should be preached in His name among all nations, beginning at Ierusalem.' So, if Yeshua died for the sins of all men and women, then He also died for Kynops. How can I, a mere man and servant of Yeshua do otherwise? Heaven is open to everyone who accepts Christos."

"But, it is Kynops," insisted Myron. "What good could he ever be for your God or His Heavenly kingdom?"

Ionnes could not be deterred. Still embraced with Myron, he moved his head to touch his host's forehead and said, "Did I ever tell you about the Apostle Paulos and his conversion?"

PATMOS

CHAPTER 30

Kynops felt the cool wind blowing over his body from the sea. It aroused his senses to finally see how damaged he was. He tried to groan. Still no go. His back throbbed where he had been kicked the hardest. His jaw still felt broken, but he seemed to be able to slowly move. Rolling over, he took much time to sit up. Each new pain became quickly accompanied by another.

The beach lay empty. Looking around, he saw Roman soldiers afar off and prisoners tending their ropes. None seemed to notice him. Well through the afternoon, sunshine still rode its merry dance, ever traveling westward to share its never-ending day with others so far away. Behind the cover of distant clouds, a breeze flowed. If he had been a flag, he would have flapped. If he had been a kite, he would have flown. He was neither and tried to crawl to the edge of the water to wash some of the blood off his face and hair and neck. The cold water revived. The salt stung each wound. He slowly and carefully rose to his feet. Oh, his back hurt to support his weight. Even if his horse remained here, he could not mount, much less ride. It would hurt way too severely. His only plan imagined the long trek home to find his bed and take time to recover.

He checked his jaw. Swelling and numbness along the left side. Not good. He tried opening and closing and found new pain. His hand shook as it pressed against the cheek. Perhaps only dislocated? He slammed the jaw upwards. His whole face erupted with pain, but as the pain gradually abated, the jaw seemed better stationed. He dared not yet try to open his mouth very wide.

Out of the corners of his eyes he saw the shadows, rumbling around him like the first bubbles of a soon boiling pot of thick stew. He sought their help but could say nothing to order them. They kept an open perimeter of distance, perhaps out of reach of his whispers. He could feel their agitation. He could hear their voiceless wails. All he had sought to destroy only collapsed in upon his own head. Well they knew it and well they would accuse him. Forgiveness never ever occurred to them.

He turned towards town and his home, so far off. Perhaps one with a cart would help. No. Weakened as he was, he would not show the weakness to accept compassion. He was Kynops the Magician. However crushed, he would rise again.

Ulysses made it back on his own. So, would Kynops.

Each step took a lifetime. He sought a stick on the beach to help him walk. None big enough or strong enough within eyesight. He pressed on, slowly and carefully. At first, he wished to avoid the sight of people who would see him crossing through town. At this rate, he might not even make town before nightfall. Well, not really. The longer summer days brought darkness around the fifteenth hour; three hours away still by his estimation. He would saunter up the beach and find a place to rest until nightfall. Hopefully, no one would take notice or worse, do him more damage.

Reaching the edge of town, he spied a chunk of driftwood, taller than himself. He tried to bend down to pick it up. His back said, 'no.' He kicked the stick along the ground to a large rock where he could place his hand and try again. Only after a dozen tries could he reach the stick. It felt mighty in his hand. Measurable progress. He was not done – not yet.

He checked the sun. At this rate, he would be all night to get home. His pride still suggested he wait. His pain argued otherwise. He sided with the pain, and slowly moved towards town. A lazy sloth would have outdistanced him in a race, but he pressed on.

Plenty of people of Phora noticed him but kept distance. An angry wizard is not someone most wished to approach, even if he appeared weak and broken. They knew the stories and deceptions of the gods. Even Zeus and Hermes walked among them as peasants by one account. Distance from Kynops seemed both prudent and preferred.

Except for one.

Kynops placed his free hand against a building for support.

"Move," he said to the young child of seven who stood, hearing nothing.

"Move," Kynops repeated, then rolled his eyes. He still could not talk.

"Read my lips," he mouthed; a useless instruction, his jaw and lips still swollen.

The child stood before him, studying the wounded man with utmost curiosity. Kynops tried to move forward. The boy would surely move, but he remained stationed before the magician. Kynops continued forward, bumping the boy with his knees. The boy kept position before Kynops, even as he was moved backwards by the bigger man.

Kynops stopped after a few such steps. His feet moved unsteadily as it was. He needed not to trip over a foolish child. He tried to shoo the boy away with his walking stick. The boy grabbed hold of it like they were playing a game. The youngster's tugs caused more cracks and snaps in Kynops' back. He moved forward to reclaim the stick, pressing it against the dirt roadway.

As they reached the edge of the building, he prepared to cross the street. Curiously, the boy raised his hand and touched Kynops' rough and injured hand, then grabbed hold of his sleeve and placed the man's hand on his shoulder. He would help Kynops to the next wall. Kynops stood a bit dumbfounded at the boy's offer, not sure he truly read it right. One step answered that question as they crossed the street together until Kynops could reach the next building. As soon as Kynops let go to support himself against the building, the boy darted off without a word. Kynops watched him a moment, shook his weary head and continued his long walk through town and home.

So many steps later, as he reached the end of the next block, the boy again appeared. In his hand was a ladle. Apparently, he had run to the water bucket to bring Kynops a drink. He raised the ladle slightly, some water trailing down his arm.

Kynops stood equally perplexed at the compassionate offerings of a young child. He was much more accustomed to people being afraid and avoiding him. He took the ladle from

414

the boy. His hands shook terribly, losing much of the water, but the bit that did make it to his broken lips felt like magic. He knew he was thirsty but did not realize how much. He slurped every drop the handled cup could give him.

The boy took the ladle back, then again offered to help Kynops across the street. Others in town started noticing the pair, and Kynops wished none of their consternations, their judgments, nor even their pities. Still so very bruised and beaten, he felt terribly vulnerable to the utmost.

"Go," he silently said to the boy, and brushed him away with a hand. The boy smiled, nodded and ran off, ladle in hand.

"He is deaf, you know," said a woman.

Kynops turned. An elderly babushka approached, cane in hand, bent slightly with a white shawl over her head to deflect the warm sun. Not a tooth in her head.

"His ears do not work, but his heart makes up for the loss."

Kynops glanced over his shoulder towards the direction the boy ran. No sign. The elderly woman remained, studying him like a chicken magnifying its eye.

"Ah!" she said, nodding. She started to search her pockets. "I know it's…. There!" With a sense of victory in her eyes, from under the folds of her dress she presented to him a loaf of flat bread.

He stared at the loaf dumbfounded.

"Here," she pressed, moving closer. "You must be hungry."

Keeping his one hand on his staff, he looked at the bread in his free hand. "No," he tried to say and pointed to his broken jaw.

"Silly man," she chided. "Dip it in hot tea until it is soft enough to eat. What did you think – that you would not eat until your jaw was fully healed?"

He blinked and nodded as he accepted the food from her hand. As much as he felt he might appreciate her gift, he had to be off. Begone, old woman. Begone. He moved passed her.

"Now, go with God," she added.

His eyes flared at her endearment. The old Kynops still lived mightily within. In anger, he almost threw down the bread onto the dirt, but his heart briefly softened, as if marinaded in hot tea – just for the moment. He nodded to the old woman and continued his arduous trip.

Many steps later, he heard a horse-drawn cart approach from behind. The road looked plenty wide and Kynops slowly continued.

"Looks like you need a ride," called a ruddy man from his cart as he halted his horse. He kept hold of reins as he hopped off the buckboard. "Come on. Let me take you home. You will be out here all night at this pace."

Kynops studied the short man with dark red hair and even freckles. Mid-thirties. Probably married with kids. A farmer of some sort, he looked.

"I brought a couple of blankets. If you cannot ride up on top, you can lay down in the back on the blankets. Here. Let me help you."

Kynops saw the man was not going to take no for an answer. He wanted to resist but saw nightfall still approaching and long parts of road with no wall to lean against.

"Come along," said the man, placing Kynops' arm over his shoulders. Both moved slowly and carefully to the back of the cart. The man ducked out from under Kynops who held onto the side of the cart. He grabbed a footstool from the back to help the wounded man step up. All pains flared at once as he tried to raise himself. His foot quivered unsteadily on the step, but he kept hold of the cart. His ruddy host kept strong hold of the arm to steady him. Another moment of pain and he sat upon the back of the cart. Less pain allowed him to move forward and bring his legs and feet up.

"There," complimented the man. "Let us get you home. That is where you are going, is it not?"

Kynops nodded.

He jumped up onto the buckboard, grabbed the reins and clicked his cheek to tell the old nag to move. The wagon bounced forward a bit as they proceeded. Kynops laid down upon the blankets and placed his arm under his head. He kept eyes out the back in case this man meant to take him elsewhere where others could do him more harm. His death may have

416

merely been deterred a short spell. Watching the road behind him, he saw the driver heading the shortest way to his home.

He was not used to letting anyone take him anywhere, but also realized if this stranger wanted to take him to his grave, there was little Kynops could do to stop him. That fear factor and the reality of being helpless shook him to his core.

The cart turning, he saw the temples. No priests present, he wondered if they would ever again seek him.

As the night approached, his shadows drew in closer. Some rode in the cart with him. Some tried to spook the driver but seemed unable to get close enough. Some zipped around from townsperson to townsperson to turn their heads towards Kynops, moving through their town. With enough agitation, they could cause another riot. They channeled through Roman soldiers, letting the resident demons know what was to come. For them, the night served as the best time to be active, and they raced to and fro as that time approached. Sometimes they snapped teeth at one another in glee, and other times they snapped those same teeth to snarl.

Darkness became full by the time the driver reached Kynops' home. He hopped down again, a lit lantern in his hand, and helped the wounded man into his home.

"Brrr!" he said, entering the dwelling. "Want me to light a fire?"

Kynops motioned no with his hand. The driver laid him down on his little cot, then brought the water bucket beside him.

"I will come back tomorrow and check on you if you want."

Kynops stared blankly at the driver. "No," his mouth said.

The driver understood and went out. The light of his lantern caught the glimmer of gold and silver in a bag on the table. He noted it only as he moved towards the door.

"May God's blessings be with you," he prayed as he exited and closed the door.

Kynops rolled eyes again but was glad to be home and in his little bed. He laid totally exhausted, but the pain would not let him sleep. Jabs and itches arose all over his body. Each moment some new nuisance would erupt. He could only carefully toss and turn without satisfaction or peace. At one moment, he opened eyes to see bulbous, yellow eyes peering angrily at him. He was not sure he knew this one.

"Begone spirit," he whispered.

The demon remained, angry and menacing. Others crowded him, and he realized they were the ones who provoked his aches and pains. He mouthed his incantations, but nothing changed. If anything, they got worse. If he could have fled, he would have. Just as he felt another barrage of demonic prods and punches, practically raising his cot off the ground, the impressions of cold, slimy fingers wrapped around his neck, cutting off his air. He gasped a spell, wheezing in just enough to remain barely conscious. His own fingers could not feel or fight against to free the beings which choked him. He rapidly and sorely tried to sit up. The squeeze remained, and he gasped for each breath, over and over. One breath felt like it might be his last. He felt the breeze tour his lungs, unable to make its final exit. He had to act, or he would never act again. He looked around his dark, gloomy room and saw it as his casket.

"No," a little thought emerged. "No," again, a little louder, floating upward near the top of his thoughts. His breath demanded escape, with or without a voice.

"No," he silently said. "No," again, but the denial seemed more and more foolish as his air departed his lungs with no plans to return. They seemed as good of dying words as any, especially when no others would be there to hear. He tried to draw air in but could not. His throat remained closed for business. His lungs demanded another breath without satisfaction. His dread and fears rose quickly to mind as his death became imminent. Falling back off his cot, he thudded against the floor, struggling forlornly until his mind eased away to fearful nothing. The pit opened up beneath him, hot and searing. The only air to move within and without him now came from his broken mouth. In his last dying moment, losing consciousness, no longer sure he was still alive, the words, "Yeshua is Lord," uttered forth, like sticky drool off his puffy, swollen lips.

His windpipe immediately opened. The fully alert, panicky feeling of air moving in and out, in and out, over and over, filled him as he frantically gasped for renewed life.

"Ahhhhhhhh!" he screamed, turning over and grabbing hold of his head. "No. No. No." he yelled. Then, without warning, the episode stopped all by itself. He waited, broken but alert.

After a spell, he opened his eyes. Only his room appeared before him. He struggled painfully to sit up. All quiet, save the sounds of his own rapid breathing. He checked the walls. No motion. He checked the ceiling. Nothing he could see up there, either. Reaching into his pocket, he pulled forth the bread given him. He took a bite. His swollen jaw protested, yet he carefully chewed. Swallowing, a sense of lonesomeness filled him; of abandonment. For years, he had never been fully alone. His shadows had never been far. Perhaps they were still here, and for whatever hocus pocus reason, he could not see or detect them. But, considering his last encounter...

He checked his clothing and his body. Still torn and broken, but no new pains. With extreme effort, he pulled and pushed himself up, back onto his cot. Collapsing with the effort, he lay quietly. His back still ached terribly, right in the center. He had numbing potions but would have had to mix one. His bed said, "No. Stay put." The severe battery of the day kept him from sleeping soundly, and the night dragged on, but he could breathe, and he could feel the softness of his old pillow against his throbbing head.

One thought seized him enough to prod his joints to renewed pain. Should Ionnes or others hear him speak, they would know he regained his vocal words by confessing Christos as LORD. That thought filled him to overflowing with detestable anguish. Audible curses followed with vulgar vengeance as he wondered how to avert others from realizing that truth. Their deaths spelled out the only answer he could choke down. His broken body challenged that reality as his dark heart continued to hopelessly scheme. Then, his nefarious musings toppled, disturbed and replaced by the memory of the deaf boy visiting his thoughts, time after time. And, the babushka. And, the ruddy farmer. Whatever compelled them to help Kynops? If they had asked Kynops for help...

He had never before been a compassionate man towards anyone.

"What does Kynops do now?" he asked aloud at one point as the first rays of morning light slid in under his closed door. Wondering, the question replaying over and over in his head, he remained still and motionless with pain and exhaustion beneath his thin blanket as he finally found a few dreamless winks of sleep.

PATMOS

CHAPTER 31

A lull settled over Phora like a thick blanket of fresh, grainy snow. The riotous uproars from Kynops' visits left its marks on the townsfolk. Some felt great shame at their actions. Some felt the anger after manipulative betrayal and deceit. Some still sought Ionnes' demise and others simply encountered confusion and uncertainty as to what to think or believe. In response, most became very polite to one another. The civility became both amazing and sad, for though all were treated rather respectfully, all also avoided discussing anything worthwhile or substantial with their neighbors. Even at the gatherings in the temples nobody spoke of the Christian Zealot and his strange duel with a scheming sorcerer.

Kynops had not been seen all week. Some thought him dead. Some still feared him. Those who knew not what to think were content to let the aftermath of the drama continue to play out.

Ionnes, on the other hand, had been seen both daily and often. Many greeted him as he walked to the shore for his daily duties. He blessed those who had been baptized, urging them to keep close to the faith of Yeshua. He shared Yeshua's Parable of the Sower a few times. Others, he at least smiled and greeted while inviting them to worship the One True God.

When Barbara returned and heard what happened, she fell at Ionnes' feet and after repeated apologies for not being there for her master, she begged him to let her kill the magician. Though Ionnes persisted and tried to lift her, she remained on the ground before him. So, he joined her, head down and flat on the ground.

She looked at him curiously.

"Good place to worship Yeshua," he smiled.

She sat up.

He sat up.

"Much better," he complimented. "Never forget," he added. "The same Christos which lives in me also lives in you. And, that means the same Spirit dwells within each of us. Never cease praying or seeking Yeshua's Spirit, and you will know Him all your days as well as see Him thereafter, in His Heavenly Realm. There is no greater gift I nor anyone else can give you than eternal life with Christos."

The following Sunday, they met again upon the Phora hill to worship. Though the group to attend was so much bigger than last week, Ionnes knew not all who were baptized attended, (and some not baptized attended). Along with Dim, Chryspippe and the others, he prayed specifically for those he remembered baptizing who were not present, then for those he could not remember. Seven Roman soldiers also attended – more than last week for the gathering had greatly grown. The soldiers clearly saw themselves far outnumbered and wished more had been assigned to their company.

As the service continued, dark clouds rolled in, threatening to begin autumn a few weeks early. Ionnes ignored them at first, then as the calm sea breeze gusted to wind, Ionnes raised arms to Heaven and praised Yeshua for the cooler temperatures. It had been so hot for months for the prisoners working the quarry.

A few drops of rain started. Then, more rain.

Everyone watched the sky. Most could see the obvious; the rain would only get stronger before it would subside.

"Come," called Ionnes. "There is shelter not far off. We can finish our meeting there." He glanced at the soldiers. None forbad.

He grabbed a walking stick and led the crowd as the rainfall increased. Not anticipating such a bold change in the weather, few had brought coats, cloaks, robes or shawls. The trail was not yet muddy as Ionnes turned off, heading along the side of the hill. They saw the cave, and all entered as the lightning flashed and thunder rumbled shortly thereafter. The rain increased to a downpour as many watched out the opening of the large cave.

"I am sorry," called Ionnes. "I did not bring candles or torch, but we have the light of Christos to bring all of us together here." He continued to pray and sing. He spoke on the love of Christos for all, no matter what any man, woman or child had done.

"God is Love," he said at one point, *"and he that dwells in love dwells in God, and God in him...*

"...Beloved, if God so loved us, we ought also to love one another...

"...For this is the love of God, that we keep His commandments...

"...We love Him, because He first loved us." (1)

And, when he finished with the final, "Amen," those in attendance surrounded him. Some asked for prayer. Some asked for healing. Some asked for more of Yeshua's word. Ionnes heard each and every one as the rain continued. Flashes of canary silver lightning occasionally lit up the small grotto. Some feared the cave might collapse with them within. Others felt confident Yeshua would never let that happen with His elect within.

Ionnes sat by the rock wall. His left hand rested comfortably on one small shelf of stone as he continued to minister to the people. He loved them so much. It scared him at times how much the Love of Yeshua filled him abundantly for this new little flock.

As the rain started to subside, all ventured forth and continued down the trail. Entering town, Ionnes stopped.

Stopped cold.

Frozen in his steps.

For just a moment.

"I cannot believe my eyes," he announced – an amazing statement considering who was saying it. "Everyone, come and meet Prochorus."

Not yet fully healed, still he raced, stick in hand, to his friend and scribe. Tears gushed like impatient geysers, blinding both men, as each gloried at seeing his old friend, still alive; still in one piece; still in One Peace. Their hug never wanted to end as the two old men reunited in ever contagious laughter.

"You would scarcely believe how we have been searching the four corners of the Earth for you. We got your message last week," said Prochorus.

"And, it took you how many days to get here?" teased Ionnes.

"The weather almost made it more."

Prochorus backed away to study his master. "Looks like you have added a few new bruises."

"You know not the half of it," assured Ionnes.

The crowd gathered around.

"This is Prochorus," yelled Ionnes. "He has been with me practically since the beginning when we were both much, much younger. He is also a disciple of Yeshua - not one of the twelve, but one of the first deacons. He also knew Yeshua and served with the twelve after Yeshua's ascension. Whenever someone asks me about all of the other disciples, his face is one which oftentimes first comes to mind."

The crowd joined in the celebration as Ionnes introduced each and every one. First Chryspippe and Apollonides, then Dim and Talor and Teos, then others. A young man approached.

Ionnes was stumped.

"You do not recall his name?" chided Prochorus.

"Hammer me not upon the anvil. He was baptized with a few hundred others only, what? Three days ago?"

"Four."

"Four days ago."

"Wish I had been there."

"We could have used your help." Ionnes smiled.

"In the holy Name of Yeshua, I have missed that smile more than you know."

"And, I yours," admitted Ionnes. "And, I yours. You came alone?"

"Aye," Prochorus nodded. "I sent word to the others throughout the region, even past the Great River Euphrates. Just before I was to leave, Papias and Polycarpus sent word they would be here, hopefully within the week or two. Ignatius sends his greetings and in one side his mouth praises Yeshua you are still alive and in the other mourns for you that you have not yet been sent home to Yeshua's bosom."

"Amen," sighed Ionnes. "If only, but it has become obvious Yeshua is not through with me, as yet. There is something else He seeks and prepares me for."

"Besides building a new church?"

"Yes," he nodded solemnly.

"Any idea what?"

"Not a clue. Not a clue."

The men continued along the road to Myron and Fona's.

"I see you got caught in the rain," greeted Myron. Fona followed and bowed to Ionnes.

"This is Prochorus," he introduced, sharing a bit of their history.

"The House of Myron is honored by your presence," said Myron, then added with an impish glance towards Ionnes, "It is not only prisoners and slaves we honor in my home."

"I see," answered Prochorus, "that he wears a new tunic. Not the regular attire for a prisoner or slave."

"Cost me a fortune," answered Myron. "I kept giving him new tunics, and he would give them to the other prisoners. Eventually, I just had a new tunic woven for every prisoner, so Giovanni would finally keep his. And," added Myron, "we will see how long this one lasts. New prisoners may arrive any week."

"Yes," agreed Prochorus. "I know how stubborn he can be."

"No more than you," countered Ionnes.

Prochorus submitted, then leaned into Myron, "I yield, but take note. You have never met a more civil mule."

"You or Giovanni?"

"Uh-huh."

"When did you say Papias and Polycarpus were coming?" asked Ionnes.

"Uh-huh," repeated Prochorus.

The men sat to dine and shared the events and activities of the past year apart, but only for a short time.

"Sir?" approached Guard Ernesto. "The men..."

"Yes, yes," agreed Myron. "Can you not tell them they are in my care?"

"Aye," answered the guard, "but that will not keep me from doing extra guard duty all night."

"Noted," scrolled Myron.

The men rose to part.

"You may lodge here as our guest," offered Myron to Prochorus.

Prochorus looked at Ionnes. "Only if you will let me earn my way."

"Then, you would not be my guest," countered Myron.

"Agreed," agreed Prochorus. "I would be a good friend who does not take undue advantage of another. I plan to be on Patmos for quite some weeks or even months."

"Scrolled," noted Myron.

Another hug, and the men parted. As Ionnes and the other prisoners exited the House of Myron, they saw Myron with Prochorus through the window of the huge dining room talking away.

"What'dya think they talkin' about?" asked Dim.

Ionnes grinned. "Either the time we hid Cephas' tunic when he went fishing all night half naked on the boat, or on Pentecost when Prochorus first tried to dodge his tongue of fire like it was an angry bee."

"Ya missed him muchly," stated Dim.

"Yes," agreed Ionnes. "More than words can speak. He is part of my family – even my closest relative. You know well also that pain of loss and yearning, my brother."

"Aye," agreed Dim somewhat blankly, keeping his emotions off his sleeve.

"Still," added Ionnes, looking out over the town and harbor below, "Has this not been an extraordinary time being with all of you? I would never trade it, but I am also happy beyond description to have been reunited with a little bit of home."

He paused for effect – something he had learned from Yeshua and others.

"...And, I earnestly and fervently pray you shall soon find your family that your joy may be full."

Dim nodded to reply for no words would do, but his thoughts recalled Ionnes' own admission that he failed often –

even every day, and it could hurt too much to arouse that much hope. Still, he noted his little dolphin bouncing about his chest as they slowly walked back to the penal colony.

(1)   New King James Version

PATMOS

CHAPTER 32

"Do you know that God loves you?" called Ionnes, standing in the town square. A few dozen Patmosites stood by, listening intently. Two thirds had been baptized the day Kynops left their company. The other third teetered or stood one toe away from the edge of commitment to Yeshua. For the most part, Ionnes could pick them out as clearly as if each wore a frightened chicken on his head. The fear in their eyes bore testimony. Some felt fear of the temple priests' disapproval. Some feared family consternations or losing family inheritance. Some tightly held onto the security of old ways, fearful how this Yeshua might change them. Some resembled owls waiting to hear more before making a valid and well considered decision. Some clung tightly to their sin while others merrily teased the apostle, pretending to be interested. Finally, some simply did not know what they believed, having lived life with the devil's modern-day thinking noise between their ears bringing its cacophony of confusion.

"Yes, He does, verily," continued Ionnes. "He loves each and every one of you, through and through, regardless of what you have done with your lives. He loved you so much he sacrificed himself on a Roman cross. What other god have you ever heard who would give up his own life for you?"

"Prometheus," answered a tall man, standing directly before Ionnes. Ionnes felt surprise at the man's response. Clearly, he was neither Greek nor Roman. His refined attire suggested Jewishness.

"Perhaps," agreed Ionnes, "if Prometheus had ever lived. But, as I recall from the story, the Titan Prometheus brought fire to man to oppose Zeus, not because he loved men more than himself."

"Did not he still give up his own life for men?" challenged the man.

"Not if he accepted the cost of his mischief to separate men from the gods. That is not truly giving up his life for men. Did not he lead the Titans in war against the Olympians? When the Titans would not support his war tactics, he went over to the Olympians and helped them defeat the Titans. Thereafter, he disapproved of Zeus and the god's selfish ways, so this clever trickster stole fire to bring to men, knowing it would enrage Zeus by further separating men from the gods."

"Well said," admitted the man.

"Bones and fat," added Ionnes, "But, I am here to speak about the living God, not a creation of man's imagination. And, I deduce by the form of your speech and the manner of your dress that you do not hold to the gods, Greek or Roman, but know of the One True God in Heaven."

The man nodded. "Filon," he introduced himself.

"Ionnes. Or for you, Yochanan."

The man acknowledged.

"And, what is your profession?"

"Lawyer of the Holy Law," answered Filon.

"Then, you know the Jewish scriptures?"

"Better than most," admitted the lawyer, "and I have questions regarding your claim that Yeshua is Messiah."

Ionnes urged Filon to continue before the crowd. They discussed the holy scriptures, sometimes passionately, Ionnes pointing out many scriptures supporting Yeshua as Messiah. Filon, a prudent debater, mostly disagreed, sometimes seeking narrower, more literal meanings to the holy words. Though Ionnes could see the Pharisaic disciplines by which Filon spoke, Ionnes likewise could not help but love and appreciate the man's knowledge of the scriptures. And, Ionnes welcomed all questions with gladness. So many men came to Yeshua from barren fields of the mind, sopping up the baptism of Christos with previously unquenchable thirst. Others responded out of loneliness and a desire to be accepted. Many came out of fear, seeing the awesome power of Yeshua, without yet seeing how much Yeshua truly loved them. Their salvation came more to avoid God's judgment than to find new life in Christos. Then, there arose those like Filon who knew the scriptures better than most. Their scales were always tipped more towards the truth of God versus the love of God. Ionnes recalled how Yeshua taught them how both love and truth needed to be equally balanced.

And, so they parted, each man to his duties of the day. And, there it ended.

Until that later afternoon.

"So," approached the lawyer as Ionnes headed for the barracks and dinner, "if Yeshua was Messiah, why did He leave His chosen people in Roman bondage? What kind of love is that?"

And, so continued the debate until each man parted to his duties of the evening.

Until the next morning.

"So," approached the lawyer as Ionnes headed for the shore, "how could Yeshua of Nazareth be Messiah when Micah said He would come from Bethlehem?"

And, so continued the debate until each man parted to his duties of the day.

Until that later afternoon.

"So," approached the lawyer as Ionnes headed for the barracks and dinner, "how do you know Yeshua was actually born of a virgin as Isaiah foretold?"

And, so continued the debate until each man parted to his duties of the evening.

Until the next morning.

"So," greeted Filon, "why would Messiah accept death on a cross? Why would Messiah come to us from humble beginnings? Why would Messiah come to us not as a great king to rule the entire world?"

And, so it continued, when Ionnes stopped.

"Dear me!" he exclaimed as they entered the town square. He glanced at Filon, then to a small group of people approaching with a man on stretcher. His body swelled and the skin around his legs sagged upon the stretcher.

"Please, sir," they arrived in haste, laying the man on the ground before him. His face showed great fear as he had heard the stories surrounding this apostle. His fear counter-balanced by a lesser fear - that Ionnes could do nothing.

"Dropsy," said Ionnes, kneeling beside the man. He looked up at Filon and invited him to kneel beside him. The lawyer resisted a moment.

"Front row seat," said Ionnes. Filon acknowledged, then came down to the ground, keeping a little distance.

Ionnes looked at Filon. "Do you believe in the power of Almighty God, the maker of Heaven and Earth, to heal?"

"Yes," nodded Filon, "though I have yet to see it."

Ionnes smiled and nodded.

"*Blessed are they who have not seen and yet believe,*" he said, recalling the words Yeshua said to Thomas after His resurrection. He looked at the man before him.

"What is your name?" asked Ionnes.

"He cannot speak," answered a woman who had brought him. "He has been close to this death for nearly six years."

Ionnes peered at her.

"Your father?"

She seemed surprised he could tell but nodded in answer. His swollen features hid most family resemblances, but they both showed the same distinct color of eyes with flecks like green chrysoprase or turquoise mixed with the brown.

"And, his name?"

"Domestia."

"And, your name?"

"Zoe."

"Well, Zoe, whose name means Life, please join me to share Yeshua's healing love with your father."

"We have money," she said, producing a small purse from under her garment.

"That is good," said Ionnes, "but share your money with those who need it. The healing gifts of Yeshua are not for sale. Eternal life He gives freely. I am only His servant; one who is unfit to loosen His sandal."

He turned towards Domestia. "Dear Domestia, may I touch you?"

He did not wait for answer, and the sick man dared not say no.

Ionnes closed his eyes as he touched his swollen feet. He felt along the feet to the ankles to the calves to the knees and on up. His lips moved, uttering the deepest of prayers Ionnes knew how to pray, but that was ever and always the only way he prayed. His hands moved up until they rested on Domestia's swollen chest.

"Ah," smiled Ionnes. "Oh, yes," and he continued to pray.

He looked at Domestia.

"And, you have pain here?"

The man nodded upon his pad.

"I can tell," answered Ionnes, keeping his hand upon the chest over his heart, he moved the other over the lower right of his stomach.

"Breathe," ordered Ionnes. "Breathe deeply. Let it happen, but you must breathe deeply and fill your body with *pneumos*."

Domestia's heart started to beat more rapidly. At first, it flubbed and strained at the effort, but the beat became stronger. Amazement filled Domestia's face. The dropsical man with no neck lifted his head off the ground to look at his chest, moving up and down as if he could see with his own eyes his heart growing stronger and becoming revitalized.

"Breathe," stressed Ionnes. "This is not done, yet."

Domestia laid his head back to look at the bright sky and clouds. He closed his eyes to concentrate upon his breathing. After a few minutes, a terrible urge suddenly took hold, and he opened eyes to Ionnes. He could not form the words, but his face spoke for him.

"Let it out," acknowledged Ionnes. "It is what you have to do."

Domestia looked around at the others. Embarrassed but no longer able to control it, he cringed within as his bladder evacuated.

More prayers. More urine. Then, even more prayers.

"Look," gasped Zoe, pointing at her father's legs. They showed some color and less volume. She pressed a finger into the skin between shin and calf. It bounced back up rather than leave an indent. The skin started to regather against the muscles right before their eyes. Filon tried to find words and realized he could not. The others started to bounce and dance a little. Townsfolk walking by stopped to watch. For the entire hour the vigil continued until Domestia raised up his head, looking down at his flatter belly and narrowing legs and arms. Tears welled, and he cried shamelessly.

"Can you speak?" asked Ionnes.

Domestia looked shocked at Ionnes, then moved his jaw like an athlete stretching to warm up.

"Yes," he gurgled, and smiled. "Yes," he said again, just as watery, and looked at Ionnes with pure and utter disbelieving gratitude. Empowered, he tried to sit up. The water cleared from his throat and he said, "How?"

"Yeshua, my son," answered Ionnes. "The power of Yeshua's Holy Spirit has brought you back to us."

Domestia looked down at himself. His tunic was soaked with pee.

"I am a mess," he apologized.

"Let us see how you can stand," said Ionnes.

Domestia shuddered.

"No," said Zoe. "Surely he is not ready."

Ionnes looked up at her and said, "He is ready if he has your help. You brought him this far. Let us help him go the rest of the way."

She started to cry and laugh at the same time and put out a hand to her father.

"Filon?" turned Ionnes.

The attorney took that moment to decipher Ionnes' request, stood and gave the man a second hand to stand as Ionnes struggled to push himself up from the ground. His legs had grown so stiff kneeling there the whole hour plus. He shook off the tension and stooped down to place hands on seated Domestia's shoulders and back.

"Come on," urged Ionnes to Domestia. "Have faith in Yeshua. Like Zoe, He brought you this far, and He will take you the rest of the way."

Domestia felt the weight of his body anew. He felt so light. His skin sagged not. He saw his slender neck in his shadow on the ground. His wet and soiled tunic felt many sizes too big. He took another big breath and let the others lift him off the ground. His legs responded with renewed strength. He felt dizzy as he found new height; so many days since he had truly stood on his own.

His corded belt fell to the ground, landing around his feet.

He looked at his beautiful daughter and laughed. The gurgle cleared away from his voice. His deep, baritone voice came forth with renewed verve and joy. It sounded so alien to their ears after all that time. He did not wait to be invited to walk. Looking down at his bare feet - wow, it had been so long since he had really seen his feet - he tried a step. Then, another, and another. He again felt amazement, to be able to walk so easily. Perhaps like riding a horse, one never forgot.

"I think I have got it," he told Zoe and Filon, withdrawing his arms. He kept them out for balance and in case he stumbled but walked through the crowd almost too easily. Moving to Ionnes, he looked with awe at the old man. Immediately, he dropped down to knees to worship him.

"No!" shouted Ionnes, bending to Domestia. "This is wrong. I am not one to be worshipped. I am only a man - a servant of the Most High God. His name is Yeshua, and He is the one who healed you. Not me."

Domestia arose, still not sure, though dared not challenge his 'savior'.

Ionnes smiled to melt his fears. "You are a healed man in body only. Now, perhaps you will let Yeshua heal your soul? It is He who is your Savior."

Domestia looked at Zoe, then others, then down at himself.

"May I first get washed off?" his wet tunic clinging to his new legs.

Ionnes missed not any opportunity.

"Would you like to be baptized?"

Domestia looked at him perplexed. He knew not what Ionnes offered, but Zoe did. She had been present during the baptisms after Kynops. She heard Ionnes speak of Yeshua. This had been her final test of his God.

"Yes," she answered for him. "I know I would." The others in their initial party agreed as well.

"Then, off to the sea," pointed Ionnes. He looked at Filon. "Coming?"

The lawyer looked shaken and his mind deeply troubled and preoccupied, but he answered, "Yes. Yes. Of course."

Others who had joined to watch followed them down to the beach.

"Here they come again," said a Roman soldier to his partner as they saw another holy parade head to the water.

"How does he do it?" wondered the other.

Both saw a man skipping along, his long tunic somehow wet. He looked a bit familiar, but neither was sure who he could be.

Ionnes entered the water. Domestia went first, then Zoe, then others. At Ionnes' invitation, Domestia stayed in the water to help with baptisms. Thereafter, Ionnes looked at Filon.

"Coming?" he invited.

"Not yet," answered the lawyer.

Ionnes waded out of the water.

Filon took his hands and said, "Will you be heading to the barracks your same path this evening?"

"I expect so," answered Ionnes.

"I hope I shall see you then," said Filon, bowing low before the apostle before turning to head back towards town.

"What else would he seek?" asked Domestia.

"I expect I will find out later today," answered Ionnes. "But listen, I am still a prisoner of Roma and must go work in the sea. Can you come with me? I can still talk while I work and would like all of you to learn more about Yeshua."

None refused, and all soaked up his words like thickly woven flax linen towels in water.

Prochorus stood on the beach as Ionnes worked in the surf.

"This is a waste of your time," he scoffed. "The last apostle of Christos should not be stuck doing such manual labor. And, for Roma no less."

Ionnes held the rope under the water as he answered, "You make it sound like a special honor to be the last apostle."

"It is not?"

"Of course not. The others got to go home before me."

He had a good laugh, then added, "and my friend, Yeshua has never left me idle. Oftentimes a man shines brightest when he must work. His accomplishments beget him and provide a sense of purpose. That is how our Creator made us, and I have no criticisms with the designs and the ways of our LORD."

Prochorus sighed. "I know. I know," his head down. Suddenly, he saw what he had been awaiting. His eyes perked, and he called to Ionnes, "Look."

The old apostle followed the direction of his friend's arm to see a small band of men walking towards them.

"Aahhhh!" agreed Ionnes. Taking his ropes out of the surf, he ran forth, ever slowly, but still as fast as his old bones would take him to the men on approach. They likewise ran to meet their spiritual father.

"Papias. Look at you," he met, holding out arms to share that long overdue hug.

"And, Polycarpus," he turned to also find the hugs he missed all those months from his protégé.

The others gathered around, and he greeted all in like. One he did not recognize.

"This is Silva Viridi, from Italia," introduced Polycarpus. "He does miracles on the lyre, the flute, and well, any other instrument we have thrown at him. And, he has a voice the angels would envy if they could."

"Welcome, welcome to Patmos," greeted Ionnes. "I look forward to worshipping with you in song."

"And so you shall," smiled Silva.

"We even once found a water organ for him to play," added Papias. "You would have thought he had played one his whole life."

Silva grinned. "They exaggerate, of course, but I am glad to share what gifts I have for Christus Yeshua and the church."

"Good," applauded Ionnes. "We meet early after sunrise in the House of Myron. Prochorus will take you there.

"Forgive me my brothers, but please follow. My Roman captors have become much more tolerant with my exceptions, but I, in turn, have agreed to promptly return to my duties. Prisoner or not, slave or not, the LORD would have me perform to my utmost. But I am happy to hear your news from abroad.

The men looked at one another and immediately became much more sullen.

"Not if you hear what we have to report," said Polycarpus.

Returning to the water and his rope, Ionnes motioned for them to continue. His eyes became saltier than the sea as he heard report after report.

"Nymphas has died," Papias first said in his typical straightforward tone. "He saw the Laodicean church faltering to gnostic thinking. He taught against the heresies, so they put him out. Theirs is a church with thick cushions to place ever resting feet."

"How did Nymphas die?" asked Ionnes.

"Roman and Jewish deviousness," answered Prochorus.

"He promptly came to me at Hierapolis," said Papias. "We talked and prayed and broke bread. Archippus joined us from Colossæ. Nymphas unloaded his heart for the church and could not find the words at times to express his frustration. He and his family stayed with us a fortnight, then he felt compelled to return. We had been in communication with Laodicea, of course, during that time, and they claimed Nymphas was ever welcome with open arms, but he should step down as bishop."

"Why?" asked Ionnes.

"That is what I asked. That is what we all asked, and their only answer was that his hour had come. So, with prayer and thanks, Nymphas kissed us in thanks and headed back with his family to Laodicea.

"Reaching his home, he found Roman soldiers ransacking his home. When he asked for an explanation, they said his thievery had been reported by Jewish authorities. His flight from Laodicea attested to his guilt, so they seized his home and hearth to repay the debt.

"He declared his innocence and demanded audience with the proconsul to face his charges. Word has it the Jewish leaders heard of his 'disgraceful fall' from the Christian sect. Without the support of the church followers, they saw opportunity to destroy him, a Hellenist with more Greek than Jewish roots. We tried to attend, but were not allowed in, so outside we prayed."

Polycarpus added, "I ran to the church, but the Laodiceans would not listen. 'He is not one of us,' I heard one say. I am young, and my voice is seldom weighted by my elders, but I rebuked them sharply in the name of Christos and reminded them that the same fate may befall them for their disregard. They turned their backs and shut the door."

Papias continued, "With no one to speak for him, the 'warthog court' went off without a broken wheel. The guards promptly took him out and murdered him in the street right before us."

"I tried to stop them," said Polycarpus.

"He did," said Papias. "We all stepped forward towards an armed band of Roman soldiers, ready to send us home to Heaven with Nymphas. He stood, strong and straight with his hands tied behind his back. They pressed him down to his knees. He looked at us and yelled, 'I will be with you beside the angels in service to Yeshua's Holy Spirit.'

"We thought they would run him through right there, but they stopped – like a pause of confusion or apprehension, and we hoped the Holy Spirit would take them all down like the Walls of Jericho, but alas, it was his time to leave this sin-filled world. He looked at his accusers standing on the fringe, huddled together like hungry, half-starved wolves, and said to them, 'I pray Yeshua Christos, your true and only Messiah, will show you the sins you commit today. Beware, but also be knownst that His love transgresses your sins. His mercy lives forever. You can still come to Him when your time comes.' His face shown like Stephanos and they ran him through and cut his throat to silence him. His eyes met mine as life left him. His mouth still moved in prayers which bore not the air to be uttered."

Ionnes stood with his ropes in hand, weeping for his brother and friend. He knew few more loving and caring than Nymphas. When Paulos had made him Bishop of the Laodicean church, he feared that others more selfishly ambitious would try to oust him. It took much longer than he would have prophesied, but their lies finally took them away from the promises of Christos.

As the day progressed, they shared other struggles and persecutions encountered by the churches throughout the region. Loss of jobs. Some discharged from the unions. Raids on the churches or some expelled from their homes. Members beaten, flogged, tortured or killed.

"And, Simon Magus deceives the very elect," added Papias. "Paulos' disciple strayed away from his divine gifts for the charlatan's stance. He leads the gnostic cause to destroy the church. Like the devil, he tries to show his disciples how to become god."

Throughout the reports, the cruelty of Roma wove through the fabric of all life in the region. Ionnes had seen many of these struggles for all the years he had lived in Christos, but the reports still crushed his heart like an irate marble cliff. There were times like this when Ionnes and the others wondered whether the struggles to share the redemptive life of Yeshua were worth it, then the Spirit's awesome power would fill them, and they would be reminded of the promises Yeshua gave them during his short years among them. They would see people healed, demons departed, sadness slain, the most sadistic soldiers coming to Christos, and amazing lives changed, oftentimes in the twinkling of an eye. Ionnes knew better than any of them the need of Yeshua's love and redemption for the world that loved its sin more than people love themselves.

"Rein in the insanity," he thought more than once. As he thought of Chryspippe, Apollonides, Gallo, Euæmon, Barbara, and others, including Domestia and daughter Zoe just that morning, he needed not look any further to the love Christos gave him for the world. Like Paulos, he would finish the race.

They dined on the beach sharing bread and fish for lunch. The visitors brought enough food for all the prisoners and guards working the salt ropes. Laughter filled each heart and they shared faux pas' and mix-ups by familiar faces and names in the churches. Ionnes could not help but absorb the love of his brethren, there to encourage him after such a year plus apart.

"We need to get you out of here," said Polycarpus. All the others became quiet.

"Why?" asked Ionnes.

"Because," answered Polycarpus as though that word explained everything perfectly. "We could arrange a boat and take you to the mainland tonight if you wish."

Ionnes loved his young student. In his twenties, Polycarpus had served Yeshua most of his life. Like Paulos saw in Timotheos or Cephas saw in Clement, Ionnes saw a powerful life in Christos for this young man.

"Aye, you are right," acknowledged Ionnes, "and I for one would love to return to Ephesus and the love of my children, but it is not the time."

"Why?" challenged Polycarpus.

"Many good reasons," answered Ionnes. "The prisoners here would be tortured to see if any knew where I went. We had one try to escape in the month of Sivan, and the tortures just about destroyed the quarry. He was found and killed. They did not even try to bring him back to the quarry to punish with a torturous death.

"Add to that, the Romans would seek me among the Asian churches, perhaps even going to Ierusalem. Many would die so I could escape a Roman penal colony? I would never let that happen."

Polycarpus wished to argue more but knew the wisdom of his rabbi's words.

"But, take heart," added Ionnes, "Yeshua has not abandoned me here. On the contrary. Despite Roman charges to take away all my rights and privileges and their plans to enslave me, I have prospered in Yeshua's Spirit. A new Christian church thrives where one did not previously exist. Listen to this. Who do you think the first to be baptized here?"

The others waited, not even shrugging.

"It was the governor's wife."

The reality took longer to settle in for some than others.

Ionnes continued. "A Roman socialite. A woman who considered prisoners and slaves dirt under her feet. But, by Yeshua's leading, He brought her to His church by His amazing love, and she was the first to ask to be baptized. That conversion matches any miracles I have ever seen in all my years as an apostle."

The others started to appreciate the old teacher's words all the more. They realized even more than expected how much they had missed him. He saw the Love of God in ways they all still struggled to see. Ionnes smiled. These men were all still growing in Christos every day, just like him.

"A woman who was born lame, Yeshua healed that day. She was the second to be baptized, and one of the prisoners, a remarkable man named Dimetrius accepted my invitation to be baptized. Then, other prisoners came forward, and the church became a living, thriving part of Patmos. The devil responded sending a sorcerer to destroy me. Not surprising, Yeshua turned it to good for His kingdom. Many were baptized that day. More are added every week; even this day.

"And my brothers, I will tell all of you, the Holy Spirit has given me His Word that He is not finished with me here on Patmos. I know not what form this blessing will take, but I await His guidance with great anticipation and joy."

He placed an old, weathered hand on the boy's shoulder.

"Be patient," he shared. "Yeshua is not done with any of us here. Not yet. Not at all. His journey for our lives will continue to amaze and awe as His grace ever blesses all we encounter. You have become one of the torchbearers to continue to share the name of Yeshua after my years here have been spent. In my last years in this world, I see your faces and am encouraged for the future of Christos' church."

<>< ><> <>< ><> <>< ><> <>< ><> <>< ><>

As the workday ended for the prisoners, Ionnes joined his friends on the beach. They joined hands in a circle and prayed together for the church, including the new church on Patmos. They prayed for Roma. They prayed for their families. They prayed for the unsaved, on Patmos and beyond. They prayed thanks to be together again. The amens could not be numbered.

Walking slowly towards town, Ionnes saw a familiar face approach.

"Filon," he greeted. "Come meet my brethren."

Filon, stood in front of three women, covered head to toe, their faces veiled – one older, and the other two clearly younger. He nodded to each of the brethren, but his attention clearly showed urgency to Ionnes.

"As you know, I had heard rumors of miraculous works by your hand in the name of Yeshua. Patmos is a small place, and everyone cannot wait to tell others what they have seen or heard, including rumors of all sorts. You know the flapping of lips, like a world of yentas living on such a small island. I stubbornly refused to be taken in, but as you spoke the other morning, I found my chance to challenge you as a fraud or verify what I had heard. Yet, after our days of debate, we were no closer to an agreement over your claim of Yeshua as Messiah."

Ionnes felt compassion for the middle-aged lawyer. The Jewish lawyer sought Adonai's wisdom with a verve Solomon would have envied.

"Filon. Filon," supported Ionnes, "the understanding of the Holy Scriptures does not need many words, but obedience and a clear heart."

"Perhaps," said Filon. "Still, let me confess. I have always heard of the love of God, but it never became more real to me than seeing that poor dropsical man healed before my eyes this very morning. And, I had to ask myself, Teacher, what is love?"

Ionnes replied without haste or from repetitive rote. "Lawyer Filon, my friend and brother in Adonai, love is God and whoever has love has God."

Filon nodded, but asked, "And, does this well filled with God's love have a bottom?"

Ionnes smiled, needing to not answer. He saw that Filon knew the answer almost as well as the other men there.

"So, what troubles you this day?" Ionnes soon said in answer.

Filon felt around his emotions before beginning. "I have always been a man of intellect. I have studied the scriptures and discussed with many much wiser than myself, striving to become their equal. My parents were Pharisees but turned to Essenes to find the deeper ways and strengths of Elohim. They taught me well, and as I matured, I saw the call to become a lawyer. My life was one of divine blessing for over a decade, but the night has followed my day, and so mine is a heavy heart that seeks a new hope that brings me to you this late afternoon."

Ionnes and the others waited a moment for him to continue.

Filon took a short step back to the veiled women with him. He touched one to bring her forward. The younger two women remained in place though the fearful concern for the older woman could still be seen in their eyes.

"This is my wife," he introduced, "and, the other two are our daughters. We all come in the utmost fear and hope." Filon paused a moment as though apprehensive how to continue. With a resigned sigh of one compelled to move forward, win or lose, he untied the veil across his wife's. All standing there saw the purpose of his meeting.

"Leprosy," they all mouthed.

"I know the scriptures and dare not tempt Adonai," said Filon, "but I still ask, can you cure my wife? I love her more than any man alive and it breaks me in half to see her suffer and deteriorate."

"Brothers," summoned Ionnes without hesitation, then looked at Filon. "Please, join us."

They encircled the woman and bowed heads in prayer. Ionnes glanced at the other two women but said nothing as he recalled the times Yeshua healed lepers. How many? He could not recall. Two came to mind - the first one their first year together. He fell at Yeshua's feet and asked to be healed. No trepidation at all. He saw his LORD and dropped at his feet shamelessly before all there. Many there stood back in fear and consternation, some ready to stone the man for his insolence to come among them. Then, Yeshua shocked them all. He reached forth and touched an untouchable. Even the apostles felt astonishment and sudden fear.

Then, he thought of Simon the leper - well, Simon the used to be leper in Bethany.

Then, how could he forget the ten lepers who called to Yeshua from afar near the border of Galilee and Samaria? As he recalled, entering town, Yeshua healed them without a second glance, then directed all to show themselves to the rabbi. They departed, all healed, yet only one, a Samaritan, returned to thank Yeshua. Yeshua never hid His love for all, even Samaritans. He asked about the other nine. The Samaritan did not know their placement. Still, Yeshua blessed him and sent him away for his faith had made him whole.

Ionnes laughed at himself. All these years, and for some reason it had never occurred to him before now that Yeshua's direction for the Samaritan to present himself to the rabbi must have sounded so odd. Rabbi's rejected Samaritans just as much if not more than any other Jews. Which rabbi would he find who would examine him? In response, the healed man turned back to the Rabbi of rabbis to give him his final examination of wholeness.

Then, Ionnes thought of other lepers he had encountered throughout the years. Few, if any, Yeshua's Spirit declined to heal when asked. Yeshua's power could never be stronger than when needed the most. The woman's features had already begun to distort, and Ionnes felt great compassion for her. She remained silent, but her disfigured face displayed her shame and fears.

He reached out to touch her. She drew back. To her surprise, another touched her backside. She spun around, perhaps fearing violation from this group of strangers, even with her husband there. She knew leprosy would keep Roman soldiers from raping any woman. She saw two strangers, Prochorus and Silva withdrawing hands. She looked at Prochorus and saw the compassion in his eyes. She looked at the other man, the musician Silva who stood, his eyes closed, with his mound of curly hair covering his head like a huge, deformed melon, rolling into his long beard. She spied Papias, around her age, smiling like a kindly uncle. Then, another face – the youngster Polycarpus in his early twenties – his beard still thin and straggly, but his eyes like an angel's. Only her husband's face seemed stern and full of fear. Her daughters had taken position behind their father to aid as needed. She loved them both immeasurably. It had been so hard to be apart from them as her disease spread across her body. Just their presence with her today aided her courage to enter the town.

Her passions became distracted as she realized a change occurring. She looked down at her covered arms. Pulling back the thin fabric, she gasped at the sight of clean and perfect skin. She could not check everywhere else on her body visually before this group of men in a public square, but she patted herself down and found no deformities where she knew they had existed. As she looked back at her husband, she saw what he saw reflected in his eyes. The tears showed true; her leprosy cured right there before them.

The men broke ring and opened up. She ran to Filon who scooped her up in his arms and kissed her refigured mouth with total renewed pleasure he had long missed. He cupped her baby skin face in his big hands as their daughters joined them. After they celebrated their newfound joy, they turned to Ionnes to thank him. She bowed low before him, and Ionnes went through his regular routine to raise her up and give glory to Yeshua.

"Now I know Yeshua is Messiah," said Filon to all there, "for no man could have healed my wife of her afflictions without the true hand of Adonai."

"Amen," agreed Ionnes and the others. He looked at the daughters. "Forgive me," he requested. I wanted you to join our circle but knew your mother would stay close to you three when she needed to fully seek Yeshua." He smiled at both, then to Filon, placing a hand on his arm.

"Ready to be baptized in Yeshua's name?"

"Without reservation," confirmed Filon.

"Then, come forth tomorrow. We will be waiting. And, be sure to go present your wife to the rabbi for inspection as Moses prescribed."

"Um," considered Filon, "there is no rabbi on Patmos."

"Yes, there is," smiled Ionnes, "and I will tell you where to find him."

<>< ><> <>< ><> <>< ><> <>< ><> <>< ><>

The next day, after Filon and his household were baptized, Ionnes stood before Prochorus, Papias, Polycarpus, Silva and the others.

"Did you bring the letters?"

Prochorus nodded. Papias and the others had brought some copies in Greek of the gospels, some of Paulos' letters, Loucas' account of Yeshua's ascension, the descent of the Holy Spirit and early missionary efforts of the church, and more.

"Very good," approved Ionnes. "Papias. Polycarpus. I need for you to return to the mainland."

Both men were surprised by the request but would head to Tarshish and beyond if Ionnes wished it.

"Of course," said Papias.

"Whatever you ask, father," added Polycarpus.

Ionnes smiled and approached both men. "I have a special mission for you to do. Pray that Yeshua leads your steps and quickly return to me."

PATMOS

CHAPTER 33

"There is a Redeemer
Yeshua, God's own Son"

Silva sang, bright and clear, before the congregation. The beauty of his voice echoed sweet life to all to absorb. He sang alone – just his voice, but it was enough. No instrument could make him sound better, save the Harps of God.

"Blessed Lamb of God, Messiah
Ho-------ly One"

Prochorus smiled at Myron and Fona. The aging couple never imagined what they brought upon their lives by inviting the new Christian church to meet in their home. New members came each week. And, now deacons and scribes and brothers from the mainland – a ready-made council of elders. All they missed - a tithing collection. Myron, the consummate businessman wondered how long such a church could continue without financial backing. Maybe they had living fountains of water speaking with the voice of many waters to bless and support their rapidly increasing congregation.

Myron nodded back at Prochorus. It had been extraordinary having this companion and scribe of Ionnes to talk to during the week. Both he and son Apollonides learned more about Ionnes, the twelve, and of course, Yeshua walking and living among them than Ionnes could share from his chained life of slavery. Initially Myron may have seen just an old man – a prisoner of Roma with one eye. Then, starting with the other eye and eventually with both eyes, he realized how boldly that impression dissolved away as he himself witnessed a blessed disciple rising way above his station by the power of his God. It was not hard to tell which of their eyes had known blindness.

Prochorus taught the congregation that day. Ionnes sat on the floor, or knelt, happy to let his friend take the reins. He reveled to absorb the day's teaching as well as the chance to grow in his faith. Even after a lifetime of service to Christos, he never lost his desire to learn and grow in his faith.

Prochorus continued, *"This is the message which we have heard from Him and declare to you, that God is light, and in Him is no darkness at all."* (1)

He pointed at the skylight, brightened by the slowly rising sun filling the dining room made tabernacle.

"But if we should walk in the light as He is in the light, we have fellowship with one another, and the blood of Yeshua His Son cleanses us from all sin." (2)

Rather than stand at the front before the crowd, Prochorus preferred to walk among them, seeing them up close and gauging their reactions. He had seen Yeshua a few times before His crucifixion but did not notice Yeshua's style of teaching before Cephas mentioned to him that Yeshua did that oftentimes. Over time, Prochorus eventually adopted the walk. Ministering with Christos practically since the beginning, some of his movements had become more habitual than practiced, but he still loved to share Yeshua among the crowd and felt closer to His LORD emulating Him at such times.

"If we say that we have not sinned, we make Him a liar, and His word is not in us. But, whoever keeps His word, truly the love of God is perfected in him. (3) *So, he who says he is in the light, and hates his brother, is in darkness until now.* (4) *He who loves his brother abides in the light. No stumbling. Whereas, he who walks in darkness knows not where he is going because the darkness has blinded his eyes."* (5)

Ionnes noticed a new figure standing in the doorway of the dining hall. He rose off the floor as Prochorus continued and with an open, pleasant smile approached his Jewish brother, Seth.

"It is good to see you," he greeted, placing a hand on Seth's big shoulder. "You are welcome to join us."

Seth paused and glanced back.

Ionnes followed the flow of his gaze and added to his already glowing, flowing smile.

"You are welcome as well," he greeted.

Rabbi Yosef hmmph'd on cue, but accepted invitation to enter the large room. He wore his old tunic, ripped into a large square to cover his head for the assembly. Both newcomers took baby steps, but still proceeded forward towards Prochorus, Silva and the rest of the group. Spying Dim, Talor and Phranc, they moved towards familiar faces.

Prochorus continued. *"Behold what manner of love the Father has bestowed on us, that we should be called children of God. (6) Whoever does not practice righteousness is not of God, nor is he who does not love his brother. For this is the message you heard from the beginning, that we should love one another, not as Cain who was of the wicked one and murdered his brother. And why did he murder him? Because his works were evil and his brother's righteous."* (7)

Rabbi Yosef felt the blind eye of Cain drop away from his face, not that he thought himself evil. But, as he saw the works of Ionnes outshine his own, he had to humbly accept the gifts of Elohim upon this man.

Prochorus continued, *"So, my little children, let us not love in mere word or tongue, but more so in deed and in truth. (8) Beloved, let us love one another for love is of God, and everyone who loves is born of God and knows God. He who does not love does not know God, for God is love. (9) And, he who abides in love abides in God, and God in him."* (10)

"Leviticus," thought Yosef. "And, Deuteronomy."

Prochorus continued, *"In this the love of God was manifested toward us, that God has sent His only begotten Son into the world, that we might live through Him. In this is love, not that we loved God, but that He loved us and sent His Son to be the propitiation for our sins. Beloved, if God so loved us, we also ought to love one another."* (11)

Prochorus closed with prayer, and Silva finished with a new song before the throne.

> *"Thank you, O, my Father*
> *For giving us Your Son.*
> *And, leaving Your Spirit till*
> *Your work on Earth is done."*

"I am so glad that you came," applauded Ionnes.

Rabbi Yosef still felt ill at ease - more so than Seth who was glad to dig into the eats provided.

"I have heard tales of your risen Savior for over a year, and your claims of prophetic fulfillments. They have given me cause to think and wonder, though I confess I mostly dismissed them. Then, you sent that lawyer, Filon, and his wife to me. I was astonished, to say the least, and give thanks to Elohim to be His minister once more according to the law."

"How was she?" asked Ionnes, already certain of the answer.

Rabbi Yosef stood dumbfounded a moment as if he had been asked why the sun became black as sackcloth of hair or the moon red as blood.

"Oh," he realized. "Um, clean. She was clean. No spot I could find."

"Good," said Ionnes.

"But I am disturbed, still," admitted the rabbi.

"Regarding?" asked Ionnes.

"Was she truly as deformed as Filon described?"

"I know not Filon's words, but yes, she showed great deformities, in her face, hands, and I know not where else. The leprosy displayed an evil twist."

Rabbi Yosef sighed. "Well, she was a lovely creature, the woman who stood before me, and I was pleased to find no spot on her."

"Praise Yeshua," said Ionnes. He checked the old rabbi's response and noted less disapproval than usual. Yosef detected the apostle's observation.

"Be ye not meddlesome, Yochanan," he scolded. "You are worse than an old yenta."

"Sometimes," admitted Ionnes. "But I learned it from you."

Seth laughed heartily. In his experience, rabbis seldom received such ribbing.

Yosef frowned, then accepted the merriment of the moment. He had been a prisoner too long.

"Verily, my rabbi, I am just glad you came to join us," said Ionnes.

"It has been a most humbling experience. I admit my folly, but not my timing, for Filon's maiden brought a new realization perhaps I could share."

"Realization?" checked Ionnes.

"About Messiah," said Yosef. He moved his hand broadly.

"Perhaps I could share what Elohim has revealed to me."

Ionnes took a quick moment of internal reflection. Live or die. Truth or lie. He would gladly give the floor to one of God's chosen. He nodded approval, then turned and yelled, "Everybody. Please come forth. Rabbi Yosef tells me he has something to reveal about Messiah."

It took some moments to get everyone to quiet down, but all ears turned to the old rabbi.

Yosef held up both hands to the group, then lowered them, palms up, in surrender.

"I am a Jew from Ierusalem and was reared to be a rabbi. My teachers included Gamaliel. I have argued tooth and nail with this old apostle for over a year whether your Yeshua was Messiah. Messiah for a Jew is greater than life, and though I saw Yeshua in the flesh when I was but a boy, I never placed Him among the prophets, much less as Messiah.

"For, we all sought one who would destroy Roma and bring us freedom from Roman occupation. We looked for another Ioshua or Gideon. Correction, we awaited King David, in a manner returned from the grave, for scripture told us that Messiah would reign again on David's throne. So, how could we see Messiah in One who became no more angry than to turn over tables of money changers?

"Then, I thought of the pain filling this world. What if our Savior was a warrior? Then, our children would all grow to be warriors. Then, our children would continue to fight, even if the war dispatched. Never would we hammer our swords back into plowshares.

"Then, I considered how Elohim knew better than any of us what we Needed to overcome our sin. We needed discipline and self-control that only God could provide. The Spirit of Messiah would continue to dwell with us thereafter and forever, ever speaking to us as our guide. So, instead of a warrior, we would become teachers and healers and those who drive out demons. We might walk on water. And, best of all, we all would receive the key to unlock the chains of our sin. And, as much as I fought against this Yeshua of Nazareth as Messiah, I had to admit we do not fight against flesh and blood, but against principalities and powers. Yeshua came to us in Spirit, in Truth and in His total Love.

"As Moses stated, I come from a stiff-necked people, so I had to swallow hard to say these words, but they demanded to be said from deep within me, and now I profess to all of you my testimony that Yeshua is Messiah."

Ionnes raised hands in praise as Yosef spoke. Heads nodded. Mouths muttered appreciably. Dim noted another reference to Moses.

Myron came forward, tapping Ionnes on the shoulder.

"I thought that I had seen everything," he said. "I was wrong. If this stubborn old codger can find in his heart the words of your truth, then who am I to argue."

Ionnes locked arms, shoulder to shoulder.

"And?" he asked.

"And, the next time you head to the shore, I will accompany you into the water."

"Amen," said Ionnes.

"Amen," said the others.

"Me, too," said Seth. He looked at Rabbi Yosef who nodded.

"Both of us."

"Amen."

<>< ><> <>< ><> <>< ><> <>< ><> <>< ><>

"If your truth be known, apostle," spouted Rabbi Yosef, "I shall declare upon this day that I come to be baptized that I have already been baptized."

The group awaited explanation. Seth, puzzled and already in the water, furrowed those big brows.

Ionnes took a moment of reflection to decipher Yosef's announcement.

"But, not by Yeshua," he deduced.

"Correct," answered Yosef. "Yochanan the Baptist baptized my family in the bubbling Spring of Ænon, near Salim.

"I know the place," smiled Ionnes. "I know it well. How old were you?"

"Barely seven – or eight. I cannot recall. My father came home with great excitement. 'Come,' he said loudly to all of us. 'Let us make haste to Ænon.' My mother looked at him like he had lost his mind, but he showed great urgency. 'I have heard Yochanan baptizes there.' 'Pack clothing and food. Load our donkey. We can be there the day after tomorrow if we leave today.'

"I recall not any other time my father showed such excitement uncontained. On the way he said he rued not finding Yochanan when baptizing in the Iordan near Ierusalem, and something inside feared he had missed his chance."

"You made quite the journey," applauded Ionnes.

"Yochanan brought Elohim's presence back to Yisra'el; that we were still His people."

Dressed in only his loin cloth, Rabbi Yosef entered the water ahead of Ionnes to join Seth and Dim. The cool fluid flowed over his feet and legs like salted silk and swirled scarlet. He shivered a bit, his old flesh suddenly bumpy. His hands flowed through the water as his waist submerged.

"What do you recall of the journey?" asked Ionnes.

Rabbi Yosef stroked his bushy beard with a wet hand as he collected memories.

"On the road, I only recall not knowing where we were, and a sense that we might have lost our way. I had to hold my brother at times. He tired of the hike and tried to squirm out of my arms. I recall sleeping along the Iordan River one of those nights. The lap of the water awakened me often and the moon rose high enough to reflect off the water.

"I know not how we found Yochanan - whether others told us or if we followed the line of pilgrims or if Elohim Himself directed our father's feet. I know not, but I recall seeing Yochanan, seated in the sun on a rock when first we arrived. He scared me, of course, not only as a stranger but also a mystery. His skin showed darker than the camel hair he wore. His hair on his face and head never knew the brush.

Still, I loved his eyes. They pierced me like the sharpest arrow when he looked at me, yet I could not look away and watched all he did with wonder.

"And, his speech. I am sure I understood almost nothing he spoke, but my father knelt before him and placed Yochanan's hand against his forehead."

"Did you feel welcome?" asked Dim.

"Very," answered Yosef. He smiled greatly and with total joy to be sharing the gift of Elohim. 'Repent!' Yosef yelled, shaking his entire body to imitate the long-gone prophet. 'Repent of your sins.'"

"And, did you?" asked Dim.

"I was seven or eight. What sins did I have to repent of?"

"Did he offer you food?" asked Ionnes, grinning impishly.

"I recall not," furrowed Yosef. "Um, wait! We spent some hours there, listening to his teachings. He drank water right from the fountain. Some of the other children there told me they saw him eating locusts and honey."

"Yum!" shuddered Dim.

Seth also looked less than enthusiastic. "Sounds like a dare."

"Crunchy & nutritious," added Dim.

"I tried them," admitted Ionnes. "The honey made them less bitter. I might not have swallowed otherwise."

"Then," continued Rabbi Yosef, "he baptized first my papa, then mama, then his parents then my aunt who lived with us, then me and my brother and sisters."

"How did that feel?"

"Funny," answered Yosef. "I could not wait to get into the water, yet as he held me in his long, thin arms, I could feel my chest pounding against his hands. He lowered me down, then brought me up far too quickly. I wanted to stay under. I kept my eyes open the whole time to see the water rush over me, the wavy image of Yochanan above me, then brought back up out of the water like mama cleaning our clothes."

Watching the briny harbor water swirl between his fingers, Rabbi Yosef smiled at the far away memory; one not recalled for many, many seasons. He gazed at Ionnes and smiled.

"And, that memory helped bring me here today. Do you recall when I said Yeshua could not be Messiah for He left us in bondage to Roma?"

Ionnes nodded as he said, "Of course."

"Then, sometime later - I cannot measure how many weeks or months, I recalled Yochanan baptizing me. I was young, but I know my papa - and mama and others praised Elohim again to have another prophet among us after so many centuries. Then, he faced beheading by Herod the tetrarch, and I recalled my family weeping. And our friends and neighbors, and well, it seemed all of Iudæa mourned his death. And as I grew to manhood and learned to serve Elohim with all my mind and heart and strength, I recalled wishing I could be the next Yochanan the Baptist. But the dream became lost amidst other childhood dreams until this week where its resurrection resurfaced boldly and brightly. I stood in awe of its return, perhaps even as you did when Yeshua appeared before all of you. I had examined the woman with leprosy and found her skin soft and pure, like a newborn's.

"Then, I recalled that I revered Yochanan, the last prophet of Iudæa. Only then did it occur to me this week that the Jews never expected him, the Baptist, to free us from Roma's grip, so why did I place that same yoke on Yeshua? No matter how much I may have wanted to see Yochanan the Baptist as Messiah, I could never see him seeking David's throne. Seated on that rock in the sun made more splendid a throne than any gold seat with amethyst cushion.

"As I came forth from the water, the feel of his hands still fresh on my body, I recalled his words. 'Repent,' he said to all of us. Repent of our sins."

The old rabbi paused and looked very far away. "Um," he stuttered, "I never considered this before. Yochanan the Baptist told us to repent, but he never pointed to the temple in Ierusalem or told us to bring an animal for a burnt offering. He merely said, 'Repent.'

"I laughed to myself at the time. What sins did a child like myself commit? Hitting my sister? Not like she did not deserve it. Stealing an extra raisin cake? But, repent we did with earnest and trusting reverence. It is that same childlike reverence I bring to you today - to trust in your words that Yeshua is Messiah - to trust in His love to bring me to my death in His glory. For many years I have been worn out worse than our old tunics - long before I stepped my first foot from the boat and touched this land called Patmos. Now I know with full certainty that I shall leave here, whether in body or spirit, reborn in Yeshua my Savior."

Ionnes took him by both shoulders and smiled with complete and unreserved approval of the old rabbi. The men smiled brightly eye to eye through old, gray beards and brows and locks and aged, brown wrinkles.

Ionnes and Dim took hold of the rabbi, carefully tipped him back then supported his weight as he entered the water. He kept eyes open and watched the two men above him. Dim began to raise him, but Ionnes gave him an extra few seconds to relish the moment before bringing him forth. He laughed beneath the water as they began to raise him up, the bubbles bursting forth announcing each syllable of his joy. He broke surface still in glee, pulled his hair away from his face, and announced, "Hineni, Yeshua. I am here and have answered your call. Like Samuel. Like Isaiah. Like Abraham. Hineni."

Glancing at both elders back and forth, Dim asked, "Who is Samuel? & what is Hineni?"

(1)	Et al
(2)	Berean Literal Bible
(3)	New American Standard Bible, et al
(4)	New Heart English Bible
(5)	Holman Christian Standard Bible
(6)	Berean Study Bible
(7)	NET Bible
(8)	Jubilee Bible 2000, et al
(9)	New Heart English Bible
(10)	Darby Bible Translation
(11)	English Standard Bible

- Hineni - Hebrew for "I am here," or "Here I am." Isaiah responded with Hineni in Is. 6:8 and again Is. 65:1

PATMOS

CHAPTER 34

"Do you know the most amazing thing about Ionnes?" Prochorus asked Dim.

Dim looked up from one of the books Prochorus had brought. Still in Myron's home after the morning church service, the congregation remained, some to socialize, but most to learn, hear and experience more about their newfound Savior. He saw the Greek words crossing the leather scroll in his lap - a letter Ionnes had written some years back in Ephesus, and the topical source of Prochorus' sermon that morning.

"He writes a lot like he talks," said Dim.

Prochorus nodded. He looked over at Ionnes, out back in the garden, on knees in prayer. The apostle had excused himself to feel the warmth of the autumn sun and breathe in the green smells of the atrium as he prayed. Prochorus thought the sun shone brighter around his friend and teacher, whether it actually did or not.

Dim looked over at Myron, near the open window, also reading one of Prochorus' books. Chryspippe sat beside her mother, leaning into her shoulder and enjoying the calm. Dim detected a bit of sadness in her eyes. Perhaps she wished her husband to be present, or she felt sadness to see Ionnes still in chains at times. Or, perhaps she did not like the table arrangements. He could not tell.

Apollonides stood to gather attention.

"Everyone, please," he began, glancing over at his father with a sly smile. "I have a confession to make - to all of you. But it is a confession of victory. What began as utter failure and my road to destruction now has become my utmost delight. It shines within me like a great star, falling from the heavens, burning within me like a torch. It still feels odd to think what I had been, not three months past. I heard news of the destruction of Apollo's temple. Walking amidst the rubble, I was shocked, of course, like all of us, but perhaps you need now know, just the previous month I met with those priests to challenge and take-out Giovanni. I knew not the demons which filled me. See here. I still bear the scars of self-inflicted damage. I placed my trust in those priests who could never heal or mend for all the years I knew them. No. But, my story has the happy ending most of us only yearn for. My healing has come, and I know the source of my salvation; the Host of my deliverance. His power destroyed the old carnal man in me, and then raised up a new man. I shall be ever grateful for that gift – a gift that keeps on giving, I pray, for years and years. I gave so much to the gods – to Jupiter and Neptune. To Mercury and Venus. Oh, yes. Lots to Venus."

He smiled.

"And, of course to Apollo – my namesake. You can all imagine Apollo racing in his fiery chariot across the sky – his countenance too bright to behold. What man can look upon that splendor? But, now I see there is a splendor brighter than the sun and it comes in the words and form and ways of Yeshua. That brightness exposed my foolishness, even if I was too blind to see it. Yes, there are those who are blinded by the darkness. Then, there are the others, like myself, who were blinded by the light. So now my eyes are made new. Yeshua gave me His new eyes. Now my new eyes have adjusted to that very light, better than any others who still seek out the darkness. And, I plead with all of you to pray that I never be thus blinded again."

All in attendance nodded and approved and applauded with their smiles. He looked around the room, smiling at all, gazing longest upon his sister, then returned to his cushiony place on the floor.

Dim watched him idly a moment, then turned to Prochorus.

"Were not ya goin' to tell me the most amazing thing 'bout Ionnes."

Prochorus almost choked on his wine.

"That is right," he coughed. "Do you have a guess?"

Dim thought briefly. "His commitment to Yeshua?"

"No," said Prochorus.

"His sinlessness?"

"No," answered Prochorus, "and let me tell you – he is not nor ever has been sinless. I said the same thing to him one time, and he confessed my ear off for the next couple of hours."

Dim considered another answer.

"Those miracles he can do in Yeshua's name. He always corrects me when I say he performed the miracle."

"No, but closer."

Dim put up his hands, stumped.

Prochorus smiled. "His humility."

Not the answer Dim expected, but let the meaning gradually take form in his mind to aptly appreciate what Ionnes' lifelong friend and associate may have meant. He nodded for him to continue.

"I know many who have done miraculous signs and wonders in the name of Yeshua. In each case when Ionnes was present, he never seemed competitive. He loves what we do and encourages us to develop all the more. There are so many I know who, if they had Ionnes' miraculous powers, would be impossible to live with. Unbearable. And, Adonai would be showing them the destruction of their pride in some very loving but uncomfortable ways.

"But, I have yet to see pride or arrogance with this Son of Thunder. He could be fiery and impulsive when he was younger, but his faith and understanding ever deepened year by year. I am an old man, but he shows me daily strength that I may never fully understand this side of the grave."

They both looked out towards their apostle, still deep in prayer.

As he knelt, Ionnes felt the green grass beneath. It prickled and tickled him. He felt its soft and cushiony loam, yet a deep and troubling agitation traveled up through his legs and into his body.

"Breathe," he responded. "Breathe."

He drew deep breaths to calm his spirit and his mind. A chafing whirlwind of thoughts and ideas racing through his mind needed diverting, like noises, thundering, lightnings and an earthquake, resistant to the changing course. Such thoughts darted about like a drunken house fly, changing directions with unforeseeable immediacy.

"Breathe," he repeated to himself. "Breathe deeply like the Holy Spirit."

He could smell the sweet scents of flowers spread about the inner atrium. Sweet violets and purple blue larkspur. Gallic roses and poppies and myrtle and heliotrope. He opened eyes to see the sunshiny yellow everlasting flower. The plush, living scenery and greenery felt so out-of-place compared with the rest of deserty Patmos. He loved visiting the small piece of Eden and praised Yeshua for the chance to come to Him there in prayer.

The scurry and tensions of his mind eased as he prayed for the many souls around him. His list ever had grown over the years, but never became tedious. His love for those Yeshua had brought to him ever added to his joy.

"Alleluia! Alleluia!" he celebrated and welcomed the presence of Yeshua's Holy Spirit to fill him to overflowing. He shuddered like a wineskin ready to burst seams as the sunlight filling the garden met a flock of clouds, slowly migrating across the sky. The shadows about him lost distinction and contrast but could still be seen. He bent forward, his face barely an inch from the delicate, green blades.

From above a voice shouted down to him from the heavens with words like a trumpeting herald.

"I AM THE ALPHA AND THE OMEGA, THE FIRST AND THE LAST!"

Ionnes shuddered deeply with sudden fear at the unexpected premonition. Still facing the ground, his eyes widened as the figure shouted all the louder.

"What you see, write in a book and send to the seven churches which are in Asia: to Ephesus, to Smyrna, to Pergamos, to Thyatira, to Sardis, to Philadelphia and Laodicea."

Ionnes considered the seven churches named. All followed a trade path like colored beads on a string.

He looked upward, squinting to see the image of one coming with the rolling clouds. Seven gold lampstands caught his eyes. In the midst of them, the Being's form took shape, looming so big above him, descending and growing bigger.

Ionnes' eyes widened, and his heartbeat rapidly sped up, soon pounding inside his chest like a huge tom-tom.

The Supreme Figure was clothed with a brilliant white garment down to His feet which looked like burnished bronze. A golden sash crossed His body diagonally. He displayed snow white hair, flaming eyes, and a voice which flowed deeply and unquenchably.

Somehow in the midst of the shocking sight above him, Ionnes recognized the face.

"Yeshua," he squeaked with renewed awe.

Yeshua raised His right hand to his disciple. In it lay seven stars, barely detectable against the blinding bright countenance, brighter than even the sun which would undoubtedly blind the apostle if he stared too long. Ionnes peered as long as he could, then looked away back to the seven golden lampstands.

At that moment he fell over, shuddering a moment before he laid still.

Dim and Prochorus noticed him fall. Waiting barely a moment to see if he moved, they then jumped up and ran outside. Others quickly followed. He moved not. Kneeling beside him, they placed hands upon him in prayer as his features began to turn blue.

Ionnes had prayed for this moment so many times uncountable – to depart the pain and fear and troubles of life for eternal life with Yeshua. As he expected, the awe and splendor and beauty filled him through and through as he tried to behold all holy activity around him. It never occurred to him to look down towards his dead mortal shell, but noticed Yeshua bend forth, reaching down, down, down with all seven stars still shining from His right hand to touch Ionnes' body. Barely a graze, Ionnes resumed breathing as he opened his eyes. Returning from death, he saw Yeshua's right hand, still holding the stars, move away from him and felt the warmth against his skin after Yeshua's reviving touch. He took in all with earnest anticipation. Later he would selfishly grieve, at least in a moment's passing, for returning to his body and again be separated by the thin, thin veil between himself and Yeshua's glory and abounding radiance.

Yeshua looked directly upon Ionnes as He again spoke.

"Fear not." His voice, still multifaceted and multi-dimensional, became a bit clearer to Ionnes' ears.

"I am the First and the Last. I am He that lives, and was dead, and behold, I am alive forevermore. Amen. And, I have the keys of Hades and of Death."

His words replayed through Ionnes over and over, reverberating through every fiber of his being.

"Write the things which thou hast seen, and the things which are, and the things which shall be hereafter."

"Past. Present. Future," thought Ionnes. He glanced again at the seven stars in His hand.

"The mystery of the seven stars which you saw in my right hand, and the seven golden candlesticks. The seven stars are the angels of the seven churches: and the seven candlesticks which you saw are the seven churches."

Ionnes replayed the list of seven churches in his mind.

The LORD looked upon His child with the greatest compassion as Ionnes heard the words he was to write to the seven churches. Tears filled his eyes at times. Joy filled his heart otherwise.

Some minutes passed. His rapid breathing subsided, but he continued to tremble. His glazed eyes moved a bit, focusing on the faces around him. He seemed terribly disturbed as he took Dim's hand and tried to sit up. Still looking at everyone, he settled on Prochorus.

"Papyrus," he said. "And, a quill. And, ink. I need to write while the memory is still fresh. Quickly, do you have some?"

"Of course," answered Prochorus, but remained beside his friend.

"Quickly," urged Ionnes, squeezing Dim's hand as he struggled to stand. "I need it now."

Prochorus arose, walked as quickly as his old legs would take him to his room in Myron's home. He grabbed the requested materials and returned to see Ionnes sitting on cushions at Myron's table.

"Thank you," he said, almost vacantly, quickly scribbling words like a madman. Everyone gave him distance, but none dared not watch him. He continued to write with great urgency and haste, then after a couple pages, took a drink of someone's wine and set down his pen. He continued writing the next hour, then stopped. Looking over the pages, made a couple changes, then looked at Dim sternly.

Dim waited, becoming a bit more uncomfortable, wondering what Ionnes thought while looking at him.

"Dim, my child," he finally said. "You were the first to be a comfort to me after I arrived on Patmos. I know that you are young in the faith, but would you be the first to see what Yeshua just revealed to me?"

Dim felt like an aqueduct just unloaded on him but took the pages from Ionnes' hand. He tried to read but felt the eyes of each person upon him.

"Relax," assured Ionnes, and glanced knowingly at Prochorus. "Take a deep breath and just read it, then Prochorus, would you read it to everyone?"

Dim acknowledged, took another breath as thus commanded by a spiritual father, and read some crazy words about Yeshua being Alpha and Omega. Being first and last. He had stars in his hands and lampstands. He read of a terrible being, larger than life, with white hair, flaming eyes, bronzed feet and a tongue like a two-edged sword. Then, carefully he handed the papyrus to Prochorus who glanced at Myron before reading aloud.

The faces in the room all told the same story. Most felt the same what-does-it-mean questions. Prochorus handed the papyrus back to Ionnes, who glanced over it again, then looked at everyone.

"Forgive me if I scared you," he started. "I was praying and feeling Yeshua's Holy Spirit filling me to overflowing. At times like that, I feel like I could take on the entire Roman army; like Elisha blinding the army that gathered at his door."

"Who is Elisha?" asked Dim.

"One of the prophets of old," rambled Rabbi Yosef. "Elijah's student, and a man endowed with double Elijah's Spirit."

Dim nodded acknowledgment and thanks.

Ionnes continued, "The image that filled and overran through my mind scared me beyond description and I fell as dead. I knew His face. I knew it better than I know my own. It was Yeshua, but nothing like I had ever seen or encountered before. Not even the transfiguration compared. Brilliant white robe and hair. Feet of burnished bronze. Eyes aflame. A voice like many waters and a tongue that could slice or defend."

"Like Daniel saw?" asked Prochorus.

"Who is Daniel?" asked Dim.

"Another prophet," answered Yosef. "He was taken to Babylon after Ierusalem fell the first time. He had great spiritual insights, including interpretation of dreams."

Ionnes interjected, "He wrote of a vision of God which matched what I have seen. So many times, I have read those words in the sacred scrolls and wondered what the vision must have been like. Now I may well know."

"So, you had a vision?" asked Myron.

Ionnes looked at Myron, a bit perplexed, then answered, "Not exactly. I have had visions before, but none prepared me for this."

"A dream?" offered Rabbi Yosef.

"In a fashion," answered Ionnes. "More like both, really. As a vision, I saw the LORD, but was also part of it, like a dream. He spoke to me. I died. He touched me, and I lived again. Daniel did the same, did not he?"

Prochorus, Rabbi Yosef and Seth all nodded.

"Then, Yeshua told me to write what I saw. So, I left the vision to finally see all of you, and I had to write it down while it was still fresh in my mind."

He sighed and felt the Spirit tugging at his heart.

"What?" asked Prochorus.

Ionnes showed no hurry.

"Let me be," he said, taking back the pages. "I feel the need to write a bit more."

He rose, taking the sheets and quill back out to the garden. He used a stone as a table and continued writing for another couple of hours. No one dared disturb him, but only two knew when he set down his pen and rubbed his old, tired eyes.

"Ionnes?" called Prochorus.

Still rubbing his eyes, he motioned for them to enter if they wished.

Dim led the way, bringing Ionnes some water. He drank it dry in one turn, then looked at Dim. "It is a letter."

"You are composing a letter?" asked Prochorus. "To whom?"

"Not I," answered Ionnes. "Yeshua. I am merely His scribe. He seeks to write to seven churches not far from here." He peered at Prochorus, thinking. "My friend and scribe? I need you to copy this letter with me. We need another seven copies - perhaps more, to send to each of the churches."

"Which churches?" asked Prochorus.

He glanced over his pages.

"Ephesus, Smyrna, Pergamos..." he glanced at Dim then continued, "Thyatira, Sardis, Philadelphia and Laodicea." Christos Yeshua has a personal message for each church. He read each message with insightful verve, recognizing the unique features for each church. He also felt awe to see words of insight and even correction for circumstances and situations that Ionnes could not have known about during his year plus as a prisoner of Roma.

"Why those seven?" asked Dim, reminded of his missing family as he mapped the direct, hooked route in his mind from one town to another. His hand habitually went up to his marble dolphin, feeling the sculpted stone and not surprised to find another tear forthcome for his missing loved ones.

"You will have to ask Yeshua the answer to that question," smiled Ionnes, his eyes alive with anticipation and more wisdom than he could convey with mere words.

Ionnes awoke, brooding. Lying on his back in the barracks, something felt not quite right. The other prisoners around him all slept, some snoring, some covering up their ears to ignore it. He sat up to look around the gloomy room, unsure of the time. It felt like at least a couple hours before daybreak.

"What is it, LORD?" he whispered, lying back. Nothing materialized above him in the nighttime shadows. The barest breeze slipped in the small openings near the ceiling like a still, small voice. His heart listened with ears wide open.

The soft, feathery waft comforted, but contained nothing he could discern.

He checked his pulse. Still alive.

He checked his spirit's pulse. Still alive.

But something seemed - he could not decide what.

He touched the papyrus beside him. After the vision last Sunday, he had decided to keep some close by. It seemed silly to bring it into the barracks. Once the door was closed for the night, even a leopard would stumble about. Nonetheless, he felt glad to have it there as the night's vigil moseyed along.

He had been an apostle long enough to know when he awoke at night, often the Holy Spirit would summon him to pray. He needed not always know the specific reason for the summons, but he knew well enough to respond. Oftentimes, the Spirit answered and directed his prayers. Sometimes not so, or at least not in words and ideas he could always fathom. He continued his prayers, reassured Yeshua would let him know when the time was right. Still, he detected a nagging grief still stirring deep, deep within. He pondered. He mulled over. He even moped a bit with frustration but could not decide what bothered him.

With another 'amen,' he turned onto his side, pulled his blanket over his head, and burrowed deeply to try again to find sleep. Listening to his breathing, he kept his quiet vigil. No reason to let any prime prayer time go to waste, even if he knew not the purpose. Eyes open or closed did not matter.

Until he saw the light.

Coming from a door.

He stood, unsure whether to proceed. Then, a familiar voice beckoned him.

"Come up here, and I will show you things which must take place."

Before the thought finished being processed in his mind, Ionnes whooshed into the Spirit, finding himself in an amazing and grand throne room. Domitian's throne room by comparison appeared totally small and insignificant. Ionnes noted around the throne the rainbow, Elohim's promise never to again destroy the world with water. Yet, it seemed dominated by emerald green hues. Lightnings and thunderings and voices all rang forth from the throne. A sea of glass, like crystal spread out before the throne.

One sat on the throne. In awe, Ionnes gazed long and hard at Him. His skin and robes resembled the reds and reddish browns of jasper and sardius. Stepping back, he saw twenty-four more chairs – or maybe thrones. They had to be thrones. The elders seated there, all wearing white, also wore crowns of gold.

Between the throne and the twenty-four thrones stood seven lamps of fire, fully ablaze. Like a moth attracted to a flame, or a man hunkered down before a campfire, he watched the seven lamps. The flames danced and flowed. Then, to Ionnes' amazement, he realized they were not just lamps, but seven Spirits of God.

Then he saw, near the throne four amazing creatures, unlike any he had ever seen or heard of. Each had multiple eyes around their heads. He saw in one a lion, and another a calf. The third a man and the fourth a flying eagle. Yet, all four had wings, six wings to be exact, singing together as one voice:

> *"Holy, holy, holy,*
> *LORD God Almighty*
> *Who was and is and is to come!"*

Then, Ionnes watched to his wonderment as the twenty-four elders left their thrones, cast off their crowns and dropped to the crystal glass floor before the LORD's throne to worship Him, saying in one voice:

> *"You are worthy, our LORD and God,*
> *to receive glory and honor and power;*
> *For You created all things,*
> *And by Your will they were created*
> *And have their being."*

Ionnes looked down in his barracks at the papyrus sheets before him. It was still midnight dark, yet somehow he could clearly see the pages. He could not tell with eyes the source of the light, but fretted not as without hesitation, he grabbed quill and ink to write what he had just witnessed and experienced as the visions continued...

Ionnes listened to the chanting repetitions, taking in the words and the rhythm. He closed eyes and let it flow through him until he became part of the praise. Eventually opening his eyes, he looked towards the one on the throne. Where there had been seven stars in His right hand now set a scroll. He held up the scroll to reveal it locked with six? - no, seven seals. A short lull followed as every being set attention upon the scroll. Ionnes, brimming with excitement, felt the sense of eager anticipation like when the lights were snuffed to begin a perfectly orchestrated stage play.

Still focused on the scroll, his attention became diverted by another mighty and powerful presence entering from above. He gasped at the pure power of the angel above him, impressive and mighty. He hovered above the scroll to address the assembly.

"Who is worthy to open the scroll and to loosen its seals?"

Ionnes' ears rung to hear the sound of his voice. He let the ring subside as he looked at all present there. No one moved forward or called out or raised a hand. For the first time, Ionnes noticed the size of the throne compared with the material world he knew. The world paled by comparison.

Since Yeshua had brought him to God's throneroom - a place in the Heavens where only the most sinless and pure could enter, he briefly - very briefly, examined himself, but fully knew he was not worthy to open the seal. No, he was still the consummate scribe for this event.

And, as he felt the sins of the world making all unworthy, tears flooded his eyes.

"No one?" he uttered in misery. He buried his head in sleeves and continued to weep until a voice interrupted. Looking up, he recognized one of the twenty-four elders, dressed in his white robe and golden crown. He smiled reassuringly at Ionnes.

"Do not weep. Behold, the Lion of the tribe of Judah, the Root of David, has triumphed. He is able to open the scroll and its seven seals."

Ionnes looked to where the elder pointed, and there, in the midst of the throne and the four creatures and the other twenty-three elders, stood a Lamb. At first sight, Ionnes gasped for besides having seven horns and seven eyes, it appeared to have been slain. Then, he looked into the seven eyes and saw glorious life; life from seven Spirits of God he somehow knew had been sent out into all the Earth. In those eyes, he recognized his LORD and friend, Yeshua, shining brightly now as the worthy Lamb who came forth and took the scroll out of the hand of the One on the Throne.

Ionnes then jumped, startled. As soon as the Lamb took the scroll, the four living creatures and all twenty-four elders fell down flat before the Lamb. Ionnes' surprise increased, knowing God and only God as worthy to be worshipped. But each now had a harp and a golden bowl full of incense. He smelled the incense and realized it was the prayers of the saints. He detected the distinct and recognizable scents of even his own prayers, presented to the Lamb. In procession to the Lamb holding the scroll, about to break the first seal, they joined together, singing another song:

> *"You are worthy to take the scroll,*
> *And to open its seals;*
> *For You were slain,*
> *And have redeemed us to God by Your blood*
> *Out of every tongue and people and nation,*
> *And, have made them to be a kingdom of priests*
> *to serve our God;*
> *And they shall reign on the Earth."*

Then, no sooner had that song ended when Ionnes heard more voices, singing with the utmost beauty. He turned to look and saw angels. Many angels. More and more angels around the throne, ever gathering. More and more, spanning his periphery to the tune of ten-thousand times ten-thousand, thousands of thousands filling the huge throne room as perhaps over a hundred million voices sang as one:

> *"Worthy is the Lamb who was slain*
> *To receive power and wealth and wisdom*
> *And strength and honor and glory and praise!"*

Then, as if that was not enough, the angels' song of praise to the Lamb gathered all creation together in one song. Ionnes looked and heard all manner of animals and sea life and even insects and other small life - so many voices he had never heard or even imagined, singing together with all humanity. He could not begin to guess how many animals he had never before seen with his own eyes before that day, and he marveled that Adam had named them all. Yet, he had little time for personal musing or questions as he heard the unnumbered earthly creatures present with one perfect voice:

> *"Blessing and honor and glory and power*
> *Be to Him who sits on the throne.*
> *And, to the Lamb, forever and ever!"*

Ionnes dared not breathe lest he miss a note as the holy choir continued in endless praise.

Then, "Amen," cried out many voices within the throne room. Ionnes again turned towards the sound of many voices in time to see the four living creatures along with the twenty-four elders call out "Amen!" So be it. They completed the song of the earthly hymn and fell forward towards the Lamb to worship without reservation or detachment. In that manner, they fulfilled the celebration for the Lamb who was slain who could open the seven seals of the scroll.

Ionnes, atop his bedroll thus wrote all he engaged and witnessed as the visions continued...

In all Ionnes observed, he realized all attention throughout the Heavens never waned away from the Lamb. All eyes witnessed as He opened one of the seals. One of the four creatures, the first like a lion, called over to Ionnes with a voice like thunder, loudly and clearly with a crack and a rumble.

"Come and see," he ordered.

Ionnes stepped forward, arriving in time to see a magnificent white horse emerge from points unknown. Its rider, equally impressive, toted a bow, and received a crown to wear as He went out as a conqueror bent on conquest.

"Yeshua," thought Ionnes as he watched the Conqueror gallop away over the entire Earth.

Then, the Lamb which was slain opened the second seal. The creature like a calf addressed Ionnes.

"Come and see," he commanded, and Ionnes followed to where he could see a rider atop a fiery red horse. Frightening flames flowed from its haunches as the rider received a great sword. Ionnes shuddered as he felt the delicate balance of peace between nations dissolve away. Who were those who rejected the Prince of Peace as nation after nation waged war against one another as testimony to their insatiable bloodthirst to slaughter one another?

Ionnes recalled Gideon's victory over the Midianites.

Still shaken by the sight of the second horse, Ionnes then saw the Lamb open the third seal. A man came forth to Ionnes, the third creature before the throne with many eyes, front and back, who also said to Ionnes, "Come and see."

Ionnes followed to see another man on a horse – a black horse this time, black as the silhouette of distant mountains against the moonless night sky. He noticed less the rider but focused on what he held – a pair of scales, perfectly calibrated to balance. Ionnes wondered what would be measured on the scales.

Then, he heard a voice. He expected it came from the rider, but no. He looked around the throne room, and though none of the four living creatures seemed to be speaking, he heard from their midst the words, "A choinix of wheat for a denarius, and three choinix of barley for a denarius."

"A day's wage," thought Ionnes. What an exorbitant price for flour! How could one feed and support his family on that?

The voice without a face continued, "And, do not harm the oil and the wine."

Ionnes received but a brief moment to ponder those words and take them to heart. After the ravages of wars by the second horseman, the aftermath of war would follow. Scarcity would drive up the price of grain, but so also economic imbalance between the classes. Yet, oil and wine would not rise in price similarly. Would Yeshua send severe rains to destroy the wheat and barley but would also water and increase the vineyards and olive groves? Would the rich still flourish while the poor got poorer? That sounded unlikely, as the LORD'S judgment on Earth applied to all.

Or did the wine and the oil show Yeshua's loving concern, leaving medicinal wine and oil to help to heal those who suffered such great loss after the second horseman who captured and withheld peace from the Earth?

No sooner had those thoughts raced through his mind when Ionnes saw the Lamb that was slain open the fourth seal of the scroll.

The sounds of a screaming eagle scared Ionnes briefly until the apostle heard him also say, "Come and see."

Ionnes followed the direction of his gaze, looked and beheld yet another horseman. Oh, how he knew that horseman by the times he himself had faced him! Death. And, Hades. He shuddered at the sight of the pale horse as he felt his own color wash away to nothing. The dreadful horseman vengefully wreaked havoc across a quarter of the Earth, destroying with swords and hunger and beasts unto ultimate death.

Ionnes found little time for tears when his grieving was interrupted as the Lamb opened the fifth seal. To Ionnes' surprise, an altar appeared in the throne room where none had been seen before. He recognized the stains of blood and first considered it the blood of animals, but as he looked closer, he saw under the altar the souls of those who had been slain for the Word of God, including their testimonies of Christos.

So many. Oh, so many.

Christians and Jews alike, their faces filled with the pain of their suffering for the Word of God. Did he see familiar faces? Cephas and Paulos and Yaakov and all the other apostles? Stephanos and Antipas and other departed disciples he had known? And, Ignatius? And Polycarpus? Though he truly saw no faces firmly, Ionnes stood stunned. The last he had heard, Ignatius was still alive in Antiochus and he had just seen, Polycarpus not many days back. Then, he reminded himself all shone as prophesy; glimpses of the things to come, in Heaven, on the Earth and under the Earth. With eyes closed, Ionnes muttered prayers of praise and veneration. The prophetic always took away his breath with awe and reverence, as the future ever became Yeshua's to design.

Did Ionnes also see prophets of old? Zechariah and Isaiah? Even Abel? They cried out in woe and pain. They called upon the LORD with a loud voice, saying, "How long, O LORD, holy and true, until You judge and avenge our blood on those who dwell on the Earth?" Their cries of anguish continued a short while, then they seemed to abate, to relax; to come to rest.

The angels gave each a white robe for their sinless devotion as the LORD indicated they should rest awhile longer until both their servants and brethren who would be killed for their faith in Yeshua came to completion.

The number of souls beneath the altar already numbered so many. Ionnes wondered how many more would complete that number?

With merciful compassion, he watched the martyrs a little longer until his eyes turned to see the Lamb opening the sixth seal. Immediately, the ground around them shook severely, splitting and rearranging topography worse than an angry, volatile volcano. The sun turned jet black above his head; black as goat hair sackcloth or the muzzle of a sheep. The land around him also darkened as during a full eclipse, but he could see that the moon did not block the sun. It merely seemed to lose its light. Darkness followed. The moon and stars came forth – the moon red as blood. Ionnes recalled Isaiah when he wrote, "I clothe the heavens with blackness, and I make sackcloth their covering."

Next the stars began to fall to Earth from the firmament like ripened figs on the tree, swept back and forth by strong winds until they let go of the branch which gave them life. The fiery rain continued some time when Ionnes noticed the entire sky rolling away like a carpet or scroll to expose nothingness above them, save the holy presence of the One who likewise sat on the throne and His awesome, majestic throneroom.

He looked down upon the darkened planet. The mountains and even islands, all out of joint and shifted by the cosmic Circus Maximus. Hordes of people seemed to be fleeing the cities and towns to head for the mountains, not unlike those fleeing Ierusalem for the mountains as Roma's army advanced and took siege. All manner of people fled, from the richest to the poorest; from kings to slaves. They sought refuge among the rocks, hiding in caves, and covering themselves not only from advancing forces on the ground, but also from advancing forces from above.

"Fall on us," Ionnes heard some cry. "Fall on us and hide us from the face of Him who sits on the throne and from the wrath of the Lamb! For the great day of His wrath has come, and who is able to stand?"

Ionnes looked up at the nothingness of the empty sky. He looked at the throne room against the nothingness. He looked back down at the fearful masses and wondered if they could see the same throne room that he could see? Could they see the Lamb that they had slain? Could they see the four horsemen? Could they see the angels and the elders and the martyrs and the four living creatures? Could they see the seven stars and lampstands and the sea of glass? What made them afraid? What illumination of mind brought them to this moment? How did they now see what they could never before see?

And, Ionnes atop his bedroll thus wrote all he engaged and witnessed as the visions dictated.

Finishing up, setting down his pen, he rubbed his eyes and heard the call for reveille. He would have to take these to Prochorus. Apparently, the letter to the seven churches was not yet done, as he first supposed.

Dim turned a few times, then sat up to begin his day. Sleepily, he looked at Ionnes. A curiosity filled his face as he saw the old man sitting with something in his lap.

"Good morning," greeted Ionnes.

"Good mornin'," Dim yawned back.

"Read this," offered Ionnes.

474

Dim took the pages but looked oddly at Ionnes. Inside the barracks, it was commonly too dark to read much of anything, even with the door open during the day.

"Did ya write this?" Dim asked.

"Just finished," answered Ionnes. "Yeshua had more to say. I must get this to Prochorus. Or Myron."

Dim moved closer to the open door and read through the words. Ionnes' penmanship was a little sloppy, making it difficult to read in places, but he got the gist of the composition.

"Got a tuna in yer tunic?" joked Dim.

"You might think so," grinned Ionnes.

"Ever been in Yeshua's throne room before?" Dim asked, returning the parchment.

"Not before last night," nodded Ionnes. "I look at my pages and know I cannot possibly cover everything that I saw, but Yeshua told me to write and write I do."

"I have never been in a throne room," admitted Dim.

"I have," said Ionnes, "or thought I had until I saw Yeshua's. Now I will never see a worldly throne room so grand ever again."

He paused, thinking; trying to recall something.

"It reminds me of somewhere, but I cannot recall where as yet."

He pondered and played it through his imagination but could not quite add Beta and Beta to make Delta. He wanted to know, but also had a good feeling it would come to him when he needed to know.

<>< ><> <>< ><> <>< ><> <>< ><> <>< ><>

"I copied those letters," called Prochorus, catching Ionnes on his way to the salt ropes. Besides two Roman soldiers escorting the prisoners, few others moved down the dirt trail to town. The autumn morning fared cooler than yesterday, faintly showing one's breath. "Seven copies, plus one to keep."

"Perfect," thanked Ionnes as they met, "but, last night I learned Yeshua has more to write."

475

Prochorus looked at his teacher questioningly, then noticed the pages in Ionnes' hand. He took them from Ionnes and read through as they walked. Brows went up, and he shuddered with both trepidation and joy as he read.

"When did the Spirit speak to you?"

"Last night. Woke me from a fitful sleep to show me more."

"I will say!" agreed Prochorus. "So, you want me to copy these, too?"

"Definitely," answered Ionnes, "but do not close the letter. I expect more from the LORD."

"Why do you say that?" asked Prochorus.

"Because there were seven seals on the scroll to be opened. I saw only six. I expect more when the time comes."

Prochorus walked along silently a ways.

"What?" asked Ionnes.

He rattled the pages in his hand a moment before answering, as though the breath of the Holy Spirit blew past.

"You actually saw all this?"

"Yes," Ionnes firmly answered. "I wrote it down as I stood before the throne and the Lamb, just as real as we are walking down this road."

Prochorus took a moment to find the right words.

"You saw this, yet I see the symbolism from scripture. The images of the throne room, the scroll with the seven seals, the Lamb that was slain, the four horses, and the martyrs."

"As do I," acknowledged Ionnes. "So, what is your question? Or concern?"

He considered his answer again. "Why now? Why give you this message at this time?"

Ionnes smiled as he considered his answer. "My guess is a simple answer," he began, rather like thinking aloud. "This is a different time than before. You yourself, Papias, Polycarpus and Silva Viridi all reported to me the increased persecutions imposed by Roma from Domitian. I have seen him and looked in his eyes. I have seen the fear that drives him to be worshipped by others. He means to test our faith. He means to test our commitment to Christos Yeshua. I believe the already terrible persecutions will get worse. Most of the other letters were composed before Domitian reigned, and for that matter before the destruction of Ierusalem. It is my guess that Yeshua wanted this letter to be misunderstood when it fell under Roman eyes."

"Do you expect that to happen?"

"Of course," nodded Ionnes. "Have they not confiscated virtually all of our other gospels and epistles at some point? My one comfort and prayer is that as they read them, Yeshua's Spirit may touch them."

Prochorus still looked a bit doubtful.

"Think about it, my brother," said Ionnes. "You read it and easily understand its meaning. Our Hellenist brethren will read it with little understanding for most of the images come from our Jewish writings as well as other letters written by our deceased brethren. Fortunately for them, you who grew up a Jew, plus have served Christos for years, can translate the messages. But, if a Roman reads it, it will be gibberish to him. He will say, 'See, those Christians are a bunch of lunatics.'"

"You want them to think of us as lunatics?"

Ionnes laughed. "No - but, well, yes as well. Mad ravings are seldom dealt with as harshly as open rebellion, and as I read Yeshua's words, I recognize His call to stay the Godly course. The sinful world will be judged in the same manner they judge us - and is being judged already. Outside of Christos, Roma as well as others who do not follow The Way open themselves to the Almighty's judgment and wrath. I pray none will fall, but our prayers for salvation to all brings with it retaliations by those who are seduced by the devil and his angels. From there, we have seen many attacks, even unto death. I pray none enter the bronze bull as our brother, Antipas. It keeps me up nights imagining that horrid, torturous death."

"Amen," answered Prochorus. He too recalled the report from Smyrna of Satan's Throne and the bronze bull used to roast a man to death. Neither he nor Ionnes had been there during the execution but received reports when Antipas' naked body was pulled from the chamber. Despite his painful death, he prayed to his last breath for the churches and the world.

His cooked face still showed the love of Christos apart from the cruelty of men.

"They know it is wrong," muttered Ionnes.

"Who knows?" asked Prochorus.

"Them," head tipped towards the guards behind them. "The Romans. And others. They kill us not out of ignorance as much as fear. The love of Yeshua cries within them and brings them to face pure truth. Those who avoid truth fear it."

"But they attack in fear?"

"Verily," answered Ionnes. "Do not men so often fear what they do not understand? Many respond by trying to destroy it, but still, they know it is wrong."

"Why do you say that?" asked Prochorus.

"Because," sighed Ionnes, "have you ever met a Roman who wanted to be crucified? Of course not. He knows well the pain he inflicts. He knows well what to avoid. He knows down to the marrow, deep within that it is wrong."

The men walked through town, turning attentions to the people. Ionnes greeted each as a good friend and wished upon all he met Yeshua's blessings. Few followed as they left town for the beach. Some were disappointed he healed none miraculously as though it had been for show.

"Anything else?" asked Prochorus, thumbing through the pages Ionnes had given to him."

"Yes," realized Ionnes. "I need more papyrus. Makes me wonder if Yeshua stopped last night because I had no more pages on which to write."

<>< ><> <>< ><> <>< ><> <>< ><> <>< ><>

Ionnes strode blindly up the hill as others followed. The wind blew furiously about them, twirling their tunics to wring out the men within.

The long, hard week of work came to a close. Ionnes spent every waking moment engaged in prayer, ever ready to listen to the message given by Yeshua's Spirit. His spirit within ached as if the pangs of labor came and went, ever increasing in intensity. With only a barren focus on life around him, he barely ate or drank. Others set food before him and he would eat, but only a bite or two before he would again be engaged by the aching torment within. He moved rocks in the quarry like a worn-out puppet. He would stand with rope and water for long periods. The ropes would be salted more than usual that week.

The Sunday morning service at Myron's passed with barely his notice. He looked like a sulking dog in the corner, staying away from everyone else. None had ever seen him like this, save Prochorus, and even that for far less time than this. When asked what was wrong, he would look surprised and weakly smile, then return to his vigil. The Roman soldiers thought he had lost his mind and felt some relief that he might become less a bother.

Partway through the service, Ionnes rose. He grabbed his stomach and headed out the door. Dim and others thought he might have been nauseous, but he seemed more intent to depart their company than empty his stomach. Prochorus nodded to Dim who followed the old man out. He left Myron's to head up the road, then finding the way to the mountaintop, he went upward. By this time, old Prochorus, Talor, Phranc, and others also followed. They looked around at the sky. Large, gray clouds tumbled, one over the other. No rain, yet, but it looked likely.

"Where is he going?" muttered Talor.

"Go ask him," answered Dim.

"Um," thought Talor, looking back and forth at Ionnes and the followers.

"Ionnes, whereya goin'?" called Teos, running up alongside.

"Ascending," answered the apostle, huffing and puffing.

"Sending?" said Teos.

Ionnes glanced at his fellow prisoner whose childlike spirit touched and influenced him over and over during his time on Patmos.

"Let the little children come unto me," said Yeshua inside Ionnes' memories. Children were not always measured in years.

"Amen," answered Ionnes, taking hold of Teos' shoulder. Locking arms, they continued together.

Topping the hill, the wind increased. Standing between the two olive trees, Ionnes knelt with a plop, raised arms and head towards the sky as he let the wind freely flow through him. Prochorus followed first, kneeling beside his friend. Teos joined and Dim as well as the others in like order. Teos mostly watched Ionnes with guileless eyes. Over a whole year they had lived together with so much Teos never would understand about the old man, yet his fascination for him never wavered or wandered.

Another hour passed before Ionnes uttered a lasting, "Amen". He turned to all in his company and smiled.

"Forgive me if I scared you," he said. "I have been brooding over many words and visions Yeshua has given me. I know that more is to come which arouses my holy fear - my awe of the Almighty. I thank you all for your patience and assure you, though I know not the time or day of Yeshua's loving touch upon my life, I know that He would not bring this message if it were not all important. So, be of good and Godly cheer. I am so blessed to see His love shining through all of you."

He rose and hugged each of them. Each he could call favorite. Each brought his own blessings in Christos.

"You must be starved," he said. "Perhaps there is still a morsel for us left at Myron and Fona's."

"Tobie said he would be ready," answered Phranc.

"Excellent!" applauded Ionnes and started the downhill descent.

As did the rain.

A few drops soon evolved into many. Many drops became a deluge. The old men hurried as they could, but their worn-out legs could go only so fast. Ionnes looked at Prochorus.

"Come," he urged, turning to the left along a narrow, muddy trail.

The men all followed, quickly seeking refuge. The cave appeared as they rounded the corner. Entering, they passed a cold firepit. No wood left for a small fire.

Some took a seat on the floor. Some stooped down to let their garments dry a bit before resting on the rocky sand.

Gathered water flowed near the entrance. Ionnes and others took a healthy drink of the rainwater. It tasted both sweet and gritty.

"The worst of the rain will pass, then we shall continue," said Prochorus.

Ionnes smiled and nodded.

"Did you bring papyrus and pen?"

"Aye," answered Prochorus, patting his leather shoulder bag. He pulled out the sheets but found no quill.

"I know there was one in here when I left this morning," said Prochorus. He searched again. No pen, nor ink.

"I must have left them on the table in my room."

Ionnes still took the tan sheets, looking at the blank pages like an artist ready to begin drawing. He went to the firepit and pulled out a charred stick. Sitting down, he took the moment to let his legs rest and catch some breath. The cave felt cold as the wind whistled in and out, chilling the wet men. Ionnes took a spot closer to the doorway and started to scribble on a papyrus sheet.

The words mattered not. He had no direction or purpose, but let the charcoal speak for him. He looked at the black in his hands and recalled the visions of destruction he had received so very recently. He looked at the men about him. He looked around the cave – its four corners deep and dark within. One stood in the corner of the cave who he did not recognize. Another in the next corner, then another before him and one beside him. He peered at them perplexed as he saw them take position at the four corners of the Earth. Their arms stretched out. Their wings spread out wider than the sky. The chilly breeze moving into the cave ceased, held back by the four angelic figures. He looked down at the Earth. All became still. The air barely moved. The seas became calm. The trees looked more like unfinished statues.

Another angel arose, flying high overhead, coming from the Asia Minor side. Ionnes saw something in his hands. It looked like a seal one would use to seal an envelope or scroll. He recognized the symbol as that of the living God.

As the angel reached his zenith, he yelled loudly. Ionnes jumped, surprised at the volume of his words. The four angels holding back the wind looked towards him as he announced, "Do not harm the Earth, the sea or the trees till we have sealed the servants of our God on their foreheads."

The four angels stood strong, acknowledging their messenger who raced off to seal the servants of Yeshua.

Ionnes paused. A voice arose from places unknown, declaring the census of those whom the angel had sealed.

"One-hundred-and-forty-four-thousand," said the voice, "of all the tribes of the children of Yisra'el sealed."

Ionnes felt genuine awe at that number. So many, yet so few. The voice continued as Ionnes wrote.

"Of the tribe of Judah, twelve-thousand sealed.

"Of the tribe of Reuben, twelve-thousand sealed."

Ionnes looked down at his page. Did he hear the voice correctly? Did he first say Judah and not Reuben? No time to dwell on it. He kept writing.

"Of the tribe of Gad, twelve-thousand sealed.

"Of the tribe of Asher, twelve-thousand sealed.

"Of the tribe of Naphtali, twelve-thousand sealed.

"Of the tribe of Manasseh, twelve-thousand sealed.

"Of the tribe of Simeon, twelve-thousand sealed.

"Of the tribe of Levi, twelve-thousand sealed.

"Of the tribe of Issachar, twelve-thousand sealed.

"Of the tribe of Zebulun, twelve-thousand sealed.

"Of the tribe of Joseph, twelve-thousand sealed.

"Of the tribe of Benjamin, twelve-thousand sealed."

Ionnes rescanned the list. Obviously not a genealogy. Only Benjamin was in proper order. And the tribe of Levi? And Joseph? Those were new ones. And where was Dan? And Ephraim? His Jewish root suddenly wanted to kick up a temper tantrum, but he squelched that voice, compelled by the Spirit to continue.

As the voice receded, he turned and looked, and beheld a huge number of people – many more than one-hundred-forty-four-thousand. A multitude too many for him to number. Nor were they all Jews. He saw all nations, tribes, peoples and tongues, standing in the throne room before the Lamb. All wore white robes and held palm branches.

Then, they cried out loudly, "Salvation to our God who sits on the throne, and to the Lamb!"

"Salvation belongs to our God who sits on the throne," the words echoed through Ionnes' mind as he wrote with his makeshift charcoal pencil. "And, to the Lamb!" His pencil rested on the last letter i. "Apvaki," he repeated. He looked up from the page back to the throne room. All fell to worship the Lamb – the twenty-four elders and the four living creatures, on their faces before the throne. Their voices sparkled of gladness as they said,

"Amen! Blessing and glory and wisdom,
Thanksgiving and honor and power and might
Be to our God forever and ever.
Amen."

A man soon stood beside Ionnes. Ionnes had not seen him rise off the throne room floor, but one of the twenty-four elders stood there to address him.

"Who," asked the man, "are these arrayed in white robes, and where did they come from?"

Ionnes looked at him a bit puzzled as he answered, "Sir, you know."

The elder acknowledged Ionnes as he said, "These are the ones who have come out of the great tribulation and washed their robes and made them white in the blood of the Lamb. Therefore, they are before the throne of God and serve Him day and night in His temple. And, He who sits on the throne will shelter them with His presence. They shall neither hunger anymore nor thirst anymore. The sun shall not strike them, nor any heat; for the Lamb who is in the midst of the throne will shepherd them and lead them to living fountains of waters. And God will wipe away every tear from their eyes."

Ionnes felt as choked-up as the multitude around him, worshipping the Lamb. Yeshua had often wiped away Ionnes' living fountains of tears throughout his years. He knew his body to be the Temple for Yeshua's Holy Spirit and thereby served Yeshua in his midst in His temple day after day. He glanced out the cave entrance to the flow of rainwater which had quenched his thirst and felt renewed peace, assured

Yeshua's well of living water ran deeper than Ionnes or any other person could imagine.

The throne room became very quiet. The silence felt so odd after the many voices – some like trumpets – some like many rushing waters – some like many thunderings – some like harps – like millstones – or, like great multitudes, all crying out to the Lamb. But, now nothing. Not even breathing. Ionnes shuddered at the deafening soundlessness. He looked at the scroll. The angel had broken the seventh and final seal. Nobody moved. Not even a breath. He imagined hearing the shadow of the sundial moving across its face. A minute. Five minutes. Ten minutes. Fifteen... Nothing. He waited with the rest of the Heavenly host. The four living creatures. The twenty-four elders. The seven angels who had broken the seals. Many other angels. The martyrs beneath the altar and the vast multitude in white. Even their palm branches dared not rustle to disrupt the sounds of silence. Twenty minutes passed. The throne room remained at bay. Twenty-five minutes. No change.

Then, as though the next act would begin on cue, an angel entered as time moved towards its half hour of silence. The seven angels who had loosed the seals moved forward towards the throne, standing before Elohim. Seven trumpets appeared before the throne, and to each angel one horn was given.

Then, another angel presented a golden censer. As he stood before the altar, another filled it with incense, ignited by holy fire. The smoke and fragrance completely filled the throne room. Ionnes breathed in the sweet scent and as he did, he detected more in that smoke than just the odor. Millions upon millions of prayers rose with the smoke. Countless prayers of praise and thanksgiving, of love and adoration, of hymns and psalms, all concentrated in each puff rising from the smoldering incense in the golden cistern on the golden altar set before the throne. It ascended before God from the angel's hand and all took in the life and beauty contained within that offering.

Then, the angel set down the censer to fill it with more holy fire from the altar. He raised it over his head and threw it, full force, down upon the Earth. Ionnes felt the effects of the prayers of all the saint cast upon the Earth. Amazing noises, thunderings, lightnings and next a terrible earthquake. The Earth groaned under the waterfall strain of blessings cast upon it opposing the dry, selfish hearts and lives of sin-filled men.

Ionnes watched the two forces grappling against one another until he heard the sound of a mighty trumpet. The first angel blew long and hard and loud. Ionnes put his hands over his ears to endure the din. Hail, fire and mingled blood fell with vengeful force to Earth. All grass burned black, and with it a third of the trees.

He watched the forests burn bright for some time when he heard the equally bold sound of a second trumpet. Looking up, he saw a huge mountain, alive with fire, flying through the air. Briefly, he thought of having the faith of a mustard seed as the mountain plummeted like a great, burning rock to Earth. It landed in the sea to where almost half the sea became as blood. Any within the bloody third died – sea creatures and ships alike.

All fell prey to the fiery mountain's enactment.

The rivers and streams flowing into the sea became blood red as they entered the sea, but before that, clear water still flowed.

Then, another trumpet sounded – the third angel at his post. Ionnes saw everyone look up, so he did the same in time to see a huge star flying down, down, down to Earth. It divided before it crashed to contaminate a third of the rivers and springs.

Wormwood!

Many died by the bitter water. Or died of thirst.

Then, another bold trumpet blast. The fourth angel called down the wrath and judgment of the LORD of Hosts for immediately the sun became dimmer, as did the moon and the stars. A third of each seemed as black as the sun covered with sackcloth of hair. Many on Earth looked upward to the sight to feel great fear for One who could blot out the sun, moon and even the very stars.

Then, against the backdrop of shadows, an eagle appeared, brightly reflecting the light of Yeshua.

"Woe! Woe! Woe!" cried out the eagle loudly enough for all the Earth to hear. "Woe to the inhabitants of the Earth, because of the remaining blasts of the trumpet of the three angels who are about to sound."

Ionnes' hand shook writing those words. As terrible as so much had been, he felt great trepidation all over for those upon the world who would endure the three judgments to come. He paused. Some in the cave had fallen asleep waiting. Some kept private vigils while all watched Ionnes to varying degrees.

He noted but kept writing as the fifth trumpet was blown.

A star fell from Heaven to Earth. The star an angel, he was given a key. Ionnes wondered what the key would lock - or unlock. He needed little time to wonder for apart from the throne room, he saw a great Abyss. A bottomless pit. The world a lost cauldron.

A huge door pressed down upon the great hole to keep those beneath contained. The fifth angel went with the key to the door and unlocked it. He opened the door. Immediately, sour smoke poured out of the pit. The mountain of smoke darkened the air. The sun became a bright spot in the nighttime. It choked Ionnes, but he kept watch and kept writing.

Suddenly, out of the smoke came huge locusts. At least they appeared at first like locusts, but they were shaped like horses prepared for battle. They wore crowns like gold adorning faces resembling that of men. They had long hair like women but teeth like a lion, and for armor, breastplates of iron.

Ionnes heard the sound of many chariots heading into battle. He looked to find the new sight, then realized the sound emerged from the many wings of the locusts. Each had tails with stingers like scorpions to complete the picture.

Ionnes heard many voices command the locusts to only harm the people who had not the seal of Adonai on their foreheads. As locusts, they were told to not harm the vegetation - only people. But even the people they could not destroy unto death, but only torment them for five long months. Most would wish for death during that time, but death would not find them.

"Oh, the great travail!" thought Ionnes, for men who feared death more than anything except the torment of life by God's judging words.

For five months they tormented anyone without God's seal. Ionnes watched the tortures continue in all fates and manners when his attention returned back to the smoky abyss. A cruel and terrible angel emerged as the locust's king from the smoke of the pit.

"Abaddon," said Ionnes in Hebrew.

"Apollyon," he said in Greek.

The Destroyer is Destruction.

The Destruction is the Destroyer.

Ionnes shuddered at his appearance, but then just as immediately, the Destroyer disappeared. Where to Ionnes could only guess. He knew they would cross paths again soon.

Then, another blast of the trumpet by the sixth angel. Ionnes heard voices in the throne room. He was uncertain at first, but the voices came from the four horns around the altar who instructed the sixth angel to go to the four angels who were bound by the Great River Euphrates. He loosed them for the hour and day and month and year to kill a third of all mankind.

Ionnes felt shock at such a holocaust.

He heard a massive army of horsemen – two-hundred million Ionnes calculated, but wrote twice ten thousand times ten thousand, the number that was spoken. The warriors bore breastplates of red, blue and yellow – fire, hyacinth and sulfur.

Even the horses' appearance changed. Their heads became like lions who blasted fire, smoke and brimstone out of their mouths which they used to kill one-third of all humankind. And, that which they did not kill the first time by the fire in their mouths, they killed by the serpent's heads in their tails.

Ionnes gasped incredulously for even after such a judgment, stubborn men still refused to repent, still choosing to worship their lifeless idols. Ionnes shook his head with great sadness at their stubbornness, their murders and sorceries and sexual immoralities and their thefts.

A bit stunned, Ionnes looked at the papyrus sheets before him. Taking deep breaths to calm himself, he tossed the remaining stub of charcoal to the ground. Carefully he folded the sheets so as to not smear the words and handed them to Prochorus who placed them in his pouch. All stepped from the protection of the cave to a drizzle of rainwater cascading from the sky to pray and sing with rejoicing for Phora.

Approaching Myron's, they were stopped by a small company of soldiers.

"Where are you going?" yelled Guard Julius.

"To Myron's," answered Ionnes.

"Not by my word," yelled Julius. "Where have you been?"

Ionnes motioned towards the mountain behind them.

"To pray," he added.

"To plan your escape," accused the guard, drawing his sword.

With furrowed brow, Ionnes glanced down at the weapon, then to the soldier. "None here seek escape or rebellion," he assured.

"We shall see," pressed Julius, then turned his attention to Prochorus.

"What is in the bag?"

"Papyrus," answered Prochorus. "Just papyrus sheets."

Julius hesitated not. He grabbed the bag from the old man, practically ripping off his shoulder. He opened the bag to produce the sheets Ionnes had written.

Glancing at the charcoal written texts, he said, "What is this nonsense?"

He looked briefly at the men, not really expecting an answer, then walked over to a nearby fire and tossed the written paged within. He turned back, his face a challenge.

"Barracks," yelled Guard Mucius to the prisoners.

Ionnes and the other prisoners glanced at each other, then went forth towards the penal colony.

"You are lucky we do not cut you down right here for your insolence," said Julius as they marched forth out of town.

Ionnes looked up towards the clouds above. He saw the face of Yeshua and His angels watching them.

"Yes," agreed Ionnes, "and so are you."

PATMOS

CHAPTER 35

Ionnes knew he could rewrite the script of yesterday but feared some misperceptions and faulty recollections. Writing fresh off the moment could never be improved. He had no papyrus or pen, so lying upon his bedroll, prayed for patience and Yeshua's timing to rewrite the prophesies exactly as Yeshua saw fit.

The night passed slowly for all. Renewal of Roman hostility always added its weighty travail to the barracks of men. Ionnes saw it as the devil's futile ways to try to disrupt Yeshua's perfect voice.

He reimagined the Lamb that had been slain and saw Yeshua. His LORD had not picked up the scroll from the One on the throne with His mouth or hoof. His hand took the scroll and sliced through each seal like a knife, thereby not damaging the scroll as each seal was broken. Ionnes wondered what had been written on the scroll. The seals all He broke, but He opened it not.

Ionnes had heard the number of those who were sealed. One-hundred-and-forty-four-thousand of all the tribes of the children of Yisra'el. Perhaps those words Elohim read from the scroll. He still wondered at the list of names. Obviously not a genealogy. Then, he recalled the end of Genesis, where Jacob, renamed Yisra'el, blessing his sons before his death. Each son he gave a prophetic word. Judah would be the tribe of kings - Yeshua's tribe, and David's. It would be first among the tribes. Reuben showed the excellency of dignity and power. Zebulun a haven. Simeon and Levi paired together for their cruelty, yet out of this Adonai mercifully chose his Egyptian hostage and his lineage of Moses along with priests and rabbis.

Issachar showed strength. Gad, triumph over foes. Asher richness. Naphtali, a graceful deer of beautiful words. Joseph, the fruitful bough. Benjamin, the meekest of Jacob's offspring to be a ravenous wolf, devouring his prey and thereby the strength against their enemies. Yisra'el's first King, Saul, had been a Benjamite.

Joseph's son Manasseh evoked personal healing – to forget one's toil and the betrayal of one's household.

But, Yeshua left out two names for Ionnes and the church. "Dan and Ephraim," said Ionnes from his bed. Ephraim had been fruitfulness in the land of one's affliction. Yeshua became their fruitfulness in the land no longer afflicted. And Dan, the judge, would judge the people no more as Yeshua would be their final judge.

As the words of the LORD softened his fears, he could drift off to sleep. The start of the work week would be short hours away. It seemed he had barely closed his eyes when he awoke to hear the guards stirring outside. The click of the bolts slid open and the garish sunlight filled the room announcing the start of their day.

"Out," yelled Guard Mucius. The men arose, one by one, and shuffled out of the building. Bright sunlight greeted them as they took time to clean up for the day. They received bread and water to break fast. Daily assignments were doled out. Ionnes headed for the quarry to collect stones and prep them for shipment. His old bones ached as the chill of the autumn morning wrapped around him. He would have preferred a shawl, but still praised Yeshua in song that the hard toil would both loosen his joints and keep him warm. Taking the last bite of his bread, he prayed, "This is my body which is given for You."

"That is too bad about yesterday," greeted Dim.

"Amen," answered Ionnes, "but take heart. Yeshua's word never comes back void. Julius' actions are but a mere and temporary setback. Yeshua's words are never lost and will still ring loudly in the hearts and mind of His people."

Later, a Roman man approached Ionnes as he piled ornate rocks upon a cart. He knew him not but smiled to receive him.

"You are the apostle?" he asked.

"Yes," nodded Ionnes.

"I am Hilarius. Prochorus sent me to you."

"That is always good news," said Ionnes, placing another rock upon the cart. The cart was little over half full, but the marble so heavy, too much would break the cart. They would soon take it to be loaded on a ship at harbor.

"Prochorus sends his greetings and good news."

Ionnes checked the young man's face. No deception indicated, plus by the term "good news", did he mean the gospel or something new to report.

"This early morning, I arrived on Patmos from Roma. Clement sends greetings and prayers. He knows your hardships and sent me to you. I found Prochorus in prayer this morning. He knew I would not be recognized, plus I am a citizen of Roma. As I said, he has good news for you."

"Go on," urged Ionnes.

"Last night when the Roman guard burned up the papyrus, Prochorus carefully fished it out of the fire as soon as you left. Most was preserved and still very readable. The charcoal you used to write could stand the heat of the fire and thereby remain intact on the pages."

"Are you serious?" checked Ionnes.

"Verily," answered Hilarius. "I saw the pages. Prochorus was careful to keep them from collapsing, and separated the sheets to copy them, but from my eyes, they looked much more preserved than any other papyrus I have ever seen upon the fire. More brown than black. The charcoal words stood out cleanly and clearly."

"Praise You, Yeshua," declared Ionnes, "and, thank you, Prochorus. Send him my love if I do not see him for a few days. The Roman soldiers seem to be on alert again. It will likely get rough. All of you must be cautious. Nurture the church if I cannot come. Build them up for they, too, shall likely endure hardships at the name of Yeshua."

"As you say," said Hilarius. He hugged the apostle like two men preparing to wrestle. Roman fashion. Ionnes felt amusement.

"Be strong and courageous," counseled Ionnes. Hilarius nodded as he turned to leave. Ionnes, with spirits lifted, watched the young man until he was out of sight. Returning to the task at hand, he noticed a thin, woven flax pouch upon the cart, gray in color. He checked the contents. Papyrus, quill and a small ceramic vial of ink topped with a molded chunk of cork. He did not notice Hilarius remove anything from his robe, but perhaps...

As evening approached, the prisoners gathered for their small ration of food and water. Ionnes accepted his portion, then moved apart from the group. He could hear their words. Some complained, but he recognized that unlike when he first arrived, many prisoners' hopelessness had been surgically removed by the Great Physician's perfect touch. He praised Yeshua for His never-ending gifts and hope.

The breeze rustled the leaves of weeds. It was cool but felt good after the hard day of labor. Ionnes plopped down and set his head back against a large stone. Though more tired than hungry, he still ate. Big, puffy clouds hovered far above. He watched them in their idle flow, moving without hurry. His mind wandered to remember his parents, Zebedee and Salome. Zeb and Sal, their friends called them, even after they were gone. Long departed to be with Yeshua, he smiled at their memory and praised Yeshua for the gift of his parents. He wondered where he would be today if cousin Yeshua had not called him to apostleship. Probably still tending his nets in Galilee if he had not been fitted onto a Roman cross during the rebellion.

"Galilee." He spoke the word. Some days it seemed so much further away than other days. Patmos was technically closer to Galilee than Ephesus, but somehow Ephesus always felt closer.

"Yaakov," he added. He always missed his older brother the most. Looking upwards to the cloudy sky, he recalled a warm spring day which blessed the two boys as they played. Their father had already arrived with the day's catch, sorted out the bad fish and sold the good ones. Mama swept the floor with a verve and a vengeance after she finished the day's baking. Their baby sister awoke from her nap, crying to be fed and changed. Their younger sister, barely five, helped mama with the infant.

Multiple layers of clouds moved overhead. Both boys laid upon the rock, still warmed by the sun.

"Look," pointed Yaakov. "A tiger."

Younger Yochanan strained to see the wild beast but found only fluffy feathers overhead.

"Look," urged Yaakov, still pointing.

"I do not see it," Yochanan finally admitted.

"Never mind," said Yaakov. "It is gone now."

"Ooh! A woman carrying a jar of water," pointed Yochanan.

"I see it," cried Yaakov. "Looks like the jar may tip at any time."

The boys watched earnestly, but the jar of clouds never tipped, and no water poured forth. Instead, the image moved along.

"Oh ho!" declared Yaakov. "There is one." He pointed. "Rabbi Silas."

Yochanan studied the sky and did see something that could resemble their beloved rabbi's son. He just was not sure it was the same cloud.

As more clouds passed, the blue of the sky sometimes hurt their eyes. It could be so intense. The boys squinted at such times. Small specks of dust and lint peppered their eyes, more visible against the clear blue. Yochanan followed one such shadowy image as it seemed to want to go left each time he stopped moving his eyes. His gaze would follow the lint, then pull it back to the center of his sight.

"That one looks like a scroll," said Yaakov.

"And, that one a treasure chest," pointed Yochanan.

More clouds moved unhurried above them.

"Wo!" exclaimed Yochanan. He pointed. He had never seen a cloud so distinct. He just about blurted out his find but pointed and waited a moment to see if his older brother could also see it.

"Wo!" agreed Yaakov. "An angel."

"Clothed in the cloud," finished Yochanan.

The image did not morph away so quickly like the others. The eyes of the "angel" looked down upon them. A smile came to its lips. Its wings quivered back and forth in the wind. They watched intently until the cloud moved beyond their sight.

Both boys sat up and looked at one another.

"Do you think?" asked Yaakov.

"Of course," answered younger Yochanan. "Who would not?"

"Yaakov. Yochanan," called Salome. "Dinner."

"Dinner," yelled Yaakov and jumped up to race his brother to the house. He always won, not just because he was older and bigger, but much more athletic. Once the rabbi had compared them to young Esau and Jacob.

"We saw an angel in the sky," declared Yaakov, entering the house.

"It was dressed in clouds," added Yochanan.

"You did?" laughed Zebedee. "I wish I had also seen it."

Zebedee and Salome shared a glance of appreciation for their two fine sons. They always saw Adonai's blessings on their poor lives, but some moments shone brighter than others.

This was easily one of those moments.

Ionnes let the memory slide through his thoughts smooth as cool river water over a flat rock. He checked the clouds floating above him with similar childlike anticipation. The clouds rearranged the sky like his mother slowly stirring the stew.

After a fashion, some clouds seemed to gather and even collide, blending together as one, then seemed to move downward towards Ionnes. He studied the phenomenon with piqued interest as the clouds became a garment for a mighty angel. A rainbow wrapped around his head like a halo. Ionnes felt the warmth radiate as his face shone brightly like the sun and his feet resembled glowing pillars of fire.

"The seventh angel," muttered Ionnes in awe.

In the angel's hand he held a small scroll. Ionnes watched him descend until he landed hard upon the Earth, huge to behold, with one fiery leg on land and the other in the sea. The waters could not quench the fire, but no steam appeared or rose. Likewise, the right leg of fire started nothing on Earth to burn. He considered Moses before a burning bush.

The angel looked up towards the sky. More clouds gathered about him as he spoke with a roar any lion would envy.

Ionnes could not make out his words, but then to his surprise seven clouds, illuminated beneath by the angel's countenance, rumbled like thunder many words in response. Ionnes started to transcribe the words he heard, but a voice from above called down to him commanding, "Seal up the things which the seven thunders uttered, and do not write them."

Ionnes looked down at his scribblings. He quickly crossed out the few words he had already recorded, covering them with ink until fully indigo.

Then, the angel standing on sea and land raised his hand to Heaven and solemnly swore in the name of Yeshua who lives forever and ever and created the Earth and the sea and all it contained, including all life that it held. "Delay no longer," the angel seemed to say that the mystery of God would be finished, as Yeshua declared to His servants, the prophets.

Ionnes heard the same voice from above speak to him. "Go, take the little book which is open in the hand of the angel who stands on the sea and on the Earth." It seemed to be speaking to him, so he arose to approach the mighty angel. It towered above him, yet in Ionnes' awe, he felt no paralyzing fear.

"Give me the little book," he called upward, assured the angel expected him.

"Take and eat it," boomed the angel.

Ionnes paused to make sure he heard right as the angel continued.

"It will make your stomach bitter, but it will taste sweet as honey in your mouth."

Ionnes put up a hand to receive the book as the angel looked down to him, bent over and gave him the little book. Ionnes looked at it in his hands and wondered what truth and marvels it contained. He tasted it, then took a bite. It was sweet as honey. He took another and another and quickly consumed the scroll.

Not long thereafter, his stomach started to convulse. The pain increased, and Ionnes bent over, hardly able to contain it. He fell to the ground hard to deal with the pain. Bitter, hurtful words came to Ionnes' mind.

In sync, the angel said, "You must prophesy again about many peoples, nations, tongues and kings."

Ionnes felt the bitter words of judgment come forth, but also knew more words would come from him in the days and even months and years to come as the LORD's Spirit led, as written on the little scroll.

After much time, his stomach settled. He sat up and checked his gut to make sure the pain had verily subsided.

The mighty angel still stood before him. He reached down to give Ionnes a reed like a measuring rod. The angel straightened up and said, "Rise and measure the temple of God, the altar and those who worship there."

As Ionnes rose, he thought of Zechariah and the man who would measure Ierusalem.

"But," continued the mighty angel, "leave out the court which is outside the temple, and do not measure it. It has been given to the Gentiles."

Ionnes nodded as he looked down at the temple, and truly saw for the first time the throne room of Adonai represented by the Inner Temples – both of the temples of Solomon and Zerubbabel.

As he measured, the angel then added, "And, the Gentiles will tread upon the holy city for forty-two months. And, I will give power to my two witnesses, and they will prophesy one thousand-two-hundred-and-sixty days, clothed in sackcloth."

"Three-and-a-half years each," calculated Ionnes between measurements. "Like Yeshua who walked with us for three-and-a-half years."

Dim and the others watched Ionnes from afar. None dared disturb him. All there noticed that the guards did not even seem to see Ionnes, as though he was invisible to their eyes. Of course, no prisoner would alert the guards to draw attention to Ionnes anymore than they to themselves.

As Ionnes completed the measurements of the Temple, the angel spoke further regarding the two witnesses.

"These are the two olive trees and the two lampstands standing before the LORD of the Earth."

"Two olive trees," wrote Ionnes, again recalling Zechariah. He also recalled many times lampstands were cited in scripture. Many, many times in Exodus, but he could not recall specifically *two* lampstands. Still, he knew the olive trees would represent the anointing oil which would feed the light upon the lampstand to light the way for all the world to see.

The angel continued, "And, if anyone wants to harm them, fire comes from their mouths and devours their enemies. This is how anyone who wants to harm them must die. These have power to shut heaven so that no rain falls in the days of their prophesy, and they have power over waters to turn them to blood, and to strike the Earth with all plagues, as often as they desire."

Ionnes heard the words of the two witnesses. Deuteronomy. The law was specific:

"One witness shall not rise against a man concerning
any iniquity or any sin that he commits;
by the mouth of two or three witnesses
the matter shall be established."

"The Truth," uttered Ionnes. "I am the Way and the Truth and the Life." The witness of the Father, Son and Holy Spirit to their children.

The witnesses before Ionnes spoke for Christos, for a witness is one who has truly seen and knows what is right. Many heard and believed, but many cursed the truth, even running forth screaming with hands over ears. As the two finished their testimony, a beast climbed forth from the bottomless Abyss to make war, ie, to kill them. The war raged by those who held fast to their lies. Oh, so many died.

Then, by the vicious lies and deceptions of the beast, the two witnesses fell upon the pavement dead. Ionnes knew well the city where the witnesses met their end. He grieved all the more to see the spirit of Sodom and the spirit of Egypt take over the city where Yeshua had been crucified. This city still reigned as the city that killed Adonai's prophets.

Ionnes briefly thought of Kynops and the beatings Ionnes had received by the townsfolk which almost removed his mortal life, sharing part of the pain of the two witnesses.

Those who followed the beast celebrated. So many peoples of different tribes and tongues and nations came from afar to see the two dead bodies, left to rot upon the roadway. A festival of debauchery followed. No more would these two prophets torment those who dwelled upon the Earth.

Then, the gala ceased more quickly than it began. Three-and-a-half days passed and the breath of life from God blew forth to enter the two witnesses. Resurrected, they stood to their feet, more fearsome than ever. Great panic filled the city, spreading across the nation, to other nations and throughout the world. The two have arisen. God's severe judgments shall begin anew.

Then, all heard a loud voice from Heaven across the sky, surrounding all who had ears to hear.

"Come up here!" the voice called the Two Witnesses.

Before their enemies, the wild winds sent forth the clouds to capture the Witnesses and carry them Heavenward. Ionnes watched the crowds gasp in despair and their courage and resolve drained from them like sand through an impatient hourglass. An earthquake followed, destroying a tenth of Ierusalem to rubble. Seven-thousand souls died in the wreckage.

Those remaining gasped in horror. The beast was nowhere to be seen. In fear, they dropped to knees to repent and give glory to the God of Heaven.

Ionnes wrote rapidly. His hand ached, trying to keep up with his mind. The words on papyrus could not come fast enough. He completed and took a moment to catch breath. He knew the Spirit was not yet done. He knew another woe would come quickly.

On the tails of those in Ierusalem repenting and giving glory to God, Ionnes heard again the trumpet blast, loud and long and clear. The seventh angel heralded the next judgment to come.

Yet, across the throne room, Ionnes heard many voices loudly crying out, "The kingdoms of this world have become the kingdoms of our LORD and of His Christos, and He shall reign forever and ever!"

Again, Ionnes saw the twenty-four elders fall down before the throne to worship God, saying:

"We give You thanks, O LORD God Almighty.
The One who is and who was.
Because You have taken Your great power
and have begun to reign.
The nations were angry, and Your wrath has
come.
The time of the dead, that they should be judged.
And, that you should reward Your servants
the prophets and the saints,
And your people who fear Your name, both small and
great.
And should destroy those who destroy the Earth."

Ionnes gasped with reverent joy. For the first time, he saw the Temple of God open in Heaven to uncover the Ark of His Covenant. Throughout his life, he knew he would never see it, so it amazed him even now all the more. With no words spoken, he knew what he witnessed.

Lightnings, noises, thunderings, another earthquake and great hail followed as the Ark became present for all in the throne room of Heaven to see.

Ionnes tried to describe the Ark he saw. No words would form on the pages. No words could his head make to race down his arms to his hands and fingers to record the indescribable images he witnessed. The quill dripped on the papyrus, but no words would form. He laid down his pen on the papyrus. He could no more draw a picture of that divine creation with true Cheribim standing guard than he could draw the rest of the throne room, the Lamb, or the One on the throne. His words seemed so inadequate; his language so inarticulate. His descriptions no more than ghostly shadows to the magnificence he witnessed beyond the veil; beyond the limits of time and space; beyond the physical, sinful world around all of them.

Nonetheless, he obeyed Yeshua's command to write what he saw.

And, then he saw her.

Clothed with the sun.

The Moon under her feet.

On her head a garland of twelve stars.

And, pregnant.

Labor pangs struck hard and she cried out, on and on. Ionnes watched the deep pain in her face under the light of twelve stars.

The pangs of labor carried on, but his attention diverted to a gruesome and terrible sight. It came not from the bottomless abyss, but from the heavens – a fiery, red dragon. Seven heads. Ten horns. Seven crowns, one on each head. As it moved about, it grabbed almost half the stars of the sky and threw them to the Earth.

But that was only its entrance for it hastened to the woman about to give birth to devour her newborn Child. It raced about with great anticipation, yet never took its eyes off its prey. Her pangs increased, and she pushed forth the male Child. Helplessly, she laid there to protect her Child. Yet, as the dragon pounced, the Child was caught up by God Himself and taken to the throne room.

The dragon growled in rage as its quarry escaped for all knew the Child would rule the nations, and rule hard like iron. Then, the dragon turned to attack the new mother, but she had fled it knew not where for Adonai prepared the place for her. She would be safely fed there one-thousand-two-hundred-and-sixty days.

"Three-and-a-half years, again," uttered Ionnes as he wrote.

So, the dragon attacked the Heavenly Host. Angels came forth from throughout the universe to engage in the battle. Ionnes saw one angel leading the army of the LORD. The name Michael could be heard throughout the warriors.

"Michael the archangel. Michael the prince," said Ionnes, recalling the Book of Daniel, "and I think Jude's letter also mentioned Michael."

The dragon and his unclean angels fought but could not prevail.

Then, Ionnes felt amazement at Yeshua's compassion, even for His enemies. They sought to find a place in Heaven for the dragon and his angels, but no place could be found to contain them. Ionnes sat incredulous of Yeshua's mercy, even after this terrible, spiritual war. He watched with great sadness as the dragon was expelled from Heaven. Still seeking whom it may devour, the madness and danger of the Earth suddenly made that much more sense. Sin came to the world, not just by Adam's sin, but by the dragon's loss; also called the Devil and Satan, the one who ever tried to deceive the entire world; the dragon's consolation after Michael and Yeshua's angels cast to Earth the dragon and his legion of angels.

Then, as the demonic forces headed for Earth, a loud voice in the Heavens called upon Ionnes to write:

"Now have come the salvation and the power and the kingdom of our God, and the authority of his Messiah. For the accuser of our brothers and sisters, who accuses them before our God, day and night, has been hurled down. They triumphed over him by the blood of the Lamb and by the word of their testimony; they did not love their lives so much as to shrink from death. Therefore rejoice, you heavens and you who dwell in them! But woe to the Earth and the sea, because the devil has gone down to you! He is filled with fury, because he knows that his time is short."

The fury of the dragon showed apparent. In rage for having lost the Child, the dragon skittered about to attack the mother who birthed the male Child. Ionnes saw the dragon rapidly approaching her when she received two wings, like of a great eagle, and she flew far, far away into the wilderness where her needs would be cared for. She would eat and drink there for another three-and-a-half years.

Then, a great flood erupted. Ionnes first thought it to be God's judgment, but when he turned, he saw the flood came from the mouth of the dragon, trying to carry away the woman.

He stood in amazement to see that much rancid water come out of the mouth of the dragon.

The water swept towards her until a vast chasm opened up in the Earth, swallowing the deluge to help the woman.

The dragon bellowed and screamed and destroyed all in its reach, then stopped. It could not gobble down the Child nor destroy the mother, but perhaps her other children. It raced off to make war with those who keep the commandments of God and have the testimony of Yeshua Cristos.

Ionnes looked at the pages he had written. The last light of day became twilight. He rose and stretched to head to bed. He knew not where he would be working tomorrow, but he wanted to be a little more rested than today.

"More visions?" asked Dim, already lying on his bedroll.

Ionnes nodded.

"Does this happen all the time?"

"No," answered Ionnes, "and yes."

Dim turned head towards the old man.

"It is not unusual to hear Yeshua's voice, but this time it has been more a journey. At first, I was part of the journey, like a man in a dream, moving from place to place. But tonight's final visions I was merely a witness. Part of an audience. I performed no part, and only played the scribe."

"Sometimes that is better," adjudged Dim.

Ionnes nodded and sighed as he gazed at the dark ceiling.

"You are right, my friend," Ionnes admitted as the gross and terrible vision of the dragon tore through his memories. He prayed, but in this he sought not comfort. He knew Yeshua wished for him to know and see their enemy.

PATMOS

CHAPTER 36

"Good morning," greeted Prochorus as Ionnes headed to the shoreline and the salt ropes.

"Greetings my brother," answered Ionnes, smiling broadly. He produced the new sheets he had recorded the night before.

"More for the letter?"

Ionnes needed not answer. Prochorus handed him a wedge of cheese as he took the sheets.

Ionnes looked at the white chunk with gladness and a tear escaped his eye. He had not had cheese since Ephesus.

"Some came in on a ship yesterday. I was able to gain some samples."

"I thank you and Yeshua for this special blessing."

He nibbled the goat cheese. A little salty, perhaps, but that could have been his own tongue. As a prisoner he ate less salt. It mattered not, and he still gave it a perfect score.

"I thought they would never take away the rubble of the temple," said Prochorus. The two men glanced over at the barren area.

"They did seek miraculous remedies first, did not they?"

"I have heard of no plans yet to rebuild."

"Probably not before I am gone from this island," agreed Ionnes.

"I wish it were today," admitted Prochorus.

"As do I, my brother. As do I - lest I am needed here." He winked.

They walked along in silence a spell until reaching the beach.

"I have work to do and you have letters to amend."

The two old men exchanged a hug, then parted company for a spell. Prochorus intended to bring lunch for all of them. It became a bit costly, but he knew it to be an effective way to help his teacher. Roman soldiers liked good, free food as well as anyone.

Ionnes watched his friend depart a moment, then headed for the beach. He felt the sand under his feet and between his toes. Cool and clammy. The breeze stirred the surf and waves lapped upon the shoreline. The blue water drew his attention. He always loved the sea and always would. High clouds feathered the sky overhead. One shaded the morning sunlight, darkening the blue sea. The sea stirred around restlessly, somewhat like a boiling pot. Ionnes watched the turbulence with interest.

Then, a tapered post rose up out of the water, larger at the base than top. Then another and another. More posts appeared – ten in all. Then, to his greater surprise, each tapered post was wrapped with fancy jewelry and gold. Soon, a giant head emerged from the water. Then, another head, and another and another, still some distance out, but moving towards him. Seven hideous heads in all moved through the water and Ionnes saw that the posts were horns and the jewelry more like crowns. Each head had a blasphemous name written upon its forehead. One of the heads looked like one who had died in battle. He wondered how that one could still be alive? Ionnes detested what seven creatures he would see come out of the water. They moved together as one, and as the heads rose forth from the sea, Ionnes discovered they were all one gigantic body. As it continued to move towards land, Ionnes then discovered it walked on four legs. Its body like a leopard, its feet like a bear and its mouth a lion. This fearsome image left the water to seduce the people of the Earth. Ionnes saw many who followed, falling down to worship the beast.

"Who is like the beast?" he heard some say. "Who is able to make war with him?"

Then one of the mouths of the beast began to speak. Great things initially to allure those of the Earth, then started to introduce blasphemies against God and Yeshua as well as the tabernacle and those who dwell in Heaven. Ionnes could see the work of the dragon empowering this one. He quickly saw its motive to make war with the saints to overcome and subdue them. The beast showed authority given to him by the dragon over every tribe, tongue and nation. Ionnes found that all those remaining upon the Earth bowed low to worship the hideous beast – those whose names had not been written in the Book of Life of the Lamb slain from the foundation of the world.

Ionnes wrote all that he saw. He sat upon the sand, so completely shaken over his visions and his words. So many dead or dying. So many deceived. How could he ever reach them all?

As he completed writing, he said, "For anyone has an ear, let him hear. He who leads into captivity shall go into captivity; he who kills with the sword must be killed with the sword."

He wrote the harsh words like an eye for an eye, but then ended them with, "Here is the patience and the faithfulness on the part of God's people."

Laying down his pen to pray, he wept for the lost; wept for those who loved their sin; and prayed for those who thought themselves wise, but still foolishly followed after the beast. Then, his tears subsided as he remembered the saints. Through them, Yeshua's hope and eternal life would ever be shared. Through them, Yeshua's love would glow.

<>< ><> <>< ><> <>< ><> <>< ><> <>< ><>

Ionnes sat alone on the beach at the end of the workday. The images of the horrible beast with the seven heads and ten horns continued to plague and disturb him. For whatever reason, he watched the water, half expecting it to come forth a second time. The water lapped tamely.

"I would have preferred to baptize the beast," decided Ionnes.

He shuffled his pages of papyrus in his lap as he prepared for Yeshua's Spirit to guide him to the next dreams. After such a sinful sight, he knew Yeshua was not done speaking to him via these visions. The beast would not be Yeshua's final word, inside or outside the throne room.

He had not long to wait for the water before him disappeared to reveal another great abyss. The great, dark hole expelled all light which tried to penetrate it. Not surprising to Ionnes, another fearsome beast came forth. This one had only two horns though its voice sounded more like the dragon. By its words and actions, Ionnes could tell it exercised the same authority as the first beast. It performed great signs and wonders which fooled so many people; even calling fire down from heaven before the eyes of all. He even commanded that men make images of the first beast to worship. Those who refused would be killed. The second beast cared nothing for the station of any man, rich or poor, slaveman or free. Those he marked with the sign of the beast on their foreheads or right hands – binding their thoughts and their actions. Those without the mark faced greater persecutions, even losing their abilities to buy or sell in the market.

On some, Ionnes saw the name of the beast. On others, he saw three numbers, or more precisely the same number three times.

"Total incompletion," muttered Ionnes, shaking his head sadly.

"Here is wisdom," he continued. "Let him who has understanding calculate the number of the beast, for it is the number of a man: His number is VI-VI-VI."

He turned away from the sad sight of people destroying their lives as well as destroying those they claimed to love. He had long been witness to the devil and his destructive ways, but with these visions, Yeshua had chosen to open the eyes of the Christian church so wide they would hurt. Ionnes never forgot that this would be shared with the entire Christian church. This letter; or this book as it had become, needed to bless the church. Know their foes, but more so know Yeshua will ultimately triumph.

Mist entered the bay. It flowed slowly towards the land. Flowing up the beach, it surrounded Ionnes. The fog was not thick, and he could still see a fair distance around him. The mist unhurriedly thickened into a cloud. Ionnes looked and suddenly beheld the sight of a Lamb standing on Mount Zion, not alone. The one-hundred-and-forty-four-thousand gathered about him, all wearing and bearing the Father's glorious name written upon their foreheads.

Music began to play. Beautiful harps playing together in harmony and unison from all directions around him. He looked all around to engage each glorious nuance of sound.

A voice joined the music - a voice that resembled the sound of many waters, or at times resembled the thunder rolling like a large, crescendoing drum after the lightning. All sang together as only a Heavenly Choir could. They sang a new song Ionnes had never heard, presented before the four living creatures and twenty-four elders. Only the one choir who were redeemed from the Earth could sing the song. Living pure and sinless lives, these were God's FirstFruits, delivered from sinful men. In their mouths, God found no deceit. Those without fault before God.

Something flew overhead. Ionnes looked up to see another unrecognized angel flying in the midst of Heaven. The everlasting gospel poured forth from him to preach to all nations as he loudly proclaimed, "Fear God and give glory to Him, for the hour of His judgment has come; and worship Him who made Heaven and Earth, the sea and springs of water."

"The hour of His judgment," said Ionnes as he wrote. He knew no better time to give glory to Yeshua and His Father in Heaven.

Next, another angel he also had not previously seen, flew overhead. The angel's announcement showed all what goodness would come as he proclaimed, "Babylon is fallen, is fallen, that great city because she has made all nations drink the maddening wine of her adulteries."

Ionnes heard "Babylon," but thought Roma.

Then, a third new angel followed the first two, adding to the heraldry. Loudly and clearly, the angel announced, "If anyone worships the beast and his image, and receives his mark on his forehead or on his hand, they too, will drink the wine of God's fury, which has been poured full strength into the cup of His wrath. They will be tormented with burning sulfur in the presence of the holy angels and of the Lamb. And the smoke of their torment will rise for ever and ever. There will be no rest, day or night, for those who worship the beast and its image, or for anyone who receives the mark of its name."

Ionnes wondered at how the church would endure. Again, he answered the question himself – by the patience of the saints.

Patience of the saints? Those who keep the commandments of God and the faith of Yeshua. As he wrote those words, he dwelled upon them and how they would unfold and bless the ever-growing church.

Soon, a voice from Heaven called down to Ionnes saying, "Write."

Ionnes paused to record the Word of the LORD.

"Write, 'Blessed are the Dead who die in the LORD from now on.'"

The call of the martyr. Ionnes peered closely at the sentence a long time after he wrote it. This would be hard for many in the faith to accept and follow. He recalled the martyrs under the altar and Yeshua's earlier word that more would be added.

"Blessed are the dead who die in the LORD from now on," Ionnes wrote as the Spirit added, "Yes, that they may rest from their labors, and their deeds will follow them."

Ionnes noted so many Heavenly beings moving and growing and living in the light of Christos. The four creatures. The twenty-four elders. Angels and the one-hundred-and-forty-four-thousand, all engaged and moving towards the completion of God's Holy Word - all but the martyrs. To them, Yeshua gave rest. Those under the altar and those who would soon join them.

"Rest, my brethren. Rest."

Then, gray clouds rolled across the sky, too many to count. Ionnes watched their movements. Suddenly, one cloud, all white, pierced its way through the pack. Ionnes gasped with reverent joy. On the cloud sat one like the Son of Man. Ionnes knew that face. Ionnes watched His every move earnestly.

He wore a glorious, golden crown upon His head. No more the crown of thorns though He would ever be known by His scars. At first obscured by the cloud, Ionnes then noticed the tool in Yeshua's hand – a sharp sickle. From the Temple of the Throne Room, another angel flew forth, crying with a loud voice to Yeshua, still seated upon the cloud.

"Thrust in Your sickle and reap," called the angel, "for the time has come for You to reap, for the harvest of the Earth is ripe." Ionnes heard it, not as a command, but more as an announcement for everyone else who had ears to hear.

Yeshua hesitated not. His hand raised the sickle, then swung it low across the entire Earth, reaping the good harvest. Not a head would He lose. He would leave none to thereafter glean.

Then, also from out of the Temple, another angel flew forth towards the Earth. This one also held a sickle, but his was not designed as the sickle Yeshua toted. He took position over the Earth and waited but moments, for another angel flew forth from the altar of the Temple in the Throne Room of Heaven. He had the power of fire radiating throughout his form. He called to the first angel, "Thrust in your sharp sickle and gather the clusters of grapes from the Earth's vine for the harvest of the Earth is ripe."

Ionnes watched with anticipation as the sickle swung down into the Earth and gathered the grapes of the Earth. Gathering his harvest, he then threw it into a great winepress to effect God's wrath. They trampled it outside of the city, pulverizing the grapes. Ionnes had seen many winepresses, so felt shock to see gobs of deep, red blood flowing from this one. Out it came, a flood immeasurable to him, rising throughout until it was as deep as a horse's bridle. A sea of blood one-thousand-six-hundred furlongs in diameter. The sea of blood would be a sea of red the entire way from Ephesus to Laodicea and back again.

Ionnes looked down at the words on the page.

"Out of papyrus again?"

Ionnes looked up at the inquisitive voice. Hilarius, the odd Roman, stood over him, then plopped down by his side. He handed Ionnes more sheets. A lot more sheets.

"Prochorus had a feeling you would need more." He looked down at what Ionnes had written.

"May I read it?"

"Of course," answered Ionnes, handing him the text.

He read without haste. He savored each word and muttered meanings. Handing back the papyrus, he nodded approval.

"Yeshua is pleased with your work."

Ionnes looked at Hilarius with a new eye. Something seemed most familiar all of a sudden. He could not quite put the face to the one in his memory, but it poked his mind over and over, demanding an answer.

"Where is Prochorus?" asked Ionnes.

"Coming," answered Hilarius. "He will be here soon." The Roman rose, then helped Ionnes to his feet. Violently slapping his dark brown tunic with his hands to expel the dirt, he added, "You have been keeping him most busy with these written words."

"It is Yeshua who has kept me busy," added Ionnes, smiling. "The visions try to frighten me, like a nightmare. They are hard to see, but I see Yeshua's hand and Spirit in all of it."

Hilarius nodded in agreement. "Ah," he said, "Prochorus approacheth."

Ionnes turned to see his friend.

"What are you doing on the beach?" greeted Prochorus. "I kept watching for you to come through town."

"Another vision," answered Ionnes, handing the pages to his friend.

"I am not sure there is enough papyrus on all of Patmos to complete these letters," joked Prochorus.

"Praise Yeshua for Hilarius," complimented Ionnes.

"Who?" asked Prochorus.

Ionnes looked at his friend oddly, then looked around to discover Hilarius was nowhere in sight.

"Hilarius. A Roman who said he was in your company. He has brought me papyrus and ink twice now."

Prochorus started to laugh. "I have no idea whom you are talking about, but I would bet a day's wage Yeshua does."

Ionnes looked at the pages in his hands and also started laughing. He had been given much more. He held up the ream of papyrus.

"Apparently, Yeshua has much more to say."

"Apparently," agreed Prochorus.

The sun started its descent behind Mount Elias. The air would cool down quickly with the loss of sunlight. Prochorus wrapped a shawl around his friend as they began the trek up the hill.

"I am pleased to be in such blessed company," said Prochorus.

"Who? Or how?" asked Ionnes.

"Your Hilarius. He said he has been in my company. I expect that was no lie."

Ionnes nodded, then stopped. He looked far away a moment, then smiled and looked at Prochorus.

"What?" asked Prochorus.

Ionnes replayed the memories through his head. He was sure he was right.

"The visions," he said. "One of the angels that flew across the sky as a herald. I did not notice it at the time, but now I see it was Hilarius."

"You are sure?" checked Prochorus.

"Glad to say, yes. Definitely," grinned Ionnes, then paused again. Roman uniform? He was not quite so sure since they came covered in the dark of night. He sighed. Perhaps he would find out when he asked Yeshua. Taking Prochorus' arm, the two friends praised Yeshua and continued the hike to the barracks in song.

<>< ><> <>< ><> <>< ><> <>< ><> <>< ><>

"*Great and Wonderful*," sang Silva Viridi, leading the congregation, "*O LORD God the Almighty...*"

No others knew the song at the start, but they hummed along and made droning undertones to join in and share. Silva Viridi's voice carried the weight of the praises to Yeshua, but the bigness of his heart and commitment in praise to Christos he pretty much shared equally with all others there.

Light raindrops pecked at the roof of the House of Myron. Ionnes looked around the room, half full of people praising Yeshua with all their worth. He knew himself to typically be a room half full person as he noted the potential to add more. He knew the Holy Spirit to provide a packed house.

Ionnes spoke one of his favorite parables which Yeshua had spoken many times through their travels. A sower who haphazardly tossed seed everywhere – on the road, among the thorns, on the rocks and on good soil. Ionnes knew from experience this was an important parable to share to a church of young and new disciples. None as yet had left the church, as far as Ionnes could tell, but he sadly knew it to be an absolute inevitability, and this parable helped to address that before any would get discouraged or be placed under persecution and thereby depart the faith. Rejection from family often caused a spiritual exodus. Even more sadly, many of those would return to the old habits, sinful pursuits and other idolatries of their previous lives.

Tobie stepped forward with drinks and food as the service ended. Lorin joined him, and Talor also stepped in to help. Ionnes looked with pride at the teen. His captors tried to make him a slave. What they obviously never saw was that he already had a servant's heart. As his trust in Yeshua and faith in the church grew, so also did his desire to serve.

Or he was trying to impress Lorin. At least one of the two. Maybe both.

Chryspippe peered at Dim. "Are not you the prisoner who became baptized the same day as I?"

"Aye," answered Dim. His eye kept watch of Ionnes, but the governor's wife was not bad to look at as well. He never would have opened any dialogue with her, (being the governor's wife and all), and was surprised when she did. "This could be interesting," he thought. "Brother in Christos or dirt under her feet?"

"How long have you been on Patmos?" she asked.

"Um, jus' over four years."

"Wow!" she said, not even trying to contain her astonishment. "Is not that longer than most pris----oners?"

"Aye," repeated Dim.

"Do you like it?"

He looked at her like, "Really?"

"You are right. You are right," she laughed at herself.

"Silly question. But something must keep you going. Am I now right? Somehow you have not lost hope. Somehow you have made this your life - as one whom the gods have ---"

She paused and slightly blushed.

"Old habit," she whispered.

Dim nodded. "I done the same error."

She recollected herself, and continued, "Somehow you have made this life into something better than just prison toil."

He considered her words. He would not have said it that way – would not have ever thought it, but her point touched his heart and opened his eyes just a little wider.

"I have Ionnes t' thank."

She glanced over at the apostle, chatting with her father. "As do I," she affirmed. "As do I."

She looked up to the left briefly as she added, "Would I have ever known Yeshua without him?"

It was not a deep thought, really, but Dim still considered her words carefully.

"In m' days under Roman toil, I know not how else Yeshua woulda reached me without one o' His own t' work by my side."

"Yeshua would have figured it out."

"Verily," answered Dim, "I may doubt my faith at times, but I never doubt that Yeshua is much smarter than I."

Chryspippe giggled. She thought the same thing just that morning during her morning prayers. She paused, then asked, "How did you two meet?"

Dim thought it through a quick moment to answer.

"If the truth b' known, I loved him the first minute I saw him. But then he raised one – um, correction – he, thru Yeshua, raised one from the dead." He grinned sheepishly. "It shook me like the trees 'gainst mighty winds, & the memory of priz'ner Gallo haunts me daily, but it also gave me great awe & wonder 'bout him & his Anointed One."

She glanced at Ionnes again.

"He scares me, too," she admitted. "Sometimes I fear that if he can bring back life so easily, perhaps he can take life, too."

Dim had not considered that, and he then looked at his teacher.

Nah!

He hoped.

Then added, "I saw him whipped & flogged within an inch o' his life. If he had that power, would not he have used it t' destroy his tormenters? I know I woulda."

Now they both looked at Ionnes.

"Maybe we should ask him?" suggested Dim.

She took a deep breath. Part of her wanted it to be true for she revered him, but part of her feared if it showed not true that her impressions of him somehow had been wrong all along.

They both looked at each other, and she took the lead, crossing the room.

"Marcellus is the greatest charioteer Roma has ever seen," argued Myron.

"Not according to Judah Ben Hur," countered Ionnes.

The two men stopped to address Chryspippe and Dim.

"Good morning," she greeted them both. "We have a question."

Ionnes loved it when someone came forward with their questions.

"W-we wondered," she stammered, "if Yeshua working through you could bring someone back from the dead, could not He also take away the life of any man by just your word?"

Ionnes' brow furrowed.

"Good question. Good question," he said, not backing away. He looked up at Myron who also showed great interest in the answer to this question.

"As our resurrected and ascended LORD, Yeshua has total power over life and death. It is true," said Ionnes, "but He is also one of great mercy. He wishes no man to leave this world apart from Him. That very point has been one of the hardest lessons for someone with a skull as thick as mine to finally understand."

He looked at all three both a bit embarrassed, but also happy to be transparent.

"Let me tell you a story. Yeshua had ascended to the Father not long and the Holy Spirit had descended upon us all. The church grew daily, in some ways as you have seen for yourselves on Patmos. We were serving those who came to us, and many sold all they had to give to the church."

He sighed. This had always been a hard memory to bear.

"One couple, Ananias and Sapphira as I recall, had a field which they sold to give to the church. It was not their only property, and they certainly would not be homeless thereafter. Ananias excelled in business and Adonai had blessed them much. Well, he came to us himself to give the money from the sale, but he held back part of the gift, then lied and said it was all that he had received for the sale of land.

"What is foolish is that he could have given us whatever he wanted. He was under no compulsion to give us the total amount, or anything at all, but the Holy Spirit told Cephas and the rest of us that Ananias lied about the amount of the sale. We were not upset by what he gave, but that he lied about it."

"Why was that such a big deal?" asked Dim.

Ionnes looked with compassion upon his friend and now student.

"Do you like being lied to?"

"No," answered Dim, then shrugged, "but it happens."

"Understood," agreed Ionnes, then continued, "Would not you agree that lying can make changes?"

The others all nodded or said, "Yes."

"Small changes?"

"And big," interjected Myron.

Dim also nodded recalling the itsy-bitsy lies that sent him to Patmos.

"Verily," agreed Ionnes. "Sometimes very big changes. Ananias' lies created big changes for though the church was blessed by their gift, they gave not out of love for Yeshua, but rather out of pride. They wished their gift to elevate their status in Yeshua's new church. Yeshua saw right through their motives, and His Spirit exposed their lies to us."

The group stood silent with anticipation until Tobie asked, "So, what happened?"

Ionnes smiled at the slave, then glanced at Myron. Ionnes certainly knew, with deafening recent clarity, the rules of being a slave. Speaking out was one of the no-nos. Myron seemed more surprised than provoked by Tobie's question –

perhaps because the same question fretted and prodded his own mind, pressing against his own lips to escape.

"Cephas verified Ananias' story a bit, then said something like, 'Ananias, why has Satan filled your heart to lie to the Holy Spirit and keep back part of the price of the land for yourself? While it remained, was it not your own? And, after it was sold, was it not in your control?' Ananias nodded acknowledgement to Cephas, as my friend and brother continued, 'Why have you conceived this thing in your heart? You have not lied to men but to God.'

"This was not the response Ananias expected. Rather, he expected great praise and appreciation from the church and his name would rise for that season above the others. I saw nothing in his demeanor that admitted his lie. He seemed more irritated with all of us for not kissing his stinky feet for his sizable gift. If a church father told me that Satan had filled my heart to lie, I would be on my knees in a Ierusalem minute begging Yeshua's forgiveness and mercy. But that display never arrived. Instead, I saw no remorse or confession in any form." Ionnes sighed, his head hung low.

After a spell, Dim asked, "Uh, so what happened after that?"

Ionnes took his time to look up to Dim and the others. Tears had filled his eyes and his voice shook as he answered.

"V-v-very quickly after Cephas' words of correction and rebuke, Ananias fell down before us all, dead. Not even a final gasp of air. His spirit fled from his body faster than a rat from a sinking ship."

The crowd before Ionnes felt stunned at the answer. For any mortal man to wield such power in Christos brought forth great fear.

"What happened after that?" asked Myron, holding a commanding head though just as fazed as the others.

Ionnes took the moment to recollect.

"As I recall, all of us did nothing for a bit, still amazed to see Ananias fall. Cephas motioned to some of the young men to collect his body. They wrapped him for burial and took him out to the cemetery."

Chryspippe thought for a moment, then asked, "How did Ananias' wife take his death?"

Tears still filling Ionnes' eyes, he answered, "She soon joined him."

All waited for him to continue.

"A few hours after Ananias' mortal repose, Sapphira arrived, looking for her husband. One of the young men alerted us of her coming. We all stood as she entered. Cephas went to her and asked about the offering and the land they sold. She replied that yes, that was the selling price, standing beside her husband's deception.

"Cephas suddenly seemed taller as his voice crescendoed.

'How is it,' he said, 'that you have agreed together to test the Spirit of the LORD?'

"I saw her face change suddenly from uncertain confusion to great fear – and transparency as though her body was made of fine glass. She looked away from Cephas to the rest of us, seeking help, or perhaps still searching for Ananias. She spoke not, but likewise did not show a spirit of repentance. Like most women, she followed the lead of her husband. In that, I weep for her, but like many, she preferred the security of money over trusting in the LORD. I believe that she wholeheartedly supported Ananias in keeping part of the money when the plan was conceived, that her comforts would be preserved. As I mentioned earlier, they were well-to-do, and she accustomed to citron-like luxury."

"So," asked Chryspippe, seeing within herself that part of Sapphira, "was she rebuked by Cephas or sent away?"

Ionnes shook his head in grief. He had already answered that question for her.

"I wish I could say it was so," he muttered, grumbling to himself until he had to clear his throat to continue. "We heard others entering the house. Cephas still stood before her as he said, 'Look. The feet of those who have buried your husband are at the door...'

"Her face turned to horror, and she looked towards the doorway. The young men entered. I believe she expected to be taken out and perhaps stoned. She knew not how her husband died. She looked back at Cephas as he added, '...and they will carry you out.'

"We saw the fear of her face drain away. She suddenly turned blank, and fell where she stood, slumping down like a pile of wet mud. Her breath left her and never returned. After the second shock of death washed over all of us, the young men who had buried Ananias came forward. They shook recognizably as they wrapped her as they had her husband, then took her out to be buried beside him."

The group again became silent, lost in their own fears and questions.

"What became of the money?" asked Myron, perhaps still trying to distance himself from the selfish fear he now felt. It surprised him, that fear. He certainly knew the days of his youth were long spent. He saw his days ahead less than his days lived. Thus, to so readily fear his mortality seemed the ultimate foolishness, but with that thought, he also reasoned one does not overcome one's fears with mere words.

He looked at Ionnes and again saw the would-be martyr who still stood before them with life and breath and spirit. Somehow he could not see the end of Ionnes' days. Perhaps he would outlive them all, even to the end of all time.

Ionnes tried to recall the answer to that question. It had been so many years.

"As I recall, and I truly am not certain, but I believe it was returned to the family, added as part of their estate. Ananias and Sapphira had no children, God bless them, but they had many relatives, and it would have been wrong for the church to keep the money."

"What was the response o' the church?" asked Dim.

Ionnes looked at Dim very seriously. "What would you think?"

"Great fear," answered the prisoner.

"You are correct," affirmed Ionnes, then added, "and great reverence for Yeshua."

"So," asked Chryspippe, "why did Cephas judge them so severely?"

"He did not," answered Ionnes. "They did not lie to Cephas or me or the church. They lied to Yeshua's Holy Spirit. They tested His Spirit. Yeshua judged them. That is why I have often told all of you, I have no power apart from Yeshua. It is Yeshua within me that gives me strength."

Dim considered the answer. "Did anyone else die like that, where Yeshua jus' took away their breath?"

"Just His own breath," answered Ionnes, somber but not mourning. "Just His own, and not for His lies or His sins, for He was sinless, but He breathed His last for all of our lies and sins."

"So," continued Dim, "ya have never called upon Yeshua t' kill someone for their lies or sins?"

"Not after Pentecost," he answered. "Not after the Holy Spirit entered to dwell within me."

"But, could you?" pressed Dim. "Were ya not tempted to call down the wrath of Yeshua upon the Roman soldiers as they flogged you?"

"Yes," admitted Ionnes. "Perhaps to my shame. I am only a man and can likewise err, but if there is anything Yeshua taught me, it is to love God by loving those who walk upon the same land I do. All of you are loved by God. Can I do any less? If I cannot love all of you whom I can see, how can I love an Almighty God whom I have not seen?

"And," he suddenly added, "have not some of those soldiers begun to seek the name of the LORD? If a cruel and vicious Roman can be forgiven and come body, mind and soul to Christos, who am I to reject any? I am not Yeshua to judge. I cannot send a man to eternal judgment before his appointed time."

He stood and brushed himself off. He felt the tug of the Holy Spirit, calling him as a loving, protective mother calls her young. The rain continued to fall as he walked without hurry to the door. Opening the door, he stood to look out at the rain. It was not anywhere near dark, yet two torches burned brightly along the walkway. Ionnes gazed at the flames, then down at the reflections of light upon the watery stones. The stones were flatter and smoother than he earlier recalled. The divots and ripples of the rock continued to melt away until he envisioned a great sea of glass mingled with fire, growing brighter and brighter.

To his surprise, he then saw many, standing on that plane of glass. How could he have missed them? Each held a harp. His ears became aware of the music flowing in unison out of the strings. It filled him to overflowing, beautiful to behold.

First, he heard the Song of Moses, Yeshua's key servant and recorder of God's old covenant with Yisra'el. Then, he heard a different song, filled with the glory of living strings giving glory to the Lamb.

"Great and Marvelous are Your works,
O LORD God Almighty!
Just and true are Your ways,
O King of the nations.
Who shall not fear You, O LORD,
And glorify Your name?
For You alone are Holy.

"For You alone are Holy." Ionnes heard that line over and over and over throughout the song.

"For You alone are Holy,
For all nations shall come and worship You,
For Your righteous acts have been revealed."

Enthralled, Ionnes remained absorbed by the music, playing over and over.

Suddenly, smoke flooded the throne room. Ionnes sought the source of the smoke and noticed the temple. Somehow, he knew it was not being destroyed by fire. The holy smoke then filled his nostrils with its sweet and powerful scent. He took note of the fog he could still clearly see through.

Some figures emerged from the temple – seven in all. They were easy to see, clothed with pure, bright linen. Each wore a golden banner, from one shoulder, crossing diagonally down across the torso. They moved away from the temple towards the throne and the four living creatures. (Ionnes still did not quite know how else to describe the unique quartet.) One of the four living creatures moved forward. From Ionnes' angle, he could not tell which one. Near the throne sat seven large, golden bowls. They were as big as the angels who would each carry one.

Ionnes strained to see what each contained. To his horror, he saw each contained the wrath of God who lives forever and ever. As each angel took the bowl handed to him, the smoke from the temple became far thicker and denser. Ionnes saw that none would be able to enter the temple and wondered how long the overwhelming, blinding smoke would flow.

Before any answer to that question would come forth, a loud voice sounded from the smoky temple, speaking directly to the seven angels.

"Go and pour out the seven bowls of the wrath of God on the Earth."

Ionnes shuddered and goosebumped at the severe command. He looked down at the seven angels still standing by the four creatures and twenty-four elders. One moved forward and flew off towards the Earth. Ionnes watched him as he positioned himself, then poured out his bowl upon the Earth. It took not long for the wails of pain to arise. Ionnes saw men, marked with the mark of the Beast, breaking out with loathsome sores all over their bodies. Nothing would ease the pain. Nothing would give them comfort, and they wailed hopelessly to announce their torment.

Ionnes looked to the left in time to see the second angel pour out his bowl upon the seas of the world. The water turned a disgusting, dirty red like the blood of a dead man. Fish popped to the surface, unable to breathe. Other sea life as well floated to the top, all dead. The sight felt sickening. Nauseating stench soon followed.

Then, his attention focused upon the third angel, flying over his head inland. The angel emptied out the bowl, turning all the waterways to the same dreadful color of dead red. All creatures in the rivers and lakes turned belly up. Ionnes licked his dry lips as he saw virtually all potable water become undrinkable. Ionnes recalled Moses on the Nile River and the Ten Plagues. Would many of these plagues – these judgments follow? How could they not?

His old covenant musings were disturbed by the angel's mighty voice still far above him.

"You are just in these judgments, O Holy One,
You who are and who were;
For they have shed the blood of
your holy people and your prophets,
And you have given them blood to drink as they
deserve."

Ionnes felt great sadness. He thought of Stephanos, the first of their brethren to taste the martyr's tears. He thought of his brother, Yaakov, and Cephas and Paulos and all the others.

So many. So many to name.

"What is a man who would destroy the life of those who brought life and light to this world?" he thought, yet he knew the answer. Those in darkness always showed blindness.

He thought of Zechariah, dragged out of the temple into the courtyard as King Josiah struck him down. From there, his blood cried out like Abel's, lamenting from the altar long after Zechariah's body breathed its last. The priests declared thereafter that the angels never again were seen within the temple.

Another voice, different from the Father's or the Son's, cried forth from the altar saying, "Even so, LORD God Almighty, true and righteous are Your judgments."

Ionnes dried his tears with his sleeve as he melodically muttered to himself, "For You alone are holy."

The fourth angel shot up like David's smooth stone from its sling, heading straight for the big, bright sun. It poured out the wrath of the LORD. Ionnes saw the sun become hotter and brighter, as the LORD's Spirit blew hard upon the fiery coals. Great fire like embers rappelled off the sun to head downward to Earth, scorching men throughout the world. The hellacious sight of the sun's fury should have awakened men to the judgment they faced. Ionnes could not see how they would not cower under the Almighty's power and penance. Would not even one accept God's refinement by fire?

Yet, to Ionnes' amazement, most men did the exact opposite. They cursed God all the more in their hearts, their mouths and even their actions. Yeshua had full power over all these plagues, yet like Pharaoh before Moses, the hardened hearts of men refused to repent or give God any glory.

Thus, another angel – the fifth, went downward to the bottomless pit and poured out his bowl on the seat of the beast. Already dark, the abyss became like the blackest ink at night.

No light could escape. A hideous black hole. Ionnes saw nothing below, but he heard the wails of those tormented. He also heard as they bit down hard on their tongues to endure their pain and darkness and fears. More blasphemies poured forth from below, their bitter plight reaching the hearts of the men above who served them and repeated their blasphemies aloud. Their pains and sores continued to drive them, for none would repent or accept Yeshua's loving mercies and grace and love and life.

Sadly, none.

"Tiber," whispered Ionnes to himself, still rapidly recording with pen and ink each vision as he saw the sixth angel fly off to the Great River Euphrates. The angel's bowl polluted the water, drying it instantly to nothing, like bitter steam off a hot rock. In wonderment, Ionnes saw this move as a call to war. The dry riverbed opened opportunities for forces from the east to attack.

In turn, to defend themselves, Ionnes saw the dragon, the beast and the false prophet all open their mouths. Demonic frogs leapt forth. Ionnes watched but could not tell which of the seven heads of the dragon nor seven heads of the beast expelled the repulsive frogs. He thought of the plague of frogs brought upon Egypt by Moses. The three persisted, performing signs and wonders to fool the men of the Earth, for at such times men would seek any strand of false hope to overcome the plagues and pains they were made to endure. Sadly, none could see the guilt of their sins brought to the justice of Yeshua's judgments. Sadly, they instead prepared for battle against the LORD God Almighty Himself.

All heads turned an ear upward as a loud voice boomed down from Heaven.

"Behold, I am coming as a thief," declared the voice. Ionnes recognized the voice as Yeshua. He recalled Yeshua when he spoke similar words during his teachings. Ionnes recalled Cephas quoting them. Paulos as well.

The voice continued, "Blessed is he who watches and keeps his garments, lest he walk naked, and they see his shame."

Adam and Eve came to mind for Ionnes, as did the Cushites when Assyria attacked during the years of Isaiah. They each sought to cover their naked shame. They each felt the exposure before a cold world.

Yet, the soldiers marked by the beast rejected the holy words spoken for all to hear. Instead, they let themselves be herded to battle like witless sheep.

Ionnes wondered where they would come together. He watched in earnest as they crossed the plains well north of Ierusalem. They looked to be heading to Nazareth, the holy town where Yeshua grew from human boy to man, but rather stopped some miles to the southwest.

"Jezreel," thought Ionnes, yet watched as they approached the northern hill. He could see Mount Tabor where Deborah defeated Sisera, but they stopped before that upon a different, smaller hill.

"Megiddo," said Ionnes. "Har Mageddon."

As the battle lines began to form in the sand, another voice flowed down mightily from the temple and throne of Heaven. Ionnes saw the seventh and final angel pouring out his bowl upon the Earth as Yeshua declared, "It is done!"

"It is finished."

Ionnes could hear those very words from the cross as Yeshua hung, seemingly helpless.

"It is done!" The wrath of God was complete.

Ionnes recalled the death knell of Christos on the cross when a terrible earthquake shook the world down to its foundation. That earthquake announced Yeshua's loving and eternal deliverance. This earthquake announced the same even though people only saw judgment and wrath.

"Roma," hacked Ionnes, but wrote, "Babylon," as he saw the great city divided into three parts. The land and water seemed to ebb and flow like the waves of the ocean shore for islands fled away and mountains disappeared. Hail began to fall, its stones growing in size and destructive purpose, bigger and bigger.

Ionnes picked up the rock-hard hail stone with both hands. Hefting it in his arms, he noted its size. So big. Big as a talent, he adjudged. What? Sixty/seventy pounds? That is a lot of ice to crash upon the ground with wrathful intent. That is as big as a bag of three thousand shekels. Ionnes could not recall ever holding three thousand shekels in his hand. He could not recall even seeing a money bag that full. He recalled when times were good as a Galilean fisherman when he could earn even a couple of shekels a day - enough to provide for most families for three or four or five days. Nowadays he had not even a gerah - or even a mite to jingle between his fingers.

He sighed sadly. More human voices arose to blaspheme God for the exceeding plague of hail. He plopped the gigantic hailstone to the ground to return to his writing. It sunk into the Earth with glacial intent.

Turning back towards the throne room, he could see some of the Heavenly Host entering the temple. As the smoke flowed forth from the glory of God and from His power, Ionnes noticed none could enter. Now that the seven angels had poured out the seven plagues, the temple opened-up again for those among the Heavenly Host to enter and be filled to overflowing with the glory and power of the LORD God Almighty.

"*For You alone are holy,*" sang Ionnes to himself as he wrote. "*For You alone are holy.*"

Continuing to scrawl the words as rapidly as his pen could scratch ink onto papyrus, he failed to notice the approaching angel.

"Yochanan," the angel called.

Ionnes looked up. An angel at full height hovered before him. As awesome to behold when flying overhead, Ionnes gasped with glee and awe at the stunning sight of the divine being. It took a moment, but he soon realized this spirit to be one of the seven angels bearing bowls. First? Second? Third or fourth? He could not quite remember.

"Come," requested the angel. "I will show you the judgment of the great harlot who sits on many waters, with whom the kings of the Earth committed adultery, and the inhabitants of the Earth were made drunk with the wine of her fornication."

No sooner were the words spoken when Ionnes felt his body lifted away in the Spirit, heading far out to a barren wilderness. No water. Cracked soil. Only scant, sickly vegetation. But, upon the scorched soil sat a woman of mesmerizing beauty riding a large, red beast. Again, the beast had seven heads and ten horns, each head spelling out many abominable blasphemies against Yeshua and the Father. The woman wore purple and scarlet garments, dressed up with gold and numerous precious stones and pearls. She held in her hand a very attractive, golden goblet. Ionnes did not notice at first, but soon saw the cup overflowing with the abominations and filthy fornications of the Earth. Her external image showed only a façade to cover her godless sins and seductions within.

Turning towards him, Ionnes noted words upon her head. They read:

MYSTERY
BABYLON THE GREAT
THE MOTHER OF HARLOTS AND OF THE
ABOMINATIONS OF THE EARTH

Ionnes quickly realized the source of her intoxication, having imbibed the blood of saints and martyrs. His body shook off her effects as he recognized her seductive wiles outshone the repulsive beast she rode upon.

The angel noted Ionnes' face, and asked, "Why do you marvel?"

As though awakened from a hypnotic spell, Ionnes shuddered and looked at the angel who nodded his support as he announced, "I will tell you the mystery of the woman and of the beast that carries her, which has the seven heads and the ten horns."

The angel pointed downward toward the beast and the bottomless pit as he said, "The beast that you saw was, and is not, and will ascend out of the bottomless pit and go to perdition."

Ionnes replayed those words. The beast that he saw, and is not, and will ascend. He repeated them a few times to make sure he got them right as he wrote.

The angel continued, "And, those who dwell on the Earth will marvel," his voice almost scolding after Ionnes' reaction to her. "And, those who dwell on the Earth will marvel, whose names are not written in the Book of Life from the foundation of the world, when the beast that was, and is not, and yet is."

"Was, and is not, and yet is," repeated Ionnes, recording the words to later dwell upon unto understanding the angel's meaning.

Ionnes praised Yeshua for bringing to clearer light the meanings of some of the visions.

The angel continued, "Here is the mind which has wisdom. The seven heads are seven mountains on which the woman sits."

"Seven mountains," scribbled Ionnes, and thought of Roma first before other places and localities.

The angel further said, "There are also seven kings. Five have fallen, one is, and the other has not yet come."

Ionnes considered the five kings as he wrote – Egypt? Assyria? Babylon? Medes and Persians? Greeks?

"One is," the angel had said.

"Roma?" thought Ionnes filling in his own blank considering the kingdom that crucified Christos and utterly destroyed Elohim's temple.

"The other has not yet come," spoke the angel.

"Another empire after Roma?" pondered Ionnes, and he wondered what this new and terrible kingdom would become. Whomever it was, they would continue for only a short time. He looked again at the seven-headed beast in a new and clearer light. Eternal damnation promised to be its fate. That included eternal pain and suffering apart from Yeshua for all time for those who bowed to it and to the harlot.

And, what of the ten horns which twisted and entwined each other, restricting the movement of all seven heads to move as one.

528

In answer as if the angel read Ionnes' mind, he said, "The ten horns which you saw are ten kings who have received no kingdom as yet, but they receive authority for one hour as kings with the beast. These are of one mind, and they will give their power and authority to the beast."

"Foolish ones," thought Ionnes, but did not write it.

"These will make war with the Lamb," said the angel, "and the Lamb will overcome them, for He is LORD of Lords and King of kings, and those who are with Him are called Chosen and Faithful."

Ionnes looked over at the throne room afar off, but within his divine sight. He considered the Lamb, the four creatures, the twenty-four elders, the martyrs under the altar, the many angels, and of course, the one-hundred-and-forty-four-thousand plus gathered around the throne to receive power and strength from the Lamb. He sized up the opponents. He knew the Almighty Father would be victorious, but having a bit of the heart of Christos, also felt great sadness at so many who would be lost to the dragon and its eternal damnation apart from Yeshua.

The angel then said to Ionnes as if to verify his grief, "The waters which you saw, where the harlot sits, are peoples, multitudes, nations and tongues."

"So many lost," Ionnes feared. "So many so sure they are right yet could never be more wrong."

The angel surprised Ionnes' musings as he said, "And the ten horns which you saw on the beast, these will hate the harlot, make her desolate, and naked, eat her flesh and burn her with fire. For God has put it into their hearts to fulfill His purpose, to be of one mind, and to give their kingdom to the beast, until the words of God are fulfilled."

Ionnes felt awestruck and for a moment considered the strange alliance of the ten horns serving the purposes of Yeshua, but then reconsidered that the horns – the ten kings may have turned on the harlot not out of righteousness or holiness, but out of simple, selfish greed for power.

"A house divided cannot stand," thought Ionnes, recalling the words of Yeshua in his own ears, oh so many years past.

The angel had one more thing to add.

"And the woman whom you saw is that great city which reigns over the kings of the Earth."

"Babylon," uttered Ionnes to himself, but in his mind he still pictured Roma, as he acknowledged the mighty angel. The two shared a gaze of absolute oneness in Christos, bound together by His Love; a Love that spread widely but not thinly across the nations. The angel nodded, then flew forth, fading away into Heaven's veil as Ionnes set down his quill to rub his eyes and wash them with an abundance of loving, gracious tears.

PATMOS

CHAPTER 37

"Still writin' yer masterpiece?" asked Dim, almost a demand. He wondered how many more times his fellow prisoner turned teacher would need to further leave his duties to grab papyrus and pen and write like a furious madman. He still did not fully understand the crazy scribblings Ionnes had composed, but he completely trusted the old man. The first episode, where it seemed Ionnes died still plagued Dim. He kept watchful eyes on alert. He had never composed a letter nearly so long. Never, and wondered how much longer until the letter was done.

Ionnes nodded as he placed a sizable chunk of marble onto an old, wooden cart. He felt the limitations of his old body but continued to move rock with purpose and even joy.

Dim's earlier evaluation of the quarry was coming true. The marble began to give way to dirt and granite. Huge sheets of gray marble were no longer available, and the prisoners mostly cut away marble chunks, some still quite large but ever shrinking in supply. Sometimes they had to brush off the dirt to determine if they were marble, granite, or some other igneous creation.

Dim and others had overheard mention that the Romans believed they would find lodes of gold or silver or precious something else if they kept digging. Probably one of Jack's jokes that went a bit too far, so now the Romans opted to find out and make sure the digs were really drying up. Nothing but ebbing marble thus far, noted Dim, swinging an axe with might and purpose into the now whittled and gradually sloping hill.

"How do you know?" Pterrkee had growled two or so years back, shortly after the angry Asian arrived.

"How d' I know what?" asked Dim, standing atop the marble cliff, pounding a wedge into the stone. He had stated the night before at dinner that the marble of the quarry would not last.

A new prisoner from Helikarrosos in Asia Minor, Pterrkee's anger peaked regularly. He would challenge prisoners just as aggressively as he would any Roman captor. His back and legs and neck displayed the bloody response from Roma to his hissing grumbles.

"Easy," answered Dim, wielding his sledge with accuracy and strength. Pterrkee, holding the wedge, waited for him to continue. Two others there also awaited answer, though remained quiet and focused on their tasks.

Dim tried to recall the two quiet workers. Neither of them shared their penal limitations any longer. Each died at the hand of a Roman soldier. Each fell beneath the Earth to flee Roman malice. He looked at Pterrkee to answer.

"We are on a hill, are we not? I went 'round t' the other side o' the hill," he pointed behind himself with a shift of his head. "There is no marble there at all."

Pterrkee glanced to the flat mesa behind them, its decline clearly seen.

"Then," continued Dim, "we checked the topsoil. See that line?" He pointed to a shallow trench in the dirt, now softened by wind and rain.

Pterrkee nodded.

"We tried t' see how far back the marble went. The end ya see is 'bout a dozen feet past where the marble shelf seemed t' end. I could be wrong, but I think the vein will dry up sooner than the dumb Romans think."

Pterrkee scoffed because that was his favorite answer to everything, but he saw the possibility to Dim's words.

"Why do you think the Romans see the vein as bigger?"

"Cuz," answered Dim, "they keep addin' men & tools & such. If they thought it would not produce marble much longer, they would not send more pris'ners."

Pterrkee scoffed again, but sort of smiled, his cheek muscles unaccustomed to such movements.

"It is a letter," answered Ionnes as he returned to grab another stone. He slyly looked about to check soldier stations. None were within earshot.

"A letter?" questioned Dim, also checking for guards.

"To the church," added Ionnes.

"It looks not like a letter," said Dim. "Ya let me read some."

"Aye," answered Ionnes. "and what did you think?"

Dim shrugged. "It is hard t' understand."

"That is because you are not Jewish, or from Jewish descent," said Ionnes. "I assure you the Jewish converts in the church will recognize the code."

Dim moved rock awhile before another question occurred.

"Why does it need t' be coded?"

Dim had to take a moment to collect the thoughts. In time he said, "I got t' read some other pages by Yeshua's church. Cephas & Paulos & Loucas. Even a couple by you. But, none o' ya wrote in any secret code. Why this time? What is Yeshua doin'?"

Ionnes knew the answer before the question could have been asked.

"It is Yeshua's will," he said, toying with Dim, fully knowing that answer would not satisfy Dim's curiosity even if it was ultimately the best and right answer. He smiled and waited a moment for Dim to give him "that look," then added, "My blessed child, I asked Yeshua the same question when first I started to see these visions. His answer was twofold."

Dim waited for him to continue.

"As you know, our captors like to intercept, read and even destroy our mail. So, when most Romans see this letter, they will say, 'See? These Christians are all lunatics, but when a Jewish born believer sees it, he will understand the meaning of the images, the numbers, the colors and everything else. It will be no more perplexing a code to him than a child learning his Alpha, Beta, Gammas.

"Second, Cæsar Domitian truly believes he is god on Earth. I can attest. I have met him. I recall only Cæsar Caligula a greater lunatic. Add to that Domitian's brother Titus and father Vespasian's attacks against the Jewish Rebellion and Ierusalem and the destruction of the temple by Titus' army. Domitian surely regards us from Iudæa as bugs to be squashed. He would like nothing better than to exterminate us, yet in Yeshua, our following grows every day. That makes a man who is sure of his own deity all the more frantic and motivated to snuff us out.

"Where the other letters you have read talk about life with Christos, this is Yeshua's letter to his children that Roma is not the last word. They may seem too powerful to overcome – for a season, but the LORD of Hosts overcomes nations in His time. He loves us who seek Him. He has not abandoned us and wants us to know His love more fully. It is because of pagan kingdoms like Roma that Adonai sent His Only Begotten Son to bring us a new freedom never before achieved."

Ionnes checked the guards once more as he grabbed another stone. The coast was clear.

"Now, if I wrote, 'Roma will fall,' then Yeshua's church would suffer all the more. But, when Yeshua through me writes, 'Babylon will fall,' the obscurity keeps Roma from performing greater persecutions - even all-out war against our people. We are far from over Roman persecution and occupation, I fear, but Yeshua promises us, validated by these visions, that Roma will be conquered and Yeshua's church set free."

"You are sure?" challenged Dim.

Ionnes smiled as he hefted a rock and winked, "As sure as the LORD God omnipotent reigns."

Dim came up from the quarry for dinner. He took time to get cleaned up after his day of dirty labor. A short cloudburst drenched everything late in the afternoon. He took advantage of the friendly deluge to wash himself thoroughly.

He became a bit chilled, but otherwise it felt marvelous to be clean. The clouds moved on and the sun moved downwind.

Others dined or chatted as he approached. Talor looked at him questioningly.

"What?" Dim's expression asked.

Talor's eyes moved towards the back lot.

Dim looked and saw Ionnes, seated upon a rock, papyrus, pen and ink in hand, but not writing. His eyes fluttered as though half asleep or entranced with a fever. Dim had seen this look before as had all. This time, Ionnes seemed more at ease than other times in the Spirit.

"No," corrected Talor.

Teos also looked concerned – an odd expression for the simple man.

Again, Dim questioned them with his eyes, and again Talor bobbed head towards Ionnes. Dim took the rein to see what troubled the teen.

Others watched him as he moved through the camp.

Rabbi Yosef and Seth fretted the most – not unusual for either. Phranc and even Minos looked concerned. Dim's curiosity increased with each man's questioning face.

He glanced at the guards. None of them seemed the least bit concerned. They chatted and told stories and laughed at their stations as usual.

Reaching Ionnes, he promptly saw the reason for their concerns. A wound the size of a sword blade crossed his lower abdomen. It looked gruesome though the blood had abated.

Dim touched Ionnes. He quickly awoke, looked at Dim and smiled greeting.

"What happened?" asked Dim, pointing to the wound.

Ionnes looked down then looked surprised.

"My my!" he exclaimed. "Where did that come from?"

Dim seemed more concerned with the injury than the man who endured it.

Talor approached behind Dim's lead; his courage hidden from him before that.

"Did ya see what happened?" asked Dim.

Talor looked a bit apprehensive and turned to see the guards who still seemed unconcerned with any of the prisoner activities.

"Ernesto," he said. "The guards saw Ionnes sitting here like one who slept. If I heard right, either a bet or dare was made by the others. Suddenly, Ernesto drew his sword, rushed forth and stabbed Ionnes in the gut. Ionnes did not so much as flinch. He sat quietly as though still asleep. Ernesto withdrew his sword. We could see the red blood inches up the shaft, yet the wound seemed to close up more quickly than I ever seen a wound close."

Ionnes looked down again at the stab.

"Wow!" he said and raised hands in praise to Yeshua.

"Does it hurt?" asked Dim.

Ionnes looked at Dim, then down at the wound. He pressed his hand around it, first carefully, then harder. He stood and carefully stretched. No. No pain.

"Praise Yeshua," said Dim. It was not an expression he heard himself say often, but when he did, it held great weight within his own mind.

"Amen," answered Ionnes and the others followed. "I am glad to still be with you. Apparently, Yeshua is not done with me here as yet."

Dim smiled. "Ya keep sayin' that."

"And, I keep meaning it, too," assured Ionnes. "Now if you will excuse me, I need to write something." He plopped down onto his rock again and started writing.

Dim watched him a while, then went to get some dinner. He kept a protective eye on his friend, though he wondered what he would have done if he had seen Ernesto attack the old man. Would he have kept to himself and even looked the other way? The old Dim most certainly would have. The new Dim felt the new life of Christos flow through his veins more powerfully than strong wine. Perhaps Yeshua was not done with Dim yet as well, keeping him busy with a rainstorm while Yeshua through his rabbi showed the Romans again he was not one they could just kill and be done with.

Meanwhile, Ionnes saw even another angel he did not recognize coming down from Heaven. The being shone brightly like the sun. The entire Earth glowed under his glory. He radiated great authority as he shouted to all, "Babylon the great is fallen, is fallen, and has become a dwelling place of demons, a prison for every foul spirit, and a cage for every unclean bird and a haunt for every unclean and detestable animal. For all the nations have drunk the maddening wine of her adulteries. The kings of the Earth have committed adultery with her, and the merchants of the Earth have become rich through the abundance of her luxury."

He peered at the angel as he heard another mighty voice come down from Heaven, commanding as from a judgment seat, "Come out of her, my people, lest you share in her sins, and lest you receive of her plagues. For her sins have piled up to Heaven, and God has remembered her iniquities. Give back to her just as she has given and repay her double according to her works. Pour her a double portion from her own cup. In the measure that she glorified herself and lived luxuriously, in the same measure give her torment and sorrow, for she says in her heart, 'I sit enthroned as queen. I am not a widow. I will never mourn.' Therefore, her plagues will come in one day – death, morning and famine. She will be utterly burned with fire, for mighty is the LORD God who judges her."

As Ionnes wrote, the herald's words reminded him of judgment of the harlot.

The voice from Heaven continued, "The kings of the Earth who committed fornication and lived luxuriously with her will weep and lament for her, when they see the smoke of her burning, standing at a distance for fear of her torment, saying, 'Woe! Woe to you, great city, you mighty city of Babylon! In one hour your doom has come!'"

Ionnes considered briefly the kings who would lament for her, but even more so considered the millions who would celebrate her demise. He glanced at the mighty angel still standing before him as he kept writing, and thought the voice completed its words, but then found it waited for Ionnes to finish writing before continuing.

"And, the merchants of the Earth will weep and mourn over her for no one buys their merchandise anymore; merchandise of gold and silver, precious stones and pearls, fine linen and purple, silk and scarlet, every kind of citron wood, every kind of object of ivory, every kind of object of most precious wood, bronze, iron, and marble; and cargoes of cinnamon and spice, of incense, myrrh and frankincense, of wine and olive oil, of fine flour and wheat, cattle and sheep, horses and chariots, and the bodies and souls of enslaved men."

"...bodies and souls of enslaved men," wrote Ionnes and stopped briefly to glance at the very men who dwelled and worked with him. How many had lost their souls, stolen by Roma, trampled beyond recognition before they could give them to Yeshua who would bless them and rebuild them and heal them and give souls back, restored and renewed.

The mighty voice lamented, "The fruit that your soul longed for has gone from you, and all the things which are rich and splendid have vanished, and you shall find them no more at all. The merchants of these things, who gained their wealth by her will stand at a distance, terrified at her torment, weeping and wailing, and saying, 'Alas, alas, that great city that was clothed in fine linen, purple and scarlet, and glittered with gold and precious stones and pearls!'"

Ionnes again saw the image of the harlot, dressed and adorned as described by the merchants.

"For in one hour such great riches came to nothing. Every sea captain, and all who travel by ship, sailors, and as many as trade on the sea, stood at a distance and cried out when they saw the smoke of her burning, saying, 'Was there ever a city like this great city?'

"They will throw dust on their heads and cry out, weeping and wailing, and saying, 'Alas, alas, that great city, in which all who had ships on the sea became rich by her wealth! For in one hour she is made desolate.'"

Ionnes felt a sense of anticipation and jubilation begin to build up from above. Sounds of joyous laughter feathered

538

down upon him. The mighty voice announced with gladness, "Rejoice over her, O Heaven. Rejoice you people of God! Rejoice, apostles and prophets! For God has judged her with the judgment she imposed on you."

The air became fragrantly sweet as Ionnes could scarcely breathe-in all the life which abounded above and before him. Then, the mighty angel turned and lifted up a mighty stone the size of a large millstone. Ionnes watched his strength with awe. The huge stone pressed upon him terribly, yet he held it aloft, flexed like a cat ready to spring then vigorously threw it into the sea. Turning back towards Ionnes, he announced to all who could hear, "Thus with violence the great city Babylon shall be thrown down, never to be found again. The music of harpists, musicians, flutists, and trumpeters shall not be heard in you anymore. No craftsman of any craft shall be found in you anymore, and the sound of a millstone shall not be heard in you anymore.

"The light of a lamp shall not shine in you anymore, and the voice of the bridegroom and bride shall not be heard in you anymore. For your merchants were the great men of the Earth, for by your sorcery all the nations were deceived. And, in her was found the blood of the prophets and saints, and of all who were slain on the Earth."

Ionnes threw down his pen, staining the page. He gasped air to take it all in. He saw the destruction of Roma like one sitting first row in the amphitheater. It brought him joy, but also greater pain for the lost.

"Clement," he cried, recalling the bishop in Roma. Then, he sighed and knew Yeshua had not forgotten His church in Roma. Even as the city burned, Yeshua's Spirit would shine brightly there.

His musings were interrupted by the sounds of a great multitude in Heaven, crying out in unison, "Alleluia! Salvation and glory and honor and power belong to the LORD our God! For true and righteous are His judgments because He has judged the great harlot who corrupted the Earth with her fornication, and He has avenged on her the blood of His servants."

Ionnes reveled in the spirit of jubilation. The celebration filled the vast spaces all around him. His feet danced merrily upon the dirt. He loved the sounds filling the heavens and the Earth and had to wipe away tears of joy and gladness as he wrote. Some joyful drops covered the pages set before him. He let the tears be. They belonged on that page more than the inked words they celebrated.

Again, they said, "Alleluia! Her smoke rises up forever and ever!"

Ionnes set down his pad and pen to kneel, then fall forward as he saw the four living creatures and the twenty-four elders fall forward and worship God who sat on the throne. He gasped with joy, again inside the throne room of Heaven. The four creatures and elders had been gone from his sight for so long, and he felt surprise to see them come forth at this time. All fell down upon the glassy surface to worship God who sat on the throne. Their voices rang out clearly and distinctly.

"Amen!"

"Alleluia!" they added in the same flow of praise and worship.

"Amen! Alleluia!" Ionnes spoke along with them.

Then, a dynamic voice exploded from the throne to all in Heaven who had ears to hear.

> "PRAISE OUR GOD,
> ALL YOU HIS SERVANTS
> AND THOSE WHO FEAR HIM,
> SMALL AND GREAT!"

Every voice around him replied in unison, like the flowing of a mighty river over many stones, pounding and thundering and together proclaiming, "Alleluia! For our LORD God Omnipotent reigns! Let us be glad and rejoice and give Him glory, for the Marriage of the Lamb has come, and His Bride has made herself ready. Fine linen, bright and clean, was given her to wear," (for the fine linen is the righteous acts of God's holy people.)

Ionnes replayed the voice through his head - a voice like many waters. A voice like Yeshua's at the first sight of his

LORD and God. But, no. It was different, though he could not rightly say exactly how.

He sighed with contentment at the sight, then realized he had scarcely noticed the angel, still beside him. He looked up to that magnificent being who nodded to affirm Ionnes' amazement and satisfaction. He pointed outward towards the Heavenly host, then down at the papyrus Ionnes held.

"Write!" he commanded, as Yeshua had commanded at the start. "Write: Blessed are those who are invited to the wedding supper of the Lamb!"

"Yeshua never married," thought Ionnes. Now he could see why, at least from his human eyes. Yeshua's marriage would never be with one woman, but with an entire church; an entire society. He felt the love again like when he laid his head upon Yeshua's bosom. No bridegroom ever loved his bride more than the Lamb that is Yeshua.

"These are the true words of God," added the angel.

Ionnes, filled with the flow of the Spirit, beheld the mighty being before him, speaking to him. He shuddered greatly to the foundations of his own being and fell forward to worship the one before him. But the angel touched Ionnes and said strongly though not sternly, "See that you do not do that! I am a fellow servant, and of your brothers and sisters who hold to the testimony of Yeshua. Worship God! For it is the Spirit of prophesy who bears testimony of Yeshua."

Ionnes raised himself up on his haunches a bit awkwardly and remembered the numerous times he had told others to not worship him. He nodded solemnly at the angel, then sat to resume writing in the Spirit of Prophesy. At one point, he shook and wrung out his hand to relieve the cramps threatening to thwart his divine stenography. He laughed to himself. This journey was beyond anything he had ever imagined or encountered, and that was saying a lot. Even better, he knew it to be far from over.

"What did it look like when Heaven opened?" mused Ionnes to himself over the many days past. Ionnes had heard the expression before and had often wondered what it could possibly look like.

Noah saw the heavens open when the rains began. Ionnes wondered what the skies displayed at that time, for Elohim changed the Earth after the flood. He knew not in what manner, but all knew the lifespan of all became shorter and shorter after Noah.

Ionnes thought of Ezekiel who saw Heaven open to bring visions of God.

Daniel probably saw the Heavens open as well, though he did not say it that way.

Then, Ionnes recalled Stephanos, just before being stoned by young Saul, seeing Heaven open and Yeshua on the throne. He also recalled Micaiah, the prophet of Israel during Ahab's reign who saw God in His throneroom with the Heavenly host.

Likewise, he recalled the words of Cephas when Heaven thrice opened to him the vision of a large cloth dropping down to reveal many animals no longer forbidden to eat.

Ionnes had seen so many awesome things throughout his life. And, now he could add how Heaven opened to release his LORD and Redeemer, Faithful and True, riding forth on a white horse. What a vision! Eyes like flames of fire. Many crowns on His head for each nation. A name showed upon Him. Ionnes could not read the words and realized no angels or men or martyrs could read the name, either.

In turn, he thought of the similar feature with the name of God - a name which no man could pronounce.

YHWH

The Rider wore brilliant, white vestments dipped in His blood. Without a word spoken, Ionnes knew His title - The Word of God.

"And, in the beginning was the Word and the Word was with God and the Word was God."

Ionnes recalled the account of Yeshua's life he had penned, starting with those very words.

Now, as the visions unfolded and moved alive before him, he noticed many soldiers who followed Yeshua, also upon white horses, and also clothed in white linen.

The Faithful and True rider leading the great army looked fiercely down at the nations of the Earth. A sharp sword protruded from His mouth, much like the original vision of Yeshua that Ionnes had witnessed. It slashed forth to smite entire nations. The sins and rebellions of so many required He rule with a rod of iron. With fierceness, he attacked like a whirlwind winepress.

Ionnes wondered that none of the other warriors attacked. They followed Yeshua into battle, but His was the only One to complete the attack. He looked again at Yeshua, riding forth upon His white horse. He could not read the written name upon His robe earlier, but now the words made sense, much like things change in a dream and the new sight just seems right.

KING OF KINGS AND LORD OF LORDS

The words shown clearly upon Yeshua's robe and thigh. He was the King of nations perhaps even more than He reigned as the King of hearts. The dark evil of the world made the truth of Christos shine that much more brightly.

"Come and gather together for the supper of the great God."

Ionnes heard the words but had to look for its source. The sun shone brightly above. The voice continued and seemed to come out of the sun itself. "Besides Yeshua God, only an angel could do that," thought Ionnes as he recorded the voice saying, "...that you may eat the flesh of kings, generals, and the flesh of mighty men, the flesh of horse and of those who sit on them, and the flesh of all people, free and slave, both small and great."

The image of the angel in the sun became apparent as he spoke, and millions of birds gathered throughout the region, filling the sky, awaiting the fulfillment of God's Word which beckoned them.

Ionnes looked down to the Earth. The beast still lumbered along as it led many. The kings of the Earth mobilized their armies. Ionnes wondered if they would war against one another.

No! They came together to make war upon the Lamb; against Him who sat on the throne and His army of angels.

The battle ensued. The angels targeted the beast and the false prophet. The kings and their armies who wore the sign of the beast saw both of their leaders captured. The warriors waited anxiously as the pair were carried away from the fields of battle.

Ionnes felt a hot blast from one side. He looked and saw a huge, deep lake alive and burning with fire. Steep, smooth walls bordered the lake, so none could escape. He looked upwards and saw the angels carrying both the beast and false prophet. They hovered over the lake of fire but a moment, then threw both of them forth. They were not dropped. Gravity would not bring them down. They were placed forcefully by the angels. The beast and false prophet tried to cling to the angels, but they were powerless to stop the eternal judgment awaiting them.

Ionnes heard their cries, but his attention soon turned back to the kings of the Earth and their armies. They ran forward to continue the war against the Lamb and His angels. They advanced full force towards Yeshua. He responded in no way idle even before His sword-like tongue flashed out of His mouth, killing the entire army and kings.

Ionnes watched the rebellious hearts enter mortality with more speed than an angel of death visited old Egypt. There were none left to bury the bodies, and the birds swooped down in great, uncounted numbers to feast upon the freshly fallen.

Ionnes saw the cruelties which made up the armies of the kings. Still, he wept for their deaths as he had seen Yeshua do for many when He walked the Earth. Justice and judgment still filled him with grief, yet he knew Yeshua's judgments broke the LORD's own heart all the more than his own.

"We named him Ionnes," said the happy father, entering the House of Myron. They had not converted to Christos but had heard Ionnes and the church met there on Sundays.

The mama beamed as she held their newborn before the prisoner prophet.

"Our parents were displeased we gave him a Greek name," he added.

"You could change it to my Jewish name, Yochanan," teased Ionnes, "though I suspect they would not like that any better."

Ionnes touched the little hands and face. The swaddled child moved a bit but kept sleeping. He made the sign of the fish on the child's forehead as he prayed, "Yeshua, give this one Your greatest love and life. He shall be," - he paused, and looked at the couple, back and forth. Looking down again at the child, he said, "He shall be - a master of horses. The stallions and mares already whisper his name." He beamed at the small being.

"Yeshua died for your sins, also," he mouthed to one who as yet knew no sin. Leaning over, he kissed the baby's forehead, and nodded his approval to the pleased and proud parents.

Ionnes gazed long and hard at the couple.

"Oh, wow!" he said, looking at the woman. "How do you feel about triplets next time?" Both parents gasped.

"Just kidding," said Ionnes with a laugh. The slaves in attendance also enjoyed the joke. "You should have seen your faces. If I could sculpt…"

He took hold of the dad's wrist.

"Still has a pulse but feels like it skipped a few beats."

The trio laughed, then hushed as the baby stirred and stretched a bit, then nestled down again.

"You should have seen the governor's face when we told him," grinned the dad. "He said, 'Does not surprise me,' but I could tell it did."

"Come," invited Ionnes. "We are about to get started. You would honor us with your presence."

He led the trio to the meeting room with an unhurried gait and a hand holding the wall for support. As the meeting started, the new father stood to address the assembly.

"Salve," he greeted all. "I see some familiar faces here, but most of you I know not. My wife and I have come to share a story with you. As you can see, we are new parents. We tried for years to start a family, but it seemed that the gods were against us. Then, about a year ago, we went to see the Governor, Laurentius. We saw he was with a prisoner, and we dared not interfere. Then, to our surprise, this prisoner - more like a fossil, and older than the back side of Janus, walked out somewhat unassisted. The guards came forth, yet they did not shackle him or manhandle him, but walked as though they were going to afternoon lunch.

"Then, even more surprising, this old lunatic stopped before us. He touched my wife, and I was about to order the guards to remove his life right there. His assault upon my wife struck me as mortally wrong. But, the guards did nothing, and before I could really react, he said to my wife that she would be a mother before the year was over. If we thought him not mad before that moment, we knew it with full certainty the next. He then muttered words of blessing us or something and moved on.

"We asked the governor who that was, and he said a Christian zealot. We considered his words, but honestly, we were mostly glad he was gone. Then, as you can all see, to our amazement and joy, his prophesy came true. We are proud to share with you our son, Ionnes, named after this crazy, old man who saw the ways of the gods."

Most heard his references to the gods and wondered if they should say anything. They looked to Ionnes who allowed him to finish.

"So, we came today to thank this prophet of the gods and to share with him the joy of our life." He turned to Ionnes.

"Thank you, dear father. Thank you with all I can give."

Ionnes went forward and the two shook arms. He nodded respectfully to the mother.

"The sight of you two with your new son thrills me in more ways than I can count," said Ionnes. "I stand as Yeshua's witness, for it was His Spirit that blessed your womb, and shared with me the good news to come."

The young father nodded but looked more serious.

"We know the gods," he said. "Of Jupiter and Juno and Apollo. And, we have heard of The Way, but all I have heard of your sect only verifies what I have thought all along – that the gods, led by Jupiter, have given you a great gift with the one you call Yeshua, and like Romulus, Remus and Hercules, he should be numbered among the great demigods. You, yourselves teach He is a Son, and we believe His father to be one of the gods – probably Jupiter."

Some gasped a bit, but most waited to see what Ionnes would do.

Ionnes placed his hands together, closed eyes, and assumed a position of prayer. When he opened his eyes, he said with earnest consideration, "It was not Jupiter or Juno or Apollo who brought Yeshua to life. Yeshua created all that is and was and will be. He is the LORD of Lords and King of kings. He is the only God Almighty. He is not made of stone or metal, to be on display in your home. He created all the universe, including all of us, yet He loves each of us more than you or even I can imagine.

"So, my friends, I am blessed to see your new son has come. Yeshua's Holy Spirit told me it would be so and be not upset that I say the gods did not bless you. Yeshua, and Yeshua, alone has given you this great gift."

The young Roman father nodded, but clearly still disagreed.

"We still wanted to honor you for your prophetic words, but we will not deny the gods." He motioned to his wife, and they departed without another word. Their son began to fuss and cry as they exited the room.

A stillness stayed with the room a spell. Ionnes knelt forward in prayer for the young couple. He had been down this road many times – many more times than any other in the room. Sometimes it took more than even a miracle for others to see the full light of Christos.

"I am sorry," said Apollonides. "Perhaps I should talk with them."

Ionnes turned and smiled at his young convert.

"That would be perfect," he said, "but, let it come in Yeshua's timing. Do not come charging in with a four-horse chariot. Invite them to dine or share a drink with them. Offer to share your time with their son as he grows. I know not how soon Yeshua will return, so take not too long, but share with them your story and your sister's and the others. Yeshua knows them better than they know themselves."

"But," argued Apollonides, "they came to argue against Yeshua."

Ionnes' compassion flowed easily. "No. They came to share their joy."

Apollonides started to get agitated.

"Apollonides!" consoled Ionnes. "I love your zeal for Yeshua – truly I do but, forget not your journey to this point. It took more than a demon deliverance to bring you to Him. Be compassionate. You already have your own powerful testimony of deliverance to share with them. And, even more, take heart. Your job is already half done."

Everyone stopped to wonder what Ionnes meant by that – the job was already half done.

Ionnes explained, "They already admit Yeshua is at least part God. Now show them the rest of Him, and they will know the truth that set free all of us here."

Apollonides nodded. Part of him absolutely wanted to charge in and demand their allegiance to Christos, so much so that his sword would take them to their gods if they refused, but if there was anything he had learned from Yeshua, it was a bit of patience. And, he had never been a particularly patient man.

He placed a hand on Ionnes' shoulder and nodded agreement. He would try his best to use honey instead of old wine vinegar to share the gospel.

Ionnes turned to the three Roman guards who attended to them each Sunday.

"My brothers," he said, "I know your duties, but I also know your flexibilities. I would appreciate some time alone this day to go upon the mountain to pray. My friend and brother, Prochorus, can continue in my absence."

Two guards looked to the leader. He nodded to one to attend and stay with the old apostle.

"Not for too long," he said as they departed.

"I promise," said Ionnes, thanking him.

The autumn wind blew with a bit of a chill, but still not uncomfortable. Ionnes breathed in the freshness and the sea salt carried with it as he waited for the Roman guard to walk with him.

"So, what do you make of all this?" he asked the soldier.

The soldier felt like he should disapprove, so Ionnes added, "Honestly?"

"Are you trying to convert me, zealot?"

Ionnes smiled. "Always."

The two men laughed.

"I still do not get it," said the soldier.

"What is that?" asked Ionnes.

"You are a prisoner of Roma."

"Yes."

"But sometimes you act like you are supposed to be here."

"You are correct. Yeshua guides my steps, and He brought me to you."

"Well," continued the Roman, "when I first saw you I woulda rather spit on ye then give ya the time of day."

"And now?" asked Ionnes.

"I will at most point you to the sundial."

"Praise Yeshua," chuckled Ionnes. "We are making progress."

The men walked along silently a spell, partially from Ionnes breathing heavily from the strain of the uphill climb. He knew where he was going before they left. He turned off the dirt trail to return to the cave. Not that it was a holier place than anywhere. No rain loomed overhead, so cover was not needed. He merely enjoyed his earlier visit, and everyone loves to explore even a small cave. He entered the rock opening and followed the shape of the cave with his right hand. Eventually, he turned back, and facing the opening, knelt upon the dirt to pray. He felt the Spirit fill him to overflowing and let the power move through his old bones like water down a steep, wooden chute.

The Roman took a load off, sitting against the rock wall. It felt good to be off his feet. He leaned his back against a wall, and before he knew it, he fell fast asleep. He could not perceive that the Holy Spirit literally put him out of commission for a spell. One moment awake. The next moment unconscious.

Ionnes knew the truth taking place behind him. He enjoyed the unhurried moment to pull out his papyrus and pen for the Spirit already told him the next words to write.

He saw the image before him and wrote, "Then, I saw an angel coming down from Heaven, having the key to the bottomless pit and a great chain in his hand. He laid hold of the dragon, that serpent of old who is the Devil, or Satan, and bound him for a thousand years. He cast him into the Abyss and shut him up, and set a seal on him, so that he should deceive the nations no more till the thousand years were finished. But, after these things he must be set free for a short time."

There appeared many thrones. Upon the thrones sat those who had been beheaded for their witness to Yeshua and for the Word of God. Ionnes saw many who remained in the grave – even martyrs, for the thousand years as the dragon was chained. The beheaded martyrs ruled as priests with Christos on high.

And, so Ionnes wrote as a thousand years passed before him with immeasurable haste. He expected his own beard to reach to his feet before the thousand years passed. He felt great joy when the dragon was bound and exiled, then anguish to see it released, even for a little while for Ionnes knew with full certainty that nothing good would come from his freedom. As Yeshua released the dragon by His own will, Ionnes completely trusted that his LORD knew what He was doing.

The dragon did not escape by its own strength or wit. The dragon did not overpower its captors. No others in homage to the dragon came to free it. Whatever lies spoken by the dragon as it found the sweetness of release, the truth of its freedom still shone exposed. The same compassion and mercy Yeshua gave to all who walked the Earth, He gave also to the dragon. He knew with complete certainty that the dragon would again rise against Him. He knew many men would foolishly follow the dragon. The dragon's release was not in ignorance or disinterest. No. No. No. The dragon would serve Yeshua's Spirit and needs, even in defiance. The dragon's war would bring the final judgment. The final judgment would bring the final and everlasting Peace upon the Earth. Each person alive would choose which everlasting judgment he or she would face.

Every human soul lived forever – they just had to decide where.

Ionnes saw the dragon race off with a vengeance to stir up the masses into a tizzy. Men and women everywhere seemed to accept the foolish deceptions Satan poured out on all flesh. For it deceived not only men but full nations, spinning and twirling and tangling anyone who would listen from the four corners of the Earth.

"Gog," muttered Ionnes, writing, "and Magog." The words of Ezekiel flooded to mind. The war of wars described by the prophet of old. Ionnes received true glimpses from Ezekiel's experience. He saw the barren lands and fallen soldiers and the LORD hid His face from them that the enemies of Yisra'el would destroy. He saw the allies to Gog from Libya in the west, Ethiopia in the south, and even Persia far to the north. He saw the armies numbered like the sand of the sea, taking position around the beloved city, Ierusalem, where the saints all prepared, encamped. Ionnes' memory recalled the fallen city only twenty-six years earlier. The temple brought to complete and utter ruin. The ark of the covenant still gone only Yeshua knew where.

Gog laid siege upon the beloved city, and all saw the approaching end.

Then fire came down, faster than lightning, out of Heaven, devouring Gog's armies. What had seemed utterly impossible only moments before suddenly became cause to celebrate.

Ionnes breathed his own sigh of relief. He had fretted for those imprisoned within the holy city. Now they could come forth without fear. They who followed the dragon watched as it was thrown into the lake of fire – this unending, sulfurous slag of heat and pain, alongside the beast and the false prophet, still there in judgment after the thousand plus years. If they thought the thousand years long, they would find that far less than the never-ending torment, void of day or night, forever and ever.

Ionnes felt his apprehensions abate. Ionnes, who feared when the dragon was released, could now praise Yeshua unfettered and free.

Then, for the first time, Ionnes saw the throne, great and white it shone, and Him who sat upon it.

"Yeshua," Ionnes sighed, shivered and shuddered. Every trial Ionnes had endured over the decades suddenly seemed insignificant and small compared to the sight of Yeshua before him.

Many stood before the throne. Many trembled. Many feared. Many gasped as the books with each man's sins were opened by the Almighty.

Then, another book was opened. Ionnes recognized it. The Book of Life. Those dead would be judged according to their works by the writings in the Book.

Many souls continued to approach the throne of God.

Ionnes saw the sea give up its dead. Then, Death and Hades came forth, delivering up the dead in their care. Each knew judgment, according to their words. Then, as Yeshua completed His judgments of men, Death and Hades were also cast into the endless and eternal Lake of Fire.

Ionnes watched with great sadness how many were condemned. He wept inconsolably as so many were likewise cast into the great Lake of Fire. The screams of torment filled the region for a spell. Their wails filled Ionnes' ears and head as he wrote his last words of the day. He set aside his pages and knelt in homage to Yeshua. He thought he knew his Savior and Redeemer. He clearly saw he had been wrong, and he gave glory and praise to this King of Kings and LORD of Lords as he tucked away his papyrus and pen.

At that moment the soldier awoke, refreshed, and apparently unaware he had been asleep. He rose, ready to move.

"Done?" he asked Ionnes.

Ionnes struggled to his feet and nodded respectfully to the soldier. The soldier did not seem to notice the lateness of the hour as they trekked down the hill back to the barracks. Ionnes expected Yeshua's mercy would be shown to this one whom He had put to sleep when he returned to the soldiers' barracks. No ribbing or correction would come to him this time.

PATMOS

CHAPTER 38

Ionnes gasped. The sky disappeared. The heavens fell away, rolling up like an old garment. No sun. No moon. No stars. No clouds. No sky. Even Yeshua's throne room, gone. Then, the very Earth beneath and around him also shriveled up to nothing. No land and no sea. He floated upon nothing. Everything he had seen became a nonexistent void and he wondered if this was the eternal abyss God had before creation.

He tried to look around but felt suspended and locked within that exact moment. No time. No space. Less than nothing.

He wondered about the other disciples who had rejected the mark of the beast. Where could they have gone? Where were the four living creatures, the twenty-four elders and countless angels? And, for that matter, what of the dragon, the beast, the false prophet, those judged and the Lake of Fire? This resembled the bottomless pit, though he knew he occupied it not.

Eyes and ears became useless instruments as did his lungs. Only his mind seemed alive.

For the immeasurable moment.

Then, he detected the light.

Small in measure, or very far away? He could not tell. His interest captured more than a dot of ink on a blank page, he watched the beautiful light spread and grow and take shape as he briefly thought of Light, Adonai's first creation in Genesis. If he had a breath, it would have been taken away as he saw the new Heaven spread-out magnificently overhead and wrap around him like an unimaginably huge feathered comforter flowing over, then cascading in and all around him. The throne room of Heaven likewise unfolded anew. He had been completely awed at the earlier visions of Heaven and God's throne room. This new encounter outshone anything he could speak or imagine. No words could come. He could only squeak indiscernible noises as the nothing became somewhere for his voice to travel.

The light flowed. New clouds formed. He looked down and realized he was standing on dry land, but the trees and mountains and everything else around him defied description. All transformed anew, he appreciated the poor, blind beggar in the Pool of Siloam seeing the daylight for the first time.

He took a deep breath. The air filled his lungs sweeter than after a thunder storm. The New Heavens and New Earth continued to move and dance and tumble amazingly about him. Then, he saw far above a huge, golden cube moving towards him. He watched with fascination, trying to figure out what he witnessed. As it continued down, growing in size and perspective, his mind shuddered as he realized he saw the New Ierusalem, the holy city, coming down out of Heaven from Yeshua, prepared like a bride adorned for her husband.

As the amazing, impressive city continued its descent, he heard a loud voice cry out from the throne room where the New Ierusalem had first appeared. Like the great herald, the voice said:

> "Behold, the tabernacle of God is with men,
> And He shall dwell with them,
> And they shall be His peoples,
> And God Himself shall be with them,
> And be their God.
> And He shall wipe away every tear from their eyes;
> And death shall be no more,
> Neither shall there be mourning,
> Nor crying, nor pain, any more:
> The first things are passed away."

Ionnes prayed for that day as his old bones creaked. He looked towards the throne, alive in its new splendor. The One on the throne looked at Ionnes, then all around as He said, "Behold, I make all things new."

Looking again at His little scribe, He added, "Write this down, for these words are trustworthy and true."

His words shot directly to Ionnes' ears. "It is done! I am the Alpha and the Omega, the Beginning and the End. To the thirsty I will give water without cost from the spring of the water of life. Those who are victorious will inherit all this, and I will be their God and they will be My children. But, the cowardly, unbelieving, abominable, murderers, sexually immoral, sorcerers, idolaters and all liars – they will be consigned to the fiery lake of burning sulfur. This is the second death."

No sooner had Ionnes finished writing the words when he became again filled with grief over the lost souls. This he learned long ago from Yeshua, and though He spoke judgment of the world from His throne, Ionnes knew it broke His heart more than any could imagine. His love for all exceeded all.

As Ionnes stewed, an angel approached. He looked up at the being and recognized him as one of the seven angels who emptied a bowl filled with one of the seven last plagues. He saw the pain in Ionnes' spirit, so spoke words of comfort.

"Come," he said. "I will show you the bride, the Lamb's wife."

Ionnes barely nodded acknowledgment when he was suddenly lifted-up on high to be carried away in the Spirit of Yeshua. Up, up, up the angel took him to the highest mountain Ionnes had yet stood upon.

No sooner had Ionnes found his footing when the angel directed attention up to the sky above. Ionnes looked upward to see an extraordinary sight – a city descending from Heaven. A new creation like everything else; one God constructed over the centuries. Nothing built in merely six days. Ionnes watched with awe as the glory of God shone brightly forth from the floating city. It hurt his eyes to see it, bright and glowing like many lights made into one, like jasper but clear as crystal.

A large, protective wall surrounded the descending city, the wall flowing into four equal sides. Ionnes saw three gates on one side. An angel stood guard above each gate. The angel took him to see each side of the city. Another three gates and angels appeared, then another three on the far side, and finally another three on the last side. Twelve gates and angels in all, east, north, south and west, and above each gate, the name of a tribe of Yisra'el. The true names, not like he had seen days earlier with twelve-thousand from each tribe of Yisra'el making up the one-hundred-and-forty-four-thousand.

Ionnes also noticed the twelve foundations of the walls. Each foundation stone bore the name of an apostle of the Lamb. Ionnes dwelled a moment longer as he saw his own name before one of the gates. He felt twinges of unworthiness and/or total humility. If he could have, he would have removed his name and placed the many names of Yeshua upon every wall foundation.

He had read each apostle name as he circled the beautiful city, but like the elusive dream, he could not recall whether he saw the name of Judas Iscariot or Paulos at the foundation. He wished to circle around again to see when his host, the angel produced a golden reed. Ionnes peered at the reed questioningly, so the angel moved forth to measure the dimensions of the city with the reed.

Ionnes gasped. He had studied the city before him for some time, now, but he still did not expect it to measure so big – twelve thousand furlongs, height, breadth and width. All equal.

Then, the angel measured the protective wall. One-hundred-and-forty-four cubits, according to the measure of a man. Or, that is, the measure of an angel.

The wall looked like it had been constructed out of jasper, but the city resembled pure gold, almost transparent like clear glass. Everything reflected everything in the golden splendor.

The foundations were also adorned with precious and semi-precious gemstones and colors. Ionnes wrote each as it broadly passed overhead as far as he could see in either direction.

The first foundation matched the wall, being made of clear, sometimes white, sometimes deep red jasper.

The second foundation a dark blue sapphire.

The third foundation whitish green chalcedony.

The fourth foundation green emeralds.

The fifth foundation dark reddish sardonyx.

The sixth foundation dark red ruby.

The seventh foundation lime green chrysolite.

The eighth foundation blue-green beryl.

The ninth foundation golden brown topaz.

The tenth foundation light green chrysoprase or turquoise.

The eleventh foundation deep, dark orange jacinth.

The twelfth foundation purple amethyst.

The array of colors both striking and beautiful.

Then, each gate looked to be made of one giant pearl. The translucent orbs made from the shed blood of one of Yeshua's sea creatures became the entranceway to the New Ierusalem. The gate opened to reveal golden streets transparent as glass.

Ionnes entered to walk with bare feet on the perfect road. As he continued to explore, he noted there stood no temple. This perplexed him briefly until he realized the LORD God Almighty and the Lamb were its temple. Likewise, the city needed not the sun nor the moon to shine, but the glory of God fully illuminated it. The Lamb shone brightly as its everlasting, eternal light.

Ionnes saw those saved enter the city to walk in His glorious light. Even repentant kings brought their glory and honor to the city. As Ionnes toured, he noticed all gates ever open, as though the pearl doors were unneeded for the gates would remain open during the forever day. No night would fill the city ever.

Then, Ionnes noted the forgiven purity of those inside. None defiled. None to speak abomination. No lies. Only those whose names were written in the Lamb's Book of Life could enter. He felt the perfect warmth of all within and wished he would never leave.

The sounds of running water somewhere close by captured Ionnes' attention. Led by the angel, they followed the sound to a pure river flowing with the Water of Life, clearer than pristine crystal. Ionnes followed the upward flow of the river, literally coming down from the throne of the Father and the Lamb. Following the river further, Ionnes and the angel came upon a large tree in the middle of the street. Ionnes looked questioningly at the angel who indicated it was the Tree of Life. Ionnes stopped to take it in. The Tree of Life, like in Eden? The tree that would make anyone to live forever? The tree forbidden to be eaten by Adam and Eve in Eden?

He studied the tree. It bore much fruit which changed each month. Twelve types of tasty, succulent fruit in all, and its leaves Yeshua created for the healing of the nations. With such healing, there shall be no more curse upon the New Earth as the Lamb shall dwell with men upon the Earth. They shall serve Him. They shall see His face and His name emblazoned upon their foreheads. And, in the everlasting day, the LORD shall reign forever and ever.

Then, Ionnes and the angel suddenly stood upon the old Earth as the vision dissolved away, but the angel spoke words of encouragement to Ionnes as he said, "These words are faithful and true." Ionnes then remembered how the LORD God sent His angels to show His servants the things which would shortly take place. He heard the words of Yeshua in his mind, "Behold, I am coming quickly! Blessed is he who keeps the words of the prophecy of this book."

Ionnes heard and shook at the voice. Looking at the angel, he fell forward again to worship at the feet of the angel who had shown him so many things. But again, the angel lovingly rebuked him, saying, "See that you do not do that. For I am your fellow servant, and of your brethren the prophets, and of those who keep the words of this book."

The angel raised his hands to the heavens.

"Worship God," he cried with great joy and exuberance. Then, he dropped his arms and turned towards Ionnes to share a serious warning.

"Do not seal up the words of the prophecy of this book, for the time is at hand. He who is unjust, let him be unjust still. He who is filthy, let him be filthy still. He who is righteous, let him be righteous still. He who is holy, let him be holy still."

As Ionnes listened, he realized his confusion. The words the angel spoke sounded like Yeshua, but he was only the spiritual embodiment as Yeshua's messenger. He spoke the words of Yeshua as Yeshua directly moved through him to speak, and Ionnes considered better understanding of the Angel within the burning bush before Moses.

"And behold," continued the angel, "I am coming quickly, and My reward is with Me, to give to everyone according to what they have done."

Ionnes considered that, for he knew they were saved by faith and not by their works. It took not long to consider Yeshua's meaning. As Yeshua's own earthly brother, Yaakov, had written, Father Abraham himself, the man of faith made his faith known by his works. Ionnes knew so many who tried to clean up their acts before coming to Yeshua. He always counselled them the same – come first to Yeshua and let Him change you into what He wants you to be. Your divine and blessed works would always follow.

He also recalled Yeshua speaking the parable of the sheep and the goats. They were judged strictly on what they did or did not do.

"I am the Alpha and the Omega, the Beginning and the End, the First and the Last," relayed the messenger of the LORD. "Blessed are those who wash their robes, that they may have the right to the tree of life and may go through the gates of the city."

Ionnes knew no sin could dwell in Yeshua's New Ierusalem, so was sad to be brought back to the present with the words, "But, outside are dogs and sorcerers and sexually immoral and murderers and idolaters, and whoever loves and practices falsehood."

Ionnes knew Yeshua would never bear false witness against His children. The devil spoke enough lies to fill the world once over again and again.

"I, Yeshua, have sent My angel to testify to give you this testimony for the churches." Ionnes, scribbling away, could not wait to share this with Prochorus who would write the copies to be sent to the seven churches of Asia Minor and beyond.

Yeshua then said, "I am the Root and the Offspring of David, and the Bright and Morning Star."

Ionnes sighed. He missed his LORD so much. It was beyond good to see Him again. The lineage of David to bring the guiding light of life. He felt the Spirit's flow through his being like the river of the New Ierusalem. He felt the love of

Yeshua fill him to overflowing. He could not contain his excitement as he heard their final words.

"Come."

The Spirit and the Bride spoke together as one.

"And, let the one who hears say, 'Come!' Let the one who is thirsty come; and let the one who wishes take the free gift of the Water of Life."

Ionnes' feet danced around with joy as he wrote those words.

Finishing, he laid down his pen. He looked at the words he had written and made a few corrections for clarity. As he reread, he knew these final words would not complete the letter to the seven churches. Yeshua had intended this to be for them and beyond. He gave them His Words to bless and correct them. Now, He had also given them these prophesies to encourage them. Yeshua never lost control. Roma would fall. Judgment would absolutely come.

He picked up his quill again. Dipping it deeply in the last of the ink, he almost touched the pen to the papyrus. He paused. What words did he need to say to close this amazing letter? A sense of warning arose in his mind for the gnostics would always try to rewrite anything Ionnes and the other disciples wrote. Yeshua's inspired words were not meant for others to edit and change to suit their personal, misguided beliefs.

Thus, by his hand guided by Yeshua's Holy Spirit, he wrote, "For I testify to everyone who hears the words of the prophesy of this book. If anyone adds to these things, God will add to him the plagues that are written in this book, and if anyone takes away from the words of the book of this prophesy, God shall take away his part from the Book of Life, from the holy city, and from the things which are written in this book.

"He who testifies to these things says, 'Surely, I am coming soon.'

"Amen. Even so, Come, LORD Yeshua!"

"Come," Ionnes said again, recalling the open invitation spoken by both the Spirit and Bride. "Come."

"The grace of our LORD Yeshua be with God's people. Amen."

Ionnes sighed again. The letter was complete. Prochorus would record the words over and over to send to the seven churches and beyond. More than anyone else, Prochorus had been deeply intrigued to see the words Yeshua brought to His last living apostle. Ionnes knew the message complete, but he felt some sadness as well. His life on Earth was not yet complete and having seen Yeshua again filled him with joy he had longed for over and over since Yeshua's ascension. He knew his LORD was never far, but these visions and dreams had brought Him closer than any other time over the sixty plus years. Ionnes' death he would welcome all the more.

For the moment, he considered punching a Roman guard or two on the way to the lockup, just to hasten that journey.

PATMOS

CHAPTER 39

"This scared me greatly," said Prochorus, seated by the window in Myron and Fona's home.

"What?" asked Ionnes, looking up from the pages he had written. The first pages seemed like so long ago when he had seen the visions. Rain fell throughout the night and now morning as the seasons began to favor winter.

"That," he pointed at the pages.

Ionnes looked down at his lap, then at Prochorus, then his lap, then Prochorus again.

"This unveiling? This disclosure? This apocalypse?"

Prochorus nodded.

"Not all of it, but much. I had much time to dwell on your words as I copied the sheets, over and over. It felt like the devil regularly tried to spill the ink to disrupt my progressions."

"It does stretch and twist a man's imagination like a mangled, old rag, does not it?"

"Amen," answered Prochorus, "and, I am just your scribe. You saw the real beings, evil and terrible to behold. The dragon and the beast and the harlot. I... I... I can only imagine..."

"It *was* terrible," shuddered Ionnes. "Much frightened me greatly as well, but more than fear, I felt great sadness and regard for those who chose sin and ignorance to Yeshua's goodness and wisdom."

Placing his chin and mouth on his fist, he took a moment to recall the many visions. He looked down at the floor as though it was very, very far away. No man takes such a journey with Yeshua Almighty without encountering big changes in oneself. Prochorus let him dwell on the thoughts and memories obviously racing through his mind. After a fashion, Ionnes peered up at his scribe, to nod, then confess,

"And, I feared not just the hideous creatures. The first vision of Yeshua scared me beyond belief, and I fell down dead."

"I recall," acknowledged Prochorus. He had held the limp body of his rabbi and friend in his arms before life returned.

Ionnes' voice broke-up and choked-up as he added, "Only by His touch did I revive. Nothing in my life prepared me for that – not even when Yeshua was transfigured on the mountain and made brighter than the sun."

"Even that must have been amazing," agreed Prochorus.

"Aye," answered Ionnes. "Cephas, Yaakov and I all fell flat on our faces when we saw Him with Moses and Elijah. I peeked over at my brother. Our faces like a mirror, such was our fearful countenance. Then, we heard Cephas blithering about building three altars. We both thought it sounded stupid and equally wished we had thought of it to say. Then, with eyes closed, I waited until a hand touched me. It was Yeshua, standing like his old self. No longer shining like the sun on Earth. No prophets of old in attendance. I looked around as he helped me to my feet. Cephas and Yaakov were already standing. We brushed ourselves off then headed down the mountain. None spoke aloud, but we all knew what the other thought."

"You said Yeshua was bright as the sun on the mountain?"

"Aye. Later some told us they saw Yeshua's light many miles away as they stood down in the valley wondering about the bright and stormy beacon of light atop the mountain."

He scanned through the first page of his writings. His brow furrowed, somehow concerned with the words.

"What?" asked Prochorus, reading his friend's features with practiced familiarity.

"Um," considered Ionnes. The words were not yet ready to come. He scanned the next page, then the next, then back to page one. "Um," he repeated. His face perked up as he realized what was missing.

"No introduction," he said aloud, to himself as much Prochorus.

"What?" checked his friend.

"Here," he pointed. "I started writing when Yeshua appeared. The first words, "I heard behind me a loud voice, as of a trumpet, saying, 'I am the Alpha and Omega, the First and the Last. What you see, write in a book and send it to the seven churches.' That is when I started writing – after He commanded.

This would be more confusing to send it to the churches this way. It is a letter and a book, so it needs an introduction."

Prochorus was not in the habit of arguing with Ionnes. He readily nodded agreement.

Ionnes took a clean sheet of papyrus, then looked around.

"Where is my quill? And, ink?"

Prochorus looked around and saw none as well.

"Myron?" called Ionnes, standing to find his host. No answer.

"Myron?"

"What is it?" entered Fona.

"Forgive me," asked Ionnes, "but I cannot find my quill or ink. Have you any?"

She smiled glad nothing was wrong.

"Of course." She turned. "Tobie?"

The slave entered, nodded, then left to retrieve the request. He had heard all before entering. He quickly returned with pen and ink in hand.

"Thank you," accepted Ionnes, and sat to write. "Did that pig give you any more trouble?"

Tobie's lips brrrrr'd. "I know not where he escapes from, but he loves our yard."

"Still digging things up?"

"Strongest snout on Patmos."

Ionnes laughed.

"Still writing your play?" asked Fona.

"Almost done," nodded Ionnes, looking down to the page. His hand hovered like an impatient falcon over the subservient papyrus, the ink threatening to drip. Not sure how to begin, he recalled some of his earlier letters. His pen touched the page.

"Ionnes, to the seven churches which are in Asia. Grace to you and peace from Him who is and who was and who is to come." He paused to consider the words, then prayerfully continued, "and from the seven Spirits who are before His throne, and from Yeshua Christos, the faithful witness, the firstborn from the dead, and the ruler over the kings of the Earth."

He continued writing. He prefaced that He made us kings and priests. Then, that the LORD would come with clouds, that all would see Him – even they who pierced Him, and some of the first words Yeshua spoke to Ionnes some weeks back as He began His divine message to the seven churches.

He paused. And thought. And imagined what Yeshua would have him say. He knew this was more than a letter. Even the extensive introduction he wrote seemed incomplete.

"What do you think?" he said, handing the script to Prochorus. His friend read the words a few times, then looked up at Ionnes.

"It seems fine to me." He handed back the pages.

Ionnes nodded his head, then changed it.

"No," he insisted. "Something is missing. Something to announce this book. Like a written herald. Like an emcee's announcement.

"Like a Preface?" asked Prochorus, "or a Prologue?"

Ionnes looked at Prochorus, running the concept through his mind before answering, "Yes. Exactly. In all letters I have composed before to the churches, I shared the wisdom Yeshua had imparted upon me throughout my life, but this one – this was more a wild and out of control ride on one of Solomon's chariots up and over the hills of Iudæa. The churches NEED to know Yeshua loves them and has sent this message directly to them."

Prochorus could not argue. He had gnawed his tongue on many of the images as he recorded it. At times, Prochorus asked his teacher about some of the visions for more detail which Ionnes clarified. Ionnes now looked at the pages in his hand, including the new page he had begun to write. Closing his eyes, his lips muttered and uttered and sputtered as he praisefully pondered the word or words which would encapsulate and entitle the letter.

"Revelation," Ionnes finally said, looking up at Prochorus.

"Say again," checked the scribe.

"Revelation," repeated Ionnes. He smiled as he pressed the point of the quill to rough sheets of papyrus.

"The Revelation of Yeshua Christos which God gave Him to show His servants – things which must *shortly* take place. And, He sent and signified it by His angel. His servant Ionnes, who bore witness to the Word of God, and to the testimony of Yeshua Christos, to all things that he saw."

Ionnes paused to reread the words. He had been blessed beyond measure by the dreams and visions. He delighted that Yeshua's church would share the same blessings. He further wrote, "Blessed is he who reads and those who hear the words of this prophesy, and keep those things which are written in it, for the time is near."

He paused as he reread, then laid down his quill and ink. Smiling, he handed the finished work to Prochorus who read the words and gave his smiling endorsement.

"The Revelation of Yeshua Christos," Prochorus said aloud. "We shall send this as the opening page, added to the other pages you wrote."

"Do not forget to include the greeting I also wrote this morning when we started. The 'I, Ionnes…' part. Then, comes the amazing vision of Yeshua. "It needs to get out to the people quickly." He knew fully well how many disciples died at the hands of Cæsar Domitian and Roma for refusing to worship the emperor. The church had been shaken to its core, over and over. Cæsar had never been particularly supportive to the Christian movement, of course, but Domitian continued to ever bring Roma to new lows. The church needed to hear these words of Christos to help keep their faith alive. Yeshua's power shone so brightly page after page. Get it out to the church. The sooner the better. Ionnes knew it. Prochorus knew it. Soon the entire church would know it.

Others entered the room to join in praise and worship to Christos Yeshua in keeping the Lord's Day.

"What will you speak on today, rabbi?" entered Seth. Rabbi Yosef entered behind him, nodded respectfully, and took a favorite position on the floor. Other prisoners arrived. Dim and Talor entered laughing.

"What is so funny?" greeted Ionnes.

"We told Jack you had one of your visions about him and were writing it down to tell the whole church. I never seen him so scared, and that is saying a lot."

Ionnes laughed and suggested they tell Pterrkee the same.

And, perhaps even Guard Octavius. Um! On second thought...

Chryspippe entered along with Lorin. Lorin took her place alongside the other slaves. Despite numerous words and insistences by Ionnes and others that they were not slaves in this room, each still maintained his or her station of human life, brothers and sisters in Christos notwithstanding.

Apollonides came from his side of the house to join the group. He looked especially dapper in full toga and greeted all like long lost friends. Ionnes beamed more and more every time he saw the young man, so much did his faith seem to grow day by day.

The baker and his wife arrived. Others from town. What started not a year earlier as a little gathering on a hill had already grown beyond most of their dreams and expectations.

Finally, the guards arrived to watch the prisoners. Ionnes greeted each soldier with a smile, then standing before the congregation said, "All are here. Now we may start."

He highly treasured the moments of prayer before he spoke to the church. They spoke to his heart the ever pressing need to hear the Word of God. He glanced around at all as he said, "Do not believe every spirit. Test them. Test them all to make sure they are from God." Such words he spoke with force and conviction.

"Did you know that you can test them? Spirits? It is true. If the spirit will not confess that Yeshua Christos has come in the flesh and is of God, trust not its words. It lies and will deceive those foolish enough to listen. And, I caution you, they are real, and they are out there waiting to pounce upon whomever they may devour.

"But, fear not. No demon or evil spirit can take away your life in Christos. And no demon is greater than Yeshua who created them all."

He took a step closer to the group as though about to convey a very special and personal idea.

"He who is in you is greater than he who is in the world." He smiled as he felt Yeshua's Spirit fill him again, within and throughout, blessing Ionnes beyond description.

"Beloved," he continued, "let us love one another for love is of God. Love may be His greatest creation. His love sent His only Begotten Son, Yeshua to us. I used to dwell upon that thought many times, and it led me to one and only one true conclusion. That God is Love. And, *that* Love was manifested to us through His Son, Yeshua, come into the world as a living sacrifice to die for us all. Our sins He took upon Himself. That is the God I love and that is the God who loves each of you."

He gave the young group of believers an extra second or two to dissect that thought, then raising his arms added, "God is Love, and he who abides in Love abides in God, and God in him." His voice continued to crescendo with intensity. "We love Yeshua because He first loved us."

He wanted to give everyone there the biggest hug of his life at that moment for he knew anew the love which lived greatly and wildly within himself came directly from Yeshua and His Holy Spirit.

Shortly after the meeting, as all were visiting and talking, one of the guards approached Ionnes.

"I have a question," he said.

Ionnes nodded for him to continue. This guard had been their escort only the previous month or so.

"You are a prisoner of Roma," he announced. "You have been beaten and tortured for this God of yours. Yet, you tell us to love even those who hate you."

Ionnes took a moment to decipher the young guard's comment into a question. "There is no fear in love," he said. "Perfect love casts out all fear. Even fear of one's captors. Even fear of one's whips and rods. Only when that fear is purged can you know Yeshua's total love." He placed a hand on the soldier's shoulder. "And, that is the same love you can have each and every day, whether you are a soldier, at war or keeping the peace."

The soldier looked at Ionnes a moment, his eyebrows moving up and down and the meanings of Yeshua's words filtered through his being. He heard a little heckling behind him from his friends, so backed off, but Ionnes smiled and could see Yeshua's Spirit bringing him forth into the kingdom, if he allowed. Then, he turned and could see young Talor talking with Lorin. The spark there was easily evident. He wondered whether it would sprout and grow and was encouraged to see little Lorin smile at times. For most of the first year he had known her, she seldom smiled and never laughed.

He looked over at Dim, sitting beside Seth. It appeared to be a one-way conversation – Seth speaking about his days in Galilee which Dim nodded at times, but really did not seem to be engaged.

Then, two men entered. The room became quiet, and Ionnes moved forward to encounter the pair, drenched and shivering from the morning rain.

"Papias! Polycarpus! My children, welcome. We have missed you greatly." All shared a hug, Prochorus joining them.

Polycarpus beamed with excitement he could barely contain.

"What?" smiled Ionnes.

"We found them, just as you asked."

Ionnes started laughing robustly until tears filled his eyes.

"Where are they?" he asked, greatly earnest.

Papias grinned ear to ear. Ionnes knew his friend well and recognized the answer. They were here at the House of Myron. They came directly with the men, so waited just in the next room. Ionnes turned.

"Dim," he called.

Dim kind of shook and shivered and stood at the summons.

"Come," urged Ionnes.

Dim, ever cautious, even with Ionnes, paused briefly, assessing. Assured any danger laid not in wait, he approached.

Ionnes placed both hands on the young man's shoulders. "We have something for you. My friends here – our brothers, have just delivered."

Dim looked puzzled, but Ionnes nodded towards the next room. Dim acknowledged, leaving the meeting hall to enter Myron's lounge. There he gasped at the sight. He totally lost all air for a moment and had to remind himself to breathe.

"Philomena," he choked as the trio came forth, running towards him faster than legs could carry.

"Papa!" the two boys yelled. They grabbed hold of their father and jumped up higher than they knew they could jump to be with him. He grabbed hold of both and held on tight. They had grown so much in four plus years, and he could not help but weep within the joy of the unexpected reunion.

Then, with two boys hanging from his neck, he wrapped the rest of his arms around his beautiful wife. For a spell, no one could move. One might have sculpted them in the marble.

He peered anxiously at his wife. She smiled, but the sadness and loss of the years showed behind her gaze. Her slender features showed the hardship without her husband's hard-working provisions. He still loved what he saw and kissed her, long and hard with the promise of forever in his heart. Briefly, he wondered how he appeared to her and what the years of hardship and torture had done to him. His little dolphin necklace bounced around his chest as if it's mission complete as Dim kept hold of his family to let their love begin the long and arduous process to dissolve the past pains.

After some minutes, he turned to look back. No one had entered behind him. They all knew this was a most private and treasured moment. He kept hold of all three, so they could barely squeeze through the doorway into the big hall.

"Everybody," yelled Dim as he entered. They were already heading his way and gathered around the tearful reunion with praise and thanksgiving in every heart. They welcomed the family with gladness and tears of joy. They knew them not before, yet reveled in the joy of Dim's loss ended, replaced by the joy of reunion.

Lastly, Ionnes moved forward to meet Dim's family. Dim placed his right hand forward to flow around the back of

Ionnes' neck and head. He tugged forth, pulling the prophet's forehead against his own. They peered eye to eye long enough to speak volumes of thanks and appreciation and the end of despair, now dashed into little pieces upon the tile floor.

As Ionnes greeted them, he said to Dim's wife, "I hear you are staying on Patmos."

She smiled and answered, "As long as my husband is here, we shall remain."

"Then, I pray it shall be only for a short stay." He smiled encouragingly. His confidence may never have been greater than it was at that very moment.

<>< ><> <>< ><> <>< ><> <>< ><> <>< ><>

"And, what is your name, young man?" asked Ionnes, taking a seat on the floor next to the two boys.

"N-N-Nikon," answered the elder, a bit stunned and suddenly looking rather nervous.

"Sophos," said the younger who was delighted to meet the old man everyone had been talking about.

"How old are you?"

"I turned ten last Poseidon." He pointed to his younger brother. "He is eight."

"Eight-and-a-half," protested the younger.

Nikon sighed. "He keeps saying that. I think he heard it from Euclid's great, great grandson." He turned towards his brother. "You do not even know what that means."

"Do so," lied the younger.

"If you know not today, fear not, young man," said Ionnes. "You will know soon enough what eight-and-a-half means." The apostle leaned towards Nikon to whisper, "I am still trying to figure out why the Romans made their silly numerals without a zero."

The boy looked at the old man with a bit of amazement. Even at the young age of ten, he felt like he should have noticed that before.

"You are old," said Sophos, studying Ionnes' features.

"That I am," agreed Ionnes, smiling at the youth. "That I am."

"Was your hair always white?" asked Nikon.

Ionnes blew upward to his flyaway hair.

"Oh no," he answered. "When I was your age, my hair was as black as yours. Even blacker, perhaps."

"Then, why are they all white now?" asked Sophos.

"Just part of getting old," Ionnes sort of said, but it sounded incomplete in his own ears. It answered not why someone's hair changed to colors different from his youth. He brushed fingers through his locks, pulling them out to look upward, studying the strands. He looked at the boys.

"Did you know each strand of hair has a name on it?"

The boys looked at Ionnes not sure either understood.

"Look," urged Ionnes. "As someone became sick or died, a strand of my hair lost its color. With each new sadness, another hair lost its color. After a while, I had more white hair than black. That was when I discovered the names." He singled out a strand of hair and studied it.

"Stephanos," he finally said.

"Sir?" asked Nikon.

"Sir?" repeated Sophos.

Ionnes looked down at the two boys. "See here. This hair says Stephanos." He grabbed another strand. "And, this one says Yaakov. And, this one spells Cephas and Paulos and many, many others who have found Heaven ahead of me."

The boys looked intently at the hair. They had never heard there were names printed on each tress or strand. Sophos came forward to see the names in the old man's hair. Try as he might, he could not see the words, but fretted not. He could not yet read. He looked at his own dark hair. Nothing he could see there, either. Maybe someday...

"Oh! Here is another one," perked Ionnes. The boys turned their full attention. Ionnes looked at some strands with great interest and intent.

"What does it say?" begged Nikon after waiting longer than he wanted.

Ionnes continued to look a moment longer, then holding the hair before his face, looked towards both boys. Their eager faces gladdened his heart beyond description.

"Dim," he answered.

The boys jerked a bit taking at that one.

"It says Dim," repeated Ionnes.

"Papa?" asked Sophos.

"Aye." He looked up at other strands. "Here is another one. And, another. And, a few more." He held the strands forth for the boys.

Nikon looked with awe and amazement even if he could not read the words. Meanwhile, Sophos concentrated all he could muster, trying to put his impressions into words.

"Um," he stammered, looking first at his brother, then at the old apostle. "Um. Mama says we give her gray hairs, but not papa. Now I know he gave them to you."

The flames crackled and popped and spit feathery flame and fleeing ash, up and over, like a gracious geyser or tidal blow hole. Four longtime friends watched the cozy warm campfire, mesmerized as they surveyed the consumed wood. Mostly orange, all rainbow colors made their appearances in the glowing pit. Only the lap of small sea waves against the sand and rock beach added to the restful, easy time. The words of men would come, but only when one felt the need to speak. That moment had not yet come.

The younger looked up at the starry sky, allowing his eyes to adjust after watching the bright flames. He always felt the sense of awe and wonderment at the beauty of night so far above. The mostly cloudless sky seemed so dark against the brightness of stars until, leaning far enough back to look upside down, he noticed Mount Elias behind him, above the town. Its black silhouette loomed all the darker, and he saw for the first time the brightness of the midnight blue sky. Straightening back up, he glanced at the fire a moment, then turned towards the hill behind him. That moment of light made his pupils close until they again had to gradually adjusted to the lack of light. He always liked to fancy himself like the leopard, or the owl, able to see clearly through the gloom.

"What else did they say?" the elder finally asked. The younger looked over at the other two to see who would answer first. Being the newest comer, he respected the position of his teachers, even if they were also his friends.

"Your letter made quite a stir," Papias finally answered.

Ionnes nodded. "Yeshua knew the pot needed stirring lest the fires of hell from beneath cause it to scorch and burn."

Prochorus added, "The Nicolaitans were expelled from both Ephesus and Smyrna churches. Practically from the whole province. Yeshua made no bones about how He felt about them, and the people finally listened."

Ionnes felt both relief and sadness.

"I have been telling them about the misdirection of the Nicolaitans since the first or second day I was with them. At first, I was puzzled that it took the churches so long to understand after I had spoken warnings time and time again. Now, as I can look back and hear your words, I finally realized the Truth of truths. The Revelation was of Yeshua Christos, not Ionnes. It was His voice they finally heard and heeded. Alleluia! Thank You, Yeshua."

"Amen," the other three said.

"Um," started Polycarpus.

The three elders looked questioningly at the young man.

He looked at Ionnes.

"You still look sad."

"Aye," agreed Ionnes. "I am sad, verily. The Nicolaitans earnestly came, seeking the truth like so many men, but they have perverted the message of the gospel to suit their own tastes. Yeshua loves them as much as all of us here, but He also knows fully well the danger of wrongful words. I continually pray for them, earnestly and fearfully."

"Amen," agreed the other two.

Polycarpus grinned impishly. "The Ephesians wanted to know more about that Tree of Life and the 'flavor of the month' fruit."

The men peeked at one another before they burst out laughing, overturning the somber mood around the fire.

"I will bet they did," chuckled Ionnes. "I will bet they did."

"Did the Tree of Life really change its fruit each month?" asked Papias.

"Verily," answered Ionnes. "For me, it was like a dream where it had one type of fruit, then the next time I looked, a different fruit. And, also different leaves. Like a dream, I saw it. I noted it. I saw it as different, but my mind still accepted it for what it was."

"But," objected Polycarpus, "you saw a full year of growth?"

"Yes. A full year and longer."

"A full year – in a vision?"

Ionnes had to smile. "Yes, and I also saw the dragon bound for a thousand years."

"Oh, yeah," admitted Polycarpus.

"But," stressed Ionnes...he paused a moment to collect his thoughts, "but, unlike a dream, I still recall everything clearly, as though a man fully awake. The memories do not fade or become obscure like when a person dreams."

Looking at Prochorus, he said, "Correct me if I am wrong. As you probably recall, the Tree of Life was in Eden. After Adam and Eve sinned and were put out of Eden, the LORD did not want them to eat of that tree lest they live forever."

"Why not?" asked Polycarpus. "What is wrong with them living forever?"

Ionnes tried to recall an answer from his boyhood. "Yeshua never spoke about this, nor do I recall prophetic utterance from His Spirit about this, and none of us twelve asked Him, so I must rely upon the lessons from my rabbi in Hebrew school. My rabbi knew not for certain, he said, but feared that if they ate of the fruit, both Adam and Eve would live forever as flesh on the Earth, and thereby never find their places in Heaven. So, being cast from Eden was as much Elohim loving his creations as a punishment for their sin."

A thought popped into his head for the first time. He played with it a moment before placing words upon his lips.

"That would also mean Adam and Eve would have still been alive when Yeshua came."

"Impossible!" objected Prochorus.

"Hey!" shrugged Ionnes. "I expect we shall never know – at least not this side of the tomb. I can only wonder. Still, the Tree of Life is also mentioned in Proverbs, as I recall, but it is not like the Tree of Life in Eden. Solomon thought of it as the fruits of wisdom, or hope, or righteous acts."

He stared blankly at the fire, dwelling upon his words and the images of the Revelation Yeshua had shown him, when another thought suddenly occurred to him. He quickly looked up.

"Elohim did not remove the Tree of Life from Eden." He became more excited. "No, no, no. Recall in Genesis where he posted an angel with a fiery sword to guard the way."

"So," asked Prochorus following Ionnes' train of thoughts,

"Do those of Ephesus have to find again Eden and the Tree of Life?"

"It would seem so," admitted Ionnes, "but no," he reconsidered, "for also I saw the Tree beside Heaven's throne room, so it would also seem that Yeshua removed it from the garden like a farmer brings in a prize potted plant out of the windy rain. Perhaps He merely had to take it through the thin veil into the eternal realm."

"Perhaps," agreed Papias. "But also, He would not want the devil to get hold of it."

"Amen," they all again agreed.

"So," said Ionnes, "in answer to your question, no they do not have to find Eden to eat of the fruit of the Tree of Life."

He paused as he looked out towards the lapping water and a few lights far off across the sea on the neighboring islands, or even the mainland.

"It is always odd for me at times," he mused. "I heard Yeshua speak to Ephesus. I have been part of that church for so many years. They have been like the flagship church of the region since I first arrived, oh, thirty some odd years past. To hear Him say they had lost their first love... it broke my heart into such small pieces. One could better reconstruct shattered glass or potsherd. Daily do I ask myself, did I fail them? Did I become blind when all I needed to do was open an eyelid to see the truth? Did their faith erode that far? The words Yeshua spoke to Ephesus were words to me as well." He shook his head sadly to let the tears come. Faces and names crossed his mind – many he had known for uncounted years. Looking at Papias and Polycarpus, he asked, "How did Timotheos take the message?

The pair looked at one another until Papias answered, "Like always, with patience and holy restraint. He has often expressed his frustrations at times by those who claim to follow the words of Christos, then write their own scrolls."

Ionnes sighed. "I always loved the name Timotheos. 'To esteem or honor God.' What a beautiful name! If I had children, I might have named my son Timotheos."

"Amen," they all chimed in again even if two of them already had sons with names other than Timotheos.

They sat quietly for some minutes when Polycarpus asked, "What is first love?"

The men all knew what he meant but nodded to continue.

"Did not you write that Ephesus had lost its first love? What is that?"

Ionnes felt pride for his young protégé. Like Clement was to Cephas, and Timotheos was to Paulos, so Polycarpus was to Ionnes.

"You know that you already know this answer," encouraged Ionnes.

"I know," stumbled the lad, "or, I think I know."

"You do," assured Ionnes as the other two offered supporting body language. "When you first came to Christos, what did you feel?"

Polycarpus could not help but feel the exuberance he had discovered not so long before. For that matter, he still rode that high cloud most of the time.

"I could not hold it in," he confessed. "Do you remember the time I told you that I was praying, and I asked Yeshua what it was to be filled to overflowing? And, when He answered, I fell back as His Spirit continued to fill me completely like a wine bag more than ready to burst. 'Stop! No more,' I wanted to say, but all I could make were weird sounds as I felt the flood of Yeshua's grace wash over me and submerse me like a limp autumn leaf washing downstream only to enter a holy, wild whirlpool. It spun me around, over and over and over, flushing out any dirt and sin I still held within."

Papias nodded. "I recall finding you on the floor and wondered if you were okay. When I asked what happened, you could not stop laughing. Tears of glee literally washed your face and ears and hair. Even when you tried to explain, no words spoke louder than your joyous laughter."

Polycarpus sighed at the recollection, then noticed Ionnes lean towards him.

"I love that you know and still can feel your first love, but what if I told you it goes even deeper than that?"

Not just Polycarpus sat up straighter to hear that explanation.

Ionnes continued, "When we speak of First Love, most people seem to think of the emotional experiences they encountered when Yeshua's Spirit first touched them. But that is just the first room within the mansion of His love. The entrance. The foyer. From there, the Spirit continues to fill and grow each one from within."

"Did Yeshua speak of first love?" asked Prochorus. He had heard Yeshua speak often, but never recalled Yeshua use that expression.

"Yes," answered Ionnes, "but you are right to ask. If ever He said the words 'first love', I cannot recall, but I clearly recall other things He said."

He looked at the men and gave them a moment's anticipation before continuing.

"All those years back, some asked Him about the commandments and Mosaic law. I never ceased feeling awe at His answers. His authority. His knowledge of Adonai's laws. Not until Pentecost did I fully begin to see His authority came because He Himself made those laws. His answer was so simple, yet completely profound, that none could argue otherwise."

"What did He say?" pressed Polycarpus, practically falling off the log he sat upon.

Ionnes loved stretching out the moment just a tad longer, but soon answered, "He said, 'Love God. Love Your

Neighbor." He gazed at Polycarpus' face in the light of the fire and saw a little, "That's all? I already know that," in his eyes.

"Hear me well," Ionnes urged, his voice increasing in tone, volume and pitch. "That is the foundation of First Love. To love Yeshua and His Father with all our hearts and all our minds and all our souls and all our strength. And, no sooner are we told to love Him who loved us more than we can measure or understand, when He told us to love our neighbor as ourselves. Those are the basic and most perfect elements which make up our First Love.

We all try to make it some mystical first experience of the Spirit, but one who loves the LORD completely and loves his neighbor as himself shows his first love in thought, word and deed. Those are the stones placed right next to the Chief Cornerstone. In that way, 'first' love does not strictly mean when a person first becomes a disciple, but rather that it be the 'first' and most important part of our walk with God. Put not greed or fear ahead of it. Put not faith or hope, even. God's love is foundational, and the first thing He asks for in our lives is our love. And, why not? It is the first thing He freely gives to us.

"And, that is what Yeshua wants the church in Ephesus to return to. Not just an emotionally charged excitement (which still has its place in Christos' kingdom), but also the depth to love God and others, even when love seems like the last thing we think we should feel. That is the beauty of His First Love for us. And hear me well. Yeshua, the Alpha and Omega - the Beginning and the End, also means that our first love is also our last love."

Ionnes took the next moment to let them filter his words as well as catch his own breath.

The men with him fell to silence to thoroughly absorb his words. After a spell, Prochorus tried to break the silence, but every word which entered his mouth seeking escape sounded shallow and foolish in his own mind. He withdrew each expression until perhaps another time.

Polycarpus rose to stir the fire. As the flames regained life, he asked, "You know what I liked?" He glanced at each as he tossed the stick by the bordering rocks. "I really loved that Christos walked among the churches."

"Like when?" asked Papias, trying to recall the passage in the Revelation letter.

"Right near the start," answered Polycarpus, "when it says Christos walks among the seven lampstands. Are not those lampstands the seven churches?"

"Aye," happily agreed Ionnes, then complimented, "Good ear."

"Then, that means He is walking among ALL the churches. When we come together on the Lord's Day, I always watch for Him. And, His angel. Now that we have a church here, we must also have an angel for Patmos."

"That we do," acknowledged Ionnes and the others.

"Have you seen him? Our angel of Patmos?"

Ionnes laughed again. "No, my son. Not with human eyes, but I know he is there just as surely as I know Yeshua dwells with us."

"I hope I get to see him someday," mused Polycarpus.

"I pray you do, too," answered Ionnes as he personally noticed the small, nimble dance of an angel in delight beside the flaming glow of the woodfire.

"Oh, yes. Oh, yes," spouted Papias in his distinguishable deep, gravelly voice while he pulled a fishing net up on shore. Polycarpus tended the other end of the net. A lot of little ones, but some big enough to be well worth the effort. Keeping the net half in the water, they sorted through, tossing the too small and inedible. Some dogs dropped by to see if anything could be scavenged.

Papias tossed some of the smaller fish their way.

"Lavraki?" laughed Papias, holding up the sea bass to toss on the beach, far enough for the flapping fish to never find the water - close enough so the dogs would not steal their treasure. "No bluefin," he searched, "but looks like a couple good turbot. Plenty for the day's meals."

Ionnes loved talking with Papias, if only to hear the bold tones of his voice.

"You were saying?" called Ionnes, wrapping the net with Polycarpus to stow for the day.

"At first, some churches were angry," he said, pulling out his knife to start cleaning the fish. "Especially Sardis. And Laodicea." The sea bass still gasped for air as it felt scales scraped from its body.

"Had Yeshua nothing good to say about Sardis?" asked Polycarpus. "And, to expose its sins to the other churches..."

Ionnes nodded at Polycarpus. "Do you recall the story of Ananias and Sapphira who gave to the church only part of the money from the sale of land? They said it was the complete price, thereby lying to the Holy Spirit?"

"Uh-huh," answered Polycarpus. He had heard that story more than a few times throughout his young life.

"Well, you are too young to have been in Ierusalem before the siege, but you have seen Jews being pretentious and even arrogant about their faith?"

Polycarpus nodded.

"We were in Ierusalem at the temple when Yeshua told us a story. There were two men praying – one a tax collector and the other a religious leader – a Pharisee. Well, the tax collector knelt down begging forgiveness from God. The Pharisee stood nearby saying his regular prayers when he noticed the tax collector praying, 'God, be merciful to me, the sinner, and beating his breast with his fists.' We watched as the Pharisee snubbed up his nose at the man while he prayed, 'See LORD?' and he reminded God that as a Pharisee he fasted twice a week and paid his tithes faithfully. He followed the law of Moses to the utmost, so was nothing like that pitiful, sinful tax collector still on the floor." Ionnes looked at both men who had stopped tending nets or cleaning fish to hear the rest of the story. Ionnes eyed both as he asked, "Which man do you think left forgiven that day?"

"The tax collector," answered Polycarpus. Papias knew the answer before Ionnes asked.

"Absolutely," answered Ionnes. "And, that is what Yeshua saw in Sardis. Pretentions. Holy façade. Yeshua did say there were a few, not specifically named, who follow Him earnestly and have held to His teachings, but most were more concerned with outward appearance than the inner man; his heart and his soul."

"Well, they did not take the message well," said Papias. "Instead of coming clean, many are withdrawing and muttering amongst themselves. That also means withdrawing from the other churches."

"No one likes to have their hands slapped," said Ionnes, "but Yeshua never corrects without love. That tongue of His whipped me worse than Zebedee's switch, I will tell you. Nonetheless, He made me all the stronger and wiser for it, and so many of His words continue to carry me forward all these years."

"But," checked Polycarpus, "what if they fall away? Does not Yeshua care about them?"

"You know He does," answered Ionnes. "If He cared nothing, He would say nothing. He speaks not to hear His own words, but for us, His children, to grow stronger in the faith while growing closer and more dependent upon Him. Of course, He cares – deeply and truly. Now the real question here is, will they repent or not? We may need to go back to Sardis to disciple and instruct them further – if they do not let their pride get in the way."

"And their shame," added Papias.

Ionnes nodded gravely towards Papias. "Their shame can be forestalled by their pride. Be encouraged. Oftentimes those who need our prayers the most become the brethren who shine the brightest in the last days."

Ionnes looked at Polycarpus and flipped his head towards the fire. Polycarpus acknowledged and went to tend it. Soon the beach would be filled to overflowing with the smells of cooking fish.

Ionnes sighed. "I felt great sadness as I wrote that part of the letter to Sardis. The message was short and brief and to the point. It is the church that had no special promise from Yeshua near the end - only to get their names in the Book of Life. That was it. No hidden manna. No eating from the Tree of Life. No avoiding the Second Death. No gift of the morning star. Nothing – just get in the Book. It grieved me, but it also made perfect sense. Yeshua clearly told them to get back to basics. He offered them truth and the road to get back upon it; to get back on their knees to the simple and authentic faith God called them to. Like the Pharisee and the tax collector, some come to Christos in arrogance and some in earnest."

"I hear both churches are buying the whitest clothing they can find," said Polycarpus from the fire. "Both Sardis and Laodicea."

"I also heard," added Papias, "that Laodicea is getting heckled by Hierapolis and Colossæ. No one likes to be called wretched, pitiful, poor, blind and naked."

"Amen," agreed Ionnes. "As I was writing the letter, I dwelled briefly on each word, and Yeshua showed me in what manner they were wretched, or pitiful, or poor, or blind, or naked. But, the Laodiceans were not like those of Sardis. Where Sardis strived to put on a holy show, Laodicea preferred the minimum of effort. Neither cold nor hot. Lukewarm. Tepid. Boring. Middle of the road. No zenith. No high highs or low lows. Blah and bland, effecting no significant changes. Satisfied with the status quo. No striving. No learning. No developing. No advancement. No seeking others into the kingdom, like an old cup of calida sitting on the window sill all night, collecting dust and hardly worth reheating the next day.

"So, much like Sardis, Yeshua had not many good things to commend to the Laodiceans. 'You think yourself rich, but you are poor.' I personally recall Yeshua speaking those words in Galilee. Those who are rich will be poor and vice versa. It seems He saw that also in Laodicea, so He told them they were wretched, pitiful, poor, blind and naked. Yet, He continued forth to lift them up. He offered them richness. He offered them warmth to cover their nakedness, and healing salve so they could see more clearly.

"I was truly blessed to pen His words. He did it perfectly. Unlike any of the other six churches, including Sardis, He told them His rebuke was out of His love for them. He urged them to be earnest and to repent. He said if they would, he would enter and dine with them. Then, he took it another mighty step higher, offering to share His throne with them. Think about how amazing that is."

Ionnes raised both arms in praise to Yeshua. His loving joy started to flow over.

"But," he continued, "first they must be no longer lukewarm. They must no longer be smugly self-satisfied with their lives. Yeshua sought only holy fervor and dynamic love in their lives. And, why would they not want to have it? If they would step out of their lackadaisical stupors, He would make them co-judges with Him in Heaven; a truly mighty and wondrous call. I loved His message. Be victorious just as Christos is victorious."

He grinned before his friends as he accepted the first chunk of sea bass. It tasted better than he had remembered, and he savored each bite like one tasting some vinter's private stock of wine for the first time. The barley loaves and greens which accompanied the meal seemed outclassed by the welcome flavor of the fish touring his palate.

As they finished, each laid back, full of fish and bread and veggies and the abundant blessings of Christos.

Papias muttered word, half to himself, half to Yeshua and half to the group. "I think I have died and gone to Heaven."

Ionnes peered up off the rocky sand at this friend.

"I hope not," he said.

Papias raised his head up to look at his friend and teacher. Ionnes explained, "If we are in Heaven, I have to have a word with Yeshua. My belly may be ready to burst, but my joints still ache a plenty. This better not be Heaven."

"Granted," nodded Papias with a grin.

"What of those at Thyatira?" asked Ionnes.

Prochorus answered, "For the most part, the church welcomed your message, but Jezebel was fit to be tied."

"Verily?" checked Ionnes. You think?

"Yep," answered Polycarpus. "Jezebel had a tantrum when she read it. She threw around everything and anything she could grab. She cursed foully and tried to divide the church right there. Maybe even crush it.

"Then, after we left for Sardis and Philly, we received word that she amazed everyone, confessing her sins and promising to follow Yeshua's teachings of the letter. Everyone, including me, were awestruck. No words could be spoken."

"I am likewise in awe that she finally listened," said Ionnes.

"She is afraid of you."

The apostle raised brows. "I am nothing without Christos. It is He she should fear."

"Aye, but you she has seen. Christos she has not seen with her own eyes."

"Yeshua told Thomas, 'Blessed are they who have not seen, and yet believe.'"

Prochorus butted in, "But, Ionnes, some say it is easier for one like you to follow Yeshua when you walked with Him for over three years. And, in your case, you knew Him most of your life."

"Oy," groaned Ionnes, placing his face in his hands. "What is wrong with that idea?"

The three again sat silently, even if they knew the answer.

"It is simple," added Ionnes. "We twelve and others, (he glanced at Prochorus) walked with Yeshua for those years, and yes, they were the most blessed time of my life. I cannot say differently, but most still fell away when the trials became too harsh and they arrested Yeshua to execute Him. Even though I remained with Him throughout His trial and crucifixion, watching through my own veil of tears as life drained away from His body, drop by drop and minute by long, harsh minute, I understood none of it until after His resurrection, and even then, my knowledge fell short of completion until His Holy Spirit filled each of us to overflowing during Pentecost. It was only then, and not until then, that we, his eleven disciples, and others like Yochanan Markos, Stephanos, and even you, Prochorus, that our faith could not be made complete before we were baptized and readily filled with His beautiful, loving Holy Spirit. The eyes and ears of a man can only take his faith so far. Yeshua's Spirit takes each of us the rest of the way in His faith and holy grace.

"So, with that said, did Jezebel finally find the gift of Yeshua's Holy Spirit?"

Papias thought about what they had seen at Thyatira. "We saw her come forth humbly on our return trip from Sardis, Philadelphia and Laodicea. Perhaps she put on the show for our benefit, but I have not reason to believe that. Others there reported that after she had her tantrum and swore to destroy the church, not many days thereafter she became impaired."

"Impaired?" checked Ionnes. "How? With what?"

"I know not for sure," admitted Papias.

"Some said it was polio," inserted Polycarpus.

"Polio?" checked Ionnes.

"We do not know that," corrected Papias, "though it fits much of what was told to us."

Polycarpus nodded agreement, but still added, "We heard she became ill, and in her bed, could not walk. The pain was terrible, and she had many days to consider her ways. Those in Thyratira came forth to pray for her often, but it was not until she admitted her sin that she began to improve."

"Um," Papias wanted to interject, "We do not know for sure what happened. We have only hearsay, but Polycarpus speaks the truth of what we were told. Some said that she changed, not only for the sickness she was made to endure, but the promised and prophesied death of her children. That shook her deeply. She finally listened to the core of her being. She herself felt the pain that she feared would be passed on to her children. She could not bear to do that to them and feared greatly that she would lose them."

"Did you see her?" asked Ionnes.

"Yes," answered Papias, "as I said, on our return trip to Patmos. She walked with difficulty."

"Did she speak with you?"

"No," answered Polycarpus. "I think she avoided us. At one point I thought she would rip your head off if you walked into the room."

Ionnes looked at Papias who continued, "Perhaps, but she came dressed in plain clothing – not the flashy, seductive colors she often wore, as a sign of her penitence. We were told that she denounced her words as a prophetess. I took her avoidance as more like shame than anger."

"Amen!" applauded Ionnes though a part of him felt every bit of the pain she had endured. "So, what shall she do for work?"

"I know not," admitted Polycarpus. All four knew of Jezebel's career. A temple prostitute when she came to Christos, she brought her livelihood to the church, oftentimes seducing the men of the church to pay life's expenses. Ionnes and the others had seen this practice before. Evangelizing in a society where temple prostitution was considered holy and certainly held its alluring attractions, the converts coming to Christos did not just shed their polytheistic ways overnight. And, as fast as the church continued to grow, it always brought new Greek converts who still wanted to practice the worship of idols, especially where prostitution and consuming tasty foods offered to idols were involved. It always took some time for most to fully accept and even more, to appreciate the constructive restrictions Christos placed upon them. Their sins could never be their salvation before they found Christos. Even less so after meeting their Savior.

"Then, we need to pray as well as follow up with the church there for her welfare and employment."

"She could marry," said Polycarpus. "A couple of the young men seemed attracted to her. They told me."

"Perhaps," answered Ionnes, though he expected that might not be the best option for either. But he also knew his own shortcomings and lacking wisdoms where matters of love and marriage brought people together. A lifelong bachelor, his words of wisdom and counsel often came back to him with teasing and mocking by those who actually had spoken the words, "I do."

And, as a mother with young children, many men were reluctant to take on a new family. And for most, their own extended families would not approve of such a union. So, with those pitfalls in mind, the four men prayed for Jezebel and her family. Then, Ionnes sent instruction with Papias upon return to counsel the church leaders how best to help her to avoid feeling compelled to return to her past sinful life.

Prochorus peered at Polycarpus for a spell.

"What?" checked Polycarpus, feeling a bit awkward at the old man's expression.

"Are not you still single?" asked Prochorus.

Papias, right beside Polycarpus, started giggling.

"That is not funny," answered Polycarpus. "Um," he looked to Ionnes, "which prisoner wanted to get married?"

"Talor," answered Ionnes.

"Maybe we should introduce them."

"I think Talor already has a maiden in mind," Ionnes smiled at the lad, "and it is just my opinion, but I think you would not make a good matchmaker – perhaps even worse than me."

"Amen," answered the other two verily as Prochorus whispered to the group with bouncing eyebrows, "Behold, our new Yenta."

Some Roman guards actually yawned watching the quarry workers. As the supply of marble clearly diminished, the workers became more like scavengers than prisoners. The stones were smaller. Rolling logs were less often needed. Carts were used more to collect the pieces. The large wall showed intrusive sections of dirt and common rock to sabotage the quality of the marble.

As the walls of marble fell and crumbled into many pieces well worth collecting, the prisoners still gathered. Some others dug away to expose and dislodge whatever marble could be found. The salt ropes were needed less and less. Thus, Ionnes mostly gathered stone, large and small, which would be carved into household idols, tiers for fountains or plates and spoons with which to eat. Some others dug away to expose and dislodge whatever marble could be found. Rabbi Yosef helped him heft a larger stone on the cart.

Placing the marble, Ionnes looked around at the brotherhood of prisoners with an affectionate eye. Big Seth, the Jewish fisherman from Cæsarea, purposely selected the largest stones to lift. He ever sought to be the strongest there if only to intimidate the smaller Roman soldiers. They were not above giving the lash but showed more reservation to flog him for lesser misdemeanors.

Euæmon from Nemesis still walked with a limp. Ionnes knew his wounds to be completely healed, such was the power of Yeshua's Holiest of Spirits, and figured Euæmon thought the guards would be more lenient to a crippled man. Having received miraculous healing made him something of a celebrity as well around the quarry. Ionnes did notice when he would change which leg he limped upon, probably to see if any of the guards would ever notice.

Jack from Sparta learned to twirl smaller stones atop his fingers like lopsided tops. Ever the jokester, he fooled Guard Octavius into admitting he spooked Kynops' horse the night the sorcerer came for crazy Apollonides.

Minos from Knosos, Creta still wore his sour expressions of gloom, but seemed less weighted since his baptism.

Ionnes would not have thought it possible, but Phranc from Assisium became even more compassionate and helpful after his conversion. Just last week, this vintner from Italia told some of the guards he would not have believed it within himself, but his new life in Christos brought him to joy in life he never thought possible, even during a good harvest year. Some scoffed. Some heard. Even those who scoffed heard as well, even if they did not admit or understand it at that moment.

Pterrkee from Helikarrosos continued to bark and growl at anyone who came near, but at times, locked in the barracks while Ionnes and the others conversed, would say, "Huh?" or "Say again?" or "What?" if he did not quite hear what they said.

Teos from Side, (or Side from Teos) found greater strength than ever he imagined in his simple faith. He loved Ionnes more than any other there and followed the old apostle like a happy-go-lucky puppy whenever he could.

Arion from Thorikos gambled a different game, seeking to become a soldier of Roma. He boasted the Roman citizenship fit him perfectly. Lucius, the Captain of the Guard, had already tested him in military tactics and fighting. Arion swore to the group he would never become as sadistic as their captors, but all there knew the truth. Once in that camp, any ideals and experiences he had would be compromised and strictly replaced with Roman brutality.

Talor from Knidos slowly approached the end of his sentence. The teen confided in Ionnes his plans for after he left the quarry and prison life. Ionnes laughed heartily and gave the lad his full blessing.

Ionnes pictured Mothcrates of Athenæ, no longer with them. The heartless quarry made its lasting demand on his life until he gratefully breathed his last to escape Roman savagery and barbarism.

"Look at you," chided Ionnes to Rabbi Yosef as each continued to pick up chunks of marble throughout the quarry. There were still sizable pieces to be cut, but more and more the smaller stones became the norm.

Rabbi Yosef dropped a large chunk on the low cart as he wiped the sweat from his face with his sleeve and peered at Ionnes questioningly.

"It is late autumn. Clouds cover the sun. The rest of us shiver and you are covered in sweat."

"Hmmmf!" replied Rabbi Yosef. "I have always been one who sweats more than the others, even when I was a child. It is thus the way Elohim made me."

"Knit in your mother's womb?" cited Ionnes, recalling scriptures. Isaiah. Psalms. Jeremiah. Perhaps others, all sharing how God formed and "knitted" a person in a mother's womb.

"Precisely," agreed the old rabbi, grabbing another rock.

"So," teased Ionnes, "you are saying that God knit you a sweater?"

Nodding, Rabbi Yosef totally missed the pun. Ionnes let it ride. He bent to pick another chunk of rock when he saw a stone about the size of a dove, pure white, unlike any other rock he had yet seen at the quarry. He picked it up to examine.

Yosef also stopped to check the interesting find.

It seemed iridescently beautiful, even exceeding an uncut diamond. He turned it over and over, each new side as beautiful as the other.

"Like Pergamos?" guessed Rabbi Yosef.

"Possibly," answered Ionnes. He looked towards the old teacher. "I never saw the white stone in my visions - just was told to write it. Holding it in my hand makes it that much more real. I half expected to see my new name imprinted."

"Like when Elohim carved the Ten Commandments before Moses?" asked Rabbi Yosef.

"Exactly," agreed Ionnes, "or God's finger carving words in the wall of the palace before Belshazzar."

"I am glad your new name is not 'Mene Mene Tekel Upharsin'," the Rabbi said.

"As am I," said Ionnes, both still examining the stone.

"What are you both doing?" yelled Guard Julius, approaching with whip in hand.

"Examining this amazing piece," answered Ionnes, holding up the white stone.

Guard Julius glanced at Ionnes' hand.

"What stone?" he demanded.

"This stone," answered Ionnes, holding it forth.

Guard Julius stared at an empty hand.

"We need no madmen here. Get to work." He held forth the whip to flog each, but paused a moment as though redirected, and his hand dropped.

"Get back to work," he repeated with a mumble and moved away.

The two looked at each other a moment, then returned to the work of the quarry.

"I think he could not see it," said Rabbi Yosef in hushed tones.

"Apparently," agreed Ionnes, loading another rock aloft. He glanced at the white rock in his hand and wished he had a large pocket. He felt tempted to toss it high into the air to see if it hovered above - or even disappeared. Instead, he set it upon the ground near the cart wheel as he continued to load marble.

"You should have thrown it at the guard," muttered Rabbi Yosef. "You could have clobbered him with no weapon to accuse."

Ionnes looked down at the white stone on the ground.

"I am not used to throwing away divine miracles," commented Ionnes.

"Divine miracle?" checked Rabbi Yosef.

"Just as much so as hidden manna."

The Rabbi nodded. The promise to the Pergamos Church; to eat of the hidden manna, kept in the Ark of the Covenant.

Manna - the bread of life. Did not Ionnes call Yeshua the Bread of Life, hidden only from those who refuse to see?

The old rabbi looked down at the white stone. A sinless stone. A forgiveness, just as Yeshua was the chief cornerstone. Verily, the white stone brightly reflected the righteous, sinless power of almighty Yeshua, given to all.

And, what shall be Yeshua's new name which only they can know and pronounce? He sighed. The new name would replace the old carnal, sinful name. Old ways pass away as each becomes a new creature in Christos. A new name for the new creation. A new identity in Christos Yeshua.

He wondered what his new name might be?

Stooping down, he picked up the white stone. Without turning it over, he saw the words form before his eyes. He knew the name he read, in Hebrew, though he had never spoken it before. The word as unspeakable as יְהֹוָה, it rapidly captured his heart to add to the new man he had become in Christos. Setting the white stone down, he dwelled upon the higher calling he had just received most plainly by Yeshua's Spirit. He had not felt so much like a young child for many, many years and he giddily giggled like one through his deep, white beard.

"The church in Smyrna is invisible, like the little mole, or autumn's breeze," said Papias. The three accompanied Ionnes along the road through Phora.

"Or," added Polycarpus, "like bugs under a rock."

"Bugs under a rock, eh?" teased Ionnes affectionately.

"Aye."

Ionnes had anticipated this reaction from Smyrna after his letter. The diaspora. Like the Jews during the Roman siege of Ierusalem. Or after Babylon's scourge. Many fled before the danger arrived. Yeshua foretold the coming calamity. Yeshua warned them to stay strong in the faith. That meant severe persecution. Sorrow and suffering. The final hammer.

Yeshua also warned them to stay strong and hold fast. He listed those meant for the Second Death - the cowardly, the unbelieving, the vile, the murderers, the sexually immoral, those who practice magic arts, the idolaters and all liars - their place would be in the fiery lake of burning sulfur; their names not written in the Book of Life.

Ionnes knew himself to be not the author of the Book of Life. That task had not been as yet assigned to him as his compassion for his Smyrna brethren flowed up and over. He felt like a dancing fountain of living light amidst the parched and thirsty darkness, but he still shuddered for those who fled for the *cowardly* were named with the others excluded from the Book of Life.

"Have all fled?" asked Ionnes.

"Of course not," answered Papias. "If anything, the church is stronger. Those short on faith have departed, or worse, returned to their old lives apart from Christos. The core who remain compel my hopes and desires to remain in Smyrna with them."

"Then you should go," directed Ionnes.

"What of Hierapolis?" asked Papias. Already he had led the church there some years.

"Is Epaphras still there?" asked Ionnes.

"Yes," answered Papias. "There or Laodicea."

"Then, you are needed in Smyrna - at least for a season. We can send word that you shall be detained for a short time. Plus, Hierapolis is right by Laodicea and Colossæ if they need anything. Smyrna needs you more right now."

Papias paused not and nodded affirmation. Like his brethren there, he faced the martyr's call without fear. He cherished the chance to stand strong in his faith for Christos. He would go to Smyrna.

It was one thing to play the messenger – to drop off a letter and soon leave. As a true believer, he knew better to remain to help when he bore harsh news.

"The Jews!" Polycarpus spurned.

"Why do you say that?" asked Ionnes.

Polycarpus knew the answer but struggled to find words.

"Fakes all," he finally blithered.

"It seems that way sometimes, does not it?" nodded Ionnes. "But most Jews are truly a blessing to the world. We see misuse of power by some, and it reflects badly upon all."

He knew well the synagogue in Smyrna before the message of the Revelation. Smyrna boasted the largest synagogue in Asia Minor. In like manner, the Jews held stronger posts in the city than anywhere else outside Iudæa. They used their strength and influence to persecute the Christian church. Oh, not they themselves. They would never get their hands that dirty. They did not have to. A few carefully chosen words by informants, and the Romans danced to their tunes to persecute the growing church.

"Hence," added Ionnes, "Yeshua identified it as the Synagogue of Satan, for the devil perverted their simple faith into a dead and fallible covenant. And like so many, they think themselves alive when they are totally dead."

"What about Philadelphia?" asked Papias. Yeshua had called both Synagogues of Satan.

"As I recall," answered Ionnes, "the synagogue in Philadelphia is not as big. They cause similar problems as Smyrna, but Yeshua foretells how the Jews there will bow to Him and His church."

"Like how every knee shall bow and every tongue confess?" asked Prochorus.

"Exactly," answered Ionnes.

Entering the town square, Polycarpus started dancing and bouncing backwards before the other three.

"Can I ask a question?"

"That already is a question," said Papias.

Polycarpus rolled eyes but awaited Ionnes affirmation.

595

"Rabbi? What did you learn from the Revelation of Yeshua Christos?"

What a perfect question! Ionnes smiled and admired the young man.

"Much," he answered.

"Such as?" asked Polycarpus.

"You mean besides the fact that Yeshua is infinitely stronger than Roma? Or that the churches need to become stronger for the trials that are to come? Or the amazing beauty of the throne room of Heaven?"

"I wish I had seen it," chirped Polycarpus.

"You will," assured Ionnes.

"But, what else?" asked Polycarpus.

Ionnes took a brief moment before answering. A huge smile filled his entire face and he looked like he might be lifted to flight at any moment.

"What?" asked Polycarpus, more intrigued than ever.

Ionnes spoke slowly and carefully. "As you know, I walked with Yeshua on this Earth for some years. We all grew up in Galilee and as cousins knew one another. Also, I took care of His mother for years after His death, resurrection and ascension, so I knew Yeshua the man as well as perhaps anyone on Earth. Still, as the years have passed - first with Pentecost, then with the Holy Spirit coming upon the Samaritans, then even the gentiles, I feared the memories and images I have long treasured of Yeshua would become distorted and no longer truth."

"How so?" asked Prochorus. Neither of the three men attending had ever previously heard this from his teacher and close friend.

Ionnes continued, "You all know how a story can grow far, far beyond its original telling?"

All three nodded.

"I ever feared that would happen to Yeshua within the church. I have always tried to tell the awesome good news of Christos with sober clarity and honesty, but now all these years past, I have seen many exalt Yeshua somewhat beyond that which was preached to them. And, I also wondered at myself. Could I distort and inflate the truth of Yeshua in my own mind after all these years gone by?"

The three barely breathed, awaiting the answer to that question.

"Asking myself that question, I realized, yes, I could indeed distort the truth, but it was not because I enlarged Yeshua.

No, no - Yeshua was already far, far bigger than anything I could imagine. The Revelation brought that home for me. I stood in the throne room of Almighty God. I saw the world attacked by the dragon and Yeshua leading the battles against the devil and its angels. I saw my LORD lead the battle against it. I saw my LORD victorious, and now I know that all I saw and preached in Yeshua was amazingly puny in light of all Christos was, is and will be. That is the most treasured part of what the Revelation brought home for me. Not that I would make Him too big, but rather that He already is so much bigger than anything I could speak or imagine. That, my child, is one of the most amazing things that I learned from the Revelation."

PATMOS

CHAPTER 40

"Question," said Dim, scraping a chunk of marble to make a Greek cross. Seated under the eaves of Myron's house leading to the back garden, the sounds of falling rainwater converted to waterfall played melodically over their ears.

Ionnes turned to hear the question, but then saw the stone's intended form.

"Such a symbol will bring certain persecution upon you and your household."

Dim looked up at Ionnes, then cocked his head towards Myron's back doorway. A Greek cross adorned space above the door.

"I always loved this shape," said Dim, "even long before I met ya. &, Yeshua. So, I am pleased t' see the Christians 'dopt it. The four equal arms. Four roads; or four directions – forward t' the east, backwards t' the west, right t' the south and left t' the north. All equal in their own way."

He carved another small chunk to chip away more rock.

"&, now it could even be yer four stories of Yeshua from ya, Mattathias & who were the other two?

"Ionnes Marcos and Loucas."

"&, which one wrote down the Acts of d' Apostles?"

"Loucas. A physician, and a man of unlimited compassion."

Dim paused from his sculpting as a moment of heavyhearted reflection weighed upon him.

"They are all dead now, are not they? All three?"

Ionnes nodded gravely. "Loucas was crucified in Thebe upon an olive tree by temple priests. Oy! Has it really been a dozen years since his execution? It feels more like just a couple/three years back."

His thoughts went to Mattathias, stabbed and chopped with a halberd in Nadabah, Ethiopia over thirty years past. And Ionnes Marcos, now almost thirty years dead, killed in

Alexandria, also by temple priests. They tied a rope around his neck and dragged him through the streets until well after he entered mortality, losing extremities along the way.

He shook with grief at the memory of his beloved friends. So many had died. He wondered how many of them would have chosen this road of life at the start if they had known what was to come? Perhaps all, for none swayed from it or bowed knee to Roma once they met the Living Word – the one true God incarnate - the King of Kings and LORD of Lords, as Ionnes wrote so recently.

Then, he readily recalled the visions of the martyrs in the LORD's throne room. He knew so many of those fallen in the name of Christos. He saw them, given rest and made complete in Christos' love.

Dim continued with his sculpting.

"Um," interrupted Ionnes, "you had a question?"

Dim stopped carving a moment to try to recollect what he meant to ask. The thought evaded him, never quite materializing cognitively. He shrugged to Ionnes and returned to his stone, scraping and crafting and blowing off the fresh dust.

"Oh!" he announced after some time. "Now I remember. In Phil'dephia, ya wrote they would be spared the 'Hour o' Trial' which would befall the rest o' the Earth. That sounds like somethin' good for them. So, what is the Hour o' Trial? Did Yeshua say?"

Ionnes recollected the vision and the words which so eloquently flowed from his fingers in the moment.

"Yeshua showed me two parts," he said. "The first time was right after the one-hundred-and-forty-four-thousand started singing. The grand choir pleased me to the core with their voices. Another angel flew past, preaching the everlasting gospel to all on the Earth, then said very loudly to fear God and give Him glory for the hour of His judgment had come. The judgment to be leveled towards Babylon. Then, later I saw merchant ships trying to come into port at Roma but were unable because the hour of trial had begun. And, as Yeshua's judgment goes out over all of Roma's empire, He promised Philadelphia that His judgment would pass far away from them.

Those who truly honored and followed Yeshua would be spared and untouched."

"&, they will stand firm?" asked Dim.

"That is always our prayer," answered Ionnes. "Yeshua called them a pillar and compared them with the New Ierusalem.

Their names would be on the walls of the new city."

"&, that will be forever?"

Ionnes nodded. Certainly. Yeshua seemed so well pleased with that church, Ionnes wished to visit and be renewed by their love and fellowship. His soul thirsted for the prayers and love of the saints just as deeply as any man.

"Did they say anythin' else? The church in Phil'delphia?" asked Dim, still chipping away at his stone.

Ionnes had to laugh. "Actually," he said, "they wanted to know more about the New Ierusalem, if Yeshua is 'coming soon,' how soon is that, and one babushka asked if the door was locked open, would not that let in the flies?"

"She did not?" questioned Dim incredulous.

"Aye. She totally did," answered Ionnes.

"What did ya tell her?"

"Me?" asked Ionnes. "Nothing. I am here, not in Philly. You know that, but I am told Polycarpus told her that if the flies did not serve Christos in her home to treat them like pagans or tax collectors."

"Well," thought Dim, "ev'ry time I saw a fly land, it quickly rubbed its hands together in prayer. That would make 'em totally welcome in my home."

"I am not sure your wife would agree," thought Ionnes.

"Sure, she would," he countered, "just so long as they wiped their itty-bitty feet before enterin'. My wife knit a few o' these dinky housefly door mats."

"Funny!" noted Ionnes.

Both stood and shook off the stiffness from sitting. Some of Ionnes' bones popped and cracked loudly.

"Ya are gettin' brittle, old man," said Dim.

"I am exactly as strong right now as Yeshua needs me to be right now," he blustered mockingly, then leaned in and comically whispered, "And, you are right."

The sounds of voices increased inside Myron's home. The two looked at one another questioningly, then went inside to see two more soldiers standing before Myron, Fona, Chryspippe, Apollonides and the rest. The attending soldiers kept watch over the group, hands on sheathed swords, but obviously strained to hear the breaking news.

Both messengers stood before Myron, noting the group gathered around them, placing both in a decidedly dangerous and less defensible stance.

Myron saw their faces.

"Out with it," he ordered. "None here will harm you."

With hands still on swords, the two turned attention on the governor's father-in-law.

"I am here to report news of a death. The emperor Cæsar Titus Flavius Domitianus has met mortality."

All in the room stood silently, taking it in. Myron broke the silence.

"When?"

"XIV.Kal.Oct., it is reported." Well over a month past. Patmos could often really be the last to know.

"Have you any details? The cause of death?

"Only rumors and other wagging tongues."

Myron's brow furrowed. He looked at Ionnes, then his family.

"You know not his cause of death?"

"Only that he was stabbed," answered the soldier.

"An assassination? Or an angry husband? Or...?"

"We know not."

"Any other news? Has another Cæsar been selected by the Senate?"

"We know not."

Myron wanted answers. Guesses and conjecture would be sorry substitutes.

Apollonides stepped forth.

"Would you have me go to Roma for our family?"

He gazed, eyes locked, towards his son. The man who a year earlier Myron would not dare trust with a front door key would now be the one to go to the House of Flavius to pay respects - IF in fact Cæsar truly met death.

"Let me consider," he answered, "but go forth to the harbor to seek news from others who have docked, and if so, seek an outgoing vessel, if one to Roma can be gained."

He turned towards the house slaves.

"Tobie. Attend to Master Apollonides' needs."

Tobie acknowledged. Apollonides nodded as a bow to his father and left their company.

"I take it the governor knows?" questioned Myron to the messengers.

"He sent us directly to you."

"My thanks," he granted, and pointed forth. "Have you dined? There is much here to eat. I am sure you are famished from your travels."

The guards bowed and thanked him, approached the table and broke fast. One hoped the wine would be better than what they typically drank.

Myron turned to the congregation.

"If you please, I would like my home to be empty for a spell to be with my family. This is a time of mourning for all that is Roman."

The group nodded and understood. Some thought to say they had all become family in Christos, but bit tongue.

Chryspippe took hold of her father's hand, then her mother's and leaned into both. Their free arms went around her in a dual hug.

"You must be with your husband," whispered Myron. "He will need your strength this day."

"Yes," she said and struggled against emerging tears as she moved from the bosom of her family. Lorin followed her mistress as they departed.

Myron turned to see some kneeling in the outer corner of the room, heads down in prayer. At first, he wondered that they had not left as he requested, then wondered at their prayers. Did they praise Yeshua for death of the emperor? His persecutions had certainly produced unnumbered enemies, but nothing unusual about that. Even the great Cæsar Augustus knew many enemies, even within Roma.

Instead, he heard prayers of comfort for the family of the deceased as well as prayers for the chaos often created whenever any emperor passed, and especially one as disliked at

Domitian. The inevitable bloodshed and destruction could only be averted by the One more powerful than any Roman emperor. And so, Myron and Fona joined them on the tile floor, soundly reminded of the amazing reasons they had come to Christos.

In time, more soldiers arrived.

"We have come to take the prisoners back to the barracks," the centurion announced.

Myron acknowledged, and the prisoners where shackled before leaving the home to walk back to the prison camp. Standard procedure. When one in the upper chain of command died or was dethroned, prisoners were collected and incarcerated to prevent uprisings, attempted escapes, and additional assassination attempts. This was even more true when the emperor died. A reshuffling of power and position was always inevitable.

Some wondered that the empire could ever stand strong with such a system in the Senate. No Cæsar ever knew his successor. If he did, he would probably kill him to maintain his place on the throne. None were ever truly groomed and polished to become the next ruler. Thus, each new Cæsar sat upon the throne with little to no preparation or training before assuming the position as the world's most prestigious and influential ruler. The sudden and extreme learning curve washed out many otherwise decent rulers before they had the chance to establish themselves or learn the rules for the one possessing the golden laurels.

Departing, the prisoners were marched up the hill to their barracks. Ionnes, coming up the rear, took especial notice. The city seemed quiet. The streets mostly empty as extra soldiers walked the streets. It felt like Marshall Law; felt like the whole island suddenly became one great, big penal colony. Their chains clanged all the louder throughout the quiet afternoon streets. Quiet enough for Ionnes to perceive and even faintly hear the prayers and praises of those around him. He joined them in prayer and led them in hymns with loving care from Yeshua Christos, the LORD.

The dark and dank barracks still reeked of dirty men and sweat and old bedding and new fears. The changing of Cæsar always bred uncertainty and fear in prisoners throughout the empire. As bad as things were, they could always be worse. As bad as things were, the new ruler could decide to send all of them to another prison worse than Patmos. Or, decide their lives on Patmos had become too lax and impose many new rules. Or, just decide their usefulness to the empire had ended and execute the lot. Ionnes thought it strange that a new emperor could also mean good changes, but most of the prisoners dwelled much more upon their fears than their hopes, even after Ionnes pointed out that such fretting would change nothing. If nothing else, it caused their sense of helpless worthlessness to become all that much more magnified.

"Arion," whispered Seth, "you were down at the docks today. Did you hear anything?"

Arion remained silent. It seemed clear that he perhaps overheard something but seemed unwilling to share.

"Huh?" pressed Seth.

Still no answer.

Minos grumbled, "You probably heard we are all to be killed, except you, and you dare not say anything."

Stone silence. For a moment, then movement.

"No," he finally rasped. "If there is any plan to execute any of us, I have not heard."

"What have you heard?" Seth re-asked.

"Nothing," answered Arion, and turned away from Seth towards Pterkee.

The grump turned towards Arion. "Do not breathe on me."

Arion blew in his face.

Pterrkee jumped upon him like a large cat. He went right for the jugular, trying to pin his neck to the bedding with his long fingers. Suddenly, to his amazement, Arion flipped him over, easy as a frying egg, grabbed hold of Pterrkee's thumb and easily kept him pinned to the ground for as long as Arion wished. His face eating part of the rough floor, Pterrkee felt his shell crack while wondering if his yolk also broke.

Neither spoke. Pterrkee would never admit defeat or beg for mercy. Arion held on more than long enough to know he effectively made his point. He let loose. Pterrkee raised up far enough to move back onto his bedroll, flopped down, turned towards his wall and mentioned something about death will be his.

Arion laid back on his own bed, hands behind his head. As the rustle of the room settled down, Arion began a personal chuckle. None asked, but certainly all wondered what amused the young man.

Again, a bit of laughter slipped out as he ah'd, then said, "I always wanted to cook a Pterrkee in Greece."

GROAN!

Countless eye rolls.

More groans, but the tension in the room eased a bit. Silence returned to the barracks.

Jack piped up, "I never thought life here could get any worse but Arion, you proved me wrong."

Rabbi Yosef looked troubled as he asked, "Did you hear who would replace Domitian as Cæsar?"

"No," answered Arion quickly. "I am told that the Senate is still in session to decide."

"Let us pray that it is a man better than Domitian."

"Amen," uttered some.

"Setting the target that low, it should be easy to find a man more capable than Domitian."

"Like Nero? Or Caligula?"

Some shuddered at the thought of either.

"Exactly," said Arion, "but odds favor the foolish. When one as evil as Domitian is murdered, the replacements typically have a very good example to avoid."

"True. True," all said, and quiet again filtered the room. Heads turned away. As those with other questions unanswerable for the night, snores started to take over. The sounds of anemic, grunting pigs toured the room. One snore always tried to compete against the next.

And so on. And so on.

"Nervæ is emperor," Apollonides announced to his parents in their home. Few days had passed since learning of Domitian's demise. Apollonides continued, "Domitian was murdered in his own bedchamber. Another cargo ship arrived today from Macedonia. They were surprised we had not heard of Domitian's death. It is old news for the rest of the world.

"No one knows for sure, but it is believed some from the Senate conspired to kill him. One bandaged his arm the week or so before to conceal the dagger. He gave Domitian something to read, and as he held up the scroll, the assassin stabbed his belly coming from underneath the scroll. Domitian paused in astonishment, then attacked with his own fury. His wound bled as the men wrestled, and he lost much blood. He called for his servant to bring his knife from under his pillow on his bed. The servant ran and found only the sheath. The assassin had thought of everything. A few more stabs and Domitian the god left this life."

"Why did not his slave defend him from the attack?" asked Fona.

"Good question," answered Apollonides. "I know not. For that matter, I know not if any of the account is truth. I can only share what has been told me. Sailors! They know how to spin a yarn better even than old drunkards."

"Anything else?" asked Myron.

"Absolutely. One of his first decrees was to release all political prisoners. If I understand his words, that means Giovanni is a free man."

The three, as well as the slaves, stood silently, stunned, as each played through their minds what might come in the days ahead. Many times before had Myron invited Ionnes to stay with them for the rest of their days when he gained his freedom. In typical honesty, Ionnes thanked him with full authenticity, yet always answered that he would go wherever Yeshua's Spirit led. If the Spirit told him to remain, he would remain. Myron pressed him for which way his heart leaned. Ionnes never swayed from his resolve. If Yeshua wanted him on Patmos, he would gladly serve. Period.

Myron knew there was more inside that old apostle's head than mindless servitude. Myron could not say for the other apostles, but he firmly came to believe Yeshua picked one of the best men in all Galilee to be this trusted disciple; part of Yeshua's inner core. In that same way, Myron knew Ionnes did not personally choose to be arrested, brought to Roma, faced and tested to overcome execution, then dragged off to exile on Patmos to mine marble. No, this aged and brittle-boned Apostle did not personally pick it, and for that matter, Myron felt fairly sure, Yeshua did not pick it either, but Yeshua certainly turned Ionnes' crushing exile and slavery into the utmost victory. Like the seed must die before it can spring forth in life. Like the aging eagle can find renewal to glorious youth.

Fona wondered what would become of the weekly visitors to her home to worship on the LORD's Day? Would they serve Yeshua thus even after Ionnes departed their company, whether back to the mainland, or even in death? Also, a smaller part of her thought it would be nice to have her home back.

Apollonides had considered following the old apostle wherever he would go. Being an orator, he knew his words could serve the kingdom of God. No sooner had that thought crossed his mind when he wondered where Yeshua would want him to go? That question had not at any time previously come to his mind.

"Does your sister know?" asked Myron.

"I know not," answered Apollonides, "but, I am sure Laurentius knows, and in that she shall know soon enough."

"How shall she take the news?" asked Fona, feeling great concern for her daughter.

Myron looked deeply in his wife's eyes as he answered, "With great joy and almost equal fear, like all of us."

She returned his gaze long enough to paint her own pictures in her mind how best to help. They be family. In the same way an entire family could be destroyed should Myron fall out of favor with the emperor, so their family needed to remain bonded together in the goodness and blessings of Yeshua Christus.

Apollonides gazed outside towards the Ægean a spell, then announced, "I sail tomorrow for Italia."

"Roma?" asked Myron.

Apollonides nodded.

"To what end?" checked his father.

"To congratulate Nervæ for our family, then to pay respects to the house of Flavius. After that, to the real purpose, bringing encouragement to the Christians who are surely in hiding in Roma.

Myron furrowed brow. "Do you think they will see you?"

"Surely," answered Apollonides. "Two weeks back when I first told you that I would return to Roma, I also mentioned it to Giovanni who gave me his blessing to go, and directed me how to contact their bishop, Clement, and others."

"You might have him compose a letter of introduction for you for the Roman church," suggested Myron.

"Good idea," agreed Apollonides.

"Are any ships harbored leaving for Roma?"

"We shall see," answered Apollonides, smiling. "You know the old saying. All currents of sea and wind lead to Roma."

<>< ><> <>< ><> <>< ><> <>< ><> <>< ><>

Rains fell as the men shivered and sloshed through the mud of the quarry. The only advantage anyone could find was that it made the ground easier to dig. And, the guards tended to stay under cover, only coming forth with the whip for more obvious or severe misdemeanors.

The wheels of the carts continually bogged down in the mud. The men pushed and used their large poles for leverage to lift the rock-filled carts out of the muck. Dim, Seth and Jack led the attacks each and every time, but all the men put what strength remained in their bodies to work together - not for Roma, but for one another. Contrary to times when they were free men, cold and rainy days seemed to bring the camaraderie of the men to full fruition. Perhaps such misery really did love company.

At mid-morning, the repeated gong of the large bell rang forth, calling the workers to gather and form ranks. The men looked to one another with concern. These formations seldom ended well. Usually, someone had stolen something. All would be severely punished if the guilty party did not step forward, or more often was fingered by other prisoners.

Jack elbowed Minos who elbowed Phranc who elbowed... The bust of Cæsar Domitian had been removed; his name also removed from the side of the guardhouse. Clearly, it appeared being prepped for different letters.

The rain continued as though dissatisfied how much water each man should hold in ratty tunics and waterlogged skin. The Captain of the Guard, Lucius stepped out into the rain, accompanied by four soldiers. All guards had already taken positions around the ranks to quash any rebellions which might suddenly burst forth. Some ever hoped for such uprisings, providing occasion to practice another death technique, or if nothing else, to divert their boredom.

"Attention," yelled Lucius in Latin. "The following men step forward. Yosef. Seth. Talor. Pterrkee. Giovanni."

The five moved to the front of the ranks and stood side by side. Talor fearful, glanced at the four senior men and drew strength from their countenance. Ionnes looked upward briefly to watch the undershadows of the raindrops falling out of the sky. As cold as it was, he appreciated the long overdue cleansing shower.

Lucius continued, "By decree of Nervæ Cæsar Augustus, those whose names were called are released from custody."

Short and sweet. No further ceremony. No "thanks for your service to the empire". Nothing. He rolled up the scroll, turned and left the quarry.

The five stood, somewhat stunned at the unexpected news. The others broke ranks to surround them.

"Lucky swine," said some.

"I hate you," joked some - perhaps.

"Good luck," said others.

Dim stood before Ionnes. "I always knew ya would leave here before me."

Ionnes felt tears rise for his friend. It seemed most unfair to leave him behind to the cruelty of Roman justice. Phranc, Minos and Teos joined them.

Phranc's passion rode on his sleeve. "As much as I want you to be free, I never want you to leave us."

Minos agreed. "My sad and sorry world became a haven of hope for the first time in my life."

Ionnes knew his words would sound empty for a spell, but still he answered with encouragement. "Your haven of hope is still within you. As Yeshua brought me forth, He will bring you forth as well. Keep His faith. His love is still here to fill and guide each of you."

Phranc agreed, but still said, "I know, but it shall still be all that much more dreary without your guidance and love of Yeshua to strengthen and teach us. I, for one, know I will work all the harder to get free if it will bring me back to you someday."

They all shared hugs of farewell. Teos wept worse than a willow. "Do not go," he said.

"My child," said Ionnes, cuddling the man, "we shall be together again. Of that I am certain. I feel it in my bones. The Spirit of Yeshua fills me with such certainty. Keep praying. Keep loving Yeshua. He loves you so much more than any of us know."

"I will. I will," promised Teos. He kept hold of Ionnes until the guard came forth to order them back to work.

"Yeshua's love and blessings be with you," Ionnes said to Guards Julius and Octavius.

"Thank you," said Octavius. Julius spit and walked away.

Octavius promptly followed in step.

A loud voice behind them caught everyone's attention.

"Ha!" yelled Pterrkee. "I rejected your Yeshua, and still I walk away a free man before those who sucked up and gave their pitiful lives to your lonely God."

"Then, you know nothing of true freedom," said Ionnes, still walking.

Pterrkee whipped the wet hair out of his eyes and pranced away to the barracks to get his few personal items.

When Roma freed a prisoner, they were given nothing to return to civilian life. Ionnes did not fear, of course, for his friends had come and would gladly take him anywhere he wished to go, plus Myron and Fona had clearly invited him to remain with them if he wished.

"What about you, Jack?" asked Ionnes in the barracks.

"Heading home to Sparta," he said. "I am certain some ship coming through will be shorthanded and need an extra hand to man the ropes. Whatever it takes, I will get there. I have been living off nothing for a long, long time. Whatever they give me will be more than I have had for years."

"Sounds good," supported Ionnes.

"What about you, Talor? Is your plan still coming true?"

"Faster than I expected now," admitted the teen. "Are you leaving Patmos right away."

"No," Ionnes said decidedly. "There are still some matters to complete before I leave."

"Good," said Talor, looking somewhat sheepish.

"What?" asked Ionnes.

"Um. I have been meaning to ask you a favor but have always been too afraid to ask."

"What favor?"

Talor looked at the others in the stinky room. He leaned forward and whispered in Ionnes' ear. Ionnes responded with a huge grin.

"I can hardly wait," he said, and gave Talor the hug of his life. Talor knew he felt the power of bolted lightning bring the charge of God's Spirit in that hug. It both warmed and empowered him. He never wanted to let go.

Rabbi Yosef entered the barracks.

"One last time," he said, looking around. "I will never miss this place."

"Nor I," admitted Ionnes, "though I have endured worse."

Yosef tipped his head to one side to admit, yes, he had, too.

"Have you any plans as yet?" asked Ionnes.

"I awoke this morning an old man. Now I stand here with resurrection in my bones. My purpose has seen me through. I shalt not betray that strength."

"Will you stay on Patmos?"

"Perhaps for a spell," he thought aloud, "but truly, my heart guides me back to Ierusalem. I have not returned since the rebellion. I believe it is time."

"So do I," agreed Ionnes. "I may meet you there some day as well."

The two also exchanged hugs of affection and parting. They gathered their few personal items and stepped out into the light. The rain reduced to a drizzle and soon not even that, they watched the clouds and walked with bare feet on cold mud and wet gravel down the hill towards town.

<>< ><> <>< ><> <>< ><> <>< ><> <>< ><>

"I heared it through the grapevine," reported Dim, "'arently, Nervæ Cæsar made some sorta decree t' free all political priz'ners that Domitian imprisoned. Of course, if their political or spiritual beliefs caused them t' commit a crime – "

"Like as an assassin?" interrupted Polycarpus. He had been walking on soft downy pillows of air since learning the news Ionnes had been freed. All were thrilled, of course, but Polycarpus just could not stop praising Yeshua, over and over and over.

"Uh, no," answered Dim.

Ionnes interjected to the young man, "Assassins and would-be assassins are promptly executed. They are seldom if ever sent to labor camps or penal colonies."

"Right," agreed Myron, swirling his goblet of wine. He, too, felt cause to celebrate. "Domitian executed and arrested so many – virtually any who caused him any trouble at all. Even members of the Senate and notable families of Roma."

"Why?" asked Polycarpus.

"Partially because he lived in fear for his life but also, he could then seize their lands, livestock, horses, gold, silver and whatever else to help him pay deficits and other spending and debts he had accrued as emperor. The richer the better became a secret expression throughout the elite of Roma and for that matter, all of Italia. I would never admit this before now, but we moved to Patmos to a great degree to avoid Domitian's notice."

"So," asked Prochorus, "will those Domitian stole from have their lands and properties restored?"

"Dead men no longer need an estate," answered Myron, "and the only land they need is their final resting place. And, when one is condemned, so also is his entire family."

"I heard," said Papias, "that Domitian liked watery graves better than land. Why waste good, fertile land on gravesites?"

"I heard that also," said Myron, "but know not the truth behind such statements. Perhaps we will never really know."

"Yeshua knows," spouted Polycarpus enthusiastically.

"Yes, He does," agreed Ionnes while the others all nodded and smiled and muttered each one's personal words of worship and respect to Yeshua.

They heard a loud knock at the door. Tobie went forth to answer. Soon indistinct words could be heard from the other room. Sounds of approaching footsteps blended with the sounds of military armor. Two soldiers soon entered the room behind the herald of noisy uniform gear that announced them. Entering the dining room, they bowed before Myron, then headed straight to Ionnes.

"You must come with us," said the leader.

"On what charge?" demanded Ionnes.

"On no charge," answered the soldier. "One of our warriors has fallen and we were sent to seek you out."

Ionnes quickly studied the soldiers, eye to eye. No deceit could he receipt.

"Can you tell me more?" asked Ionnes.

"I can tell you on the way. We were sent in dire haste."

"Who sent you?" asked Ionnes, grabbing his cloak to accompany them.

"Lucius, the Captain of the Guard."

Ionnes again studied the men's faces. Hard. And officious, but no targeted hatred. He looked at his companions.

"Dim? Polycarpus? Care to accompany me? I could use some prayer warriors if we are to do the LORD's work."

Polycarpus already stood, but Dim had to mentally coax then compel himself. He had zero love for anything Roman, so sometimes had to twist his own arm to compel his actions to follow this sometimes insane Christian ideology. Probably the very reason Ionnes requested his company.

Dim recalled conversation with Ionnes back in the quarry the day after his baptism.

"I just want to gather up everything Roman and toss it into Vesuvius' gaping mouth," Dim had said to Ionnes.

"I understand," said Ionnes, and he did. He again recalled the time he and brother Yaakov suggested Yeshua call down fire and brimstone upon Samaria. He knew his repulsion for all things Samaritan, but only after he walked with Yeshua did he face how bloodthirsty his contempt. And, no Samaritan had ever done more to him than glare at him as they passed widely apart on some dirt road.

He also recalled his most recent scourging.

"Yet," counseled Ionnes, "I saw Yeshua beaten and destroyed and crucified far worse than I had ever imagined, yet His love never wavered, even from the cross. Even when He spoke to us after His resurrection, I never heard Him condemn Roma. We were all such dodos. Even then, we all wanted and even expected Him to lift Ierusalem and all Iudaæ out of the filthy dust of our squalor to become the glorious kingdom both King David and King Solomon ruled. None dared defy either – David for his strength and Solomon for his wisdom. Only after Solomon's death did Yisra'el rebel against the very disciplines and godly ways which made us strong. By their own words and actions, they made themselves weak. For many generations thereafter, they continued to reject Adonai's counsel to build Yisra'el and Iudaæ into one kingdom of strength and glory. Now, all these years gone by and we still yearned to see David's kingdom reestablished. Yet, when Yeshua returned from the grave, still He did not set-up Himself as a worldly king. That would have been a serious demotion in rank at very least. I can see that now. It amazes me that I could not see it at the time. It seems so obvious.

"So, although Roma seems to do everything it can to destroy us, they also ever remind us that they need Yeshua more than any others on Earth. Just before Yeshua ascended into the Heavens, He commanded us to make disciples of the entire world, baptizing in the name of His Father and of Yeshua, the Son, and of His Holy Spirit. At no time did He tell us the Romans were to be excluded. Oh no. Just the opposite.

"I can still see His face as He looked at all of us. There we were – all eleven of us and more with Yeshua standing alone on Mt. Olivet. That would be the last instruction He would give us from His flesh and blood body. He looked at me the longest.

He always could look right through a man as though he were a sheer woven cloth of the thinnest threads, and I felt His words fill me like the tide takes over the shore. Thus, I felt great fear."

"You?" challenged Dim.

Even Polycarpus seemed surprised to hear that.

"Verily. Intrepid fear. Do not forget, just a few weeks earlier, we saw Him arrested, scourged and beaten and crucified. Every dream we ever found in Yeshua got crushed that day. Then, He returned to life, more alive and real than you and me standing here. We took it all in and praised Elohim for sending Him back to us. We all had our eyes opened painfully wide to see how much we depended on Him. When He was taken to the cross, we were lost. Then, He resurrected, and our hopes resurrected with Him. He shared so much with us those forty days. We were filled fuller than the floods that lifted Noah's Ark. Then, He was taken from us again – this time not in anger and destruction, but in gladness and victory. I recall walking beside Him up that hill, knowing fully well He would be taken from us again, but as much as we trusted Him, we also feared being alone again after He returned to Heaven and His throne though that is where He is meant to be.

"So, yes, I felt great fear. But the good news did not stop there. We praised Him over and over, in song and word, clinging to one another like children preparing for the storm. The Romans knew He was back. The Jews knew He had risen. Yet, they all seemed ready and willing to let us carry on. Romans and Jews alike kept distance those forty days. We would see them. They would see us. But, if they had something to say, they did not speak the words."

"Why not?" asked Polycarpus.

"Oh, probably fear as well, assessing their actions. Everyone likes to think he acted best. That is why it is hard for so many to confess when they sin against another and need ask God's forgiveness.

"So, we reached the top of the hill. He gave each of us a long and lasting hug and commissioned each of us to continue to share His message to the world. Then, before our eyes, He started to rise off the ground, just a bit at first, then more rapidly. He looked down at us at first, then raised His hands and face to the Heavens. Up, up, up He went, finally disappearing into a cloud. All of us kept looking for Him, straining with everything our eyes were made with for just even one more glimpse.

"Suddenly, we heard some voices. Two men we knew not stood upon the hill with us. We were busy with Yeshua, so perhaps could have missed them climbing, but I believe they were two angels Yeshua sent to us from above."

"What did they look like?" asked Dim.

"Honestly," answered Ionnes, "they looked like regular men."

"Then," checked Dim, "how do ya know they was angels?"

"Good question," said Ionnes.

"Did not you say we see angels all the time?" asked Polycarpus, "but usually know it not?"

"You are correct - both of you," answered Ionnes. "Truly, we saw nothing remarkable about their appearances, save that their countenances showed calm assurance. Their robes were stone washed white and they knew Yeshua had ascended upward way into the sky. So, they challenged us, 'Men of Galilee, why do you stand gazing up into Heaven? This Yeshua who was taken up from you into Heaven, will so come in like manner as you saw Him go into Heaven.'"

Ionnes stopped to dwell on the moment. The event wanted to replay through his mind over and over like the lapping of creek water over babbling stones.

Dim watched him a spell before asking, "So, ya still think Yeshua will come back t' us?"

Ionnes paused a moment, still lost in thought, then finally heard Dim's words, replayed somewhere in the back door of his mind. He looked at Dim, found and used a new smile as he answered, "Absolutely. I know not when, but every day I watch for Him."

Dim replied, "Then, I will watch with ya. Did not ya say He said He was comin' soon?"

"That He did," answered Ionnes. "That indeed He did, but I will also warn you."

"What?"

"Every time I think I understand Yeshua's words, I commonly find my understanding is not full, and even sometimes downright wrong. Still, I watch for Him coming down as we saw Him rise."

Walking down the road towards the soldier barracks, Dim's fear continued to increase with each step – not only for himself, but even more for Ionnes. This smelled of a trap. Word had it the soldiers were none too happy with Governor Laurentius for letting Ionnes walk. Orders from Cæsar were often wide open to the governor's interpretation, and he had often granted special favors to this religious zealot for reasons which probably made the guards more envious than anything. Likewise, the proconsul Makrinos made no bones about wanting Ionnes dead along with rumors of disapproval towards the governor's leniencies. Add to that, Ionnes staying in the House of Myron. Every soldier in the realm coveted such favor. Retaliation might could come from them at any moment. Even if Ionnes walked no longer a prisoner, it did not exempt him from soldier cruelly. If anything, the soldiers might even be more inclined to kill such a good man now that he lived no longer under their watchful eyes as a prisoner of Roma.

The two soldiers spoke not a word as they walked, not even to each other. Another sign to Dim that something was amiss. They walked rapidly, then waited for the aged apostle to catch up. Dim knew they would normally be pushing their prisoner along with the whip or the tip of their spears.

As the soldiers walked on ahead a bit, Dim touched Ionnes' arm.

Ionnes turned to look at Dim and saw the fear in his eyes.

"Somethin' is wrong," he said.

Ionnes nodded, then placed a reassuring hand on the younger man's shoulder. Not that he could see every plot of Roma against him before it sprung, but if his spirit truly detected anything dangerous, he would send Dim and

Polycarpus away. Especially Dim for his family. Ionnes would not have invited Dim along if he foresaw danger. For the soldiers to request his assistance in such a manner seemed odd enough already. He would attend them as far as his feet could take him.

A question occurred to Dim. "Did Yeshua ever help non-Jews like me?"

Ionnes collected a few memories as he answered, "Yes."

"When? Whom?"

Ionnes tried to recall the times Yeshua was asked by gentiles to heal.

"As I recall, a Roman centurion had a sick servant in Capernaum. He approached Yeshua right in the middle of the day and before a large crowd and asked Yeshua to heal his servant. He would not ask Yeshua to come to his home, as at the time we thought that would make Yeshua unclean to enter the home of a gentile. So, Yeshua granted his request, and his servant fully recovered that very hour."

Polycarpus raised his hand like one in a classroom.

"What about the Canaanite woman?" he perked.

Ionnes paused a moment for further recollection. "Oh yes," he thought aloud. "And the??? Oh, no." He struggled to remember the face of the other woman - perhaps a year earlier, between Tyre and Sidon. He spoke as one trying to remember as words departed his mouth.

"That Canaanite woman shouted for Yeshua's help for her demon possessed daughter. She bantered with Yeshua a bit. Yeshua saw the love in her from her answers and healed her daughter that same hour. We never even met the daughter until quite some years later when she introduced herself to Phillip."

"Who is Phillip?" asked Dim.

"One of the twelve."

"Tribes or 'postles?"

"Apostles."

"Aha!" said Dim. "I am sure ya told me that before."

"Oh yes," affirmed Ionnes. For that matter, all the other disciples had given stories and accounts for Ionnes to share, not only with Dim, but with all there who would listen.

Entering the Roman base, they strode across the parade ground towards the barracks. Soldiers stood, silently watching the group until they passed. Their muttering voices whispered from behind them as though they would sneak in behind them unnoticed.

Arriving at the soldier's barracks, Ionnes and Dim could barely see movement of the few soldiers within the shadowed doorway. They entered and had to let their eyes adjust a moment to the darker room. Guard Ernesto stepped forward.

"This way," he said, heading past the stock of weaponry to the sleeping quarters. They were led to a bed where a man lay, barely moving. A blood-soaked tunic covered his broken body. Both Ionnes and Dim recognized him immediately.

"What happened?" asked Ionnes. "Looks like a chariot accident."

"Yes," nodded Guard Ernesto with no further explanation.

Ionnes knelt beside the bed. "Julius," he said, placing a hand on his shoulder.

Guard Julius took a moment before opening eyes to see who spoke. His face took long moments before showing recognition.

"No," he croaked and moving as little as possible, turned his head away.

Ionnes prayerfully considered best action at this moment. Two ideas occurred to him. First, if Julius rejected his prayers for healing, Yeshua usually did not heal. In turn, Ionnes could pray for Julius until his eyes popped out of his skull, but if Yeshua did not heal the soldier, his friends might end Ionnes' life with the flick of a sword. Even then, any soldier might claim Ionnes refused to heal because Guard Julius had scorned his faith as well as flogged and beaten the old apostle many times. Like most pagans, compassion outside of their faith typically measured in small portion. Again, they would reward Ionnes with a gut full of sharp steel. That idea did not disturb Ionnes so much as that they would likely do the same to Dim and Polycarpus.

The second thought seemed more constructive. He could pray for the injuries to Julius' body, but it meant little if the man inside remained totally broken, so first he would pray for Julius the man. Of course, Ionnes wanted Julius to be completed in Christos, like for any man, but he also knew that the Roman's holy conversion was not required for Yeshua's loving, healing touch to be made complete.

"I will stay with you awhile," said Ionnes.

Julius did not respond.

Ionnes nodded to Ernesto and the other soldiers. The two escorts departed. Ernesto wondered if he left, would this old zealot finish off his friend. In his experience, most ex-prisoners certainly would grab the chance, but over the year and a half he had guarded Ionnes, he found neither a violent nor retaliatory bone in his body. As a Roman soldier, such an attitude disgusted him.

He normally saw it as weakness, but he had never met another like Ionnes. He had taken many Christians with the sword without remorse or question. Then, this frail, old man came along and turned upside down and inside out everything else he had ever done before to God's people. It was not Julius' summons that brought Ionnes to the barracks, but Ernesto's as his only hope to save his friend.

He sat on the bed across from Julius and watched.

Ionnes remained on round, knobby knees, uttering words Ernesto could only sometimes understand. Ionnes held hands together, or fell forward on the wooden deck, his breath puffing the dirt beneath his face. Ernesto had seen more than his share of temple priests praying. Some spoke passionately. Some loudly. Ionnes he saw praying genuinely.

Dim knelt beside his friend and teacher. He also prayed but seemed more like a puppet watching which string the master would pull next. Polycarpus took position on Ionnes' other side. Some hours passed as the men continued praying. Soldiers came and went - some snickering - some scoffing - few if any approving. Some hoped Julius would die, if only to blame Ionnes.

As the late sunlight of the day bid its adieu through windows, Julius spoke.

"Water," he said weakly.

Ernesto raised his head, then rose off the bed. He plodded over to the cistern near the front door and half-filled the ladle. Returning, he carefully lifted Julius' head to let him sip. No hurry. They were going nowhere anytime soon.

Julius finished drinking, then looked at Ionnes.

"Come to gloat?" he charged.

"When is the last time you saw me gloat?" answered Ionnes.

Julius answered with silence, but kept eyes locked on the old apostle. He still growled as he spoke. "Then, why?"

"To pray for your healing," Ionnes answered plainly.

Dim recalled Ionnes' admission the previous year, that he had failed many times. He wondered if this would be one of those times? Then, he promptly wondered if his fretting would not somehow jinx Ionnes. He started to rise to leave, but Ionnes placed his hand behind him to touch Dim, assuring him without words that his presence there Yeshua (and Ionnes) dearly wanted. Dim glanced at young Polycarpus who seemed cast in stone against Ionnes' side, and only until that moment resolved to be the opposing supporting wall.

Ernesto held his breath to hear Julius' response to his question. None in the barracks cursed and maligned the name of Yeshua and His sandal-licker Ionnes worse than Julius. He recalled Julius anxiously jumping to the head of the line when Captain Lucius assigned guards to flog Ionnes within or even beyond an inch of his life. He also recalled how shaken Julius felt when Apollo's temple crumbled to rubble. He had to see it for himself, and his rage at Ionnes thereafter boiled without limit. Even his critical words, spoken in private against Governor Laurentius and Chryspippe regarding Ionnes, caused Ernesto to check over his shoulder more than a few times. Only Makrinos seemed to approve and conferred with Julius at times to cause Ionnes more pain.

All could see the words touring Julius' mind as he considered answer. His condition restricted many words.

"How much?" he finally said.

"The gift of Yeshua's healing Spirit has always been a gift," answered Ionnes. "Even then, like all gifts, you still must accept it. Yeshua gives you choice to accept or reject His awesome gifts of life."

Julius licked his lips a bit before saying, "Then, begone."

Ionnes remained unhurried. He looked at Ernesto a moment, then Dim, then back at Julius.

"Then, I leave you, Julius, with this promise. Yeshua has told me He wishes to heal your body, but first to heal your soul. If you call, I shall return, but Yeshua also wishes for you to know, if you call upon His name at any time, you shall be healed. He gives the gift of your life back to you. You only have to ask."

Julius spoke crudities to send them away.

Ionnes looked at Ernesto. "Are we now free to go?" Dim and Polycarpus knew this moment to be the key time when they might be released or destroyed.

Ernesto looked at all three men, then Julius, then back and nodded sadly. Ionnes arose off the floor. Dim and Polycarpus followed, both stretching a moment. Ionnes turned to go, then stopped and turned back towards Ernesto.

"I know you have not given yourself to Christos, but He also just told me that you, too, can pray over your friend and he will recover. Yeshua's mercies come in many forms, many colors, and many different words. He will hear your prayers as well as if Julius asks."

Ernesto nodded solemnly, but thought such words utter foolishness. He had heard such absurdities from Ionnes many times before. He knew to expect them today as well. Only the hope to see his friend fully recovered compelled the soldier to keep his judgments at bay.

Ionnes led the way through the sea of uniforms, all parting to let through the trio. Again, muttering words followed behind them. This time, they sounded louder. Words of criticism. Words of failure. Words of fraud. Words that they should be killed for stubborn failure to help Julius. Words that Ernesto and any other man was a fool to call that old fossil into the barracks in the first place.

Ernesto heard their words but said nothing. He would not waste his breath. Instead, he attended to his friend, giving him another drink of water, and cleansing his open wounds for the last time of the night. As he dabbed, he noted Julius looking at him.

"You fool," Julius said.

"I know," answered Ernesto, and kept to task nursing his friend.

Another hour or two and all slept save those on guard duty and the one with never-ceasing pain in every joint, muscle, and sinew. Ernesto snored softly on the cot next over. Julius laid flat and broken, very thirsty and needing to pee. Never before much of follower of the gods, he already felt hypocritical having since prayed to Apollo, Jupiter, Diana and any others who might be out there listening. If this Yeshua of Nazareth could heal him, *de facto*, why would he refuse it? His pride? His anger? He never had been one who worried about upsetting the gods, but if anything could upset them, praying to another deity seemed pretty high on that list.

The long seconds ticked on and on and on, plodding along through Julius' mind with perpetually painful torture. His heart began to race. Against the pad he laid upon, he could feel his pounding heartbeat in his left ear. His breathing increased to meet the frantic beat. Cold sweat followed. The room became darker as his pupils slowly caved-in. Uncounted cold fingers moved upward to wrap around his body; his head; his legs and feet; his neck, constricting. The rapid breathing became labored and choked. He tried to sit up, but his broken body flatly refused. Even turning to his side seemed impossible.

"Ernesto," he coughed.

No response from his friend.

"Ernesto," he repeated, his voice cracking off into small shards more than cohesive sound.

The stranglehold fingers ever tightened like the strings of overdrawn bows. As the darkness increased, he no longer knew if his eyes were open or shut. He purposely shut them to find out and found the answer mattered not. The initial, frantic panic started to ebb. As life waned, so also did his fear. Little images suddenly popped up in his mind as though to distract it from the dire straits of mortal exodus. Images of his life, as a child in Pescara living with his mother and two older sisters working an olive orchard. As a teen whipped again and again by the orchard overseer for any infraction, real or imagined, he chose the life of a soldier to escape the fetters of family on the backside of Italia's knee. On foot he walked, and even half ran to Roma. There he would distinguish himself as a soldier of the regiment. The eagle's blood became his, and as time went on, he got a little bit older, a little bit colder.

His comatose dream rolled scroll without warning. There he faced the face of Ionnes, naked and tied to the post to be flogged without mercy. He hated that old face, hideous and repulsive as he flung his strong arm with all he had. The lash made its many marks, digging into flesh like a fishmonger's filet knife; his only regret that the whips held not pieces of potsherd or metal. Over and over, he and Ernesto whipped the defenseless man. His face shone the torment with each new strike, yet he wept not. Julius, about to afflict another blow instead looked in Ionnes' eyes. As ept as a tick, the old zealot's gaze dug in, thick and deep. Ionnes managed a weak smile. Then, his face began to shine like sunny reflections on water.

Still dreaming, Julius looked at Ernesto. His big friend also stood dumbfounded and after a spell even dropped his whip. Ionnes' face became that much brighter except it was no longer Ionnes' face. A face he did not know topped the same body. The shining eyes seemed to look through him. He knew the face belonged not to Jupiter or Apollo or.... A ring of brambles circled his crown. Julius strained to see through the bright lights and thought he could see two other figures standing behind, or nearby their prisoner. Dressed in white brilliance, he perceived they were not of this world – perhaps from Olympus? Perhaps atop Palantine Hill? Perhaps atop the emperor's palace itself or the Circus Maximus? He watched them with childlike interest and curiosity until his eyes hurt from the blinding bright. As he looked away, all faded into cold darkness rapidly closing in all around him. He felt his breath leave his lungs with no plan to return. All strength resigned to surrender his life in one final flop. He yielded to the darkness without dissent or protest.

From both corners of his eyes, he detected light. Though far off, it contrasted the darkness, yet evaded when he tried to look towards it. He settled for periphery, measured against his departed breath, this time encountering the beauty of the Heaven.

He yearned to go to the light but saw no road or path from his mind's eyes. The chasm of darkness divided them completely. He tried to call out. The Divine Being pointed back to mortal life to find the only road to Him. Julius watched the vision as long as he could. He felt forgiveness. He felt mercy. He felt love unlike any he had ever seen or encountered as a man. He tried to make it last as long as he could.

Until the pain aroused him.

Cracked ribs dug into the muscles surrounding his lungs. The lungs obstinately pulled in raspy air. The unexpected pain jerked him back to reality. He opened one eye – barely – but enough to see Ernesto pressing upon him with both of those big hands of his, shaking him, and urgently yelling his name. Julius expected Ernesto awoke the whole barrack, but from his deep, myopic pit, he could neither tell nor care.

"Awaken," ordered Ernesto most loudly. "Julius. Stay with me."

He continued to move the broken man until Julius croaked, "Stop. I here."

Ernesto checked his friend.

"I thought I lost you, buddy."

"You did," moaned Julius, turning his head to find any position less painful. His bed felt weird. Cooling wetness around his groin. He realized his bladder gave up while he sought eternal sleep and relief from the pain.

"Eyore!"

"What?" asked Ernesto.

"Wet."

Ernesto checked, then wiped his hand on his tunic.

"I will get you cleaned up."

"Good." Julius' lips buzzed like a trumpeter's as his nose tried to repress the smell of urine.

Ernesto ripped off the wet tunic, set towels under Julius' body and fed him more water. Covering him with a wool blanket, he knelt beside the bed and asked, "Is there anything else I can do for you? Anything else you need?"

Even in the dark room, Julius looked at Ernesto a long time before answering.

"What?" asked Ernesto.

Julius closed eyes a moment, letting the pain and discomfort move through him without resistance, then looked at his friend and forced out the words, "If you can, pray for me."

"I have been," said Ernesto.

"To Yeshua?"

Ernesto looked surprised. "Um, no. Of course not."

"Do," said Julius, and with eyes closed, rested his head against the bed pad.

"Um," Ernesto protested.

But Julius just repeated, "Do."

Ionnes felt the prayers of the saints. He did not always feel them. Oftentimes, he felt nothing, and thus needed to totally trust AND have faith in Yeshua's loving dominion over all. But this night he felt the presence of His Holy Spirit on Patmos, sliding through the night's quiet with perfect grace. From his soft bed, his eyes saw nothing but the dark pitch of the room where sleep should have been. He watched the darkness for a spell as the flows of the Spirit continued to gush through his room. Eventually, he rose. The House of Myron kept quiet as his calloused, bare feet felt their way along the tiled floor. Stepping out the front door, cold wind from the north slid down to cover him with its chill. He responded with a quick shiver and considered returning for his cloak, but waited, expecting he would not be outside long. The street also seemed quiet, and the bit of downhill view of Phora also seemed content to rest. Whatever the purpose of Yeshua's Spirit and ministering angels, he felt content to raise arms of praise and join in with his still, small voice. Great changes against principalities and powers often occurred at night when frail humans slumbered.

The strength and urgency of the impressions ebbed away as they always did after a spell. He needed not know the reason for Yeshua's call. He only knew to respond. He knew not what he prayed for. He only knew his voice was requested.

He would not have been surprised to hear after daylight other saints and disciples who were aroused from their slumbers that same hour. He knew not how far away the need of the prayers, but also knew that mattered not. Distance never interfered with God's will.

Demons interfered? Yes, like the Prince of Persia.

Foolish men who followed after sinful ways interfered? Yes, and often, for their hearts ever remained closed to the One True God. But, distance and topography? Never. The omnipresent Creator of all never had to go far to be with those He ever loved. And, there lived none He did not love.

Ionnes continued in prayer, moving lips in praise and thanksgiving for that which Yeshua touched that night. He slipped back in, quiet as a thief, returned to his bed, and let more prayers carry him back to sleep. He fretted not. He only knew Yeshua sought the voice of His child to move with His Holy Spirit in unity. Ionnes knew it more fitfully perfect than feeling the warm blankets on the soft bed wrap around him snugly to lead him back to blessed sleep.

Ionnes and Prochorus sat upon stone benches of the town square sharing a loaf of bread and wine.

"Yes," affirmed Prochorus, "I awoke as well, and rose to pray. At first, I just tried praying from my bed, but it became obvious this needed more attention, so I dropped off the bed to my knees on the floor to share in the LORD's call to pray. Of course, I wondered for what purpose Yeshua beckoned us."

"It matters not that we know," said Ionnes. "He will tell us if we need to know."

Prochorus already knew that. Ionnes knew Prochorus already knew that. Yeshua knew they both already knew that. Over the length of years, both men had often been called to holy vigils. Many callings they knew why. Some, like the previous night, they knew not, and it mattered not one bit for both reveled to be part of Yeshua's kingdom in any capacity. They felt honored to receive Yeshua's holy summons.

"I marvel that Yeshua succeeded in awakening you," teased Ionnes.

Prochorus shrugged. He knew his reputation as one who slept more deeply than a corpse. Some of the brethren razzed him that he would sleep through Yeshua's return.

Together they watched the shoppers and laborers moving through the square. Some hastened like vexed turtlenecks ducking into the next shop. Some strolled like a careless heiress. Some showed off their latest treasures or feasted on the day's baked goods.

Ionnes noted a young family of three. The Roman couple with their precious son. It lightened his heart to see them so happy. They saw the old apostle, held up their bambino and grinned all the bigger. Ionnes replied with an approving thumbs-up.

Ionnes wondered, "It seems busier this morning than usual."

Prochorus nodded and said, "Yep. I hear an Egyptian ship came through yesterday. Quite the haul. Linen and papyrus. Even glass. And, Nubian gold jewelry."

"Any beer?"

Prochorus laughed. "Of course. Have you ever heard of a beerless Egyptian ship? I know I have not."

"Nor I," agreed Ionnes.

They noted Myron and Fona departing the seamstress' store. A young woman walked behind them.

"New slave," said Ionnes.

"I heard," answered Prochorus.

Ionnes added, "We met yesterday. From Pergamos. She is an accomplished loomstress."

"Must be why they are leaving the weaver's shop," said Prochorus. He narrowed eyes to peer at her. She looked vaguely familiar, but he often thought that. Still, he did not perceive they had previously met.

"Quite the imagination, that woman," applauded Ionnes. "Speaking yesterday when we met, she sought a new loom, but none like I have ever heard."

"Like how?" asked Prochorus.

Ionnes furrowed his brow to try to imagine it. He knew the words, but not how it would actually work. "She said she devised a loom with two heddles."

"Like two looms?" asked Prochorus.

"No. No," answered Ionnes. She went into a most elaborate explanation, yet honestly I only understood the words without a picture in my mind to make it real."

"So, it has two wefts?" asked Prochorus.

"No. No," replied Ionnes, "and that is where she lost me. It still has only one weft, but two warps. She claims the final fabric would make tapestries envious."

"So, Myron and Fona are there to buy one?"

"No. No," again said Ionnes. "The one thing I did understand is that it is a new invention. Something she has conceived but has not yet tried to build. I know not what she said to her new masters, but I am guessing they visited the weaver to seek materials to perhaps try to make one."

"I pray they succeed."

"As do I," nodded Ionnes. "As do I."

A stir of voices arose up street followed by the sounds of horses' hooves galloping with speed and urgency. The two men looked at each other briefly, then turned attention towards the forthcoming action. Roman soldiers on horse popped out from between buildings, their horses protesting a bit, but dutifully moving wherever the reins and sandaled heels demanded. The group of five, all in full soldier uniforms, paused in the square, scanning the pedestrians throughout the square. Spying Ionnes and Prochorus, one kicked horse haunches to hasten the group forward.

"Looks like we have company," said Prochorus.

"Obviously," answered Ionnes. "Perhaps we should have brought more bread and wine."

"Obviously," agreed Prochorus as both wondered if Ionnes would be hauled away again on some new trumped-up charge. For that matter, they could just as well grab Prochorus. Get two for one.

The soldiers rode up with verve, yanking back on the reins just in time to halt the horses before the pair of old men. Ionnes and Prochorus looked again at one another, then saw one soldier jump off his horse, landing securely on the pavement with both sandals and slightly bent knees. His skin scuffed and bruised and scraped, he still moved most ably. He stepped forward towards Ionnes, removed his helmet and fell forward to his knees to bow. The others also jumped down from their horses, fell in behind the leader and genuflected onto one knee, helmets removed, and heads bowed.

The leader looked up at Ionnes, his eyes full of tears.

"Julius," identified Ionnes, breathing in the sweet delight and joy of the Spirit which loved loved loved to fill him to overflowing when he became witness to Yeshua's amazing love.

"Forgive me, I beg," cried Julius. "I am a stupid man."

The bruises and scabs of his wounds still showed, but the man who last night could not move had found the sweet favor of Yeshua's healing Spirit.

"Please tell me what happened," requested Ionnes. Only then did he look at the other four and noticed Ernesto in their number coming up beside his friend.

Ernesto looked at Julius, asking permission to speak first.

Julius bowed again in answer.

"I saw death in his eyes," said Ernesto. "He could no longer move, and his bladder could no longer hold. I saw him fade away, so I attacked him, slapping him and begging him to come back. He refused, and I knew I had lost him. Then, I saw life's spark sneak back in. He turned his head and tried to open eyes. 'Pray,' he said."

"No," corrected Julius, turning head sideways toward his friend. "I asked if you had been praying for me."

"That is right," corrected Ernesto. "Then..." He paused, perhaps wondering if he should continue.

Julius took the reins of the account. "I asked if he had prayed to your lonely God, Yeshua."

Ionnes sniffled with joy as soon as the words left Julius' mouth. The little gasp of air barely opened his lungs and he shuddered as a tear covertly snuck into one eye. A quick glance over the bowing soldier, he noticed the townsfolk all stopped to watch as usual. Equally typical, none came closer, but their faces showed sheer amazement to see Roman soldiers bowing to a released prisoner, even if it was the famous old holyman.

Ernesto said, "I said, 'no,' of course. And, Julius said 'do.'"

"Do?" checked Ionnes.

"Exactly," affirmed Julius. "Something in my short death grabbed hold of my mind tighter than a tugged and tangled rope knot. I cannot tell you what I saw. The memory evades me worse than a lost dream. My brain is dumbly muted and cannot speak but I knew I had to hear the word Yeshua again, even if I slipped away thereafter to the sleep of death and lost my grip on this life. So, now I come to beg your forgiveness."

On both knees, breathing hard, he again bent full forward; his forehead almost touching the ground.

"Why do you ask forgiveness?" asked Ionnes, asking as much for Julius and the others as for himself.

Julius kept his head forward. His breath disturbed the loose dirt resting on gray stones. Ernesto followed his friend's lead, bowing farther down. The others remained on one knee with heads still up to watch the drama unfold.

Julius wrestled hopelessly to find the right word, and wallowing in his grief, instead wept. No matter how embarrassed he might have felt, he could not help but release his sorrow with tears.

The three soldiers shifted uneasily as Julius' sobs filled the air around them. There for support, they still felt oddly vulnerable and conspicuous. One fleetingly imagined hoping some leathernecker behind them would speak snide words, so he could rise and lop off the gawker's head.

As the lament ebbed, Julius looked up at Ionnes. He expected harsh judgment. He expected cold blood. He expected icy consternation for that described exactly what he would have done, even only yesterday. He did not expect compassion or forgiveness, even though he begged for it. Such clemency had never been part of his being before, and he knew not how to behave thus. He only saw for the first time his foolishness. The new eyes he tried to see with did not yet fit or feel right and would need time to break-in like a new pair of sandals.

"Why do you ask forgiveness?" repeated Ionnes, or the question once again rang through his ears without Ionnes actually speaking it.

"Because I am a foolish man," he choked out the words, still looking downward. "I tried to break you with the whip. I tried to tear your backside off piece by piece. I hated you and your God. I wanted you and your kind dead. What a dog I have been."

Then, he saw for the first time that Ionnes had already left the bench to kneel before Julius on the pavement. He placed both hands on the soldier's shoulders. Julius looked up, the two eye-to-eye barely inches away. Ionnes looked intently at the Roman, his dark hair and dark brown eyes and whiskered face.

"If Yeshua can forgive you, so can I."

"Can Yeshua forgive me?" checked Julius.

"Did you ask Him?"

Julius nodded.

"Did you mean it?"

Another nod.

"Then, it is already done."

Julius reconsidered Ionnes' words. As a soldier, he always strove without mercy for anything he wanted. Each battle became part of his journey. Now, this Yeshua offered forgiveness without a sacrificial price. Could it really be that easy?

"Yes," answered Ionnes as though he could read the soldier's mind. "Yes, it really is that easy."

Ionnes looked over at Ernesto. "The same goes for you." He looked at the other three. "All of you. Yeshua loves all of you. Come meet Him. It matters not what you have done to any man before today. Yeshua still invites you to be baptized and join Him in everlasting life."

Julius knew he could not refuse. Not this time. He nodded to Ionnes, then looked over at his friend. Ernesto had been there. He had stumbled along reciting prayers to an alien God, and in awe became witness to Julius' resurrection and rapidly miraculous healing. How could he refuse?

"Would you join me again in prayer right now?" asked Ionnes. Prochorus had joined them on the pavement before Julius.

Julius and Ernesto nodded. The other three seemed less sure, but they had seen Julius, racked with pain and broken body parts, his life's breath bankrupt, suddenly healed and rising from his bed as though he suddenly had a leg cramp and jumped up to put weight on the gnarly muscle. If this strange Diety could do that, they also wanted to know more, so they rode with him that morning without reservation or purpose of evasion.

Julius placed a hand on Ionnes' hand, still stationed on his shoulder. He placed his other hand on Ernesto. Together the men shamelessly prayed in the town square. Together five Roman soldiers came to know Yeshua anew and rose from the pavement new creations. Each shared a hug with Ionnes and Prochorus. Ionnes saw Myron and Fona watching them. Ionnes seeing Myron's eyes, even across the court, could read his amusement. Every time Myron thought he had seen it all, Yeshua showed him something new.

Julius reached for a bag on his belt. It jingled with coins.

He picked up Ionnes hand to place the bag upon.

Ionnes closed his hand to a fist and said, "I thank you for your offer, but the eternal life of Yeshua is free. Neither gold nor silver can pay for the blessings He gives you today. Likewise, I am only His servant as well. If you wish to pay anyone, you would have to pay Yeshua."

"I cannot see Yeshua," protested Julius, "but I can see you."

"Verily," agreed Ionnes, "Verily. And, you know what? Now I also can see Yeshua in you."

He beamed again as he witnessed right before him the cold, hard heart of the soldier and guard continue to melt and soften. Julius started to feel the tears rise again. He fought to hold them back, but part of his brain shook and wriggled his psyche, screaming, 'You have never felt like this before. It feels pretty good, does not it?' He shuddered to accept and even cling to the feelings as long as they would steam and bubble within. He sighed with peace never felt as he settled for grateful acceptance of Yeshua's love. He found it the night past as new life entered his broken body, healing and making whole. Seeing old Ionnes before him inspired him to know he would ever see Yeshua's peace thereafter.

"I do not believe it!" exclaimed Dim, jumping and leaping around Myron's large meeting room like an uncovered skillet of sorghum, crazed and popping. "I am free? Like really free?"

Ionnes and others laughed with him and affirmed the news.

"How?" Dim asked, catching his breath. Part of him truly cared not just so long as it was true. Grabbing his wife, Philomena, they reveled and danced around together in absolute glee. She giggled more than he. He scooped up their boys and swung them around. He trusted the source of the news, but still feared its fabrication. How many sad nights had he counted? How many long, lonely prayers finally answered?

Settling down to encounter the reality of his release, he kept hold of Philomena as he awaited explanation.

"Penelope," called Ionnes.

The new slave entered apprehensively, wondering who called her and why.

"Penelope," Ionnes directed to bring her to them. She approached, then seeing Dim, her eyes widened with recognition.

Dim returned her gaze perplexed. She looked not familiar at all.

"She knows of you," said Ionnes. "A recent acquisition from Pergamos."

Dim's hometown.

Ionnes continued, "You told me the story of your capture and arrest? How you were working at a home when some of the mistress's jewelry was stolen, and you were lined up with the slaves?"

"Uh-huh," confirmed Dim. "Two o' the slaves claimed I entered the home & stoled it."

Penelope stepped forth. "You know me not, I know, but I know you. I saw you arrested and taken away for I was there, serving the home of my mistress. I knew not who had taken the gold. Then, over the next month, it became known how the two who accused you were not the thieves, but they lied to protect their brother – another slave in our home."

Dim suddenly felt numb. "Did yer mistress learn the name o' the thief?"

"Verily," she answered. "They hanged him that same day along with his brothers."

Dim plopped down in grief. Looking up at Penelope, he asked, "So, my innocence has been known for over four years while I slaved here?"

Penelope paused a moment, thinking of nicer answers, but nothing she could think of would ease the pain of her answer.

"Yes."

Dim felt the anger of betrayal. Briefly, he wondered if it had been better to not know the truth. Somehow the feelings and impressions of lost years seemed more painful and extreme attached to the truth. Yet, he had long past learned that even the worst truth became better to know than any unanswered mystery.

Ionnes interjected, "She recognized you as soon as she saw you and reported to Tobie who told Myron the tale. He approached his son Laurentius who verified her story with the next ship. Your release became immediately granted. You have been fully exonerated."

Dim felt great anger billowing within. He wanted justice – a foolish notion he knew but wanted it still. The injustice of his imprisonment had been known perhaps even before he stepped off the boat on Patmos. In that, nothing changed.

He felt both grief and euphoria – the release grinding against the truth of his harsh years of imprisonment and fearful separation from his family. Gnashing his teeth, he punched his fist into his palm a few times.

Then, he looked at Ionnes.

The old apostle had been imprisoned for less than Dim's charge yet counted not the years as lost. His heart lightened. Philomena took hold of his hand and clung to her husband's strong right arm. Would he have found Yeshua without his imprisonment on Patmos? Possibly, but he never would have met this amazing man – a man who believed in him when he failed to believe in himself. A man who Yeshua brought to Patmos and used mightily, even as an enslaved prisoner.

The whirlwind of thoughts continued to play through his mind, including one reminding him it would be awhile before any of it finally made sense, but his breathing and heart slowed noticeably. He saw hard days ahead to deal with the pain of his lost years but took heart for he would not have to face them alone. Ionnes and friends brought his wife and family to him. More important, they showed him joy in Yeshua, regardless of the pain. He would let the pain and grief work their way away with love and support as his allies. He would find new joy in the new life ahead.

"Like Yosef," said Ionnes.

"Which one?" asked Dim. "Rabbi Yosef?

"No," answered Ionnes. "Yosef from scripture."

"Which one?" repeated Dim, though he felt sure this time Ionnes meant Yisra 'el's son.

"Yisra'el's son."

"I thought ya was gonna say that," said Dim. "The one ya mentioned in the Revelation letter when Yeshua named the tribes o' Yisra'el?"

"Yes."

"Why Yosef?"

Ionnes pounded the table as he answered, "Yosef's own brothers sold him into slavery in Egypt. He served both Potiphar the Captain of the Guard, and Adonai. By equal injustice as you have been given, Yosef faced unjust charges and was sent to prison. But Adonai stayed with him, blessing all that he did. Eventually, he became the ruler over all of Egypt, second only to Pharaoh."

"I see not myself rulin' Egypt," said Dim.

"Nor I," agreed Ionnes. "Nor would I want to, to be honest but Yosef, who did nothing sinful, continued to rise above the terrible life others pressed him into. Then, as he came to greatness, he forgot the pain of his imprisonment. He married and had two sons, Manasseh and Ephraim. Those became the bodily witnesses of his healing. And, now you share in your kinship with Yosef as one who has known great injustice and pain, yet can move forward, a free man with the LORD God to guide you and love you."

Dim's anger still smoldered within. He expected it would take time to lose its bite, but he felt greater hope for the future than he had felt in all the years on Patmos. He turned to Penelope.

"Thank ya - deeply," he bowed. "Ya have brought me great joy & deliv'rance with yer words. I can only 'magine that Yeshua Christos brought all this together."

"Amen," answered Ionnes.

Penelope returned a thin smile.

"Amen," avowed Dim. "Alleluia & amen."

The biting winter now past, the warmth of spring began its annual cycle to settle in and revive the island. The strange group gathered upon the hilltop as nuptials were promised between the loving couple. Chryspippe looked at her husband a moment, remembering their wedding day. He stood a bit stoically; he had never cared for weddings but felt tugs from the back of his mind reminding him to be glad he came. Not really reading her mind, he still gave her his reassuring and supportive smile.

Dim and Philomena leaned against one another like mountain stones immovably propped against each other as they watched the ceremony.

Myron and Fona, the patriarch and matriarch of the affair, stood on each side of the loving couple to be joined. Ionnes officiated. The eclectic gathering of Romans and Greeks and Jews and such, all brought together as one in Christos, shared their prayers and love and support for the young couple.

Talor glanced at Dim who nodded his support and approval for the young man. If the ear-to-ear grin on the lad's face became any wider, it would separate his jaw from the rest of his head. He took Lorin's hand as Ionnes led them in their vows to one another. She remained shy and somewhat embarrassed to be the center of such attention. At one point, she looked down to see their shadows, connected one with the other. She moved to test the shadow to see if it would truly follow her. It did, and she considered how the shadow ever faced enslavement like herself, save the shadow followed its master without grief or complaint. She watched the moving lips of Ionnes on the dirt. She watched the flow and curves of each silhouette move effortlessly upon the ground. She blinked a few times to watch her own eyelashes. She smiled. Her smile showed up not in the shadow, but she knew it was still there.

When Ionnes sealed the ceremony with Yeshua's blessing, both bride and bridegroom felt the flush of love fill each. Together, they found one of Yeshua's sweetest gifts - the gift of divine marriage.

All trapsed down the hill to Myron and Fona's where they gathered to celebrate. The party began. Slave and prisoner both, yet as brother and sister in Christos, they found family with which to celebrate. Being slaves, the party would not last the whole week like so many others had reveled, but they still felt great honor and appreciation for those who shared their happy occasion.

As the party continued, Ionnes sat upon the sidelines and watched all. Young Talor had completed his sentence at the quarry. To take a bride, he agreed to an indenture to learn leather work on Patmos from Daniel the tanner. The governor signed the recommendation and allowed him to live and serve under their roof with his new bride. He knew not what to expect in the governor's home. His courtship with Lorin had been hit and miss whenever they could get together, and she would never divulge a critical word regarding her mistress. He accepted that he would find out soon enough.

Ionnes watched the young couple. His sense of satisfaction weighed both deep and high. Talor, the teen, would quickly learn the ways of men. Lorin, the slave, would learn all the more to serve her husband. Those who start with so little always drew strength from one another. He felt comfort at that thought. He had seen so many with so much more riches turn their lives into greater pain and grief than joy or blessing. It seemed so often those with the least had more to give to their mate. He watched them share happy words across the room. He could not make out the words. It mattered not at all. His heart felt encouragement and joy just to watch them become one under Yeshua.

Then, he thought of the bride of the Lamb whom he had recently seen and written about. If he could share anything with young Talor, it would be how the Lamb loved, cherished and treasured his bride. Ionnes knew his words could only take Talor so far. The rest he would have to discover on his own. He dwelled upon that thought, and realized Yeshua did the same, instructing and loving and sharing His Spirit, but each still had to walk upon their own feet through each day. And, that seemed the way Yeshua made each of them. At that moment, all the pain and sorrow the world had to offer melted away to nothing compared to the joy and love Yeshua gave all on Earth who opened hearts to accept.

PATMOS

CHAPTER 41

Polycarpus ran into the home of Myron, excited. Even giddy. As he entered the lounge, Ionnes and Prochorus stood to meet the lad.

"We found a ship." He had to stop to catch breath before continuing. "It sails for Miletos within the next day or two."

He paused, thinking to himself whether he should say anything. Okay, he would add the other find.

"And, another ship heading to Ephesus, but it does not depart for at least a week. Perhaps two."

Ionnes looked over at Myron, lounging on his favorite cushion. "Do you think you can put up with us for another week or two?"

Myron did not hesitate to answer. "My home is blessed by your presence and company. I can put up with you for another lifetime or two."

Fona, seated beside her husband, fretted.

"What is wrong?" asked Ionnes.

"The spring storms approach. It is not the best time to sail. What if your ship sinks?"

"Yes," agreed Myron. "It is almost miraculous to have two ships sail to the mainland this week. I can see you heading out to sea and ending up on Malta or somewhere else remote."

Ionnes grinned. "I think we are already on that remote island you are warning me about."

Myron laughed. "Yes. Yes. I guess no one comes to Patmos unless he must."

Ionnes said to Polycarpus, "Please secure our passage for Ephesus. At least the three of us to start. I shall speak with Dim and Philomena. They may join us as well."

Polycarpus showed he understood and skipped out, heading back to the docks.

Ionnes recollected, "It has been some years, but I have taken the road from Miletos to Ephesus. No thank you. These old bones would prefer to float to Ephesus."

"I concur," said Prochorus.

Ionnes looked at his friend. "Were not you with me last time we took it? We said, 'Never again.'"

"No," answered Prochorus. "No. Not me."

"Are you sure?" asked Ionnes. "I would have testified it was you."

"Uh-uh," assured Prochorus. "Maybe you are thinking of Gaius?"

"Perhaps," considered Ionnes, then looked more intent. "No, my friend. I know it was you. Remember that inn we stayed at near Anala? They had the moldy bread they 'fresh baked' that morning? You asked if they used moldy flour?"

"Oh, yes," giggled Prochorus. "And, those lentils had to be over nine days old."

"That is the place."

"Now I remember. And, I agree. Never again. You have my hand to sail rather than walk."

"What shall you do for the week until you leave?" asked Myron.

Ionnes replied with all seriousness, "It shall not go by idly. I have a church to equip and prepare for after I am gone."

Myron said earnestly, "They are welcome to meet here as long as we are on Patmos. We know not how long that will be, but they shall be ever welcome."

"In Yeshua's name, I thank you, my friend. You have truly been a blessing not only to me, but to all who honor Yeshua's name."

He smiled.

"I have much to do, but you know, there is goodness being brought here a prisoner. It makes packing to leave a snap," he snapped his fingers. "I came to Patmos as a prisoner with nothing. Look at all I have gained for Yeshua. In that fashion, I leave with much, much more than I came with."

"I have secured work here," said Dim, standing amidst the crowd on the beach. Myron and Fona. Talor and Lorin. Chryspippe, looking sadder and sadder than Ionnes ever recalled seeing her. Tobie and other slaves. The baker and his wife. Julius and Ernesto and other soldiers. Jack from Sparta. The young Roman couple with their son, Ionnes. Silva Veridi. Filon with his wife and daughters. Domestia and Zoe, and others.

Philomena stood beside Dim, supporting her husband though part of her clearly wished to return to Pergamos. Like all who travel and live part of life in different locales, she came to love the people of Patmos not unlike her homeland. In that way, she knew they would prosper more than ever on the little island. And, if Yeshua decided elsewhere..."

"Masonry?" checked Ionnes.

"Aye," answered Dim. "There is much brickwork for me here. We have been blessed with a decent home & a decent life here - a good place for my boys t' grow."

He looked down at both and beamed, then stepped in closer to Ionnes. Speaking aloud, he acted as though whispering in the old man's ear, "When the temple priests heard I was stayin' & did brick masonry, they asked if I would help rebuild 'pollo's temple?"

"Verily?"

"Amen."

"And, what answer did you give?" asked Ionnes.

"Silly question. What d' ya think? I told them I was engaged elsewhere & would not be 'vailable t' work on the temple. T' be honest, I am sure they knew me t' be Christian. Made me wonder why they would ask. I would think they would wish t' keep me as far away as possible."

Ionnes considered a moment before answering. "I know not for sure, of course, but I have often seen those from the temple try to lure new believers away from the faith and back into their old ways. It is an old ploy."

"Ya may be right," answered Dim, and shuddered all over as though shaking off a pesky misgiving.

"Also," added Philomena, "my husband also wishes to stay here to help the prisoners still working the quarry."

Ionnes felt a tear of appreciation come right up and out.

"That is – impressive. Even amazing," he said in sincere admiration. "We both know how many ex-prisoners flee this island as soon as they can, to put as much distance as they can between there and here."

Both thought of Rabbi Yosef and Seth, long gone to Ierusalem.

"Will ya feel the same way when ya sail away?" asked Dim.

"Not even close," stated Ionnes. "I have been planting and nurturing churches for Yeshua since I was younger than you. Moving back to Ephesus will be just another part of the journey. I will miss you all as much as I have missed everyone at every other church I have been part of - and that is very, very much."

They all shared a hug. The boys, Nikon and Saphos jumped in to share the moment. No hurry. The tide not yet in, Ionnes knew to give himself much time for this farewell sendoff.

Talor and Lorin moved in next.

"Father," said Talor, "we shall miss you more than you know. You have brought the two of us together and we will never forget you."

"And, I will never forget either of you," assured Ionnes. "It has been my delight to see both of you together these months. Lorin, I never thought I would see you smile so much." The slave smiled with embarrassment in response.

"And Chryspippe," he turned, "I am ever blessed that you would see an old man off."

"It is I who have been blessed by you," she answered. "You introduced me to this crazy God of ours, and my life has yet to be the same. And, for the better. I share more with my parents. My husband has become my closest and dearest friend. By the way, he apologizes for not being here, but he wished me to tell you, your passage to Ephesus has been paid for. You are his guests."

She dimpled, "He also wanted me to tell you he is pleased to be rid of you. Hence, the gift."

643

Ionnes recognized the joke. "You tell him, just for that I will keep praying for him, and if I hear that Patmos is falling apart again, I will return just to spite him."

"I will tell him," laughed Chryspippe. She knew it improper, but chose to not heed Roman social etiquette, and stepped forward to give him a long, hard hug. She knew she would never see him again. He returned the gift, then backed away enough to place both his rough hands over her painted cheeks.

He smiled some more, and said, "You have been the first child of Patmos called by Christos, and His love for you will see you each and every day for the rest of your life. I see that you shall be here only a little longer. I know not your next calling – back to Italia I believe, but that is only an impression. In turn, I charge you to seek the believers wherever Yeshua takes you. He truly will always be with you, and He knows that you have so much love to give. Now that you know the true God of Agape Love, you will fly higher and farther than any bird you have ever seen. Be blessed, little Chryspippe. Fear not and fly."

The soldiers – Julius, Ernesto and others saluted.

The baker and wife gave them bread for their journey.

Others shared hugs and tears, and as the tide came up, so also did the sailors.

"Ready?" yelled a mate from the rowboat.

"Aye," answered Ionnes. He turned to Prochorus. "Have you everything?"

Prochorus patted the pack he bore containing the holy writings on papyrus or leather that they had all grown to love.

The three men entered the small boat as the mate shoved off. The water of the harbor lapped forth into a star pattern. Some on shore noted it and pointed as others waved.

Stepping upon the deck of the ship, Ionnes felt both great joy mixed with equal heartbreak and sorrow. It was always, always so hard to leave those he had grown to know and love, but Patmos would be the hardest, yet. The remarkable touch of Yeshua on the small island continued to hold Ionnes in awe. His love for his LORD never waivered, but times like now he felt even closer to the wildly beating heart of God.

On board, oarsmen pushed the ship forth to sea as Ionnes, Prochorus and Polycarpus stood along the stern waving good-bye one more time. Those on the shore watched the ship leave harbor, then looked at each other. Each possessed their own personal sense of loss. Hopefully, they would seek each other to share their sense of loss and grow together all the more.

The fabled trio noticed more Roman uniforms farther up the beach, watching their send off.

"Makrinos," pointed Prochorus. Ionnes had already seen him.

The air blew crisp and cool, but the skies were clear. Leaving harbor, they set sails and moved eastward to clear the top of the island. Continuing over the top of Akrites Ins, they continued northward and were able to make Samos before nightfall. All bedding down on board, Ionnes felt the hard boards beneath his mat and smiled. The stench of dead sea life and the sweat of men filled the hold. Around the eighth hour of the night, the wind stirred, rocking the boat all the more. A sense of chill pressed through the boards of the hull as those aboard slumbered.

Rising, Ionnes and Prochorus shook off the stiffness of the night to venture topside. Though Samos seemed not the best harbor, the captain and first mate agreed to stay anchored until clearer skies appeared. In turn, the trio took advantage to go ashore and visit with the local church of believers. They were able to encourage and break bread with the dozen odd disciples who were more than thrilled to have the old apostle bless their little home. Weather dictated they remain in harbor some days. Ionnes made sure they were days well spent in the company, sharing tales of his days on Patmos, his release and heading back to Ephesus.

The disciples had not yet read the message of the Revelation, so Prochorus went to work copying sheets to leave with them.

Early one morning, Ionnes awoke on board to realize the boat had drawn anchor and was underway. They proceeded through the Mycale Strait easily. Ionnes loved seeing the beauty of the land on both sides. The narrow passage lent an ample breeze to take them home all the faster.

Another twenty-five miles, and they would be in Ephesus. The captain never tarried. He knew the route as well as he knew his wife and hastened with all the sails would give him. The mid-afternoon sun continued to shine as they drew near Ephesus and entered harbor. The ground seemed just a little firmer as Ionnes stepped onto the dry mainland. Well over two years had lapsed since he had stood upon that spot, and he raised hands in praise to Yeshua for the entire life's journey – its pitfalls and dangers – its beatings and pains – and most of all for its triumphs and blessings, built by the new church Yeshua and the Holy Spirit planted there.

Walking along the road, Ionnes took in the Ephesian scenery and the memories it conjured.

"What happened to the tanner?" he would ask.

"Run through by marauders one night," someone would answer.

"They moved the tax collection."

"Aye, verily. They found a site closer to the gate."

Some faces looked familiar as Ionnes greeted all they passed.

The group heard grumbles coming from Prochorus.

"What bothers you?" asked Ionnes.

"It is nothing."

"Does not sound like nothing." They all well knew their friend and his sounds.

"It seems like a perfect day," Prochorus eventually said. "We received the layover in Samos giving ample time to bless our brethren. Then, after only a second day of sailing, here we are strolling to Ephesus."

The others felt a bit perplexed.

"So then, what is wrong?" Polycarpus eventually asked.

Prochorus grumbled a bit more like a baby rockslide until he said, "I have seldom sailed such a journey so quickly. Are not we supposed to be attacked by storm and wind and rain and wild wave? Should not we engage the storm for many days as slave to the tempest, praying with all our might while the crew tosses cargo overboard to lighten the ship only then to run aground against some rocky sandbar where waves crash and pommel the prow until she breaks up and we are forced to abandon ship? Then, we jump into the surf and with great struggle make it to shore, worn and spent and in need, only to find the bite of the poisonous asp upon one's hand as we warm ourselves by the fire.

But, no, we had nothing like that. We shall be welcomed back where others will kill the fatted calf to celebrate."

"I still do not get you," puzzled Polycarpus. "What is so wrong?"

"Everything," barked Prochorus. "All is too perfect. I feel like we blindly walk towards a trap. Who knows who awaits in the shadows to pounce upon us when the time arrives?"

Ionnes placed an arm around his friend's shoulders. "Feeling some catapult shock, are you? Seeing Roman soldiers everywhere and in greater number with nothing else leading their lives than to kill and destroy?   Waiting for the unforeseeable snare to catch each of us and leave us hanging from the broad limb?"

"Precisely," answered Prochorus.

Ionnes and Polycarpus stopped to consider his words.

"Are you being prophetic or just overly cautious?" asked Ionnes.

Prochorus shrugged. "You know my gifts of prophesy have never been that precise, so probably just being overly cautious."

"We shall see. We shall see," said Ionnes.

"That is why you are the apostle and I the scribe," he said, lightening up a bit.

"Teacher, which do you hope it is?" asked Polycarpus, "prophetic or overt cautiousness?"

Ionnes answered without hesitation. "Good question. If I pray it is prophetic, then more harm will come to some if not all of us. If I find our brother is merely being overly cautious, then the harm may pass by us all like the hawk flying overhead who fails to see the mice hiding in the tall grass. So, though I certainly hope to avoid further catastrophe, I still prefer prophecy to caution."

"Why?" asked Polycarpus, amazed by the answer.

"Because, my son, one is rooted in fear and the other in divine love. Even if the news appears bad, I would rather it be utterance in Yeshua's love than the solitude of avoidance by my own misguided fears."

Prochorus paused to consider the phrase, "solitude of avoidance by his own misguided fears."

"Are you busy later?" he asked Ionnes.

"Why do you ask?"

"Sounds to me like I have some confessing to do." He smiled a bit.

"As you wish," answered Ionnes, "but for now, sit back and enjoy the moment. Man's destruction will return to us soon enough."

Ionnes breathed in deeply and shouldered his small load for the short walk to town. Heading east along the Arcadiane, Polycarpus ran on ahead to alert the body of believers. Soon they came forth, little by little as word quickly spread.

"Ionnes is back. Ionnes is back. He is here in Ephesus. Come all. Yeshua's Apostle is back."

With tears and joy, hugs were shared, greeting one and all with holy kisses. The city wondered at the small parade which brought these men through ornate streets dedicated to the multiplicity of Greek and Roman gods and goddesses, as well as Roman emperors. But, the only true God filled to overflowing His beloved group of believers celebrating the return of their bishop.

"There is another one," pointed Polycarpus to where Domitian's name showed missing. Throughout the Roman empire, anything with Domitian's name or face had been removed, like he had never been emperor.

All nodded, then Ionnes saw familiar faces.

"Timotheos!" he yelled, turning along the Marble Road.

Both old men laughed and cried, holding arms together to see one another as though neither would ever let go. Walking through the city, Ionnes noticed the idol shop closed. The Agora looked about the same as did the Celsus Library, but the Private House seemed closed.

Ionnes looked towards everyone and flipped his head towards the Private House questioningly.

"Yes, it is closed," someone said, "for now."

"I heard the whores all walked out and went to Notion or Colophon," said another.

"I heard," added Demetius the Silversmith, "an epidemic of genital condition requiring strict abstinence for a spell undetermined. I, for one, praise Yeshua it is closed and pray that it never reopens."

Timotheos sighed. "It took many prayers for that one to be answered."

"Sometimes it does, does not it?" answered Ionnes. "I see the Celsus still stands."

Timotheos flinched a bit in answer.

"That bad?" asked Ionnes.

"Oh, no. No," answered Timotheos. "Yes, the library is still there, growing it seems every day. Word is they hope to exceed Pergamos within the decade."

"Then, why did you flinch?" asked Polycarpus.

"Oh!" recollected Timotheos. "Just my stomach giving me fits."

"Still?" asked Ionnes.

"Always. It used to bother me that Yeshua never healed it. It also befuddled me how I could not ingest the LORD's healing, yet He used me to heal others. Never fully made sense but was true all the same. So, I still follow Paulos' advise and have a little light wine before a meal. It helps."

They turned up Timotheos' lane. Slowly walking along the hill, Ionnes' right knee kept bothering him. He had to stop at times to loosen it, like a horse shaking away a hoard of flies.

"It bothered me not yesterday," he considered. "Perhaps I slept upon it wrong. Or, wrenched it by the shifting waves."

The group arriving at Timotheos' home, they slowly climbed the long flight of stairs.

"These stairs never will get shorter, will they?" chided Ionnes.

"Some days I still wonder why I moved here," answered Timotheos.

"It has a good view of the sea," answered Prochorus.

"And the river."

"Yes, it does," agreed Timotheos. "It is a picture – or more so, Yeshua's artistry which never I tire to see."

More greetings and chatter as they settled in. Wine was brought. Then cheese and bread and grapes. Timotheos wanted to butcher a lamb to celebrate, but Ionnes suggested they save it for another day. He knew weariness after his journey, and as darkness already started to overtake the day, he looked forward to a warm and comfy bed more than a stomach full of lamb.

"I shall be the first to say it," opened Timotheos. "I know I may candidly speak for all here. We feared we would never see you again."

Many there uttered and nodded the same.

"As I look back on the day of your arrest and saw you taken in chains to the brig, I fell upon my face before Yeshua and begged to be taken in your place. Later, we learned you would be taken to Roma before Domitian, and even though we may believe in wonders and miracles, we have seen too many of our number destroyed in the name of Roma."

"You were right to consider," admitted Ionnes.

"I thought of my father, Paulos, and barely breathed words of hope for you, such was my torment."

Ionnes rose from the floor cushion, stepped forth and helped raise Timotheos before him. He placed an arm out over Timotheos' shoulder to share a blessed and thankful hug. Others rose and joined in to share the feeling and love in oneness. The circle of believers collected like a cluster of grapes joined to d'vine. All felt the Holiest of Spirits bind them together with the hardiest strings of His love.

Ionnes kissed the foreheads of those he saw. Their holy names appeared before his eyes at times, and he praised the LORD of Hosts with every completed breath.

Some unhurried minutes later, all returned to their places as Ionnes confirmed, "You heard correctly. Domitian did sentence me to death."

Timotheos' eyes perked up like a flock of startled starlings collectively taking flight. "So we were told. Clement sent word from Roma of your adventures. They verily poisoned you, then dropped you in hot oil?"

Ionnes nodded. "In Flavian's Amphitheater they prepared the cauldron."

"But it harmed you not?"

"To my amazement, no. In praise to Yeshua I did not cook."

"How did it feel?" asked a young man, shuddering at such a horrible idea of execution.

"It felt hot," answered Ionnes, "but no true discomfort.

As I recall, I danced around a bit with joy in the liquid."

"How hot was it?" asked a woman.

"Hot enough to fry bread and fruit." He recalled watching a grape or olive boiling before him as he stood in the cauldron. "Certainly, hot enough to kill a man without Yeshua's miraculous protection."

Prochorus piped up, "Causes me to recall Shadrach, Meshack and Abednego in the fiery furnace walking unharmed with the angel of God."

"Same here," said Ionnes. "I thought of them as I stood in death's abated grip. I found new voice as I stood before the assembly of Romans and yelled to all there to come to Yeshua. No drama in any amphitheater held a more rapt audience."

Tears returned as he recalled the others there sent to their deaths. The mental pictures of their bloodstained and maimed bodies vividly returned; the pacer and the woman who committed her life to Yeshua and others he saw piled up on the battlefield, freshly dead and limp; his prayers for them ever renewed.

Continuing the accounts of the two years, Ionnes and Prochorus reported to their brethren and sisteren all that occurred on Patmos. The Ephesians praised Yeshua mightily and fervently to hear such tales and promised to help the young church any way that they could. After some hours while most of Ephesus already slept, the group heard call of their own beds.

"We shall share more tomorrow," said Ionnes, and departed as he said, "Good night." He placed his right hand along the hallway wall to lead him to the guest room where he would spend at least a few nights. Timotheos had not mentioned the house Ionnes lived in until his arrest. He wondered about his little home but fretted not. Yeshua would guide him as He always did.

PATMOS

CHAPTER 42

Some months later, Ionnes sat near the window as a late summer day moved into play. His eyes still saw clearly enough but needed more light than in his youth. A small dried camel dung fire struggled to warm the cabin. His joints ached with the chill and he reconsidered moving south, perhaps to Ierusalem, or at least his birthplace near Capernaum and Bethsaida and the north shore. His aching, old bones suggested even warmer climes like Egypt or even Ethiopia.

He reread the papyrus sheets upon his lap. His heart shared the pains of his friends at Patmos. Dim reported the struggles of the fledgling church now that Ionnes had departed. Ionnes' presence had maintained a kind of fearful reverence from the Romans. His celebrity status had reduced Roman and Greek caution for only a season. Roman persecutions retested the holy waters not long after he sailed away.

Likewise, Laurentius would be replaced as governor. Makrinos, the proconsul, took the reins like one intending to clean up the Christian mess Laurentius let slide. Chryspippe would leave the island with her husband. Myron and Fona would also be gone. Likely Talor and Lorin as well.

He looked with disapproval at his letter. The words seemed so incomplete and trite compared with the struggles he knew the Patmosite church presently encountered. He laid the sheets upon his stepstool which served also as a small table to support the pages and steady a new tremor in his hand. Feeling their pain across the Ægean, he folded hands to pray again for Dim and the church. He also sought Yeshua's council whether to return to Patmos.

Yeshua smiled at little Ionnes with the utmost love and assured him Yeshua's Spirit still flowed and filled the church there like living blood through a pounding heartbeat. The disciple Yeshua loved breathed a sigh of thankfulness for his LORD's ever-present compassion and support.

Still on knees in prayer, he also prayed for the Ephesians. So many lives lost without a clue of the judgment and pain to come. Back on Patmos, he always knew he would return to Ephesus if given the chance. Now that he had made it and had time to resettle in, Yeshua's Spirit reminded him again how lost was so much of the city. Two years earlier, he had become accustomed to the many lost souls serving non-living gods. Likewise, his time away dulled even those memories a bit. Now back, the harsh realities of a city still lost came to bear upon his shoulders like never before. There was still so much to do and say.

He peered over at Prochorus, still asleep. A smile visited Ionnes' face. His lifetime friend and scribe could saw logs just about anywhere. Always an early riser, Ionnes often enjoyed taunting Prochorus with a cheerful, perky voice to awaken his friend. He recalled one time he made up a little song to taunt and tease his friend.

"Time to rise and time to shine," he sang with impromptu acapella. "It is the bright and early time. No cause for mourning just 'cuz it is morning."

Prochorus would have punched Ionnes if so disposed. He usually slurred a sleepy, "Go away," or, "I am going to get you - later," as he turned away, wrapping the blanket all that much tighter around himself before burying his head, contending to ignore Ionnes' mischievous provocations.

As Ionnes rose, he heard dogs barking along the street announcing a pedestrian, perhaps coming, perhaps going. He glanced out the window to see an elderly man approaching. He looked closer. Him! It was Him!

He smacked Prochorus as he yelled, "Get up! We have company." Racing out the door, he raced like, well, an old man trying to run to the street. Prochorus turned almost halfway over before giving up.

"Ionnes," called the man, also speeding up at least the top half of his body while feet and legs moved not much faster.

"Ignatius, my brother," replied Ionnes, enjoying both the senses of urgency and hope as they hastened forth. Hugs and holy kisses and unfettered excitement. Ionnes studied his student, now teacher and bishop of Antiochus.

"Antiochus sends all their love and prayers," he joyfully greeted. "There, I got that out of the way."

"Gratefully received," accepted Ionnes. "All of you are ever in my prayers as well."

"You look good," said Ignatius. "Better than I was led to believe."

"Yeshua has given me this time to heal. You look good, too. How old are you now?"

"Sixty-one this year."

"Still just a kid," joked Ionnes.

"Compared to you, fossilface?"

"How is the church in Antiochus?" asked Ionnes.

"Doing well enough for me to come see you. Since Domitian died, we have entered a good season. I feared that it would not last, but after reading your last letter, it seemed the church would have lasting peace as Yeshua defeated the devil and Roma."

"I pray that you are right," said Ionnes, "but, my impression is that much would happen before Roma would be destroyed. This season of peace is not an immovable rock. Not a Pillar of Hercules."

"You mean Mons Caipe?" said Ignatius.

"Exactly," agreed Ionnes. "The devil is still at work. As you know, we battle not against flesh and blood, but against principalities and powers. Roma dances to the devil's music, and the devil often finds a new and seductive tune."

"Yet did not Yeshua tell you Himself if you had the faith of a mustard seed, you could toss Mons Caipe on its head?"

"Verily," answered Ionnes. "Do you think Africa would want her?"

"No more than Mons Abila belongs in Iberia."

"Well said," said Ionnes as they heard the dogs again barking. Peeking out his one small window, he saw Timotheos and others hastening his way.

Smacking Prochorus, he said, "Up. We have more company coming." Prochorus tried to sit up, this time succeeding – at least for that moment. He saw Ignatius and nodded, scratched his head, behind his ear, and a few other places before rising.

Ionnes opened the door as Timotheos approached. He clearly saw the look of concern on his face. Then, he recognized another face he never expected to ever see again.

"Pterrkee?"

"Yeah," Pterrkee grumbled, holding his tattered cloak over his head just a little tighter.

Ionnes was just about as flabbergasted. "What? Um, it is good to see you."

"I wish I could say the same."

Odd thing to say, but totally Pterrkee? No, his face showed anxiety and concern. Not a common look for him.

"What is wrong?" asked Ionnes.

"Damn you," said Pterrkee. "I should be in Helikarossos exploiting my father's home and enjoying my escape from Patmos, but your accursed Yeshua told me to come find you."

"Why?" asked Ionnes, finding again his emotional bearings.

"It is Dim. The new governor, Makrinos…"

"Makrinos, the Proconsul?" asked Ionnes.

"Yes. As you know, he never approved of your work, or religion – or whatever you called it, on Patmos. I know not if the catalyst was your exit, but Roma presented new orders which sent Laurentius and Chryspippe packing."

"Are they in ruin?" asked Ionnes.

"Not that I know of. They did not seem disturbed or upset when they left."

"Myron and Fona with them?"

"Of course. They seemed fine, too. Even glad to be leaving. I heard tell Apollonides was still in Italia at the family estate."

"But you came for Dim?" asked Ionnes.

"Aye. Makrinos had him arrested."

"Do you know the charge?" checked Ionnes.

"I wish," said Pterrkee. "You know how it is. You cannot just walk up to one of the Roman soldiers and say, 'Hey, what are you arresting him for?' If they do not run you through right there, they very well may take you in with him to find out."

"Best guess?"

"He is a mason who found work, so chose to stay on Patmos. But he refused to help rebuild the temple to Apollo. My guess is that mixes in there somewhere. Whatever it is, I know it is serious."

"Why? Did they send him back to the quarry?"

"No. He is in chains with two guards assigned to him. To my way of thinking, that always spells e-x-e-c-u-t-i-o-n."

Ionnes' face became downward and dark. His head drooping down against the palms of his shaking palms, he prayed first and foremost for guidance. The answer came quickly. He looked up, firmly sure what he must do.

The others all looked anxiously awaiting his words.

"What father?" asked Timotheos.

He looked at all their faces – on Prochorus and Ignatius and finishing on Timotheos.

"I must go back to Patmos."

"You shall be killed," said Timotheos. "I would suspect a trap – something to bring you back to Patmos."

"Then," urged Ionnes, "we must make haste. Makrinos is not a patient man, as I recall. He will not leave his trap set for long."

Ignatius took hold of Ionnes' arm. "I know not this Dim."

"He is from the quarry. He was the third person baptized on Patmos."

Ignatius sighed. "Then, I shall go as well."

"And I," said Timotheos. Others nodded as well.

Ionnes looked over at Prochorus, still seated on his bed; his white hair disheveled.

"Why are you even asking?" asked Prochorus. "You already know my mind."

Ionnes looked at Pterrkee. "Would you return with us?"

"Not on your life," answered Pterrkee. "I swore I would never return to that God forsaken island. Never! And second, I have taken more risk than I care to think just coming here to tell you."

"Thank you, all the same," said Ionnes. "I owe you a great debt for your words. And Yeshua thanks you as well."

"Good," answered Pterrkee, and with that he left the small dwelling as abruptly as he had entered.

"We need to secure passage," said Ionnes, looking around the room making mental notes what to pack.

"Um, Ionnes," said Ignatius. He looked over at Prochorus who nodded to continue. "Dim may already be dead."

Ionnes did not stop even a second as he said, "Perhaps. I have not Yeshua's eyes any more than the rest of you, but I shall not wait here praying to find out if there is any chance, I can save my friend and brother."

The others shared agreement.

"And," he added, "Philomena and others may also be in danger and need help from us, His church."

Most heads nodded. A couple of amens also added to all in agreement.

"Can you check the harbor?" Ionnes asked Timotheos who nodded towards one of the brothers who immediately obeyed, heading out the door for the harbor. He would be back within the next hour or two, hopefully with good news. They would have to wait until he returned, but they would not be idle. Even without Ionnes' lead, all knelt together as one in prayer to petition the love of Yeshua for their friend and Christian brother and new disciple of the Almighty Christos Yeshua.

Amen.

<>< ><> <>< ><> <>< ><> <>< ><> <>< ><>

Ionnes looked upon the harbor of Phora with new eyes. The first time he had seen it, he wore chains. The first time he stepped upon the rocky soil of Patmos, he felt the strongholds of the enemy, the devil, filling every nook and crooked cranny. Those first steps he took felt so heavy with great weight piled high upon him.

His heart felt great weight this time, as well, but with different purpose. Even if deadly poison or boiling oil or grueling labor or the heartless scourge failed to remove his life, his heart, broken in two by the pain of loss and grief, could cease to beat for a moment or a day or a year or even further on towards forever. He wondered at each day left before him.

Did he lose an able step or two each given day here on out? He engaged such selfish introspection like all men yet counted his life bankrupt if he did not give all to Christos Yeshua. Against the crushing weight of concern for Dim, he smiled and looked at his companions. Together they would share that same weight with holy joy and gladness of heart.

Thank You Spirit!

Hosanna in the Highest!

For unlike his first time, he came not alone but with those he loved and trusted; brethren of the utmost.

The short journey by boat had already gobbled up eleven days since Pterrkee brought the news of Dim's arrest, shipboard travel being what it was. Storms came and went. Not the kind of journey any sane man intentionally chose. Plus, Patmos shared no major shipping lanes. Only by the number of passengers did the captain reroute his intended course to deliver them. They remained close to the mainland until Miletos, then headed westward by Tragia and Akrite and Hyetousa Islands, the latter to harbor for the night. None slept well. Hyetousa had a nice harbor, but no fresh water. To remain there long would be suicide. Plus, they were so close to Patmos, Ionnes thought he would swim the rest of the way if the captain balked.

But, true to his word, they were delivered, whole and healthy. The captain shoved off right away to continue to Kos, his intended destination from the start.

A crowd cheered as he entered the town square. Ionnes expected he would be quickly recognized; he had not been gone that long, but still hoped to find some of the local church before word spread of his return. Roman interference often altered a man's plans and direction of travel.

Many came forth with hugs and kisses of greeting. Even many who had rejected Yeshua seemed genuinely pleased to see him. He stopped to greet each and every person with Godly joy of heart and blessed many in the name of Yeshua.

He noticed the temple of Apollo still a pile of rubble, though obvious that some work to clean up was already underway. No temple priests appeared. He also noticed the Roman soldiers standing along the perimeter of the town square, apparently content to watch and act only if any indication of more serious disturbances arose.

Silva Veridi broke through the crowd to get to Ionnes

"Praise Yeshua!" he greeted, hugging Ionnes like he would never let go. "You are here. I cannot believe my eyes. You are here." The joyous song in his voice rang forth with each syllable.

"Does Dim still live?" called Ionnes loudly to be heard above the din of the surrounding crowd.

"He does, verily," answered Silva, "but he still wears Roman chains."

"What of Philomena? And their boys?"

"They are safe. I will take you to them. It is not far."

"Good," answered Ionnes. Nothing on Patmos was far, he thought, but bit his tongue. Slowly they moved through the crowd. Ionnes still took time to greet and bless each. Some brought forth their sick and crippled to be healed. Many confessed they regretted not coming forth for healing last time. Seeing Ionnes brought renewed hope. They would not wait lest they lose the chance again.

Ionnes prayed as the Spirit led, healing all he touched, and sharing the name of Yeshua with each man, woman and child who came before him.

Prochorus, Ignatius, Timotheos and others prayed with the old apostle, sharing Yeshua's Spirit of healing and renewal with each. Silva first wished to hasten away, but when it became obvious they would go nowhere anytime quickly, he knelt with his elders to join in. (Later, he chided himself. Here, the best evangelical meeting he had yet encountered, and he preferred to watch the sundial.)

They needed not leave the town square. Intrigued by the noise and activity, Philomena appeared. Seeing Ionnes, she also raced forward, struggling through the crowd to get to him. Before him, she fell to her knees and clutched his tunic-covered legs. She used the edge of her wool shawl, wrapped around her shoulders, to catch the long string of tears that emerged, on and on.

Raising her to her feet, Ionnes held her hands as he asked, "Tell me what has passed. Tell me all."

"Not here," she answered, and he acknowledged.

They continued to slowly maneuver through the crowd until they reached her home. Only after Ionnes disappeared inside did the crowd eventually move on. Some would play the sentry and watch for him to emerge.

"Pterrkee found me in Ephesus and told me Dim had been arrested."

"I know," she answered. "I sent him."

"And, he went?" asked Prochorus, not yet ready to believe it.

"Yes," she answered. "Truly, it took very little insistence upon my part. As I look back, I am not sure he did not suggest it. Did he return with you?"

"No," answered Timotheos. "He said he would never return."

"Oh?" considered Philomena. "That surprises me. He has been working with Dim right up until the arrest."

"Then, he has something else in store?" guessed Prochorus. "He always kept his own secrets. Perhaps this was the chance he opted for to flee Patmos."

"Perhaps," said Ionnes, "but as you said, he always had his own agenda running through that dour brain of his, even if nobody else could yet see it. If he singly purposed to flee from Roman hostilities, his legs would not have brought him directly to Ephesus and my home. A move like that could incur Roman wrath."

Ionnes knew another explanation warranted, even if he knew not what (and might never know).

"Tell me about Dim," he requested.

Philomena checked the walls to make sure their ears were deafened. She spoke in hushed tones even those in the room with her could barely hear.

"I knew we should have left Patmos," she began, holding back more tears. "But we also felt welcomed by those in the church. The island needed a good mason. Dim was known by the locals, including many who still wished to treat him like prisoner scum, but in a short time his quality work started to become known."

She paused to breathe deeply before going on.

"Then, he came home one day last month to tell me the temple priests had again summoned him. They were preparing to rebuild the temple to Apollo as summer approached and wanted to hire him."

"What did he tell them?" asked Ionnes.

"At first, he said he would think about it, though he truly knew his answer before they asked, but he came home to discuss it with me. We knew the power of Yeshua in our lives and knew we could not be such a major part of our old lives. To rebuild the temple – the temple you destroyed no less..."

"...Yeshua destroyed," corrected Ionnes.

"Of course," she said, "but, you know what I mean. You tell them Yeshua destroyed the pagan temple, but they still see Ionnes."

"Of course," he allowed. "And, what happened next?"

"We know not for sure. He wondered what persecutions might they do for refusing to help rebuild the temple. He tried to avoid them for some days, but they finally came to him demanding an answer. He apologized but said he could not."

"What did they say?" asked Timotheos.

"Nothing," she said, turning towards him in a startled fashion. Replaying the story, she lost sight of where she sat and perhaps saw only Ionnes before her.

"They did not press him and said not another word as they turned and walked away. Dim told me it felt eerie. Strange and mysterious. He started to wonder what troubles they would create. We even considered leaving Patmos right away, or after he finished his present job, so we would have money for passage. Those at the church prayed with us and counseled us to leave Patmos if we felt in danger. Then, I saw something in Dim I had never seen before."

The men waited for her to continue. She looked down to consider her words before speaking, or perhaps wondered if she should say anything. She looked at Ionnes. His kind eyes gave her strength to continue. Well she knew she was in safe company, but a reminder absolutely helped.

"Ionnes, he loves you so much. He spoke of you often. Every day. He missed your words of truth and your inner strength, and he strived to be more like you when he faced hard moments. This moment promised to be difficult. He knew that you would stay to face your adversaries in the name of Yeshua. He said you had no family to look out for, but before Yeshua, our family never knew the love of the church. What I mean to say here is that we stayed because he knew you would stay.

"So, the following week, as he and Pterrkee worked on a house, Roman soldiers arrived to arrest him. I heard two of them were even soldiers he knew from his years at the quarry. They threatened to kill him right there. One of them even said my husband should have left Patmos when he had the chance."

"So, what is the charge?" asked Ionnes.

She peered towards the window before whispering, "Unholy service."

"?????"

"Yes," she insisted. "You heard right." Her voice still a secret.

"It sounds serious," said Timotheos.

"Punishable by death," Philomena heaved as new tears appeared.

"Yet, still he lives?" asked Ionnes.

She nodded between her sobs and trying to dry her eyes.

"How long has he been held?" asked Prochorus.

"Over a month," she answered.

The men looked at one another questioningly. No one lasted a month. Dim should already be dead. All there knew Romans classically did not hold prisoners for any longer than needed when fated for execution.

Just then, they heard the sound of heavy footsteps and metal clanging together in cadence with the footsteps. A pound on the door, and uniformed men entered.

"Guard Octavius," greeted Ionnes. "I knew it would be you. And, Mucius. How have you been?"

"Good," answered Mucius.

"This is no social visit," said Octavius, stepping towards Ionnes. With swords drawn, they moved through the small room to take Ionnes into custody.

"We are not armed," said Ionnes with empty hands held forward for inspection. "No reason to take life here," he assured.

Octavius glared at Ionnes, then changed to bewilderment. He never quite understood the old apostle the whole time he lived in the penal colony. That old feeling immediately emerged, chasing away whatever dutiful resolve and purpose he had conjured when given orders to arrest Ionnes.

"Shall we go?" asked Ionnes, putting out a hand like a gracious host.

"This way," answered Octavius, then realized he followed Ionnes out the door.

Ionnes motioned to the others with hands held together, then pointed upward. They understood.

The men stood dumbfounded a moment before Prochorus spoke.

"Come. Let us see if this was planned."

"Should not we pray first?" checked Timotheos.

"We can pray along the way," answered Prochorus. "I know for a fact you prayed often with Paulos on the road, especially after you were chased out of a city."

"Yes, we did," acknowledged Timotheos.

The parade of prayer warriors left Dim's home with renewed purpose. They watched the soldiers taking away Ionnes from a distance to see where he would be taken. After a spell, Prochorus and Philomena looked at one another. Their eyes verified what both earlier suspected. Ionnes had been taken before the new acting governor, Makrinos.

<>< ><> <>< ><> <>< ><> <>< ><> <>< ><>

"Good to see you again, Giovanni," mocked Makrinos.

Ionnes felt the hard shove on his back moving him forward.

"Good to see you, too," answered Ionnes.

Makrinos could not tell if he was being insulted or not. He almost had the guard slap him for insolence but waited.

There would be plenty of time for pain later, now that he had the holy sorcerer in chains.

"That was quite an elaborate trap you set," said Ionnes. "Having Pterrkee come all the way to Ephesus to find me. You knew if I learned Dim's life was in danger that I would come."

"Well said," complimented Makrinos. "Very clever. I am thrilled to see my scheme worked."

"Perhaps," said Ionnes.

"I have you, have I not?"

"Just my body. My spirit belongs to Yeshua. That is the greater part of me you can never chain."

"Yeah. Yeah. So, I have heard."

Makrinos took a healthy swig of wine and said, "But, now that I have you, what shall I do with you?"

Ionnes looked at him straightly. "It has been my experience that as Romans, you typically choose death as the first answer."

"You know us Romans well," Makrinos snidely said, "But, in this you are wrong. I did not bring you back to Patmos just to kill you. If that was all I wanted, I would have had you assassinated in Ephesus or wherever."

"Not so," countered Ionnes. "You very much wanted me here. You mean to destroy me before the very people who hold me in esteem."

"I love how you think," said Makrinos. "You go out of my way to make my job all that much easier. But my statement still stands. If I wanted you dead, you would already be dead."

"Even as proconsul?" challenged Ionnes. "I understand that you, as acting governor, do not practice all governmental duties and authority. Likewise, I have been brought here with no formal charge. What is my charge?"

"You have no charge," answered Makrinos, almost smugly.

"You are here only upon my request. Think of it as my guest."

"Do you put chains upon all your guests?" challenged Ionnes, holding up his shackles.

"Only the most special guests," he answered. "but fear not. Death is not my most immediate design for you. And as far as formal charges, you will receive them if you fail to pass my test."

"You put me to the test?"

"That is why I brought you."

"What is the test? Back to the quarry?"

"Oh, no. Nothing so dreary. The quarry is just about dead, anyway. We would merely free you or kill you or ship you to another penal colony, however Roma decides."

Ionnes stood his ground. "As proconsul and acting governor, you would be reprimanded to take my life without formal charges or a trial. That would look bad on your service record and your future in Roman government."

"True. True," he said, "Sometimes too true. But that is not why I brought you here."

"If you wanted me to return to Patmos," said Ionnes, "you could have just done a friend's request."

"Right again," snapped Makrinos, "though somehow I expect you would have declined my invitation. No. I knew if you heard your friend was in trouble that you would come to help."

"And, you are correct," said Ionnes. "So, where is Dimetrius? Does he still live?"

"He is being held nearby. And yes, he is alive - for now. That is the test."

"Test not the LORD your God," said Ionnes.

"Why not?" challenged Makrinos. "What is your lonely God going to do to me if I test Him? I would think He would want to be tested. He is not a very strong God if He cannot stand up to a few inhuman tests."

"So, what is this test?" demanded Ionnes.

Makrinos looked at Ionnes disapprovingly, but still managed to smile. "I want the people of Patmos to know you as fraud. Dim shall die, and if you cannot raise him back from the dead, all here on the island will know you are a fraud."

"Fortunately, it is not that simple for you," contended Ionnes. "I have known many who died whom Yeshua did not return to us their lives, yet Yeshua's Spirit and church continue to grow. Someday Yeshua will be revered in Roma itself. I know. I have seen it."

"Not in my lifetime," challenged Makrinos. He stood up from his chair to approach Ionnes. "You mock Roma with your ways and your words," he shouted into Ionnes' face. "I stood back and watched as you hexed Laurentius with your magic."

Ionnes tried to speak, but Makrinos kept yelling, "Well, Laurentius is no longer here to protect you, so Giovanni, here is my game. Dim dies. If you raise him, you all may leave. If you fail, you die with him."

Ionnes wiped flecks of spit off his face with his chained hand.

"That is quite the gamble for you," said Ionnes. "When Yeshua raises him, the people will flock to Yeshua all the more."

"I am willing to take that chance," said Makrinos. "Not that you truly have a choice, but are the terms accepted."

"They are understood."

"Good," said Makrinos. "Then you will understand why we hold you until after Dim is dead."

Ionnes stood motionless, yet indicated he understood. "You know not the power of the LORD, creator of the Heavens and the Earth."

"And, you know not the means of execution," said Makrinos.

Ionnes waited.

"Oh, I have not quite decided. Beheading or cut him in half."

Tears appeared in Ionnes' eyes, mostly for Dim and his family.

"Take him away," said Makrinos to the guards. They moved forward and grabbed Ionnes by both arms.

"Yeshua knows the evil in your heart," said Ionnes.

"Then, pray He explains it to you better," quipped Makrinos. "I expect you are going to need it."

He looked at the guards. "What are you waiting for?"

The guards grabbed an arm each and led Ionnes down and outside. Just next door stood the holding prison. Ionnes had seen it many times but had never actually been inside. Unlike the Carcer Tullianum in Roma, the holding cells were less dark and damp. They were still quite small. Maybe four by five feet – too small for a man to fully lie down when came time to sleep. And, where to put urine and feces? The guards did not even provide a pot.

"Dim!" shouted Ionnes as he passed his tiny cell.

Dim looked incredulous. Running to the door, he yelled, "Ionnes! What are ya doin' back here?"

"I heard you were in trouble," said Ionnes as they shoved him into the cell opposite Dim and locked the door.

"&, who is gonna come help ya?" said Dim.

"Yeshua, of course," answered Ionnes.

Dim placed his forehead against the small, barred window of his cell door.

"Ya should not have come," he muttered, half to himself. "Now both o' our deaths will be upon my shoulders. That is a weight more than I or any other man can bear."

He shifted away from the door and wept shamelessly. Ionnes well knew the signs – those of a man made hopeless. Ionnes himself knew the feelings that Yeshua had abandoned him, battling against the fear to dare hope again. Ionnes' presence brought Dim's hope crashing back, even as the old apostle himself entered a prison cell. Both now encased behind locked doors, yet the odds immediately became two-or-more-in-prayer-to-Yeshua versus whatever and whomever.

"How long have you been here?" asked Ionnes.

Dim took a moment to stop weeping and pull himself together. His voice cracked as he answered, "I know not. At least a month. Did ya see Philomena & my boys?"

"Yes," answered Ionnes. "They are well. Silva and the others have attended to their needs for you."

Dim felt the tears return, this time mixed with a little gladness. He let the waves of emotion pass over him like the repetitive, breaking surf, then looked over at Ionnes in the small window of the dark room.

"Damn ya!" he spouted. "I never shoulda entered the water. I would not be here. This totally blows. Taken away from my family. Arrested for whatever. Stuffed in this cell t' rot. &, where is Yeshua in all this? He ain't anywhere in this cell with me. I knows. I have searched for Him over & over, & all I can see is darkness & cold. All I can smell is the stench o' my waste. If yer beloved Yeshua really loved & cared about me, as you claim, I would not be here."

Ionnes sighed. "And, where would you be? Were not you a prisoner when we met? You are merely a prisoner again, but this time you are guilty of your crime. This time you are preserved; not left to rot. Yeshua shares the cell and the pain with you, whether your eyes can see Him or not. This time, you stand as a light in the darkness, and the darkness hates the light." Ionnes waited a moment to gauge Dim's reaction.

"Jus' words, old man." He turned away to slump down on his cold, stinky floor. "Jus' do me a favor & stay away from me. I am a loser. Run for your life. Get back. Let it be." He muttered a few more syllables Ionnes could not make out, but the elder asked not. Much discouragement makes a man deaf. Ionnes certainly knew discouragement as well as any man, so knew from experience he just had to let it run its course for a bit. Just as a man's thoughts ran a linear course to conclusion, so also his emotions. He knew Dim knew the truth of Christos and thereby hoped he would soon return again to His first love. He knew Dim's time was short. Dare he tell Dim of Makrinos' mad plan? Falling on roughened knees against a rock-hard floor, he again chose the proactive comfort of prayer to his Friend and Savior. All the better, he rejoiced, knowing fully well those in the church also prayed for them fervently. His first prayer asked to blend his words with the sweet incense of praise and petition that his brethren shared.

Still deep in prayer, Ionnes heard a stirring across the way.

"Was not I bait?" called Dim.

"Aye," answered Ionnes.

"They used me t' get ya here?"

"Verily."

Dim cursed again.

"Ionnes, how could ya be so stupid?"

"What do you mean?" asked Ionnes.

"I mean, how could ya be so stupid t' fall int' their trap?"

"It was not hard," he answered. "If you were in Ephesus and word came that I had been arrested, would not you have come?"

Dim thought a moment before answering.

"I guess."

Silence again.

"How did ya know?" Dim eventually asked. "Who contacted ya in Ephesus?"

"Pterrkee," answered Ionnes.

"Pterrkee?" yelled Dim. "Pterrkee? The lowly dog! I knew I could never trust him."

Ionnes could hear Dim pacing around in his small cell.

"He did not come back, did he? He is not here?"

"No."

"Damn him," said Dim.

"No," corrected Ionnes. "His betrayal is horrible, but do not call on Yeshua to send him to eternal damnation."

"Why not?" challenged Dim.

"Because you know not the inner workings of the man's heart. You know not why he betrayed us. Or even if his motive was betrayal. I know not as well, and so I shall not judge him."

"I still would kill him if I saw him," swore Dim.

"I understand," answered Ionnes. "Truly I do. And, if I was a younger man, I might feel the same way, but as I stand here in chains, I am compelled to put my trust in Christos all the more - not to look for another to blame."

Quiet suddenly settled in as their words took time to sink in. The thick silence, thicker than the stone walls, labored heavily between them.

"Ya did not come alone," said Dim, breaking the mute moment. "Who else is here? Prochorus? Papias? Polycarpus?"

"Yes, no and no," answered Ionnes. Papias went back to Hierapolis and Polycarpus to Smyrna."

"Ya sent them both?"

"Yes. But, in answer to your question, Timotheos is here."

"Timotheos?" checked Dim. "The bishop of Ephesus that Paulos brought to Yeshua?"

"The very one. Also, Ignatius came."

"Who is Ignatius?" pondered Dim. "I remember the name, but not what ya told me 'bout him."

"He is head of the body of believers in Antiochus. In Syria."

"The one who considers his life in Yeshua not complete lest he is martyred?"

"The very one," verified Ionnes.

Dim suddenly felt humbled to be in such company, even if he had not yet met them. He would not have felt more touched if Moses and Elijah landed on the island with Ionnes, (and he would not have put it past Ionnes to bring those two prophets of old as well).

"Damn!" Dim repeated.

"What?" asked Ionnes.

"Nothing," said Dim. "I jus' feel like a fool. I know not if ya can help, but ya came t' my aid. Makes me feel foolish a bit..." his words trailed off.

He paced around some more, thinking and thinking and thinking. Finally, he asked, "So, why did Makrinos set such a trap t' bring ya back?"

Ionnes sighed, "Makrinos means to test the LORD Almighty."

"How?" asked Dim warily.

Before Ionnes could answer, the door to the prison could be heard being unlocked and opened. Four soldiers entered, crowded tightly in the narrow hallway. They unlocked Dim's door. Two reached in and yanked Dim out. He tried to fight until a sword became planted against his throat.

"Just try that again," challenged the guard, his eyes afire with hatred.

Dim kept eyes on the man a spell. The sword withdrew, and he felt strong hands lead him into the stark, blinding sunlight.

No sooner was he brought out when he saw four other soldiers entered the small prison. As Dim stood blinking against the midday sun, the soldiers eventually emerged with Ionnes chained to them. Ionnes looked about but saw none of the followers of the The Way within eyeshot. Rough hands pressed them forward to a closed courtyard behind the governor's berth. High white walls rose on all four sides with only one way in and one way out. No direct sunlight ever touched the dirt bottom.

A lone tree stump stood near the center of the courtyard. Dim knew the courtyard's purpose all too well after his years on Patmos. He looked at Ionnes frantically as fear suddenly seized him in its stranglehold. The four soldiers held him all the tighter, well-practiced for this purpose. Beheading never played out like some Greek drama where the prisoner dutifully laid his head on the stump. They had to be held down by rope or chain only to fight and struggle right up to the bitter end.

Just then, Makrinos entered the inner court. An insidious smile dressed his face. He stared triumphantly at Ionnes, then at Dim.

"Make him ready," he said to the soldiers.

The harsh hands promptly dragged Dim to the stump, forcing him down. He slipped away a few times, but never found full freedom as the ropes were fastened around his neck and shoulders to hold him fast.

"Ionnes," called Dim.

"Pray," said Ionnes. He knew it sounded hollow to Dim, but no other order could stand taller or move stronger. "You are on your knees. Pray to Christos Yeshua with all your heart and mind and soul and strength."

Dim strained against the ropes awhile longer without success. His skin rubbed raw against the rough hemp, yet he pulled all the harder. Suddenly, strangulation sounded somehow better than beheading and he inconsequentially struggled all the harder. Makrinos watched the display with pleasure.

Along the way he spied Ionnes, also on knees, bound but praying for his friend.

"Let us see if your prayers save your friend this time," he taunted.

Ionnes looked directly at Makrinos. The test this proconsul saw being played out sadistically, certain Ionnes would fail, and his own neck would share the same fate as Dim.

Ionnes started to weep with compassion for his friend. Salty sweat bled from both, mixed with the tears. Makrinos watched just another minute, then made a slight wave of his hand. One soldier stepped forth.

"Yeshua, blind them," said Ionnes, but none stopped.

"Demons depart in the name of Yeshua Christos," he ordered, but the soldier continued.

Ionnes looked quickly around the courtyard, seeking an army of angels to call forth. None materialized.

"Yeshua, break the blade," said Ionnes desperately, looking back as the soldier raised the long sword over his head. Dim turned his head to try to see Ionnes. The two met eyes as the sword made its long trip to Dim's flesh and bone. It drove not through despite full force. Dim flinched in great pain, but refocused fearful eyes on Ionnes. Blood flooded forth from the wound. Another hack of the metal blade drove further into the neck, then another and another, and the head left the body. Blood ran forth from his open neck to drench the ground. The eyes seemed to express shock a brief moment as the head rolled onto the dirt as his life expelled and its light dissipated from his eyes.

Ionnes wailed and fell forward, hitting the ground almost as broken as the limp body before him. The sobs held him fast in its grip. His entire being shuddered with uncontrollable grief.

"Now it is your turn, priest," mocked Makrinos. "Bring him back or share his fate."

Ionnes forced his lamentations to allow him speech. A still, small voice whispered deeply within his mind.

"Have I permission first to mourn with his wife and family and to bury him."

Makrinos smiled in delicious consideration. He looked at the soldiers.

"Free him."

The guards paused to make sure they heard him correctly.

"You heard me," barked Makrinos.

One pulled forth keys and unlocked Ionnes fetters. Ionnes rubbed his wrists, but his heart still mourned the terrible loss of his friend. He stared long and hard at the lifeless body while seeking Yeshua's wisdom how to pray. "Philomena," the voice seemed to say.

Ionnes stood and brushed himself off. His back still racked and his countenance dark and broken, he looked at Dim's body as he said, "Others shall come to remove the body and bury it."

"Today," said Makrinos.

"Of course, today," answered Ionnes, looking at and through Makrinos. His eyes saw the black side of the proconsul's soul. The name upon his forehead spelled a terrible horror and Ionnes shuddered at the dreadful image. Slowly he stepped forward to exit the courtyard, keeping his left hand against the wall for stability and support. Four soldiers followed as he slowly and numbly walked onto the cobbled street. He looked about but saw no one familiar. Gradually moving towards the Kastelli Acropolis, countless dozens of thoughts popped in and out of his brain without rhyme or reason. Some accused. Some questioned why. Some shared his brokenness. He recalled no time since Yeshua's crucifixion and death that he felt such extreme pain for the martyrdom of one of his own, save his own brother, Yaakov. So many had died by the martyr's fate - apostles and disciples all, but this felt more like the death of a beloved son. He looked up to the blue sky with its visiting white clouds and contemplated how Elohim felt when His own Son met the heartless pain of death.

Still slowly moving, his thoughts started to collect more singularly. Prayers never ceased passing through his lips. His grief still weighed him down heavily, but he also started to see Yeshua's hand here though he would be the first to admit he completely knew not how this would serve Yeshua's glory.

Then in recollection, he reentered the throne room of Almighty God. Under the altar gathered the martyrs with special love for those beheaded. He thought he could see Dim there with the others. The thought comforted him as one who steps out of the dark dungeon to the light of day, or as one lost in the desert who finally finds the oasis.

"Ionnes," he heard a woman's voice call.

Looking up, he saw Philomena racing towards him. His eyes flooded again to see her. He knew the grief in store for her, and it broke his heart into shattered shards and jagged fragments.

"Ionnes," she met him, out of breath. "Have you seen Dim?"

He nodded. She swallowed hard as she saw the pain in his face. Others quickly joined them including his traveling companions.

"Philomena," he said, his voice shaky and broken. "I am a man of deepest sorrow. I could not save him."

Her eyes welled-up as her head turned back and forth, denying the meaning of the words his lips expressed.

"No," she said, then again, "No," as she slumped down on the street and sobbed violently. Those passing by watched the scene without compassion. The soldiers laughed coldly from behind them. Ionnes ignored them and their foolishness. He looked at Timotheos, Ignatius and Silva.

"We must bury our brother." He heaved with grief, then said, "Together."

The group stood as one and gathered arms around one another to share in the mourning and anguish.

"Where is Dim?" asked a voice.

Ionnes turned towards the sound of the alien voice. When he saw the source, he almost choked with surprise.

"Pterrkee!" he slurred. "What are you doing here?"

"I came as fast as I could," he said. "I knew not how Makrinos used me to bring you here. I came to try to break free my friend and steal him away from Patmos, but I see I am too late."

He bowed low before Ionnes asking forgiveness. Raising up, he said, "May I help bury my friend?"

Philomena continued to cry. Ionnes nodded at Pterrkee, then dropped to his knees before Dim's wife.

"Woman," he said, "go home and get your children. Meet us on the hill. We must bury your husband this day."

She stayed planted on the stones.

"Woman, please. Go get your children. We need you to join us on the hill in the next hour."

Still sobbing, she shuffled along towards her home.

"Go with her," Ionnes ordered the baker's wife and the other women. "Quietly," he added, then turned towards his companions. "We need cloth and herbs to dress the body. We need shovels to dig."

The men understood and went off to get the needed items.

Old Ignatius, Prochorus and Timotheos stayed with Ionnes as they led the young men to the body. Others joined them with cloth and herbs. Together they entered the closed courtyard. All gasped at the sight but went forth to prepare the body right there for burial. As they wrapped the cloth around Dim's limp body, one took the head. The weight of the head kept it from staying put within the flax cloth.

"We could pin it," said one, and off he ran. Soon he returned with small nails. Only the most stamina could take hold of broken, blue skin and stretch it against the skin of the body, joining the flesh together with the nails. The sword had cut the skin in different places with each hack, leaving two holes in the skin of the neck where pinning with nails would not hold. Some puked and could not watch.

Keeping support of the head, two were able to wrap the body as a whole. One had to keep hold of the head as they raised up the body. One brought a woven mat to carry Dim out. Six held the body as they proceeded out of the court and through town, singing hymns and dirges. Some tried to wail with mock grief, but Ionnes placed a finger against his lips to silence them. They stopped, perhaps a bit confused, but followed the old apostle's instruction.

The four soldiers continued to follow cautiously, spears or swords in hand. Ionnes saw Makrinos in the window above, his face stiff. No cocky smirk. No pleasure even as his plan played itself out.

Without hurry, the procession moved out of town. Philomena and her boys joined, walking blankly near the body. The boys cried without consolation as they held their mother's hands. Roman soldiers completed the procession.

The graveyard loomed ahead. Men continued to dig as they approached. Setting down the body on the dry weeds and ground, they continued to pray and sing in mourning as both the attendees and the grave continued to grow. Ionnes looked at Ignatius as he replayed his words.

"My life in Christos is incomplete if I know not the martyr's death."

That message rung through his thoughts over and over. Men climbed out of the hole in the ground and threw aside their shovels. Others picked up the wrapped body of the deceased, and supporting the head, carefully lowered it down into the pit. From there, they climbed out and stood awaiting further instructions.

Philomena knelt before the grave, her head down. Her boys clung to her like burrs and buried their heads in the folds of her garment.

"We should pray," said the baker, looking first at Ionnes then the others. The suggestion seemed moot. Most had been praying since the procession began.

"We should pray," the baker said again. He cocked his head towards Dim. "We should pray for him to rise."

Ionnes said a private amen as he rose and looked inquisitively at the baker. How well that man knew that a little yeast leavened the entire loaf and made it rise. Any baker could tell you that. Did he mean Dim needed a little leaven and he would rise? What did that even mean? What did that look like? Ascend up to Heaven?

His entire body shook with grief as he spoke the words, "As Yeshua has brought life back to many I have touched, I know no man who has been beheaded ever came back to life." He looked at all, settling on Timotheos.

"What of Lazarus?" said Timotheos. "Four days he laid dead. No man ever raised one four days in the grave."

"As well as the man born blind," said Prochorus. He himself still recalled looking in the stranger's new eyes as they washed off the mud in Siloam. Every person there that very day received new eyes for Yeshua as well. That had been the day that ultimately changed the course of Prochorus' own life.

"How about the man with the withered hand?" said Ignatius.

"Or feeding the masses with fish and bread?" said Silva.

"Or healing lepers?"

"Or calming a storm?"

"Or healing the woman with the issue of blood?"

"Or raising Jairus' daughter?"

"Or catching the fish with a coin in its mouth to pay taxes?"

"Or walking on water?

"Or cursing a fig tree that it quickly withered and died?"

"Or restoring Malchus' severed ear?"

"Or those who were healed when Cephas shadow passed over them?"

"Or...."

Ignatius looked at Ionnes as he said, "You know better than any of us that we worship the Creator of all things, seen and unseen. He created all with just the utterance of His voice. He held back the waters of the Red Sea. He fed how many thousands with manna in the wilderness. He caused a young virgin to conceive who had not yet known a man. It is His and only His will to do so, but He can bring life back to the dead, no matter how they died."

Ionnes felt the humbling love of Yeshua ever surging through his bones and being. He hugged his friend. Over Ignatius' shoulder, he spied Pterrkee who stood outside the crowd as had always been his way.

"Then, let us pray," he agreed, and stepped forth to the graveside. Others joined him, all holding hands or folding hands while others placed hands on arms or shoulders or backs.

Again, he looked at Pterrkee.

"Join us, please," he requested.

Pterrkee remained apart. Ionnes nodded to him as he looked back towards the open grave.

Philomena remained on the ground before them. Ionnes leaned down to her and said, "Please join us. Your prayers are needed, too."

She stayed planted a very long minute, then arose and took both hands of her boys. The still body of their father, wrapped in flaxen linen, seemed so far, far away down in the shaded hole. Her eyes still stubbornly refused to see her husband's body held within the wraps.

The wind stirred upon the hill, almost blowing some over. Ionnes looked Heavenward to watch the swirling leaves above. Words arose in his mind – something he wrote quite some years earlier. Words he thought he understood at the time but found over and over new meaning. Something Yeshua said right after he washed the feet of the twelve. Ionnes felt the words move upward and out through his lips.

> *"Very truly I tell you, whoever believes in me will do the works I have been doing, and they will do even greater things than these, because I am going to the Father. And I will do whatever you ask in My name, so that the Father may be glorified in the Son. You may ask Me for anything in My name, and I will do it."*

He replayed the words through his mind over and over.
"Greater works than these."
"Because I am going to the Father."
"You may ask Me for anything in My name, and I will do it."

The assembly, led by the Spirit of Truth and Light, joined together in prayer. Eventually Philomena shared in the praises, rubbing harshly against her suffering to smooth it out. All shared the same words for their fallen brother. All clung to each other as one.

Ionnes felt a new hand on his back.

Some minutes passed as all prayed, and the words of petition started to rest in the quiet. The body below still still. Arms and hands returned to their owners. Some gave hugs to console. Some stooped down reflectively, looking down the hill towards the city and the harbor.

Ionnes turned to see Pterrkee behind him. He had a "See? I told you" look on his face but said nothing. Ionnes thanked him with his eyes, then went to join those in introspection. He felt the heaviness of death still, as he recalled the days in the quarry and how many times Dim had helped and accompanied him.

"Have you ever failed," Dim asked just a short year back.

"Many times," answered Ionnes.

He sighed.

"Many times, my friend," he said aloud to his fallen friend in the hole as the sun started its descent behind the hill they stood upon. He saw the Roman guards nearby. They would come to take him away any moment. Grieving, he welcomed their harsh hands. Perhaps it really was time for him to depart this life. He would share the same fate as his brother, Yaakov...

Philomena knelt again before the grave, each of her boys wrapped in one of mommy's arms.

"I love you, my husband," she choked out the words. "I wish you would come back to me."

Her tears found new trails down her cheeks. She moaned with great pain and travail in her grief, paralyzed to rise for that moment.

"Um, hey," someone said.

The moment passed.

"Um, help," the voice again spoke.

Philomena looked down in the hole. The arms imprisoned within the linens started moving. The head rolled to the left and then the right.

"I am stuck. &, I cannot see."

"DIM!" yelled Philomena, falling forward to the rim of the grave and reaching down, her arms not long enough to reach him.

The others around her raced up. They heard his voice as well and knelt beside in astonishment.

Dim tried to sit up, hampered by the wrap and fifty pounds of herbs and spices.

Philomena jumped down into the hole and grabbed hold of her husband. Two young men also jumped down in the hole.

"How do you feel?" one asked.

"Helpless," answered Dim, his voice muffled as his mouth moved against the tightly wrapped cloth.

They helped Dim sit up as they sought to unwrap him.

"Here it is."

"No, here it is."

"I cannot find it," they bantered, seeking the end of the cloth. One finally found the end, and they unwrapped hastily, at one point practically pulling Dim's head off as Philomena struggled with everything in her being to not hold onto him while the cloth moved round and round upward.

"Take it easy," he said, looking at all three with the top half of his head now uncovered. He looked upward at the line of faces watching him from above and smiled. Ionnes and Ignatius praised Yeshua aloud and with shouts of praise as they waited. This occasion demanded loud voices for all to hear.

Before much longer he was able to stand. Philomena helped him to his feet, then grabbed hold and would not let go. Both could hear the sounds of their children on all fours, leaning over the side of the grave straining to reach their papa.

Many hands stretched forth to help all four out of the hole, starting with Philomena, then Dim. The group wrapped themselves around the ecstatic couple to celebrate Yeshua's mighty power once again at work in them all. Ionnes examined Dim's features. Everything seemed fine, though a series of scars wrapped around his neck. Ionnes first noticed the pattern of the scars resembled a necklace of fish:

<>< ><> <>< ><> <>< ><> <>< ><> <>< ><> <>< ><> <>< ><>

"Your neck is strong?" asked Ionnes.

Dim moved his head around in full motion.

"Everythin' seems t' work," he answered, then looked back down to the open hole. "Guess I almost found out what it feels like t' be a worm."

"*Eyore!*" exclaimed one of the soldiers behind them. Ionnes checked to see them, standing there with their teeth in their open mouths, unable to fully fathom what they just witnessed. He took hold of Dim's arm as he broke through the pack to address the soldiers.

"Here is another proof that Yeshua is LORD," he said to them in holy triumph. "You go tell Makrinos what has happened. We shall depart Patmos when we are ready to go."

The soldiers stood a moment before nodding and turning to race down the hill to the acting governor.

Dim kept an arm around his wife and practically tripped over his own children grabbing hold on each side. He laughed elated as he felt the love of his family wrapped around him tighter than the funeral cloth.

"Let us go home," he said to her. Her tears of joy continued to flow as she laid her head against his blood-stained shoulder and began an unhurried migration back to town.

Pterrkee stood to the side to join the group heading down, but Dim stopped before him.

"Are ya ready t' be baptized now & tell e'vryone that Yeshua is LORD?"

Pterrkee almost scoffed in selfish exasperation, but placed a hand on Dim's shoulder and said, "Yes, my partner. You talked my ear off about Yeshua as we worked. When we shared the cell with Ionnes, I saw so many things I could not believe already, but your rebirth takes the pita. I will race you to the harbor. I wish to be baptized before another Roman nobody schemes how to destroy another one of us."

Dim smiled with agreement then turned to Ionnes.

"You old goat," he said.

"Old Sheep," corrected Ionnes.

"Old sheep," smiled Dim and sighed. "It all happened to me and I still cannot believe it."

"How does it feel to be beheaded?" asked one of the young men.

"Terrible," Dim answered, "but I will tell you, not as bad as I 'xpected. I found the fear was greater than the pain. I remember seein' the ground roll around me as my head fell off my shoulders." He shuddered. "But the pain quickly vanished, and I felt my spirit leave my body. It was amazin'. Only my love for my wife & children compelled me t' accept Yeshua's invitation t' return t' life."

"You saw Yeshua?" asked Timotheos.

"Amazin'ly, yes," answered Dim. "In a glorious place unlike any I ever seen, with a huge throne & golden crystal all 'round. I saw four weird creatures & a huge choir o' angels all singin' praises t' Yeshua. There stood a big, square table & many came forth from there t' welcome me. I felt safe as I went b'neath the huge table. Perhaps it became an altar where all

682

received a brick load o' comfort. I would have gladly stayed there forever, but I heard Yeshua call m' name. 'Come,' He beckoned. As I moved forth, He told me t' prepare."

'Prepare?' I questioned, though no one there feels perplexed. He motioned with His fiery eyes & I knew He wished me t' return t' Patmos. I knew my head was gone, but it never 'curred t' me that He went ahead t' prepare the place for my soul t' return. I felt the darkness o' sleep move through me & when I 'woke from dreamless slumbers, I found myself wrapped in cloth & hardly able t' move. As I found my bearings, I heard the voices of all 'o ya above. I knew they were not out o' Heaven, so I called for help & have found Yeshua's most special blessin' in all o' ya, here t' bring me back."

He sighed as he recalled the visions of Heaven. Then, he looked at Ionnes.

"I know ya know much of Yeshua & God, but I got an odd question for ya."

"Continue," said Ionnes.

"When I visited Yeshua's throne room, I was invited t' remain under the big table with others who got martyred. By the way, Cephas & Yaakov & Stephanos & Didimus & Paulos & others all send their love. Oh, & Yochanan the Baptist, too."

"Amen!" laughed Ionnes. "I hope to see them all soon." He paused. "It could have been today."

"Yeah, indeed," agreed Dim. "But here is my question. I died the martyr's death t' remain with those already martyred, but Yeshua brought me back. If I die not a martyr's death the next time, will I still be with my brethren under the huge table, or with the hoard o' disciples, too many t' number?"

"Good question," said Ionnes. "I know not, but I do know whichever it is, we will be there with Yeshua for all eternity. That is the promise I rest upon each and every day."

"Then, I shall do the same," agreed Dim and leaned in towards Ionnes with renewed gladness of heart. His despair from the time in the cell and execution had thoroughly dissipated. He only felt Yeshua's love and saw more real than ever before that that was more than enough to last for an eternity.

Amen.

<>< ><> <>< ><> <>< ><> <>< ><> <>< ><>

The ship left harbor with a happy compliment of passengers. The brisk breeze slightly chilled the bones, but none felt greater warmth in each other's company. Ionnes and Dim stood upon the bow, watching the waves part before them. Dim ran his finger along the scars on his neck and throat.

"How is the neck?" asked Ionnes.

"Fine," answered Dim. "Sometimes it itches, but I think that is more from me messin' with it than additional healin'. Lyin' in bed, sometimes I just run my fingers 'long the grooves."

The salty wind blew past them as they cut through the waves. Dim quit fiddling and covered his neck with his cloak.

"Ya know what bothers me most?" pondered Dim.

Ionnes looked at him to answer.

"Who would ever believe me?" He stood upright, peacock proud and mock boasted, "I had my head cut off & died, but Yeshua reattached it & brought me back t' life." He shrugged towards Ionnes. "What man, woman or child with an ounce o' sanity will believe it, no matter how true it is? I lived it & scarcely believe it meself."

Ionnes empathized. "I know, I know," he answered. "I have received the same responses over all these years when I testify to what Yeshua has done, and what Yeshua has done through me. There are so many who make up boastful, elaborate stories. Fortunately for many, truth still has a way of entering a man who is open to the gospel. You will figure it out."

Dim leaned against the railing, looking aft as they turned away from harbor northward. It had been nearly five years of his life spent on Patmos. He saw the white buildings placed against the rise of the mountain to the west, and he realized he saw it this time with new eyes versus the imprisoned, broken man who beheld the island years earlier.

"Think ya will ever come back here?" Dim asked Ionnes.

"You know the answer to that," goaded Ionnes.

"Ya shall go as Yeshua leads," his voice plodded along by rote.

"Exactly," smiled the old apostle. "What about you?"

"I hope not," answered Dim, "but with that, I know Makrinos will not always be actin' governor. The days will bring changes like the winds bring & take the clouds. If I return, it will be for reasons I cannot now see."

"Verily," agreed Ionnes.

"With that said," added Dim, his countenance rising, "I still laugh at the look on Makrinos' face when I 'pproached him. He looked like a man frightened out o' his sanity. Shoulda named him Kaspar. I expected him t' flee like a one-winged fly before us."

"Indeed," said Ionnes. "I pray fervently that he learns and soon comes to Yeshua."

"Do ya think he will?" asked Dim.

"We shall see. I have seen men more evil than Makrinos come to Yeshua. Let the one who does wrong continue to do wrong; let the vile person continue to be vile; let the one who does right continue to do right; and let the holy person continue to be holy.

"We know not the day or the hour of Yeshua's return. For myself, I will ever seek to hear His summons. The Spirit and the Bride call me daily, saying, 'Come!' When I thirst, I will drink from the free gift of the Water of Life."

"What 'bout the rest o' us?" asked Dim.

The disciple whom Yeshua loved grinned with missing and crooked teeth, a thousand wrinkles covering his weathered face, wisps of white hair which refused to remain brushed, thin, leathery tanned skin covering old bones, and those gray-brown eyes that pierced holes in a person's being faster than a Roman spear.

"Yeshua said it best," he quipped as the sea pitched them back and forth with the swells. Each tightly grasped the rail.

Dim waited with anticipation.

"You heard Him yourself in Heaven, my son," said Ionnes.

Dim smiled and nodded.

"He said, 'Come!'"

GLOSSARY FOR PATMOS

Abaddon	Hebrew word. Means Destruction.
Aceto di Cato	Latin for Cato's vinegar.
Acropolis Kastelli	The civic center of Phora on Patmos.
Æ or æ	a digraph or ligature, also called an "ash", appearing in Latin and Latinized Greek words. In English words of Latin or Greek origin, *ae* is now usually represented by *e,* except generally in proper names (*Caesar*), in words belonging to Roman or Greek antiquities (*aegis*), and in modern words of scientific or technical use (*aecium*). Reportedly discontinued in the 12th or 13th centuries, but I recall seeing it used often in literature when I was a schoolboy. Nowadays, not so much.
Almah and Betulah	(עַלְמָה 'almāh, plural: 'ălāmōṯ עֲלָמוֹת) is a **Hebrew** word for a maiden or woman of childbearing age who may be unmarried or married. ... The Septuagint version of the Old Testament renders both Hebrew words almah and betulah as the same Greek word parthenos.

Amicis	Latin word for Friends
Apvaki	Hebrew, meaning "mindful". Used in Ps. 8:4, (What is man, that you should be <u>mindful</u> of him?"
Asklepion in Pergamos	A healing center specifically in ancient Pergamos where they gave their patients a mild drug to cause sleep. While asleep, nonpoisonous snakes were let loose to wander over the sleeping body. After the patient awoke, they reported their dream(s) to identify the problem area(s) in their body.
Aureus	A very valuable Roman gold coin.
Calida	Warm water and wine. Common daytime winter drink in Italy and Greece.
Caput Bove	The name of Laurentius' Arabian horse. Latin for Ox Head
Carcer Tullianum	The prison in ancient Rome, believed to have been built even before Rome became a city.
Castra Legionaria	The Roman military base on Patmos.

Celtic Vertragus	A Roman dog breed.
Choinix	Greek. Dry weight measure equal to about a quart.
Dominus	Latin for Lord.
Flavian's Amphitheater	The original name for the Roman Coliseum, named after Domitian's family name, Flavius.
Galinthias	In Greek mythology, **Galanthis** or **Galinthias** was the woman who interfered with goddess <u>Hera</u>'s plan to hinder the birth of <u>Heracles</u> in favor of <u>Eurystheus</u>, so she was changed into a <u>weasel</u> or <u>cat</u> as punishment for being so insolent as to deceive the goddesses of birth that were acting on Hera's behalf.
Halberd	A spear with a sharp ax attached.
Har Megiddo	Another name for Armageddon, a physical location in ancient Israel. Har means 'mountain.' Megiddo could have been named after an ancient city Tar Megiddo.

Hastatus	Spoken by Chryspippe to a Roman soldier, the singular of <u>hastati</u>, a class of infantry in the armies of the early Roman Republic who originally fought as spearmen. Chryspippe calls one of the young Roman soldiers hastatus.
Hineni	Hebrew alliteration, means "I am here, LORD." Used throughout scripture to respond favorably to the LORD's call.
Iberia	Spain, or rocky structures between Spain and Portugal.
Krikri	A rare mountain goat, found mostly on Crete.
Kurios	Greek alliteration for LORD.
Latrunculi	Also called Tali, or in English "Knucklebones," a gambling game similar to dice.
Lavraki	A sea bass.
Legate	Military commander of any Roman base.
Maspik!	Spoken by Rabbi Yosef, means "Enough" in Hebrew.

Mea Culpa	Latin, spoken by penitent people asking God's forgiveness. Literally means "Through my fault."
Middad	Hebrew, meaning "Be gone!"
Mons Abila	Mountain on the north African coast of the Mediterranean Sea opposite the Rock of Gibraltar, (aka Mons Caipe or Pillar of Hercules).
Palæstra	A Gym or Spa for physical work-outs. Ancient Roman soldiers commonly used them for warrior practice.
Palatina Hill	The part of Rome where the Cæsars lived.
Patricide, aka Parricide	The crime of killing one's parents, especially fathers. Penalty of being beaten and flogged, then sewed into a large leather bag with a dog, rooster, viper and monkey, then all trapped inside are thrown into deep water to drown while the animals all fought and scrambled in fear to escape.
Pillar of Hercules or Mons Caipe	Roman/Latin names for the Rock of Gibraltar.

Psittacula Parrot	Parrot common to Ancient Rome and Greece.
Salve	A Latin greeting or endearment.
Skybalon!	Hebrew word spoken by Rabbi Yosef – means 'rubbish' or 'dung'.
Terni Lapilli	A game created in Rome around 100 BC, similar to Tic-Tac-Toe.
The Forum	Civic center of ancient Rome.
The Paraclete	The Holy Spirit as counselor or advocate. The presence and power of God intended to come after Yeshua departed the Earth.
Voltrys	Greek word, spoken by Kynops, it literally means "You Are Blowing."
XIV.Kal.Oct	Latin - The date Domitian Cæsar died, (Sept. 18, 96 AD)
YHWH Tsuri	Spoken by Ionnes at the quarry. Hebrew, means "God is my Rock."

Thank you for Reading Patmos – An Apostle in Exile – A Planet on Trial

I pray that you enjoyed and were greatly blessed by the book. I have been exceedingly blessed by St. John's life, over and over.

You are welcome to contact me with any questions and concerns at Albedobooks@gmail.com

A Thumbs Up is also very much appreciated.

May God's blessings be with you, always and all ways,
David Stoeckl, Sequim, WA, USA

www.ingramcontent.com/pod-product-compliance
Lightning Source LLC
Chambersburg PA
CBHW070341030726
47504CB00001B/33